I0733388

OTHER BOOKS BY ANNA DURAND

Willpower (Psychic Crossroads, Book One)
Intuition (Psychic Crossroads, Book Two)
Kinetic (Psychic Crossroads, Book Three)
The Mortal Falls (Undercover Elementals, Book One)
The Mortal Fires (Undercover Elementals, Book Two)
The Mortal Tempest (Undercover Elementals, Book Three)
The Janusite Trilogy (Undercover Elementals, Books 1-3)
Obsidian Hunger (Undercover Elementals, Book Four)
Unbidden Hunger (Undercover Elementals, Book Five)
The Thirteenth Fae (Undercover Elementals, Book Six)
Cyneric (Undercover Elementals, Book Seven)
Echo Power (Echo Power Trilogy, Book One)
Echo Dominion (Echo Power Trilogy, Book Two)
Echo Unbound (Echo Power Trilogy, Book Three)
The Complete Echo Power Trilogy
Passion Never Dies: The Complete Reborn Series
Banished in the Highlands (A Hot Scots Prequel)
The Notorious Dr. MacT (A Hot Scots Prequel)
The British Bastard (A Hot Scots Prequel)
The MacTaggart Brothers Trilogy (Hot Scots, Books 1-3)
Gift-Wrapped in a Kilt (Hot Scots, Book Four)
Notorious in a Kilt (Hot Scots, Book Five)
Insatiable in a Kilt (Hot Scots, Book Six)
Lethal in a Kilt (Hot Scots, Book Seven)
Irresistible in a Kilt (Hot Scots, Book Eight)
Devastating in a Kilt (Hot Scots, Book Nine)
Spellbound in a Kilt (Hot Scots, Book Ten)
Relentless in a Kilt (Hot Scots, Book Eleven)
Incendiary in a Kilt (Hot Scots, Book Twelve)
Wild in a Kilt (Hot Scots, Book Thirteen)
Unstoppable in a Kilt (Hot Scots, Book Fourteen)
Valentine in a Kilt (Hot Scots, Book Fifteen)
Lachlan in a Kilt (The Ballachulish Trilogy, Book One)
Aidan in a Kilt (The Ballachulish Trilogy, Book Two)
Rory in a Kilt (The Ballachulish Trilogy, Book Three)
Brit vs. Scot (A Hot Brits/Hot Scots/Au Naturel Crossover Book)
The American Wives Club (A Hot Brits/Hot Scots/Au Naturel Crossover Book)
A Novel Secret (A Hot Brits/Hot Scots/Au Naturel Crossover Book)
The Dixon Brothers Trilogy (Hot Brits, Books 1-3)
One Hot Escape (Hot Brits, Book Four)
One Hot Rumor (Hot Brits, Book Five)
One Hot Christmas (Hot Brits, Book Six)
One Hot Scandal (Hot Brits, Book Seven)
One Hot Deal (Hot Brits, Book Eight)
One Hot Favor (Hot Brits, Book Nine)
One Hot Bash (Hot Brits, Book 10)
Natural Obsession (Au Naturel Nights, Book One)
Natural Deception (Au Naturel Nights, Book Two)
Natural Passion (Au Naturel Trilogy, Book One)
Natural Impulse (Au Naturel Trilogy, Book Two)
Natural Satisfaction (Au Naturel Trilogy, Book Three)

THE PSYCHIC CROSSROADS

SERIES COLLECTION

Psychic Crossroads, Books 1-3

ISBN: 978-1-958144-50-3 (paperback)
ISBN: 978-1-958144-51-0 (ebook)
ISBN: 978-1-958144-52-7 (audiobook)

Jacobsville Books
www.JacobsvilleBooks.com

Publisher's Cataloging-in-Publication Data
provided by Five Rainbows Cataloging Services

Names: Durand, Anna.
Title: The psychic crossroads series collection / Anna Durand.
Description: Marietta, OH : Jacobsville Books, 2024. | Series: Psychic crossraods, bk. 4.
Identifiers: ISBN 978-1-958144-50-3 (paperback) | ISBN:978-1-958144-51-0 (ebook) | ISBN 978-1-958144-52-7 (audiobook)
Subjects: LCSH: Psychic ability--Fiction. | Amnesia--Fiction. | Man-woman relationships--Fiction. | Family secrets--Fiction. | Psychokinesis--Fiction. | Mental healing--Fiction. | Romance fiction. | BISAC: FICTION / Romance / Paranormal / General. | FICTION / Romance / Suspense. | GSAFD: Love stories. | Romantic suspense fiction. | Occult fiction. Occult fiction. | Romantic suspense fiction.
Classification: LCC PS3604.U724 P79 2024 (print) | LCC PS3604.U724 (ebook) | DDC 813/.6--dc23.

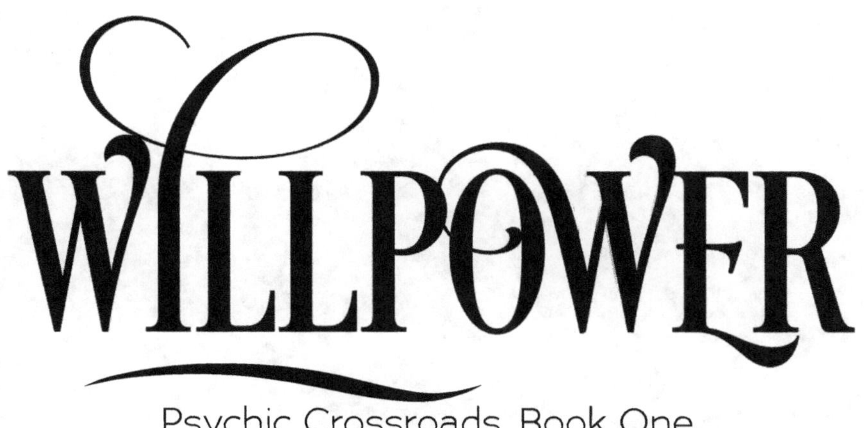

Psychic Crossroads, Book One

CHAPTER ONE

T HE LAST TENDRILS OF SUNSET SPREAD OUT ACROSS THE SKY AS THE OLD Pontiac Sunbird swerved into the driveway. The car's front bumper sideswiped a bush, spraying greenery over the hood.

Grace Powell gritted her teeth, her pale knuckles clamped around the steering wheel. She stared straight ahead as if a taut string connected her eyes to the garage door. The glow of the headlights reflected off the big metal door, forcing her to squint at the sudden brightness. It pierced her vision like needles shoved straight through her eyeballs into her brain. The car jerked to a stop inches from the garage. Grace uncurled her fingers from the steering wheel. Her head throbbed, and pains in her neck stabbed upward into the base of her skull. Christ, the migraine was getting worse.

She shut off the engine and extinguished the headlights, bringing blessed relief from the glare. When she unhooked her seatbelt, her fingers slipped, and the retractor sucked the belt back into its housing with a *thwack* that made her wince. She eased the door open, dragged herself out and onto her feet, and shut the door gently.

The garage stood attached to her home, a two-bedroom brick number with dirt-brown trim that matched the dirt-brown garage. A single light burned on the porch beside the front door. Stains dotted the cracked strip of concrete that led from the driveway to the front entrance. The house squatted in the center of a one-acre lot on the southern outskirts of Lassiter Falls, one of many Texas towns that hovered on the brink of becoming a city.

Not that the property was hers. She rented the dump—okay, maybe "dump" was an exaggeration, though only a slight one—because she couldn't afford anything else. Even tiny apartments in this town cost more than her unreliable stream of income could handle.

Grace leaned against the car for a moment, enjoying the ever-deepening twilight, a respite from the knife-sharp headlights of other cars on the freeway and the sterile bulbs in the doctor's office. Her body ached from the hour-long drive back from Fort Worth. The trip had proved fruitless, netting her nothing but a burgeoning migraine and another visit to a specialist who could offer no explanation for her headaches—and no relief from them, either. Doctors invariably asked questions she couldn't answer, then eyed her with a mixture of curiosity and pity as they offered excuses couched as possible explanations. Sure, the doctor today had written her a prescription for some pills. She didn't bother to fill the prescription because she knew the medication wouldn't work. Nothing worked.

The doctor had called her a "strange case." How comforting.

She rubbed the back of her neck, but the pain refused to relinquish its hold on her. With a heavy sigh, she pushed away from the car and trudged around its front bumper toward the concrete path.

The nape of her neck tingled. A current of frigid electricity rippled through her body. She froze mid-step and listened for… something.

Someone is watching.

For months now, at odd moments, she'd felt a gaze fixated on her, trailing her movements, always hidden in shadows, hovering just beyond her comprehension. Of course, she dismissed the sensation as paranoia. Stress-induced. Temporary.

The hairs all over her body stiffened.

A claw scratched at her shoulder from behind. She swung around, hands raised in defense, a shout lodged at the back of her throat.

A skinny, hunched man stretched out one bony hand. His fingers clawed at the spot her shoulder had occupied a second earlier. His brown eyes, wide and dilated, darted back and forth. A sheen of sweat glistened on his skin. His hair must've been trimmed with a chainsaw, considering the way it stuck out in matted clumps, and he looked like he hadn't seen a shower in weeks, maybe months.

Grace scuffled backward.

The man stumbled forward.

"P-please," he said, the word punctuated with a burst of spittle. "Don't run. I need to talk. To you."

"You've got the wrong person."

"Grace Powell."

She ought to run inside, lock the door, and call the police. But all she could manage to do was inch backward toward the front door. "What do you want?"

"Talk. To you. Please." He glanced over his shoulder and bit his lower lip, drawing a bead of blood. He dropped his voice to a hoarse whisper. "Inside. Hurry. They're coming."

"Who?"

"Inside. *Now.*"

She stared at the little scarecrow of a man as she edged closer to the door—and to escape. This guy was probably a drug addict who got hold of some bad crack or crank or whatever people called it these days. With those pupils, dilated beyond the effect of darkness, he must've been high on something.

Think, Grace. What do you do when a drugged-out scarecrow wants to talk to you?

Damned if she knew.

Grace slipped a hand into her purse and clasped her keys. Drawing them out behind her back with one hand, she snaked the other hand out to feel for the doorknob. The serrated ends of the keys poked out between her fingers. If forced to, she might use them as a weapon.

The scarecrow whimpered. "Please. They're getting closer. *In my brain.*"

His eyes bulged as if they might pop loose from their sockets at any second. He panted and glanced around with jerky motions of his head.

"You wait here," Grace said. She closed her hand around the doorknob. "I'll go inside and make sure they're not in the house."

She twisted the knob and shoved the door inward.

"No!" he screeched. "No!"

He rushed at her, his arms flailing. Spittle sprayed from his mouth as he sputtered objections at her, nonsensical phrases peppered with the words "no" and "please." She slashed at him with the keys and felt the metal catch on his flesh. Blood oozed from the cut, dribbling down his cheek into his mouth.

He clutched her elbow.

Wrenching her arm free, she threw herself backward through the doorway. Her shoelace snagged on the jamb. Her legs flipped out from under her. When her tailbone smacked into the floor, a lacework of pain fanned out through her hips and legs.

The scarecrow lunged at her.

She kicked at the door. Just as it banged shut, the scarecrow hit it with his full weight. The wood trembled. His cry, muted by the door, sounded more like the wail of a dying animal than the ranting of a madman.

Grace sprang to her feet. She flung herself at the door and closed her fingers around the deadbolt, fumbling to move it. Finally, she shoved the lock into place.

Aftershocks shook her entire body. Her tailbone smarted. Her heart pounded fast and hard, in syncopation with her gasps.

Outside, the scarecrow wailed. "They want your mind!"

Despite the thick wood separating them, his cry vibrated her eardrums with an intensity that rattled her brain.

Abruptly, silence descended.

She stood immobile, the keys still clenched between her fingers, the metal digging into her skin. The doorknob jiggled. Fingernails scraped at the bricks. An image flashed in her mind's eye—the dead, risen from their graves, scrabbling to get inside the mortuary. In the vision, the mortuary bore an uncanny resemblance to her house.

Scratch-scratch. Jiggle-jiggle. Scratch. Jiggle.

Silence. The dead had returned to their graves.

Her heart knocked against her rib cage, wanting out of her chest as badly as the scarecrow had wanted to get inside the house. She took a slow, deep breath. For a long moment, she stood there propped against the door, her entire body shaking. She was afraid to move, to make a sound, to think about what had happened.

Maybe the scarecrow had left.

She needed to know for sure. Cautiously, she settled her forehead against the door with her eye lined up with the peephole.

The scarecrow's face, distorted by the lens, filled her view. His eyes glimmered green.

Weren't his eyes brown before?

In the half cone of light created by the porch bulb, she might've mistaken brown for green. Hell, she might've mistaken up for down when the scarecrow jumped her.

He leaned forward, his green eye staring back at her through the hole as if he saw her.

She swallowed against the tightness in her throat. The shimmering of his eyes was... preternatural.

His body convulsed. He squinted and chewed his lip, oblivious of the blood trickling down his chin. His eyes glistened.

Was he crying?

His body convulsed again. In the wake of the tremor, he stilled and tensed his body. All expression vacated his face. Maybe the drugs had worn off.

Without a sound, seemingly in slow motion, he hurled himself at the door.

The concussion slammed her forehead into the wood. She stumbled backward and lost her balance. For the second time tonight, her buttocks hit the floor hard.

She shouted a wordless cry of pain.

Footsteps clapped outside, fading as the scarecrow fled the vicinity.

And just like that, it was over.

Chapter Two

S HE SLUMPED ON THE FLOOR, STUNNED. THOUGH HER TAILBONE smarted, the pain began to lessen. At first, her body seemed to have turned to stone, and she couldn't make her muscles move, but soon that sensation also diminished. Her pulse calmed, beat by beat, as she took slow breaths. With every second that ticked by, her body eased back into its usual state. Now if the rest of her would follow, she could pretend to feel like a normal person.

Hauling herself onto her feet, shuffling to the door, Grace peeked through the peephole. The scarecrow was gone. What he wanted, why he picked her, those questions would remain unanswered unless the lunatic returned later to explain himself. Yeah, like right before he ripped her heart out barehanded and tossed it onto a barbecue grill.

Leaning against the door, she closed her eyes. It was over. Whatever the scarecrow man had wanted, he'd given up on getting it, at least for now. He wouldn't come back.

She hoped.

Every hair on her body prickled. She sensed something nearby, like a magnet pulling at the atoms of her body. Her chest tightened. The air seemed to push against her, simultaneously compressing her chest and trapping the breath inside her. She willed her eyelids to part.

A man stood across the room from her, near the kitchen doorway. He held his arms at his sides, his head tilted to the left.

This man was not the crazy scarecrow. No, the stranger watched her with a steady gaze, his blue eyes studying her face and then examining her body. His gaze felt neither sexual nor threatening, more curious than alarming. The irises of his eyes glowed like sapphires lit from behind by an unseen source. A breeze ruffled his blond hair.

Somehow, she knew he meant her no harm.

Crazy. He must've broken into the house. She ought to scream for help.

Instead, she blurted out, "What do you want?"

His gaze settled on her face. Standing there as still as a boulder, he scrutinized her with unblinking eyes.

Grace heard a car speed past on the street and peripherally saw its headlights slash through the interior of the house. Her focus stayed locked on the strange man, who kept watching her. His blue eyes seemed to catch fire in the flare of the headlights.

"Who are you?" she asked.

He ducked around the corner into the kitchen.

A gale tore through the house. Her hair whipped against her face. The gust whisked a newspaper off the coffee table and fluttered it in the air before releasing it to settle on the floor.

Grace rushed into the kitchen. If the man came in through a window, it would explain both the wind and how he got inside the house. No one was in the kitchen. The window above the sink was shut. She spotted the window's latch, which was engaged. Moving to the back door, she twisted the knob. Its lock resisted.

She searched the house room by room. Every closet, every nook, and every dark hole became a threat, a possible hideaway for the intruder, even the foot-high space under her bed. All the windows were shut and locked from the inside. Since the back and front doors were also secured, with dead bolts, the man could not have slipped in through any window or door. How had he entered the house?

Grace spun around.

Behind her, the door to her bedroom hung open. In front of her, the hallway stretched into darkness. She hadn't dared turn on any lights during her search. Now the shadows loomed all around, grasping at her with claws of darkness and spitting shadow flames from their nostrils.

Call the police.

Her inner voice virtually screamed at her. But the man might still lurk in the house, perhaps trailing behind her to hide where she'd already looked. The idea sounded ridiculous. Yet the man had broken into the house without cracking a window or jimmying a lock. Anything seemed possible. She needed to call for help.

The house had one phone. In the kitchen.

Between here and the kitchen lurked phantoms of every shape and size, plus one very real monster.

"Dammit," she muttered.

Grace bolted down the hallway.

In the kitchen, she switched on the overhead light, vanquishing the phantoms. No intruder awaited her. Nothing lurked there except air and light and the telephone. She snatched up the cordless handset and, fingers trembling, dialed 911.

When the operator answered, Grace's voice failed her. Yet when she did speak, her tone sounded calm, almost confident, despite the quaking in her limbs and the typhoon raging in her gut.

"Send the police," she said. "There's an intruder in my house."

THE DEPUTY AIMED HIS BEST LOOK OF CONCERN AND PITY AT GRACE, with a hint of irritation creasing the skin around his eyes. Grace slumped in the recliner across the coffee table from the sofa. With her foot, she rocked the chair in a ferocious rhythm.

The night had gotten worse. An intruder, she thought, must be the worst that could happen tonight. Then the deputy arrived, and her day sank deeper into the cosmic toilet.

The sheriff's deputy, Reilly Skidmore, knew her. She had a vague recollection of him and his clique of science-obsessed friends who looked down their noses at everyone else. Back then, Reilly had worn eyeglasses thicker than the arctic permafrost. Tonight, he sported no glasses. And his skin had cleared up.

He did, however, retain that certain quality that made her want to deck him.

"About this intruder," Reilly said, "are you sure it wasn't the same guy who jumped you outside?"

"Positive."

"Maybe your eyes were playin' tricks on you," Reilly said. "Stress can affect a person in funny ways."

His Texas drawl oozed like molasses, slowing down some words and truncating others. Despite having lived in Texas since high school, Grace had never adopted the drawl and therefore never quite fit in with the natives. Even if she'd consciously tried to sound Texan, she still would never fit in here. She didn't fit in anywhere.

"I did not imagine it," she said, struggling to keep the anger out of her voice. "And there's nothing funny about confronting an intruder."

"Okay, okay. See, it's just that I didn't find any footprints other than yours and the first guy's. But those tracks don't prove anybody attacked you, only that someone was around. There's no sign of a break-in either."

She squinted at him. Tonight, his Texas twang irked her for some reason, though it never had before. Every time Reilly spoke, his voice awakened a chorus of imaginary fingernails scraping across a blackboard in her mind. She found herself gritting her teeth and rocking the recliner even harder. The chair's base lifted off the floor slightly with each push backward, smacking down again with the forward motion.

"Maybe it was a black panther," Reilly said with a smirk. "Guy last week claimed one of them killed his cat. Turned out it was a black Rottweiler."

Grace huffed out a breath. "So, I'm either crazy or stupid."

"That ain't it at all. I'm sayin' eyes can play tricks on us."

She glared at the wall. The conversation had spun in tornadic circles for twenty minutes. *You're crazy. No, I'm not. Yes, you are.* Reilly had searched the interior and exterior of the house, questioned neighbors on both sides of the street, interrogated Grace, and resolved nothing.

She was crazy. End of investigation.

"I'll keep an eye out for the guy who jumped you," Reilly said. "But I reckon he's long gone."

Grace absently wondered how Reilly had wound up as a cop. In high school, he bragged about winning a scholarship to Harvard, or maybe it was Stanford. Ivy Leaguers didn't generally wind up as sheriff's deputies.

She'd ended up barely scraping by as a book designer when her dreams of becoming a teacher were dashed by budget crises at schools across the country, so her teaching certificate hung in the bathroom as a piece of abstract art. She had retrained herself in book design and set out into the desert of self-employment. Oases were few and far between. The point was, she understood how people found themselves in jobs that bore no resemblance to their schoolyard dreams. She shouldn't think less of Reilly because his plans didn't pan out either.

Reilly rose and clomped around the sofa to the front door.

Grace followed, opening the door for him.

As he pushed past her, Reilly shoved a business card into her palm. "Anything happens, call me."

She noticed he didn't say if anything *else* happened. Clearly, the man assumed nothing had happened tonight. A weirdo had accosted her, but by Reilly's logic, the guy was probably a homeless man who meant no harm. Nothing worth fretting over. Although Reilly might not have said those precise words, Grace felt them bobbing just below the surface of their conversation tonight.

She took the business card. "Thanks."

With a curt nod, Reilly strode out the door.

As Grace lingered in the doorway, watching him cross the lawn, a breeze kissed her face. The warmth of it hinted at the summer heat that would set in soon. This was April in Texas, after all.

Reilly climbed into his cruiser and drove away. The taillights of his vehicle receded until they vanished altogether.

Grace shut the door, snapping the dead bolt into place, and yawned. The action seemed to breach the dam that held back a deep reservoir of exhaustion. The fatigue flooded through her, carrying with it a chill that penetrated her to the core. Today had really, really sucked. Strangely, though, the events of this evening served to extinguish her migraine. She couldn't recall when the symptoms had dissipated, but she thanked heaven they had. She could do without another brain-crushing, nausea-inducing headache.

On her way to the bedroom, she stopped off in the kitchen to double-check that the overhead light was off and that the back door was locked. Once inside the bedroom, she eased the door shut and engaged the lock. Hiding behind a closed door alleviated the tension in her gut, though she had no idea what she was hiding from or how a door might protect her from an intruder who apparently wielded magical powers. Sometime between calling 911 and seeing Reilly's cruiser pull into the driveway, she'd realized something important and indeed magical had happened to her. Not sweet, fairy-tale magical. Demonic, terrifying magical. The idea was ridiculous. Still, in her gut, she felt the truth of her revelation.

She'd experienced a life-altering event. She glimpsed the otherworld that existed within this reality, the realm of ghosts and demons and super-natural forces.

Maybe she ascribed too much value to the incident. She might have, as Reilly suggested, suffered a stress-induced hallucination or a bizarre kind of mirage. The stranger she confronted inside the house never spoke or touched her. Maybe she had imagined it.

Sure, and maybe she'd suffered a narcoleptic seizure, dreaming the whole thing while remaining upright through some quirk of gravity.

Grace flopped onto the bed. All the windows were locked, the back door too. The intruder snuck into the house and out of it again without using doors or windows. Maybe he teleported himself, like in a science fiction movie. Maybe he was a ghost. She believed in neither ghosts nor teleportation.

Yet she believed the incident was magical.

The intruder got inside somehow.

Unless she'd imagined him.

A chill shimmied up her spine. If she could imagine an event that seemed real, if she could give in to a hallucination so completely, she must've lost all sense of reality. She must've gone insane.

Oh yeah. Today really, *really*, really sucked.

CHAPTER THREE

LYING ON HER BED, GRACE GAZED UP AT THE CEILING WITHOUT SEE-ing it, without seeing anything. She replayed tonight's events in her mind. Nothing made sense. A scarecrow accosted her. An intruder broke into the house as if by magic. The scarecrow man she understood. The world hosted many psychos who needed no reason to torment another person. They did it for drug money. They did it for fun. They did it to satisfy the voices in their heads.

But she saw no rational explanation for the intruder.

Well, one explanation did fit. The last tether between her mind and reality might've snapped. Maybe the stress of her medical situation affected her more than she wanted to admit. Self-employment brought more pressure, as she struggled to stay afloat in a sinking economy. Working as a freelance book designer gave her freedom, but it also meant she never knew how much money she'd make in a given month. Her fluctuating stream of income meant she couldn't afford health insurance, so she paid for her doctor visits and prescriptions out of her own pocket. Those visits had become more frequent in the past few months. Three times in as many weeks, she found herself squirming in an uncomfortable chair waiting for a nurse to call her name.

Yeah, she had some stress.

In retrospect, calling the cops tonight was a bad idea. She had no one else to call. Her parents and grandfather, the only family she knew in her whole life, were gone. She'd lived away from them for years, but to lose them completely, to have them ripped from her life forever...

She was alone.

When a weirdo assaulted her, and a shadow man invaded her home, she had no one to call but the authorities. It had still been a bad idea. Now someone she sort of knew from years ago, someone who currently worked in law enforcement, thought she was a total whackjob. Though other people's opinions meant little to her, the opinion of a sheriff's deputy might matter if she ever needed real help. Worse, she recalled that back in high school Reilly liked to gossip. Thanks to her failure to think ahead, soon every cop in North Texas might know about the crazy girl in Lassiter Falls who imagined intruders.

At least the footprints out front proved a real person had assaulted her. Still, as Reilly pointed out, the footprints didn't prove the man attacked her. They showed simply that a person other than Grace approached the house. So yeah, she was on her way to becoming the Lassiter Falls loon.

Tears welled in her eyes. She touched the corner of one eye, feeling the warm liquid dribble down her finger. Crying signified weakness, self-pity, all the things she loathed. Squeezing her eyes shut, she willed the tears away, but instead, they flowed faster.

The curtains billowed. The door rattled against the jamb. A breeze tousled her hair. She glanced at the window, but it was closed and locked. Down the hall, the air conditioner clicked off, and silence pervaded the house.

The curtains rippled. The breeze whispered in her ear.

I'm not alone.

The thought exploded in her mind. The tingling she'd experienced earlier resurfaced, stronger and sharper. The air grew heavy and dense around her as if she sat on the bottom of a deep swimming pool. She gulped in breaths, her chest aching from the effort. Air, she needed air. Leaning sideways, she struggled to unlock the window, but her fingers slipped. The latch scraped her knuckles. She fought to breathe as the pressure of a hundred hands pressed against her chest and the air congealed in her lungs. Darkness flickered at the edges of her vision.

The door burst inward.

Air rushed into the room. She slumped onto the bed, sucking in blessed oxygen, her entire body shaking.

In an instant, the air felt normal again.

She pushed up off the bed. Her muscles quivered as she scuffled to the door. The jamb had splintered where the lock fit into its slot. Fragments of wood littered the carpet, and the door itself had warped inward at the center. She touched the distorted wood. The damage proved something happened in the bedroom. She hadn't hallucinated this time.

Unless she was still in the grips of a delusion.

No, she could not be *that* far gone.

When she tried to shut the door, it refused to latch. The bulge at the door's center distorted the whole thing so much that it wouldn't fit in its frame anymore. Replacing the door meant incurring another expense. *Terrific.*

Grace shambled to the bed and crawled under the sheets, rolling onto her side as she pulled the sheet up to her chin. Sleep wouldn't come, she accepted that fact. She thanked God for it. Sleep meant dreams, and so she prayed for insomnia.

Sleep came for her anyway.

———

A CORRIDOR. BEIGE WALLS. TWILIGHT. RED PINPOINTS OF LIGHT LINE THE corridor at floor level. A bland female voice speaks from nowhere and everywhere.

"Night mode on."

Further down the corridor, on her right, she spots a familiar door. Her heart skips a beat. Her stomach flutters. A force seems to draw her toward the door. One scuffling step at a time, she crosses the corridor.

Voices approach from somewhere beyond sight. Footsteps clap.

She freezes. Her gaze lands on the shape reflected in the mirror-like floor. She stares at her reflection, entranced by the shimmering image of her face, pale and indistinct.

Footfalls draw her attention to the corridor ahead of her. Two men are advancing toward her.

She glances around for a place to hide, but she knows the doors are locked.

The men walk past, oblivious of her, chattering to each other.

"That's right, man, crazy."

"Think he'll do it?"

"No way."

"Escapees should get the harsh stuff."

"I agree, but..."

Their voices diminish as they disappear into the twilight of the corridor's depths.

She waits. Listens. He is calling to her, not with his voice, but rather with his soul. She inches closer to the familiar door. Why does she sneak when they can't see her? Shaking off the question, she settles her hand on the knob.

The corridor vanishes. Now she floats in the void of space, surrounded by stars. With one hand she reaches out to the stars, stretching a fingertip toward one in particular. The one that calls to her. His star.

The light explodes, engulfing her in blinding brightness and scorching heat.

Sand. Cold. Noises. Darkness blankets her. Nearby but out of sight, a snake hisses. Coyotes howl from far away. Dirt invades her mouth and nostril, and grit burns in her eyes. She lies facedown on the ground. Levering up onto her knees, she gazes at the sky where stars glimmer. The moon smiles down at her. She senses its presence drawing nearer and watches its mottled face swell. The light glows pure white, infusing her with a sense of familiarity.

The night spins around her. She grabs a bush, fighting to keep her balance. Thorns slice across her palm. She feels a warm liquid oozing across her flesh. Blood.

A figure rises out of the sand. A hand reaches out for her. Green eyes gleam.

"There you are," says the figure, though not in words, in thoughts.

Hot fingers clutch her arm. Sear skin. Tear at flesh.

Pain rips through her.

———

GRACE WOKE WITH A JERK. FOR A MINUTE, MAYBE LONGER, SHE HELD still and listened to the metronome of her heartbeat. *Thump-thump. Thump-thump.* Quick, but slowing with each exhalation. A powerful ache throbbed behind her temples. The darkness around her seemed alien. She squinted as she struggled to discern shades and contours. Where was she?

In bed. Of course.

Her left palm burned. She explored the flesh with one finger, gently prodding at the sore spot. A warm wetness coated her fingertip. *Blood.*

She floundered for the lamp on the bedside table. Her fingers bumped the switch, and she twisted it. Light cascaded over her. She winced at the sudden brilliance, at the pain that stabbed through her eyes into her brain. The throbbing worsened into a pressure that spread from her temples to her forehead, into her jaw joints, and behind her eyes. Nausea welled up in her gut as a wave of dizziness overtook her.

She clutched at the sheets and stared at a small stain on the ceiling until the dizziness abated.

The migraine had returned, stronger than before. Though she let go of the sheets, she lay motionless for several minutes, until the nausea subsided too. Then, slowly, she pushed up onto her elbows. When that seemed all right, she dared to sit up. The light hurt her eyes, and she winced yet again. With her eyes half-closed, she slid off the bed and stumbled across the room to her dresser. In the top drawer, she found a scarf made of thin fabric. Back at the bed, she draped the scarf over the lampshade to dim the light. Only then did she settle onto the mattress again, flat on her back.

Even if she hadn't suffered a migraine earlier today, she would've experienced one now. Every time she had that dream about the strange twilight corridor, she woke up with a raging headache. In the dream, a certain doorway always beckoned her to enter, or at least it felt that way. This time, her dream self left the corridor before entering the room. Most often, she did go inside. After awakening, she never could recall what happened inside that room.

Occasionally when she dreamed of that corridor and that door, she sleepwalked. She might wake in the morning to find her lamp on when she knew she'd turned it off before going to sleep. Once, she awakened to find her handgun lying on her stomach. For a terrifying moment, she'd imagined that in her sleepwalking state she'd killed someone. But she had quickly realized the illogic of that idea. If she'd killed someone, surely the police would've caught her. At least that was what she told herself. She kept the gun in her dresser, which meant she didn't need to sleepwalk very far to retrieve it. The dream that night had been frightening, though the details of it blurred in the morning.

She lifted her hand to study her palm in the muted lamplight. Dried blood outlined a cut two inches long.

A cut. Like in the dream. *Ridiculous.*

She made her way to the bathroom, homing in on the glow of the night-light plugged into an outlet above the sink. Leaving the overhead light off, she searched the medicine cabinet for a box of adhesive bandages. Once she found the box, she applied a dab of antibiotic ointment to the cut and covered it with a small bandage.

Back in the bedroom, she changed into a cotton nightshirt and crawled under the sheets. The haze of sleep clouded her mind. In the morning, she might find the cut had been a dream too, vivid as hell, but just a dream. Maybe she was still dreaming.

Her mind drifted into slumber.

Just a dream…

Chapter Four

WHEN HER CLOCK RADIO BUZZED AT SEVEN FORTY-FIVE THE NEXT morning, Grace hit the snooze button. Twice. Dreams, not exactly nightmares but disturbing anyhow, fractured her sleep. She fought to stay awake, yet always succumbed to slumber. Her dreams couldn't have been weirder or more disturbing if Salvador Dali designed them.

Her jaw felt tight, her eyes grainy. Post-nausea hunger growled in her gut. She'd forgotten about the migraine. Thanks to a miracle or a quirk of biology, she had fallen asleep again while the headache raged. She wanted to stay in bed, wrapped in her cocoon of blankets, free from thoughts of last night, assuming she could escape the dreams. She had to get up, of course, and face life. Face the scarecrow man, and the ghost man, and the Vincent Price movie her life had become.

Her eyelids grew heavy. She drifted back into sleep.

A sharp knock at the door jolted her awake.

Grace rolled out of bed and onto her feet before she realized the knock came from the bedroom door, not the front door of the house. What the hell? As she blinked the sleep out of her eyes, she stumbled to the bedroom door which, warped from the previous night's weirdness, couldn't latch properly.

The door crept open a few inches.

Grace froze. Her pulse quickened. She glanced at the dresser, trying to gauge whether she could reach the gun in the top drawer before an attacker surged through the door at her.

Silence reigned, save for the thudding of her heart.

The door did not move.

She leaned sideways to peer through the gap between the door and the jamb. The hallway looked empty. She tiptoed closer, grasped the knob, and thrust the door wide open.

Empty space greeted her.

The warped door had probably drifted open on its own. She'd let paranoia get the best of her, a bad habit she seemed to have developed lately.

After changing into jeans and a T-shirt, she wandered into the bathroom. Fatigue hung over her like a heavy cloak. When she examined herself in the bathroom mirror, her malaise mutated into disgust. Her hazel eyes were bloodshot. Her dark-auburn hair, foregoing its usual curls, hung in greasy strands around her face. She slid her hands through her hair, but the action served only to exacerbate the problem. A shower would help with the hair, but as for the rest of her body and mind, it would take bathing in bleach to cleanse the mildew.

She had transmuted into walking mold. Algae with a skeleton. So long had she languished in financial and emotional limbo that her soul moldered and became encrusted with gook. Now the yuck inside was showing on the surface, in the tangles her hair had woven itself into, in the pallor of her skin, and in the frown that had nestled into a permanent home on her lips. She looked like hell, which seemed appropriate since she felt like she'd moved into a basement apartment in the nether regions.

Twisting the faucet on, she grabbed her toothbrush. Though she couldn't eradicate the spiritual mold in five minutes, she might at least look clean. Gazing into the sink drain, she scrubbed at her teeth.

A shape flashed in the mirror. She lifted her head to look.

He hovered behind her, silent, unmoving. The intruder who had sneaked into the house without breaking a window. The magical shadow man.

Their reflected gazes met.

He stepped back, gesturing with one hand, confusion flickering on his face.

She whirled to confront him.

The empty shower stall gaped back at her.

A gale swept through the bathroom. The roll of toilet paper flapped in its holder, and towels undulated on the rack beside the shower. Her hair lashed against her face.

She must've imagined seeing the intruder. The stress of everything triggered yet another hallucination. She needed to relax. No one had been there. The wind came from... the air conditioner, a window, or a freak indoor vortex. She was grasping at shadows, desperate to accept any answer, to grab hold of anything that might explain what she witnessed.

To hell with logic. A phantom man was not logical.

Out of the corner of her eye, she glimpsed the closed window.

A coldness burrowed into her belly. Wind did not erupt in a closed room. Well, if she'd accidentally tripped a circuit in the universe that opened the doorway to the beyond, anything could and would happen. Wind without source. Men who vanished. Air vacuumed out of a room.

If a huge rabbit bounded into the house and slapped a wet kiss on her, she'd commit herself to the nearest hospital. Until then, she would deal with her new reality. Make that *sur*reality.

Or plain old insanity.

She gave up on showering, settling for rinsing her hair in the sink. Two voices shouted inside her head—one warning of impending lunacy, the other urging her to give in to the new reality. The first voice grew louder until she no longer heard the second. Its litany about the otherworld became a memory, a paranoia to which she'd almost succumbed. Almost. There was no magic. No secret world. She hallucinated the intruder, both last night and this morning. The rest was remnants of nightmares. She suffered from an excess of stress, nothing more.

Yet the intruder had seemed familiar to her.

Oh sure, she knew him. He was *her* hallucination after all. Of course she recognized him, from her delusions and crazed dreams.

The dream.

She turned her hand upside-down, exposing the bandage that veiled her palm. Ripping it off, she tossed the bandage onto the counter and touched her skin. Not a scratch, not even a pinprick, scarred her palm. What had she expected, a gaping wound? From a dream? She remembered seeing a cut on her palm last night. That was why she'd bandaged her hand. This morning the cut was gone, so she must've dreamed the injury.

A spot of color on the counter drew her attention to the discarded bandage. A maroon blotch stained it. She reached out to touch the bandage, then yanked her hand aways and cradled it against her body.

The bandage was bloody.

Preserve the evidence, a voice inside her urged. She jogged to the kitchen where she retrieved a sandwich bag from the cupboard. Back in the bathroom, she tucked the bloodstained bandage into the bag, sealed the zipper lock, and stuffed the bag into the pocket of her jeans. Crazy, saving a bloody bandage. The blood had meaning, though, a significance she could not yet grasp.

Save the bandage, the inner voice urged.

So she did.

CHAPTER FIVE

G RACE WANDERED INTO THE KITCHEN. NORMALLY, SHE'D POP A BOWL
of oatmeal into the microwave for breakfast. The post-nausea hunger
still growled, but the idea of putting food in her mouth appealed to her
about as much as swilling antifreeze. A toaster pastry, stale and washed
down with root beer, sufficed.

A rapping at the front door interrupted her last bite of pastry. Tossing the empty can of pop in the trash, she hurried to the door and squinted through the peephole. A man with gray-flecked chestnut hair stood on the porch, adjusting his navy tie, which matched his navy suit. His white shirt looked crisp and unwrinkled. Reflective sunglasses shielded his eyes.

His tongue darted across his lips.

Grace opened the door a few inches, enough to poke her head into the gap. The man was of average height, with a trim physique fleshed out with muscles. He smelled of something stale and vaguely unpleasant, an odor she couldn't quite identify. A scar slashed across the right side of his neck, below the ear. His eyes, dark as coffee, locked on hers while his wide, thick lips parted into a smile. A subtle undercurrent in his presence unsettled her, like the rush of cold air when a ghost passed through a room.

"May I help you?" she asked.

"You must be Grace," he said. "Deputy Skidmore gave me your name."

She eyed him warily. No drawl colored his baritone voice, and he spoke in precisely articulated syllables. His jacket bulged under the left breast, a small lump that might indicate a cell phone or a day planner. Or a gun.

Christ, she'd gotten so paranoid.

He reaffirmed his smile. "Is everything all right?"

Trouble. The word echoed in her mind. Yet he looked harmless—a little too harmless.

"How may I help you?" she asked again, keeping the door wedged between the two of them.

"It's about the man who approached you last night." He lunged a hand through the doorway. "I'm Henry Winston, by the way."

She shook his hand. His skin was warm, almost feverish.

"What man?" she asked.

"The lost soul who approached you outside this house last night." Winston adopted a solemn expression. "It's a matter of some delicacy. May I come in?"

"No," she said, and guilt flushed her cheeks. If Reilly sent this man, then the matter he wished to discuss must bear some relation to her ordeal last night. This man might offer her a few answers. She ought to invite him inside, but that odd undercurrent within him set her nerves on edge.

Winston removed his sunglasses, tucking them in the inside pocket of his suit jacket. "I understand. A woman alone at home, a stranger at the door, and so forth."

She stared at the crown of his head. The hairs, short and thinning, poked up like fresh-cut grass, with Old Spice substituted for the aroma of turf. The cologne failed to mask that stale odor. She estimated his age as late forties.

Twice in their brief conversation, Henry Winston had referred to "the man who approached" her, as if the incident involved nothing more sinister than a handshake. Winston's phrasing irritated her, but she supposed he was trying to be diplomatic. If he knew anything about the scarecrow man, the information might help her understand why the weirdo accosted her.

Ignoring the unsettled feeling in her gut, she swung the door open. "Come on in."

Winston strode past her, swerving left into the living room. He glanced at the sofa and then opted to settle into the armchair across from it, propping one ankle atop the other knee. Linking his hands over his abdomen, he gazed at Grace with a neutral expression.

She lowered herself onto the sofa, perched on its edge. Her hands she dropped to her sides, with the fingers tucked under her legs.

Henry Winston swept his gaze over her entire body as if assessing a racehorse before making an offer to purchase the animal.

"What's this about?" Grace asked.

"The man you encountered last night. His name is Adam Hansen, and he escaped from a private clinic outside Dallas several days ago. I'm his psychiatrist." Winston rested his arms on the chair. "I need to find Mr. Hansen before he harms himself or someone else."

She waited for him to continue, but a long silence ensued. Finally, she asked, "What does this have to do with me?"

"I hoped you might be able to provide some clues as to his where-abouts."

"Sorry." She hunched her shoulders. "He babbled nonsense and then he left. I didn't ask for a forwarding address."

"What precisely did he say to you?"

Memories flashed through her mind. The creepy little man lunging at her. His claw-like fingers scratching at her. His voice, hoarse and fraught with anxiety.

They want your mind.

Her throat tightened. She swallowed against the constriction, focusing on Henry Winston. He watched her—and waited.

"Um…" She floundered for a believable lie because she certainly would not tell Winston the truth. "I don't remember what he said. None of it made sense."

Winston sat forward. "Deputy Skidmore mentioned that you claimed a second man broke into your home immediately after Mr. Hansen left."

She stared at him, unable to form a response. Reilly had told this man, a complete stranger, the details of what happened to her last night. She understood Reilly sharing information about Adam Hansen's attack on her, because Winston did claim to be the scarecrow man's psychiatrist. But her encounter with the shadow man? Reilly had no business telling Winston about that.

So much for privacy.

"Tell me about this other man," Winston said.

Like hell, she thought but said nothing. If Winston was a psychiatrist, after hearing about her encounter with the disappearing intruder, he'd drag her off to his so-called private clinic and pump her full of enough drugs to put an elephant in a coma.

Next time she saw Reilly Skidmore, she'd slug him.

Which would get her arrested for sure. *Brilliant idea, Grace.*

"There's nothing to say," Grace told Winston. "I was mistaken."

Leaning back in the chair, Winston stared at her. She felt his attention focused on her like the hot glare of a high-wattage bulb aimed directly at her face. The urge to flee rushed through her, but she suppressed it. Her involuntary reaction to this man was ridiculous. Though he was rude and strange, those traits hardly qualified him for membership in Maniacs Anony-mous.

"Perhaps you were mistaken," Winston said, drumming one finger on the chair. Then he broke eye contact and added, in a casual tone, "I under-stand your parents and your grandfather passed away last year."

Grace went stone-still. A cold pit hardened in her gut. Reilly couldn't have told Winston about the deaths of her parents and her grandfather be-cause Reilly didn't know. No one knew.

Except for Grace.

"Your parents died in an auto accident," Winston said, "and your grandfather in a plane crash. Is that correct?"

"How could that possibly be any of your business?"

He shrugged. "It speaks to your emotional state at the time of your encounters last night."

The cold pit melted into boiling anger in her gut. She clenched her teeth. It spoke to her emotional state? His words sounded like code for "you're nuts, lady."

Winston fixed his stare on her once more. "Do you sometimes wish you could join your loved ones?"

"Join them where?"

"In the hereafter," he said. "Do you ever wish you could die and be reunited with your family?"

She gaped at him, unable to respond. As if trapped in a bad dream, she listened from a detached viewpoint deep inside herself.

"Or perhaps," Winston continued, "you don't believe in the afterlife. In that case, you are completely alone, and death offers the promise of oblivion. Freedom from life and struggles, from everything."

Grace snapped back to reality with a jolt that shook her body. This man either had a cruel sense of humor or he *was* the lunatic in this room.

"Tell me," Winston said, "how did you spend last summer?"

"None of your damn business."

He arched an eyebrow. "Are you unwilling to tell me or unable to?"

She leaped to her feet. "I'd like you to leave, Mr. Winston."

A smirk tightened his lips. Without a word, he rose and headed for the door.

Grace followed close behind him.

Winston swung the door open, stepped outside, and turned to face her.

She stood with one hand on the door, ready to shut it in his face.

He leaned into the doorway. "It was lovely meeting you, Grace. Thank you for your hospitality."

She scowled at him.

The smirk widened. He pulled away from the threshold.

Grace slammed the door. She started to walk away but then stopped. A shiver tingled down her spine. She swung back around to press her face to the door, aligning her eye with the peephole.

Henry Winston gazed at the door, expressionless, green highlights glowing in his dark-brown eyes. He bent forward to peer through the peephole.

Grace jerked backward.

The dark circle of the peephole lightened.

Slowly, she leaned forward to look through the lens.

Henry Winston had backed away from the door. Patting the bulge in his jacket with one hand, he waved at her with his other hand. Was he letting her know he had a gun? Certainly, he wanted to intimidate her, though she had no clue why. She'd done nothing to him. They'd never met until today as far as she remembered.

Which left plenty of room for doubt.

He turned and sauntered down the cement walkway.

She rushed to the living-room window, adjacent to the door. Parting the curtains a couple of inches to get a view of the walkway, she watched Winston amble across the lawn and down the sidewalk, out of sight.

She bit her lip and let the curtains drop closed. For a little while, she'd let herself believe things couldn't get more bizarre, but they just did. The motives of Henry Winston, and indeed his purpose in coming here, eluded her every attempt to comprehend them. Grace hugged herself, rubbing her arms. One thing she did know for certain.

Winston had been sizing her up.

But why? Who was he? What did he want? Was his name even Henry Winston?

More questions without answers.

Chapter Six

An hour later, after much wondering about Henry Winston's visit but without arriving at any conclusions, Grace gave up on solving the mystery, at least for the moment. She changed into a beige pantsuit with a cream-colored blouse and flats that matched the suit. After a brief but futile attempt to improve her bedraggled appearance with makeup, she drove to Professional Personnel in downtown Lassiter Falls.

The head of the employment agency had expressed an interest in publishing his own book about job-seeking strategies. He wanted an estimate for book design but insisted that Grace present her quote in person. The man apparently harbored a Luddite streak that ran deeper than the Grand Canyon. When she'd suggested emailing the quote would save them both a great deal of time, he'd snorted.

"I don't trust email," he'd said, in a tone that matched his derisive snort. "And I don't do business with somebody 'less I meet 'em in person first."

How quaint, Grace had thought, but kept the sentiment to herself. That was how she wound up traipsing all the way to downtown Lassiter Falls when she would much rather have stayed home to nurse the aftermath of this morning's migraine. She needed this client.

Professional Personnel occupied a suite on the second floor of the newest structure in town, a two-story office building one block from the town square. Grace parked along the street. Several other cars occupied spaces along the curb, however, few vehicles traveled the street that served as one of the main arteries in Lassiter Falls. The courthouse, a historic site dating to the late nineteenth century, loomed up ahead. Its clock tower jutted above the surrounding trees. At night, the clock glowed orange. On St. Patrick's Day, it glowed green, and throughout December its face burned a festive red.

The courthouse reminded her of a Gothic castle. Its spires resembled turrets, and its clock tower seemed perfect for imprisoning a deposed queen. The traffic circle surrounding the courthouse gave the illusion of a moat. Grace envisioned a dungeon hidden beneath the courthouse, knights dueling on the front lawn, a desperate lady waving a white hankie from the tower's apex.

Grace sighed. She wasn't destined for the tower, but for the office building in front of her. Tearing her gaze away from the majestic courthouse, she approached the modern, and to her mind, depressingly sterile structure known as Market Street Plaza. A pair of glass doors hissed open for her automatically. When she entered the building, cold air enveloped her as the doors hissed shut behind her. Goosebumps prickled her arms. Ahead, a wide staircase curved up toward the second floor. She followed the stairs to the second-floor landing, letting her loafers drag across the carpeting. She imagined herself gliding on a cloud, floating toward the gates of heaven—until the clickety-clack of someone typing in one of the office suites popped the bubble of her reverie.

At the landing, she turned left and trudged down the hallway to a composite-wood door emblazoned with the logo for Professional Personnel. A handwritten sign taped below the logo declared, "Come on in, y'all." She pushed through the door.

The waiting room was vacant. The reception desk at the far end of the small room also stood unoccupied, the chair behind it turned to one side, a file lying open on the desktop. A light on the telephone blinked red.

Behind her, in the corridor outside, soft voices drew nearer.

Grace marched to the desk.

A woman emerged from a door to the right. She held a manila folder tucked under one arm. Flumping onto the chair, she slapped the folder down on the desktop.

"Are you here to sign up?" she drawled.

"No," Grace said. "I have an appointment with Ron Petrovicz."

"Oh." The woman shuffled papers on her desk. "Ron was supposed to be here today, but I'm afraid he got called for jury duty. Would you like to reschedule?"

Grace felt a scowl creeping into her features. She forced a polite smile to cover it. "Why don't you just ask Mr. Petrovicz to call me when it's convenient for him. We can discuss rescheduling then."

"I'm real sorry about this."

Grace made a noncommittal sound. The receptionist wasn't to blame for her boss's rudeness. Petrovicz should've called Grace to cancel.

"I'll give Ron the message," the woman said.

"Thank you."

The woman reached for the phone. The conversation was evidently over.

Pressing the blinking button, the receptionist said, "You still there, Sally?"

Grace walked out of the office into the hall. This was just what she needed after the events of the last twenty-four hours. Wasting a good hour and a half driving to and from the business district of Lassiter Falls swallowed up time she could've spent on paying projects. Besides, her irritation at Petrovicz's failure to cancel their appointment churned up the acid in her gut. She felt her migraine threatening to resurface too as pangs erupted behind her eyes.

All her life she'd believed certain events occurred for a reason. Why she believed this, she couldn't explain. But whenever she tripped over a pothole in her life path, the notion of fate soothed her, mostly. Sometimes, like today, the notion also disturbed her. Why did fate want her to feel sick, delusional, severely aggravated, and utterly alone?

Lately, she'd realized fate was an illusion. So was control. She no more controlled her life than she controlled the programming on television. Just like networks would air drivel no matter what she wanted, her life would also bump and skip forward without her consent. Chaos governed the universe.

Still, she occasionally felt destiny's hand nudging her. Maybe she'd watched too many movies.

Grace tramped down the staircase toward the lobby. Maybe one look at her had convinced the receptionist she wasn't their kind of book designer. "Sally" on the phone might've been Ron Petrovicz hiding in his office, awaiting a signal from his receptionist. Thumbs up, come on out. Thumbs down, lock the door. Grace's attire was professional, she thought, but her hair looked like straw laden with grease. She'd been too exhausted, and too harried, to take a shower.

Groaning, she shook her head at her pessimism. Her looks, her clothes, none of that condemned her. Ron Petrovicz was occupied with jury duty today. She had no reason to doubt the receptionist's veracity. Yet she did.

She doubted everyone.

Paranoia was the devil on her shoulder, whispering dark notions in her ear. She needed an angel to kick his ass off her shoulder.

She had good reason for a modicum of paranoia. Her brain had become a bit Swiss-cheesy in recent months.

Grace pushed through the doors and into the daylight. Halting on the sidewalk, she half-closed her eyes as she let the sun melt the ice encrusting her soul. Birds chirped from the bushes. The heat still slumbered, though its eyes had begun to open, releasing a sticky breeze.

A man darted out from between parked cars, careening toward her.

She jumped sideways.

He brushed against her. His hand, warm and rough, clasped hers for an instant before he vanished around the corner of the building.

Grace felt an object in her hand, smooth with sharp edges. She uncurled her fingers. The man had shoved a piece of paper into her palm, a small sheet ripped off a notepad and folded into a square. The sheet's corners jabbed her skin. She unfolded the paper.

Someone had scrawled a message on the sheet. "Meet me at Ray's Country Café. Twenty minutes. Urgent. Your grandfather was murdered."

⸻

THE BRUNCH CROWD HAUNTED BOOTHS AND TABLES THROUGHOUT the old building that housed Ray's Country Café, an establishment that, despite its cutesy name, was a traditional greasy spoon. The diner hunkered alongside the interstate on the outskirts of town like any self-respecting greasy spoon would. The crowd hardly qualified as a throng of people, but it was large enough to quell the churning in Grace's gut. If the man who had passed her the note attacked her inside this diner, she would scream. Surely, one of these people might rush to her aid.

Grace chose a booth near the entrance, in the corner, a few feet from the picture window at the front of the diner. Hand-painted lettering on the glass announced today's special—chicken-fried steak with mashed potatoes, country gravy, and black-eyed peas. From the jukebox in the far corner, a country-western singer crooned a love song. Chatter from the back of the diner drifted forward on the breeze from the air-conditioning system, and the smell of frying burgers tantalized her senses. She hadn't come to Ray's in years, since before her parents moved to California, yet she could still taste the burgers and curly fries, and the special sauce that made the diner famous locally.

The door chime jangled.

A man stepped over the threshold.

Was this the man who gave her the note? Maybe. Out on the street, he'd darted past her so quickly she didn't notice what he looked like, not even the color of his hair or the kind of clothes he wore.

The man surveyed the diner. When his gaze intersected hers, he hesitated.

She returned his stare.

He shifted his attention to the window. Apparently satisfied, he ambled toward her.

Grace stiffened. The guy might be crazy. He *must* be crazy. No one had murdered her grandfather. Edward McLean died when the jet he'd chartered crashed over the Kansas prairie. Grace read the official reports in the papers, talked to the police, and watched TV news stories that played an amateur video of the crash over and over until the images had burned themselves into her mind. A plane crash was an accident, not murder. Even if the pilot was drunk or the charter company got lazy with its maintenance, those actions didn't qualify as murder. Manslaughter, maybe. But not murder.

For the millionth time in the last two months, she replayed the crash video in her mind. A teenager had been filming his buddies doing donuts on their dirt bikes when the jet screamed into sight over their heads. The plane plummeted from the sky so fast that the video needed to be slowed down for the shape of the jet to be discernible, but what came next required no manipulation. Flames erupted. Smoke plumed upward. The explosive concussion of the impact drowned out the terrified voices of the teenagers.

The fire. The smoke. The anguish.

Her stomach churned. Her ears rang. She took an uneven breath. The fire and the smoke, she knew of those from the video footage. The anguish she'd imagined, in vivid and horrifying detail, for weeks afterward every time she closed her eyes. Footage of the crash site taken hours after the accident revealed debris scattered over farmland, smoke curling up from the twisted and shattered wreckage. According to the authorities, the plane depressurized for unknown reasons, leaving everyone on board unconscious or dead when the plane ran out of fuel and smashed into the earth. The bodies were burned beyond recognition.

Grandpa had worked as a neuroscientist, first at a university, and later for a private research foundation based in California. His later work formed part of a secret project, maybe for the government, though he wasn't allowed to tell her anything about it. His area of expertise had centered on consciousness research, the same topic his daughter, Grace's mother, studied as well. Christine Powell followed in her father's footsteps, to the point that she left her university post to join the same secret project where Edward McLean worked. Grace's father, Mark, had been a computer scientist specializing in artificial intelligence. He too joined the mysterious project in California.

Grace knew nothing about the work her grandfather and parents did. She felt relatively secure, however, in her belief that no one murdered any of them. Why should anyone want to kill three scientists who shared a passion for neurology? The man walking toward her must be crazy. Edward McLean was not murdered.

She suspected the mystery man was nuts from the get-go, but she came to the meeting anyway. Maybe a tiny part of her needed to believe the plane crash and auto accident happened for a reason, more than bad karma or pilot error or a manufacturing defect. She needed a reason, a tangible shred of evidence, a crumb trail to guide her out of the woods and into the open space of clarity.

The man slid onto the bench opposite her. He clasped his hands on the table.

He must be nuts. But she wanted to believe his claim. The conflict within set her stomach to roiling.

"I assume," she said, waving his note at him, "you're the one who gave me this. Would you care to explain?"

"You're Grace Powell?"

"Naturally. And you are?"

"Brian Kellogg," he said, examining his hands. "I worked with your grandfather."

"Did you know my parents?"

"No, they died before I joined the project."

Grandpa never mentioned a Brian Kellogg to her. He hadn't mentioned any of his colleagues. Whenever she had asked him about his work, he'd snapped at her to mind her own business or hung up on her after a curt brush-off. His odd behavior started after her parents' deaths seven months ago, so at first, she dismissed it as grief-related except it got worse rather than better as the months passed. She struggled to understand the change in him, to no avail. After her parents' deaths, he was the only person she could talk to, which made his withdrawal from her all the more painful. She needed a connection to life, through someone she trusted. Edward McLean had provided that link.

Until he cut her out of his life.

A month before his death, he'd canceled a trip to visit her. She'd tried calling him to ask what happened but got no answer at his home or office. She left messages that he never returned. His sole response came in the form of a terse message on her answering machine, left two days before his death. In the message, he warned her not to call him because he would be unavailable, and he had nothing to say anyhow. Besides, he'd said in a rough voice, she needed to learn to get by without his support. At the time, she took the statement as an insult. After his death, however, she wondered if he knew he was about to die.

She had many questions. Brian Kellogg might hold the answers in his twitchy brain.

He looked to be in his mid-thirties, although his brown hair and tanned skin made him appear younger. He was trim, not skinny. Thick eyebrows sheltered his caramel-colored eyes. He wore a heavy watch, the kind with two time zones and fifteen alarms, and he frequently checked its digital readout. He wore gray slacks and a white shirt with a gray tie loosened to accommodate his unbuttoned collar. Despite his one slip into the casual, his collar was starched to concrete.

She looked under the table, pretending to drop her fork.

His pants had sharp creases ironed into them, and he'd double-tied his shoelaces.

Grace straightened in her seat. Shadows darkened the skin under Kellogg's eyes. His hair looked odd as if he'd glued Barbie's fur coat on top of his head. Men. They just had to have something resembling hair on their heads or they'd hide in a closet. She'd allocated all of two minutes to detangling her locks and pinning them back with a barrette. Looks hardly seemed important when she was losing her mind.

Possibly losing her mind.

A crash echoed through the diner.

Kellogg jumped.

As laughter erupted from the back of the diner, a waitress stuttered apologies for dropping a glass.

Kellogg exhaled, massaging his hands.

"Mr. Kellogg," Grace said, "are you all right?"

"Sorry. I'm tired and… anxious. If they find out I've come here to see you, I'm dead."

His tone resounded with finality. She couldn't believe anyone would kill over her. She simply wasn't that important.

"They killed Edward," he said. "Dr. McLean. He was going to expose them."

"Expose who?"

"He found out they'd been lying to him. So they had him killed. The crash was a cover."

"*Who*, Mr. Kellogg?"

"Call me Brian."

She slammed her fist on the table. "Who are 'they'? I'm not psychic, and I hate riddles."

An odd, almost confused look flashed across his face. He seemed to be waiting for her to say something, but when she didn't, he cleared his throat and muttered, "This isn't easy for me."

"Not my problem."

"I'm sorry, I'm doing it again. Please forgive me."

She stood halfway.

Kellogg grabbed her wrist.

She glared at him.

His face reddened as he released her arm.

"I don't know who they are," he said. "Edward never told me and I never asked. All I know is what I found out afterward."

She plopped onto the bench.

Afterward. After Grandpa died. She swallowed a glacial lump. She'd had two months to get used to the idea she wouldn't see her grandfather again. She boxed it all up in the back of her mind, sealed with five layers of duct tape, blanketed in steel, chained to the farthest reaches of her psyche. Now Brian Kellogg tore through her security measures and ripped the box open. She felt naked.

"Edward was going to Washington," he said. "To talk to a senator he knew. He had evidence. He was determined to stop the experiments."

"What experiments?"

"It's hard to explain."

She fisted her hands, suppressing the urge to strangle him. He lured her here with a sensational statement that he had yet to explain or prove.

"Try," she said. "Or I'm walking out that door."

His gaze flitted across the diner, his head bobbing with a motion reminiscent of a gazelle listening for lions. "Not here. It's too public."

A waitress, approaching the table, asked if they wanted to order.

Kellogg threw a panicked expression at Grace, who batted it back to him with a roll of her eyes.

The waitress tapped a pen on her order pad.

Kellogg sat robot-stiff, lips compressed.

If they didn't order something, they might get kicked out of the diner. It wasn't a public meeting hall. Grace ordered a chocolate malt and curly fries.

The waitress scribbled the order on her pad and trotted away.

"Why did you want me here?" Grace asked. "If you're not going to tell me anything, I mean."

Kellogg leaned forward. Sweat rolled over his temples, down his cheeks. "Edward was murdered. I can prove it. I have evidence."

"Show me."

"It's at my motel room."

She blew a breath out through her nostrils, certain that flames erupted from them.

He shifted in his seat. "He was dead before the plane hit the ground. Everybody on board was. They were murdered. The crash destroyed the physical evidence. The investigators identified pieces of all the bodies, except Edward's. Wasn't much to identify."

"Nobody knows if they were dead or unconscious."

"I know."

"You claim to have evidence."

"That's not the main reason I came. I have to warn you."

"About…"

"They want you."

Grace tapped her boot on the floor in a drum-roll cadence. She'd had enough of hearing about the nebulous "them." She should leave now, before Kellogg told her "they" were aliens from the planet Beta Zappa, come to Earth to kidnap humans for use as sex slaves.

"Nobody," she said, "would waste time coming after me."

"They think Edward gave you something."

"Unless you count DNA, he gave me nothing."

With a sigh, Kellogg launched into a stammering, unspecific monologue about an "item" Grandpa had left her, something vital, something worth killing for, something "destined to change humanity forever." Whatever the supposed item was. Kellogg offered no answer, of course.

If she believed him, which she did not, she had to wonder why Grandpa chose her to bear his secret. She didn't deserve the honor of dying to save the world. Or to save a cockroach. According to everyone else on the planet, she was delusional, not heroic.

This was insane. No one murdered Grandpa.

She checked her watch. She'd wasted fifteen minutes listening to this garbage.

The scarecrow man.

No, that incident had no connection to Kellogg. One nut accosting her did not signify a conspiracy. Besides, Kellogg's assertion of murder was too much. If she accepted it, her notions about life and justice and security would vanish, like shooting stars.

"Sorry," she said. "I don't buy any of this."

Kellogg reached into his pocket.

Grace tensed. An image of him withdrawing a gun and firing a round into her head flashed in her mind.

He pulled out a pen.

She almost laughed.

Grabbing a napkin, he scribbled on it. "This is where I'm staying. If you decide to believe, come by. I'll be waiting."

Kellogg handed her the napkin.

Then he got up and hurried out of the diner.

Chapter Seven

After leaving the diner, Grace headed for the Oak Hills Mall, the one concession Lassiter Falls had made to consumerism. Five years old, the mall housed the usual novelty shops, department stores, and jewelers.

She needed time to think. The encounter with Kellogg renewed her sense that her life operated by someone else's design—whether that someone was a human being or the force of fate—and infused her with a new sensation of foreboding. She needed people around her, without the obligation of talking to anyone or pretending to care about their problems while they yammered at her as if she were a therapist at a free clinic. She needed anonymity in a crowd.

College kids ambled down the corridors, chatting loudly, listening to music through headphones. Older people speed-walked amid the throngs.

As Grace meandered past the novelty stores and jewelry chains, she remained aware of the noise around her even while tuning it out. The cacophony calmed her. It blocked her thoughts and drowned out the anxiety. No worries about her loss of sanity. Just a background of laughter, talking, and the ka-chunk of vending machines dispensing their wares.

She almost felt alive.

A pack of kids slammed into her. Nodding in response to their apologies, she veered toward the escalators. Part of her envied those kids. They had vitality, innocence, possibilities. She was no more than seven years their senior, yet she felt much older. Ancient. Half buried. Suffocating.

As she stepped onto the down escalator, out of the corner of her eye she noticed a man stepping onto the track behind her. He moved onto the step directly above her. Great, a tailgater. She hopped down two steps to get a little distance from the creep.

He moved down two steps.

She hopped four steps, taking them two at a time.

He hesitated, then closed the gap and stopped one step behind her.

Grace glanced back at the creep. Her heart thudded. *Him.* The shadow man.

No, it couldn't be.

She checked again. Him. Definitely.

"Don't look at me," he said.

His voice was deep, soft, and… familiar. Ridiculous. This entire situation was ridiculous. Men could not appear out of and disappear into thin air. Either she was insane or at this moment she was lying in a coma at a hospital somewhere, suffering bizarre and disturbing dreams.

"Why are you acting this way?" he demanded, though his tone stayed calm.

Her instincts urged silence. Never knew what might set off a stalker. "Hello" might be the word that triggered a killing spree that started with her. She had no desire to get her throat slashed today. Tomorrow, maybe.

He let out a sharp sigh. "I know you can see me."

Of course she could see him. Everyone could. Right?

"Say something, dammit," he hissed, the nonchalance vaporizing.

Now her hallucinations cursed at her. Jeez, her mental state must've deteriorated at lightning speed for her mind to create visions that swore at her. Or perhaps this was her mind's way of dealing with anger at herself. She could take a little verbal abuse from her own psyche. Except this didn't feel like a hallucination.

Well, did hallucinations ever *feel* like hallucinations?

She fixed her gaze on the bottom of the escalator. *Almost there.*

"Fine, don't talk," the man said. He leaned over her shoulder to murmur in her ear. "Just listen. You have to be careful. They're after you."

"Leave me alone or I'll scream," she said in an equally soft voice, and instantly regretted speaking. But she couldn't help it. The guy was ticking her off. Hallucination or not, he needed a serious dressing-down.

"Someone has to warn you," he said.

"That's novel. A stalker warning his victim."

Each time he spoke, with his lips so close to her ear, his breaths whispered across her skin and sent a shiver rippling down her spine—an oddly stimulating shiver that didn't feel like fear.

She ought to move down another step. Her muscles refused to obey.

He sighed, the warmth of his exhalation setting off a flurry of goosebumps. "I'm not a stalker."

She laughed. The tone echoed hollow and stark in her ears.

"They're coming for you," he said. "Be careful."

She twisted her torso to face him. "If I hear the word 'them' one more time—"

"Sh." He tilted his head, apparently concentrating on a sound only he heard. "I have to go."

"Wait."

He vanished.

A blast of air tossed her hair into her face. She brushed the locks aside. He had disappeared, like a light winking off, gone faster than the speed of a spinning atom.

During their brief conversation, something inside her had changed inexplicably. The notion of a shadow man no longer bothered her, she realized. He disappeared at will. Couldn't everybody? Maybe not everybody vanished, but in a bizarre way, she accepted that this man, whoever he was, possessed that ability. It seemed perfectly natural.

Shit.

The notion did make sense if he was, after all, nothing but a hallucination. A part of her believed that, but another part believed he existed as a real person, made of flesh and blood and bone. The split in her psyche gave her a stomachache.

And the start of another migraine.

He stepped off the escalator. People meandered through the concourse, chatting back and forth, window-shopping, oblivious of the supernatural happenings around them. No one had seen the man on the escalator. No one else *could* see him. Her mystery man seemed unsurprised that she could see him even when no one else could. She avoided wondering why.

But she'd felt his breath on her. Warm. Tantalizing.

If no one else could see him, how on earth could she feel him?

The concourse split around a fountain, dividing into three walkways. Grace chose one at random and picked up her pace. She wanted to hide, anywhere, get out of sight where no one would find her. When she was little, she used to hide up in the branches of an old oak tree in the backyard of her family's home. She'd found safety in that tree. Camouflaged by the leaves, alone with her thoughts, she would sit cocooned in a blanket of greenery. The perfume of the flowering bushes below calmed her nerves.

In a mall, she wasn't likely to find an oak tree.

Ahead, a department store entrance gaped wide as a dragon's mouth. She hurried through the entrance, past rows of sofas and dining-room sets, through the electronics department, up the escalator to the second floor. She pushed through aisles of clothing. A saleswoman thrust a bottle of makeup in her face while blathering on about its benefits for her skin. Shaking her head, Grace rushed past the woman.

A row of fitting rooms lined the far wall. A retail version of caves. Better than a tree. She veered toward the fitting rooms.

A cashier observed her. The girl canted her head in a cat-like expression of curiosity.

Grace halted. She couldn't jump into a fitting room to hide. The cashier would get suspicious and probably assume Grace was shoplifting. She needed an excuse.

Her hands trembled. Her face tingled. *Calm down*, she admonished herself. Squeezing her hands into fists, she took a deep breath.

The cashier stared at her. The curious expression tightened into concern.

Grace relaxed her hands. With as much composure as she could muster, she strolled between two racks of blouses. She pretended to examine the seam on one blouse. Glancing sideways, she watched the cashier turn away to pick up a stack of jeans. The girl carried the garments to a group of display shelves where she began to refold and stack them.

Grace snatched two blouses off the rack and took them into the first fitting room. After pulling the curtain closed, she hung the blouses on the provided hooks and collapsed onto the bench. After taking off her suit jacket, she drew her knees up and wrapped her arms around them. Her short-sleeve shirt exposed her skin to the cool air.

Her life had flipped upside-down and rolled sideways. She might've believed she'd lost her mind, except for a few pieces of evidence to the contrary. First, there was the sincerity of Brian Kellogg. He said someone murdered her grandfather and swore that he had proof, which he would give her when she contacted him at his motel. Her main reason for thinking she might've cracked up was the shadow man. Yet a real, physical force warped her bedroom door. She didn't imagine that event. The cut on her hand had been real too as evidenced by the blood on the bandage.

Something was happening. She must find out what.

She ought to see Brian Kellogg. Find out what he knew. If the whole thing was a trick to lure her into his motel room for a Rohypnol cocktail, she'd castrate him. She'd had enough lies and evasion.

As she rested her forehead on her knees, the smell of clean cotton fabric filled her nostrils. She would interrogate Kellogg tomorrow. Right now, she needed a rest. Oh lord, did she need it.

Her eyelids fluttered shut. One by one, her muscles slackened. The murmur of the ventilation system lulled her into a kind of trance where all thoughts and worries slipped from her mind. A glorious peace settled over her.

The curtain fluttered.

She raised her head.

He stood before her, inside the tiny booth, his body a foot away from hers.

She sprang to her feet.

The toes of her shoes bumped into the toes of his. Her bosom grazed his chest. She found herself literally face to face with the man, though she was several inches shorter than he was. Her nose brushed across his chin as she wobbled on her feet. He bent his head to look down at her, and she couldn't resist tilting her head back so she could meet his gaze.

He looked like an angel. A tall, muscular angel.

She couldn't move. His eyes, with those dark pupils ringed in shimmering sapphire, mesmerized her. The irises glowed like nothing she'd ever seen before. Without meaning to, but unable to stop herself, she leaned into him. The heat of his body radiated into her. His gaze held hers as he lifted his arms to cradle her in them, and everything inside her tensed in anticipation. The sensation wasn't entirely unpleasant, but it was tinged with a need she didn't understand. A desire to stay close to him. To take comfort from his presence.

He spoke softly. "I'm not leaving until you hear me out."

"I'm listening," she said, unsure of how she managed to speak.

"You're in danger. Very nasty people want something they think you have."

"I have nothing. Unless they want my bad credit."

"They want a flash drive."

She furrowed her brows. "What?"

"A flash drive, a kind of external memory card that plugs into a computer. Edward left it for you."

Brian Kellogg had mentioned an unspecified thing that her grandfather supposedly left for her. Now this man, whoever he was, mentioned a flash drive.

She pushed away from him. The spell had broken, and that delicious tension evaporated the instant she severed their physical contact. She felt a pang of disappointment as if she'd just given up something she wanted badly. But what?

He reached for her, trying to wrap her in his arms once again.

The tension rose inside her.

Oh hell no. She did not want this. Whatever this was.

She slapped both hands on his chest and shoved him backward. He stumbled, bumped into the wall, then righted himself. His mouth quirked with what looked like annoyance.

He was annoyed? Screw that.

She folded her arms over her chest. "I know what a flash drive is, but I don't have one. My grandfather left me nothing."

Except for a cryptic phone message that had sounded like a warning. Of what, she didn't know. Maybe he'd known this man would come for her.

"He must've hidden it," her stalker said. "Someplace where only you would find it. Whatever you do, don't give it to anyone. Destroy it."

"Yes, *sir*. Any other orders, commander?"

The hint of a smile flickered on his face. He raised a hand to touch her cheek with one finger.

She jerked backward. Her legs hit the bench, buckling her knees. She threw her arms back to catch herself, but her hands slipped.

He grasped her arms, steadying her. "Careful."

His hands felt warm, the skin surprisingly soft. He was too close again. Much too close. She felt the heat of him on her skin, smelled his masculine scent—

She shook off his hands. "Who are you?"

"Listen to me," he said, pulling her closer. "Don't trust anyone. You have no idea how badly these people want that flash drive."

Her heart pounded. Indefinable feelings coursed through her body like electrical currents.

"Destroy the flash drive," he said. "It's the only way."

He held still for a moment. His fingers encircled her arms in a firm yet gentle grasp. His eyes locked on hers. She sensed a familiarity in his gaze, akin to a half-remembered dream. Her lips parted as her brain fumbled, unable to hold on to a single thought.

Without a word, he released her.

And then he vanished.

THE OLD PONTIAC GOT HER HOME, THAT MUCH GRACE KNEW, THOUGH the details of the drive blurred into one big slab of missing time. They called it highway hypnosis. She remembered reading the term in a magazine or newspaper. Her mind shifted into automatic pilot, operating her muscles without her awareness of the actions. That was how she arrived home with no memory of the trip.

It was creepy.

She wanted to hide. She needed answers. No one vanished at will. No one vanished, period. She'd taken physics in college and understood the laws of nature. A mass didn't go poof without releasing some kind of energy.

The gusts of wind.

Was a burst of air enough to account for the energy of a vanishing human being? Damned if she knew. And she'd bet even the top scientists in the world would be damned if they knew.

They'd call her nuts anyway.

Slamming the car door behind her, she scuffled across the driveway and down the concrete path to the front door. As she slipped inside the house, easing the door shut after her, the old weariness seeped into her body once more. She wanted to sleep until everyone and everything she knew crumbled into dust and a fresh, sane world sprouted from the remains.

A new world without inexplicable phenomena. A place where she might feel normal and competent, both in her mind and in real life. As she turned the corner into the hallway, she avoided glancing into the kitchen. If the shadow man awaited her there, she did not want to know about it. Her brain needed rest, not vague warnings of impending peril delivered to her by an anonymous stranger.

An attractive anonymous stranger.

The memory of his scent filled her nostrils. Her skin tingled as if his warmth still kissed her flesh. From deep inside her soul arose a sense of familiarity, of memories long forgotten, of things she ought to recall but that stayed buried inside her. Each time she saw the shadow man, she experienced this sensation of knowing but not remembering. She knew him. Yet he was a stranger.

She did not know him. Her life was an open book, of the boring variety that no one wanted to read unless they were stuck in a dentist's office and her life was the only reading material available in the waiting room. The tale of her life, at least thus far, excluded all adventure and risk-taking—and certainly all romance. She'd never met a man like her seemingly invisible stalker.

Except she might have. Her Swiss-cheese brain left big enough holes to fit even a tall, muscular man.

Down the hallway she trotted, ducking through the open bedroom door. Without thinking about it, she kicked the door shut behind her. The latch refused to engage, thanks to the door's warped center, the aftereffect of the inexplicable change in air pressure last night.

The door creaked inward.

Grace grabbed the chair that sat by the window and dragged it toward the door. She jammed the chair under the knob to brace the door shut. No barricade would keep out the shadow man. She knew that. He appeared anytime he liked, wherever he liked, regardless of privacy or courtesy. Maybe the barricade would keep out "them," whoever they might be, or at least slow them down to give her time for a prayer before they sliced-and-diced her.

Tired. She was so tired.

Crawling into bed, she settled onto her side with her knees drawn up close to her belly. Within minutes, sleep overwhelmed her.

She dreamed of the faceless man. In a voice both inhuman and intimate, he urged her to stop fighting, to give in, to let him have what he wanted. She had no clue what that thing was, but she knew he wanted it. His need infected her, hot and dark and cloying.

Give in, give up.

More than anything, she wanted to obey the command. She wanted to give herself over to him because that would be so much easier. So much simpler. Sink into the depths of his need and lose herself in the scalding darkness.

Give in.

She twitched awake. Her heart hammered against her rib cage. She glanced around the room, certain she was not alone. Yet she was. It had been a dream, nothing more. Dreams could seem so real, but they weren't. She couldn't keep fighting the shadows in her dreams. She lacked both the time and the energy for it, and she needed all her strength to battle the real shadows that lurked outside. She must insulate herself from them.

She sat up. Them. Who? Her head ached from thinking about it.

The bedside clock gave the time as four in the morning. She flopped back onto the bed.

For the next three hours, she slept in fits and starts. The dream returned each time she dozed, the same as before, like a movie played over and over and over. The man's voice echoed through her mind, low and distant.

Give up. You want to.

Like hell.

If they wanted her to give up and give in, they'd get a serious shock. She would not abandon herself to insanity or collapse on the floor in a shivering, weeping lump. She would fight—until the invisible forces were defeated. Or until she was defeated.

One way or another, this craziness would end.

CHAPTER EIGHT

HER BOOTS MADE A SOFT CLOPPING SOUND ON THE PAVEMENT AS Grace marched down the sidewalk. Yesterday, she'd walked with slumped shoulders and bowed head. Today, she held herself straight and tall, or at least as tall as she could get, being of average height. Something inside her had shifted. Doubts still niggled at her, but much less insistently than before.

At four o'clock this morning, she'd experienced a revelation. She was not insane.

Despite sleeping less than well, she felt energized. She had a mission. Find Brian Kellogg, see the evidence he claimed to have, and evaluate his claims about her grandfather's death. If the claim proved credible, she'd follow wherever the evidence led her.

Okay, so she had a mission but no plan. A mission was a starting point.

Which was far more than she'd had yesterday.

As for the shadow man who cornered her in a fitting room... Well, she'd sort that out later. At least today she had a destination.

The Bed & Bath Inn.

It was the cheapest motel in the vicinity of Lassiter Falls, situated along the interstate to take advantage of exhausted motorists. Though Grace had never patronized the establishment, from the outside it looked like a dingy, beat-up building divided into tiny rooms.

A chill shimmied down her spine.

Grace stopped. The sensation of being watched lingered, though the chill had dissipated. She twisted her head around to glance over her shoulder.

No one there.

She had wanted to drive to the motel. Then she realized she'd forgotten to gas up the car yesterday and it probably didn't have the juice to make it the ten miles or so to the interstate. The migraine had impaired her thinking, or maybe her encounter with the shadow man left her dazed. She'd intended to stop at a gas station on the way home. She forgot.

That was why this morning she found herself walking to the nearest bus stop.

Someone is watching.

The thought burst into her mind. She stood there for a moment, facing forward again, and let the thought sink in as she listened and waited. Nothing happened. No stalkers leaped out from behind bushes. No footfalls clapped behind her. She found no logical reason to believe she was being tracked. Still, she patted her purse to feel the hard outline of her .357 Magnum revolver inside, snug in the holster sewn into the purse.

Yet as she started off down the sidewalk again, the uneasy feeling stayed with her. It haunted the recesses of her mind even after she boarded the bus. By the time the bus turned onto Main Street a few minutes later, the sensation had lessened but not disappeared.

The bus delivered Grace into town amid a cloud of oily smoke and a throng of people who looked as hopeless and helpless as she'd felt for the past two months, until her pre-dawn epiphany. Maybe she would sink back into the malaise later when Brian Kellogg turned out to be delusional and her shadow man proved to be a hallucination.

No. She was not crazy. If it took every ounce of strength she possessed to keep her head above the morass, she would never again allow herself to drown in a quagmire of self-doubt.

Never.

At least not today. At least not until lack of a decent night's sleep caught up with her.

Stop it.

The bus deposited her in front of the truck stop that hunkered at the base of the freeway on-ramp. The two-block trek from the truck stop to the motel, along the edge of the on-ramp, gave her time to organize her thoughts. She tried to organize her thoughts, anyway. What could she say to Kellogg? What *should* she say? "Gimme the damn evidence right now, you scumbag" seemed inappropriate, though it suited her mood. She was sick of feeling helpless and hopeless. She wanted to prolong the empowered feeling she'd woken up with this morning. Yet the closer she got to the motel, the less empowered and invigorated she felt.

Damn.

Just as she veered off the sidewalk and into the motel parking lot, she glimpsed a shape darting out of the ditch on the other side of the on-ramp.

Grace spun around to face the road.

The scarecrow man rushed across the single lane, heading straight for her.

She tore open the purse's main compartment, seized the revolver, and whipped it out. Leveling the gun at the scarecrow man, she shouted for him to stop.

He jerked as if she'd shot him. She hadn't. Her finger wasn't even over the trigger but resting on the barrel above it.

His face contorted into a frightened expression. He mumbled to himself, the words indistinct. When his gaze fell on the gun, his eyes bulged. The poor little loon seemed more scared than she was.

To hell with this. She lowered the gun to her side, aimed it at the ground, and waved her free hand in a casual greeting. "Hi, it's me. Still want to talk?"

His lips worked soundlessly.

"Well?" she asked.

"Not here," he said. "They see. They know."

"Here or nowhere."

He hesitated. "All right."

Dragging his feet, he moved off the road and halted half a dozen feet away, to her left and slightly in front of her. He cringed and flitted his gaze back and forth as if watching for demons from the fiftieth dimension to suddenly appear and suck him into their hell-world. He paced along the road's periphery but maintained a discreet distance between them. Fine with her. She wanted to stay clear of him too.

"I'm only trying to warn you," he said. "Someone has to."

Someone has to warn you. The shadow man had said that to her yesterday.

The scarecrow took a step toward her. "He tries to stop me. But I push him out. Free. For a while."

"Who tries to stop you?"

He bit his lip so hard it turned white and spat one word. "Them."

"Who is 'them'?"

"The—ones. Who want me. And you. He tries to make me do things for them. Bad things. I don't want to. I want to help. Not hurt. Never hurt." He choked back a sob. "Please don't let him take me. Please, please, please."

His voice rose to a crescendo as he repeated the word please a dozen more times, faster and faster with each iteration. His cheeks flushed. His body trembled.

She must calm him down before he lashed out, enmeshed as he had become in a frenzy of syllables. She had no desire to become the object of his terror. Fear could easily shift into violence, especially in someone as deranged as this little man.

"I know you want to help," she said in a soothing tone. "I believe you."

He choked, coughed, choked again. His breaths came shallow and fast.

"I believe you," she repeated. "I understand."

"Understand? You do?"

"Yes. What's your name?"

He looked at the ground. "Andrew."

Henry Winston told her this man's name was Adam Hansen. Yeah, she needed to fight hard to control her shock at realizing Winston lied to her.

"You wanted to warn me," she said. "What about?"

"They're after you now. *The man with evil eyes. Darkness inside.* His name…" Andrew thumped the heel of his hand on his forehead. "Can't remember. All fuzzy."

She waited, unable to think of a thing to say.

Andrew smacked his hands to his temples. Squeezing his eyes shut, he rocked back and forth on his heels. "Fuzzy, so fuzzy. Must clear."

Grace took a step backward and tightened her grip on the gun. "Why are they after me?"

"What Dr. McLean gave you. They want it."

"Dr. McLean. My grandfather."

"Uh-huh."

This loony little man said the same things Brian Kellogg had said, that Grandpa gave her something, an object that strangers wanted to steal. The shadow man claimed it was a flash drive. If so, she had no clue what the drive might hold. Maybe she shouldn't assume this lunatic could piece together enough coherent thoughts to tell her the truth. She should mistrust him—and the shadow man.

Unless the three of them worked together, in a conspiracy to confuse and irritate her, she had to believe them. Three people told her Grandpa left her something.

Andrew thrashed his head. "Don't give it to them. Don't."

If she ever found "it," she would give the thing to no one. She wouldn't destroy it either. Whether it was a flash drive or something else, the object must contain the answers she sought. She needed those answers, desperately.

Whether or not Andrew could assist her, he most assuredly needed help himself. Maybe she could help him. Together they might shed light on the shadows.

How had he found her here? Had he followed her? That might explain why she'd felt like someone was watching her ever since she left the house. She supposed he could've snuck onto the bus after she climbed aboard. This cloak-and-dagger stuff was new to her, after all. She had no training in counterespionage, or whatever spies called it when they tried to evade other spies.

Checking the surroundings for strangers with "evil eyes," she slipped the gun inside her purse, tucking it into the holster. She had to trust someone. Since she would no way trust Henry Winston, that left her with a choice between the shadow man and this twitchy nutball.

She'd take the nutball.

"Andrew," she said, "will you come with me to meet someone?"

He wrapped his arms around his torso like a self-made straitjacket. "I don't know."

"Do you trust me?"

"Yes."

"Then come with me, Andrew. Maybe I can help you."

"Go. With you. Yes."

Turning away from him, she marched across the parking lot. The sound of footsteps behind her made Grace look back.

Andrew had fallen into step behind her. He clutched his arms, head bowed, shoulders hunched.

She slipped her hand into her purse until her fingers grazed the gun. Safe. Maybe.

As she approached the door to Kellogg's room, her stomach twisted into a pretzel knot. A pang erupted behind her eyes. When she raised a hand to knock on the door, the pang stabbed deeper into her brain. God no, she could not handle another migraine. Not now.

Andrew shuffled up behind her, staying an arm's length away.

Hand hovering in midair, she hesitated. Took a deep breath. Let it out slowly. Repeated the deep breathing twice more. The pang faded. Her stomach still burned with acid, but at least she'd staved off the potential migraine.

She rapped on the door twice.

Grace had never gone inside one of these rooms before. She had noticed the Bed & Bath Inn many times as she drove past and read the sign advertising "a cheap, clean place to sleep." The sign made no mention of cable TV, room service, or other amenities. The bulbs inside the motel's sign flickered at night, and in the daytime, the sign looked cracked and faded. Graffiti slashed across the doors to several rooms.

Icy worms slithered inside her gut.

Behind her, Andrew sniffled.

What a pair they made. She rapped on the door again.

Kellogg's voice came through the scarred metal. "Yes?"

"It's Grace Powell."

The lock clicked. Kellogg swung the door inward. He motioned for her to go inside.

When she stepped into the room, Andrew started after her.

Kellogg's mouth dropped open.

Grace started to speak. "This is—"

"Andrew Haley." Kellogg ushered the pitiful scarecrow into the room and shut the door. To Andrew, he said, "What are you doing here?"

Andrew's lower lip quivered.

"You know him?" Grace asked.

Kellogg nodded. "We both worked with Edward."

"What?" Grace felt a jolt of dizziness, as if the earth beneath her feet had tilted. "Andrew worked with my grandfather?"

"Uh, yeah." Kellogg guided the other man to the bed. "Why don't you watch TV, Andrew?"

"TV," Andrew said, perching on the bed's edge. "He's not in the TV. Good."

Kellogg walked to the television and punched the power button. A talk show appeared on the screen. Two women were screaming and pulling each other's hair, their profanity bleeped out while the host nodded and gestured, his expression laden with contained glee.

"Couldn't you put on something calmer?" Grace asked.

Kellogg switched the channel. Mickey Mouse cavorted with Donald Duck.

Andrew giggled.

Crossing the room in two steps, Kellogg opened the door and pushed Grace outside. He followed, shutting the door but not latching it. Traffic on the interstate rumbled in the background.

"Where did you find him?" Kellogg asked.

"He found me."

Kellogg stared at her.

Grace stared right back at him.

"That's not possible," he said. "Andrew's been locked up in a mental ward for almost a year. He couldn't escape."

"Obviously, he could."

"He doesn't have the capacity to plan ahead. He can't remember things. Not anymore."

"I don't have to justify myself to you, Mr. Kellogg," she hissed through clenched teeth. "*You* contacted *me*."

He averted his gaze to the pavement. "Sorry. I'm nervous."

Scared to death, she would've said. But if he wanted to play down his fear, she couldn't blame him. After all the strange things she'd seen in the past two days, she liked the notion of chopping the fear into bite-size bits too. She'd had enough riddles and evasion, though. She wanted answers. Now.

"You said my grandfather was murdered," she said. "Prove it."

"It's hard to explain."

A groan escaped her throat. She clenched her teeth and bit the inside of her lip, tasting the tang of blood. Her jaw ached. Massaging the joint, she tried to relax the muscles. Though she sympathized with Kellogg, she'd slug him if he didn't produce evidence that supported his claims. Soon. Like in the next five seconds.

She forced a less-than-pleasant smile. "Please try."

"I've made you angry." He slumped his shoulders. "I apologize. But I… I know you won't believe me. Sometimes I can't believe it."

"Try me."

"We—Edward, me, Andrew, and others—worked in a research facility in California. A pharmaceutical company funded the project, or so I was told. Publicly, we were studying how the brain works so the company could develop new and better drugs to treat mental disorders."

"Publicly?"

"Only a tiny part of the facility was devoted to that research."

"And the rest of you were studying…"

"Parapsychology." The wind gusted, and he paused to adjust his hairpiece. "Psychic phenomena. You know, telepathy and the like."

"Why would a pharmaceutical company care about that?"

"I'm a subordinate. They tell me what I need to know, nothing more. The area I worked in wasn't strictly related to parapsychology, but it had relevant applications. I studied hypnosis as a means of manipulating a person's thoughts and self-hypnosis as a means of inducing certain psychic phenomena."

He spoke so quickly that her brain whirred at high speed yet failed to interpret the meaning of each word before Kellogg launched into the next.

"What does that mean?" she asked.

"Oh God." His mouth dropped opened once more. His body tensed. His eyes focused on something beyond her face.

She looked around but saw nothing. "What's wrong?"

"Get away," he hissed at her. "Go!"

Grace shook her head.

With both hands, he shoved her backward.

She stumbled, nearly landed on her butt, then found her balance.

Kellogg choked, his eyes widening. He pawed at his throat. His tongue lolled out of his mouth as he gasped and clawed at the air in front of his face and his knees buckled.

Grace rushed forward to grab his arms.

In the instant her fingers brushed his sleeve, his feet were hoisted off the ground, seemingly by an invisible force. He dangled in midair as if hanging by a noose. Saliva gurgled from his lips. He thrashed his legs, clutching at his throat.

She grabbed his abdomen and yanked him down. Despite an effort that choked the breath out of her, his body refused to move. He hung there, stiff and flailing, sputtering and grunting.

His body went limp. He crumpled onto the concrete walkway.

She collapsed with him, entangled in his limbs. For a moment she just lay there on top of him, too stunned to think and too out of breath to move. The second her strength returned, she extricated herself from his arms and legs.

She felt for a pulse in his neck. Nothing. She bent over him, pressing her ear to his chest. No sign of breathing or a heartbeat.

Brian Kellogg was dead.

He couldn't be dead. She jammed her finger into his neck again. Nothing.

Grace slumped against the wall of the motel. Though it was the last thing she wanted to do, she raked her gaze over Kellogg's corpse. A person did not spontaneously choke to death. Something on his body must offer a clue to the real cause of his death. Of course, she was no medical examiner. What did she know about determining how someone had died?

Then she saw it. A series of bruises had formed on his neck. Two big purple marks discolored his throat near the larynx. while smaller bruises dotted the sides of his neck. The contusions resembled the size and contour of fingertips.

Someone had strangled him.

Impossible.

The man had levitated half a foot off the ground. He'd grasped at his throat and wheezed, clearly struggling to breathe. Now bruises had formed. Exactly like someone had strangled him.

Kellogg had studied psychic phenomena. Could someone have used extrasensory mental abilities to kill him? The idea sounded ludicrous, but so did the idea of a man vanishing into thin air. She could believe almost anything now, or at least consider almost anything.

Frozen wide open, Kellogg's eyes stared outward with the blankness of death. With the tips of two fingers, she eased the lids down over his eyes.

Strands of hair stuck out from beneath his hairpiece. Hair under a toupee? No, the hairpiece must've shifted position. A man wouldn't wear a toupee if he had natural hair.

Grace tugged on the hairpiece. It slipped off in her hand.

Thick hair covered Brian Kellogg's head.

The hairpiece lay stiff in her palm. She flipped it over. A key was taped to the underside. Prying the tape off, she removed the key and held it close to her face. A number was engraved into the metal. The key might unlock a post office box, a locker at a bus station, anything.

She stuffed the key into her pants pocket.

On the interstate, sirens ululated.

Two police cars sped toward the motel, tires squealing as they swerved from the freeway onto an off-ramp. Within half a minute, they would careen into the parking lot.

Brian Kellogg's body rested at her feet, his neck bearing the signs of strangulation. Another tenant of the inn must've seen her with Kellogg, witnessed his death, and called 911. The police were coming for her. She knew that. Even if the witness remained anonymous, the cops would find her standing over Kellogg's body with no evidence that anyone besides her and the dead man had been in the area.

Shit.

Grace threw open the door to Kellogg's room.

Andrew was gone.

No, he couldn't have left. He would've walked right past her and, despite the chaos of Kellogg's attack, she would've noticed.

Someone whimpered.

Andrew. The sound came from the other side of the room, if eight feet away counted as the other side. She trotted around the end of the narrow bed, into the two-foot gap between the bed and the wall.

Andrew huddled on the floor, mashed up against the wall in the corner. Tears streamed down his cheeks as he held his hands clamped over his ears. Tremors shook his body.

The sirens howled outside, louder, closer, seconds away now.

Seizing Andrew's hands, she yanked him to his feet.

He gasped in a breath and fought her pull.

"Come on," she said. "We've got to go."

"No, no, no. He's out there. It was him."

"The cops are coming. We have to go, Andrew. *Now.*"

"No! He'll get us too. Please."

The whine in his voice grated on her eardrums. She hauled him toward the door, but he planted both feet on the carpet and leaned back with all his weight. Despite his scrawny build, the change in momentum knocked her off balance. Her feet skidded across the carpet.

Andrew keened. His wrists slipped from her grasp.

The sirens wailed. Voices shouted outside.

Andrew crumpled to the floor and curled up in a ball.

She couldn't carry him out of here. She couldn't stay either. The police would want to know who strangled Brian Kellogg. She could tell them an invisible man did it or maybe the ghost of Jack the Ripper, but somehow, she doubted the police would buy either explanation. Without another suspect, they would level their sights on her.

And pull the trigger.

She poked her head out the door.

The police cars had parked at the far end of the building. Two officers were talking with a man in a bathrobe. The man waved his arms in her direction.

Andrew sobbed.

She couldn't leave him here alone.

No choice. She tiptoed out the door, hopped over Kellogg's body, and slunk past two more rooms toward the end of the building. A field sloped down the hill away from the motel, into the woods half a mile distant. Rounding the corner, she continued up the opposite side of the building. Another row of rooms filled this side, identical to the others except in the numbers on the door. Three cars occupied spaces in front of the rooms.

She stopped. The police might search this side of the building. She couldn't just mosey past them. The man in the bathrobe must've seen her. Even if he hadn't, the police would likely stop anyone who attempted to leave the motel.

The air felt sticky and warm, yet her teeth chattered.

Dammit. She angled off into the field.

———

HE RETURNED TO BLACKNESS. THEY SHUT OFF THE LIGHTS WHEN HE traveled. He'd given up asking why a long time ago. They would only refuse to answer. "That's classified," they'd say, as if they were secret agents. These jerks liked to pretend they worked for the CIA or the military, spouting terms that meant nothing in the private sector, treating him like a prisoner.

No, they viewed him as more of a slave than a prisoner, someone who obeyed their commands without questioning, without thinking, like a robot made of flesh and blood.

"I'm back," David announced.

The electrode wires tickled his arms. The chair felt cold, hard. When he shifted position, the straps around his ankles, wrists, and forehead chafed his skin.

The lights came on in a burst of white. He blinked in the sudden glare.

One of the technicians jiggled the doorknob from the other side. It had become a ritual. They jiggled the knob before entering the room to ensure that he hadn't pulled a Houdini, unlocking the door and escaping without triggering any alarms. Next, they'd peek through the tiny window set into the metal door, in case he'd somehow manipulated the surveillance cameras into displaying an image of him seated in the chair while, in reality, he hid near the door waiting to ambush them. Never mind that he knew nothing about cameras or alarms and had no clue how he might manipulate those devices.

Finally, with reasonable assurance of their safety, they would enter the room accompanied by two armed guards. Never knew, he might spontaneously acquire superhuman strength that allowed him to break the leather restraints, leap the fifteen feet from his chair to the door, and butcher them all with his bare hands.

They thought he was an animal.

In some respects, they overestimated his abilities. Yet in other ways, they underestimated him. They had no conception of what he could do if he chose to. If they knew, they'd realize no precautions would protect them. They also lacked one piece of information that might ease their minds.

He had given up on escaping.

Satisfied that he hadn't tricked them, the technician unlocked the door and swung it open for the man who entered the sterile white room. Tesler, the lead scientist, was a tall and wiry man in his sixties, with short-cropped gray hair and freckles that hinted red hair had once crowned his head. He wore a lab coat with a name badge pinned to the lapel. The lump in his pocket marked the location of his tablet computer.

All the technicians at the facility carried tablets instead of pens and paper. Handwriting was passé.

No guards accompanied Tesler. *Strange.*

David arched an eyebrow. "Would you mind unstrapping me?"

Tesler approached him. The older man eyed David's restraints for a couple of seconds, then reached out to unbuckle the forehead strap. Clasping David's chin in one hand, Tesler forcibly twisted his head from side to side, scrutinizing his subject's face. He released David's chin and seized his wrist, measuring the pulse with two fingers.

On a metal table positioned near David's chair, the heart rate monitor showed his pulse. They kept him hooked up to so much equipment, various kinds of monitors and meters, that he felt like he might physically meld with the machines one of these days. Still, Tesler always ignored the heart rate monitor and checked David's pulse himself.

"Normal," Tesler said. He sounded disappointed.

David glared at him.

As Tesler released the other straps, he asked in a faux-casual tone, "How was Seattle?"

"Dark and dreary. You'd love it."

Tesler ripped the electrodes from David's head.

Hairs dangled from the sticky patches, and his scalp burned where the hairs had torn loose.

A smile flickered on Tesler's face. "The guards will take you to the debriefing room."

"Don't make me go, I'll miss you too much."

Tesler unhooked the straps that bound David's wrists. He pulled handcuffs out of his pocket and secured them around David's wrists. "Where did you go today?"

"Seattle."

Tesler released the straps around David's ankles. "Where else?"

"Outer Mongolia. I heard it's nice this time of year."

Tesler leaned over him, placing a hand over each of David's forearms. The scientist's lips twitched. "David, don't lie to me. You were gone for five hours. Where else did you go?"

"I got lost."

Tesler pressed the weight of his body down on David's arms. The metal of the chair pinched his flesh. David stared into Tesler's eyes as the man's fingernails dug into his skin and his thumbs pressed into nerves. David's arms throbbed from deep within the flesh. He wanted to belt Tesler. He wanted to repay the man for all the pain he'd caused. All the pain he would cause.

Get off me.

Tesler's eyes widened. He flew backward, limbs flailing, a cry choked off in his throat. His face turned bright red.

With a thud and a gasp, he hit the concrete wall.

Tesler blinked. Though he opened his mouth, no sound came out.

Well, that was a new one. Not that he believed the ability had come from him. It was borrowed power for sure, and he knew exactly where it had originated. He must never let Tesler figure it out.

David rose from the chair. Even he didn't know the full extent of his abilities. No one did.

"You tripped," he said, striding toward Tesler to offer his cuffed hands to the man. "Better be more careful."

Tesler ignored David's offer of help and pushed himself up off the floor. Smoothing his lab coat, he straightened his spine and rolled his shoulders back.

When he spoke, a sharpness edged his voice. "Nice, David. Try that again and I'll put you in a coma."

David swallowed the smart retort that bubbled up inside him. He'd probably aggravated Tesler enough for one day. The bastard could do whatever he liked to David, so long as he got nowhere near Grace.

David moved toward the exit.

Tesler knocked on the door.

It swung inward as a guard outside opened it. The guard and his partner, both armed with bulky semiautomatic handguns, stepped onto the threshold.

Tesler glanced at David's handcuffs. "Maybe you need shackles on your feet too."

Both guards guided David out into the hallway.

As he paused to glance over his shoulder at Tesler, David smiled and said, "You can't shackle my mind, Tesler."

"Yes, I can," Tesler said. "With the serum. Test me and I'll prove it."

David's smile faltered. They had given him the serum before, though not to suppress his abilities. He had no idea if any drug could interfere with his powers, though Tesler seemed convinced. He might've been lying. Of course, they might've tested a new version of the serum on their other subjects.

Dammit. If they had drugs to stop him...

Grace would die.

CHAPTER NINE

S HE WAS LOST. GRACE CURSED HERSELF FOR LETTING THAT HAPpen. She had headed into the middle of the woods, where the trees formed a canopy overhead, blocking out the rays of the sun. An ambient radiance guided her through the woods. Underbrush choked the ground. Briars nipped at her arms and her pants.

She'd avoided the roads in case the cops fanned out in search of her. She assumed they knew about her. Call it intuition. Or just common sense. Or paranoia.

Maybe a little of all three.

Either way, she sensed the danger. Someone had known Kellogg would confide in her and opted to frame her for his murder. The good citizen in her urged her to turn around, report to the police, tell them everything—how she met Kellogg, what little he had told her—and then explain to them how he died.

Gee, Mr. Policeman, it was a ghost that strangled him.

The police had no way of knowing her name. The person who called them couldn't know her. She was safe.

Unless Andrew talked.

God, she had to stop torturing herself. The sensible thing to do was to go home, think, and formulate some kind of plan to save herself. A plan to fight off invisible killers? No problem. She'd whip one out in five minutes flat.

More than a plan, she needed rest. Her body cried out for a break. Her mind slogged through the facts, unable to siphon off the relevant data. Her eyes were gritty. She pushed through a clump of briars, and the trees thinned, opening into a clearing. Twenty feet away, a deer paused in its grass-munching and looked up at Grace. She took a step toward the animal.

It darted into the woods. The white tuft of the deer's tail bobbed through the brush until the creature melded with the darkness of the deeper woods.

Across the clearing, Grace spotted a woven-wire fence, camouflaged by vines and briars. The fence spanned that side of the clearing and disappeared into the trees. She trotted across the clearing. The fence was chest high and corroded, with a strand of barbed wire strung along the top. The barbs looked rusty. If one of them nicked her, she'd need a tetanus shot.

She wasn't up to testing the structural integrity of her fate. Not today. It might collapse under her.

The fence lured her into the trees again. It must lead somewhere, to a road or a stream, something she would recognize. From there, she'd find her way back into town.

Or she'd upset a hive of killer bees and die from hundreds of stings.

Way to think positive.

She had to stop visualizing the worst possible outcome of every situation. Start picturing the happy endings. Even if she never made it to the happily ever after, at least she could nourish her psyche with the fantasy.

Half an hour ticked by before the woods opened onto a dirt track. Not exactly a road, the track cleaved the earth where vehicles had driven through an opening in the woods. Grass, sparse as a balding man's hair, had cropped up between the tire tracks.

She glanced up and down the track. One direction led toward town, the other out into the hinterlands. If she could just tell which one led to town...

The sun had started its westward descent through the sky.

North led to town. Studying the sun's trajectory, she guessed that taking the road left would aim her back toward civilization. Either that or some rancher would find her desiccated body lying in the woods a decade or two from now.

She followed the road leftward.

Twenty minutes later, a stream blocked her passage. The dirt track had vanished into the shallow waters, reappearing on the other shore. The water was cool and relatively clear.

She coughed. Her throat burned and tickled with each inhalation. Her tongue was parched. She'd be in trouble if she didn't drink something soon, even if it was partially muddy water. Kneeling at the water's edge, she cupped her hands together, scooped water from the stream, and took a sip. The water tasted faintly of dirt, but it soothed her parched throat, so she gulped in the liquid.

A twig popped behind her.

She froze. Water dribbled down her chin.

Another twig snapped.

Slowly, she rose to a crouch and slipped the gun out of her purse. She squinted into the trees, searching for the source of the noises. The cracks had sounded close, somewhere behind her, but she couldn't tell for certain. She'd been concentrating on quenching her thirst, not inspecting the woods for enemies. No one could've tracked her out here. She would've noticed another person clomping through the thickets.

A twig cracked. Closer now, a few yards from her, the sound so loud it echoed in her ears.

The hairs on her neck prickled.

Gripping the gun in her hands, vise-tight, she whirled around.

The track was empty. In the trees to her right, a beast growled.

"Who's there?" she demanded.

Rustling. Soft growling.

"Come out or I'll shoot."

The weeds parted. A dark shape slunk out of the shadows and onto the road.

She swung the gun toward the shape.

The black cougar halted in the middle of the dirt track, ears flattened back, upper lip curled, a growl reverberating in its chest.

Grace held still, the gun directed at the cat. Although she'd heard tales of black cats showing up in the area, she hadn't seen one herself. The stories always sounded like rural legends to her.

Now she crouched face-to-face with the reality of those tales.

The cougar watched her. She watched it. Maybe it wasn't a cougar, but some other kind of large cat, like a jaguar. It hardly mattered now. Whether it selected her as its next meal mattered a hell of a lot more. Her heart hammered inside her chest.

She didn't dare move.

Suddenly, the cat dashed into the woods. Twigs splintered in its wake, the sounds fading into the distance.

Her heart still pounded, so she sat motionless for a minute or two, drawing in deep breaths until the rushing of blood slowed to a more sedate pace. Then she hopped across the creek.

And stumbled to a halt.

He stood there. In the middle of the dirt track. Straddling the strip of grass that bisected the trail.

She blinked. Nope, he was still there. His blond hair glistened in the filtered sunlight.

Grace frowned at him. After their encounter in the mall, she had hoped he might leave her alone. But then, she couldn't expect a hallucination to heed her wishes. Problem was, she no longer believed he was a figment of her screwed-up mind.

She raised the gun. "Get out of my way."

"You don't want to shoot me."

"Don't push me. I'm having a bad day."

He pointed up the road. "You're going the wrong way."

"I'm going north."

"Not anymore. The road turned."

Reluctantly, she took her gaze off him and glanced up at the sky. The sun had shifted. It now hovered behind and to the right of her. She was facing southeast, approximately.

Damn. She hated admitting he was right. The ache behind her eyes burgeoned anew.

She lowered the gun. "I would've figured that out. Eventually."

"When you got to Cuba?"

He stepped closer to her.

She raised the gun, finger on the trigger.

He shook his head.

"Thanks for the help," she said, "but I can take it from here."

"Have it your way."

She spun on her heels and marched down the track in the opposite direction.

He cleared his throat.

She paused mid-step.

"You need to go through the woods," he said, "or you'll end up going south again."

Grace clenched her fist around the butt of the gun. Saying nothing, she veered off the track into the trees.

SHE SENSED HIM TRAILING HER. THOUGH SHE NEITHER SAW NOR heard him, she felt his presence in the air, like rain about to pour down from the heavens. Not that she equated her shadow man with rain. She loved the rain and the smell of damp earth afterward that permeated the air. No, she did not equate her stalker with rain.

That would mean she liked him.

Up ahead, a trail cut through the trees. Animals had worn down this path through the landscape—deer, cows, horses, she assumed. Humans might've used the trail as well, though she saw no footprints to indicate it. The boughs of the trees curled over the trail. Although the sun's glow bathed the woods, the orb itself, her compass, stayed hidden above the canopy. The sun's heat nonetheless warmed her skin, drawing a sheen of sweat from her pores. She stopped and tilted her head backward, squinting at the treetops.

"This way."

His voice murmured behind her, too close behind. She sensed him move even closer until his body felt mere inches from hers, though she didn't dare look back to see if her estimation was correct.

"Go left," he said, his voice soft and deep.

And sexy. A shiver snaked down her spine. The shiver wasn't creepy, but rather...

Oh, she absolutely would not finish that thought.

He grasped her shoulders and gently turned her leftward. Now she could see him out of the corner of her eye. Tall and handsome and so very close.

She shook off his hands and snapped, "I know left from right, thank you very much."

"Then move."

Good idea. She fully intended to move. Her muscles, however, seemed to have gone on strike.

He scrunched his eyebrows. "You don't remember me, do you?"

"Sure, I remember. You cornered me in a department store fitting room yesterday."

She marched past him down the trail.

Fifteen minutes had passed since he first appeared, ostensibly to guide her, and she had yet to see any evidence that they traveled in the right direction. He might have a worse sense of direction than she did. Or he might have a reason for keeping her lost.

She continued down the trail. Not like she had a choice. Stand still and die of heatstroke, or follow the directions given by a shadow man and possibly die anyway. At least moving gave her a chance of finding civilization.

Her stomach growled. Her throat went dry again. Stabbing pains behind her eyes exploded into a headache. The sun dipped behind the trees, shining between the branches, scorching her eyes. The temperature dropped a little, though not enough to make a difference.

The birds silenced. Crickets chirped in the underbrush.

She held the gun in one hand. The sensation of metal against her skin did little to calm the creepy feeling building inside her. She disliked the idea of wandering through the woods, alone, after dark, but she had no choice. The sun was setting, and she still had no clue where she was. The daystar gradually slid below the horizon, and soon its glow would abandon the earth as well.

The ground collapsed.

Her right leg twisted sideways, wrenching her knee. She threw her hands out for balance and the gun flew from her grasp. She hit the dirt face-first.

Her knee throbbed, a charming accompaniment to her growing migraine. She rolled onto her back. Pain radiated out from her knee, making her wince and gasp. In the twilight, she spotted the obstacle that had thwarted her—a pothole.

The air seared her right arm. She touched the skin above the elbow. It was raw and damp with blood. She had a feeling these injuries wouldn't heal themselves overnight. This was no dream, unfortunately.

She had no time for injuries. She was lost in the forest, something she thought only happened in Grimm Brothers stories. She'd explored the woods countless times as a teenager, without getting lost. Back then, she stayed in the areas she knew. She should never have sauntered off into unknown territory. How could she have been so stupid?

Bracing herself against a tree, she tried to stand. Pain ricocheted up her leg. Her knee buckled. Her buttocks hit the ground hard as the back of her head smacked into the tree.

She shouted a curse.

Night settled over the woods like a blanket.

Grace struggled onto her knees. All the muscles in her leg cramped at once. Her arm scraped against the tree as pain screamed through her body and tears welled in her eyes. She blinked them back. No, she would *not* cry. She would crawl if she must, but she would never concede to the pain.

Of course, now that she needed a hand, her shadow man had vanished. Typical.

She avoided thinking about the insanity of using the word typical in reference to a man who appeared and disappeared at will, poof, like magic.

A breeze wafted over her. Goosebumps raised on her arms and neck.

Grace stood, gritting her teeth against the pain. She retrieved her key chain flashlight from her purse and flicked the power switch. A cone of wan yellow light illuminated the trail, the light glinting off the barrel of her gun. When she bent down to pick it up, pain jabbed her knee as if a thousand needles pierced her sinews. She bit back a yelp.

Gun in hand, she straightened. Her hand shook. She couldn't carry the gun. Holstering it inside her purse, she flung the bag over her neck and shoulder with the strap cutting a diagonal across her torso. Then she trudged along the trail, inch by inch, her knee screaming at every movement. The breeze irritated the abrasion on her arm.

The flashlight flickered.

She tapped it. The beam died. She smacked the thing against a tree. The light flashed once and died. Tossing the flashlight into her purse, she slogged onward, testing the ground ahead with her toes, feeling for obstacles with her hands.

After an eternity, she stumbled out of the woods onto a paved road. A double yellow line traced the road's center. It was a highway.

She shuffled to a halt on the shoulder.

Headlights popped into view in the distance as a vehicle topped a hill. As the lights drew near, she heard the grumble of an engine. Though she dreaded hitching a ride, she couldn't walk to town.

The vehicle neared.

Grace waved her arms.

The vehicle, a late-model BMW, pulled up beside her. The driver rolled down the window.

A man, his face obscured by shadows, said, "Need some help?"

The voice. She knew him. She bent over to peer inside the car, the movement shooting pains through her leg in a web of agony. Through gritted teeth, she said, "Henry Winston."

"Imagine running into you out here." He flicked a switch, and the door locks popped up with a thunk. "Hop in. I was on my way to your house."

She stepped back. Henry Winston happened to drive down this highway. On this night.

"I live down the road," he said. As his gaze traveled over her bloody arm, his expression darkened. "We'd better get you to a hospital."

He ignored the obvious questions—*How did you get out here? Why are you standing alongside the road in the dark? Why are you bleeding?*—that any normal person would've asked. He'd met her once. He should treat her with suspicion. Yet the man studied her with a thoughtful expression that lacked any hint of skepticism, concern for her condition, or even curiosity about her situation.

Winston leaned across the passenger seat to push the door open. "Come on."

"I'm fine. Just getting some exercise."

He scrutinized her through half-closed eyes. "Get in, Grace."

His voice, deeper and calmer than the waters of the Atlantic Ocean, elicited shivers in her belly. She stumbled backward. Her heel caught on the edge of the pavement. She sailed down the slope of the shoulder, landed on her butt, and tumbled backward until her head hit the ground. Her feet flipped up, almost went over her head, but then flopped down again. Her knee screamed. Her head throbbed. Tears trickled from her eyes as she clamped her jaw tight against the pain.

Staring up the slope at the car, she watched Winston slide into the passenger seat. He swung one leg, then the other, out the open door.

The gun. She reached for her purse. It was wedged under her hip, so she pushed up onto her elbows. White-hot pain scorched the raw flesh on her arm. Biting back a cry, she fumbled for the purse's zipper. Her fingers felt big and clumsy. The zipper slipped out of her grasp.

Winston's shoes clapped on the pavement. "Come on, Grace. You need medical attention. Let me help you."

"You killed Edward McLean."

The thought had burst into her mind and so she spoke it. Before now, she'd overlooked Winston as a suspect. As she uttered the words, though, they made a kind of sense.

In one step, he reached her.

She scuttled crab-like away from him, ignoring the pain that ricocheted through her body. The purse. She had to get it open. Seizing the bag, she clawed at the zipper. The indirect glow of the headlights stung her eyes. Squinting, she spotted the zipper pull, took it between her thumb and forefinger, and yanked. The zipper opened with a zzzt sound.

Above her, at the slope's pinnacle, Winston stood eerily still, backlit by the headlights. The faintly blue glow lent his eyes the luster of faceted onyx.

He thrust a hand toward her. "I won't hurt you."

Yeah, right, she thought and plunged her hand into the purse. Her fingers touched metal. She found the gun's grip, closing her fingers around it.

Winston's hand hovered above her head. He wiggled his fingers. Even in the moonlight, he was a shadow, a dark wraith. His eyes gleamed, though his face was obscured by the darkness that enveloped him from this side. The light that wreathed him from behind petered out before revealing his front.

A shiver as cold as liquid nitrogen raced through her body. She sat there, tears dribbling down her cheeks. Tears of pain, not defeat. She gripped the gun, keeping it inside her purse for now. He looked unarmed, except for that suggestive bulge under his suit jacket. Even in these lighting conditions, she made out the unnatural shape that snuggled in the hollow of his left shoulder.

Winston growled.

No, she must've imagined the sound. Probably the wind.

He yanked his hand back. "The hard way, then."

Winston slipped a hand inside his jacket.

Gritting her teeth, Grace pulled out her gun and sprang to her feet. Her knee gave out. She crumpled to the ground, lost her balance, and tumbled sideways down the slope. Winston shouted at her. When she hit the base of the slope, she shoved herself up onto all fours. By some miracle, she still held the gun tight in her fist.

Winston loped down the hill after her with an oblong object clasped in one hand. He stumbled, cursed, and trotted toward her as fast as he could. In a minute, he'd be on her.

She leaped to her feet. Pain tore through the muscles from her knee straight up to her hip. White lights danced in her vision. Her ears rang. *Breathe, dammit.* She sucked in a breath and, teeth clamped over her bottom lip, she limped along the hill's base.

Winston bounded off the slope. He spun in her direction, breaking into a fast jog.

Thirty feet separated them. Not enough.

Her knee slowed her progress. She pushed harder, grimacing and panting from the pain as much as the exertion. Faster, faster, she must move faster. The road followed the curve of the hill, so she did too, pushing harder. A wave of dizziness crashed over her.

She listed right, then left. The night tilted around her. Nausea swelled inside her as she tripped and stopped.

Behind her, shoes clomped through the sandy loam. Breaths grunted. Clothes rustled.

The world spun.

No, no, no.

"Ack!"

Her limbs morphed into stone. Her heart switched rhythms with a skip and a hop. The strangled cry had come from over her shoulder.

She wanted to turn to look, but the spinning forced her to stay rooted in place. The sound of footfalls had ceased. She took slow, deliberate breaths, focusing on a single star in the sky. It gave her a center of focus, something for her massively screwed-up sense of balance to home in on. And then she waited.

Silence.

The spinning diminished into rocking.

Crickets chirped.

At last, the dizziness subsided. She turned in a half circle.

Henry Winston lay sprawled on the ground. One knee was bent, his arms askew, the oblong object still clutched in his hand.

Just beyond Winston's head, a figure loomed in the moonlight. His pale hair glistened in the silvery glow. Her shadow man. He must've attacked Winston. Knocked him out. Or killed him.

Her knees shuddered. Her tongue had turned to sandpaper, and her throat burned while the embers in her stomach ignited into a conflagration.

Her hero stepped over Winston and advanced on her. Just as Winston's eyes had glowed darkly in the moonlight, his shimmered with the blue of a Caribbean inlet. When he halted several paces from her, the weakness in her legs spread through her hips into her belly, up through her chest, and into her heart. Stepping closer, he reached for her face. She flinched but did not move away. He gently ran his thumb across her cheek to wipe away the tear stains, his skin warming hers.

A vehicle passed by on the road above. In the flare of the headlights, she saw his face was ashen and his eyes were bloodshot.

"You need a doctor," he said.

"No," she said, though her voice wavered. "I'm fine."

Her knees buckled. She dropped onto the dirt. A tear trickled down her cheek onto her lip, seeping into her mouth.

No. Enough crying.

Her ears rang as the twilight world dipped and twirled around her once again. She lay down on the earth, which felt cool against her back, and let her eyelids flutter shut.

A pair of arms slipped under her, hoisting her body off the ground.

She opened her eyes just enough to see, through the darkness encroaching on her vision, the unearthly blue fire in his irises.

He carried her past Winston.

Grace's head flopped sideways. The object Winston had held in his hand, she spotted it now. It was a cell phone.

She passed out.

CHAPTER TEN

THE LIGHT BLINDED HER. SHE SQUINTED AS VOICES WHISPERED AROUND HER and machines beeped and clicked. While her eyes adjusted to the light, the scene shifted into focus. A young man in a green outfit—the kind worn by doctors and nurses—bent over her leg, scrutinizing her knee with his lips pressed together and his eyes half-closed. Red hair spilled over his forehead in stringy locks. His skin was pale. His hands were thin and long with pronounced knuckles. He didn't notice her watching him or didn't show his awareness if he did notice.

Hovering his hands just above her leg, he swirled his palms over the contours of her knee. A warmth spread through the joint. Not painful warmth. The soothing kind.

The young man jerked his hands away and looked at her. He was a kid, no more than seventeen by her estimation. But then, some people retained their youthful features even into middle age. In the movies and television, some actors who played teenagers were actually in their late twenties. This kid might be older than he looked, and more threatening too.

"Are you a doctor?" Grace asked.

He flattened his palm against her forehead. His skin felt warm. He closed his eyes as he inhaled long breaths and let each out slowly.

Opening his eyes, he withdrew his hand. "It's done."

Her eyelids lowered partway without her permission as weariness descended on her. She did not want to sleep. Well, okay, she *wanted* to sleep. But she refused to give in to the urge.

The boy backed away from her, retreating behind the curtain that surrounded her bed.

Somewhere to her left, on the other side of the curtain, someone coughed. She must've been in the emergency room.

Grace tried to speak in a forceful tone, but her voice emerged as a slur. "Wait."

"Sleep," he said.

Her eyelids shut. She couldn't sleep, not now, not yet. She sensed something important had just happened and she must investigate, not take a nap. The pain was gone—the pain everywhere, she realized, even the migraine—and she had too much to do, too many questions that needed answering. She could not laze around in bed.

Can't sleep…

Something touched her wrist. With great effort, she parted her eyelids just enough to peek through her lashes.

A nurse stood beside her, taking her pulse. The woman released her wrist and scribbled on a clipboard.

Grace cleared her throat. "Don't you have machines for that?"

The nurse smiled and drawled, "I was double checkin' the machine. Never hurts, ya know?"

Grace blinked several times, trying to clear her mind. It still felt enmeshed in cobwebs.

The nurse patted her arm. "Welcome back, hon. I was wondering when you'd rise and shine."

She didn't feel shiny. The nurse looked that way, however, with her bright smile and rosy cheeks. Dark-blonde hair, cut short, curled in ringlets around her face. She was probably a few years older than Grace.

"Where am I?" Grace asked, raising onto her elbows. "Who are you?"

"I'm Hannah Martin," the woman drawled, "but you can just call me Hannah. You're in Lassiter Falls Community Hospital. You had a little whoopsy."

"A what?"

Hannah giggled. "An accident, hon. You remember what happened?"

In her memory, the incident had taken on the haze of a dream. "Vaguely. I feel okay."

Hannah glanced at Grace's leg, looked away, and then glanced back. Her expression went blank. Moving only her eyes, she turned her gaze on Grace.

"Something wrong?" Grace asked.

Hannah tapped Grace's knee. "The wound. It's gone."

Grace leaned forward to touch her leg. Her knee no longer ached. The leg of her jeans had ripped and frayed around the knee, yet despite the flesh showing through the holes, she saw no wound. No blood. Not even a scratch. She flexed her leg. No shooting pains. No stiffness. She could've executed a cartwheel off the bed if she wanted.

"How long was I asleep?" she asked.

"Couple hours."

From the grit in her eyes, the taste of sleep in her mouth, and the mud coating her brain, she would've guessed her slumber lasted days. No injuries healed themselves in two hours. She felt fine, though, like nothing had happened. Even the paranoia and anxiety that overtook her earlier had dissipated. Though deep down she knew the ordeal had happened hours ago, she could almost believe days or even weeks had elapsed.

What the hell had come over her?

"Tell me what happened, hon," Hannah said.

Winston coming at her, gun in hand. Certainty slamming into her in the form of one thought—*he killed Grandpa*. Then running. Winston on the ground, cell phone in hand. Phone? It had to be a gun. Hands lifting her. Darkness.

"How did I get here?" she asked.

"A nice young man brought you in," Hannah said. "Wouldn't give his name. Said he found you alongside the highway."

Her stomach fluttered. "What did he look like?"

"Blond hair. Beautiful blue eyes. Cute as a button, but real serious."

Grace stared at the curtain. Blond hair. Blue eyes. He saved her life. Events appeared to support that notion, yet she couldn't believe appearances anymore. Brian Kellogg appeared to have been strangled. Her leg appeared to have healed. Her shadow man must've killed Brian Kellogg and now he wanted her dead.

Then why had he carried her to the hospital?

He might've needed her alive until she gave him the flash drive or he figured out where Grandpa had hidden it. But his concern for her seemed genuine and, in the darkest corners of her mind, she recognized that he meant no harm. He could help her. She should trust him. She knew him.

Ridiculous.

If he didn't kill Kellogg, then she had another invisible man to deal with and no clue how to do that.

She flopped back onto the bed, nestling her head on the pillow. The bed was raised so that it held her in a semi-upright position.

"You know him?" Hannah asked.

"Who?"

"The man who brought you in."

"Not really."

Hannah fluffed the pillow behind Grace's head. "The doctor'll be in soon to take a look at you."

"Again?"

"He ain't seen ya yet, sweetie. You've been asleep."

"But I woke up, and he was here. Looking at my leg. He told me to sleep."

"The doctor's been busy with a critical patient. You must've dreamed it."

Grace said nothing. No point in arguing.

The nurse eyed her with a curious expression. "You've been to the ER before, haven't you? With real bad migraines."

Grace's breath caught in her throat. How did the nurse know about her headaches? *Oh, duh.* She'd come to this emergency room and seen doctors whose offices were in this hospital. Of course they'd have her records.

"Still havin' those migraines?" Hannah asked.

Limited honesty seemed like the best policy right now, so Grace told the woman, "Sometimes. I've got medicine for it."

"Good." Hannah turned to leave, then glanced over her shoulder at Grace. "You need anything, you be sure to let me know."

Grace tried to relax, but she hated hospitals. And doctor's offices. And needles. And blood pressure cuffs. The one wrapped around her arm right now, taking her blood pressure at regular intervals, pumped itself up again for a new reading. The pressure on her arm pinched harder and harder.

She squirmed on the bed. A sharp object dug into her hip. She shoved a hand into her jeans pocket and felt the key tucked inside it. Kellogg's key. Tugging it out of her pocket, she turned it between her thumb and forefinger. Bits of lint stuck to the tape residue on the key, along with a tiny breath mint. Her pocket wasn't exactly a sterile environment. She flicked the mint off the key. It flew past the nurse's left eye.

Grace winced. "Sorry."

"Don't worry," Hannah said. "I've had worse things thrown at me. What was that anyway, a TicTac?"

"Uh… yeah." Grace fiddled with the key. "Wintergreen flavor."

Hannah grinned. "My favorite. You got any more?"

"No. Sorry."

As the blood pressure cuff deflated, releasing its grip on her arm, Grace let out a breath. She adjusted her position on the bed and promptly dropped the key on the floor.

Hannah snatched it up, glancing at the key as she handed it back to Grace.

With the key once again in her hand, Grace closed her fist around it.

"Don't worry about your mail," Hannah said. "Store's closed, anyhow."

"What?"

The nurse patted her arm. "My hubby keeps a box at Mail 'N More too. He gets off work at five thirty, so he always has to rush to make it there before the store closes at six."

"Oh. Right." Grace tried to act nonchalant, though her heart was beating faster. The monitor nearby registered ninety-eight beats per minute. "I just realized I forgot to pick up my mail today, that's all."

"Store opens at eight in the mornin', sweetie."

"Thanks."

"Sure thing. Now y'all take it easy till the doctor comes."

The nurse winked at Grace and then departed. The curtain settled back into place behind her.

Grace tucked the key into her pocket again. She knew what the key unlocked now. Tomorrow morning, she would go to the Mail 'N More franchise and find out what Kellogg had hidden there. He must've hidden something in the box. Why else would he bother concealing the key? Maybe some of the answers she sought awaited her there.

The heart rate monitor read one hundred and five beats per minute.

Grace ran her hands over her injured knee—her *formerly* injured knee. She had not dreamed the man, or boy, who examined her leg. He existed. Once in a while, a person had to accept the truth no matter how impossible it sounded. She had witnessed the evidence, touched it, smelled it. Men existed who could appear and disappear whenever they chose, commit murders while remaining invisible, and heal injuries with their bare hands. Or their minds. She hadn't decided which made more sense, although trying to find sense in the chaos seemed futile. The truth no longer made sense while sorcery became believable. In this bizarre new world, logic was extinct.

She must protect herself or risk her own extinction.

Monitors beeped nearby. A patient snored next door.

Stay alive. That was her priority. Finding answers to the many questions bouncing around in her brain, that might prove the only way to keep herself alive.

Near the foot of the bed, the curtain billowed as if someone had walked through it.

A draft chilled her skin. She rubbed her arms and scrutinized the empty air around the bed. No one was there, of course. At least, no one she could see.

Hardly comforting these days.

She relaxed against the pillow. Well, she tried to relax, anyway.

Stay alive.

Leaning back against the bed, she closed her eyes. From past trips to the ER, she knew the doctor wouldn't let her leave until her heart rate dropped below ninety. *Relax*, she commanded herself. She pictured the oak tree behind her house, her favorite place to sit and take it easy. Listening to the birds chirping, feeling the grass beneath her, those things eased the tension in her on a normal day. This day was far from normal. Still, she imagined the scene. Let her muscles go slack. Let her mind empty of all thoughts.

Sitting under the tree. Leaning against the trunk. Watching little cumulus clouds scud across the sky. Feeling a hand grasp hers, their fingers intertwining. She let herself imagine muscular arms sliding around her, drawing her into an embrace, surrounding her with human warmth. She knew who it was now, who she needed, though she didn't understand why. Just this once, she didn't worry about why. The sensation, even the imaginary version, imbued her with a kind of serenity she'd never felt before.

Grace opened her eyes a crack to check the heart rate monitor. It read eighty-four beats per minute.

She closed her eyes and drifted back into the fantasy. His effect on her was uncanny and totally illogical. Right at this moment, she didn't care.

Blue eyes. Blond hair.
Who are you?

———

AN HOUR LATER, GRACE SHUFFLED OUT OF THE HOSPITAL INTO THE night. She needed a taxi or a bus to get home. Spotting a bus stop on the other side of the parking lot, she trudged toward it.

Despite the ordeal of the day, she wanted to do something. Had to do something. Waiting for truth to find her didn't work. Success stemmed from action, therefore she must take action. Right now. The night camouflaged shadows and shadow men. It also concealed humans. She could sneak somewhere and accomplish something.

Great plan. Sneak somewhere. Do something.

Reaching the bus stop, she dropped onto the bench. She had no idea when the next bus might arrive. It gave her time to think, she supposed, but no great thoughts occurred to her. Studying the lines on her palms lulled her into a semi-trance.

A memory catapulted from the depths of her mind. Winston striding down the hillside. Urging her to go with him. The gun—no, the cell phone in his grasp. The memory mutated. Winston sprawled on the dirt.

He killed Grandpa.

The thought exploded in her mind. She'd accused Winston of murdering her grandfather back on that roadside, seconds before she ran—okay, limped—away from him. At the time, he said nothing in response. No denial, no angry retort, no confused look on his face, no shouted expletives. He simply took one monstrous step toward her.

She had thought, when he reached for his cell phone, that he would pull out a gun. Going for a phone made no sense. Unless he thought he'd whack her with the device, he couldn't stop her with a phone.

Maybe he was calling for backup.

What kind of backup? The cops? Men in white coats to drag her off to an asylum?

A shadow fell over her.

She jerked her head to look up.

Henry Winston stood in front of her, an arm's length away. A nearby streetlight cast a sallow glow on his face and glinted darkly in his eyes.

"Need a ride?" he asked, as casually as if she bummed rides from him every day.

"I'll wait for the bus."

"My car is more comfortable."

She forced a bland smile. "I'm going green. Saving the planet one bus ride at a time."

They stared at each other in silence for three heartbeats. He broke the silence first.

"Come with me," he said, his tone sharpening into a dangerous edge. "I won't ask again."

She glanced at the suspicious bulge under his jacket. Too big for a cell phone.

Winston took a step closer. "We need to talk."

Right now, his eyes reminded her of a doll's, reflective but lifeless.

She resisted the urge to shimmy sideways on the bench, away from him. Showing fear seemed like a bad idea at this particular moment. So instead, she asked, "Talk about what?"

"Everything." He hesitated, and she could almost hear the gears clicking in his brain. "I suppose it's time I came clean. I work for the FBI."

"And I'm the reincarnation of Cleopatra."

Winston looked straight at her. Like a covered pot, his face revealed nothing of what simmered beneath the lid. His expression was cold, or maybe her bias colored her perceptions. She trusted no one.

Especially not him.

What a dark and lonely place in which to find herself. No one to trust, no one to lean on for support or comfort, no one to counsel her. The isolation had once frightened her. No more. That was her advantage over people like Henry Winston. They believed they could squeeze her into a hole and she would beg for light. They were wrong. She'd found herself in this place before. She knew it well and recognized the contours of the walls, the texture of the bars, the depth of the shadows.

The dark no longer frightened her.

"May I explain?" Winston asked.

"Why not. I could use a good laugh."

From an inner pocket of his jacket, he extracted a thin wallet. Flipping it open, he handed it to her so she could see the ID badge inside that had the letters "FBI" on it. The badge could've been real or a good fake. She would hardly know the difference.

She returned the wallet to him. "Nice forgery."

A muscle in his jaw pulsed. "As I said, I work for the FBI. I'm investigating your grandfather's death."

"Uh-huh."

Grace searched Winston's expression and his body language for a clue to his veracity. Maybe she had attributed evil to him where none existed. She let paranoia take root in her psyche, braiding its limbs around her mind, blocking rationality with its dense foliage. The sensation of someone watching her, hidden in shadows or crowds of people, stayed with her even now. The feeling swept over her at intervals, like the beacon of a lighthouse. Sometimes she felt a presence right beside her and swore she felt a hand graze her skin. Other times, she sensed the presence coming closer, moving away, dissipating.

Paranoia had become her best friend.

She couldn't dismiss her gut feelings. They had served her well in the past.

If she trusted her gut, then she was wrong about one very important thing. She wasn't without allies. Deep inside, she knew she could trust one person.

Her shadow man.

Returning her attention to Winston, she said, "My grandfather died in a plane crash."

"I'm afraid not."

"You have a theory."

He rubbed his chin. "He was murdered. By a co-worker."

She had zero reasons to buy his story or to believe any explanations he offered, yet she could reject nothing at this point. When options melted away, the ridiculous became reasonable.

"The killer broke into your house," Winston said.

"To borrow my lipstick, I suppose."

"He wants a flash drive. He thinks you have it."

A flash drive. She was damn sick of hearing about the thing. "He's mistaken."

"Doesn't matter. He'll kill you anyway."

———

AN EIGHTEEN-WHEELER ROCKETED DOWN THE ROAD, FAR EXCEEDING the speed limit. The air displaced by the truck blustered over Grace and flapped Winston's clothes. Pebbles kicked up by the big truck's wheels ticked on the sidewalk. The headlights splayed across them both for just long enough to blind Grace temporarily.

For five minutes, she'd listened to Winston's story. He provided her with a solid, rational explanation for almost everything. Part of her longed to accept the story. Most of her knew she could not. It was a lie.

He hoped to seduce her with his lies—not seduce her into bed, but rather into lowering the drawbridge and admitting him into her personal fortress.

Winston had explained that Edward McLean had worked on a secret project for a pharmaceutical company, studying how the brain worked to help design better drugs. Her grandfather had been on the cusp of a major breakthrough, according to Winston, until one of his assistants grew jealous of his accomplishments and killed him.

The scenario made sense. Kellogg had mentioned both the pharmaceutical company and the study. She might've accepted Winston's version. Asked no questions. Fretted no more.

She couldn't. Kellogg had insisted the study was a facade. He'd insisted—and now he was dead. He had died because he knew the truth. Because he tried to tell her.

"So," Grace said, "why was my grandfather going to Washington?"

"To receive an award."

"Why wouldn't he tell me about it?"

"Maybe he wanted to surprise you. Drop by on his way home."

Clever. A bit too clever. Somehow, he knew Grandpa had liked surprising her with his visits. The statement sounded innocuous, but she had trouble seeing it as nothing. Everything Winston said struck her as contrived.

With every word, he nudged her toward the conclusion he preferred.

Both Brian Kellogg and her shadow man told her someone had to warn her. About what, they didn't say. Maybe about Henry Winston. Of course, they might both be crazy. She might be crazy. Winston might be the sane one.

Sure, he might be sane. But sane did not automatically equal honest or trustworthy.

Winston slipped a photograph out of his shirt pocket and handed it to her. "This is David Ransom. He's a sociopath, a master manipulator, and a murderer. He killed your grandfather."

She took the photo. The paper was limp, the gloss degraded. The snapshot captured a young man standing on a beach, probably along the ocean. The sunset blazed behind him as he smiled at the camera, his blond hair ruffled by a long-ago breeze, his blue eyes focused on the camera.

David Ransom. Her shadow man.

She shoved the photo at Winston.

He arched an eyebrow. "You recognize him?"

"Nope."

"He's extremely dangerous, volatile, unpredictable." Winston stepped closer and knelt in front of her. In a voice that sounded a bit too earnest, he said, "If you see him, call me. Do not approach him or talk to him."

"Yes, sir."

The sarcasm in the statement eluded him, she thought, because he gave her a satisfied half-smile and rose to his full height. He expected everyone should obey him. Most people probably did. They fell for his pseudo-concern, ignored the subtle signs of darkness beneath the surface, and trusted what they heard rather than what they saw.

Winston had called David Ransom a master manipulator. Maybe he'd been talking about himself.

Retrieving car keys from his pocket, Winston said, "I understand why you don't trust me yet. But I can't help you without your trust. That's the key."

The key.

She jammed a hand into her jeans pocket. Her fingers contacted metal. It was the key Brian Kellogg had taped to the inside of his unnecessary hairpiece. She now knew it led to a mailbox in the local Mail 'N More franchise. Kellogg's key might prove, well, key in more ways than one. It might be the vital clue that unlocked the entire mystery. Or not. She wouldn't know until morning.

Her pulse quickened. Winston must never find out about the key. Of that, she was certain. Why she was certain, she couldn't explain.

She pulled her hand out of her pocket but left the key safely inside.

"You must come with me," Winston said. "For your own protection."

"I appreciate the offer, but no. I'll manage on my own."

Winston hooked his thumb through the key ring and flipped his keys in a circle. Once. Twice. He let them dangle then, clinking against each other.

"Where do you live?" Grace asked.

Winston frowned at her.

She arched her eyebrows. "You're the one who said you wanted to come clean and you want me to trust you. Answering a few questions might help with both."

The frown morphed into a tight line. "I live in Los Angeles, but I've been camped out here in Lassiter Falls for nearly six weeks."

Which meant he'd arrived shortly after Edward McLean's death. She tried to sound nonchalant as she said, "Why didn't you tell me all of this when you came to my house the other day?"

"Because I didn't."

She met his gaze. "That's not an answer. Tell me who you really are."

His eyes were narrowed to slits. His entire face had tightened into a mask of contained anger. Lines fanned out from his eyes and creased his forehead. He clutched his keys so tightly in his fist that his hand trembled a touch.

Her throat constricted. She swallowed, but it felt like trying to gulp down a rock.

The anger tightening Winston's features slackened into a smirk. "All right, if you want honesty then I will give it to you. Just remember you asked for it." He folded his arms over his chest, tilting his head back to stare down at her through narrowed eyes. "My name is Xavier Waldron. I've come to retrieve something my employer wants, which we know Edward McLean gave to you."

"You're mistaken."

Waldron chuckled, though it sounded in no way jovial. "You are coming with me this instant, Grace. Your only choice is whether you walk on your own or I carry your limp, unconscious body to the car."

He was three feet away from her. He lifted one foot to move toward her.

She threw herself sideways, sliding across the bench.

Waldron grabbed for her.

Grace leaped off the bench and bolted. As she fled down the sidewalk, she heard Waldron calling after her.

"You can't hide, Grace. I know your secrets."

Did he know? Maybe. Even she didn't know all her secrets. She might've met Xavier Waldron before. Her screwy brain left a lot to the imagination these days. They might've encountered each other during the eight months of her life she couldn't remember.

She ran—and she didn't stop until she'd jumped onto a bus headed for her neighborhood.

Maybe Waldron did know her. Maybe David knew her too. Some part of her might know which of them to trust, if she could trust either man. The knowledge was buried deep in her unconscious, like a treasure trove in an undiscovered tomb.

Amnesia sucked.

Chapter Eleven

Mail 'n More resided in the corner space of a building on the courthouse square, beside the smaller of the two movie theaters in town. The building, constructed in the nineteen twenties as a theater and remodeled once in its entire history, had the reputation of being haunted. The movie theater boasted two small screens, dilapidated seats, stairs that creaked, and sticky floors. In stark contrast to the theater, Mail 'N More featured shiny floors, a stars-and-stripes color scheme, and neatly arranged aisles stacked with neatly arranged merchandise of the office supply variety.

At three minutes past eight in the morning, Grace walked through the store's glass-enclosed entryway and between the automatic doors that whooshed open before her. An electronic doorbell bonged, alerting everyone inside that a new customer had entered the premises. A smiling employee trotted to her. The girl looked barely old enough to vote.

"May I help you?" the girl asked, her tone a little too energetic for first thing in the morning. Her nametag identified her as Ashlee.

Grace cleared her throat. "I'm interested in getting a mailbox. Do you have a pamphlet or something?"

"Sure." Ashlee trotted to a nearby display of informational brochures, nabbed one, and brought it back to Grace. "Our rates are listed on the back page."

"Thanks." Grace surveyed the store with one long glance but failed to spot the boxes. "Where are the mailboxes, anyway?"

"Let me show you."

Ashlee hustled out the automatic doors, waving for Grace to follow. They turned left toward a door Grace hadn't noticed before, set back in the corner of the entryway. A modest sign above the door announced MAIL-BOXES 24-HR ACCESS, with a down arrow suggesting they lay inside this doorway. Ashlee pushed the door open and led Grace into a short hall-way that dead-ended at a longer hallway. Rows of mailboxes lined the longer corridor, which stretched rightward along the store's wall. The hallway was brick, rather than glass, with mailboxes of various sizes set into the wall. They looked just like post office boxes. A door at the far end of the hallway was marked EMPLOYEES ONLY.

The other sign had said "24-HR ACCESS." Nurse Hannah had been wrong, or maybe the store changed its policy recently. Either way, Grace could've stopped by last night and avoided the hours of tossing and turning as she tried to sleep while simultaneously wondering what Kellogg's mailbox held and worrying Xavier Waldron might abduct her from her bed. She'd gotten a little sleep but nowhere near enough.

Ashlee was reciting the benefits of the store's mailbox services.

Grace raised her hand, interrupting the girl's spiel. "Thanks, I think I've got all the information I need."

Along the wall opposite the mailboxes, a long table held pens—chained to the table, naturally—and free pads of paper. Grace marched to the table. She picked up a pen and began circling items in the brochure. She hoped it looked like she was considering her options. She also hoped Ashlee would take the hint and leave.

Fortunately, the girl had decent manners. She told Grace to "come and catch me" if she had any questions, and then she left.

Grace was alone. At last.

She fished Kellogg's key out of her pocket. The number engraved on it was 208. She wandered among the boxes and, finding 208 in the middle, unlocked the box.

Her shoulders sagged. The box was empty, save for a small tin of breath mints.

Picking up the tin, she studied the image of mint leaves engraved on the lid. She popped off the lid but saw only mints hidden inside the tin. *Damn.* She'd hoped Kellogg stashed the flash drive inside his mailbox. The key had been her only lead. Either Kellogg had kept the key as a decoy, or he'd died before hiding the flash drive in the box. Maybe he'd never intended to hide the flash drive there. Maybe he had no evidence, no flash drive, nothing more important than a grocery list to give her.

Shoving the mints in her purse, she shut the box and headed out of the store.

On the sidewalk, she paused. A plan would help. A psychic flash would be great. She had neither. As she took in her surroundings, something caught her attention. To the right of the Mail 'N More entryway, nestled against the brick facade, stood a newspaper vending machine. Inside the machine, the headline on the front page of the *Lassiter Falls Gazette* declared, "Tourist killed in botched mugging."

Grace edged closer to the machine. Below the headline was a photo of Andrew Haley, handcuffed, being shoved into a police cruiser by two stern-looking policemen. Andrew's eyes bulged. His mouth hung open. In the background, she could make out the Bed & Bath Inn.

She dug quarters out of her purse and fed the machine to retrieve a copy of the paper. Back in her car, doors locked and engine idling, she read the article.

The story claimed a mental patient had strangled a tourist who carried no identification. Andrew, they said, had escaped from a hospital in California. For unknown reasons, he hitchhiked two thousand miles to Lassiter Falls, where he lived in alleys and abandoned buildings. The attack on the tourist appeared unprovoked.

Where had the reporter gotten his information? Andrew couldn't carry on a conversation, much less dictate his biography. The police must've released the information. Where they got it from remained a mystery.

Maybe Waldron told them.

She must know for sure. And she needed to know more about Waldron. Like, oh, why he wanted to abduct her and what "secrets" he knew about her.

David Ransom might know the answers to her questions.

She must find David. An invisible man could hide anywhere he wanted. He could've been watching her right then, sitting beside her, laughing at her confusion, plotting ways of killing her. No, she couldn't believe he would kill her. He had saved her life. Besides, last night she'd realized she trusted him. She had no clue why, but at this point, she had to trust her instincts. They were all she had to go on.

Waldron maintained David was dangerous. She trusted Waldron about as much as she trusted a coyote not to kill a rabbit. She shouldn't trust David Ransom either.

But she did. Which was crazy.

Maybe she *had* lost her mind.

———

FIVE MINUTES LATER, SHE STILL SAT HUNCHED IN THE DRIVER'S SEAT OF the Pontiac. This morning she'd remembered the gas can she kept in the garage, stuffed into the corner behind the leaf rake. A hike to the nearest gas station got her enough gas to drive the Pontiac back to the station and fill up its empty tank. She couldn't face another day of bus rides.

The mailbox had been empty. Where had Kellogg hidden his evidence? Where the hell was this flash drive everyone wanted?

Kellogg had concealed the mailbox key. Why would he bother hiding it if the box held nothing?

She dug the tin of mints out of her purse. Popping open the lid, she gazed down at the round mints inside the tin. She poked the mints with her fingertip. The tin's metal bottom shifted.

Crappy construction in a mint tin. What a shock.

Hold on. She poked the mints again. The shiny metal beneath them moved, but the tin itself remained intact.

The tin had a false bottom.

She tipped the tin until the mints tumbled out onto the passenger seat. The false bottom shifted but stayed inside the tin. She used her fingernail to pry up the slim metal sheet, which someone had cut to fit the box, as evidenced by the sheet's sharp edges.

Grace removed the false bottom, setting it on the passenger seat. In the space now revealed inside the tin lay a microcassette of the type designed for small recorders used in dictation. Most people nowadays used digital voice recorders instead. Microcassette recorders were going out of fashion.

Taking the microcassette between her thumb and forefinger, she examined it. If Kellogg had concealed it with such care, he must've deemed the microcassette important.

She needed a microcassette player. Since she didn't have one at home, she'd need to buy one.

Mail 'N More sold office supplies.

Jumping out of the car, she locked and shut the door, and then half walked, half jogged back to the store. The same sales associate pounced on her as soon as she crossed the threshold. Grace asked about microcassette recorders, and Ashlee escorted her to the correct aisle. Grace figured she must've looked annoyed, or at least harried, because Ashlee excused herself more quickly this time, with the excuse that she saw another customer in need of assistance.

Grace chose the cheapest microcassette recorder and grabbed a package of batteries. Two customers got to the checkout line ahead of her. Their purchases seemed to take an eternity to ring up, and then the credit card reader malfunctioned. Grace drummed the toe of her boot on the hard floor. Her pulse accelerated with every second she waited in this line. She had possible evidence in her purse and no way of listening to it. What did the tape contain?

If it was nothing more than Kellogg's favorite pop songs, she'd scream.

The cashier struggled with the credit card reader.

Grace gulped back a groan. If this line didn't progress soon, like in the next nanosecond, she'd scream right here and now.

At last, the machine consented to read the other customer's card. A quick signature completed the transaction, and the customer moseyed out of the store. The next customer paid quickly—with cash, thank heavens. Grace did the same.

A minute later, she was back in the car. Shoving the key in the ignition, she started the engine. The temperature outside was rising, along with the humidity. She turned on the AC but refrained from cranking it up to maximum. The noise of the blower would make it difficult to hear much of anything. So instead, she aimed every vent directly at her.

Then she ripped open the packaging, freeing the microcassette recorder. Inserting the batteries took three tries. The damn icons showing how to insert them were so small she needed an electron microscope to read them properly. With the batteries finally inserted, she shoved the microcassette into the recorder, cranked up the volume, and hit the play button. The tape whirred.

On the recording, someone sighed. A crinkling noise followed, calling to mind pages being turned.

"Where should I start?g" a voice said.

Grandpa's voice. The cassette must be his audio journal. He had kept a journal of his thoughts, recording them throughout the day whenever he felt the need. Though he kept the contents of his journal private, he had told her of its existence. She'd forgotten about it. He'd also preferred microcassettes over digital recorders, she recalled. He wasn't averse to the digital revolution, but neither did he rush to adopt new technologies.

The sound cut in and out.

"—the beginning," Edward McLean said. "This morning, I made a decision. I should've exposed them long before now. I—"

Bumping and rattling noises obscured his voice. She waited it out. After a couple of seconds that felt like hours, Grandpa's voice resounded in the car once again.

"—ever realized it would go this far. I'm the only one who can stop this. Everyone else has an agenda, some connection, or else they've been frightened out of their minds by his thugs. I've talked to Senator Faulkner, and he assures me he'll help stop this madness. I hope to God they haven't gotten him as well."

A bang. Muffled shouting.

The tape hissed. Had the recording ended or was this more noise?

A chill whispered over the back of her neck. *Someone's watching.*

She surveyed the area outside the car. No one on the sidewalk. Her Pontiac sat on a slight hill, parallel parked fifty feet from Mail 'N More. No cars were parked behind her, and only a smattering of other vehicles occupied spots in front of her car or on the opposite side of the street. Every other car sat empty, however.

The chill spread down her body, raising goosebumps from head to toe.

Get out of here, a voice inside her urged. She grabbed the microcassette recorder, punched the stop button, and yanked the keys from the ignition.

Thunder grumbled.

Beyond the windshield, the sun burned in a clear sky.

She shoved the microcassette recorder into her purse and slung the bag's strap around her neck, over her shoulder. She grabbed the door handle.

Thunder rumbled. No, not thunder. Almost like a voice. Low and grumbling and speaking words she couldn't understand.

She pulled the handle and thrust the door outward.

A blast of cold smacked into her. The door slammed shut in her face. The lock thunked into position as if the car had a mind of its own. The air grew hot and thick around her. Each inhalation strained her chest. Her lungs wanted to expel the air, but the pressure somehow clogged her lungs too, until she couldn't breathe at all.

No, no, no, this was wrong. An instinct she couldn't explain warned her not to give in, to fight the pressure by breathing. Darkness speckled her vision. Her pulse thundered behind the ringing in her ears.

Breathe.

Clenching her teeth, she tried to breathe. At first, her lungs refused to operate. She shut her eyes, struggling to block out the ringing in her ears and the burning in her chest. *Fight,* she willed herself.

The first breath came in ragged gasps. She hissed it out between clenched teeth, one molecule at a time. The second breath was easier, though not by much. The pressure inside her lungs eased a little more with each breath. The air around her cooled as the pressure let up.

The engine revved.

She held the keys in her hand. Didn't she? Opening her eyes, she glanced down to spy the keys clenched in her fist, the metal glistening in the sunlight that streamed through the windows.

The door handle was frozen in place. The lock was engaged but, though she clawed at it with her fingernails and yanked the handle hard, the door stayed shut. Pulling the handle should've released the lock, yet it refused to disengage. She used a key as a lever to push the lock upward. Still nothing. The mechanism was jammed.

She shoved her finger on the rocker switch that activated the electric windows. The window rolled down a few inches.

The switch rocked upward under her finger. Though she depressed it so hard her finger ached, the switch stayed in the up position. The window slid closed.

She banged her fists into the glass.

A voice—close, almost inside her head—chuckled in that low, gravelly, inhuman tone.

Then the voice spoke. Each syllable was drawn out for a second or two, which made the sound that much creepier.

"You are mine, golden girl," the voice rasped.

The gear shift lever clicked.

She turned her head to look at it. The lever had shifted into reverse.

In the rearview mirror, she saw several empty parking spaces and then…

A massive full-size pickup. It was the brick wall, and she crouched inside a tin can, one that might rocket backward at any second.

She swung her feet around and on top of the steering column.

The engine revved again. The brake pedal, depressed as far as it would go, began to lift slowly.

She pulled her legs back, took a deep breath, and slammed her feet toward the windshield.

The accelerator sank to the floorboard. The car shot backward.

The force hurled her into the steering column. Her torso crushed her legs into the wheel. Lightning glanced inside her head. Hot threads of pain, sharp as razor wire, webbed through her, and she cried out. She gritted her teeth and flung her body sideways onto the passenger seat.

In the rearview mirror, the image of the full-size pickup swelled larger and larger. She drew her knees to her chest and kicked at the windshield. The glass cracked. Pain ripped through her as if something inside her were cracking too. She kicked again. The glass buckled outward, breaking free of the frame in gummy clumps. She rose into a crouch on the passenger seat and propelled herself through the window. The instant she cleared the window, she rolled off the hood.

Her hip struck the ground first, setting off a cascade of pain. She clenched her jaw as tears stung her eyes.

The Pontiac smashed into the pickup with an explosive crunch. The car's back end crumpled.

She winced, though not in pain this time. Her insurance had a high deductible because she couldn't afford higher payments. She rather doubted the insurance company would agree to go after the responsible party since he was invisible and had apparently controlled her car through paranormal means. If she claimed a ghost caused the accident, they'd shoot her up with enough Thorazine to put Godzilla to sleep.

Shoes clapped on concrete. Pushing up into a sitting position, she glanced toward the Mail 'N More entrance.

Two security guards were trotting out of the building toward her.

She looked at the Pontiac.

The car was totaled. If she had stayed inside it, she would've died.

Something tried to kill her.

The security guards reached her. They knelt beside her, expressions grave, both staring at her as if her head had torn loose of her shoulders. She pressed a hand into the nape of her neck. Strands of hair tickled her hand. With her fingertips, she probed the base of her skull. Nope, still attached.

"Are you hurt?" one of the security guards asked.

She managed to shake her head without grimacing. "I think I'm okay."

The men helped her stand.

"What happened?" the second guard asked.

The car tried to kill me. She kept that to herself and said, "I don't know."

"Did the gas pedal suddenly go down? Cuz I saw a story on CNN 'bout that."

"That's exactly what happened."

It wasn't a lie, not really. The gas pedal had gone down suddenly. She couldn't tell the officer that a demon had possessed her car and floored the accelerator. She sincerely doubted he would understand the invisible-man defense.

Sometimes, a lie sounded more honest than the truth.

———

STAN ARNOLD, THE CNN FAN, DROVE GRACE HOME AN HOUR LATer. He and his partner had waited with her for the tow truck and the police to show up. The cops had questioned her politely but thoroughly about the accident and decided the gas pedal had malfunctioned, like in the CNN story Arnold mentioned. Grace said little, letting the men reach their own conclusions. She had no desire to tell them the truth.

After Arnold parked at the curb outside Grace's house, he took a few minutes to offer her advice on how to deal with her insurance company. She let him talk and nodded her head at the appropriate moments. He was being nice, which she appreciated, especially since everybody else seemed to want to abduct or murder her. No point in telling this nice man she couldn't afford her deductible, and therefore would be without a car for the foreseeable future.

Finally, Arnold bid her goodbye. She thanked him with genuine gratitude but then forced a smile as she exited his car. The brave face pinched a little more than usual today.

She waved as Arnold drove away.

Breathing deeply, she winced as the bruises on her chest, abdomen, and thighs flexed. Maybe that somber young man would come back to fix her up again. Whatever he'd done to her had seemed to drain him, though, and she didn't want to hurt, even inadvertently, one of the few people who had tried to help her. So maybe he should stay away. Bruises weren't life-threatening.

Sighing, she trudged into the house. After the security guards had summoned a tow truck, she'd sneaked into the Mail 'N More restroom. She hadn't needed to relieve herself. Rather, she needed to see what evidence the invisible attacker left behind. There, in the flicker of a crackling fluorescent bulb in a bathroom that no one had cleaned since President Truman left office, she'd surveyed her entire body.

Large purple bruises had formed on the backs of her thighs. Matching bruises dotted her chest and abdomen. Blood had caked at the edges of several fingernails. All those injuries must've resulted from either her struggle with the door or the backward thrust of the car. None proved what she knew had happened.

Someone tried to kill her. An invisible someone who wielded paranormal powers.

It sounded insane. But it was true.

As she shuffled into the kitchen, each movement tweaked her muscles, irritated the bruises, and elicited a faint grimace accompanied by a half-suppressed groan. She moved without lifting her feet from the floor because each step twanged her injuries. While breathing was no fun either, she relished it compared to walking.

In the bathroom, she found an old bottle of prescription anti-inflammatory pills and swallowed one, washing it down with water slurped straight from the bathroom tap. After that, she applied antibiotic ointment and an adhesive bandage to a small cut on her arm. That was all she could do, for now, so she headed into the bedroom.

A man sat on the bed.

Grace froze.

Waldron gazed at her without expression.

She needed a second, but only a second, to gather her courage and her thoughts. "What the hell do you want?"

His voice sounded calm, yet hard as concrete. "You know what I want."

"I'm not going anywhere with you. And if you try to force me, I'll kill you."

He laughed.

Not a chuckle. Not a derisive snort. A full-out guffaw.

Grace stared at him, feeling certain her face resembled that of a cartoon character emoting shock. Waldron laughed as if they were good buddies and she'd just told him a whopper of a joke. He even looked... happy.

A shiver swept through her, frigid and sharp.

As quickly as his laughter had erupted, it ended. The stoic, vaguely threatening expression returned.

Waldron stood and took two steps toward her. "Don't make this worse than it needs to be."

He was six feet from her. She scuffled backward into the doorway.

In one swift motion, Waldron whipped a semiautomatic handgun out of a holster inside his jacket and with his other hand pulled a pair of handcuffs out of his hip pocket.

She'd known that bulge under his jacket had to be a gun, not a cell phone. Being right about it hardly seemed important, though.

"Last chance," Waldron said. "Come willingly or—"

She spun around and bolted down the hallway.

Waldron took off after her. She heard his footfalls but didn't dare look back. As she ran, she unzipped her purse and curled her hand around her gun.

A hand seized her left wrist.

Waldron wrenched her backward into him. He wrapped his other arm around her torso, pinning her arms as they bounced to a halt. His lips brushed her ear. "Stop fighting. It's easier."

His fingernails pinched her skin. Grace struggled against his embrace even as he cinched his arm tighter around her torso. She fought the urge to kick and flail because she knew that wouldn't help. He was stronger and bigger and armed with both a gun and powerful muscles that felt as unyielding as steel wires. She couldn't wrench free of him. But she refused to let him know she had given up and refused to look as weak and helpless as she felt because he would just love that.

Her right hand was still clamped around her gun.

Waldron's arm was clinched around her just above her right elbow. She looked down at her feet. Waldron's much-larger shoes straddled hers. If she moved her hand a little to the right...

He released her left wrist to reach into his jacket pocket. Peripherally, she saw him withdraw a long, thin object.

A syringe.

She pulled the trigger.

The shot boomed through the house.

Waldron jerked and bellowed. Despite the deafening effect of the gunshot, she heard his cry. His mouth was inches from her ear.

His grip loosened just enough. She rammed her elbow backward into his gut and he stumbled backward. She yanked the gun out of her purse, whirled on him, and fired another shot.

Waldron dived sideways through the kitchen doorway.

She bolted out of the house.

No car. Jesus, no car. She had to get away from him *fast*. She ran down the sidewalk as swiftly as her legs would carry her, gritting her teeth against the pain of too many bruises. If she made it to the bus stop, and if there just happened to be a bus waiting there, she might have a chance. No, dammit, she had a chance either way. *Think*.

She fled past a car parked along the curb. A car with a man inside it. A man watching her. Through the open passenger window. He must've heard the gunshot and seen her fleeing. Yet he looked interested, perhaps even a little excited, rather than disturbed. No time to think about that.

Around the corner. Panting. Praying.

No bus. Only an empty bench.

She kept running.

Chapter Twelve

G RACE LOST TRACK OF HOW MANY BLOCKS SHE RAN BEFORE SHE FI-
nally caught up with a bus. She boarded along with two other people who paid zero attention to her. The driver glanced at the hole in
her purse, arched an eyebrow, and said nothing. The gunshot had torn
straight through the leather, and her previous escapades had left the bag
scuffed and stained. The combined effect lent her purse a postmodern
apocalyptic chic.

The bus transported her to a stop within a couple of blocks of the
Prairie Grass Motel. The establishment's name had always seemed odd to
her. Sure, they had grass here in Lassiter Falls, but this was hill country,
not the prairie. Today, however, she didn't give a damn what they called
the place as long as they gave her a room and let her pay cash. The pleasant, gray-haired man in the office granted her wish.

Inside the room, she locked the door and closed the drapes. By the
window, two chairs bookended a small round table. She hauled one of the
chairs over to the door, bracing it under the doorknob for extra protection. Then she tossed her purse onto the bedside table and collapsed onto
the bed.

The mattress was blissfully soft, and the quilt featured a patchwork of
soothing pastel colors. She rolled onto her side. Letting her muscles relax,
at last, she absently ran her fingers over the quilt's pattern. Everyone wanted
the flash drive. They all assumed she had it or knew where to find it. If
she didn't find the flash drive soon, whoever killed her grandfather would
kill her too. If the presence in her car had been the same someone, then
he'd already tried to kill her once. No, he could've killed her any time if
he'd wanted to. He—based on the disembodied voice, she assumed it was
a man—wanted to frighten her, probably hoping that would induce her to
cough up the flash drive.

Andrew Haley had mentioned a particular him. What had he said? The man with evil eyes. Darkness inside. Unfortunately, Andrew had been unable to remember the man's name or offer a more detailed description. Xavier Waldron's eyes definitely qualified as evil, and without a doubt, he harbored darkness inside him. But given the skimpy description, she shouldn't assume Waldron was the man Andrew mentioned. Surely if Waldron could attack her in absentia, he wouldn't bother harassing her in her home. Then again, she didn't understand the mind of a psychotic.

She rolled onto her back, gazing straight up at the ceiling.

A draft swirled through the room.

The accommodations looked nice, but this place clearly wasn't well insulated. Her musings about the motel couldn't keep her mind occupied, though, and her thoughts spiraled back to the flash drive.

Goosebumps popped up on her arms. The draft had turned chilly.

Look at the door.

The back of her neck tingled. Overcome by a sensation that she was not alone, she moved only her eyes to look at the door. The chair stood braced under the door handle, two of its feet tilted up off the floor. She shook her head. No one there, of course.

Grace yelped when *he* materialized near the door.

He just sort of…blurred into sight. Within half a second, the blurriness gave way to high definition, and he appeared as solid as any object in the room. If she touched him, he would feel solid and warm and alive. She knew that. She *felt* it.

David Ransom focused his blue eyes on her, and excitement tingled over her skin.

His mouth twitched at the corners as he crossed half the distance between them and halted.

She sat up, folding her arms over her chest. "Are you trying to kill me?"

"No. Someone else."

"Who?"

"I don't know."

"Come on, David."

His expression remained stoic.

Damn, she'd hoped to surprise him with the revelation that she knew his name and to somehow make him show a little emotion, if only for a second. She never knew what he was thinking, good or bad, and never could discern his intentions. His actions, like phrases heard out of context, gave her clues she struggled to decipher. She longed for an emotional outburst or a flash of anything on his face to help her decipher him. Instead, he looked her up and down as if assessing her physical state—not in a medical way, but rather in a concerned manner tinged with something else she couldn't quite identify. Something familiar and far more personal.

Familiar? Please. She knew nothing about him except his name.

As far as she remembered. That phrase left her feeling less than certain.

She scooted backward until her back met the headboard. Clasping her hands over her belly, she eyed him with an expression she hoped conveyed dispassion. "You know the guy who visited me in the hospital, don't you? The redhead who looked barely old enough to vote."

"I don't know what—"

She gave him a don't-screw-with-me look.

He stared at her for a few seconds. "Yes. I know him."

"Is he invisible too?"

David furrowed his brow. Finally, some emotion.

Grace rolled her eyes at him. "For pity's sake, would you please drop the strong-and-silent routine? It's getting old. I know who you are, David Ransom, so you might as well talk to me."

"My name isn't who I am."

She snorted. Not the most feminine sound, but it made the point.

Motionless, he watched her.

She watched him right back.

After a moment, he broke eye contact and cautiously settled onto the bed near her feet. "Do you have the flash drive?"

"Screw the flash drive."

They exchanged stares again. If they knew each other, she might've thought her rudeness surprised him. They did not know each other. He couldn't know she rarely spoke her mind with such bluntness, for fear of offending someone. Impolite behavior betrayed three things she avoided displaying—anger, fear, and weakness. Sure, she felt them sometimes, but nobody needed to know. Once people knew your weaknesses, they could exploit them.

That meant his look of confusion couldn't stem from shock at her rudeness. Her refusal to follow orders baffled him, no doubt, because he expected to get his way. He confided as little as possible in her while demanding her complete trust. She never granted her complete and unconditional faith to people who refused to reciprocate.

"You told me to destroy the flash drive," she said. "Now you want it. Give me one good reason why I should trust you."

He laid a hand on her ankle. The gesture, like much of his behavior toward her, felt intimate and oddly familiar. "I thought destroying the flash drive would protect you. I was wrong."

She couldn't look away from his eyes. Blue as jewels. Backlit by a fire within. The cool hue ignited a warmth in her belly that spread outward to infuse her entire being.

"I'm trying to help you," he said. "Did you destroy the flash drive?"

"I don't have it." She hesitated, then asked, "Why do you want to help me? I could be a criminal or a devil worshiper or something."

He shook his head. "You're a good person. The best, in fact."

About to speak, she froze with her mouth open. His voice, soft yet firm, divulged a deep and inexplicable belief in her basic goodness, a faith beyond what his words conveyed, beyond anything anyone had shown her in all her life. If he was acting, he deserved an Academy Award. Her instincts told her he wasn't lying. He meant exactly what he said.

Maybe she could trust him. A little.

Yeah, she kept waffling on the trust thing.

"If you honestly want to be useful," she said, "then help me get the flash drive."

"I don't know where it is."

"Of course not."

She regretted the sarcasm in her voice the instant she spoke the words. David sat stone-still, his head cocked to one side, those luminous eyes fixed on her.

Then he rose, turned toward the door, and stepped *through* it.

He actually stepped through the closed door. Through a solid object.

A chill shimmied up her spine.

Before she could wonder where he'd gone, David stepped back through the door into the room. He seated himself on the bed again, this time much closer to her. His hip nearly brushed against hers when he sat down, and he could've reached out to touch her face.

Another wave of warmth swept through her. When she spoke, her voice came out a little more breathless than she'd intended. "You walked through the door. How did you do that?"

He shrugged. "I thought I sensed activity out there. It's all calm, though."

She straightened her spine and toughened her voice. "Don't ignore my questions. I want to know how you can walk through solid objects. What the hell are you?"

"Later."

"No, now."

He leaned toward her, so close his breath wafted over her. It smelled like cinnamon. How odd that a ghost should have nice breath. Or any breath at all.

"Are you dead?" she asked.

"No." He grasped her shoulders. "Listen to me. You are in danger. The people who want the flash drive will stop at nothing to find it—and I mean nothing. Blackmail. Torture. Murder." He pulled her forward until their noses almost touched. "We must find the flash drive. *Now.* Maybe then we can find a way to stop our enemies."

We. He kept using that word, as if they worked together or…something.

His breath tickled her lips, and she had the strangest urge to kiss him.

Instead, she asked, "Who are our enemies?"

"I don't know. I've met their employees, but never the person or group in charge."

The man with evil eyes. Grace swallowed against a newly formed lump in her throat. "I don't know how to find the flash drive."

David released her shoulders. He dropped his hands and folded them over hers, which she still held over her belly. His skin felt hot on hers. She hadn't realized how cold her hands were.

"I'll help you," he said.

"Okay."

He squeezed her hands, then let go and pulled away from her. "Did your grandfather leave you anything when he died?"

"Um, no."

"You didn't receive any of his effects?"

She thought about that for a moment. "Just a box of clothes and stuff."

David raised his eyebrows. "What stuff?"

"Mementos."

He jumped up, sending a little earthquake through the bed. "We should check all of Edward's effects. He might've hidden something in them."

She saluted him. "Yes, sir."

A smile threatened to rupture his stoicism. He regained control just in time, however—which was a shame in her opinion.

She clambered off the bed and onto her feet.

David started for the door.

"Wait," she said. "Someone attacked me in my house. He might still be there."

"I'll check."

He vanished.

Grace stood there, feeling more perplexed than at any other moment in her life. People did not disappear like that. He must be a ghost, but he'd denied being dead.

Suddenly, she wished she drank alcohol. Getting soused appealed to her right now.

David snapped back into view. She'd blinked and—poof—he was there again.

"The house is empty," he pronounced, and motioned for her to come. "Let's go."

She didn't move.

He gestured again. "I'll answer any questions you want later. For now, we have to go."

"Fine."

Grace slung her dilapidated purse around her neck to hang across her torso. David watched as she marched to the door, shoved the chair aside, unfastened the lock, and flung the door open. He followed her outside as if he needed a doorway to get out of the room.

She strode to the bus stop.

"Where's your car?" David asked.

She sat down on the bench. "My car is trashed."

"What now, then?"

"We wait for the bus."

———

GRACE RODE THE BUS ALONE SINCE DAVID DISAPPEARED AGAIN FIFteen minutes later, right before the bus pulled up to the stop. The trip seemed to take forever, probably because she spent the entire ride thinking about Waldron and the flash drive and going back to the house where more than one someone had attacked her recently. Andrew Haley struck her as harmless. Waldron was far from it.

She wanted to go back to the house slightly more than she wanted to lie down in the middle of the interstate at rush hour. David was right, though, and it was annoying as hell. She needed to go back so she could search through her grandfather's effects. Everyone else believed he'd left her the flash drive. If so, then he must've hidden it in his belongings, among the things he knew she would receive upon his death.

Which meant he'd known he would die. Or at least, he'd known somebody wanted to kill him.

The bus pulled up to the stop in her neighborhood. She disembarked, heading down the sidewalk toward home. As she turned the corner onto her street, she slipped her hand inside her purse to grasp the gun. She had four bullets left since she'd fired two at Waldron. God, she hoped he was in pain. Lots and lots of pain.

The car she'd seen earlier was nowhere in sight. Either it had nothing to do with Waldron, which seemed improbable, or Waldron and his buddy had left the vicinity. Maybe the other guy drove Waldron to the hospital. Maybe he'd be laid up for days, safely out of her orbit.

Or maybe he'd found a better place to park his car, where she couldn't see it.

Might as well be positive. He probably left, at least for a while.

She kept her hand on the gun anyway.

When she reached the house, she hesitated with her hand on the knob of the front door. She'd left the door wide open, more concerned with escaping than locking up the house. Waldron must've closed it. *Creepy.*

She twisted the knob. It turned in her hand. Waldron might've shut the door, but he hadn't locked it. Well, given that she had invisible beings trying to kill her, worrying about the unlocked door seemed pointless.

Shoving the door inward, she walked into the house.

Quiet. Still. Vacant.

Grace wandered into the kitchen, and then down the hallway. Empty.

A memory flashed in her mind. Waldron's arms around her. Hauling her backward.

She blinked away the mental images. Jeez, she couldn't remember eight months of her life, eight months she desperately needed to remember, but she recalled in vivid detail events she would've preferred to forget.

Down the hallway. Into the bedroom. No one there either.

She swung open the folding doors that concealed the closet. Behind her shoes, at the back of the closet, sat a cardboard box sealed with clear packing tape. She'd opened the box once, glanced at the contents, and sealed it up again. They weren't her belongings. She had no use for them, and she didn't like looking at them. The items inside the box reminded her of Grandpa, of how much she'd lost. She hadn't been able to deal with those feelings on top of everything else.

Back when the box had arrived, "everything else" had meant amnesia and migraines. Now the term referred to a hell of a lot more. Too much more.

No choice. She had to suck it up and keep moving. Falling apart was not an option. It would get her killed.

Pushing her shoes out of the way, she reached for the box.

A hand grasped her shoulder.

She yelped and jumped. Glancing backward, she saw David crouched behind her.

"Let me do that," he said.

Well, she couldn't see the harm in letting him carry the box for her. He might disappear with it, she supposed, but she doubted it.

Why she doubted it, she couldn't explain. She just did.

She scuttled backward, out of the way.

David picked up the box and carried it to the bed, where he set it down on the comforter.

Grace met him at the bed, seating herself beside the box, on the edge of the mattress. The comforter felt soft and cushy under her. Even better than the motel mattress. She longed to stretch out on the bed and take a nap.

Not yet. Suck it up, girl, and keep moving.

David ripped the packing tape off the box. It made a zipping sound.

The box's flaps popped up a little. Grace folded them back, revealing the contents. A sweater her mom had knit for her grandfather lay on top. She lifted it out, setting the garment on the bed. No flash drive there. David lifted out three framed diplomas representing Edward McLean's degrees—bachelor's, master's, and doctorate. There was a scarf, also knit by Grace's mother, and a photo album filled with images of their family. Grace lifted out a Christmas tree ornament, one of three she'd made in the fourth grade. One was for her parents, the other two for her grandparents. The last item in the box was a trophy from her grandfather's high school days when he'd won a swimming competition. Packing peanuts filled the rest of the box. Grace rifled through the peanuts but found nothing hidden within them.

She propped herself up with one arm, surveying the Styrofoam peanuts that lay scattered over the bed and the floor at her feet.

David settled onto the bed, on the opposite side of the box. He placed the three framed diplomas back inside it.

Grace stared at the frames. Something tickled her brain. Knowledge just beyond her reach.

She grabbed the diplomas and deposited them on her lap. Turning each over to examine both sides, she compared the three frames. One had a slight bulge on its backside where the cardboard backing had warped. The bulge was visible only when the light struck it a certain way. Maybe it was a manufacturing defect.

"What is it?" David asked.

She raised a hand to silence him. Setting aside the other two frames, she took hold of the third and carefully turned the little metal prongs that held the backing in place. The cardboard came free. She eased it out of the frame, laying it on the bed. In the space now revealed, she saw a small, thin black rectangle of plastic.

Grace picked up the little object. A smile broke across her face as triumph buoyed her spirits. The object in her hand was a flash drive.

She grinned at David, waving the flash drive in the air like a minuscule flag.

"You found it," he said, sounding surprised and impressed at the same time. His almost-smile morphed into a slight frown. "I should go. I've been out too long."

"Out? What, are you a fugitive?"

"Something like that."

He rose from the bed and stepped backward. She knew that meant he was about to disappear again.

Grace lunged off the bed, grabbed the front of his shirt, and dragged him closer.

"Oh no you don't," she said. "You promised to answer my questions."

His face was inches from hers. She felt the warmth of his body through his shirt. A ghost couldn't feel warm, and anyway, he said he wasn't dead. If not a spirit, then what?

"Are you an alien?" she asked.

He smiled a little and chuckled softly. "No."

"Then what are you?"

"A messenger. Someone has—"

"To warn me." She let go of his shirt. "Yeah, yeah, I've heard that already. I have no idea what I need to be warned about, but I sure as hell know I'm supposed to be warned."

"Take the flash drive to Senator Faulkner in Washington. He'll know what to do."

"Destroy it, keep it. Go away, do me a favor. Make up your mind."

He brushed a finger across her cheek. "If you don't do this, they'll kill you."

"Fine, I'll take it to Senator Falcon."

"Faulkner. Elias Faulkner."

"Whatever." She pushed away from him. "Just tell me one thing before you—"

He was gone. Wind gusted through the room, swirling toward the center. The damaged door rocked on its hinges.

People kept ordering her around, demanding information from her, trying to kill her. None of them bothered to tell her what the blazes was happening. They expected obedience without question.

Grace flopped down on the bed. It was mid-afternoon, though it felt like at least two o'clock in the morning. Her body hurt all over, from bruises and weariness. She could no more fight villains right now than she could scale Mount Everest. An anthill might prove too much for her.

Sleep. She must get some sleep.

Not here. The house felt...tainted. Waldron might come back for a rematch, and this time he could win.

She tucked the flash drive in her jeans pocket. Picking up the document frame, she slid the cardboard backing into place and locked it there with the metal prongs. The diploma inside the frame was her grandfather's PhD. She gazed at it for a moment, her throat tightening, then returned the frame to the box. Scooping all the packing peanuts back into it, she resealed the packing tape. In case Waldron did return to the house, she lugged the box back to the closet and stowed it behind her shoes.

At her desk, she plugged the flash drive into the USB port on the front of her computer. A message popped up on-screen.

ENTER PASSWORD.

A secondary message below that one warned she had three attempts before the drive would be permanently locked. *Terrific*. She was too tired to figure out the password. Maybe after a decent nap, her brain would function better.

She stashed the laptop in its carrying case, slinging the strap over her shoulder, and left the house via the back door. An alleyway separated the houses on her street from those on the next street. She decided against going to the same bus stop as before. This time, she walked in the opposite direction, to a bus stop a little farther away. The wait seemed interminable, but finally, the bus pulled up and she boarded.

This bus had a different route. The closest stop to the motel was three blocks away.

She lost track of time as the bus chugged down the streets, pausing at stops along the way. Eventually, she made it back to the motel and into her room. She tossed her purse onto the bedside table and set the laptop case on the other table by the window. After bracing a chair under the door handle, she kicked off her boots and collapsed onto the bed without bothering to pull back the quilt.

Her mind plummeted into sleep.

GRACE WOKE AS A GASP EXPLODED OUT OF HER. *THE DREAM.* FOR NEARLY a year, it had recurred every night. Until a few days ago, she hadn't dreamed of the corridor in months. Certainly, she had *never* dreamed of a faceless man until this week. Now, the dream had changed again. She had seen the mystery man's face.

He was Xavier Waldron.

The corridor. The room. The *man.*

Waldron. Her mind could've inserted his face into the dream because of her encounter with him earlier. The creep had assaulted her and tried to drug her. Had the figure in the dream always belonged to Xavier Waldron? Had he somehow hidden his features from her until tonight when, through a process that bewildered her, she unmasked him? In a dream. With her thoughts. Three days ago, the notion would've made her laugh. Today, she had no frigging idea if it was possible.

Or maybe someone else wanted her to think the faceless man was Waldron.

If Waldron had invaded her dreams, he was no FBI agent. He wasn't even human because no human could torment her by invading her REM cycle. Yet he seemed human enough. Totally evil, but human.

Questions and suspicions. Riddles and mysteries.

If he wanted her dead, why didn't he just do it? She hated being the duck in the shooting gallery, hearing the shots, uncertain which bang would signify the bullet that shattered her head. Waldron could've killed her anytime he pleased—strangled her, shot her, pushed her in front of a bus. Instead, he tormented her and tried to abduct her.

He wanted the flash drive. Seemed like everybody did.

David had said someone else was in charge of Operation Drive Grace Insane.

A headache pushed against her skull with the force of ten hammers pounding inside her head. Even the pale-yellow glow from the bedside lamp pained her eyes. Another migraine. Why did the dream give her migraines? Why did everything have to be so hard?

She covered her face with her hands. Light seeped between her fingers. She rolled onto her side, her back to the lamp. She did not want to turn off the light. Never knew when a psycho might break through the window to assault her. So instead, she draped her arm over her eyes. It worked a little better than her hands.

What awaited her in the future remained a mystery, a gift she preferred to leave wrapped. Not that she had a choice. The gift would open itself, and a nightmare version of a Jack-in-the-box would pop out to throttle her.

And it was all happening because of a tiny plastic rectangle.

The memory of the dream whispered through her mind in the form of a man's inhuman voice. He didn't urge her to give in, like before. Instead, he murmured something far more disturbing and bewildering.

You are mine, golden girl.

CHAPTER THIRTEEN

G RACE WOKE TO THE SOUND OF AN ENGINE GROWLING OUTSIDE THE window. She didn't remember falling asleep again. The sunlight no longer trickled in through the gaps between the drapes and the window frame. She glanced at the clock on the bedside table. It was nearly eight o'clock. She'd slept for…a long time. Since she couldn't recall what time she'd made it back to the motel, she had no clue how long she'd slept.

Pushing off the bed, she stood. Her bruises were firmly set now, but they hurt less than before. She walked toward the window, tripped, and knocked into the table hip first. Pain lanced down her thigh. A little grunt burst out of her. Okay, the bruises hurt less *except* when she banged them.

At the window, she parted the drapes a crack and peered outside. The parking lot was quiet, save for a big old four-door sedan that sat idling in front of the third room down from hers. A middle-aged woman slumped in the passenger seat holding a road map, which she studied with intense interest. No one else was in sight.

Not that seeing nothing meant nothing was there.

Grace let the drapes fall closed. She tossed her purse onto the bed and grabbed her laptop case. Once she'd settled into a comfortable position on the quilt, she unzipped her purse. The gun lay snug in its holster. She brought it out and set it on the quilt beside her. She hadn't wanted to turn off the bedside lamp for safety reasons, but she forgot to keep the gun with her. Her brain had been more exhausted than she realized.

Digging in her purse, she located the microcassette recorder. Before tackling the password problem on the flash drive, she needed to hear the entire recording. It must contain vital information, otherwise Brian Kellogg wouldn't have taken such pains to conceal the tape.

She pressed play.

The tape hissed. "What's going on in there?"

Grandpa's voice sounded distant and strained, as if he had laryngitis.

Thump. Another voice croaked, "No."

Knock-knock. It sounded like someone rapping on a door. Interference whined on the tape. *Creak.*

A gasp. "Holy mother of God…"

On the recording, thunder exploded. Wind howled. Grandpa screamed.

Grace's throat constricted. Tears stung her eyes, but she blinked them away.

Interference whined again in the recording. Someone wheezed, probably her grandfather. She bit her lip, shut her eyes, sucked in a breath. She must listen. She must know.

Laughter grumbled close to the recorder. "Say good night, Edward."

Every molecule of liquid in Grace's body seemed to freeze. She opened her eyes, glancing around the room. Nothing had changed. But the voice on the tape sounded exactly like the disembodied voice she'd heard in her car.

The tape continued, this time with her grandfather's voice. "Stop this, please. You want me, the others are innocent. Let them go, take me inst—"

He cried out, the shout choked off by hands that, though she could not see them, she felt around her neck as she listened to the strangled gasps and gurgles emanating from the tape. He'd suffered. Some invisible bastard had murdered him, and he had suffered.

She choked back a sob.

The inhuman voice growled, "I'm coming for Grace next. You can't protect her anymore. I will have my golden girl."

The recording ended with a click.

Grace massaged her throat. A tear trickled down her cheek. *He suffered.* She studied the cassette player as if it might sprout a mouth and chomp off her hand. She could no longer call such an event impossible. Anything was possible. The universe had gone insane. Grandpa had been murdered by a ghost, a demon, something evil beyond comprehension.

And now it wanted her. It killed her grandfather to get to her.

Golden girl. The disembodied voice in her dreams had called her that. In the last nightmare, Waldron had called her the same thing. The evidence seemed to connect Waldron to the disembodied attacker, but if he had that kind of power, why assault her in such an old-fashioned physical way, as he had in her house? Unless she was right that the person or thing actually behind all this madness wanted her to believe Waldron was her top enemy so she'd stop looking for another culprit. She couldn't know for sure.

She knew almost nothing for sure.

The tape whirred inside the player. She pressed the stop button.

Her throat was so dry it hurt. She trudged to the bathroom where she found a shrink-wrapped plastic cup. After a brief battle with the shrink-wrap, she freed the cup and filled it from the tap. The water was lukewarm, but it quenched her thirst. She gulped down the cup's contents, refilled it, and took her beverage back to the bed. She booted up the laptop. Plugging in the flash drive, she waited for the password message to appear.

She understood why her grandfather had taken precautions. Still, she wished he hadn't made accessing the drive so difficult. How he expected her to know the password—and what he expected her to do once she accessed the drive's contents—she didn't know. He'd entrusted her with a secret that others would kill to possess. He'd believed she would know what to do about the mess, how to clean it up, where to seek help, who to trust.

He credited her with greater intelligence than she had. Her skills of deduction and logic couldn't solve the mystery and save the world. If she had those skills, she would've figured things out by now.

Forget the self-pity. Take command, girl. Grab the wheel and steer the damn car. So what if demons could take control of the car anytime. Don't make it easy for them to kill you. Claw. Scream. Fight.

Self-delivered pep talks weren't ideal. With nobody else around to bolster her flagging enthusiasm, however, she had to make do with the tools available to her. *Stop whining*, she chastised. Whatever must be done, she must do it. Whatever force kept foiling her, she must expose and neutralize it. Wherever she must go, she would get there somehow.

In front of her lay a precipice. Behind, an army of demons. The time had come to jump.

The password. Grandpa must've programmed the drive with a phrase he felt certain she would know. How? Without any clues, she couldn't narrow down the possibilities. The password might be anything.

He would have left a clue.

She shut her eyes, thinking back to when she'd found the flash drive hidden inside the document frame. No clues there. The frame had looked normal, just glass and gold-colored metal. The diploma housed inside the frame was nothing special either. It held sentimental value, of course. Edward McLean had kept all three of his diplomas in his apartment, mounted on the wall in the living room right next to a photograph of Stonehenge. She'd asked him once why he kept a picture of an ancient monument on his wall.

"It's simple," he'd said. "Stonehenge is a mystery that modern experts believe they've solved, but in reality, they've misinterpreted much of the evidence to fit their preconceived ideas. It's the same with the human brain. Scientists believe they understand a great deal about how the mind works, yet they've misinterpreted or outright dismissed the most important evidence."

His answer still confused her. Comparing the brain to an ancient monument seemed like an apples-to-oranges issue. She'd told him as much.

But had only smiled and said, "The bluestone, Grace, the bluestone. It's the key to everything. People prattle on about the Rosetta Stone, but it's the bluestone that matters. Once we find the brain's bluestone, we'll have a real clue to work with."

"Bluestone?" she'd asked.

"Yes. Stonehenge contains a type of rock called bluestone, which the ancients quarried hundreds of miles from the Salisbury Plain, where Stonehenge was constructed. Those ancient people transported the stones from the mountains down to the plain, supposedly without the wheel or beasts of burden."

"But what's that got to do with the brain?"

"We won't know until we find the neurological bluestone."

She never had figured out what he'd meant. He could be outrageously cryptic when he felt like it.

Bluestone.

She looked at the computer screen, and the ENTER PASSWORD prompt displayed on its screen. Could that be the answer? It seemed too arcane.

Exactly the kind of thing Grandpa had loved. The arcane and mysterious.

She typed BLUESTONE into the password field and hit enter.

The box on-screen disappeared. A new message popped up in its place. This one didn't ask for a password. It displayed a single paragraph of text.

"This flash drive is dangerous," the note said. "Get rid of it ASAP. Contact Senator Elias Faulkner and arrange to transfer the drive to his custody. He'll know what to do with it. Then GET OUT of it, Grace. Do not get involved any further, I mean it. I'm sorry I had to involve you, but I had no way of getting the flash drive to Senator Faulkner myself. Please forgive me."

The note was signed "Grandpa."

Get out of it. Why the vehemence? He'd died before anyone or anything came after her. If he'd known demons would try to kill her, he would've suggested she grab a shotgun and blast them into itty-bitty pieces. He would've warned her. And why give her clues that helped her figure out the password for the flash drive if he didn't want her to read its contents?

The note ordered her to stay out of it. David had issued the same command. Like she would obey a stranger. One who refused to explain himself. One who disappeared at will. Yet the more time she spent with him, the less he felt like a stranger.

The note was outdated. Given her predicament, Grandpa would want her to continue. Probably. She thought. Either way, his wishes no longer mattered. The situation had escalated too far for her to back out now, and she doubted she could back out, anyway. Waldron seemed unlikely to leave her alone simply because she promised to stay out of his way, especially if she failed to turn over the flash drive. Edward McLean must've had more enemies than he realized.

At least now she had a plan, sort of. She'd call Senator Faulkner, tell him what had happened, and ask for his help. If he refused, if he demanded that she relinquish the flash drive, she'd hang up on him. The drive was her bulletproof vest. Possession of it warded off her enemies, for now. If she gave up the flash drive, nothing stood between her and the forces that wanted her dead. She already had an invisible someone who wanted her dead. She didn't need more demons nipping at her soul.

She closed the little window that displayed the note. A new window opened, this one a list of files contained on the flash drive. The files looked like spreadsheets or databases of information, along with a handful of text documents. She double-clicked on a file called "test sites." The spreadsheet that opened listed locations all over the world, from New York to Singapore, with abbreviations beside the place names—RV, AP, TK, PC, GP. The letters meant nothing to her, and the spreadsheet offered no explanation. Each location also had been designated as "active" or "inactive," but she couldn't tell what that meant either. As she scanned the list again, she realized only one of the locations was labeled "active," and that one wasn't a true location, anyway. It was simply called "primary facility."

Brian Kellogg had mentioned working at a research facility. Could this "primary facility" be the same one?

She closed the file and opened one of the text documents. Fifty pages of dense text documented, in scientist-speak, the "protocols" for initiating "test episodes." Grace skimmed the document, but the sentences made no sense to her. She closed the file and tried another.

This text looked like a report of some kind, written in technical jargon way outside her expertise. The text was peppered with Latin phrases and extremely long words supposedly drawn from the English language, though she couldn't figure out what they meant. She tried looking up some of the words in an online dictionary, but the terms must've been so arcane that they didn't appear in a normal dictionary. The document also liberally used the abbreviations found in the spreadsheet.

She closed the document and browsed the rest of the files. More gobbledygook. The last file was a database called "Interim Results." She selected a portion of the database labeled "RV" and scrolled through the contents, watching table after table of data roll across the computer screen. She saw numbers, symbols, incomprehensible text. Graphs interspersed between the tables and text illustrated "Rates of Incidence," "Projected Accuracy vs. Real-Time Accuracy," "Levels of Impulse Strength Over a 24-Hour Period," and more data that sounded like nonsense.

Giving up on the database, she opened the second to last file. It contained two pages scanned from a *Time* magazine profile of a man named Jackson Tennant, founder of Digital Prognostics, a company that produced security software for corporate, government, and consumer use. The company claimed their software detected potential security problems before they happened, hence the company's name. Prognostic meant "able to predict the future."

Behind the article text, a two-page photo spread featured Jackson Tennant himself. The photo showed a young man, perhaps thirty, lounging on the beach with a laptop computer beside him. A wind displaced his dark hair. Sunglasses masked his eyes. The sunlight on his face brought out the golden tones of his skin. He was attractive, in a spoiled-rich-boy way. The smirk on his lips seemed to intimate a disdain for the camera mingled with a craving for the attention it bestowed on him, as did his torn jeans and his T-shirt emblazoned with the logo for his company.

Digital Prognostics. What did the company have to do with anything? Her grandfather wouldn't have included the article on the flash drive unless it had some relation to the mystery at hand. She read the article again, more closely this time. Nothing relevant. Not that she could see, anyhow. The journalist salivated over Tennant's wealth and charm while criticizing his company's domination of the security software market, although Tennant also owned several subsidiaries involved in everything from manufacturing to, of all things, a cruise ship line. The article elucidated the government's anti-trust lawsuit against the company, which Tennant dismissed as "so completely lame." Charts illustrated the conglomerate's growth over the past five years, its current market share, and other information irrelevant to her problems.

She glanced over a quote from Tennant, then doubled back to reread the statement.

"I want to change humanity forever," Tennant says. "My software is the tool I use to implement that change."

The statement struck her as odd and vaguely creepy, but she couldn't deduce a connection between the flash drive, her grandfather's research, and Digital Prognostics. Though Jackson Tennant might be a weirdo, that didn't make him a psychopath.

Something destined to change humanity forever.

Kellogg had spoken those words when describing the "something" her grandfather had left for her. At the time, she'd dismissed his words as the ramblings of a nutjob. Maybe she shouldn't have.

She double-clicked the last file on the drive.

Scrolling down. Tables. Data. Nonsense, all of it. She stopped at a table that listed names of "travelers," their "designations," and a number described as "accuracy." The list named two dozen people. Each name was a hot link to a page on a website identified only by a string of numbers and dots that she recognized as an IP address. Scanning the names on the list, she froze. One was familiar.

Traveler: David Ransom. Designation: RV (Level 10). Accuracy: 97.9874.

She clicked the link. Even a cheap motel like this one offered free Wi-Fi, so her laptop had already detected the connection. The website loaded. A dialog box popped up requesting a username and password. *Wonderful.* Another secret code.

A light flickered on her computer, indicating the hard drive was working. The username and password appeared in the dialog box. User name: Hermes. Password: Elysium.

The reference to Greek mythology baffled her. Hermes had been the messenger of the gods, Elysium a paradise akin to heaven. The password for the flash drive had been related to Stonehenge. What did any of it mean? Maybe nothing. Maybe her grandfather was just being arcane.

She hit enter. The password box disappeared, replaced by another dialog box. This one delivered a warning: "Access to this page requires fingerprint ID. Please place your thumb on the reader."

She doubted the word "reader" referenced a connoisseur of books. Damn, she'd left her fingerprint reader in her other purse, along with her retinal scanner and DNA tester.

Her laptop's hard drive whirred to life. The message on-screen changed. It now said, "Loading fingerprint file." A couple of seconds ticked by, and then the dialog box closed. The web page loaded.

The page was titled "Status report." A subheading identified the "traveler" as David Ransom and repeated his designation. She read the next line.

The air in her lungs seemed to turn to cement. Her skin tingled as every hair on her body stiffened. No invisible assailant caused her symptoms this time around, though. Goosebumps raised on her arms because of what the next line of text said. It gave today's date, but what came next left her feeling cold and warm at the same time.

Status as of 0800 hours: In transit at main facility, Mojave Desert, California. Vital signs normal. Excursion ends 1200 hours.

Her vision blurred and refocused. The document claimed David was not a ghost, not a demon, not a hallucination. He was real. He lived and breathed somewhere in the Mojave Desert. He was "in transit at main facility," but the statement made no sense. How could he be "in transit" if he was at a facility? Maybe they got the wording wrong and meant he was in transit *from* the main facility.

She stared at the text on the web page. Vital signs normal. Excursion ends 1200 hours.

Excursion. Traveler. In transit. What in the hell had Grandpa gotten mixed up in? What had he gotten *her* mixed up in?

A chill curled around her throat. She wasn't alone. With her finger hovering over the laptop's touch pad, she looked at the door. No one there. The chill deepened, and she rubbed her arms through her jacket.

She whispered, "David?"

The cold slithered down her spine, around her chest. A breeze, like the breath of a ghost, touched her hand. She couldn't breathe, couldn't move. Her finger, poised over the touch pad, jerked.

She had not moved her finger. Not on purpose.

Grace felt downward pressure on her finger. Fighting the pressure didn't help. Her fingertip depressed the button on the touch pad, and on the screen, the web browser closed.

She tried jerking her hand away. It ignored her commands and moved without her consent. Her finger clicked the touch pad button again. And again. The file window closed. The mouse pointer on-screen spun across the desktop and clicked an icon. A message announced that the media had been ejected successfully.

What the...

Her hand lifted off the touch pad and reached for the flash drive plugged into the USB port. She struggled against the force that had taken over her hand. Her arm froze, trembling. She gritted her teeth and concentrated her every thought on regaining control of her hand. Her arm shook harder. Muscles cramped up. Pain fired straight up her arm into her shoulder.

She gasped. Her breaths came shallow and fast, almost hyperventilating.

Her arm jerked.

She shivered from head to toe. Her teeth chattered. Her arm burned.

A voice cried out.

Her arm dropped onto her lap. She slumped against the headboard, panting, and looked around the room. No one was nearby.

A human had cried out. She'd heard the wail.

Maybe the voice had been hers. No. The voice had sounded male, young, and frightened—and eerily close.

The hairs on her neck stiffened.

A voice spoke inside her head. "I'm not supposed to let you look. I'm sorry."

The same voice that had cried out before.

He spoke in a soft, uneven tone. "I promised to watch over you. Not let bad things happen. That's why you can't look."

She glanced around using only her peripheral vision. Maybe the kid was hiding in the bathroom. She leaped up to check there, but the room was empty. No one lurked in the shadows. She knew he was nowhere in the building. Nowhere in the state of Texas. He probably lived at the "main facility" in the Mojave Desert with David. Didn't take a clairvoyant to conclude that much. The voice belonged to the young man who'd healed her back in the hospital.

Standing beside the bed now, she listened for the fragile voice.

"Understand?" he said.

He was pleading for her agreement. She opened her mouth to speak but stopped. The kid could talk to her in her mind. Maybe she could communicate with him the same way.

Sure, I'll just beam my thoughts to him like a goddamn radio transmitter. No problem.

Bullshit. She was no psychic. Her only option for communicating with other beings was to do it the old-fashioned way.

"Who are you?" she asked.

Silence.

Frustration boiled inside her, but she slammed a lid on it. "I'm Grace, but I think you already know that. Please tell me your name."

His voice echoed in her mind as real as if he stood before her. "Sean Vandenbrook."

"Are you with David?"

"Not supposed to say. Said too much already."

He was gone.

She sensed his absence rather than his departure. Couldn't explain why. Couldn't explain anything. She had conversed with a boy named Sean, in her head, over a distance of more than a thousand miles.

Grace shivered.

She grabbed the flash drive, tucking it inside her bra. No man would think to look there, or at least she hoped they wouldn't. Sean said he wasn't supposed to let her look. At what? The flash drive, she assumed, since Sean had forced her to eject it from the computer. The order had come from David, no doubt. But she couldn't figure out why he sent a kid to stop her from looking at the flash drive. Until now, he had watched over her. Annoyed her. Evaded her questions.

Saved her life.

Maybe he was in trouble. Not that she cared. Her concern didn't signify anything personal. She wanted no one to get hurt, not Sean, not David, not anyone.

Excluding the person who murdered Grandpa. She prayed he would suffer.

David sought to prevent her from looking at the flash drive. He wanted her uninvolved. To hell with what he wanted. She needed answers. She needed the truth. She needed to ensure the murderer paid for his crime. To accomplish that, she needed more information.

She must look. She had looked, a little, and none of the information she saw made sense.

How could she expect it to? Nothing added up anymore.

Thoughts spun in her brain with almost dizzying speed. Invisible assailants. Telepathy. Neuroscience. Digital Prognostics.

Something destined to change humanity.

Her grandfather, a neuroscientist, had studied something so earth-shattering that dangerous people would kill to possess it. For the first time in days—no, months—she understood the root of her problems. The data on the flash drive, combined with everything she'd experienced, added up to one thing.

Her grandfather, and her parents, had studied psychic phenomena.

And someone wanted their research. Someone who would kill to get it.

CHAPTER FOURTEEN

GRACE RUBBED HER NECK. HER EYES FELT GRITTY, HER MOUTH dry. She sipped water from the cup on the bedside table and then she returned her attention to the document on-screen. Though she'd unplugged the flash drive, her computer was still logged onto the mystery site. She scrolled down the list of names until she found the one she wanted.

Traveler: Sean Vandenbrook. Designation: TK (Level 9). Accuracy: 93.725.

Clicking the link, she waited for the web page to load. When it did, she read the status report that, like David's, consisted of one short paragraph.

Status as of 0800 hours: In transit at main facility, Mojave Desert, California. Vital signs normal. Excursion ends 0900 hours.

In transit. At the facility. David's status report had said the same thing. It made no more sense now than it had a few minutes ago.

She reached for the touch pad, intending to close the browser window. A line of text at the bottom of the screen flashed. She hesitated. The text, a link to another page, flashed again. *View current excursion data (real time).*

She clicked the link.

The page switched to a chat-room-style window. As in a chat room, the text appeared line-by-line on the screen. But rather than being attributed to the screen name of the person typing the text, each segment was attributed to an abbreviation. The text seemed to be a real-time transcription of a conversation between someone designated TK24 and another person identified as LEAD.

"I can't do it," TK24 pleaded, "I want to sleep."

"Time's not up. Keep going," LEAD said and then, after a pause, added, "You're restrained. You can't get up, so stop trying."

"I can't do this anymore. Please."

"Tears accomplish nothing." Another pause in the text, and then: "Give him the lorazepam. He's useless now."

"Please no," TK24 begged. Grace could imagine the fear in his voice, despite the sterility of the typed words.

Suddenly, LEAD asked, "Who's logged on?"

A third individual, TECH3, responded. "JT's monitoring."

"Who else?"

"Nobody."

"What's that?" LEAD demanded. "Someone else is logged on."

TK24 said, "I'll do it. I'm okay now."

"No, it's too late," LEAD told him. "Session terminated."

The page went blank. A message glowed on the screen in bold red letters. "Unauthorized access. Tracking…"

The last word blinked.

And the message changed: "Re-initializing real-time link."

The chat window reopened. A single line of text, sent by LEAD, glared at her from the screen: "Identify yourself."

The cursor blinked on the screen, below the text. They demanded a response. She hovered her fingers over the keyboard. This could be a trap. Refusing to respond communicated weakness and fear. Responding would let them know she had control, or at least that she wasn't cowering under the bed. Even if that was what she felt like doing right at this moment.

But they didn't need to know that.

She typed two words, which appeared on-screen identified as GUEST. They could, no doubt, track her IP address or something. Better keep this brief.

"You first."

"Did you really think you could sneak in here?" LEAD asked.

"Looks like I did."

"You don't understand what we can do to you."

"The ignorance is mutual."

"You're not as clever as you think. Give up. It will be much easier on you."

She punched keys one by one, mouthing the words as she typed. "Go to hell."

"Hello, Grace."

She stared at the letters on the screen. This guy was up to something. He used her name as if he thought it might intimidate her—it did not—but she couldn't figure out why he waited until now to show that he knew her.

Why did she assume LEAD was a man?

The person on the other end of the virtual conversation entered another phrase.

"We have you."

Tilting her head, she considered the words. He wanted her to think they'd located her. But had they?

With everything that had happened lately, testing her fortune seemed unwise. She tried to close the browser window on-screen. Nothing happened. She tried again. Nothing.

In the chat room, another message appeared. "We have control of your computer. Stop fighting us."

To the screen, she muttered, "Screw you."

"We have you surrounded. Give up."

Although they might've been lying, she couldn't take the risk. She tried to shut down the computer. It ignored her commands. She held down the power button for five seconds, which should've turned off the computer no matter what. Nothing happened. For several panicked seconds, she didn't know what to do.

Then she tossed the computer onto the bed, grabbed her gun, leaped to her feet, and bolted out of the motel room. Her purse she nabbed on her way out, slinging it over her neck. The room door slammed shut behind her.

A car swerved into the parking lot. The headlights raked over her as the sedan braked hard and whirled toward her, tires screeching. The car rocked to a halt, angled across the two empty parking spaces in front of her.

She spun to the left and ran.

Footsteps pounded behind her, advancing with each thunderous clap. She pushed her legs to move faster, her muscles to strain harder, until her thighs burned and her breaths shortened into gasps. It wasn't enough. The footsteps echoed louder and closer.

Further away, tires squealed, and an engine roared.

A powerful hand seized her hair. White-hot pain ripped through her scalp. The force of the action flipped her feet out from under her. Another hand, as big and powerful as the first, clamped around her upper arm, holding her up with bruising strength. Her feet hit the ground again.

The man holding her yanked her head backward. Pain shot out across her scalp and lanced into the backs of her eyes. She gritted her teeth. Darkness flitted at the edges of her vision. No, no, no, she would *not* pass out.

The man gripped her right arm. Her left arm was free.

She rammed her elbow backward into flesh hardened by taut muscles. The man grunted but held his grip on her. She raised her arm for another try.

He let go of her left arm. Just as she slammed her elbow down, he clamped his arm across her torso, pinning her against him. She recognized the feel of him, the unyielding hardness of his body, the steel-bar quality of his arm fastened over her.

"Waldron," she hissed through clenched teeth.

His voice growled so close to her ear that she felt his breath on her cheek. "Did you think I'd let you go that easily? Your lovely body has quite a bounty on it, you know."

Her scalp burned. Tears welled in her eyes, squeezed out by the pain rather than her emotions. Oh, she felt plenty emotional right now, but she refused to let it show. She would not cry, even from the pain.

Blinking away the tears, she said, "Bounty? What the hell are you talking about?"

"My employer will pay me a great deal of money to bring you in."

The sedan pulled up in front of them. They stood at the end of the building where the sidewalk dead-ended at the grassy strip that separated the motel property from the interstate on-ramp. The sedan had veered onto the grass to stop directly in front of, but sideways to, the pair of them. The jaundiced glow of the parking lot lights revealed the car's driver. It was the man she'd seen parked along her street inside the same nondescript sedan he drove now.

A smattering of stars glittered overhead. Only the brightest ones could punch through the secondhand smog from Fort Worth and the radiance of Lassiter Falls.

She still held the gun. In her right hand. The one pinned tightly under Waldron's elbow.

The memory of their previous encounter flashed through her mind. Except for the setting, that incident was virtually identical to this one. For a couple of seconds, she wondered if she'd slipped through a crack in time and emerged back in that very same moment. Had she learned nothing from the first time Waldron attacked her?

Or maybe he hadn't learned. The bastard seemed to have a limited playbook when it came to assaulting women.

She couldn't shoot him in the foot this time. Her arm was too tightly pinned, and her foot was in the way.

"Stop fighting," Waldron murmured, his tone almost seductive. "You can't keep running forever, and when you stop, I'll be here to catch you."

If anyone else had said those words, she might've taken it as an offer of aid and comfort. Okay, if David had spoken those words she would've taken it that way. From Waldron, the statement echoed as a threat rather than a promise.

The car door swung open. The dark-haired man climbed out of the sedan and trotted to them. The new guy held a syringe in one hand.

Grace's throat tightened. She swallowed hard.

Waldron jerked her hair, tilting her head sideways, exposing the tender flesh of her neck.

The new guy lifted the syringe and stepped closer.

She wriggled in Waldron's grasp.

He cinched his arm tighter around her and leaned close again to whisper in her ear. "Relax, dear child, soon you'll be with David again. Well, you'll be in the same facility—but you'll never actually see him again. You belong to someone else now, and he has great plans for you."

The man with evil eyes. Grace shuddered.

Waldron chuckled softly.

The night felt colder, despite the warm wind, thick with humidity.

"What about the flash drive?" the new guy asked.

"It's either in the room or on her person," Waldron said. He ran the back of his hand down her neck and across her shoulder. "We'll search every inch of both until we find it."

Nausea swelled inside her. She choked back the bile. No time for revulsion. She must find a way out of this. Right now.

First, she needed to ask a question. "Was that your boss on the website? The one who calls himself LEAD?"

"He detected your clumsy attempt at espionage." Waldron nodded to his cohort. "Now, Lopez."

The other man lifted the syringe to her neck.

Panic shot through her. She could not let them inject her. Even if the drug simply knocked her out, that would give them a chance to do anything they wanted to her. Anything. She would be defenseless.

The needle grazed her skin.

She kicked out, but sandwiched between the two men, she couldn't get enough leverage.

Lopez flinched. The needle scratched her but didn't penetrate her flesh.

Waldron snatched the syringe from Lopez.

Grace squeezed her eyes shut, wishing with every ounce of her willpower that the needle would break or Waldron would drop the syringe or—

Waldron jerked and gasped.

She opened her eyes.

Lopez stared past her shoulder, his eyes wide.

Waldron's hold on her slackened. He stumbled backward, out of her peripheral vision.

Lopez shook his head, slowly at first, then faster and faster.

Thump.

Grace stood motionless, afraid to move. She wanted to look behind her, but at the same time, she did not want to see.

Lopez had stopped shaking his head. He choked back a whimper as he focused his gaze on her.

She opened her mouth to speak, only to realize she had no clue what to say.

Lopez whirled and ran for the car. He flung himself into the driver's seat, slamming the door.

As if in slow motion, Grace turned around to look at Waldron.

He lay crumpled on the concrete walkway, eyes closed. The syringe protruded from his neck. She knelt beside him. Her hand trembled as she reached out to feel for a pulse in his neck. The blood surged against her fingertips in a slow but steady rhythm.

She had wished for a miracle. And it happened.

David must've done it. Or Sean.

Yet if one of them had helped her, he would've shown himself. Wouldn't he?

Rising, Grace turned away from Waldron. Fifteen feet away, inside the sedan, Lopez stared at her from behind the glass of the driver's window.

She ran past the car, across the parking lot into a grassy expanse that separated the motel from a little strip mall. Lopez didn't pursue her. She kept running, aiming for the strip mall. The back of the building looked bleak and lifeless. The sickly glow of sodium-vapor lights, mounted on tall poles surrounding the mall, guided her to her destination. What she would do once she got there, she hadn't a clue.

A small loading dock stuck out from the mall's backside. As her feet hit the pavement, she veered toward the loading dock. No vehicles were parked back here. The place looked dead. She halted at a set of steps that led up the side of the loading dock. Breathing hard, she sat down on the second step.

What now?

"I don't know," she muttered.

Leaning her head against the metal railing, she stared at the pavement beneath her feet without seeing it. Her vision had drifted out of focus. Her nap earlier had done little to relieve the exhaustion that seeped into every cell of her body and left her feeling like a cotton ball floating on the ocean. Soaked through. Limp. Adrift.

"You don't know what?"

Grace jumped. She jerked her head up, rotating her head to the left, toward the voice that had startled her. She knew the speaker's identity without looking at him, though.

"David," she said because her brain refused to cough up anything better. Her conversation skills were mediocre on a good day. This was not a good day.

"Are you hurt?" David asked.

"No…"

He walked toward her, stopping a couple of feet in front of her. Even in the yellowish light from the sodium-vapor bulbs, his eyes flared a bright sky blue. The color was unnatural, almost inhuman. Every time she saw his eyes like that, it set off a chain-reaction chill inside her.

As he crouched before her, the strange radiance in his eyes dwindled. The irises were blue now, bright blue, but they lacked the burning quality.

"Thank you," she said.

He scrunched his eyebrows. "For what?"

"Helping me escape. Waldron deserved to get a needle jammed into *his* neck for a change."

David just watched her, his brows furrowed.

"What?" she demanded.

"I didn't help you. I only got here a minute ago."

"No." The world listed beneath her, and she clamped a hand around the railing. "You must have. He didn't stab himself with the needle, and syringes don't move on their own. Maybe Sean…"

David shook his head. "Sean can't. Not without help."

The ground settled back into the horizontal plane. She still felt a little lightheaded.

Leaning closer, David rested a hand on her knee. "It was you."

She blinked slowly. "Excuse me?"

"You must've moved the syringe."

"I never touched it."

He squeezed her knee. "Not with your hands, maybe."

"What?" She shook her head with such violence that her hair lashed her face. "No, that's insane. Even if I understood what you're saying, which I don't, it would be impossible."

He smiled just a little. "You wouldn't be so upset if you didn't understand what I mean. You have the power."

She didn't want to ask, but the words came out anyway. "What power?"

"Extrasensory mental powers."

"Huh?"

He patted her knee. "Psychic abilities."

"Psychic…" Her voice trailed off, along with her thoughts. Several seconds ticked by before she collected her normal sensory abilities enough to speak. Then, in a tone far more confident than she felt, she declared, "That's insane."

He laughed. The sound was low and masculine, devoid of mockery. If she had to describe the quality of his laughter, she would have to label it affectionately amused.

She pursed her lips. "Why are you laughing at me?"

"Because you know it's true. You used your telekinetic ability to save yourself." He smiled—not just a little this time, but a full smile that made his beautiful features even more attractive. "It's a good sign. If your powers are coming back, then maybe your memory will come back too."

He looked entirely too happy about the prospect. Something stirred inside her, a feeling akin to dread mixed with anticipation. Right now, the dread was stronger, but she felt the anticipation blossoming.

David slid his hand over hers.

She swallowed against the lump in her throat. "Do we know each other? I mean, did we know each other before you showed up in my house the other day?"

"Yes."

"How well?"

"Very well."

His throaty tone set her stomach to fluttering. She tried to withdraw her hand but found she couldn't move or breathe. Her heart raced. He caressed the back of her hand, igniting an ember of heat there. The warmth flooded through her entire body in the space of three rapid heartbeats. She felt her cheeks flush.

"What do you mean?" Grace asked.

Her voice sounded pathetically breathless. She couldn't summon the will to care. She could do nothing except gaze into those blue eyes.

David raised his hand to her cheek. "We were engaged."

His hand felt cool against her flushed cheek.

She forced herself to breathe. "Engaged?"

"To be married."

The fire inside snuffed out.

She leaped to her feet. Shoving past him, she stumbled a few steps and halted, then spun to face him. Her cheeks grew warm again, this time heated by the anger erupting inside her.

"That's ridiculous," she spat. "I'd remember if I—if we—"

"You don't remember anything from last summer, do you?"

Eight months of her life she couldn't remember. She wanted to scream or kick something. Most of all, though, she wanted to remember. She wanted to know for certain he was lying.

Except that a small part of her hoped it was true. A small part that grew bigger every minute. The insane part of her.

The anger fizzled. Her shoulders slumped. When she spoke again, her voice was calm and even.

"I wouldn't do that," she said, feeling not at all certain. "Get engaged to someone I'd only known for eight months. I'm way too cautious for that."

He strode toward her. "You changed during those eight months. You learned things about yourself, things you couldn't believe at first, things that tore apart your sense of order and stability. What you thought the world was, you found out it was something entirely different."

"That makes no sense."

"Explanations won't convince you. Only experience will."

"I'm not psychic."

"Yes, you are."

She felt the anger bubbling up again, about to boil over if she let it. Fear lit the fire under the pot, she knew. Fear was supposed to be cold. Instead, it heated her insides. Common knowledge could be oh-so-wrong.

Maybe that was David's point.

Ugh. She did not want to know any of this.

"What are you?" she asked, unable to stop the words. "You say you're not dead, but a living person can't appear and disappear like a ghost. Either I'm hallucinating or you're not human."

"You're not hallucinating."

"I know, which means you must be dead."

He surged forward, grasped her upper arms, and crushed her to him as he kissed her hard. With his mouth demanding a response, the heat of her anger ebbed into a tingling warmth. She relaxed against him. Just as she was starting to enjoy the kiss, he pushed away from her.

"Do I feel dead?" he asked.

No, he didn't. He felt very much alive. She bristled at the annoyed tone in his voice, but she had to admit the truth. He was a real, flesh-and-blood man.

"Okay," she said, "if you're not dead, then how do you do it? The vanishing thing, I mean."

"Astral projection." He shrugged. "That's the common name for it. In practice, it's a combination of remote viewing, telekinesis, and thought projection."

She felt unsteady and disconnected as if her body were melting as her head floated away into space.

"It's hard to explain," David said.

"No shit."

He raised a hand toward her.

She scuffled backward.

"I'm sorry," he said. "I wish I knew how to help you accept all of this."

"I won't accept things that cannot be true. Whatever your game is, I am not playing."

He exhaled a loud, drawn-out sigh. "You weren't nearly this stubborn the first time around."

"Leave," she said.

He stared at her as if she spoke an alien language.

"Get out of here," she said, squeezing the words out through clenched teeth. "Leave me alone."

"No—"

"Yes." The syllable came out as a hiss.

His mouth dropped open. He shook his head.

She shouted, "Go!"

A gust of wind swirled around them.

David raised his hands in a compliant gesture. "Calm down, Grace."

"Do not tell me what to do."

The wind intensified, snatching up paper scraps and dirt, twirling the debris inside a mini vortex that danced around them.

"Don't do this," David said.

She scowled at him. "Don't do what?"

"Push me out. Please, give me a chance to—"

Get out. In her mind, she screamed the words.

The vortex slammed into him, and he vanished. The little tornado evaporated.

In the aftermath, the silence felt unnatural as if she'd just gone deaf. In the distance, though, a dog barked. Her knees quivered. Everything seemed to tilt and roll around her. Gasping, she dropped onto her knees.

David was gone.

She'd killed him.

Chapter Fifteen

AVID RETURNED TO BLACKNESS, LIKE USUAL, BUT THIS WAS NOT A normal end to an excursion. His forehead smacked into the floor. Phantom lights flashed in the dark, a figment of his mind brought on by hitting the concrete face-first. The bare floor chilled his skin through his clothes, and he couldn't move.

Strangely, he felt no pain now. He remembered the agony from seconds ago. His mind ripping. His body screaming. Blinding light. Two words blasting through his head.

Get out.

Grace's inner voice had shouted at him so loud his ears hurt. His brain hurt worse. Yet as soon as he'd slammed back into his mind, the pain dissipated. He still couldn't move, though, and he fought the instinct to panic. That never helped. At least he could breathe. And see. And hear.

His body twitched. Saliva dribbled from his lips. His heart pounded at a rapid clip. Like an invalid, he lay on the concrete with his face pressed into the hard surface, unable to control his own body. Nothing like this had happened before. He'd traveled thousands of miles and viewed hundreds of sites. No one had pushed him out before.

And she didn't even realize she'd done it.

Their conversation must've sounded quite normal, if not exactly cordial. She was angry with him—and scared, though not of him or because of him, he sensed. She wanted him to answer her questions. He'd intended to but, well, he was concerned about her reaction when he shared the full truth with her. The news about her abilities had shocked her more than he'd expected, which made telling her more seem like an unwise option. She didn't remember any of it. Hearing the facts from someone she viewed as a stranger might not convince her.

He must convince her. Fast.

She'd gotten so frustrated with him that she struck out, unwittingly, in a way even she failed to see. She'd tapped into the invisible streams of power that permeated the universe. He'd seen her do it before, but given her current memory problems, he hadn't been sure she could still do it.

Until the pressure hit him. A wave of unseen energy as powerful as a tsunami.

Then he knew. Grace was forcing him out.

The twitching ceased. David held still, gasping for breaths. The air was cold yet soothing. He pushed up with his hands, raising his body off the floor. His arms trembled. Gritting his teeth, he struggled to hold himself up. His arms gave out, and he collapsed back onto the floor. *Dammit.*

A throbbing erupted in his head, a pulsating kind of pressure, as if his head were a balloon inflated to near the breaking point. He marshaled enough energy to slide one arm across the floor so he could rub his temple. Even that small effort left him shaking.

Behind him, the doorknob jiggled.

He must get up. *Now.* If they found him in this state…

David rolled onto his side. With both arms, he levered his torso off the floor until he was sitting. For a few horrible seconds, he felt as if he might pass out. The sensation faded, though, and he shifted into a kneeling position. His strength grew with each passing moment. He prayed it returned fast enough.

His body tipped sideways. He flung his hands out, seizing the metal chair he'd occupied during his excursion. Since it was bolted to the floor, the chair offered a secure handhold. With the chair as his crutch, he managed to rise from the floor into a hunched standing position. Electrode wires, their ends ripped free from the chair, dangled from his head.

The lights clicked on with a buzz and a flicker.

David squinted. The chair. He rubbed his eyes to clear the fuzziness. The electrode wires were attached to the chair, or at least they were supposed to be. He must've torn them free when he flew out of the seat. But something else bothered him far more than the electrode wires.

The leather restraints. Some force had rent them apart, scattering the buckles across the floor. He couldn't have done that. The same force that hurled him out of the chair must've severed the restraints as well.

Grace had forced him out with a hell of a lot of power. More than he'd ever seen before.

The door was slammed inward. Shoes clapped on the concrete.

David twisted around to look at the doorway.

Tesler raced across the room to him. "What happened to you?"

David heard nothing resembling compassion in Tesler's voice. Rather, he spoke in an irritated, accusing tone.

The room tilted. David gripped the chair harder. "I don't know. I did what you told me to."

"Your vitals were off the chart," Tesler said. "A routine excursion shouldn't kill you."

"I'm not dead."

Tesler harrumphed, shaking his head. "You look like walking death."

"Thanks." David suppressed a chuckle. "Guess that makes you the grim reaper."

Grasping an electrode wire, Tesler yanked it. The electrode ripped away from David's temple.

He winced. Pale hairs clung to the sticky surface of the electrode.

Tesler gestured toward the chair. "How did you remove the restraints?"

David looked at the chair and shrugged.

"You know what happens," Tesler said, "when you don't cooperate."

"But you still don't understand." David took a step toward Tesler. "Nothing you do can stop me. Not even the drugs. Eventually, I'll be free."

"One thing would stop you."

David didn't need to read Tesler's thoughts to know what the man was thinking. He had the ingenuity of a fungus.

"Go ahead," David said. "Kill me. See how far you get reconstructing eight years of your damn research without me. Your leader won't be pleased with you then."

Tesler tilted his head back and examined David over the tip of his nose. They both knew he could reconstruct the data without David like he could exist without his heart pumping lifeblood through his veins.

Oh, wait. That assumed he had a heart.

Tesler flicked his wrist.

A pair of guards trotted through the doorway and around Tesler. They grabbed David's arms, secured his hands behind his back with cuffs, and shackled his feet. As they hauled him past Tesler into the hallway, David twisted his torso to glance back at Tesler.

"I told you," he said, "that I won't kill for you."

"Then you will die for the research."

Both guards dragged David down the corridor toward the elevator. He let his feet drag on the floor. Why make it easy for them? Cooperation had gotten him nowhere and nothing, except separated from Grace. No more easygoing lab rat. He would fight them with every step, every breath, every ounce of power within him—even if it drained the very life out of him.

One of the guards kicked him in the shin.

Pain shot through his leg. He clamped his jaw shut and swallowed the pain. He already felt as if a tornado had sucked him into its vortex, shaken the life out of him, and spit him out again. Fighting took energy.

Well then, he'd get some. All he needed was a little rest.

In the elevator, the guards relaxed their grips on him. The one called Battaglia, a huge man with a thin mustache and the eyes of a Pekingese, chatted with his partner about the outdoors. The two men agreed that it "totally sucked" to be stuck inside the facility for weeks at a time. The shorter guard, a young man named Norris whose frame resembled a troll's, lamented the lack of large-breasted women in the facility.

David kept his gaze on the elevator doors.

Norris jabbed him in the ribs. "Hey, freak. You ever had a girl?"

David concentrated on the doors. He had learned long ago that interacting with the guards provoked them. They had the brains of rabbits and the tempers of killer bees.

Right now, he had no strength to deal with them.

Norris jabbed him in the small of his back. Pain branched up his spine. His knees shook. He stumbled backward, bumped into the elevator's rear wall, and slumped against it for support.

"Well, freak?" the guard said. "You like girls?"

David gritted his teeth.

Battaglia sniggered. "Maybe he likes you better, Norris."

The elevator eased to a stop. David pushed away from the wall.

A chime rang. Through speakers in the ceiling, a recorded female voice issued instructions in a neutral tone. "Access to this area requires handprint identification. Please place your palm on the reader."

A panel beside the doors slid open to reveal a cavity that housed a square of smooth plastic etched with the outline of a hand.

Norris slapped his palm onto the reader.

The chime sounded. The voice intoned, "Thank you."

As the panel lowered, the doors slid apart.

Both guards dragged him into the corridor. The three of them moved past rows of closed doors. A number on each door represented the room's tenant—or more accurately, the room's inmate. David and his colleagues had no names here, just ID numbers to help the guards and technicians tell them apart. No one cared who they were, how they felt, or what happened to them after the tests were completed.

Lights along the floor illuminated the corridor. Security cameras, hidden in every tenth light, observed their progress. David had discovered many of their "secret" security measures. Guards babbled about everything when they thought they were alone. Why on earth they felt safely alone inside a facility populated with psychics, David couldn't fathom.

Battaglia unlocked the door to David's room. Norris shoved him inside, then clomped through the door behind him. Battaglia followed them inside, shutting the door.

Norris removed the cuffs. "Get in bed."

David complied. His head throbbed again, his muscles felt weak and heavy, and his throat was parched.

"Water," he croaked.

Battaglia observed as Norris shackled David's wrists and ankles to the bed rails. A single lamp burned in the far corner.

"Water," David repeated.

The guards left. The door lock clicked as they engaged it from the outside.

"Are you all right?"

Sean shuffled out of the shadows. His voice was soft, his face pinched. The glow of the lamp lent his red hair a liquid quality, like molten copper.

"I'm alive," David said. "Thirsty and tired, but alive."

"You were gone a long time."

"I know."

He had volunteered for extra tests, so he could use the time to help Grace. Edward had asked him to watch out for her, and though he'd promised not to interact with her, he'd also promised to do whatever he could to help her. He would keep that promise, despite Tesler's suspicions, despite the damage it inflicted on his body.

Despite how much it worried Sean.

The boy had no one else to trust. He'd come to the facility two years before but, despite amazing progress, he hadn't lived enough to know how to handle Tesler and his goons. He hadn't developed the willpower.

He was only sixteen.

These days, Sean looked much older. His cheeks were sunken and worry lines creased his forehead.

Sean slouched beside the bed. "They're gonna kill you."

"They won't."

"But they'll give you the stuff."

David met the boy's gaze. "It'll be all right."

Sean hunched his shoulders and looked at the floor.

"Need a favor," David said.

"Sure, anything."

"I need you to keep looking out for her."

"I'm not good at it," Sean said, "not like you."

"You can do it."

Sean contemplated the linoleum.

David knew he was pushing Sean to the limits of his abilities and beyond. Although the kid possessed an amazing talent for healing, he could travel only with assistance, and interacting with the world was impossible for him—without an intense boost of power from someone skilled in that area. David knew Sean disliked traveling. It was intrusive and unsettling, even for a veteran. Pushing Sean over a threshold he feared crossing troubled David.

He had no choice. Grace was alone out there.

"Okay," Sean said, sounding miserable. "But she won't see me this time."

This time. The phrase set off alarms in David's head. "What do you mean this time?"

Sean stuffed his hands in his pockets.

David shut his eyes. Sleep beckoned him with its siren song, but he forced his eyes to open.

"She saw me when I healed her," Sean said, the words tumbling out in a rush. "I don't know how, I swear, I can't do that without your help."

"Doesn't matter," David said, though he knew the answer. Grace had made it happen. "Just watch out for her."

"Okay."

Sean left.

David sucked in a deep breath. He needed rest, but he sensed he must wait a little longer before giving in to sleep. He counted the panels in the ceiling instead. When that failed to banish the drowsiness, he focused on spotting patterns in the swirls and dots on the ceiling panels. One group looked like Abraham Lincoln.

A few minutes later, Tesler entered the room. He stopped beside the bed, gazing down on David with a slight smile as he brandished a syringe in his right hand. The needle glistened in the twilight of the room.

Tesler leaned over the bed and murmured, "You never could follow directions. Tell me where you really went. Perhaps I can keep them from killing you."

"I viewed the target."

"And?"

"That's it."

"David," Tesler said, wagging the needle in his face. "We both know you went somewhere else. Tell me where."

"Tahiti. It's nice this time of year."

"Have it your way."

Tesler tapped the bubbles out of the syringe.

Let them drug him. He would never tell, never let them intimidate him the way they intimidated the others. Tesler should've known better. The drug might shackle his body, but never his spirit. He could wait. Grace had the flash drive, but her enemies seemed unaware of that fact, so she would be safe for a while longer. Once she found the flash drive, she might decide to come here, to confront them herself. She was far too determined to just sit back and let events unfold around her. Too determined and too willful. She'd march into a nuclear reactor if she thought "the truth" awaited her inside its walls.

She thought she was meek. Lord, if only that were true.

No. He liked her willful and determined. Even if it made his self-appointed job next to impossible to complete. Most of the time she kept to herself and gave the world the impression she was... well, not exactly meek, but she certainly hid her true nature deep inside. He'd seen it. That intimate knowledge made it hard for him to reconcile the woman he knew with the suspicious, self-doubting persona she displayed now. Maybe if she remembered those eight months, she'd shed her insecure shell and reveal the powerhouse underneath.

Amnesia left her vulnerable, but she was safe—for now. He had time.

Tesler squirted a jet of liquid from the syringe. He jabbed the needle into David's arm and depressed the plunger.

Eventually, Tesler and his cronies would run out of options. Then they'd awaken him. And he'd have one more chance to save himself and Grace.

His eyelids fluttered shut.

———

GRACE WANDERED THE STREETS OF LASSITER FALLS IN SEARCH OF A telephone. She needed to call Senator Faulkner. Even if he couldn't help, she had an obligation to contact him. Her grandfather had asked one favor of her, and she must do it. She owed him that much after all he'd done for her.

Everyone wanted her to do things for them. Even her grandfather issued post-mortem orders. Andrew Haley wanted to babble at her. Waldron wanted her, though for what purpose, she couldn't say. She decided she probably didn't want to know, anyway. The knowledge would only creep her out more than she already was.

Waldron could've killed her. He needed her alive. She possessed what he wanted. What everyone seemed to want.

The goddamn flash drive.

Gimme, gimme, gimme. Those seemed like the only syllables anyone knew how to speak anymore. That and "do what I say right now." Only one person behaved as if he cared about what happened to her.

David.

Her throat constricted. Oh God, she'd killed him. Hadn't she?

Everything whirled around her as if the sidewalk had transformed into a carnival ride. Her stomach lurched. She staggered to the nearest tree and propped her shoulder against it until the dizziness faded. Pushing away from the trunk, she stood there for a moment.

Was David dead? Could she kill someone with her thoughts?

She'd been so angry. No, not angry. She'd been terrified that everything he said was true, which made her lash out. Her mind replayed the moment. David's pleading expression. The swirling wind.

Don't do this.

Don't do what?

Push me out.

At the time, she'd barely heard his words. One thought had ricocheted through her mind, drowning out everything else. *Get out.*

David claimed she had psychic abilities. But what had he meant when he begged her not to push him out? It made no sense. Push him out of what?

Her mind.

The truth hit her like a punch in the gut. He had been in her mind, or connected to her mind, through some sort of psychic channel. No, that was impossible.

Except...

It made a bizarre kind of sense. She'd pushed him out of her mind. Forced him to go away. Why shouldn't she? He had no right to invade her thoughts, to make her see him and speak to him whether she wanted to or not. It was rude.

A harsh bark of laughter burst out of her.

She was criticizing a man for rudely invading her mind. How utterly insane.

Her neck ached. She rubbed it, to no avail. The neck pain was only the precursor. Next would come the headache and the nausea and a new swell of dizziness. Soon she'd sink into the mire of a quicksand migraine, and no amount of struggling would pull her out of it. She needed to find a safe place to wait it out. A relatively safe place. If one existed.

She still had time before the quicksand dragged her under, time she must use wisely.

Grace marched down the sidewalk, squinting because she swore the streetlights had gotten brighter all of a sudden. It was just the migraine, of course, making light seem sharper and harder as if it were composed of a thousand tiny knives that pierced her brain.

David was not dead. She knew it, or maybe she hoped it was true. For now, she must assume whatever she'd done to him had caused no permanent damage.

She halted in front of a pay phone. It was bolted to the brick wall of a convenience store. No privacy whatsoever. An ever-present stream of people strolled into and out of the store, some clutching monstrously large fountain drinks, others twirling their car keys, and still more munching on fried foods that looked full of enough preservatives to outlast the mummies of the Egyptian pharaohs.

Someone might overhear her phone conversation.

Waldron's buddies might've bugged the phones.

They could not possibly have bugged every public phone in Lassiter Falls. No one could. The thought failed to comfort her. She couldn't know for certain, not anymore. "Anything goes," that was the new order of the universe. If David and his network of psychic friends and enemies vanished, invaded her thoughts, and took control of her body, then surely Waldron's friends could tap the public phone system.

The phones were hooked up to computers, weren't they? Waldron's pals had tracked an internet connection back to the motel and seized control of her laptop.

Okay, the pay phone was too risky. She'd endured enough danger to satiate an adrenaline junkie for a lifetime. Minimize the risk. She must adopt those words as her new motto.

Not that her enemies gave a fig about her wishes. Or her sanity.

As she continued down the street, the trees on either side thinned. The buildings segued from businesses to houses. Ahead, the street intersected the main highway. Cars on the road roared across the intersection at full speed, their headlights slashing through the night. The traffic signal burned red like the eye of death glowering at her.

Get a grip, girl.

She paused at the corner to rest and think.

On the opposite side of the highway sat Mesquite Hill Center. The strip mall housed a health club, a restaurant, a dollar store, and an electronics outlet. The dollar store was closed for the day, but the other establishments stayed open late, as evidenced by their glaring open signs and interior lights. A poster taped to the window of Bronco Electronics announced "dirt-cheap rate plans" for mobile phones. Sign up today, the sign urged, and get a free phone. Another sign in the store's window advertised prepaid cell phones. "No contract, total freedom," the sign declared.

A prepaid phone. Unconnected to the local system. Unconnected with her.

She jogged across the highway into the parking lot of the shopping center. Five vehicles occupied parking spots. The center's restaurant, Ruth's Tex-Mex Grill, had curtained windows. Through the picture windows of the health club, she saw two elderly men lifting weights and a woman riding an exercise bicycle as if a rabid pit bull were pursuing her. She tromped down the sidewalk, past the restaurant and health club, to the doors of Bronco Electronics. A bell jangled as she pushed through the doors into the store.

A salesman in a Hawaiian shirt scurried out of a back room.

"May I help you, ma'am?" he asked in his Texas drawl.

She pointed toward the display of prepaid phones. "I want one of those. Please."

"You sure? We got some real fine deals on full-service plans—"

"Just the prepaid phone. Now, please."

Fifteen minutes later, she departed the store with a prepaid flip phone in her hand. The device weighed a few ounces at most and, when folded shut, fit in the palm of her hand with room to spare. The casing was gray and nondescript, which suited her fine. She'd paid cash, and the phone required no contract or account sign-up, so she felt reasonably sure no one would know she had the phone. To know if the phone was truly safe, however, she'd have to use it. The thought sent a chill up her spine.

Before she could use the phone, she needed a number to dial.

She chewed her lower lip for a minute, then shoved the phone in her jeans pocket. She turned around and strode back into the store.

The same salesman approached her. "There a problem, ma'am?"

He looked genuinely concerned. Maybe he'd get in trouble if a customer returned a phone five minutes after purchasing it.

She smiled and said, "No-no, it's fine. But I was wondering if I could try out one of your computers. I'm thinking about replacing mine, and I'd like to see how good the newest models are."

It wasn't entirely a lie. She did need a new computer but, lacking any funds beyond the ten bucks and change in her wallet, she couldn't exactly pick up a new laptop today. A computer might come in handy, though. Maybe if she ran to the nearest ATM and withdrew—

No, ATMs had a limit of $200. Besides, if she accessed her bank account, then Waldron and company might notice it.

"Sure thing," the salesman said, his expression brightening. "Let me show you the one we just got in this week."

He led her to a display table that housed a desktop computer with a huge wide-screen monitor attached. Using the mouse, he opened programs and chattered about the computer's built-in features.

"Um," Grace said, "could I play around with it for a few minutes?"

"You bet."

He released the mouse and stepped back.

Grace walked up to the computer. Glancing at the salesman, she asked, "Can this get online?"

"Oh yeah. We have broadband."

He stood there watching as she opened the web browser.

She hesitated, chewing on the inside of her lip.

The salesman folded his arms over his chest and kept on smiling and watching.

Grace plastered on her best smile. "I don't want to take up all your time. You must have other things to do, and I can fiddle with this on my own."

"You sure?"

"Positive." She broadened her smile. "Thank you so much for all your help. It's nice to know chivalry isn't dead after all."

The salesman blushed.

A phone rang, and he trotted to the sales counter to answer it.

Grace's smile evaporated. Jeez, being cheerful had turned into an endurance sport. It used to come so easily.

In the web browser, she navigated to a search engine, typed in Faulkner's name, and hit enter. The results popped up within seconds. Oh, she coveted the store's broadband connection. Her internet was glacially slow in comparison. Not that it mattered much since she'd probably get bumped off by an invisible villain without ever seeing her home again.

She glanced at the search results and froze.

The first link was titled "Senator Dies in Auto Accident."

Below the title, the search results printed the first couple of lines from the news article. "Senator Elias Faulkner," the text said, "was killed early this morning when a drunk driver struck his car in a head-on collision."

Dead. Another person involved in this mess was dead.

She'd intended to look up the phone number for Faulkner's office. No point in that now. Her grandfather had said to contact Faulkner and mentioned no one else as trustworthy. She wouldn't know who else, if anyone, she could trust at Faulkner's office.

Closing the web browser, she hurried out of the store, past the health club, toward the opposite end of the building from where she'd entered the property. On the corner, a newspaper vending machine squatted at the edge of the sidewalk. She stopped there, her gaze inexorably drawn to the words printed on the front page, which was pressed against the machine's clear door. The headlines meant nothing to her. Something about local politics followed by mention of a fundraiser at the hospital. The rest of the text was below the fold, out of sight.

Some instinct made her fish three quarters out of her purse, drop them into the slot, and extract a newspaper from the machine. She flipped it over to see the stories on the lower half of the front page. Her skimming ended when she spotted the one-paragraph story at the very bottom.

"Inmate Dies in County Jail," the headline said. The story began, "Andrew Haley died overnight of self-inflicted wounds while being held in connection with the death of Brian Kellogg, a tourist who was found dead at the Bed & Bath Inn yesterday."

Self-inflicted wounds. Sure. Andrew was nuts, but given recent events, she doubted he'd offed himself. The same invisible villain who'd attacked her and strangled Brian Kellogg most likely took care of Andrew as well. And Senator Faulkner.

And her grandfather.

Grace let the newspaper slip out of her hands. It fluttered to the concrete at her feet.

So many deaths. All over what? The results of secret research into psychic phenomena? Anyone who would kill for that information must've been either insane or evil or both.

David.

His face flashed in her mind. Would he be the next victim? Her chest tightened as if an invisible hand squeezed her heart. She felt tears pooling in her eyes, hot and stinging. She did not want David to die. She didn't want anyone else to die, but especially not him.

Maybe he'd told her the truth. Maybe she felt this sickening dread at the thought of him falling prey to her enemies because they had known each other before. If she could remember those missing months, she might understand her own feelings better.

Her cell phone rang.

It wasn't the new phone she'd just bought. The old one warbled from deep inside her purse.

Digging out the phone, she answered the call on the fifth ring, one ring before her voicemail would've taken the call.

"Hello," she muttered.

"Grace."

That voice. She recognized it. One word provided all the evidence she needed because she'd heard the same voice before, whispering in her ear, too close.

Waldron.

"You may have scared Lopez," Waldron said in a calm tone laced with malice that triggered ice-cold tremors inside her. "I don't frighten so easily. You look rather upset, though."

The tremors stopped. Everything around her seemed to have frozen as if time had skidded to a halt. The sole evidence of life was the thudding of her heart. He was watching her. She felt it, an inexplicable sensation of his gaze on her, as tangible as the feel of his hand around her neck.

Waldron's voice murmured into her ear. "Gotcha."

She dropped the phone and ran.

CHAPTER SIXTEEN

GRACE RAN AS FAST AS HER LEGS WOULD MOVE. MAYBE WALDRON didn't know where she was, despite what his one-word message implied. He might've lied to torment her. She couldn't risk it, so on and on she ran. She didn't stop moving until the shopping center was out of view behind her, over the rise of a hill, and she'd passed from the commercial zone into a region of town filled with mostly vacant lots. Abandoned homes slouched on a few of the properties. They looked as bedraggled as she must look, as she felt.

When she realized no one was following her, she stumbled to a halt.

No car engines grumbled. No footsteps pounded behind her. The only sound was an owl hooting in a nearby tree. The mournful sound made the desolation around her feel even more desolate.

Rubbing her arms against a sudden chill, she turned in a circle to survey the area. Not a single human being was in sight. No animals either. Nothing but dying grass, a handful of trees, and empty shells that had once been homes. The streetlights washed the landscape in shades of jaundiced yellow.

She stood there for several minutes, her mind blank. A deep weariness settled over her. She fought the urge to lie down on the cracked sidewalk. The throbbing in her head had joined forces with the pain in her neck that stabbed up into the base of her skull. The combined misery left her weak and exhausted and nauseous. Her knees began to quiver. If she didn't find a safe place to collapse and find it soon, her body would make the decision for her.

Waldron and company would find her lying in a human puddle on the concrete.

She considered each of the abandoned houses in turn. One looked about ready to collapse. Two others had boarded-up windows. No way could she break down the doors or the window boards, not in her current condition. The last house looked relatively intact, though in need of a paint job. The windows weren't boarded.

Summoning the last of her strength, she crossed the street to the little stucco house. The chain-link fence was falling down, the gate halfway off its hinges. She sidestepped the gate and shuffled up the concrete walkway toward the front door. Fault lines as deep as the San Andreas cleaved the concrete. She hopped over the gaps and the knee-high weeds that jutted up through them, reaching the closed door. She grasped the knob and turned. Locked. *Damn.*

The window beside the door was cracked, but not broken. Under the window, bricks that had once formed a border for a flower bed lay jumbled and half swallowed by the weeds. She picked up one of the bricks and used it to smash out the glass. Once she'd knocked out the last shards, she swung one leg through the window, braced herself against the inside wall, and swung her other leg inside.

The room she found herself in was dark, except for the light coming through the window. She stepped away from the wall, crunching glass under her boots. She cursed herself for not keeping a small flashlight in her purse. The one in her car's glove compartment was of no use now.

The house smelled of mildew and dust. The floor creaked as she tiptoed further into the room. Slowly, her eyes adjusted to the darker environment and recognizable shapes emerged from the gloom—a ramshackle easy chair tucked into the corner and a blanket or sheet mounded in the center of the room. She kicked at the fabric heap, just to make sure it didn't hide anything living. The front door was behind and to the right of her while straight ahead two more windows offered a view of the lifeless backyard. She slunk across the room and through a doorway on the left side, into what looked like a combined kitchen and dining room. A couple of wooden chairs lay toppled on their sides, refugees from a dining room set. Another doorway took her into a large, empty room replete with shadows. An overgrown bush blocked the view from the only window. Even in the gloom, she could make out a pair of bifold doors that stood half open, revealing the pitch-darkness inside the closet.

Lightning burst in the sky, silhouetting the bush outside the window. At the same instant, a gust of wind swirled past the house, shaking the bush. The shadows inside the room undulated.

Grace plunged her hand into her purse and curled her fingers around the grip of her gun.

Another stroke of lightning lit the room. She saw the closet was empty, then the darkness reclaimed the space.

She scuffled to the corner farthest from the door where she could still keep an eye on the doorway but maintain a buffer zone between herself and the opening. The window was at the opposite end of the room. She leaned back against the wall and let her body slide down until she was sitting on the floor. Although the carpet had lost its bounce, it provided enough cushioning to ease some of the aches in her body. Each flash of lightning stabbed into her eyes like a large-bore needle. She turned her head into the corner, to shield her eyes as much as possible, which wasn't much at all. She shut her eyes and tried to relax. Though the muscles in her thighs and abdomen no longer twanged when she moved, the tightness lingered.

Thunder rumbled, distant but resonant. The window glass rattled.

Big empty houses gave her the creeps. As a child, she had been convinced monsters lived in the shadows. According to her childhood theory, then, an abandoned house must harbor hordes of demons. Like the ones pursuing her now. Those childhood fears might not have been so silly after all.

The floor creaked.

Just the house settling. The thought failed to alleviate the churning in her stomach or the slight quickening of her pulse. She slid the gun out of her purse and placed it on her lap, one hand resting on the grip with her index finger over the trigger guard.

Fatigue settled over her once again. Her muscles felt heavy and limp. Her eyelids refused to stay open. Her pulse slowed, her breathing grew shallower, and she sank into sleep.

———

GRACE WOKE WITH A JERK THAT THUMPED HER HEAD AGAINST THE wall. She grunted, massaging the back of her skull. She felt… weird. An odd sense of pressure made her feel as if a very heavy sack rested atop her head, sinking over her body, first pressing down on her shoulders and then over her chest. She resisted the panic welling inside her. Somehow, she knew that staying calm was the only option that would leave her intact. She took a slow, deep breath.

Intact? What the hell did that mean?

The sensation of pressure oozed down her body, over her hips and legs. Within a few seconds, the sensation passed through and out of her.

She swallowed, straightened her back, and glanced around the room.

Lightning flashed, dimmer than before. The storm must've slipped around to the south.

The room was still empty, except for her. The weird feeling of pressure was completely gone now. The dreams were nothing new, but it had been different this time. Never before had she remembered the dream so vividly after waking. Never before had she remembered what happened after entering the locked room. Never before had she woken to feel an invisible weight pressing down on her, almost as if she were being shoved back into her body. Normally during the dreams—if she could call the bizarre episodes normal—she felt as if she inhabited someone else's body or mind, as if she were merely an observer rather than a participant. This time, however, she had felt completely herself. Yet the most disturbing part had been the sense of…

Traveling.

She sat forward. Travelers. Excursions. She had read those words in the research data on the flash drive. According to the data, David was a traveler. He claimed to have psychic abilities, and he claimed she had them too. If the term traveler referred to a psychic, then she had just been on an excursion.

She'd been traveling for quite some time without knowing it. Traveling while she slept. Taking excursions to see David. And she could think of only one reason why she might do that.

Everything David said was true. They had been… involved.

She closed her eyes. The memory of her excursion came back to her, unbidden and unwanted. David lying in a hospital-type bed, unconscious, still as death. The only sign of life had been the almost imperceptible rising and falling of his chest. She remembered feeling for his pulse and being rewarded with the slow but insistent surging of blood through his veins. He was alive. Comatose, or at least unconscious, but alive.

He could do nothing to help her anymore. It was up to her now.

She must save *him* this time.

Everyone remotely connected with the flash drive had not only died but had been murdered by unknown villains. Her grandfather, Andrew Haley, Brian Kellogg, Senator Faulkner. They were murdered. She needed no evidence to tell her that. Whoever pulled Waldron's strings also killed anyone who came near the secrets contained on the flash drive.

Anyone who came near her.

She knew this. Felt it, actually. And she no longer questioned her instincts. Lately, she'd doubted her intuition, her motives, her feelings, afraid those instincts would lead her into oblivion. Maybe she was crazy. Maybe she was paranoid. Maybe she was narcissistic. Those doubts had governed her life.

No more.

Drawing her knees up to her chest, she rested her arms on her knees. The thunder had faded into silence, and lightning no longer pulsated in the sky outside the abandoned house. With her back pressed to the wall, she felt a little safer than she had out on the street. Yet she realized she couldn't stay cocooned here forever.

She needed answers. She could wait for one of her pursuers to hand them to her, or she could dig them out of the ground herself. The answers lay deep. She'd need a backhoe to excavate them.

The answers awaited her in California. David and Sean were being held somewhere in the Mojave Desert. Her grandfather had worked for a company in California. Her parents had moved there two years before their deaths. In her mind, the dots connected, though the picture they formed remained unclear because she couldn't see many of the dots. Revealing them demanded a trip to California. A trip from which she might not return.

She would return. She had to.

Either way, she must go. David needed her.

Okay, so she didn't even remember the guy. That fact had made her leery of him before, but her latest dream—mental excursion—had convinced her that he told the truth. The feelings stirring inside her, once frightening, now seemed almost comforting. Someone cared about her. Someone needed her. She could not leave him to rot in a drug-induced coma inside a windowless facility hidden in the desert.

What if the coma wasn't drug-induced? What if she had caused it? She'd used her powers on him, to make him go away, though she'd had no concept of what she was doing at the time. What if she'd hurt him?

No. She was not to blame. It was *them*.

And she needed to know who they were.

Grandpa had worked for a company called ALI, Advanced Laboratories Incorporated. He kept the details of his work, and the location of ALI's facility, a secret. Knowing the details hadn't mattered to her back then. Now, she cursed herself for accepting the secrecy, the evasion, the lies. Grandpa had *lied* to her, about more than his job. She understood the secrecy of his work, since ALI probably made him sign a confidentiality agreement, but lying to her about her own life…

She didn't know if she could forgive him for that.

He must've known David. He must've known about her relationship with him. She could no longer deny the deception. Edward McLean had insisted everything was fine and convinced her they both led normal lives when obviously neither one of them had. How long had he known he was in trouble? Months, she'd guess. He should've confided in her. They might've solved his problems together. Instead, he'd plugged her ears and slipped a bag over her head.

Worst of all, he let her believe nothing important happened during the eight months she'd lost to amnesia. Getting engaged wasn't nothing.

And what about her psychic abilities? How long had she had them? Since she remembered everything outside of those eight months last year, she knew she'd had no such powers at any other time in her life. They must've emerged during those eight months. How had it happened? Who wanted to capture her now? Grandpa must've known the answers to those questions and many more, yet he'd kept the information from her. Even at the end, when he must've known she was in danger too, he said nothing. Instead, he gave her a flash drive that every bad guy in the western hemisphere wanted to possess.

If she discovered her grandfather had a good reason for lying, her unease might lessen. But if peeling back the skin of lies revealed a tumor beneath, it just might kill her.

Nothing could undo the past, not for her, not for anyone. She must live with the truth.

She grabbed the prepaid mobile phone and dialed directory assistance. Two minutes later, she scribbled the number for ALI's job hotline on a scrap of paper she'd found in her purse. The company listed no other numbers and no address. She punched in the digits.

The call was picked up. A recorded voice intoned, "The ALI employment hotline is available twenty-four hours a day for your convenience. To hear the latest job openings, press one. To hear all job openings, press two. To search by category, press three. To speak with an ALI human resources specialist, press four."

Grace pressed four.

The same recorded voice said, "We're sorry, ALI human resources specialists are available during normal business hours only, seven a.m. to seven p.m. Pacific time, Monday through Friday."

She punched the zero key, hoping to get an operator. The recorded voice began reading off the initial menu options again. She kept punching zero.

Silence. Then, the voice announced, "Thank you for calling ALI. Goodbye."

Click. The damn machine had hung up on her.

She'd have to call back in the morning—after nine a.m., since Pacific time was two hours earlier. She checked her watch. It was 12:48 a.m. More than eight hours to go before ALI's employees arrived at work. Too much time. Waldron seemed unlikely to allow her an eight-hour hiatus before he resumed hunting for her.

Though she hadn't expected to get all the answers she needed from a jobs hotline, she had hoped for a little more luck than this. Something had to go right sometime.

She might have to accept that she wouldn't find the facility. Accept defeat.

Never. There must be a way.

Sean might help her. He seemed like a good kid, kind of like an abused puppy who craved affection while fearing it at the same time. Maybe she could talk him into disclosing the location of the facility. Though the plan niggled at her conscience, and she had no experience in enticing information from people anyway, she had no other options left. She had to try.

If she knew how to contact him.

Sure, no problem. She'd call him on the phone and ask him to pop in for a visit. Even better, she could stand on the roof and shout over the Rocky Mountains to him.

She had forced David out by thinking about it, by wishing for it with every iota of willpower she retained. By concentrating. Through psychic power. The tactic might work for conjuring Sean or at least sending him an SOS.

Just yesterday, the notion would've made her laugh. Tonight, she prayed not only that psychic powers existed, but that she knew how to tap into them. Right now.

Strange that she'd stopped wondering how Sean and David materialized out of thin air and disintegrated into it again. The question, once vital, lingered in the recesses of her mind, but she now rated other questions above it. Questions like who wanted the flash drive, who tormented her, who murdered all those people. Another question held within it the power to reveal all the answers.

What did "they" protect and why?

At this moment, however, she needed the answer to another, more mundane question. Where was the Mojave Desert facility?

She closed her eyes, focusing her thoughts on Sean. His face filled her mind's eye.

Come on, kid. Come out and play. I need your help.

Squeezing her eyelids shut, she took in a deep breath. As she released it one molecule at a time, she let her muscles slacken and her mind open. She didn't know how to do the last part, but she gave it her best shot.

Come on, damn it. This has to work. Please, Sean, I need you.

A chill washed over her. She opened her eyes.

"How'd you do that?" whispered a voice from the opposite corner of the room.

Sean huddled there, kneeling, hands on the stained carpet. He kept his back to the wall, his head turned toward the doorway.

He glanced at her sideways. "Normal people aren't supposed to do that."

"I'm not normal."

"Are you like me?" He lowered his gaze and picked at the carpeting with one fingernail.

She shrugged one shoulder. "Doesn't matter how I did it. I need to talk to you."

"I'm not supposed to. David'll get mad."

A knot cinched tight in her gut. The first sting of tears pricked the corners of her eyes, and she bit the inside of her lip to stave off the flow. No crying. Not now. Too much was at stake. David would be okay because she would find him.

David had hidden the truth from her too, at first. When he'd finally shared it with her, or at least part of it, she'd shoved him away with so much force it kicked up a small tornado. She could apologize to him later. When she rescued him. Then he would need to thank her.

Grace didn't care if he was grateful. She wanted him alive and conscious. Here. With her. Annoying the hell out of her as usual.

She scuttled across the carpet toward Sean.

His eyes bulged. "Don't touch me."

She froze. A couple of yards separated them.

"I won't touch you," she said. "I didn't mean to scare you."

He hugged himself, biting his lower lip, and fixed his gaze on the carpet.

She sat down cross-legged and rested her hands on her knees. Sean wouldn't help her if she scared him. The kid had sore nerves.

"Listen," she said, her tone soft, "I need your help."

"Me?" He lifted his head to look at her.

"David's in trouble, isn't he?"

Sean shrugged one shoulder, averting his eyes again. "Can't talk about that stuff."

"I can help him. If I know where he is."

"Nobody can help us."

"I can."

A lock of hair drooped over his eyes. He sketched invisible lines on the carpet.

"I can help you," she said. "But you have to tell me where you are."

"Why would you wanna help us?"

"I know what it's like to be alone."

He turned away from her, facing the wall.

She needed his cooperation, but her stomach burned at the thought of tricking him into telling her the location. Deceptions would make her no better than the people who sought her. She preferred that he volunteer the information. That was why she hadn't lied to him. She did know how it felt to be alone, powerless, plummeting from a precipice without a parachute. The people with the power, the kind of power money granted, enjoyed watching others flail and clutch at any handhold, however narrow or weak. She had been that victim once. Not anymore. Since her days on that precipice, she had learned one basic truth.

Power could shift hands.

Besides, not all power came from money or privilege. Some power originated deep inside the mind. No one could take away that kind. They might suppress it temporarily with drugs, as she somehow knew they'd done with David, but the power always resurfaced.

She had the power. In more ways than one.

Sean stood. "I didn't tell."

The kid vanished.

Her one chance had just disintegrated. Dammit, one break wouldn't upset the balance of the universe. One lousy break.

She thumped her fist on the carpet.

A shape on the wall drew her attention. She scuttled closer, examining the baseboard.

She smiled.

There, in the dust that coated the baseboard, Sean had scrawled a message. 50 miles NE of Reston on Dry Lake Rd. Dirt road to left. Eyes and ears everywhere.

He had given her the location without saying the words. He could assure David that he hadn't told her. *Clever kid*. He'd given her what she'd asked for, and the rest was up to her. For the first time in more days than she could keep track of, she knew exactly where she was headed.

Reston, California.

CHAPTER SEVENTEEN

S IRENS WAILED IN THE DISTANCE, DRAWING CLOSER. THE SHRILL SOUND woke Grace in increments—first her ears awakened to the noise, then her mind surfaced into consciousness, and finally, she eased her lids apart to take in her surroundings. Dingy carpeting. Dusty, mold-stained walls. A window blocked by an overzealous shrub.

The memory of last night returned to her as gradually as wakefulness had. Her stop at the electronics store. Waldron's phone call. Running.

She rubbed her eyes. At least the migraine had left. Her brief nap before Sean came had taken care of that problem. Her mouth felt cottony, her neck ached a bit, and she felt as if she'd slept on a gravel road, but otherwise, she was just peachy.

Glancing at her watch, she saw the time was 6:42. The sun was up already, its glow filtering through the bush's foliage to cast faint streamers of light into the room.

The sirens wailed closer.

She snatched up the gun and scrambled to her feet. At the window, she tried to peer through the branches to see beyond the foliage, but to no avail. She trotted through the house, unlocked the front door, and rushed outside. At the broken-down gate, she stopped.

The sirens had withdrawn into the distance again. Within fifteen or twenty seconds, the sound died out completely.

A mourning dove cooed in the treetops nearby. She listened to the song as she calmed herself with three long, slow breaths. The cops were not coming for her. Waldron might be searching for her at this very moment, but she seriously doubted he'd involve the authorities, despite his former ruse of pretending to work for the FBI.

She headed off down the sidewalk, back toward the center of town. She must've taken a different route from last night, not that she recalled much about her flight from the strip mall, because she wound up passing through a small park she'd never noticed before. Probably because she rarely ventured into this part of town. Not much out here except an elementary school and a park that consisted of one city block covered with trees and manicured grass, plus a smattering of manicured bushes and flower beds. Two concrete paths led through the park. She chose one and walked at a brisk pace.

When she came upon a park bench situated alongside a drinking fountain, she suddenly realized how parched she was. Bending over the fountain, she pressed the button. A thin stream of water jetted out of the nozzle. She guzzled the lukewarm metallic liquid, quenching her thirst in an unbroken series of gulps. Despite its flavor, the water soothed her throat.

She dropped onto the park bench. A breeze cooled her face, ruffling her hair. Reston, California. She must get there. The answers awaited her there. She felt it.

David awaited her there.

Sean had given her directions to the facility, whatever the place was. Now she needed transportation.

An airplane would get her there quickest. Right, fly and get killed like Grandpa. His death hadn't given her a fear of flying—until she'd heard the tape of his last moments. Though the idea of flying didn't scare her, the idea of locking herself in a tiny space, high in the atmosphere, did. Grandpa had died because he couldn't escape. He'd underestimated his enemy. She must learn from his mistakes.

Ruling out air travel left cars, buses, trains, and feet. The invisible assailant had totaled her car. A bus would take days as would a train. She needed a car. Renting was out of the question. Rental agencies required a credit card, and using her card announced her whereabouts as surely as painting the coordinates on a billboard. If her enemies could find her at the strip mall, probably using the GPS in her regular cell phone, she felt sure they could track her credit card purchases too. Even if she told the rental agency she wanted the car only to drive in the local area, she had a feeling Waldron would guess her real destination. And he would know what kind of car she was driving. He'd know the license plate number too.

Waldron and his cabal had killed everyone who so much as considered helping her. They whittled down her options until she held nothing but a sliver in her hand.

Her fate called to her from California.

Whatever she did, they would find out.

Grace started off down the concrete path again. When it met the sidewalk along the street, she turned right toward the center of town. She passed by the elementary school where children frolicked in a sandy playground. The scenery turned from vaguely industrial to residential as she made two turns in her route, hoping she was guessing correctly about which way to go. The houses looked old but mostly well-kept. Cars were parked along the street here and there. As she passed a beige Ford Taurus, she noticed a sign, of the plastic kind bought in a store, taped to the inside of the windshield. It announced the car was for sale.

This might be her answer. If she paid cash for a used car, buying it from an individual rather than a dealership, the transaction might remain unknown to her enemies, at least for a while. The sign on the window gave the price as four thousand dollars.

So much for that idea. Even if she emptied her bank account, she didn't have four thousand dollars. She rather doubted the seller would accept five hundred and some change. The car looked in good shape, which meant it was worth more than five hundred bucks. She needed a car. Most of all, though, she needed help.

She couldn't force Sean to help her again. The poor kid had looked seconds away from a nervous breakdown. David was… unavailable. She had to figure this out on her own.

A memory unreeled in her mind. The encounter with David last night, when she'd gotten so angry that she pushed him away with the force of a tornado. A lump hardened in her throat. He wasn't dead. She believed it because she'd seen him, lying in a bed, limp and unresponsive. Oh no, he wasn't dead, just drugged into a coma.

She swallowed hard and focused on the memory of what happened before she pushed him away. He'd said something about how he managed to appear and disappear at will.

It's a combination of remote viewing, telekinesis, and thought projection.

What did that mean? Telekinesis meant moving things through the power of the mind, just by thinking about it. She didn't know what remote viewing meant. Thought projection, however, seemed self-evident. It must've meant that a person could project their thoughts into the mind of another person, to make the other believe the notion was their own. David used a combination of the three abilities to effect his disappearing acts, and he also said she was pushing him out—of her mind, she'd later realized. So he must've projected into her mind the thoughts that made her believe she could see him and talk to him when in reality she was conversing with him through some kind of psychic ability.

It still made no sense. She'd done more than imagine him standing in front of her. She'd touched him. She'd laid her hands on a real, physical man.

Ugh. She would never understand this psychic mumbo-jumbo.

Still, if thought projection was possible, then maybe she could use it to her advantage. After all, she had lured Sean to her merely by willing him to come.

An idea occurred to her, but her sense of common decency balked at the prospect. Right now, she saw no alternatives. She'd atone for her sin later.

Grace marched to the door of the house and punched the doorbell button. The muted tones of an electronic bell sounded inside the home. A moment later, the lock clicked, and the door swung inward just enough to reveal the wrinkled face and bleary eyes of a man in his seventies.

In a voice that sounded as sleepy as the gentleman looked, he asked, "May I help you?"

"I'm sorry to bother you, sir," she said, trying for a nonchalant tone, "but I saw the for-sale sign, and I'd like to buy your car."

The man rubbed his eyes, yawned, and straightened. "What?"

"I want to buy your car. I'll pay the full asking price if you'll accept cash."

He perked up at the mention of cash. A faint smile brightened his face as he stepped aside and swung the door wide, gesturing for her to enter.

"Cash'll be fine, missy," he said.

Now came the awful part.

Grace strolled into the house. The man shut the door.

He proffered a hand to her. "I'm Leroy Bevins."

She took his hand and dived straight into the lies. "I'm J—Janet Austen."

The lump reemerged in her throat. She'd almost said Jane Austen, then caught herself just in time to avoid becoming the worst liar in the entire universe. Janet Austen sounded slightly less deceitful, or maybe she was rationalizing. Either way, her mind could come up with no better pseudonym on the fly.

Leroy squeezed her hand and let go.

Grace extracted her wallet from her purse. Flipping it open, she fingered the bills stashed inside the wallet. Two fives and a ten. Not exactly four thousand dollars.

Steeling herself against what she must do, she whipped out the bills and offered them to Leroy. He started to take them.

And then he noticed the denominations. His brow furrowed. His lips puckered.

She focused all her willpower on one thought that she repeated in her mind.

This is four thousand dollars. This is four thousand dollars.

Fixing her gaze on Leroy's, she pictured the thought as a laser connecting her pupils to his. The imaginary beam shot directly into his brain, delivering the thought she needed him to believe.

This is four thousand dollars.

She concentrated with such force that her jaw trembled. Her eyes burned because she no longer blinked. A drop of sweat beaded on her forehead, dribbling down the bridge of her nose. She envisioned the laser growing brighter and narrower, intensifying.

Leroy's brows smoothed out. His puckered lips relaxed into a loose smile.

Taking the bills, he said, "I sure appreciate this, Miss Austen. Cash is a might easier to handle than a check. I just hate goin' to the bank. Do you know they charge me if I wanna talk to a real, live person instead of a machine?"

Grace relaxed a bit. Though she felt a tad woozy, she didn't dare let up too much on whatever she was doing to this poor man, at least not until she drove away in her new used car. She had no clue how long the effect might linger after she stopped actively forcing the man to believe her lie.

A knot cinched tight in her gut. She hated herself right now.

Leroy stuffed the twenty bucks in his pants pocket. He walked to a nearby table, opened a drawer, and plucked a key chain out of the tangle of objects inside the drawer. Approaching her again, he handed her the key chain. A tag emblazoned with the Ford logo dangled from the silver ring, along with a single key.

Grace took the key chain.

"I need to sign the title over to you," Leroy said, heading for the door.

As he opened the door, Grace laid a hand on his arm to stop him from stepping outside. Leroy furrowed his brow again.

You already signed it over.

She fired the thought into his brain through the imaginary laser. A headache was blossoming behind her eyes, but she ignored it and concentrated as hard as she could.

Leroy smoothed out his brow and chuckled. "Guess I already did that, didn't I? Forgetfulness seems to come with gettin' older."

Christ, she absolutely despised herself.

Leroy held his hand out to her. "Well, you enjoy the car, missy. I sure enjoyed meetin' such a pretty little thing as you."

She shook his hand and rushed out the door. When she heard the door click shut behind her, she risked a glance backward. Only the scummiest scum on earth would do what she had just done to that poor man. She had no choice, she told herself. There was no other way to get a car without alerting Waldron to her intentions.

When this was over, if she survived it, she would return the car to Leroy Bevins—with a big wad of cash stuffed into the glove compartment.

Never again would she use her powers to manipulate an innocent person. Never.

Unless she hit another roadblock on the way to California.

Inside the car, she jammed the key into the ignition and jerked it. The engine started up. She buckled the seatbelt, released the parking brake, shifted the car into drive, and headed off down the street in her new ride. The car she'd tricked an old man into selling to her for twenty bucks.

Oh yeah. She was the scummiest scum on earth.

———

THE INTERSTATE WAS DESERTED. GRACE DROVE WEST AT EIGHTY MILES AN hour, seated comfortably in the Taurus with the air conditioning blowing a constant stream of cool air at her. The headache had faded as soon as she stopped concentrating on laser-beaming her thoughts into Leroy's mind. As for her speeding, if a cop pulled her over, she'd accept the ticket. For now, she concentrated on a single goal.

Get to California.

That single need branched out into others—stop whatever was happening, free David from his captors, help Sean if she could—but everything else depended on her achieving the topmost objective. She must find the Mojave Desert facility. Then and only then could she move on to the number-two goal.

Stop *them*.

She still had no clue who they were. But she must stop them, her enemies, from doing whatever the hell they were trying to do. Although she didn't know their ultimate goal, she sensed nothing good would come of it. Anything that involved bad guys, of the visible and invisible variety, experimenting on people with psychic abilities could not result in a smiley, happy ending for the world at large.

Before leaving Lassiter Falls, she'd stopped at the bank to withdraw the entire balance of her checking account, about five hundred dollars. It should give her enough to make it to her destination. She did not want to use her credit card to pay for gas or food because that would leave a digital trail. Her enemies might've guessed her destination, but they didn't know her exact route or the timing of her arrival. Total surprise was impossible, she figured. Partial surprise was the best element available to her.

The sun arced across the sky inch by inch as the scenery became lonely stretches of wooded hills, not a house in sight, not a light to signal other life existed in the universe. She was alone. Completely alone. She'd gotten used to the isolation of having no family, no friends, not another soul in her life who cared what became of her. But this new isolation—alone in the world and hunted like an animal, isolated in spirit and in reality—affected her like an injection of liquid nitrogen into her bloodstream. Every cell in her body had turned to ice, it seemed. The only part of her that felt anything other than icy fear was the metaphysical heart of her being, the unseeable place inside her where emotions and instinct overruled everything else.

The part of her that felt... something for David.

She drove for hours, stopping occasionally to stretch her legs or grab a bite to eat. Caffeine from pop coupled with the urgent sense of danger nipping at her heels kept her going through the miles. By nightfall, she'd crossed the border into New Mexico and passed by Las Cruces. During the hours of cruising down the mind-numbing interstate, weariness had seeped into her at an ever-increasing pace until she knew she must stop for the night, despite the looming threat. The act of using powers she hadn't realized she possessed had sapped her energy more than seemed possible. It depleted her at a level so deep within that she wondered if she'd drained away her very soul.

Half an hour outside Las Cruces, she pulled off the interstate into the parking lot of an independent motel. She spotted three other vehicles in the parking lot. After paying cash in advance for a single room, she relocated her car to the slot directly in front of her assigned room. Thick curtains concealed the interiors of all the rooms, but around the edges of the curtains, the light from a TV flickered inside one room, three doors down from hers. All the other rooms were dark.

Inside her tiny hideaway, she found a small TV so ancient it belonged in a museum, a dated but clean bathroom, a small bedside table equipped with a lamp and a worn-out alarm clock, and a bed fitted with sheets that looked surprisingly fresh and clean. A floral pattern decorated the white sheets while a plain brown bedspread covered the whole thing. The lamplight washed the room in a pinkish glow.

Peeling off the bedspread, she slumped down onto the bed in a pseudo-sitting position. She was too exhausted to hold herself upright. She untied the laces of her boots and kicked them free of her feet, then stripped off her coat, which she tossed over the foot of the bed. It landed half on the bed, half hanging over the edge. She took the gun out of her purse before dumping the bag on the floor. The weapon she set on the bedside table.

Expending her last bit of energy, she laid down on her side with her head on the pillow and hugged herself. She was alone. Like an astronaut marooned in space. Cold. Hopeless.

Tears stung her eyes. She swiped them away with the back of her hand. More tears welled in the corners of her eyes. They came faster and faster while her eyes burned and her nose began to run. Her body trembled with half-suppressed sobs.

Crying. Like a wuss. She'd turned into a puddle of weakness and self-pity. She hated crying, but no matter how hard she fought it, she couldn't stem the flow of tears.

The air temperature plummeted. A draft ruffled her hair.

Goosebumps cropped up all over her body, and she rubbed her arms for warmth. Her heartbeat quickened. She pushed up onto one elbow and scanned the shadows.

"David?" she said.

A figure detached from the shadows in the corner.

Sean halted by the TV. "It's me."

"What are you doing here?" she mumbled as she slumped back onto the bed.

"David said you needed help but he couldn't come. So he sent me. Are you mad?"

He gazed at her, forehead wrinkled, wringing his hands and chewing the inside of his cheek.

"I'm not mad," she said. "I was surprised to see you, that's all."

He shuffled closer to the bed.

Though her arms shook from the modest effort, she pushed up into a sitting position, with her back braced against the headboard. She patted the mattress. "Sit down. It's okay."

He perched on the end of the bed, touching the mattress as little as possible while still counting as sitting on it. He averted his gaze to the floor.

She wanted to hug him, which was strange because she had never been the hugging type. Sean looked in need of comfort, though, and she felt something akin to maternal instinct urging her to give him that comfort. She didn't dare touch him. The kid would probably scream.

"David told you I needed help?" she asked. "I thought he was drugged. How could he tell you anything?"

The kid shrugged. "He told me, ya know, in our heads. I think it took a whole lot of energy to do it, but somehow he broke through the drugs enough to tell me you needed help."

Of course. In their heads. They conversed psychically. Well, she no longer had the luxury of doubting such things were possible. She knew they were.

"Okay," she said. "Why does he think I need help?"

Not that she didn't need help—because she absolutely did, more than anyone could know and in ways she couldn't even articulate—but she had to ask the question anyway.

"Don't know," Sean told her. "He said come, so I came."

"I'm on my way," she said. "To help you and David."

"I know. He'll be mad at you for that."

Yeah, she'd just bet he would. Do this, don't do that. David loved issuing orders without explaining why she ought to do what he said. Well, she was coming to save him whether he liked it or not.

"Tell him it's no use trying to stop me," she said. "I've made up my mind."

Sean's mouth twitched upward at the corners. Almost a smile. "I get it. But he won't."

To hell with him, she almost said. She kept her mouth shut, though, because she was talking to a kid—a sweet, scared kid. Decorum was a bitch. She didn't want David to go to hell, anyway. Sometimes she wanted to scream at him or throw small objects at him, but consigning him to hell was no longer on her to-do list.

"I'm not helping," Sean said, "am I? You need him, not me, right?"

She wanted to blurt out an emphatic yes, complete with spraying spittle. Instead, she gathered the threads of her dignity and told him, in the most ladylike fashion she could muster, "David's an adult who knows what he's getting into. You're just a boy, Sean. I can't let you risk yourself for me."

"I get it."

He looked so dejected that she wanted to say something reassuring. Nothing sprang to mind. Her brain felt as sluggish as her body.

"If you're really okay," Sean said, "I better go."

She gave him a weak smile. It was the best she could pull off. To her amazement, her voice sounded convincing when she said, "I'm really okay. You can go."

Without a word, he vanished.

Grace settled down onto the bed again, on her side, facing the curtained window. She closed her eyes. David's face filled her mind. The image zoomed out to reveal him lying on a bed, unconscious, a needle plugged into the back of his hand while an IV dripped unknown drugs into his veins. This was no daydream, she sensed, but a real-time vision of his condition. She had to help David, but she was too exhausted to reach him.

Dammit, she needed rest. She must push those thoughts out of her mind. Time gave her no leeway. Her enemies raced after her, probably not far behind with her luck, and they would not pause to let her contemplate her feelings. Besides, self-pity was a quagmire she might never extricate herself from if she willingly traipsed into it. Later, she could dole out the blame, to herself and others. Tonight, she must sleep.

She willed the thoughts away. Her mind descended into slumber, drifting into the plane where dreams lived.

Share your golden light with me, or I'll take it from you any way I can—even if it kills you.

The voice, fraught with a dark intensity, shocked her out of the dream as her mind rocketed up from the depths of slumber. With a gasp, she slammed through the barrier into wakefulness. Her eyes flew open.

Seconds ticked by as she struggled to sort out where she was. In the motel room. Somewhere in New Mexico. Reality trickled into her mind as the scene around her sharpened into focus. She lay on her side on the bed, her chest heaving with each ragged breath. Her right hand was wrapped around an object. She glanced down at it.

Her hand gripped the gun. Her index finger was curled around the trigger, and the barrel was jammed into her mouth.

She flung the weapon onto the floor.

The man in her dream, the one whose face looked like Xavier Waldron's. He had done this to her. With some type of psychic manipulation, he had made her put the gun in her mouth. If he could force her to do that, then…

Christ.

She no longer felt certain her revelation about the shadow man's identity had been genuine and not another psychic manipulation. Anyone who could convince her to put a gun in her mouth might trick her into believing anything he wanted. To truly unmask him, she must find him in the real world.

And she knew exactly where to look.

She must get to California. *Now.*

CHAPTER EIGHTEEN

GRACE BIT THE INSIDE OF HER LOWER LIP AS SHE SCRUTINIZED THE road atlas. Twenty minutes ago, she'd given up on sleeping anymore and jogged over to the gas station next door to the motel. After buying the road atlas, she'd returned to her motel room. Now she sat on the bed with one leg folded under her and the other dangling off the edge of the mattress. The road atlas lay on the bed in front of her, open to the two-page spread showing California.

The bedspread was lumped on the floor at the foot of the bed. Both the sheets and blanket were shoved aside, just as she'd left them after her second attempt to get some sleep. The first attempt ended when she woke to find a gun in her mouth. The second ended when she gave up after nearly an hour of tossing and turning, unable to get anywhere near slumber. It was hard to relax knowing that her enemy could manipulate her thoughts and actions.

But if he could make her do whatever he wanted, why hadn't he?

He probably wanted the flash drive, like everyone else. He also wanted her to give him… What had he called it?

Her golden light.

In previous dreams, he'd called her "golden girl." She had no idea what he meant by either term. The point was, he wanted something from her. Possibly more than one something. Although he'd threatened to kill her more than once, he hadn't done it or even come close to it. The incident in her car had terrified her at the time, and it had felt like attempted murder. When she thought back on the incident, however, the truth seemed far less obvious. He could've killed her. Yet he didn't. Instead, he frightened her into believing he wanted her dead.

Maybe he would kill her, eventually, after he got what he wanted. For now, he seemed to need her alive.

Which meant she had a chance. A slim one, but hell, she'd take any chance the universe offered her.

Grace tapped her pen on the map, on the spot where she'd drawn a big black circle around her destination. Reston, California, was a tiny dot identified with tiny text.

A cool draft rushed over her.

He's here.

Her pulse beat faster as she looked up from the map.

David stood at the foot of the bed, hands in his pants pockets. He wore a gray T-shirt and blue jeans. His eyes were a crystalline blue, not the fiery azure she'd seen on other occasions. The drape of the T-shirt revealed hints of the muscles underneath.

An image flashed in her mind. David's bare chest. Her fingers tracing the contours of those muscles.

Oh, for pity's sake. Very bad people wanted to capture or kill her, and she was fantasizing about some guy's pecs.

Not just some guy. Her ex-fiancé.

Were they ex? He'd never mentioned a breakup.

"You pulled out the needle," David said.

Grace dropped the pen. It rolled into the little valley where the facing pages of the atlas met. "Did I?"

"Don't you remember?"

"I remember wanting to do it, but I couldn't."

"Well, you did," he said. "I felt you there with me. Thank you."

"You're welcome. How are you feeling?"

"Better. Clearer."

"Glad to hear it." She glanced down at her left hand, then back up at him. "If we were engaged, where's the ring?"

He shrugged. "I don't know. Maybe Edward hid it when he realized you had amnesia. When he decided to keep the truth from you for your own protection."

"Yeah," she snorted, "I've sure been protected good."

Walking around the corner of the bed, he sat down directly in front of her. Only the road atlas separated them. She thought about squirming backward to get some more space from him, until she realized, with a suddenness that made her heart skip a beat, that she didn't want more space. She liked sitting near him, gazing into those crystalline eyes. She felt safe.

It was insane, of course. She had only his word that they knew each other at all, much less with the intimacy implied by their alleged engagement. Whenever he was around, two parts of her battled for control. Half of her needed to doubt what he said while the other half believed without reservation. The contradiction left her feeling off-kilter. That was why she tried not to think about it.

She studied David. Maybe she had contradictory feelings about him because her instincts were trying to tell her he wasn't who he claimed to be. The figure in her dreams, the real shadow man, wielded the power to control her, to make her believe what he wished.

Apparently, he wielded that power. She didn't understand this psychic stuff.

David lifted his eyebrows. "Are you all right?"

"Huh?" She blinked, realizing her gaze was aimed at his mouth. She raised her focus to his eyes. "How does all this psychic stuff work?"

"What do you mean?"

"How do you do this?" She waved a hand, palm out, in his general direction. "I mean, you're not in this room, not physically. You're in California. But it looks like you're here"—She patted her palm on his chest—"and it feels like you're here."

She let her hand linger on his chest. The warmth of his body filtered through the fabric of his T-shirt to warm her palm. He looked down at her hand, then back up at her face.

"When I asked you before," she said, "you told me it was a combination of telekinesis, remote viewing, and thought projection."

"Yes."

She let out a sharp sigh. "Please elaborate."

"You know as much about it as I do, if not more."

She yanked her hand away and glared at him. "I have amnesia, dammit. I don't have a clue what you're talking about, and I need you to explain it to me."

His lips worked as if he were trying to remember how to form words. "It might be best if you remember on your own."

"I don't have time for that. Very bad people are hunting me, and some of them appear to have psychic abilities. I can't protect myself if I don't know how the hell this works."

"Fine." He settled a hand on the bed, leaning against it for support. "This is all theoretical, you understand. No one knows how it works."

She rolled her eyes. "Just get on with it."

"Telekinesis is the ability to move objects without touching them. It seems to involve affecting matter at the molecular level—for example, shifting air molecules to make an object move. Thought control is, well, influencing another person's mind to convince them to believe or see what you want them to." He paused, frowning. "Remote viewing is harder to explain. Essentially, it's the ability to visualize any location, object, or event anywhere in the world—past, present, or future—simply by thinking about it."

"Like looking at a photo?"

"Sometimes it's like that, but it can also be much more." Without looking down, he lowered his index finger onto the road atlas like a needle dropping onto a vinyl record. His fingertip traced the blue lines of interstates. "A powerful remote viewer can send his mind to the desired location. He can float around, like an invisible bird, to get a broad view of the area and even to listen in on conversations. That's why we nicknamed it traveling."

He closed his eyes.

Grace watched his finger moving around on the map. Despite his apparent lack of vision, his finger continued to trace the road lines on the atlas.

"A traveler can sense things," he said, "without knowing where or when it is. RV is a type of ESP, similar to clairvoyance."

"Are you doing it now?" she asked. "Remote viewing, I mean."

"In a way. I'm sensing the lines on the map, though I wasn't trying to. When you use psychic abilities on a regular basis, you start to do things without realizing it. The powers become second nature." His mouth twisted into a crooked smile as he met her gaze. "Convinced yet?"

She folded her arms over her chest. "That's a nice party trick, but how do I know you're not peeking?"

"Here." He took her hands and lifted them to his face, placing one of her palms over each of his eyes. "Now I definitely can't see."

At first, his skin felt cool against her palms. Second by second, his warmth seeped into her hands, setting off a chain reaction inside her. He was close enough that if she leaned forward a little, her lips would brush against his.

"Satisfied?" he murmured.

Oh no. She wasn't satisfied at all, not that she would ever admit that to him.

"Well?" he said, sounding irritated.

She suddenly remembered the map and the point of this little exercise. With her hand still covering his eyes, she glanced down at the atlas. His fingertip was tracing the twisting, arching paths of roads.

His breath tickled her wrists. Against her will, her gaze wandered back to his face. To his lips.

Grace's cheeks warmed. She yanked her hands away from his face.

He opened his eyes, looking straight at her. "What's wrong with you?"

"N-nothing."

Time to change the subject. Fast.

Clasping her hands on her lap, she cleared her throat. "I get the remote viewing thing, I think. But how do you make yourself a body? Or is that a trick? Influencing my thoughts to make me think you're a solid object when you're not even actually here."

"It's not a trick. Not the way you mean."

"Then what is it?"

"Remember what I said about telekinesis? It's the manipulation of matter. And remote viewing is kind of like an out-of-body experience or astral projection. The third element, thought projection, is pretty much what it sounds like."

"So you are screwing with my mind."

"No."

David spoke the word with such vehemence that she felt the need to apologize, until she remembered he was the one avoiding her questions.

His voice softened as he said, "I wouldn't do that to you even if I could. I can suggest that you see and hear me, and you decide subconsciously whether to let it happen. If you let me in, then I continue to project my thoughts into your mind, which you interpret as spoken words. It's a conversation, not an intrusion."

She opened her mouth to ask another question.

He raised a hand to silence her. "I'm getting there. Once I've knocked on the door, so to speak, and you've let me in, then I can affect matter in the environment to build a physical form."

"You make it sound like you're baking a cake."

"I've given you a simplistic explanation of an extremely complex and esoteric process that involves multiple psychic faculties and requires an enormous amount of energy. Even I don't fully understand how it works, and I do this all the time."

"Seriously? All the time?"

He shrugged one shoulder. "In the past few days, it's been all the time."

"Before the last few days, how often had you done this creating-a-body thing?"

"We call it manifesting." His finger, still on the map, began drawing invisible, random spirals on the paper. "I've done it several times before, but not since last summer."

She wanted to ask the question but feared the answer. At the same time, she craved the answer. Last summer fell squarely into the blank spot in her memory. If she had known David during those eight months, then anything that happened to him during that time could involve her. She wanted to know, yet didn't want to know. She *needed* to know.

Oh, what the hell.

"Why not since last summer?" she asked.

"That's when I learned how to manifest." He straightened, his gaze fixed on hers. "You taught me how to do it. I've never used the ability with anyone else."

A shiver rippled through her. A strangely warm shiver.

"Oh," she said, her throat suddenly tight. "That's... sweet. I guess."

He watched her, not saying a word.

She slapped her hands down on her knees and stared at the atlas. Lines of different colors snaked across the page, intersecting and diverging, some dead-ending and others stretching onward toward the edge of the map. Human lives did the same thing. Her life's path had intersected David's, but would it dead-end or continue onward?

For now, she knew one thing. Her path would take her straight into the Mojave Desert. Where it went after that remained a mystery. *If* it went on after that.

She glanced up at David. "How do you find me?"

"Via remote viewing. Even if I don't know where you are, I can sense you. It's like there's an invisible string between us and, if I let it, the string will guide me to you." The crooked smile returned. "Or sometimes you drag me here."

She felt her lips curving upward, just a touch. "I drag you here. Right. I'm so good at making you do anything I want."

"You're more powerful than you realize."

"Oh please."

"It's true." He lifted a hand to touch her cheek. "You were the strongest of us all."

The lovely sense of warmth and security evaporated in an instant. She thrust his hand away.

He scrunched his forehead.

"What do you mean 'us all'?" she demanded. "What aren't you telling me, David?"

"You and I were part of a scientific project funded by a multinational corporation. The objective was to prove psychic abilities exist and to figure out how they work."

She felt ice forming at the core of her and, as much as she did not want to, she asked, "For what purpose?"

"Originally, the goal was strictly to expand scientific knowledge."

"And now?"

"I don't know. After your parents died, things got even worse."

"What do my parents have to do with anything?"

He shoved a hand through his hair and stared into the corner. "They were the driving force behind the project."

SILENCE FILLED THE ROOM AS IF THE LACK OF SOUND EXERTED AIR pressure. David watched Grace's expression for some clue to how she'd handled the avalanche of information he'd dumped on her. The revelation about her parents must've hit her especially hard. It was a lot for anyone to take.

But she wasn't just anyone. She never had been. When he'd called her strong, he meant more than her psychic abilities. She could handle almost anything the world threw at her.

He still worried. She'd been through too much already.

Every time she treated him like a stranger, he wanted to smash the nearest breakable object. Anger had never been an issue for him before. Although he had his moments like anyone else, in general, he maintained his calm no matter the situation. When Tesler shot him up with a homemade drug cocktail, or when the guards manhandled him like a sack of grain, he kept his cool. Each time he visited Grace and butted up against the wall of her mistrust, he lost his temper—and he hated that.

She trusted him whether she realized it or not. Deep down in the place where her memories were sequestered, she knew the reasons why she trusted him. If only those memories would break free, everything would be fine.

Probably.

It *would* be fine. He had to believe that her memory would return and things would go back to normal because he couldn't accept the alternative. That she might never remember. That she might push him away—physically, psychically, emotionally—for good this time.

The thought made his gut twist and his jaw clench.

He refused to accept the possibility. Whether she embraced him or tossed him out the door, she needed to reclaim her memories. Amnesia seemed to have stripped her of the power she innately possessed, or at least it had suppressed that power. Without it, she was far too vulnerable. And the next time she got herself into trouble, he couldn't guarantee he'd be around to protect her.

Not that he'd excelled at protecting her so far, as she'd helpfully pointed out to him a few minutes ago.

He would do better. He must.

Grace drummed her fingers on her knees. "You're lying. My parents would not hold people hostage in the desert."

"I know that. The darker side of the project emerged only after someone else took over."

"Who?"

"I don't know. He never shows himself because he prefers to control things through his minions."

"Like Xavier Waldron."

He shrugged. "And others, I'm sure. I don't know all of them."

Grace stared at him for a moment. Her cheeks were faintly pink, her eyes a little red. Half-moon shadows darkened the skin under her eyes. Her lips looked a touch pale too. She was exhausted, physically and mentally. If she didn't get some rest...

Here came the hard part. Somehow, he must convince her to believe the one thing she seemed utterly incapable of accepting right now.

"No," she said as if she'd heard his thoughts. Then she shook her head so emphatically that her hair flopped around her face. "It makes no sense. Why would my parents study psychic stuff?"

"Because that's what scientists do," he said. "They study things. Eventually, it also became a way to help you understand your powers."

"That's ridiculous. I never had any powers until—"

Her expression went blank. Her mouth fell open as her eyes widened.

Ah-hah. The triumph flooding through him must've shown on his face because she clamped her mouth shut. Her expression tightened into a scowl.

"You've used your powers," he said. "Recently."

She froze. Her scowl melted into a look of distress like she'd just committed a terrible crime by accident. The triumphant feeling flooded out of him as quickly as it had arrived.

He laid his hand over hers. "What happened?"

She bit her lip, bowing her head.

He squeezed her hand. "You used your powers, didn't you?"

"Yes," she whispered. "I tricked a nice old man into selling me his car for twenty bucks." The words now tumbled out in a rush. "I needed a car, but I couldn't risk using my credit card to rent one and I didn't have enough money to buy one, so I practically stole one instead. From an old man."

"Maybe he was happy to sell his car to a beautiful woman for twenty dollars."

She shook her head and sniffled. "I made him believe it was five thousand dollars."

A drop of water fell onto his hand. No, it was a tear.

He hooked his finger under her chin and lifted her head until their eyes met.

She averted her gaze.

"It's okay," he said, rubbing his thumb across her chin. "You had no choice."

"You're wrong," she said. "It's not okay. I used a psychic power—thought projection, I guess—to manipulate an innocent person. I'm evil."

He almost laughed, though he felt nothing close to mirth. "Evil" was the last word he would ever use to describe her.

"Look at me," he said.

She didn't.

He tapped his thumb on her chin. "Please."

Slowly, she turned her eyes to look at him. Tears overflowed her now-bloodshot eyes.

Releasing her chin, he wiped the tears from her cheeks with his thumb. No more spilled from her eyes, but she still looked stricken. It made his chest ache.

"If you were evil," he told her in a soft voice, "then you wouldn't have any qualms about bending others to your will. I'm sure when this is all over, you'll find a way to make it up to the old man."

She sniffled. "I thought I'd return the car, secretly, with a wad of cash in the glove compartment."

He snatched a tissue from the box on the bedside table and handed it to her. "That proves it. You are not evil."

She took the tissue, blew her nose, and tossed the wadded-up tissue into the nearby trash can.

Leaning closer, he kissed her forehead.

"Are you sure about that?" she asked.

"Positive." He kissed the tip of her nose. "You're not evil."

Her cheeks were pink now. Her eyes were dry, though red.

She gave him a slight smile. "Neither are you. Evil, I mean."

The flush of triumph cascaded through him again, stronger this time, infused with a nearly overwhelming desire to pull her into his arms and never let go. Unlike the first time, the triumphant sensation stemmed not from smug satisfaction that he'd been right, but rather from an ecstatic relief that she had just told him, in her own way, that she trusted him.

Maybe she hadn't declared her undying devotion to him, but it was a start. More than that, though, it was…

Hope.

***

GRACE GAZED INTO HIS BLUE EYES, FEELING A BIT MESMERIZED. HIS irises didn't glow as they often did when he first came to her. She wanted to ask him about the fiery-eyes thing, but her voice refused to work. Her body felt paralyzed and tense, though in a strangely pleasant way, infused with tingling anticipation.

David flipped the atlas shut. He picked it up and tossed it onto the bedside table.

His gaze never wavered from hers.

She felt a tightening deep inside her, a yearning for something so close yet out of reach, until this moment. Right now, what she wanted sat inches away from her. From the first time she'd seen him, she had wanted to trust him, to take comfort from him, to touch him.

David stretched out a hand, laying his palm on her cheek.

And still, she couldn't move.

He slid his hand into her hair, around the back of her head, and drew her closer as he leaned forward. His lips met hers, softly at first, then with more pressure.

Fire swept through her body, the most delicious kind, and her eyes fluttered shut.

He deepened the kiss, sliding his hand down her throat. His other arm wrapped around her, pulling her against him. She slipped her arms around his neck and abandoned herself to the kiss, relaxing against him and parting her lips to let his tongue sneak between them.

Time seemed to stop. She heard nothing except the thundering of her pulse in her ears.

He peeled lips away from hers. His embrace loosened a touch.

She kind of woozy, but somehow, she managed to open her eyes.

He watched her with furrowed brows.

"What's wrong?" she asked. Her voice came out as a throaty whisper, but at least it worked this time.

"Doesn't it bother you," he said, "that I'm not actually here?"

Maybe it should have. It didn't, which probably should've bothered her even more. Right now, she felt nothing except warmth, anticipation, and total security.

Grace reached down to take hold of the hem of his T-shirt and lift it to expose his abdomen. Muscular, just as she'd imagined, though not in a freaky bodybuilder way. As she lifted the shirt higher, she laid one hand on his chest and met his gaze. "Feels to me like you're here."

He exhaled an uneven breath.

She laid both hands on his chest, tracing circles with her palms.

The worry vacated his face in an instant, replaced by a sensual smile that heated her up on the inside. He stripped off his shirt and pulled her tight against him, all those muscles she'd admired suddenly pressed to her body. Her shirt went next, fluttering to the floor. The remainder of their clothing followed suit, until they both wore nothing but skin. They kissed again, and again and again, as their hands explored each other with growing hunger. The kisses grew more passionate, the touching more intimate, until he spread her on the bed and took her body, gliding in and out with slow, powerful strokes. Pleasure swirled through her, intensifying with each glide of his flesh inside hers until she soared out of herself into a vast field of stars. The sensation of flying pushed her over the edge, and she felt him go with her.

By the time she drifted back into herself, a barrier had broken inside her mind. Memories flooded through her on the final crest of pleasure.

She remembered him.

Her body felt languid, relaxed, like her muscles had melted into a warm pool of satisfaction. Her mind sank into a light slumber.

The jostling of the bed roused her. She parted her lids just enough to see David sitting near the foot of the bed, already half-clothed. He was pulling on his T-shirt. The lamplight dimmed as it neared the foot of the bed, leaving swathes of shadow where David sat.

The bedside clock told her she'd slept for about ten minutes. Her mind felt fuzzy, her mouth cottony. Yet her body still felt deliciously languid.

Sitting up, she drew the sheet up to cover her chest.

David, now fully clothed, turned to look at her. He smiled almost shyly.

For a moment, she'd remembered him—not in the sense of recalling how they'd met or when he'd proposed to her, but in the sense of knowing him on a visceral level. Everything he'd told her about their relationship was true. The luxury of doubt had evaporated along with, apparently, her self-control. A blush fired up in her cheeks. What they'd just done…

She pushed the memory aside and asked, "Why bother getting dressed? I mean, can't you will your clothes to be on you again?"

"It doesn't work that way. Manifested or not, it's still clothing." He tugged the hem of his shirt. "You have to handle it like real clothes."

"Damn. It would've been so convenient to able to create my own outfits like…" She swept her hand up through the air, ending the gesture with a flourish. "Like *whoosh*."

His smile broadened. He chuckled softly. "Sorry to disappoint you."

Oh no, she was not disappointed. Not in any way.

He slid across the bed toward her, and the lamplight spilled across his features.

Grace's chest tightened. Dark circles under his eyes. A pallor beneath his skin.

Dropping the sheet, she grasped his face in both hands. "Are you all right?"

He shrugged. "Running out of energy, that's all."

She studied his eyes, which looked dull and tired.

"I'll be fine," he said, taking her hands in his. "But I have to go. I'm sorry."

She wanted him to stay. Forever. "I understand."

David kissed her right hand, then her left. "I love you."

Her entire body stiffened. "What?"

The word came out sounding hard. For a second, she thought it wasn't her voice at all. But it was. She tried to summon an emotion, any emotion. Nothing came to her. She felt cold and empty, like the void of space.

Soaring into a void. Stars all around.

I love you.

Grace yanked her hands away. "Don't say that."

He didn't speak. His eyes had taken on a glassy quality, and a single drop of sweat rolled down his temple. His voice weak, he mumbled, "I'm sorry."

His body jerked.

"David?"

He sat immobile, silent, deathly pale.

Oh God. He was dying.

———

A CHILL CRASHED OVER HIM, LIKE A WAVE OF ARCTIC WATER. EVERYthing he'd felt tonight—joy, passion, contentment, and finally regret—fizzled out in a heartbeat as soul-drenching weariness pervaded every molecule of his body.

No. Not yet.

The regret niggled at him, a remote and disconnected sensation. He didn't regret what had happened with Grace. He regretted blurting out the three words most likely to make her flee in the opposite direction as fast as she could. For a moment, she'd trusted him. For a moment, they'd connected. It had been perfect—until he screwed it all up by telling her the one truth she couldn't yet handle. What in the world had he been thinking?

Another chill inundated him. The call to return tugged at his essence, and he could ignore it for only a few minutes more, ten at most.

"I have to go," he said, unable to keep the weariness from infiltrating his voice.

She nodded, her expression unreadable. "You should go, then."

He didn't want to go, but his wishes could not overcome a lack of energy. When he fell back into his body, the real one, he'd sleep whether he wanted to or not.

"Where will you go?" he asked.

She looked at the window, seemingly focused on the folds in the drapes.

A deep sense of foreboding crept into him and cinched tight around his heart.

He couldn't say why, but he glanced at the bedside table. The road atlas lay there, its cover shut. She'd been studying the map when he first arrived. He picked up the atlas, dropped it onto the bed between them, and flipped it open to the page marked by a disposable pen.

Grace let out a soft grunt of surprise.

As David gazed down at the atlas page, that ominous feeling grew stronger. This was a map of California. A circle of black ink marked a spot in the desert. Reston, the text said.

Something deep inside him twisted into big, hard knots that burned him like fire.

"Where are you going?" he demanded.

She gave him a confused look. "California."

The need to leave tugged harder, but he fought the pull with everything he had, which wasn't much.

"Are you insane?" he asked. "That's the last place on earth you should go. Get as far away from California as you can. Go to South America, I don't care, just *stay away from Reston*."

She got that look on her face, the one he knew meant she would do the exact opposite of whatever he told her to do.

The tug strengthened. Soon, he wouldn't be able to ignore it anymore. He couldn't leave yet. He must convince her and make certain she would stay the hell away from the facility.

Grace slapped a hand down on the map. "I will do whatever I please, with or without your permission."

"Please listen—"

"Go to hell."

He had just enough power left to do one thing, though given his swiftly depleting energy level, he couldn't be certain how long the effect would last. No other options were viable. He must try this and pray that desperation imbued the effect with more punch.

"I thought you were leaving," Grace said. "Or do I have to push you out again?"

"No," he assured her. If she did that again, it might kill him, but he'd keep that information to himself. "I'll go."

He grasped her shoulders and bent close to whisper in her ear. "I'm sorry for this, but it's all I can do."

Before she could respond, he did it. The last bit of energy pulsed out of him into her.

She gasped. Her stunned expression lasted only a second, then she passed out.

He caught her as she slumped backward and settled her limp body onto the mattress, placing her head on the pillow. Rising, he pulled the sheets up to cover her. Stray hairs had fallen across her face. He brushed them away. She looked peaceful, innocent, safe. Maybe the first two applied. The last one, however, was nothing but an illusion. When she woke up, she'd be angry with him. She might never speak to him again. If his actions kept her alive, he would gladly accept the blame.

The energy was gone. He felt himself melting as the molecules that gave him form lost their cohesion, scattering into the air.

No choice now. He must go.

His vision went black. The tether pulled him backward, through a field of star-like lights, down a tunnel of blackness, and back into his body.

At the instant before he plummeted into sleep, he had time for a single thought.

She's going to die.

Chapter Nineteen

THE INTERSTATE STRETCHED OUT AHEAD OF HER THROUGH MILES OF desolation. Tumbleweeds danced across the road like ghosts of the towns and people who'd once populated the countryside during the frontier days. Few humans lived out here now. Aside from a coyote that dashed across the road in front of her, she saw no signs of life.

Grace had woken up in the motel room, alone and wearing nothing but a sheet. Six hours had elapsed while she slumbered in a state of rest she felt certain David had forced on her. How, she didn't have a clue. Why, she could guess. To keep her away from the facility.

As if she had a choice anymore. She must go there.

He'd made her so angry, ordering her to run off to South America or wherever. Running would do her no good since her invisible stalker seemed able to find her anywhere. Why wasn't the creep here now to torment her when she was at her weakest?

David had run out of energy. It forced him to stop using his psychic abilities, at least temporarily. He'd mentioned that the things he did required an enormous amount of energy. After she'd projected her thoughts into the mind of Leroy Bevins, she'd experienced a crash too. Maybe her stalker dealt with the same downside. If so, their common weakness might give her an opening.

She needed every advantage available to her, especially after she'd lost six hours on a forced nap. Whatever David had done to her, it knocked her out good. When she first woke up, she was so angry with him she wanted to manifest right next to his hospital bed just so she could slug him. After a couple of hours on the road, though, she'd lost the anger. Fear crept back in, inspiring morbid thoughts about what David's captors might be doing to him. If they found out his IV was disconnected, if they knew he'd visited her, they might get very, very upset.

Tears burned in her eyes. This time, they were tears of rage instead of despair. She needed anger to fuel her right now, and anger toward her enemies felt a whole lot better than anger at David. Not that she'd forgiven him. She simply had bigger problems.

Their last conversation had been an argument. She'd told him to go to hell.

A void. Stars. David.

I love you.

His words kept replaying in her mind at the most inopportune moments. She'd almost run off the road once thanks to the automatic stereo replay. Recalling the words brought back the feelings, both physical and emotional, she'd experienced with him last night. She'd remembered him, or at least she'd remembered the feelings he inspired in her. The intense, wonderful feelings. The visceral memories of what they'd shared once, and again last night. She trusted him, in a way she'd never trusted anyone. So much still eluded her, though.

Eight months of her life still eluded her.

Maybe that explained why she'd lost it when he told her how he felt. Feeling the truth of it, knowing it on an instinctual level, that was far different from actually remembering. She needed more than gut feelings. She needed real memories too. Recalling those feelings had instilled in her a sense of certainty—at least, it had last night. The light of day had burned off that certainty, leaving her with a disquieting sensation of floating on the ocean without a compass. Nothing made sense. One solitary goal, more of a desperate need, kept her going.

Answers. She must find them. In California.

She'd driven for three hours without stopping, her eyes locked on the road, both hands clamped on the wheel. By then she was beyond exhausted. Against her instincts, which urged her to get to California fast, she started making hourly pit stops. At each stop, she gassed up the car, got a snack and a beverage, and forced herself to lie on the backseat for ten minutes, eyes closed, not expecting or wanting to sleep but knowing she must rest. If she could teleport herself to California, like in STAR TREK, that would solve one problem. Unfortunately, as far as she knew teleporting was not possible. Manifesting a pseudo-body would work too, except for the whole enormous-energy requirement. So no manifesting. She settled for speeding across Arizona in a car she'd virtually stolen from a nice old man. Fortunately, her current bout of fear and anger overwhelmed her guilt over that incident.

You're not evil.

David's reassurance had, strangely, made her feel much better. It didn't make up for what he'd done, with his little psychic sleeping pill. Yeah, she knew he probably thought he was protecting her, but she still wanted to throttle him for it. Compared to eight lost months, six hours wasted on sleeping hardly qualified as a tragedy, except for the minor issue of the bad guys on her tail and the creepy shadow figure in her dream who wanted her "golden light." Although she had no clue what that meant, she felt reasonably secure in assuming it was not good for her future well-being.

Weariness surged through her. She turned on the radio and hit the seek button. Finding only mariachi music, she shut off the radio. Her thoughts would have to keep her awake. Problem was, her thoughts kept returning to the menacing figure in her dream. She focused on the road, but it stretched out ahead of her in a straight, hypnotic line. Her eyelids grew heavy. She turned on the air conditioner, full blast. The noise and cold air shocked her out of drowsiness, though she doubted the effect would last long. If a six-hour nap that ended ten hours ago could not sustain her through the trip, then a blast of cold air wouldn't last long either.

Think about something else. Anything else.

Okay, she could do that.

Since listening to the tape of her grandfather's last minutes, she'd shoved it out of her mind. The information the tape imparted induced fits of anger mixed with panic every time she thought about it. Someone had murdered him, slowly, painfully. No mercy. No guilt. Edward McLean had gotten in the way, and so he had to die, just like Andrew Haley, Brian Kellogg, and...

Her parents.

When Grandpa's plane had crashed two months ago, the authorities had deemed it an accident. Something went wrong, the cabin depressurized, and the occupants died. No foul play, they said. She had demanded to know how the crash happened and exactly what sort of accident could cause the plane to depressurize. They gave her a vague explanation that she knew was a cover story, though the reason for the cover-up had remained a mystery. With no recourse, she'd accepted the findings. She almost managed to convince herself Edward McLean's death had been an accident.

She knew he'd worked for a company called Advanced Laboratories Incorporated, or ALI, and that her parents had relocated to California two years ago to work for the same company. Why, then, had the flash drive included a scan of a magazine article about a different company, Digital Prognostics? That company created computer software. ALI was a privately funded scientific endeavor that revolved around the study of the human brain. On the surface, the two companies shared nothing in common.

Her grandfather would not have included the article for no reason.

She needed to take a closer look at the information on the flash drive. The last time she'd accessed it—the only time she'd accessed it—her enemies used it to track her down at the motel. It had seemed like they could only track her once she logged into their website. If she stayed off the internet, they might not be able to zero in on her.

Right now, she felt like she was driving straight into danger while blindfolded. The flash drive might give her the information she needed to gain an advantage. She must risk it.

Seven months ago, her parents had died in a car accident. Two months ago, her grandfather died in an apparent plane crash, though she now knew it had been no accident. Could her parents have been murdered too? Already, she felt as if everything she'd known or thought she'd known was an illusion.

David claimed her parents not only ran but were the driving force behind the project in which he had participated. She sensed his involvement had been voluntary in the beginning and later turned into captivity. Why on earth would someone hold people hostage?

Control, that was why. The people she knew were being held prisoner, David and Sean, both had psychic abilities. The unknown person or persons now in charge of the research project must view those abilities as a commodity worth killing for. But why? What did they hope to gain from imprisoning and drugging their subjects?

Give me your golden light.

Her stalker had spoken those words in her dream. It had been far more than a dream, she knew. It had been a psychic experience. The stalker had invaded her mind, though he seemed oddly limited in what he could do to her. Lack of energy, perhaps. Or lack of power. It would make sense that every individual with psychic powers had different aptitudes, or at least different skill levels. If David were here, she could ask him.

She was alone.

What if he never came back? Her resolve to find the Mojave Desert facility had ticked him off so much that he knocked her unconscious. No, his reaction had stemmed from another emotion, not anger. He'd been scared. Of what?

That she might find the facility. That she might encounter the people who held him prisoner. The people who wanted her. The murderers who took away her family. He was afraid she would get hurt.

Or killed.

David was with them now. He might die first.

The thought of her own death punched a spike of fear through her chest. But the thought of David's death sent her spiraling down into the freezing-cold depths of terror. She could not let him die.

She would save his life even if she had to hogtie him to do it.

HIS EYELIDS WOULDN'T OPEN. THEY FELT LIKE LEAD APRONS OVER HIS eyes. David tried moving his arms, his legs, his toes, anything. Each responded to his instructions, though with a sluggishness that dismayed him. His last visit with Grace had drained him so thoroughly he wondered if he'd ever regain his full strength.

Fortunately, he no longer needed to worry about the drugs inhibiting him. When he'd woken to find that someone had unhooked the IV from his hand, he knew it must've been Grace. Even while unconscious, he'd been able to sense her presence in the room. She had left by the time he roused.

He'd realized immediately that he must conceal the fact the IV was no longer pumping drugs into his bloodstream. The piece of tape that had once held the needle in place was, by a miracle or sheer luck, still tacky enough to adhere to his skin. He'd broken off the needle's tip and taped the broken end to his skin so that it appeared as if the IV were still in his vein—provided no one looked too closely at it. The liquid medicine from the IV line dribbled over his skin and onto the blanket. By repositioning his arm and the blanket, he'd managed to direct the barely perceptible flow down the side of the mattress instead. He prayed all his efforts would pay off, at least for a time. When he glanced down at his hand, he saw the needle remained in place, even all these hours later.

The room had no clock. His wardens didn't want him to know the time or the date. They liked keeping him drugged and confused until they decided to perform another experiment with him as their guinea pig. Then and only then did they want him alert. The outside world had become a sort of dream to him.

Grace was out there. Alone. He sensed her drawing closer. Despite his warning that she must stay away, she was coming. Even before the amnesia, when she'd known him, she rarely listened to his warnings. When she set her mind to a task, her stubborn determination kicked in, and only with great patience and his own stubborn determination could he dissuade her. These days, the problem was exacerbated because she still considered him a stranger. She bristled at everything he said, shutting him out before he could explain.

Back in the motel room, there had been a moment when he felt she trusted him. Several moments, in fact. It all ended the second he uttered those three words, followed by a command to stay away from the facility. It was his fault, and he knew it. Everything had been so easy before. Now he couldn't survive ten minutes alone with Grace without the conversation devolving into an argument. She mistrusted him. She mistrusted everyone, with good reason. Amnesia notwithstanding, the events of the past year and a half had changed her, he knew. Once he'd felt certain nothing could change her so much that he couldn't get through to her. He was wrong. She hid behind veils of anger, suspicion, and pain that he'd never seen before.

He wouldn't give up. He couldn't.

No place was completely safe, but the facility was the last place on the planet that she should attempt to infiltrate. The bastards in control here knew techniques Grace couldn't imagine, much less comprehend. Even if she regained her memory, she'd left before the project and the facility as a whole descended into the depths of hell. Once the bastards found her, they wouldn't ask if she wanted to go home. They'd shackle her body and her mind, toss her into a dark room, and proceed to squeeze out of her every drop of psychic energy they could.

It would kill her.

He sensed her getting closer, nearing the point of no return. He must try again to convince her, if he could summon the energy for traveling. Remote viewing, though less energy-intensive than manifesting, still drained him, albeit at a slower rate. Although the drugs no longer bound his powers and clouded his thoughts, he felt sluggish in every respect.

Pain sliced through his chest. He bolted upright in the bed.

Grace? No, she was too far away. The psychic call had come from close by.

A voice shrieked through his mind. "Please stop!"

Sean.

David sucked in a breath. Sean's agony and terror ripped through him with near-physical force. Wincing, he swung his legs over the edge of the bed. Shadows writhed in the corners.

His chest tightened. He gripped the bed's edge.

Sean's voice echoed in his mind, the words half-choked by sobs. "Please don't. I didn't do—"

A scream echoed down the corridor outside.

Jesus, no. Not Sean.

David leaped off the bed. Wires snapped free of the electrodes and sensors attached to him. He ran to the door and grasped the knob. It wouldn't turn. Locked.

Another scream reverberated down the corridor outside the door.

He yanked the knob, but the lock held. He kicked the door and pounded his fists on it. He'd never get to Sean this way. Leaning against the wall, he let his lids flutter shut. However weak he might be, he had no choice.

Flying out of his body. Through the field of stars. Down a black tunnel. Into a pool of light.

An exam table stood in the center of the room. There, strapped to the table with leather restraints, lay Sean Vandenbrook. Tear tracks stained the boy's cheeks. Blood trickled from his nostrils. The flesh beneath his eyes had turned unnaturally dark while the rest of his skin had taken on a frightening pallor. Sean's entire body trembled.

David watched, silent and unseen. He tried to think of what to do. There would be guards posted outside the doors to this room. They would rush inside if David tried anything, and Sean might be killed in the struggle. If David did nothing, Sean would die anyway. Tesler would make sure of that.

Clenching his hands into fists, David glared at the so-called scientist.

Tesler hunched over Sean, a syringe in his hand. "We know you visited her. Tell us what you told her, or I'll have to pull it out of you."

Sean swallowed hard. His voice quavered. "I didn't s-see anybody. Just the site. That's all, I swear, the site. I did what you wanted."

"You're lying." Tesler pressed the tip of the needle to Sean's arm. "Liars must be punished."

"Please."

Tears flowed anew from Sean's eyes. He bit his lip, drawing blood.

And Tesler plunged the needle into Sean's arm.

David lunged across the room toward Tesler. He seized the needle, ripping it from Sean's arm. Shouting for the guards, Tesler swung his arms up in self-defense, waving them around as if he were blind. Tesler couldn't see him, David realized.

He spun around and stabbed the needle into Tesler's neck, thrusting the plunger downward.

Tesler's mouth gaped, the cry caught in his throat. His eyes went glassy, and he crumpled to the floor.

The door lock chunked as one of the guards released it.

David concentrated on the lock, visualizing it snapping into position. The mechanism chunked. Metal scraped as the guard struggled to turn the key. The lock held. David gritted his teeth, unsure how long he could hold back the guards, which meant he had no time to waste.

Unfortunately, he had no clue what to do with Sean.

"Who's there?" Sean asked in a tremulous voice.

David leaned over the table so the boy could see him. *If* Sean could see him. Tesler obviously could not.

"It's you," Sean said, his attention focusing on David's face.

Sean could see him after all. He assumed that, in his weakened state, he lacked the power to project his thoughts into the mind of anyone except another individual gifted with psychic faculties. He hadn't manifested, but he had the strength to affect objects as if he had conjured a body. Grace was feeding him power, though he doubted she knew that.

"Did you see her?" David asked Sean.

"Yeah."

David unbuckled the restraints. "Did she see you?"

"Wasn't my fault."

"Dammit, I told you not to show yourself."

"I don't know how it happened. I didn't do it, I swear."

David's hold on the door shattered. He stumbled backward.

Sean slid off the table onto his feet.

The door exploded inward. Four guards rushed into the room. They halted a dozen feet inside the doorway. Jerking their guns back and forth, they surveyed the room as if searching for a ghost. Meanwhile, a technician hurried into the room and made a beeline for Tesler. The young man knelt beside his supervisor and felt for a pulse in Tesler's neck. Discovering one, the technician ordered two guards to help him carry the man out of the room.

While the others attended to Tesler, the remaining two guards grabbed Sean's arms.

David recognized the men as his old friends, Norris and Battaglia. Norris pulled out a pair of handcuffs and moved to clamp them around Sean's wrists.

The technician and the two other guards carried Tesler out of the room.

David threw himself at Norris. He didn't need to hurl his astral body at the guard since, without manifesting, he didn't have a body in the physical sense. His actions served as more of a focusing device. It still felt good as he knocked Norris to the floor. The man's hand popped open, sending the handcuffs skittering across the concrete.

Battaglia grabbed for Sean's arm.

David hurled himself at the man. Battaglia flew backward, smacking into the concrete wall. Dazed, he slumped sideways.

Norris started to get up.

David slammed his foot down on the man's chest, pinning him to the floor. He glanced back at Sean. "I can't hold them for long, and I can't help you escape. I'm sorry."

Sean nodded. "It's okay. I know a place to hide."

"You do?"

The boy managed a faint smile. "I kinda explored this place while they thought I was asleep. A lotta times."

An odd feeling of pride swelled inside David's chest. Sean wasn't as meek as their captors thought.

"Run," David said.

Sean ran.

David wanted to follow him, to make sure the boy reached his hiding place. He couldn't risk draining any more of his energy. So instead, he issued a silent prayer and returned to his room.

His lids opened. He was standing in front of the door, like before, with his hand resting on the knob.

Outside, footsteps resounded in the corridor.

He trotted to the bed and hopped onto it. After taping the broken IV needle to the back of his hand again, he reattached the wires to the electrodes on his head and the sensor clamped around his finger. The wires fed data to the machines that monitored his brain activity and heart rate. Plugged in again, he settled onto the mattress and pulled the sheets over his legs and hips. His heart was racing. He rested his head on the pillow and took several deep breaths to calm his heart rate. The staff seemed to have slacked off lately in the monitoring of their subjects, and he hoped that held true today.

Footsteps approached the door to his room and stopped.

Maybe his luck had run out.

He couldn't think like that. Unlike most people, he had the power to change his luck.

Willing his muscles to relax, he focused on the signals traveling down the wires into the monitoring equipment.

A key thunked in the lock. The hinge creaked as the door swung inward. Through his closed eyelids, he saw the room brighten as light spilled in from the corridor.

Someone tiptoed closer to the bed.

The man's breath wafted over David. It smelled of spearmint.

The visitor clucked his tongue. "Still napping, eh? I told Westcott you couldn't have been responsible for freeing the boy, and I was right. It must've been Grace."

David resisted the urge to reach out and grab the man by the throat. He recognized Tesler's voice.

The bastard laid a hand on David's arm. "We'll have your girlfriend in custody by midday tomorrow."

His girlfriend. If Grace heard Tesler call her that, she'd shove a prickly pear cactus down his throat.

"I'm sure you're wondering," Tesler said, "how we know where she is. It wasn't hard to guess. She's coming for you, naturally."

It took every ounce of self-control David had not to lash out at Tesler. For the time being, he must convince everyone in this facility that he was still drugged. He had to lie there and listen to Tesler's crowing while simultaneously controlling the machines that monitored his vital signs.

Piece of cake.

"I doubt you can hear me," Tesler said, "judging by your EEG readings. But if you can hear me, listen closely. You can't save her, so don't even try." The bed creaked as Tesler leaned closer. "Even if you manage to fight off the drugs we've already given you, we have much stronger ones available to us. I should warn you they have some nasty side effects. Cause any trouble and we can turn your brain to mush."

David struggled to keep his breathing regular. If he could've decked Tesler, he would've felt much more relaxed. As it was, he had trouble keeping his jaw from tensing. It took all his concentration and self-control to keep the monitors from alerting Tesler to his state of wakefulness.

Tesler leaned even closer, his breaths washing over David's face. The man clucked his tongue. "Your life would be so much easier if you had done as we asked from the beginning. Deal with a few strangers. Why should that bother you? Too bad, you could've been the best on our team."

Tesler left. The door clicked shut, and the lock thunked into place.

He'd hoped for more time. If they knew where Grace was headed, then he had hours at most, maybe minutes, to reach her and warn her. If she would listen. If he could break through that wall of stubbornness. If he could make her trust him again. Tesler and his lackeys didn't know David had overcome the drugs, which gave him an advantage, however tenuous. Soon, they might realize he'd woken up. He shouldn't risk traveling.

Grace was alone. He had so little time.

To hell with it. He'd go to her. He'd convince her. And all the while, he would somehow maintain control of the monitoring devices attached to his body. No problem.

Grace might never understand how far he would travel to protect her, what obstacles he would surmount to find her, how many enemies he would battle to reach her when she needed help. He must make her understand the danger.

Once her enemies located her, they'd bring her to the facility, and the unseen puppet master, the one who controlled Tesler and his goons, would take control of her. Once, David had thought they meant to kill her. The truth he'd come to realize proved far worse.

They wanted to keep her.

She couldn't grasp the implications of that. He knew all too well what it meant, and he would never let them get their hands on her. He must protect her, no matter the cost.

He would die for her.

———

GRACE HURTLED OUT OF A DREAM, PANTING, CLAWING AT THE AIR. SHE was awake. Where? She rolled to the left and nearly tumbled off the backseat onto the floor of the Taurus. Flinging her hands out, she braced herself against the back of the driver's seat, halting her fall. She rolled onto her back, held in place by the angle of the seat.

They're dead. Mom and Dad are dead.

Her throat constricted. Tears streamed down her cheeks. She took several deep breaths, fighting back the sobs that threatened to overtake her. She would not break down. Not now. Not with so much at stake. She didn't have the luxury.

The nightmare, a vision of the car accident that had killed her parents, had felt like a memory. Yet she could not possibly remember the accident because she had been in Texas at the time.

No accident.

A disembodied voice had murmured those words to her in the dream. What had the voice meant? Nothing, of course, because it had been a gut-wrenching nightmare, not reality.

The voice that uttered those two words had sounded different from the voice of her invisible stalker. She didn't recognize the voice in her nightmare.

Sitting up, she examined her surroundings. The car was parked in front of an abandoned gas station along a desolate stretch of highway. Desert extended around her on all sides.

Grace got out of the car, stretched, and strolled toward the edge of the road. A snake slithered across the two-lane highway—heading away from her, thank goodness. She watched the creature ooze off the pavement and onto the desert floor where it swiftly vanished from sight.

The wind spat dust at her. She lifted a hand to shield her eyes. The sun was dipping low in the sky, a portent of the looming night. She would've preferred to make her foray into Hell in daylight, but she loathed waiting out another night. She wanted this over with.

The flash drive Grandpa had left her contained sixty gigabytes of data. A lot of information, though not an extraordinary amount these days. Edward McLean must've chosen the data carefully, copying only what he deemed most important. But what did it all mean? Why did strangers want the data so badly that they'd kill her for the flash drive? Why had Brian Kellogg said the data would change humanity forever?

If David were here, she could ask him.

Butterflies awakened in her stomach. She wanted to see David, and she wanted to avoid seeing him. Everything had changed between them last night. She didn't know exactly how or what it meant. Though she trusted him, she didn't know if she should. He'd knocked her out cold, simply because she refused to do what he wanted. Good intentions notwithstanding, his actions had cost her precious time.

She gazed across the desert. In the distance, a pair of vultures circled over a Joshua tree. An animal must've died there. Now its carcass would feed the coyotes and their leftovers would nourish the vultures. She felt a kindred bond with the deceased animal. Carnivores of another ilk were stalking her too. When she fell, *if* she fell, they'd pounce.

Back in the car, she started down the road again. An hour later, she found a real gas station and pulled in to fill up the tank. The station was small, with just two pumps, but everything looked clean and well maintained. No option to pay at the pump, though. The pump was locked too. She waved at the attendant, who stood inside the tiny store holding a phone to his ear. The middle-aged man waved in response and then dropped his hand as if doing something below the counter. Grace tried the pump again, and gas flowed into the car's tank.

While she waited for the tank to fill, she surveyed the area. No other customers were in sight, but a van sat parked alongside the building. A little further down the road, a smattering of buildings clung to the two-lane artery. No sign had announced the town's name. She did remember driving past a dilapidated billboard that advertised a motel located somewhere nearby. The establishment boasted free HBO and in-room microwaves.

Oh lord, a bed sounded wonderful. Sleep sounded heavenly.

No. She straightened, realizing she'd slumped against the car while entranced by her daydream about a passable mattress and a nice, long nap. No sleep. She must keep going. Her enemies would not declare a timeout so she could catch up on her sleep.

The pump stopped with a click. Grace replaced the handle and wandered into the store to pay her tab. Not feeling hungry, she grabbed a bottle of water and headed for the cash register.

Her cell phone warbled.

She jumped. From inside her purse, the phone warbled again.

The middle-aged attendant squinted at her. "You okay, lady?"

Swallowing the hard lump in her throat, she nodded.

The phone rang a third time. No one knew the number. The prepaid phone had no tie to her. Yet someone was calling.

Digging the phone out of her purse, she flipped it open and gingerly held it to her ear. She had the ridiculous thought that the phone might explode or send an electric shock into her brain. After everything she'd seen lately, nothing seemed impossible anymore.

"Hello?" she said into the phone.

"I've missed you."

The voice. The man who invaded her thoughts, who spoke to her in her dreams. The man who, she felt certain, had done his damnedest to terrify her by ramming her car backward into a full-size pickup truck at top speed. It had worked too.

"What do you want?" she asked.

"I know where you are."

"How exciting for you." Through the window, she scanned the area around the gas pumps, the road in front of the station, and the empty desert beyond. "I'm not cringing."

"You will."

"No way."

In a surfer-dude voice, he said, "Way."

"What's your name?"

"God."

She rolled her eyes. "I'll assume you're dyslexic and you mean Dog."

"You can call me JT."

"What do you want?"

His voice changed, deepening into an almost-supernatural timbre that made the hairs at the nape of her neck stand up. "Your golden light, of course. Give it to me now and I just might kill you quickly. Fight me and you'll suffer. A lot."

"I'm not afraid of you," she lied, injecting her voice with what she hoped sounded like confidence.

"David will suffer more. You'll watch him die in the slowest and most painful way I can imagine—and trust me, I've got a vivid imagination."

A wave of nausea crested inside her. She gulped against it. This man meant what he said. She knew it. She felt it. What he'd done to her so far had been nothing but a teaser.

Oh God. David.

She clenched her teeth and hissed, "If you know where I am, then come and get me, you coward. Stop hiding behind remote viewing and telekinesis."

He chuckled, and his voice changed back to his surfer-dude persona. "So you remember the lingo. Cool. Won't help you, though."

She fought the urge to spew a host of obscenities at him. He'd probably like it.

"Soon you'll be mine," he told her in a matter-of-fact tone. "And then we'll play. Can't wait to see ya, babe."

Her lip curled. Babe? Was he kidding? This guy either had a split personality or he thought this was foreplay.

"I will stop you," she said.

"Come on, baby—"

She hung up and started to slide the phone into her purse.

He knew the number now. He might be able to track her through the phone. She couldn't risk it.

She tossed the phone into a nearby wastebasket. If he wanted to torment her, he'd have to find another method of communication. She wouldn't stand here and absorb his crap through the airwaves. She had no time for it. Of course, he knew other ways to torment her, ways that required no phones or computers.

The attendant whistled to get her attention. "You paying cash or credit?"

She tried for a smile. It faltered, so she gave up and sighed, "Cash."

Wiping sweat from his face, the attendant accepted the bills she offered him. A patch sewn onto his shirt identified him as Earl. He punched buttons, eliciting beeps from the machine, and the cash drawer popped open.

"By the way," Grace said, "where am I?"

Without looking up, Earl replied, "Middle of nowhere."

"But which town is it?"

Earl pushed the cash drawer shut and met her gaze. "Welcome to Reston, California."

CHAPTER TWENTY

GRACE TRIED NOT TO LOOK STUNNED. SHE WAS WITHIN FIFTY MILES of the facility, or at least the road that led into the facility. Her journey was almost over. The battle, she knew, was about to begin.

How had JT found her? The prepaid phone should've been untraceable.

Waldron had tracked her to the shopping center, using the signal from her regular cell phone. He could've easily canvassed the businesses in the shopping center to inquire if anyone had seen a woman matching her description. If Waldron had put on his FBI airs, the guy in the electronics store probably would've answered any questions, just to avoid running afoul of the government. Waldron knew how to intimidate people.

Handing over her change, Earl raised an eyebrow.

This time she managed a genuine, if strained, smile. "Do you have a computer I could borrow?"

His brow lifted a little higher. His eyes darted sideways to glance at the wastebasket. He was wondering, no doubt, why she didn't use her cell phone to get on the Internet. Practically everybody did that these days. Her prepaid phone, however, lacked the bells and whistles.

Rather than trying to explain that to Earl, she said, "My phone's dead, and I need to check my email."

He stared at her.

She bit the inside of her lip. Thought projection might work again. Oh hell, she might as well call it what it was—brainwashing. She was loath to employ the technique again, and not only because it made her feel like scum. It also left her exhausted. She needed every iota of energy.

Time to try the old-fashioned way.

"I'll pay you," she said. "To rent your computer for half an hour. How does a hundred bucks sound?"

"Um…" He eyed her with a narrowed gaze. "You look okay, I guess. But don't plug anything into the computer, like CDs or external hard drives. Stuff that might infect it with viruses or worms or what have you."

"Whatever you say."

"And don't download anything either."

She nodded. "Deal."

He waited until she handed over two fifty-dollar bills, then he trotted into a back room.

She hadn't lied… exactly. He'd said not to plug in CDs or external hard drives. The flash drive wasn't technically an external hard drive. At least, that's what she told herself. Besides, a white lie was far better than hijacking the guy's mind.

Earl returned a minute later, carrying a laptop computer under one arm. As he held out the computer to her, he waved his free hand toward a table at the opposite side of the store, next to the self-service beverage dispenser.

"You can take it over there," Earl said.

Grace thanked him and took the laptop. She marched down the candy aisle, aiming for the table. Once there, she set the computer on the tabletop and settled into one of two plastic-and-metal chairs. When she flipped the computer's lid up, she discovered the laptop was already booted up and waiting for her commands.

Slipping a hand into her jeans pocket, she felt the flash drive.

Earl had left the counter. He was sweeping the floor in front of it, casting an occasional glance in her direction.

Damn. She needed privacy.

She refused to manipulate him psychically. Her conscience couldn't take it. But maybe she could manipulate the situation in another way.

Glancing around the store, she spotted a door marked "restroom." It was located in the corner farthest from her.

She closed her eyes and visualized a toilet. Water swirling inside it. Rising, rising. Spilling over the rim, pooling on the floor. She needed more. Something to attract Earl's attention to the restroom. She opened her eyes and stared at the restroom door, imagining a fist poised to rap on the wood. And then…

Bam.

Earl jumped. He twisted around to look at the restroom door. His expression turned befuddled. Dropping the broom, he trotted around the aisles to the doorway at the back of the store, which now hung ajar. His attention dropped to the floor.

"Crap," he blurted as he peeked into the restroom. "What in tarnation?"

Grace whipped the flash drive out of her pocket. She plugged it into a USB port on the side of the laptop just as Earl tiptoed into the restroom grumbling curses. If she had any luck at all, the toilet would keep him busy for a good while.

Turning back to the computer, she opened the list of files on the flash drive. Now that she knew something about the project, the files might make a little more sense to her. That was her hope, anyway. She opened the "test sites" file that she'd looked at before. The spreadsheet contained the names of cities paired with abbreviations—RV, AP, TK, PC, GP. The first three abbreviations matched terms David had told her. Remote viewing was RV, astral projection would be AP, and telekinesis was TK. The letters PC and GP still meant nothing to her. Interestingly, GP was not paired with the name of a particular city, but rather with the designation "Universal." Unless it referred to the Universal Studios theme park, she had no idea what the designation meant.

She closed the test-sites spreadsheet and opened a different one. This was the file that listed "travelers" and contained links to a password-protected website. She would not click the links this time, but she wanted to have another look at the list of so-called travelers. David and Sean were both on the list, which included about two dozen names. The first time she'd looked at the file, she had skimmed it and pretty much stopped when she got to David's name. None of the other names had meant anything to her. Now she scanned the list more carefully. At the bottom of the spreadsheet, she noticed two small tabs that had escaped her attention the first time around. One tab was labeled "Current," while the second was labeled "Former." The spreadsheet she was looking at now must include only travelers currently participating in the project, if participating was even the right word. They seemed more like prisoners. The second sheet must contain the names of travelers who had left the project, whether willingly or forcibly.

Her mouth went dry. She had a feeling forcibly meant one thing—dead.

Unscrewing the cap on her bottled water, she sipped the cool liquid and clicked the tab labeled "Former." Another list of names appeared on-screen.

Her heart thudded. The first name on the list was "Janet Austen."

When she'd told Leroy Bevins her name was Janet Austen, she'd thought the name popped into her head at random. Jane Austen, the name that had first come to mind, was a famous writer. Grace had read her books back in high school, so she assumed the name surfaced from the depths of her mind in the random way memories often did. The other day when she'd looked at this spreadsheet, she hadn't noticed the tabs at the bottom and, therefore, hadn't seen the second list of names. It seemed far too much of a coincidence that the name Janet Austen both appeared on the list of travelers and randomly occurred to her when she needed an alias. It must mean something.

She must've seen the list before. Months ago. During the period obscured by her amnesia.

Lifting a hand to touch the screen, she ran her fingertip under the entry in the spreadsheet.

Traveler: Janet Austen. Designation: Unknown, suspected GP (Level unknown). Accuracy: 99.99859.

She desperately wanted to click the website link. If she did, JT might track her as he or his minions had done before.

Hell, they knew she was coming, anyway. And if she took a quick look at the web page, maybe they wouldn't have time to pinpoint her location.

She clicked the link. The website loaded and, as before, software installed on the flash drive logged her into the password-protected page. It was a status report for the traveler called Janet Austen, similar to the status report she'd seen for David. But this one did not record the traveler as in transit.

Status unknown. Location unknown. Priority target, reacquisition in progress.

Her mouth went cottony again. She swigged water, but it didn't help. *Reacquisition in progress.* What the hell did that mean? And why did it bother her so much? She was not Janet Austen.

She went back to the list of files on the drive. Most of them had unhelpful names that looked like random letters and numbers. She opened one. Gobbledygook. It was some kind of computer code, she guessed, or else an alien language. She opened two more files but found similar garbage. Well, it was garbage to her, anyway. This was no help. She switched back to the spreadsheet of travelers' names.

Janet Austen was suspected to have GP, whatever that meant. Since Ms. Austen was a "former" traveler, did that mean Waldron or some other goon had killed the poor girl? No, they were reacquiring her, which sounded like she was still alive.

Raising her hand, she touched the letters on-screen that spelled out Janet Austen.

"It's you."

Grace jumped six inches off her seat but managed to squelch the yelp that tried to burst out of her. The voice had come from behind her. She turned to see David standing there, gazing down at her with a neutral expression as if he hadn't just scared the bejesus out of her.

"How long have you been there?" she asked, unable to suppress the annoyance in her voice. She got a little testy when every nerve in her body snapped simultaneously.

"A minute," he said, kneeling beside her chair. "You looked engrossed. I didn't want to intrude."

"Since when do you care about not intruding?"

He looked down at his hands. "Since last night."

Oh. Last night. She felt a blush rising in her cheeks.

A change of topic was in order. Immediately.

"What do you mean it's me?" she asked.

He met her gaze, his features tightened in confusion.

"A minute ago," she said, "when you surprised me, you said—"

"Oh." He pointed at the computer screen. "Janet Austen. That's you."

She frowned. "There may be a lot I don't remember, but I do know my own name."

"Janet Austen was a pseudonym."

"Why on earth would I use a pseudonym?"

As soon as the words left her mouth, she realized one awfully good reason why she might—to evade the monsters who were chasing her at this very moment. Yet those monsters ran the project.

No, at first her parents had run the project, at least that's what David said. She needed to know a lot more about the evolution, or devolution, of the research project begun by her parents.

She glanced over her shoulder toward the restroom. Though she couldn't see Earl, she heard banging and thumping, accompanied by muffled curses, emanating from the small room. Below the other sounds, the rushing of water continued.

David still hadn't answered her question.

She turned to him. "Explain to me about this project and why I used a pseudonym when I participated in it. Come to think of it, I don't have the slightest idea why I would've participated in the project either, so explain that too. Please."

He pursed his lips.

She folded her arms over her chest. "Tell me. I don't have time to re-member on my own."

He stared at the computer screen for a few seconds, then let out a sigh that seemed to deflate him. When he spoke, his tone was resigned. "I've only been trying to protect you. As you've pointed out, I've done a terrific job of it."

The bitterness in his voice made her want to hug him. Instead, she reached out a hand to touch his arm. Her fingers went through him like he wasn't even there. Which, technically, he wasn't. Every other time he'd visited her, he'd manifested a body.

Grace tried to touch him again, with the same result. Fingers through air.

When he noticed her efforts, David released another sigh. "I didn't manifest. It takes a great deal of energy, and I don't want to waste any. I might need it very soon. Besides, I need your help to manifest."

She clasped her hands on her lap. He might need all his energy very soon because she insisted on breaching a super-secret facility run by a psychopath and his merry band of homicidal puppets. The fact that David had tried to protect her and achieved something less than resounding victory was hardly his fault. It was hers.

Stop it. The blame lay not with her or David. It lay squarely on the shoul-ders of JT, whoever the psychopathic punk was. He must be stopped.

"Project Outreach," David said, snapping her attention back to him. "That's what it was called in the beginning. Christine and Mark, your parents, became the lead scientists on the project after they started working for ALI. Edward had brought them into the company. It was a legitimate enterprise with noble goals, and the three of them did a lot of good work there. Outreach was designed to explore the limits of psychic abilities."

Grace watched his face as he spoke. The tension had dissipated, replaced by a look of... fond remembrance seemed the best description. He must've liked the project back then, back when her parents and grandfather held the reins. He had clearly liked *them*, anyway.

"You see," David continued, "other scientists had conducted studies that resulted in compelling evidence for the existence of psychic abilities. Humans could influence computers, for instance, by changing a random sequence of numbers so that it was no longer random. Christine and Mark wanted to expand on the existing research rather than conducting another study trying to prove psychic faculties are real. They spent a year searching for test subjects, screening and rescreening them until they felt certain the group they'd assembled had genuine extrasensory faculties." His lips curved into a faint, almost wistful smile. "Everything was good at first. Thirty of us participated, voluntarily, as test subjects. The scientists—Christine, Mark, Edward, and half a dozen others—treated us with respect. It was like a family." He glanced at her sideways. "Then you came."

She squirmed in her chair. Despite what had happened between them last night, she still wasn't sure she wanted to hear about their previous relationship. It was too weird. But she must hear about it. She must know everything.

"You came for a visit at first," he continued, "but your parents got permission to show you the facility. It was out in the desert, underground, to limit interference from radio waves, human thoughts, and basically anything that might affect psychic abilities." He shifted position as if an incorporeal man could get muscle cramps. "Anyway, you thought it would be fun to take one of the basic screening tests, just to see how it worked. Christine and Mark indulged you. No one expected the results to be positive. But they weren't just positive, they were off the charts."

Grace tucked one ankle under the opposite knee. A feeling of tightness started in her chest. If she didn't get a grip on it soon, the tightness would escalate into panic. She knew how this story ended.

A road. A deer. Blood.

She swallowed her discomfort. "And then..."

"We got to know each other. You joined the project, as a test subject, against your family's objections. You wanted to understand your powers. And so did they, though the thought of experimenting on their own daughter was a little unsettling. But you insisted." He smiled at her, that sweet and sexy smile that made her insides turn to Jell-O. "You were always stubborn."

She couldn't help smiling back at him. "Like you're not."

They looked at each other, their gazes fused, and The memory of last night flowed through her as a warm river of emotion and sensory recall. Though his expression stayed the same, she sensed that he was experiencing the same memory. She wanted to kiss him, but they were in a gas station and he had no physical form.

"What happened next?" she asked. "I mean, things went bad at some point."

David's smile disintegrated. "A year and a half ago, ALI was bought out by a multinational corporation called—"

"Digital Prognostics."

"Yes. How did you know?"

She knew because the scanned articles on the flash drive had told her. A man named Jackson Tennant ran Digital Prognostics.

The truth hit her like a brick to the head. *Duh.* How could she have overlooked it before? Her telephone tormenter, JT, must be Jackson Tennant. A psycho owned and operated Digital Prognostics, the company that ran the Mojave Desert facility.

"How did you know?" David repeated.

She shrugged. "Grandpa told me. I take it things changed after the new owners took over."

He nodded, his expression darkening. "Most of the scientists were fired and replaced with wonderful fellows who saw no ethical dilemma in using drugs to control us, the test subjects. Sessions that had lasted an hour at most were lengthened to several hours. We were pushed to our limits and beyond, no matter the physical or mental consequences. Some died. Some went insane. A group of eight tried to escape from the facility." His jaw tightened, and a muscle jumped. "They were gunned down in the desert. Another benefit of a remote, secret facility is that there are no witnesses."

Grace felt sick. She took a sip of water, which didn't help. Eight people had been murdered, and that was only the beginning.

A man's face flashed in her mind and she asked, "Did you know Andrew Haley?"

"Yes. He was one of the subjects who went mad."

"He escaped. I met him."

David shook his head. "Nobody escapes. Edward managed to smuggle Andrew out of the facility and to a mental hospital. Our masters didn't know where, and Edward refused to say. It made them...testy."

"Why only Andrew? Why didn't Grandpa help anyone else?"

"There wasn't anyone else, except for me and Sean. The eight were the first to die, but not the last."

He looked straight into her eyes, and the blue fire in them burned as intensely as it had on the first night she'd seen him—the first night she remembered seeing him. Every time he focused on her like this, she felt a connection to him, an intimacy beyond the physical. He knew her. She knew him. Maybe she couldn't recite his favorite foods or pick his favorite movie out of a lineup, but she knew him.

"Sean and I were okay," David said, "so Edward left us behind to keep an eye on things. He was already afraid for your safety."

"Why did I use a pseudonym? My parents ran the project."

David lifted a hand as if to touch her and then pulled back, apparently remembering he hadn't manifested. "From the start, Christine was worried their research could be used for unsavory purposes. Mark thought she was paranoid, but he agreed to keep your name out of all records."

"What about the rest of you?"

"We knew the risks. Well, we thought we knew them, anyway. No one could've predicted what would happen after the new management took control."

She felt a little weak from the dread swelling within her. She pressed on anyway because she had no choice anymore. "How did my parents die?"

"We have to go back a bit further for you to understand." He stood and began pacing between the front windows and the table. "The real trouble started two months before they died."

Nine months ago

CHRISTINE POWELL STROLLED DOWN THE CORRIDOR, THE HEELS OF HER penny loafers slapping on the floor. Under her right arm, she held a clipboard tucked against her body. In her left hand, she twirled a silver-colored metal pen. The corridor lights reflected off the pen, shooting slivers of brilliance onto the walls and floor. Amid the twirls of light, her reflection shimmered on the smooth flooring like a spectral mirror image.

She kept her chin raised as she focused on the doorway ten feet in front of her on the right side of the corridor. The door hung open, the lights inside throwing a rectangle of yellowish light onto the corridor floor. Voices murmured within the room.

At the doorway, she hesitated. Her fingers slipped, letting the pen clatter to the floor. As she bent to retrieve the pen, she whispered a mantra under her breath. "You can do this, you can do this."

Straightening, she stuffed the pen into the breast pocket of her lab coat. She *could* do this. It was nothing sinister, just a meeting to introduce the new head of security.

Then why did she feel as though she'd swallowed a lead weight?

A familiar voice from within the room called to her. "Come in, Christine. We've been waiting for you."

Edward McLean's voice bolstered her resolve, and she strode into the conference room. Her father sat in a leather chair positioned at the far end of a long table that stretched the length of the room. He motioned for her to take a seat. Though he tried to smile, the expression faltered, which only served to deepen the lines around his mouth and eyes. Christine marched down the table to lower herself into the chair nearest him. He had saved the seat for her. He always did.

At her left, Mark slumped in his chair. Worry lines wrinkled his forehead as he squinted into vacant space. With his elbow propped on one arm of the chair, he tapped his index finger against his lips.

Behind her father, a serious-looking young woman hunched in a folding chair. Her hands hovered over the keys of the notebook computer that balanced on her knees. Her name was Vanessa or Theresa, or something like that. The girl had worked at the facility for less than two weeks, and Christine was terrible at recalling names.

It was Vanessa, she decided, because she needed to attach some name to the efficient but stoic secretary.

Across the table from Christine, a man with short gray hair sat straight as a column. His elbows rested on the table while his hands were intertwined to support his chin. Freckles dotted his face. A smirk tugged at the corners of his mouth. Beside him sat another stranger. The second man had dark-brown eyes, chestnut hair peppered with gray, and a muscular physique somewhat disguised by the loose-fitting suit he wore. His face, like a movie screen before the show started, displayed nothing yet held the prospect of coming attractions.

Her throat tightened. She had the oddest feeling that whatever lay ahead, she must avoid it at all costs.

Mark fidgeted.

She leaned close to him. "Who are those men?"

"Don't know."

"What's this meeting about?"

Mark sat up, smoothing his shirt and lab coat. His tie was askew. "Must have to do with the buyout."

Yes, Christine supposed he was right. A much larger corporation had recently purchased ALI, in what her father had characterized as a hostile takeover.

Edward cleared his throat. "Now that we're all here, let's begin. We have some new colleagues to welcome."

Face pinched, he glared at the newcomers.

Confused, Christine awaited the introductions. Perhaps then she would understand the tension electrifying the atmosphere.

Edward waved at the dark-eyed man. "This is Xavier Waldron. He has something to say."

Waldron rose. Strolling behind the chair in which the gray-haired man sat, he settled his hand atop the chair's back. The other man stiffened, though he tried to hide it under a pretense of adjusting his posture.

"Let's skip the pleasantries," Waldron said. "I know your names, I know what you do here. Now let me explain my function."

His gaze locked on Christine's. Her throat went as dry as the desert sand. Under the table, she clutched a handful of her skirt.

"This is no longer your playground," Waldron said. "I'm here to make this project profitable."

Mark stared at the tabletop and chewed the inside of his lip. Edward stared at the wall, face blank.

Someone had to speak, for heaven's sake.

Christine clasped her hands on the tabletop and looked straight at Waldron. "This is a research facility, not a McDonald's. We work for results, not profit, and what we do is for the good of humanity."

"Finding ways of controlling psychic impulses does not benefit humanity, Christine. It benefits you."

He'd used her first name. She puckered her lips, trying to avoid swearing at the cretin. She had a sick feeling she knew where the conversation would end up, and she didn't like it one bit.

"It benefits everyone," she said, rising to lean on the table with both hands. "We don't want to control these impulses. We seek to understand where they come from and how they can be managed so that the individual might function normally within society. I used to think psychic faculties were aberrations that drove the afflicted insane or turned them into monsters. Since founding the project, I've come to realize these people are gifted, not cursed." She locked gazes with Waldron. "The government would love to use them as spies or assassins, but I will *not* let that happen. I will not let you use them to line your pockets, either."

"Money is the last thing on my mind."

"But you said—"

"I said I'm going to make this facility profitable. I did not say *monetarily* profitable."

She bit her lip. What did he mean? She wanted to know but feared the answer.

"They are research subjects," Waldron said. "ALI owns them. Which means I, as director of operations, own them."

"You're not the director of operations."

Waldron gave her a vicious smile. He nodded toward Edward. "Ask your father."

She gave her father a questioning look. His shoulders drooped. He averted his gaze to his lap. She felt her mouth drop open as he slowly nodded.

Still slumped over his chair's arm, Mark slid one hand over his face to cover his eyes.

"This is Dr. Tesler," Waldron said, gesturing at the gray-haired, freckled man, "the new head of research and development."

Tesler smirked at her. She fisted her hands, sure she'd leap across the table and strangle both of them if she didn't control her anger somehow. What the hell was happening? Why was she the only one questioning the situation?

Waldron glanced toward the corner of the room adjacent to the doorway and flicked his hand. A man detached from the shadows behind the door and shut it with a sharp click. She hadn't noticed the man before. His black clothing melded with the shadows. He was Norris, one of the new guards brought in last week, but he wore a black outfit instead of his usual brown uniform. Black gloves covered his hands. He wore black combat boots too, and under one arm, he held a black full-face helmet.

She glanced at her father.

Edward had shut his eyes, and the wrinkles on his face had deepened into canyons. He pressed his lips together. When he opened his eyes and met her gaze, a chill slithered down her spine.

Waldron spoke again, his voice dripping with arrogance. "After studying the security at this facility, I've come to one unpleasant conclusion." He settled his hands on the back of Tesler's chair. "It is a complete failure."

"We've done fine so far," Christine said. "No one knows we exist."

"Except everyone who works here and everyone they speak to outside the facility."

"They signed confidentiality agreements."

"Paper and ink." Waldron massaged the chair, flexing the sinews in his hands. "Every one of them is a potential breach, and this is not a discussion. Measures have been taken. More will follow."

Christine looked at her father again.

He had closed his eyes again, his expression unreadable.

Waldron pushed away from Tesler's chair. "From this moment forward, no one will enter or leave this facility without my express permission."

"We are not prisoners, Mr. Waldron."

"Correct. You are vassals and I am your lord."

Waldron flicked his wrist, and Tesler hopped out of his chair. As Waldron sauntered around the table, Tesler trailed behind him like a loyal pet. As they moved past Norris, Waldron flicked his wrist once more, and the guard fell in step behind Tesler. If they'd begun to goose-step, the fascist image would've been complete.

Christine swallowed against the tightness in her throat. She had no clue how things had changed so abruptly, and so terribly.

Oh, yes, she did. The takeover was far more hostile than anyone had realized.

At the door, Waldron paused but did not look back. "Understand this. Anyone who challenges me, anyone who shows the slightest hint of disobeying me, will be silenced. Permanently."

The trio exited the conference room. The door clicked shut. The ventilation system whirred overhead. In the space of a few moments, they had become prisoners.

Mark cursed under his breath. Edward released a long, defeated sigh.

Christine flopped into her chair and stared at her father. "What's going on?"

"I've lost the war."

"What war? Who bought us out?"

Though she stared at him and waited for his response, he said nothing. His gaze was fixed on the far wall—or a sight beyond the wall. A sight inside his mind. A vision of what the facility would become, a slave regime focused on one goal.

Mining the human mind for profit.

Except Waldron claimed to have no interest in money. To him, profit meant... what?

Control.

Mark rose from his chair and tugged her hand. He wanted to go. She didn't want to leave her father, but he wasn't there, anyway, not mentally. She let Mark lead her out of the conference room, down the shadow-infested corridor, and to the offices that occupied the end of the corridor furthest from the elevator. Standing in the false twilight, holding hands, they exchanged tense looks. He seemed as numb as she felt.

After a moment, Mark entered his office through a door marked with his name and the title "Director, Information Systems."

She stumbled into her office. Though she glanced at the lettering that spelled out her name and the designation "Assistant Director, Research & Development," her mind registered nothing. The words slipped through her brain unprocessed. Perhaps they had never meant anything. No, they had once held meaning. The title had signified her father's faith in her intelligence and dedication, the importance of the work she performed here. Now it signified nothing.

She sensed what would come. Her intuition warned her, like a tornado siren whooping as a twister headed toward the heart of town. This tornado struck in the darkest night. She couldn't see it coming. She couldn't stop it.

The phone on her desk rang. She jumped.

Snatching the phone from its cradle, she mumbled, "Christine Powell."

"Turn on your computer," a male voice instructed.

"Who is this?"

"Do it."

The voice. She recognized it. "What do you want, Waldron?"

"Do it."

Her chest tightened as if a python had wrapped its body around her. Hands shaking, she wiggled the mouse to wake her computer from sleep mode. She drummed her fingernails on the desk. Through the phone, she heard Waldron breathing.

"It's on," she said.

"Watch."

A window opened on the screen, the video feed from the RV room. She recognized the pale blue walls, the bulbs that simulated natural light, the plush recliner positioned in the center of the room. Eggshell-colored carpeting covered the floor. Another chair, a new chair, sat beside the old one. It resembled a dentist's chair, minus the comforts. The secretary, Vanessa, reclined in the new chair.

No. Not reclined. Christine leaned closer. The girl was strapped to the chair with leather restraints that crossed her forehead, wrists, and ankles. The feed had sound too, which emanated from her computer speakers with a tinny quality.

The girl sniffled. "Please let me out."

An explosion thundered.

The girl shrieked. Her body jerked, then sagged.

As the camera zoomed in on her, blood began to soak her blouse in the center of her chest. Her eyes stared, vacant.

"This was a warning," Waldron said through the phone. "Don't expect another."

Click. The dial tone buzzed in her ear.

Christine dropped the phone.

CHAPTER TWENTY-ONE

Present Day

GRACE SLUMPED AGAINST THE CHAIR. AT THE BACK OF THE STORE, inside the restroom, metal banged on metal as Earl struggled to repair what she had broken. A twinge of guilt rippled through her. She didn't know exactly what she'd done, so she had no idea how badly she might've screwed up the works. Later, she'd find a way to make it up to the poor guy.

If she survived until later.

She couldn't understand why her family, the people she had known and trusted her whole life, would let criminals take over their life's work. Why they'd let Waldron and Tesler bully them. Why they had just accepted the situation.

"Why didn't they stop Waldron?" Grace asked.

"He assigned armed guards to watch them," David said. "They were prisoners, controlled in every aspect of their lives and work. They practically needed written permission to take a deep breath."

"But why? What was the goal? I don't get it."

"Waldron showed them what would happen if they rose up against him. The secretary was a stand-in."

"For what?"

"Not what. Who." He hesitated, his gaze intent on her. "You."

She closed her eyes. Waldron had killed an innocent woman as a warning to her parents. If they resisted, he would do the same, or worse, to their daughter.

Grace opened her eyes. The threat must've worked. She now knew, however, that Waldron could not kill her. His boss wanted her alive.

"Why would my mother tell you all this?"

"She didn't have to. I followed her to that meeting, psychically. No one knew I was there."

"You like following women, hey? Or is it only the ones in my family?"

He averted his gaze to the tabletop. "I heard Norris talking to another guard. He mentioned Waldron and said the facility was about to become a fun place. Coming from Norris, that's not a good thing. He was fresh out of maximum-security prison when he came here. I went to the meeting so I could find out what was going on."

"My grandfather would not hire dangerous criminals."

"He didn't know. ALI hired new guards after the buyout, and he had no say in it." David hovered a hand over hers, and oddly, the action comforted her. "After that initial meeting, I followed Christine, Mark, or Edward as often as I could without being detected."

"Then tell me the rest."

Still kneeling beside her, he sat back on his heels. "This is where it gets nasty."

Eight months earlier

CHRISTINE HESITATED, ONE HAND ON THE KNOB, HER GAZE FOCUSED on the sign that now adorned the door. The workmen had replaced the "Off Limits—Under Construction" sign with a new one that read "Isolation Chamber 1." How many more rooms had they converted into isolation chambers? And what precisely were these chambers for?

Three weeks ago, Waldron had ordered the RV room and all the other travelers' suites renovated. She'd argued that they had remodeled the suites the previous year to create the kind of quiet, calming atmosphere the travelers needed to invoke their abilities. The suites needed no makeover. She still cringed when she recalled how Waldron had fixed his dark eyes on her and said, "No more coddling, Christine."

Never had she given him permission to call her Christine. Everyone except Mark and her father called her Dr. Powell. Of course, Waldron asked no permission before taking such liberties. She couldn't imagine him asking permission for anything. The man took whatever he desired, from liberties to lives. Still, she despised her name when it rolled off his tongue.

The renovations had taken less than the month originally estimated. Now, as she stood outside the "isolation chamber," the tremors in her hand jiggled the knob. She breathed deeply, struggling against the fear that clawed at her psyche. It was a room. Four walls, a floor, and a ceiling. A room couldn't hurt her, or anyone.

She twisted the knob. Locked.

Digging her keys out of her coat pocket, she inserted the one for the RV room. The key didn't fit. She tried all the others on her ring. None fit. Waldron couldn't lock her out. She had gold clearance, which gave her access to every room in the facility and every file on the computers.

She was a vassal now, not a scientist. Waldron let her retain the title of Assistant Director, but it meant nothing anymore. The facility belonged to Xavier Waldron.

The hell it did. She whisked her tablet computer out of another pocket and punched in a direct message to Waldron. "Please send me key to iso room 1."

A locked door hinted at a secret. Waldron didn't want her to see the room. Why? What had his men done in there? She envisioned the possibilities, and her skin prickled.

At the end of the corridor, the elevator doors parted. She glanced sideways at them.

Waldron stomped out of the elevator toward her. "I was coming to see you when I received your message."

"You've changed the locks."

"How observant of you, Christine."

"Give me the key. I have access to all the rooms."

"Afraid not."

She clenched her jaw. "I have gold clearance."

He fingered the ID badge clipped onto her lapel. "I've reevaluated all clearances. Yours is now blue."

She bit the inside of her cheek. He had bumped her down two rungs on the clearance ladder. The act would lock her out of most of the labs and all the traveler suites—or the isolation chambers, as they were now designated.

"What are you hiding?" she asked.

"You're very pretty, Christine. Very desirable." He seized a clump of her hair and yanked her closer. "But much too curious for your own good."

She winced at the pain in her scalp. Her eye level fell slightly above his nose. Their gazes locked as he flattened his other hand into the small of her back and crushed her against him until her nose smashed into his. His lips grazed hers.

Her stomach flip-flopped. She grimaced, struggling to push away from him, but his arms were too strong, enveloping her like metal restraints.

Waldron chuckled. "We could come to an agreement, Christine."

"I'd rather be gnawed to bits by piranhas, Xavier." She emphasized the name with a near snarl in her voice.

He mashed his mouth to hers.

She sank her teeth into his lower lip.

Maintaining his grip on her hair, he touched the reddening spot on his lip. His voice grew rough. "You want to see, Christine? You want to know? I'll show you."

He withdrew a set of keys from his pocket and then jerked her head backward.

She bit back a cry and spat at him.

Waldron unlocked the door, thrusting it inward. Darkness cloaked the interior.

He hurled her through the doorway.

Christine landed on her hip. Pain stabbed down her legs as a gasp exploded from her.

Stalking into the room, he flicked a switch, and light flooded the interior. The floor, the walls, and the ceiling had been reduced to bare concrete. A single fluorescent panel had replaced the natural-light bulbs. In the center of the room, an austere metal chair sat where the recliner had once stood. The barest amount of cushioning softened the seat, and leather restraints dangled from the arms and legs. A metal table occupied the nearest corner of the room, its surface home to devices she didn't recognize. But in her soul, she perceived their purpose.

The concrete exuded a chill that infected her flesh. She rubbed her arms.

Waldron towered over her. His arms hung at his sides, and he'd clenched his hands into fists and compressed his mouth. The fluorescent lighting glinted off his eyes.

She avoided thinking about the shiver she'd gotten the first time she saw him. She avoided thinking about the violence with which he'd thrown her into this room. She avoided thinking about what might come next. Her thoughts concentrated on one image—the young girl, Vanessa, strapped into the chair that occupied this room, her face a blank oval, tears staining her cheeks, eyes red, skin white as a corpse's. She'd begged her captors for mercy, knowing they would grant death instead and praying it would come quickly, painlessly, but knowing it would not. When death came for her, it had rent her flesh, contorted her muscles, and wielded a pain beyond agony.

Christine swallowed, but the mass in her throat remained. Was she thinking of Vanessa, or herself? Neither, she realized with a jolt. The face that replaced the secretary's in her mind's eye belonged to Grace.

Waldron slammed the door shut. "Let me demonstrate this room's function."

"I know what it's for."

"Get in the chair."

"Are you insane?"

In one step, he reached her. He grabbed both her wrists and hauled her off the floor, across the room, and to the chair. The concrete scraped her bare knees as her skirt rode up her thighs. She flailed her arms and legs but found no purchase, no advantage. She couldn't reach him.

He shoved her into the chair.

She lashed out at him. He smacked her so hard her head snapped back into the chair's headrest. Lights popped in her vision, phantoms of the pain ricocheting through her head. Waldron secured the restraints around her arms, legs, and forehead.

"If you kill me," she said, "it will be the end of you."

"You think your husband will avenge you?" He straightened, studying her without expression. "Or your father? They've already given up."

She strained against the leather straps. They held tight.

"It's irrelevant," Waldron said, "whether they would or not. I've no intention of killing you."

He sauntered to the door. As he swung it inward, he clicked off the overhead bulbs. In the light shining through the doorway, he looked back at her.

"No, I won't kill you," he said, stepping into the corridor. "Not today."

He shut the door.

The light from the corridor shrank into nothing, consumed by the darkness within the room. The cold stung her skin. The dark caressed her. She felt the room tilt and sway as her ears rang and her stomach lurched. She gulped back her gorge and, digging her nails into the chair's arms, concentrated on breathing. In, out. In, out.

The dark. The cold. Buried alive.

Directly above her, layers of concrete. Beyond that, earth and rock and sand. The weight of cars and human bodies and wild animals all rested atop her head and shoulders. An image of the roof collapsing flashed through her mind.

Buried alive.

The room whirled around her. The temperature plummeted, and wind gusted through the room.

"No," she mumbled. "Don't, they'll know..."

The restraints popped off her wrists and ankles. The forehead strap loosened and slipped free.

The room tilted. Her breaths came short and fast. She tried to stand, stumbled, and landed on all fours. The ringing in her ears got louder as her muscles grew weaker. Her arms trembled.

With great effort, she forced herself to breathe normally. In, out. In, out. The ringing lingered, though softer than before. Though she still felt weak, her muscles regained enough strength to push her up and onto her feet. She careened through the pitching, spiraling darkness toward the door—or where she thought the door was. She floundered into the wall, her cheek smacking into concrete.

Cold. Hard. A crypt.

She whimpered.

The door was flung inward. It crashed into the wall, bounced twice, and stopped.

A wedge of light shattered the blackness. Scuffling into the light, she collapsed onto the floor, panting. Sweat trickled over her lips into her mouth. The salty tang seeped over her tongue.

The room leveled. The ringing in her ears faded away.

She clambered to her feet and staggered into the corridor. Squinting, she palpated the back of her head. Her vision adjusted, and she spotted a figure across the corridor.

Waldron stood near the opposite wall. He folded his arms over his chest, sneering at her.

"You were trapped in a car trunk as a child," he said. "Suffered heatstroke before your aunt found you. Since then, you've had a paralyzing fear of dark, confined spaces."

"How could you know that?"

"Before you were cleared to work here, you underwent psychological testing."

The muscles in her neck and jaw cramped. She massaged her nape. "That was supposed to be confidential."

"Nothing is as it was supposed to be. Wouldn't you agree?" He strode across the corridor toward her. "I knew much about you before today. Now I know everything."

"You know nothing." She resisted the urge to take a step away from him. "What was the point of this little exercise?"

"To see if someone would rescue you." He took her chin in his hand. "And someone did. The test was not for you, Christine, but for our subjects."

He mashed his mouth to hers. She wriggled out of his grasp, hit the wall, and groaned as a torrent of nausea broke over her.

"You see," Waldron said, "they've been refusing to cooperate in our testing. I've read the reports written by you and your father. I know what these freaks can do. Since they weren't responding to Tesler's methods, I thought an experiment of my design was in order."

Moments earlier, the darkness had ripped fear through her soul like a serrated knife. Now, another kind of darkness exerted the same power over her. The memory of the isolation chamber would linger for a while. But the memory of Waldron's dark, soulless eyes would stay with her forever.

She shivered.

"Which one was it?" Waldron asked. "I want the name. Was it Janet Austen?"

"Go to hell."

A drop of sweat trickled down her temple. Waldron touched it with his fingertip, letting the drop roll onto his skin. He ran the back of his hand down her cheek.

"I know Janet Austen is a pseudonym," he whispered, "and she's been missing from the facility since I took control a month ago. None of the other subjects will reveal her true identity." He patted her cheek. "You, however, will."

She glowered at him but said nothing. He would not goad her into blurting out the information in a fit of anger.

His smile made her stomach twist. He growled, "You will tell me her name."

"You should've killed me."

"Locking you in that room…" He shook his head slowly. "It's not the worst I could do to you."

He strolled down the corridor, entered the elevator, and was gone.

Christine dropped to her knees and cried.

Present Day

GRACE STARED AT THE COMPUTER SCREEN WITHOUT SEEING THE words displayed on it. The world around her had become a kind of dream, detached and blurry. The more she learned about her mother's ordeal, the deeper the numbness infiltrated her. Although she understood David's words and recognized their meaning, she felt nothing in response. Nothing.

And that frightened her more than anything else.

Maybe she was too exhausted to feel anything. Maybe the truth overwhelmed her.

She had asked for the truth—no, demanded it—and now that David had told her, she wondered if she really wanted it. Her life might end today. What did the truth matter?

It did matter, though, a great deal. Despite the numbness, despite the ice spreading through her veins, she needed to understand.

"Was it you?" she asked. "Did you rescue my mother? And what took you so damn long? He was torturing her."

"I wasn't there. Tesler had me conducting RV sessions at the time and, well, I couldn't sense anything outside of the session parameters. Later, Christine told me what had happened because, like you, she assumed I was the one who helped her. But it wasn't me."

"Then who was it?"

"You."

She glanced at him sideways. "Me?"

He nodded. "Your parents had sent you back to Texas, but even from that distance, you felt your mother's anguish and couldn't keep from intervening." His lips twisted into a wry smile. "You always have been stubborn."

A warm feeling melted the ice inside her. It wasn't desire this time, but something gentler and more meaningful. Comfort. Familiarity. Affection.

"What else did you see?" she asked. "While you were spying on my mother, I mean."

"I wasn't spying."

"Yes, you were. It's not a criticism, just a statement of fact."

He made a face, one she'd learned to interpret. The one that conveyed exasperation and fondness simultaneously. The one he gave her quite often.

"Tell me what you saw," she said.

"A month after the scene with Waldron, I sensed a psychic disturbance, a big one, and I followed it." He hesitated. "Into Andrew Haley's room. Christine and Mark were there."

She swallowed, but the rock that had formed in her throat wouldn't budge.

"I watched them die," David murmured, "and I did nothing. I couldn't—"

He shifted sideways, turning away from her.

She cleared her throat to regain his attention, but though he tensed, he refused to look at her.

"I couldn't manifest," he said. "Without that, I can't affect the environment. To manifest, you need a connection between the host and the traveler. I didn't have that with Christine or Mark. I've only ever had that with you."

"But Sean manifested for me too. I don't feel very connected to him."

"He didn't manifest. At least, not on his own."

She opened her mouth. No sound came.

"You understand," he said, finally turning to face her again. "Don't you?"

Her throat was dry, her voice paralyzed.

"It was you," David said. "Without knowing it, you helped Sean manifest. You don't need a personal connection to manifest because you are the most powerful of us all."

She managed a weak "uh" before her voice choked off.

Snap out of it. The mental order yanked her back to reality, and she met David's gaze.

He arched an eyebrow.

"Fine," she said, "I'm the queen of psychic crap. Doesn't help me much right now."

"Well—"

"Hang on," she interrupted, as a realization hit her. "If powerful psychic stuff requires a connection to the host, then this other traveler, the slimeball who attacked me in my car, has a connection to me? That's impossible. I don't know him, and I don't want to."

"Sometimes when you follow someone around for a while, you can develop a connection with them. It's rare, but it happens. And he's obsessed with you, for sure, so I guess it's possible the intensity of his obsession somehow forced a connection between the two of you."

"You're saying he's been following me. Watching me. Stalking me."

"Maybe."

"Yuck." She froze. "Maybe?"

"There's another possibility. He might be so strong that he doesn't need a connection to affect the environment."

Her stomach churned at the idea. "Great, he can break into my head anytime he wants."

"I don't think so. To break into your mind like that, he must've needed a tool for picking the lock, so to speak."

"A connection."

"No, something else."

The creep and his "tool" could wait. She had other things on her mind right now.

Knowing the facts of her parents' deaths would give her a clue. To what, she didn't know. She simply knew she must hear the story and understand the events before she proceeded with whatever she would do next. Well, she knew she must find the facility. After that, her plan got a little fuzzy. Okay, a lot fuzzy.

"Finish the story," she said. "Tell me how they died."

Seven Months Earlier

INSIDE HER POCKET, THE TABLET BEEPED. CHRISTINE PULLED OUT THE DE-vice and brought up the message that awaited her perusal. "RV15 agitated," the message read. "Need your assistance—Tesler."

Andrew was acting up again.

She stuffed the tablet in her pocket. Rubbing her neck, she thanked God the facility had gone into night mode an hour ago, plunging the corridors into twilight. Even that half-light, however, stung her eyes and made her squint. Her head throbbed, and her neck ached. The day, which had begun at dawn, now dragged on past dusk. Ever since Waldron and his gang had taken over the facility, the term workday had ceased to mean "working in the daytime." These days it meant working whenever and for as long as Waldron commanded. He hadn't been exaggerating for effect when he'd called the facility's employees his vassals. They were more like indentured servants whose terms of service Waldron could extend for as long as he liked.

Christine scuffled down the corridor. At Andrew's room, she unlocked the door and entered. The lamp in the corner bathed a quarter of the room in milky light. On the bed, within the cone of illumination, Andrew lay still. No one else was in the room.

Tesler had sent the message. He'd summoned her here.

In that message, sent mere seconds earlier, Tesler had called Andrew "agitated." She crossed the room, stopping at the bedside. Andrew's eyes jiggled beneath his closed lids. His chest rose and fell in a shallow rhythm.

Agitated? He was asleep.

As she reached into her pocket for the tablet, the door opened. Mark stumbled into the room, leaving the door open as he shuffled to the bedside. Shoulders slumped, eyes bloodshot, he stopped beside Christine.

"You called me?" he said.

"No, I got a message from Tesler to come right away."

"Message I got said it was from you."

She brushed a strand of greasy hair from his forehead. "Honey, you look tired. Go get some rest. I'll handle this."

"It's him."

"What?"

Mark stared at Andrew. He stood immobile and stiff, his unblinking gaze locked on the man who slumbered on the bed.

"Get out," Mark hissed. "Run."

"What?"

"Dammit, Christine, *run*." Mark lifted his gaze, eyes wide and staring into an empty, shadowed corner of the room. "He's coming."

She took a step backward. A voice inside urged her to heed his advice. She couldn't leave, though, couldn't abandon her husband. Who was he talking about? Who was coming? *What* was coming?

Her gut twisted. Deep in her mind, she knew. Oh God, she knew.

Andrew's eyes opened. He turned his bleary gaze on her. His eyes shimmered green as if lit from within. When travelers engaged their psychic abilities at a high level, it caused an eerie glow in their eyes, but only in the eyes of their astral bodies, not in their real eyes.

She wanted to back up to the doorway, turn, and run out of the room. Her body refused to obey her commands, though, staying frozen to the spot beside Andrew's bed.

"He comes for you," Andrew said, his voice rough and dry as sandpaper. He thrust a hand out to her, and she stumbled backward another step, out of his reach. Andrew's fingers worked as if trying to find her by touch. "He wants the golden girl. Save her. The golden light is too bright. Save her."

Christine stared at Andrew. Her heart pounded so hard against her ribs that her chest ached. She felt lightheaded, but oh dear heaven, she could not pass out. Not here. Not now.

Andrew jerked. His eyes rolled back in his head. In a strangled voice, he shouted, "Go! Go!"

Then he collapsed onto the bed. His eyelids fluttered shut as his body went still.

Mark seized her arm and dragged her toward the doorway.

The door slammed shut in front of them, and a chilly wind gusted through the room.

Goosebumps rose on Christine's arms. Mark grasped the doorknob and twisted. It refused to move. He yanked on it until his face turned red from the effort, but still the knob would not budge.

From behind them, an inhuman voice spoke. "I know your secret."

The hairs on the back of her neck stiffened. She turned sideways to search the shadows for a silhouette but saw none. A traveler had entered the room, though not one of the travelers she knew. Only three remained at the facility, and of those only David could've managed to track her. But even if he had, he wasn't adept enough to manipulate the environment. This new traveler, she sensed, called upon more power than anyone except Grace.

"Give her to me," the voice demanded. "The golden girl is mine."

Christine hugged her arms to her chest. Golden girl. She had a horrible feeling she knew exactly what the traveler wanted. No way in hell would she grant it to him. Her life didn't matter. She could not let this man, whoever he was, have what he wanted. She must stop him. He must never get his hands on her daughter.

Stop him how? He wasn't here. Come on, Christine, think of something.

Andrew's limp body lay crumpled on the bed. He'd tried to warn her.

"I won't help you," she said to the empty air.

Mark stopped fighting with the doorknob. "No, Christine, don't—"

"You came when I called," the voice said. "I am more powerful than you can imagine."

The message on her tablet. The traveler had sent it.

He knew how to control electronic devices and the environment, both of which indicated high-level abilities. And the green glow in Andrew's eyes...

Suddenly, she understood. This new traveler must've taken control of Andrew, and somehow that action triggered the paranormal glimmer in Andrew's eyes. But the new traveler seemed to have lost control of Andrew quickly, a fact that gave her a smidgen of hope. The new traveler couldn't read minds, she knew. No one could—or rather, no one *would*. She had one chance. Tracking her at the facility was easy because it was a confined space. Most travelers, the experienced ones, could track someone through a finite area like a building, especially a building well known to the traveler. Once a target got outside the traveler's familiar, confined areas, things got more complicated.

"All right," Christine said. "I'll tell you how to find her."

Mark turned his wide eyes toward her.

She gave him a tight little smile. After twenty-nine years of marriage, he ought to know what that look meant. It was a request that he trust her and not interfere.

Narrowing his eyes, he frowned. Oh yes, he understood. But he wasn't happy about it.

"Who is she?" the traveler demanded.

Christine took a quick breath. "Her name is Allison Monroe, and she's hiding out in the Salmon River Mountains in Idaho. That's all I know. For her safety, I wouldn't let her tell me more. I knew you'd come after her eventually."

She hadn't known, and still didn't know, who he was. But she knew what he wanted from Grace.

Power.

And dear heaven, if he got it, the world was doomed. No living being should have the kind of power this traveler craved. She didn't even know for certain it was possible to achieve a state of such awesome power, much less survive it intact. The level of psychic energy required must've been astronomical.

The feasibility hardly mattered right now. The traveler wanted Grace. He must never get anywhere near her.

"You lie," the traveler hissed.

Christine squared her shoulders. "If you want her, you'll have to search the Salmon River Mountains. That's where she is."

The air stilled. Silence descended over the room like a heavy curtain.

Her college roommate's family had owned a cabin in the Salmon River Mountains. She couldn't explain why that name had popped into her brain when she needed a location far from where Grace lived. She only prayed that the traveler would take the bait she'd dangled in front of him.

A draft tickled her skin.

"Tell me more," the traveler growled. "Where to find her. I need more."

Only four people knew the true identity of Janet Austen and where she lived now. She, Mark, her father, and David served as the sole guardians of the secret. From the beginning, they had concealed Grace's identity because Christine insisted on it. The others had thought her paranoid, but she heeded the soul-deep instinct that urged her to protect her daughter. Since the first time her father had told her about Project Outreach, she'd seen the potential for good—and for evil.

A gust of wind tore through the room, nearly knocking her off her feet. Mark caught her, and they floundered into the door with a dull thud.

"Where is she?" the voice shouted.

"I told you all I know," Christine said. "Go there. You'll sense her."

Please go. Please, please, please.

A dark shape separated from the shadows in the far corner. The shape was vaguely humanoid, though far from human. When the being spoke, his voice burned with a quiet intensity that prickled every hair on her body.

"I will go," he said, "but if you lie..."

His voice trailed off, but she heard the silent threat that punctuated the statement.

And then he was gone.

The air changed, though not in any way she could quantify. The difference was intangible, inexplicable.

The door lock clicked.

Mark eased her away from him and reached for the knob. It turned in his hand. He yanked the door open, and they fled through the opening, down the corridor. Mark grasped her hand so tightly it began to ache, but she clamped his just as hard.

At the elevator, they halted. Mark pressed the button to summon the car.

"What are we doing?" Mark asked.

"Running." She watched the numbers above the elevator door light up one after another, tracing the car's path up the shaft. "What about Dad? He's on his way back from Washington."

"We'll call him once we're on the road."

She shook her head. "We can't take our cell phones or computers. They're trackable."

"We'll find a pay phone along the way."

The elevator stopped with a soft thunk, and the doors parted.

He led her into the car, pressing the button for the basement level where the parking garage was located. The doors slid shut.

Christine watched the numbers count down the floors until the car eased to a stop and the doors opened again, granting them access to the basement level. An alarm bell clanged in the back of her mind, warning her that something was off. Where had all the guards gone? Why was nobody trying to stop them? They weren't allowed to leave the facility, yet so far, they'd encountered no resistance.

The guard shack outside the elevator stood empty.

And that alarm clanged louder in her mind.

She yanked Mark's hand, hauling them both to a stop.

"Where is everyone?" she said. "Even with the staff reductions, we should've run into guards. So why haven't we?"

"I don't know."

A figure stepped out from behind the guard shack.

Christine jumped, but then she recognized the man.

"David," she said, his name coming out as a heavy sigh. "What are you doing here?"

He stopped several yards away. "Something is wrong. You need to leave immediately."

"Yeah," Mark said, "that's what we're trying to do."

"You can't take your car. It's probably been outfitted with a tracking device."

Christine groaned. "Great. How do we get out of here, then?"

David pointed toward an SUV parked three spaces down the row. "Take that one."

"Why?"

"It's Waldron's. He'd never let anyone track him."

"Keys?" she asked.

"Don't worry, I'll start it for you. Once you're far enough away, you'll need to switch cars. Don't use your credit cards or access your bank accounts—"

Mark held up a hand. "Thanks, we'll manage."

Christine scrunched her eyebrows, looking at David. "You can start a car?"

He shrugged. "Probably. It'll take a lot of energy, though, and I may not be able to help you anymore after this."

"We understand."

David hesitated, his gaze flitting between her and Mark. "Be careful."

With a curt nod to David, Mark seized her hand and dragged her toward the SUV. Once they were inside, with the doors locked, David strode in front of the vehicle. He raised his hands over the hood, hovering them in midair, and closed his eyes. His expression tightened into a grimace. She knew he wasn't touching the car because he couldn't manifest on his own, but David had always mimicked physical gestures as a means of focusing his power.

The tendons in his hands bulged as if he were lifting a heavy object.

It was too hard. He should stop. They could find another way.

She reached for the door handle, intending to fling the door open and shout for him to give up.

The car's engine sputtered, caught, and grumbled to life.

David opened his eyes, dropped his hands, and stumbled backward into the wall. He lifted one hand in a weak gesture for them to go.

Mark backed the vehicle out of the parking space. They sped out of the garage without seeing another person, dead or alive. Minute after minute ticked by as they raced down the dirt road that accessed the facility, passing through the invisible gateway. A network of infrared sensors and motion detectors, buried underground, formed an invisible fence around the facility. Trespassers would see nothing but open desert, yet their presence would be detected, and any possible threat would be assessed long before they reached the facility itself.

No other vehicles intercepted them. The SUV jounced over the asphalt lip onto the highway, and Mark swerved the car into the right lane.

All seemed well. They were beyond the facility's perimeter. They could make it to safety.

Deep inside, though, Christine felt a primal instinct warning her that something was coming for them. Power. Darkness.

Death.

Chapter Twenty-Two

Present Day

WHERE WAS EVERYONE?" GRACE ASKED. "HOW DID THEY ESCAPE SO easily? Did you follow them after they left the facility?"

"Slow down," David said, holding up a hand as if he could push back her questions. "The facility was empty. It was already at minimal staffing levels because it was the weekend. When I triggered the perimeter alarms, I made sure sensors went off on every side so that all the guards had to be deployed. It was the best chance I could give Christine and Mark."

"Why didn't you try to stop the traveler when he cornered them in Andrew's room?"

David's shoulders slumped as his head bowed slightly. "I couldn't. The traveler was too strong. If I'd expended all my energy on fighting him, I never would've been able to clear the facility. I made a conscious choice to leave them in that room while I set about triggering the perimeter alarms. I was fairly certain the traveler wouldn't kill them until he had you."

"Fairly certain?"

She regretted the edge in her voice the instant the words left her mouth.

David lowered his head, eyes closing, and ran a hand through his hair.

Grace noticed the tightness around his eyes, the furrowing of his brow and forehead, the darkening of the skin under his eyes, and the paleness of his lips. Christ, he must've burned a tanker-load of energy on coming here and sticking around long enough to answer all her questions.

"I'm sorry," she said, reaching out to stroke his hair before realizing she couldn't. His appearance was an illusion. So instead, she told him, "I know you would've done more if you could."

"I didn't save them." He spoke in a hushed voice, almost a whisper, keeping his eyes closed as he continued. "I followed them, but I couldn't stop the—"

"Car crash," she finished for him. "Are you saying it was an accident after all?"

He shook his head. "I don't know. Given the circumstances, I doubt it. But I can't know for sure. I had to whip up a localized windstorm to slow down the guards who were on their way back to the facility, to keep them from seeing which direction Christine and Mark went. By the time I got to them, the car was upside down on the side of the road. It was over."

They were already dead. That was what he meant. He'd gotten there too late to help them. She could see the guilt etched on his face and feel it rolling off him in psychic waves.

Maybe that was *her* guilt spinning through the air around them. Her parents had died because of her. Why had she hidden in Texas while a lunatic with supernatural powers hunted them? What kind of person was she?

"It's not your fault," he said, tilting his head up to look at her. "You wanted to stay, but your parents insisted you leave and have no contact with them until the situation settled down. It never did."

She wanted to wrap her arms around him. She wanted to close her eyes, bury her face against his neck, and forget about everything. Unfortunately, thoughts kept bubbling up in her brain.

"If you left them alone in Andrew's room," she said, "how do you know what happened in there?"

"When I got to the site of the accident, Christine was still alive, barely. She had just enough time left to tell me what happened and to make me promise I'd watch out for you."

Another thought bubbled to the surface, and she paused to consider it before speaking. "If my parents and grandfather were prisoners in the facility, how could Grandpa go on a trip to Washington?"

David shrugged. "I wasn't privy to everything."

"Hmm." She decided to let that go for now, considering that he was psychic, not omnipotent. "What's the deal with this 'golden girl' and 'golden light' stuff?"

"I'm not sure."

She resisted the urge to question him more. His face had gone pale, further darkening the shadows under his eyes.

He shut his eyes, sitting motionless and silent for so many seconds that she wondered if he'd gotten too weak to see or speak to her. When he finally opened his eyes, he did not look at her.

"There is a story," he said. "It's more like a myth, but it concerns a power that trumps all others. It would make telepathy and manifesting seem like nothing—if it existed. Some of the older RVs, the ones who worked for the CIA back when they toyed with psychic espionage, talked about this power. They feared it." He tilted his head up higher to gaze at the computer screen, which still displayed the list of former participants in the facility's research. "They called it the Golden Power."

She leaned forward, resting one arm on the table. "Why did they fear it?"

"Two reasons." He paused as if collecting his thoughts. "First, they were afraid it would turn out to have dire consequences for anyone who tried to use it. There is precedence for that fear. Reading minds sounded like a great idea, especially in espionage circles, but it turned out to be so overwhelming for the mind-reader that no one will even attempt it anymore."

"Why not?"

"Because it will drive you insane." He glanced at her. "And I'm talking completely, irretrievably, frothing-at-the-mouth insane."

"Oh." She gulped back the lump in her throat. "I won't try that, then."

He returned his attention to the list on-screen. "The second reason the older RVs feared the Golden Power had to do with the old saying that absolute power corrupts absolutely." When she opened her mouth to ask what he meant, he held up a hand to silence her. "Patience, I'm getting there."

She pressed her lips together.

A faint smile flickered across his face, vanishing quickly. "First, you need to understand how our psychic abilities work. Our powers emanate from something we call the crossroads. It's where everything in the universe—thoughts, feelings, knowledge, memories—all come together, like roads intersecting. When we access the crossroads, we usually experience it as a field of stars."

Grace felt the blood drain out of her face. A field of stars. Last night, she'd soared out of herself and into a dark expanse peppered with stars. Floating there, she'd felt free and yet tethered to her body, alone and yet surrounded by... something. No fear. Just a sense of completeness.

"You've seen it," David said. "You remember."

"I saw it once, recently." The blood rushed back into her face, no doubt turning her cheeks a cherry red, as she remembered what they'd been doing when she'd experienced the crossroads. "Um, uh, I didn't realize what it was at the time."

David smiled as if he knew exactly when she'd spun out of her body and into the crossroads.

Her blush grew hotter until she wanted to splash water on her face.

Clearing her throat, she said, "If it looks like a star field, then why do you call it the crossroads?"

"Because when you're inside it, if you concentrate you can resolve the field of stars into a network of bright dots linked by multicolored strands. Sort of like a map."

She didn't know what to say to that, so she kept quiet.

"The crossroads is like a network of interconnecting highways," he continued, "but they're lined with chain-link fencing. You can see there's more out there, but you can't get to it. The story goes that only someone with the Golden Power can veer off the crossroads into the uncharted territory beyond, where everything that is known, was known, or will be known exists simultaneously."

"What does that mean?"

"The Golden Power grants omniscience."

All thoughts had stopped bubbling in her mind. Her brain had gone utterly blank.

"Anyone capable of accessing that power," David said, "would know everything—past, present, and future. Can you imagine what someone like our mystery traveler would do with that knowledge?"

"I'd rather not imagine it."

A door slammed shut.

Glancing backward, Grace saw Earl had closed the restroom door and was heading back toward the checkout counter. When she looked back at David, she noticed the redness in his eyes. Strange how an incorporeal man could look so physically drained.

"You should go," she told him. "Rest up."

He gave her a pained look. "Not yet."

David said nothing as she yanked the flash drive out of the computer, tucking the little stick into her jeans pocket. She carried the laptop back to the counter, handed it to Earl, and thanked him for letting her use the computer. Of course, she'd paid him for the privilege, so it wasn't like he'd loaned it to her out of sheer kindness. But she felt bad about the restroom debacle. An exuberant thank-you seemed only polite under the circumstances.

Earl seemed wary as he shook her hand.

Maybe she'd gone a little overboard with the exuberance. There was a fine line between atonement and overcompensation.

When she glanced back at the table where she'd sat a moment earlier, David was gone. Her exuberance, feigned as it was, deflated. She trudged out to the car and settled in for the fifty-mile drive to wherever. Sean's directions, scrawled in the dust, had simply told her to find Dry Lake Road and look for a dirt road on the left. He'd also warned her about "eyes and ears everywhere." He must've meant the invisible perimeter, delineated with sensors, that David had mentioned.

How she'd get past the sensors, she didn't know. David was far too weak to help her now.

"You want to get inside the facility."

She yelped at the sound of David's voice. Gasping, struggling to regain her composure, she cast an annoyed glance at him. "Must you always do that?"

"Apparently."

He still looked weak and tired, almost sick.

She reached out for him but her hand passed right through his illusory form. Fearing the answer, she asked, "Can you die from using too much psychic energy?"

"Probably." He managed a wan smile. "But don't worry, I'm not there yet."

"That might be more convincing if you didn't look like—" Her throat constricted, choking off the words. Tears threatened to spill from her eyes. She swallowed hard, blinked away the moisture, and steeled her voice. "I need you alive, so don't go dying on me."

"I need you alive too, but I've given up on keeping you away from the facility."

"Good."

"I know I can't stop you. So listen."

She let silence be her response.

"Dry Lake Road," he said, "is fifty miles the other side of town. Turn left there, drive several more miles, and look for a black mailbox at the end of a dirt road. Follow that road to an arroyo. If you sit there for thirty seconds, the weight of your car will trigger a device that raises a keypad from a pole in the ground." He closed his eyes, slumping forward. "Punch in the number 43709. Wait five seconds *exactly*. Then type in 000."

"Then what happens?"

His image rippled and winked out. Cold air blasted through the car, lashing her hair across her face. The air burst out of her lungs in one explosive gasp. She tried inhaling but her muscles froze, and it felt like someone was sucking the air out of her body through a straw. She huddled in the driver's seat, her mouth open so far her jaw ached. Her ears rang. Darkness invaded her vision.

And her ears popped.

She gulped in air. Her vision cleared as her ears stopped ringing. She pulled in breath after breath until her breathing normalized. The same thing had happened to her when the mystery traveler attacked her in her old car, the one the traveler had totaled. It must've had something to do with air pressure in a confined space.

Rooting around in her purse, she pulled out a pen and a scrap of paper. An old gas receipt was all she could find. She jotted down the numbers David had told her. These days, she didn't trust her memory.

Driving straight into town, she took a detour off the main highway to find the post office. A sign on the main road had alerted her to the post office's location, two blocks off the highway. She pulled into one of three angled parking spaces in front of the small, dilapidated wood building. A faded sign identified the structure as the United States Postal Service of Reston, California. Inside the little building, she found a table loaded up with postal supplies and pens chained to the tabletop. She chose a Priority Mail envelope, tucked the flash drive inside it, and sealed the adhesive flap. Next, she scrawled her name and address in the appropriate box on the envelope. A few minutes later, she'd bought postage for the slim package and sent it on its way.

The flash drive would be safe for a few days. By the time it arrived at her home in Texas, she'd either have dealt with her enemies or she'd be dead. The thought of dying no longer frightened her, which seemed bizarre and wrong and yet somehow necessary. She had no time to waste on pondering the implications of her newfound equanimity.

Back in the car, she found the highway again and headed out into the desert. When she spotted the sign for Dry Lake Road, she swung left onto the two-lane strip of blacktop. The paving soon transitioned into gravel. Twenty minutes passed before she saw the black, unmarked mailbox and veered left onto the nameless road. After a few more miles, the gravel segued into a two-track dirt path. The car jounced over potholes and rocks. Dust plumed up behind the car, obscuring her backward view. A tumbleweed rolled across the track in front of the car. In the fading daylight, she spotted Joshua trees dotting the barren landscape and a humpbacked butte that jutted up in the distance, seeming farther away than the moon.

A person could get lost and die out here. Nobody would find the body for weeks or months, if ever. She pushed the thought out of her mind. No use dwelling on worst-case scenarios.

The car's headlights powered on automatically, detecting the waning daylight. Night seemed to fall swiftly as she drove at what felt like a snail's pace, hindered by the bumpy road and her fear of driving straight off the edge of the arroyo David had mentioned. Up ahead, a tall and narrow shape jutted up from the ground.

She stomped on the brake as the headlights swept across the object. Mounted on a metal pole, the dusty white sign offered a warning in thick black letters: "PRIVATE PROPERTY. Trespassers will be prosecuted. Deadly force authorized."

Oh, yeah. This was the right road.

She hit the gas pedal, and the car sprang forward, jolting over a series of potholes. The headlights revealed nothing except the narrow two-track ahead of the car and the vast, empty desert surrounding the road. Small eyes in the brush reflected the headlights. The darkness was complete now, oppressive and as deep as outer space. To the right, far in the distance, a bluish-white light glimmered.

Despite the warm air flowing from the vents, goosebumps cropped up on her arms and neck.

GET A GRIP, she told herself. *It's just wildlife.* She'd gotten paranoid living in the city. She hadn't seen wildlife in so long she freaked out over it.

But that flash off to the right...

She gripped the steering wheel tighter. She'd sailed right past the point of no return a long time ago.

Ahead, the road fell away into blackness. A stream, she might have thought, if she weren't in the center of hell. In the desert, thunderstorms unleashed rivers in the form of flash floods, carving out channels that stood dry otherwise.

The dark patch loomed nearer.

Shadows.

Grace jammed her foot on the brake. The tires slid. The car fishtailed, then finally gripped the road once more and lurched to a stop, thrusting her hard against the seatbelt. Dust erupted around the car. Unhooking the seatbelt, she flung the door open and hopped out. Leaving the door ajar, she tiptoed toward the front bumper. The headlights illuminated the obstacle.

Inches from the front tires, the earth dropped away. An arroyo cleaved the desert, its walls steep and tall, its basin wide and littered with small cactuses. In the darkness, she could barely make out the other side of the arroyo. It stretched farther across than the headlight beams could penetrate.

Back in the car, she slammed the door shut. Had thirty seconds elapsed yet? Nothing had happened while she examined the arroyo. David's captors might've changed the protocol to stop her from getting into the facility this way.

She rolled down the window to peer down at the ground. Nothing. Retracting her head, she drummed her fingers on the window frame.

A noise erupted nearby, a cross between rustling leaves and a mechanical hum.

She poked her head out the window, squinting down at the ground.

A patch of dirt shifted. Sand poured away as a pole emerged from the ground. The pole, metal and four inches wide, rose to a height that placed its top at her eye level. A panel slid open, revealing a cavity inside the pole. The opening housed a numbered keypad, just as David had told her. Above the keypad, an LCD screen stared at her.

A phrase blinked on the screen: "Enter access code."

She retrieved from her purse the receipt on which she'd scribbled the numbers David had dictated, then leaned out the window to punch in the code. She counted off the seconds—one-one-thousand, two-one-thousand, three-one-thousand. At the precise instant she got to five, she punched in the last three digits.

The pole retreated into the sand.

Ahead of the car, the earth groaned. Metal clanged. The ground trembled.

Two halves of a bridge rose up from the walls of the arroyo, joining at the center. Struts, unfolding beneath the bridge, braced the structure.

It must've been a mirage. Any second the wind would blow away the illusion.

A gust buffeted the car. Clouds of dust curled up from the depths of the arroyo and swirled around and over the bridge.

She glanced away. When she looked back, the bridge still spanned the arroyo.

All righty, then.

Easing her foot down on the gas pedal, she steered the car toward the arroyo. The rear tires cleared the bridge's lip with a thunk. She pressed the gas pedal harder, and the car sprang forward, clearing the opposite side of the bridge with a softer thunk.

She decelerated. Taking the bridge in one rush had the chance to fret over its construction and the fact that it had arisen from the sand and God only knew how long it had lain there, unused, rusting, rotting.

A groaning sound drew her attention to the rearview mirror. She watched the reflected image of the bridge duck below the level of the road. Dust puffed up from the arroyo.

If she turned around, would the bridge rise again to grant her passage out?

Didn't matter now. She would not turn back.

The road stretched out into the vast desert. Overhead, the first stars twinkled in the ever-deepening gloom of the night. Mountains hid behind a veil of haze, maybe fog or a far-away dust storm. If she followed this road until it ended, would her journey end in some magical kingdom of fairies and trolls and knights on white steeds?

She pictured David perched atop a white horse, clad in armor, wielding a gleaming sword.

The car hit a pothole. Her teeth snapped together, erasing her fantasy.

Pow!

The car shimmied. The steering wheel trembled faintly. She gripped it tighter, glancing in all the mirrors to find the source of the explosive noise. It was too dark, though, and the headlights' glow couldn't illuminate the car's rear, where the sound had originated.

The steering wheel trembled harder. The vibrations bled into her hands, triggering pain in her wrist and forearm. She braked and eased the car to a stop. A sick feeling settled over her as she swung the door open and stepped outside. Even in the gloom, she spotted the problem right away.

The left rear tire had blown out.

A chill washed through her. Blown out? Or shot out?

Turning in a circle, she squinted into the night. The bluish-white glow she'd seen before had divided into two parallel lights that bobbled in the distance from the direction of the arroyo, coming closer with every second that she stood there gaping at the shredded tire. A purring, faint and intermittent, escalated into grumbling.

She leaped back into the car, twisted the key in the ignition, and barely waited for the engine to catch before slamming her foot down on the accelerator. Damn the blown tire. She had bigger problems than the damage she might do to the wheel or the axle or whatever.

The car heaved forward. The steering wheel vibrated viciously beneath her hands. She gripped it as tight as she could, fighting to keep the car aimed down the two-track.

Pow!

The right rear tire.

She couldn't hold the steering wheel. The car angled off the road, bounced over a small cactus, and bogged down in a mass of brush. The engine sputtered and died.

Oh shit.

The vehicle jouncing down the road toward her enlarged until she recognized the shape as a Jeep Cherokee, black with tinted windows. She couldn't tell how many people hid inside the Jeep.

Or how many guns they carried.

If she ran, they'd catch her. If she crouched in the dirt, they would see her. They had spotted her already, or they wouldn't have sped straight toward her.

The Jeep bounced over the pothole she'd hit a few minutes ago.

She grabbed her purse and leaped out of the car, fleeing down the two-track. Behind her, the Jeep swerved around the rear end of her car, which stuck out into the road. The Jeep's tires slipped in the sand. The vehicle shimmied. The tires found traction again, and the Jeep rocketed after her, its engine roaring.

Her legs cramped. The soles of her feet burned as if she ran barefoot across hot coals. She needed a hideaway. She needed a machine gun.

The Jeep, swerving off the track, sped across the rough desert to circle in front of her.

A cloud of dust enveloped her. She choked, coughed, blinked. Tears blurred her vision. Somewhere within the cloud, tires spun in the sand, whirring and kicking up bits of earth. A pebble smacked her in the cheek.

She froze.

The dust cleared.

Twenty feet ahead, the Jeep had stopped cross-wise on the track. The doors were flung open. Half a dozen men in black commando outfits, their faces covered by helmets, poured out of the Jeep. They toted guns of varying sizes. Their boots clomped on the dirt.

She thought about going for her gun, but every one of theirs dwarfed hers, and she suspected their weapons were automatics too. They could perforate her with a volley of bullets before she even got off one shot.

Her thoughts came fast and jumbled. She had no bright ideas, no plans, no goddamn talent for subterfuge. When the commandos stomped past the Jeep's fender, she bolted. A snake hissed, its head snapping up from the dirt. She leaped over the creature, tripped on a rock, stumbled forward, and hit the sand face-first.

Footfalls pounded behind her. Men shouted.

Her cheek stung. She pushed up onto her hands and knees. Her face had sideswiped a cactus, and a few needles had embedded themselves in her cheek.

The snake rattled nearby. One of the men shouted a curse.

Grace tore the needles out of her cheek, sprang to her feet, and fled.

Boots clomped in the sand behind her. Men shouted to each other. The voices issued from everywhere as they closed in on her from all sides.

She pulled the gun out of her purse.

A commando jumped out from behind a Joshua tree. As his feet landed squarely in the sand, he leveled his gun at her.

She swung her weapon up and pulled the trigger.

He ducked behind the tree. The shot splintered a branch.

Grace veered left.

A shot exploded.

Something hit her from behind, an object too large to be a bullet, knocking her legs out from under her. The commando wrenched her onto her feet. Twisting her arms behind her back, he clamped one hand around her wrists to pull her close against him. His helmet pressed against her face.

"Gotcha," he growled. Then to his buddies, he shouted, "Over here."

She could claw him, kick him, bite him, get away somehow. Then what? He had five well-armed buddies. They could call in reinforcements. She might run until her muscles gave out on her, thirst overcame her, or she passed out in the sand. They could wait inside their air-conditioned Jeep, sipping Perrier and playing bridge, until then. She would have no energy leftover for escape. Better to give up now.

Hell no, her instincts screamed. She must fight the bastards with every watt of energy inside her.

The commando twisted to face his buddies, dragging her with him. The others were still thirty yards away. Her gun had landed nearby, its muzzle buried in the sand.

She wriggled in the man's grip.

The commando's hand tightened into a steel clamp around her wrists.

Grace bit her tongue and grunted. The tang of blood dispersed through her mouth as he yanked her wrists. Pain ricocheted between her shoulder blades. She'd had enough of strangers trying to kill her, chasing her across the country, demanding she give them things she didn't have and tell them things she didn't know, murdering anyone who helped her. They showed no remorse, no hesitation. Their cruelty knew no limits.

Enough.

She kicked at his legs.

When her heel connected with his shin, he bellowed, his grip loosening.

She wrenched her wrists from his grasp. Clenching her teeth against the pain in her shoulders, she whirled toward him and rammed her knee into his groin.

His back arched as a grunt burst out of him, but he snatched at her anyway.

She kneed him again, then slugged him in the gut.

Doubling over, he dropped to his knees.

She grabbed her gun and bolted.

"Get her!" the commando roared.

More shouts erupted behind her. Gunfire detonated. Sand plumed upward like tiny volcanoes, and small cactuses exploded while something buzzed past her head. Her legs pumped as fast as they could, but she knew she couldn't go much farther. Ducking into a stand of Joshua trees, she paused long enough to deduce she had no options, as usual. No houses nearby, no cars she could conveniently steal, as if she had a clue how to steal anything. Should've apprenticed with a master criminal instead of attending college.

The shots discharged closer, louder.

Leaving the shelter of the Joshua trees, she sprinted across the wasteland, from nowhere to nowhere. No one to save her now. Nothing to do to save herself.

She kept running. Her leg muscles burned, her chest ached, and her breaths came fast and hard.

The Jeep's engine revved.

Risking a glance backward, she saw the Jeep hurtling after her.

Then the ground dropped away beneath her, and she sailed into the void.

CHAPTER TWENTY-THREE

HER FEET HIT THE BOTTOM. HER LEGS CRUMPLED, AND SHE TUMBLED backward. Her head struck a hard surface—the arroyo wall, she realized, as phantom lights danced in her vision. She'd fallen into another arroyo, or maybe an offshoot of the one that blocked the road.

A figure leaped into the arroyo from above her head.

The commando landed directly in front of her, spun around, and thrust his gun in her face. She lurched sideways to squeeze around him. A starburst of pain behind her eyes stopped her mid-step as she fought back a retch.

The commando seized both her wrists in one massive hand. Threads of pain shot up her arms into her shoulders.

Not like this, they could not take her like this, so easily, so quickly. *Fight, dammit, give them hell.* She couldn't. Her body felt as limp as towels linked together with string. Her tongue was parched and bloody. She breathed hard, fast, unable to swallow enough oxygen. The first sharp pain of a migraine blossomed behind her eyes, and a twinge in her neck stiffened into the sensation of a steel rod jammed up her neck and straight into her brain.

She needed help. God, she hated admitting it, but she could no longer deny the truth. She needed somebody somewhere to somehow help her. No one was around. Just a battalion of commandos operating on orders to capture her.

Anybody. Anywhere. Somehow.

A bright light popped on, aimed straight at her face. A flashlight.

The pain behind her eyes burst into a full-fledged migraine. The light hit her with a physical force, driving the pain deep into her brain. The sound of her own breathing hurt. Her stomach heaved, and she gulped back her gorge.

The commando spoke. His words pierced her brain, sharp as needles, though she couldn't comprehend the meaning. She squeezed her eyes shut. *Please, anybody, help me.* No, not just anybody. His name wisped through her as a fleeting thought and she grabbed it, holding onto it like a mental life preserver.

David, help me. I need you.

The migraine bulldozed all thoughts from her mind. She pressed her hands against her temples. The commando yelled. Calling his friends, she realized between waves of dizziness.

David, please.

He came.

She sensed his presence, though she couldn't open her eyes. The flashlight beam was too bright, the pain too intense. Despite bouncing on the waves of nausea and dizziness, struggling to stay afloat, she felt better. Safer.

The commando grunted. Feet scuffled. Sand sprayed her face.

Silence.

Voices shouted above and behind her. The other commandos.

Arms cradled her body and lifted her. She chanced opening one eye a sliver. David carried her down the arroyo, his face stern, his arms strong beneath her. He was holding something in his left hand, an object that bumped against her every so often. She shut her eyes as he broke into a trot. Rather than exacerbating her symptoms, the bobbing motion of his gait soothed her. The glow from the flashlight weakened and faded into blackness. A chilly breeze wafted over them, and she huddled closer against David, absorbing the warmth of his body. The pain in her head ebbed as a tide of weariness swept in behind it.

David halted.

Commandos shouted, their voices distant.

"Where is she?" one asked.

"I dunno," another answered. "Didn't you see?"

"She couldn't have disappeared."

"Look! Donaldson's down there."

"Check him out… We'll go this…"

The voices diminished until she could no longer distinguish the words. The grumbling of the Jeep's engine grew fainter.

The migraine was almost gone now, vanishing in record time. Yet even when she'd been engulfed in the pain, she'd felt safer than she should have, safer than logic allowed. Commandos hunted for her. They would find her and, when they did, they would capture her and take her to their master. That fact didn't bother her. The intense weariness, an aftereffect of the migraine, skewed her thoughts. She wasn't thinking clearly. She had trouble thinking at all.

David bent his head beside hers. "You're safe."

Too exhausted to speak, she pressed her face against his chest, curling her fingers around the neck of his T-shirt.

No more shouting. No footsteps. No engine noises. The commandos were out of earshot, maybe even gone altogether, having given up the search. She harbored no illusions that they'd give up permanently. They would be back. Soon. With a lot more men.

—

DAVID POKED HIS HEAD OUT INTO THE ARROYO. EMPTY. CARRYING Grace, he knew he could never outrun the guards. Carrying her while clutching the guard's helmet and trying not to trip in a hole or smack into a big rock was even harder. A crack in the arroyo wall, four feet deep and three feet wide, had offered refuge. Their concealment was aided by a large cactus growing at the apex of the arroyo wall, which shaded the fissure. Although the commandos had scanned this crack in the earth visually, it wasn't obvious, especially in the dark. The cactus cast a long shadow on the arroyo wall so that, at a glance, the crack looked like a part of the shadows, not a fracture in the wall.

He knew this landscape the way he knew his own mind. Months of exploring the vicinity of the facility, psychically, had given him an intimate knowledge of every slope and gully, every rock outcropping and cluster of Joshua trees. He knew the locations of three abandoned homes, nothing more than shacks now, and the path of every arroyo within fifty square miles. His travels had acquainted him with the creatures that inhabited the desert, both human and animal. No one knew this area better.

Except, perhaps, the architects who had built the facility.

Grace clutched his shirt tighter and moaned.

The bastards had hurt her. He didn't know how, couldn't see a wound or a mark, but he knew they had done this to her. Pain had possessed her body like a parasite, eating away at her strength, and he had no idea what to do for her, if anything could alleviate the pain. She seemed unable to speak.

She needed a doctor.

He couldn't trust anyone in Reston. He wasn't sure she'd make it to the next town, over a hundred miles away, even if he magically conjured a car and drove two-hundred miles an hour the whole way. Her face had gone pale. A bead of blood had formed on her lip where she'd bitten it, and scratches drew red lines across her cheek.

Dammit, help her. Don't just stand here.

The arroyo snaked eastward about two hundred feet, then forked northeast and southwest. At the fork, the walls sloped at a more oblique angle and animals had worn a path up the slope at that spot. He could at least get them out of the arroyo there. After that, he knew exactly where to take them. The route ran through his mind, a series of lines on a mental map, leading toward the one safe place he knew.

He lunged out of the fissure.

Grace huddled in his arms, her body limp, as he traversed the arroyo and found the trail up the slope. Once he'd climbed out of the hole, he paused to check her pulse. It beat strong and steady against his finger. Her breathing was slow and shallow, and she seemed to be sleeping rather than unconscious. He relaxed a little. Rest would do her good.

While the sun dipped ever closer to the mountains, David strode across the desert toward a house he couldn't be sure still stood. He hadn't seen the place in six months.

His arms quivered. Sweat trickled down his brow. Even in a manifestation, he could exhaust himself, and he was no good to Grace if he couldn't walk. Besides, he might grow so tired he'd snap back to the facility, back to a locked room miles away from her. He would not abandon her.

Not after what she'd sacrificed to get him here.

He halted in an area populated by rocks and dropped the helmet. Kicking aside some rocks, he cleared a spot and lowered Grace onto the sand. She didn't stir. God, she looked weak. Vulnerable. If they found her like this, she wouldn't be able to defend herself. Tesler might haul him back to the facility at any moment by administering drugs or an electric shock to break the connection. He must see her through whatever injury or illness had seized her, because she would never survive alone, not like this.

Grace opened her eyes partway. Red veins webbed the whites of her eyes. She sniffled as her gaze settled on his face.

He wanted to hold her but feared he'd cause her more pain. Instead, he smoothed the hair away from her face.

When she spoke, her voice was hoarse. "It's over."

She's dying. He bent over her, peering into her eyes. "What happened?"

"Migraine. It's going away, though."

The tension flooded out of him in a long sigh. She had meant the migraine was over. He shook his head and almost laughed. Grace wasn't dying. Though the migraine had weakened her, she would recover. She looked much better already. Her cheeks showed a slight pinkness rather than the frightening pallor he'd seen when he found her in the arroyo.

"I'm okay," she said.

Sitting down beside her, he managed a weak smile as he stroked her hair. "I was afraid they'd hurt you."

David slid his hand down to her cheek, the one without scratches on it.

"How are you here? I thought you were too weak to manifest."

"I was," he said, taking her hand in his. "You gave me some of your energy. That's probably what caused your migraine."

"What?"

"You wanted me here, and you made it happen." He squeezed her hand gently. "Now be quiet and rest. We still have a ways to go."

Grace shivered. The chill of night had settled over the desert.

In one motion, he scooped her into his arms and rose. As he started down the path outlined in his mind, she looped her arms around his neck. Whatever happened, they would deal with it together.

Whether she liked it or not.

———

SIZZLE. CRACKLE. GRACE OPENED HER EYES. THE MIGRAINE HAD ENDed. She was tired, weak, hungry, and thirsty, but no longer in pain. She lay on her side, on the floor, where David had set her down... How long ago? The memory seemed more like a half-remembered dream.

The wood floor felt rough and cold against her skin. A draft swirled over her, eliciting a shiver. Something thunked. A door closing, she thought, unable to muster the energy to lift her head and look. The draft ceased.

Across the room, a fire burned inside an old fireplace. Two logs crackled. Flames licked upward from them.

A figure passed in front of her.

She pushed up into a sitting position, supporting her body with her arms.

David kneeled by the fire. He held twigs and broken boards under one arm and, piece by piece, tossed them onto the fire. She watched him stoke the blaze with a five-foot metal fence post. He had carried her here and started a fire. He was taking care of her. No one had done that for her in a long time.

He turned toward her and sat down, patting the floor beside him. "It's warmer over here."

She scuttled toward the fireplace. Sitting several feet from him, legs crossed under her, she studied the flames. Orange and yellow tongues darted up from within the pile of wood, flickering and dancing.

David scooted closer to her and clasped her hand in both of his.

She turned sideways to rest her head on his shoulder. He felt so solid, so real, that she had forgotten what he was—an illusion. Sure, he existed, in a building out there in the desert. But in reality, he was not here with her, not touching her hand, not giving her a look of earnest concern.

His face was haggard, his lips pale. As he exhaled, he let his shoulders sag.

She shifted her attention to his hand, cupped over hers. It looked real. Everything looked the opposite of how it was these days. Her life looked normal. People looked like people, even the ones she now knew were not people, but instead humanoid mirages. She nudged David's hand with one finger. His flesh gave under the pressure until her fingertip bumped the bone. His skin felt warm and pliable, the bone firm, the muscles taut when flexed and soft when relaxed. Beneath her finger, she detected the coarseness of hair, the texture of skin, and even the surge of blood flowing through veins. David's explanations did nothing to allay her confusion or the surreal quality of the situation.

She scraped her fingernail lightly across his hand. "Can you feel this?"

"I feel everything." He reached up with his free hand to lift her chin, aligning their gazes. "You ought to know that after last night."

She felt like curling up in his arms again, feeling his warmth surround and infuse her.

Instead, she looked away from his intent gaze, focusing on the fireplace and the embers glowing beneath the half-consumed wood.

"When you left me in the car," she said, "there was wind and pressure. It made my ears pop. What was that?"

He slipped his arm around her shoulders. "Breaking the connection too abruptly can cause a sudden expulsion of energy. It's often experienced as a localized shift in air pressure. Inside a confined space, it's more noticeable. We call it backfire."

"Right." She'd pretend that made sense because if he offered more details her head might implode. "You said I gave you energy."

"Yes."

"How?"

He shrugged and tried to laugh but coughed instead. "I don't know how you do it. I can't do it, and neither can anyone else I've met."

The firelight no longer illuminated his face. Now, it seemed to draw the energy out of his body as fuel for its flames.

"Are you all right?" she asked.

"I will be. The shot of energy you gave me is almost gone, though."

"Maybe I could give you more."

"No." His expression hardened to match the tone of his voice. "It's too dangerous."

She said nothing. Her gut told her the same thing, but she didn't like seeing him weak and virtually defenseless. "You should go."

"I don't like leaving you alone."

"I'm used to it."

"They'll find you. One against a dozen, maybe more." He brushed his thumb across her cheek. "Not good odds."

"Odds can be beaten."

He didn't scowl, though she expected he would. Instead, he turned his head to study the fire, his expression not blank, but simply inscrutable. "You're inside the perimeter now. If you try to leave, they'll find you. If you stay in this house too long, they'll find you. You might reach the facility, and I might be able to help you get inside it, but—" He met her gaze, the intensity of his making her shiver. "What do you hope to accomplish there?"

She lifted one shoulder. "Not sure. I'm trusting my instincts here, and they tell me the answers I need are inside that facility."

"We've already established I can't stop you." He stared down at the floor, tapping one fingernail on the scuffed wood. "I know the grounds around the facility. Sean knows the interior better than anyone except the engineers and architects who built it. He's hiding inside the facility now, but I can find him and get his help with sneaking you inside."

"Thank you."

Reaching into his back pocket, he brought out a yellowed and wrinkled piece of paper that was folded in quarters. As he unfolded the sheet, he held it out to her. "I found a pen in your purse and an ancient sheet of paper wadded up in the corner there." He pointed over his shoulder. "So I drew you a map."

She took the paper and ran a fingertip over the black ink lines drawn on it. One zigzagging line ducked between and around shapes and words he'd scrawled across the page. Landmarks, she realized, and explanatory phrases to guide her.

"It isn't the most direct route," he told her, "because the direct route is too exposed. This way will take a little longer, but it should get you there with the least risk of being spotted."

She noticed he didn't say zero risk, just less risk. Complete safety no longer existed for her.

"Your gun is in your purse," he said. "I picked it up back in the arroyo."

"Thanks."

Bending sideways and leaning backward, he retrieved an object from the shadows behind him. When he straightened, he offered her the object.

It was a full-face helmet like the ones the commandos wore.

"Take this," he said, thrusting the helmet at her. "Traveling at night is difficult, and the facility's security force isn't the only danger out there. If you step on a rattlesnake or run into coyotes…" He grasped her right hand and folded her fingers around the helmet's bottom rim. "These have built-in night vision capability."

She accepted the helmet. When he gestured for her to put it on, she did. Darkness swallowed her.

"In daylight, the visor acts like sunglasses," David said, his voice coming through clearly, if a bit softer. "This button turns on the night vision."

He guided her finger to a switch on the bottom rim.

She flicked it.

The world transformed into shades of green. The fire was blinding on the night vision screen in front of her eyes, and she swiveled her head to peer into the darker recesses of the room. She made out the individual boards that formed the walls, the outlines of the window frames, and even a Joshua tree that stood maybe twenty feet beyond the window.

As she shut off the night vision, she removed the helmet. "Thank you."

"Stop thanking me," he muttered. Then he pressed his lips to hers in a brief, tender kiss. "Just be careful."

And he was gone.

A breeze whistled through the old house. The floorboards creaked. The windows rattled. Inside the fireplace, flames whipped back and forth, dwindling until only the embers remained.

The storm ended in a flurry of dust. Flames burst up from the embers in the fireplace.

David had broken the connection more carefully this time, or else the room was big enough to dampen the backfire.

She was alone. Again.

———

M OVE AND I'LL SPLIT YOUR HEAD OPEN. DON'T CARE IF YOU ARE female." The maw of a shotgun gaped at her, nearly kissing her nose. A man loomed above her, shadows masking his features, and a faint grumbling issued from behind him while a bright light from outside silhouetted him from behind. The front door hung wide open.

Still groggy from sleep, since she had woken up seconds earlier, Grace struggled to make sense of the images. Gun. Man. Light. She had fallen asleep in front of the fire, that she remembered.

The man gesticulated with the gun. "You're trespassing. Just 'cause I don't live here don't mean you can break in."

"I thought the house was abandoned."

"Yeah. But I still own it."

Grace yawned. She couldn't help it. Her brain needed oxygen. The landlord, however, took her action the wrong way.

He jammed the gun into her forehead. "I said don't move."

"It was a yawn, not an act of war." To hell with this. She slapped the gun away, pushing up onto her knees. "My car broke down. I was lost, so I started walking and came to this place. Since it looked abandoned, I decided to sleep here. Sorry I offended you."

She hopped to her feet.

He swung the gun toward her. The barrel bumped her chest. "How'd you find me?"

"I told you, I got lost."

"Carlos sent you, didn't he?"

"I don't know any Carlos. I got lost."

"Sure." He shuffled backward. "The stuff better be here. If it's not, your pretty little face is gonna wallpaper this room."

Drugs. The word popped into her mind as the man kneeled, keeping the shotgun sighted on her head, and pried one board loose from the floor, then another. He dragged an olive-green canvas bag out of the hole and plopped it on the floor. She waited for an opening to run, but he kept the gun pointed at her. Though his aim varied by a few inches, he wouldn't need a straight trajectory to her head for the shot to kill her. If the blast hit her shoulder or her chest, she'd probably die all the same.

The commando helmet lay near her feet. Her gun was inside her purse, which also lay nearby. To grab either, she'd need to duck way too close to the shotgun's muzzle.

The man unzipped the olive-green bag. She glimpsed white bricks wrapped in plastic. Duct tape secured each package. Cocaine. Maybe heroin. She'd seen enough cop shows to recognize the stuff.

How did this creep get inside the facility's perimeter?

There were no fences. Anyone could walk across the perimeter, ignoring the warning signs. The sensors would detect the intrusion, however, and commandos would be dispatched.

Everything inside her went cold. The commandos had shown up quickly when she'd breached the perimeter.

Through the window and the grime encrusting the glass, she saw a vehicle with its headlights blazing. The grumbling she'd heard was the engine idling.

Her heartbeat quickened.

"Lucky for you," the man said, zipping the bag and dropping it into the hole, "it's still here."

"I told you, I just got lost."

"What were you doing out here in hell's back forty? You know this whole blasted desert is owned by some nasty corporate types."

"I—" She couldn't think of a good lie. She couldn't think of a *bad* one either.

With his foot, he maneuvered the floorboards back into place. They snapped into position.

She felt the earth liquefying beneath her, in a metaphorical sense, at least so far. If she moved too quickly, she'd plunge into the mire. If she waited too long, it would swallow her. Neither option appealed to her.

"It's silly," she said. "I was looking for UFOs. Took a wrong turn and got lost."

"That's the worst-smelling load of bat guano I ever heard. Carlos, you scumbag!"

The gun trembled in his hand. His trigger finger wobbled.

She dove sideways just as he jerked the trigger.

The shot detonated with deafening force. Wood splintered and sprayed across the room. Bricks around the fireplace crumbled.

The man bellowed a wordless cry of rage and anguish.

Grace snatched up the helmet and her purse, scrambling for the door.

Another shot boomed behind her. The doorframe exploded into projectile slivers.

She crawled out the door on all fours.

Footsteps crashed behind her.

She yanked the gun out of her purse, rolled onto her back, and aimed the muzzle at the doorway.

The man stomped into the opening, his shotgun leveled at her head.

She pulled the trigger.

As the shot resounded in the air, the man jerked, seemed to freeze for a split second, and then tumbled backward to hit the floor with a concussion that shook the cracked glass in the window.

Had she killed him?

The thought triggered a swell of nausea, and she rolled onto her side, afraid she might vomit. The nausea passed in a few seconds, though, leaving her trembling and sheathed in a cold sweat. She had to make sure he was... not a threat anymore.

Still gripping her gun, she clambered to her feet. The man lay motionless a few inches inside the threshold. On her tiptoes, she approached the doorway.

His eyes were open. Blank. Sightless. Dead.

She'd killed a man.

He was a drug dealer. How many lives had he taken, through murder or from the drugs he peddled? He had tried to kill her after all. She did nothing more than defend her life.

Whirling around, she sprinted for the vehicle, a black Land Rover. She flung the door open and jumped inside, tossing her purse and the helmet onto the passenger seat. Maybe she wouldn't need the helmet after all. Plucking David's map out of her purse, she set it on the seat beside the bag and slammed the gear shift lever into reverse.

Easing her foot down on the accelerator, she turned the Rover around to head in the direction indicated on David's map. Soon, the dark outline of the old house vanished from sight in the rearview mirror.

That was a little too easy.

The thought niggled at her as the Rover bounced over the terrain. She had to ignore the concern because getting to the facility as quickly as possible was the top priority. The drug dealer had undoubtedly triggered the perimeter sensors, drawing a horde of commandos who were swarming the old house at this moment. The Rover left tire tracks, which the commandos could follow.

She would drive the Rover until she was within easy walking distance of the facility and then abandon it to finish her journey on foot. It seemed the best, and fastest, plan.

Less risk, not zero risk.

Grace relaxed into the seat. The supple leather cradled her body, and the vents bathed her feet in warm air that leeched the chill out of her flesh. The radio, its volume turned down, murmured classical music. Between the front seats, a cell phone sat in its cradle. The fuel gauge registered three-quarters of a tank. Attached to the dashboard, a

GPS unit showed the car's position as a mobile dot superimposed over a satellite image of the desert.

Stopping the car, she took a few minutes to compare David's map to the GPS display. As she set off again, she felt more confident in her ability to find her way. The universe had granted her a measure of good luck, at last. Angering a drug dealer and being forced to shoot him hardly counted as good luck, but the fact he'd left the Rover idling did. Thank heavens. She needed a break almost as much as she needed dinner.

The Rover bumped over a rut. Her buttocks lifted off the seat, but she held onto the steering wheel, keeping the vehicle on course.

The phone rang.

Her grip on the steering wheel loosened, and the Rover swerved toward a Joshua tree. She jerked the wheel to avoid the tree, stomped on the brake, and gasped as the car slammed to a halt.

The cell phone, cupped in its cradle, rang a second time.

She picked up the phone but did not answer the call. The phone's LCD screen said "caller unknown." While the phone rang a third and fourth time, she debated answering. No way in hell, she decided. It might've been Carlos, and she had a feeling she did not want to chat with him.

The phone rang once more and stopped.

Grace stared at the LCD screen. Her heart was beating so fast she could barely catch her breath.

The phone made a *bloop-bloop* sound. "New text message," it announced on the screen.

Biting her lip, she tapped the screen to open the message. It contained three words: "I see you."

Could he? She had no idea.

The Rover's engine died. She twisted the key in the ignition. Nothing. The door locks clunked into position. She yanked on the handle, but it was locked. So she pressed the button that lowered the windows. Nothing. The phone rang. She reached for it, but then hesitated with her hand resting on the device. It rang two, three, four times more.

She answered.

On the other end of the call, a man snarled. "You're mine."

"Excuse me?"

"I wasn't dead. Did you see any blood, lady?"

She flashed back to the man lying flat on his back, eyes open but sightless.

At least, she'd thought they were sightless. Had she seen blood? In the murky conditions, she couldn't say for sure. The voice on the phone sure sounded like the same drug dealer.

Through the phone connection, the man growled, "Think you can steal my car and get off scot-free? Think again." He paused. "Tell Carlos I'm onto him."

"I don't know any Carlos." The desperation in her voice surprised her, though she couldn't imagine why. She *was* desperate. "You can have your car. Just let me go."

"Uh-uh, lady. I'm comin' to punish you."

"How? I've got your car."

"You ain't gone far, and I've got a GPS app on my backup phone that lets me track the car from anywhere." He sniggered. "You can't do nothing except wait for me, missy. You're trapped."

He hung up.

You're trapped. Like hell.

She scrambled into the backseat headfirst, dragging her body after her as she glanced around in search of anything that might help her escape the vehicle. When she saw nothing, she scaled the backseat too, landing in the rear cargo area. Empty garbage bags. A gasoline can. A small toolkit. A jack. And a short-handled shovel.

She grabbed the shovel and climbed back into the driver's seat. There, summoning all the anger and frustration she had bottled up inside her, she slammed the shovel's tip into the windshield.

Cracks webbed through the safety glass, transforming it into a gummy sheet. She swung the shovel harder. It punched a hole in the sheet, admitting a breeze that chilled the sweat beading on her skin. She struck the glass again, widening the hole. Using the shovel's blade, she folded the glass out of the way. The opening was just large enough for her to squeeze through it.

First, she tossed her purse and the helmet out the hole. Stuffing the map under her waistband, she crawled over the dashboard and shimmied out the hole headfirst. Once on the hood, she turned around to slide off it, with her boots hitting the ground first.

A series of booms echoed across the desert floor.

She looked back in the direction she'd come from, back toward the old house. Bluish-white lights twinkled there, low to the ground. Headlights. The commandos must've arrived. The booms must've been gunshots.

The drug dealer probably was dead this time. She didn't know how she felt about that. Some comfort came from knowing that at least *she* hadn't killed him.

In the beams of the headlights, she consulted the map. Choosing the direction she thought was right, she started away from the Rover at a brisk pace. She'd find the facility, or she'd die from exposure, or maybe a snakebite.

Either way, her journey ended tonight.

CHAPTER TWENTY-FOUR

GRACE TILTED HER HEAD BACK TO STARE UP AT THE STRUCTURE IN front of her. The green hues of the night vision display in the helmet revealed a bulbous shape seated atop tall metal scaffolding. It was a water tower, seventy or eighty feet high.

Turning, she surveyed the desert one more time. She hadn't seen any headlights for a while, but that fact didn't make her feel any better. The commandos had night vision helmets identical to the one she now wore. If they had opted for stealth, then she might never see them coming.

She detoured around the water tower. The landmark appeared on David's map, which told her to head straight for the humpbacked butte in the distance. She wouldn't reach the butte, according to the map, but its silhouette would guide her in the right direction. Thank heavens for David's remote viewing, because without it she'd have no chance of finding the facility. A few days ago, she would've dismissed the very concept of extrasensory abilities as bunk. Her life had changed so radically in such a short time that she marveled at the fact she held onto her sanity. Of course, her life hadn't really changed. The amnesia had tricked her into believing she was a normal, boring girl.

Now she knew better.

The ground sloped upward at an ever-steepening angle. Her thighs ached as she mounted the rise, halting at the crest. Ahead of her, the ground sloped downward in a gentle grade. She stood on the rim of a bowl-shaped depression that, when viewed from the lower terrain surrounding it, looked like yet another flat expanse of desert. Only from this vantage point could she see what the depression contained. There, perhaps a quarter mile away, sat a dark shape that she recognized as a low, sprawling complex of interconnected buildings.

The facility.

She stifled a triumphant cry. At last, she had reached her destination.

The night vision display flickered. The words "low battery" flashed on the screen.

Great. Well, at this point, she probably didn't need the high-tech guidance, anyway. If she walked straight down the slope, and straight across the depression, she would run into the facility.

Switching off the night vision, she removed the helmet. With it tucked under her arm, she lifted her foot to step off the summit.

"Hold it right there."

Her heart thudded at the sound of the male voice issuing from behind her. She lowered her hand to her unzipped purse, slipping her fingers inside to grasp the gun.

Something hard and cold rammed into her back, right between her shoulder blades.

"Don't," the man said in a stern voice, "or I'll blow a hole straight through you."

She froze.

"That's right," he said. "Now raise your hands and turn around, slow and easy."

She complied.

A helmet covered the man's head and face. Nothing on his black outfit identified him or his employers. The man towered several inches above her, his physique packed with enough muscles to give him a threatening aura even if he hadn't been pointing a weapon at her. With both hands, he gripped a bulky gun with a huge clip that contained enough bullets to rip her into confetti.

He clicked a button on the two-way radio clipped to his jacket. "I got her."

A gruff voice came through the radio. "Hold her there. We're on our way."

The other commando hadn't asked where this guy was. They must've had a tracking system, like GPS, to keep tabs on each other in the field.

She glanced down at the helmet tucked under her arm. Did it contain a tracking device that had led this commando to her? It might've taken them a while to realize she had one of their helmets. Either way, it didn't matter anymore. She was caught.

The commando jabbed his gun into her ribs, just below the sternum.

She winced and scuffled backward half a step, her right heel tipping over the sharp crest of the hill. She teetered but held onto her balance.

The commando jabbed her in the ribs again, harder this time.

She grimaced, clenching her teeth.

"You better hold real still," the man said. "My trigger finger's starting to itch."

"Your boss wants me alive."

The man snorted. "Accidents happen."

Wonderful. she got caught by a maverick with an itch to shoot her. With his gun's muzzle embedded in her abdomen, there wasn't much she could do.

She had psychic abilities, for pity's sake. Those abilities could surely help right now if only she could remember how to use them.

Wait a minute. She'd visited the facility in her dreams countless times, traveling there psychically to visit David. She'd used her powers to push David away. Those incidents told her that, somewhere deep inside, she still knew how to access her abilities. Her conscious mind had blocked the memories and convinced her she was powerless.

David had shown her the truth. He'd given her the information she needed to regain what she had lost. It was up to her to make use of the information.

Now or never.

She kept her eyes open, but let her vision drift out of focus. With an effort, she relaxed every muscle and banished all thoughts from her mind. The whisper of the breeze, the rustling of the commando's uniform, even the beating of her heart, it all faded into silence. The blurry world around her melted into blackness. She felt her consciousness rising, floating, pulled toward something she could feel but not see.

A point of light shimmered. Then another. And another.

She surfaced in a field of cool white stars. Hovering. Weightless. Free.

David. He called to her. Not in voice or thought, but in spirit.

Though she wanted to go to him, wanted it so badly her soul ached from the need, she couldn't give in to it. Other matters needed her attention more urgently.

Turning away from his call, she sank downward out of the field of stars, back into the real world. Floating above the desert, she gazed down at her body and the commando standing in front of her. She must do something. Anything.

She focused her mind, gathering energy from… somewhere.

The gun flew out of the commando's hands. It sailed through the air, hitting the ground thirty feet away.

The commando shouted. He floundered backward as if he'd been kicked in the chest.

She'd intended to fling him backward with only as much force as she'd used to discard the gun. Her control was faltering. She felt it. Doubts niggled at her, barely noticeable at first, but growing louder and sharper as panic iced through her.

The commando tripped. He flopped onto his butt, dazed.

Grace slammed back into her body with a force that rocked her off balance. She teetered backward. Her right foot slipped off the precipice. Though the drop wasn't steep, she lost her footing and tumbled to the ground. The momentum sent her rolling down the slope sideways.

Automatic gunfire chattered overhead.

She rolled down, down, down. Vegetation scraped at her. Rocks bruised her flesh. Nothing slowed her descent until the ground leveled out and she lost momentum. Hitting the ground face-first, she came to a halt sprawled on her belly.

Everything hurt. Her head felt like someone was sitting on it. She flailed her hands to push the weight away from her head but found nothing there. Searing pain erupted behind her eyes. The flavor of dirt and blood tainted her mouth as she pushed up onto her hands and knees. Nothing seemed broken. Opening her eyes, she ran her hands over her body in search of wounds. Nothing serious. Scrapes and cuts and sore spots that would mature into bruises. A cut near her mouth accounted for the tang of blood on her tongue.

Sitting back on her heels, she swept her gaze up the hillside.

The commando stood silhouetted against the night sky.

She didn't move. Maybe he couldn't see her. Yeah, right. He had night vision, and she had crappy psychic abilities that only half worked and left her drained and saddled with a burgeoning migraine.

At least she'd made it to the crossroads, on purpose this time. And she'd used her telekinesis with moderate effectiveness. Not bad for her first conscious attempt.

The commando leaped off the crest of the hill. She lost sight of him on the shadowed slope.

Scrambling to her feet, she took off in the direction of the facility.

THE DOOR CLICKED SHUT. DAVID OPENED HIS EYES TO FIND THE ROOM empty, though he'd already known it would be. He both heard and sensed the departure of the tech, a nervous young woman sent by Tesler, who was probably busy plotting the horrors he would inflict on Grace once they captured her.

The young tech's mind was shockingly pliable. No wonder they'd hired her. She would accept any story, comply with any orders, simply to avoid confrontation. Maybe she'd been abused as a child. Maybe she lacked character. The reason made no difference. She'd helped Tesler inflict untold pain and torment on their test subjects. Despite her crimes, David felt a twinge of guilt over influencing her mind so that she believed he was still in a drug-induced coma. He hated manipulating people.

When Grace had told him how desperation had forced her to trick a man into selling her a car for twenty dollars, he'd understood her anguish over what she'd done. He felt the same guilt every time he was forced to bend a pliant mind to his will. He should've told her that. Instead, he'd told her the one thing he should not have said, not yet.

He'd said he loved her.

It had been a mistake. He meant it, but she wasn't ready to hear it. Confused by her amnesia, frightened by the current situation, she'd shut down at the very mention of a certain four-letter word. He couldn't take it back now. He wouldn't take it back.

Pushing back the sheets, he sat up and swung his legs off the bed. He didn't need to get dressed, because even in a coma he still wore his jeans, T-shirt, and socks. Tesler and his lackeys didn't care about their subjects' comfort. David bent down to pluck his sneakers from the floor where they'd been tucked under the bedside table. He shoved the shoes onto his feet, tying the laces as fast as his fingers would move.

Grace was coming.

He must help her. He must find her. Despite receiving a gift of energy from Grace, he didn't have enough of a reserve leftover to reach her psychically. Not in a way she would understand. If she remembered how this all worked, he might attempt to guide her obliquely. In her current state, she wouldn't get it.

Sean would. If it took his last ounce of energy, he must contact Sean and enlist the boy's help. Sean wasn't as drained as David was. He ought to have enough energy to help Grace.

Sliding off the bed, David straightened and walked to the door. The knob felt cool when he laid his hand on it.

One chance. That might be all he had. All they had. Whatever happened, he and Grace would see this through together.

Twisting the knob, he eased the door open and stepped out into the corridor.

———

RUNNING, RUNNING, RUNNING. SHE DIDN'T LOOK BACK. FOCUSED ON the terrain ahead of her, discerning faint outlines as her eyes adjusted to the darkness, she pumped her legs as fast as possible. Looking back would distract her, and she might trip. If the commando was closing in on her, she couldn't do much about it, anyway. Shooting him in the dark while running full speed would've been a waste of a bullet. Stopping to take aim and fire gave him a chance to catch up, and she still might miss the target. She was no sniper.

It was too dark. The commando blended into the night.

Ahead of her, the squat silhouette of the facility enlarged as she drew closer and closer. She saw no lights to give her a clue where there might be an entrance. A wild guess was her only option.

David had said Sean would help her. Neither of them had shown up yet.

What if they couldn't? What if, at this very moment, both David and Sean languished in drug-induced slumber?

No. She felt David. The sensation made no sense, and it left her feeling a bit uneasy, but she knew that the slight pull she felt was him. Alive. Aware. Somewhere close by.

Not close enough.

Running, running, toward the facility. Her head throbbed. The ambient light seemed too bright, and the glow from the crescent moon rising directly in front of her struck her eyes like invisible needles. Though the cold wind generated by her motion felt good, her muscles screamed for a break that she couldn't give them. Not yet.

The building loomed nearer, larger, blocking out more and more of the sky. The moon vanished behind the hulking structure. The darkness grew deeper. She wanted to draw on her powers, to see what her eyes couldn't. If she did that, her migraine might get exponentially worse. She could not risk it.

The crack of a gunshot echoed behind her. Too close.

Dirt erupted to her left. Way too close.

Twenty feet from the building, she realized there were no doors in front of her. She skidded to a stop, whipping her head left and right, searching for a door-shaped outline in the gloom.

Behind her, footfalls slapped on earth.

She spun around, the gun in her hand.

A shape darted toward her from less than fifty feet away.

She aimed for the humanoid blob and shouted, "Freeze or I'll shoot!"

The shadow hesitated, then straightened into a man-size outline. Thirty feet away. Maybe less. *Dammit.* Judging distances was next to impossible out here, with shadows swarming everywhere.

The commando sniggered. "I got mine sighted on you too, sweetheart."

He meant his gun, she realized. The big one filled with enough bullets to take out a herd of elephants.

Could she hit him with her first shot? She'd fired on a human being only twice before, when she thought she killed the drug dealer and when she shot Waldron in the foot. Her confidence in her aim was less than inspiring.

So was her confidence that this creep wouldn't kill her for the thrill of it.

Accidents happen, he'd said before. And David had told her the facility hired dangerous ex-cons as security guards.

"Drop the gun," he ordered. "Or I'll make sure you can't run away again."

"No."

"I said drop the gun."

"And I said no."

She could practically feel his disbelieving stare. It probably resembled the look David gave her every time she refused to do what he wanted, except without the underlying fondness. Men expected her to obey their orders, and she was sick and tired of it. Besides, without Sean or David to help her, she had no clue how to get inside the facility. The commando was her way in.

He wanted to kill her if he could get away with it by framing it as an accident. Maybe she should put the gun down, so he couldn't claim he shot her in self-defense. If she dropped the gun, he might still shoot her and label it self-defense by planting the gun in her lifeless hand. It seemed to her that keeping a loaded weapon trained on the commando gave her the best chance of survival.

"I've shot one man tonight," she said. "Do you seriously think I'll feel bad about shooting you?"

"You screwed that up, sweetheart. The loser was wearing a Kevlar vest under his shirt. Now, if you'd shot him in the head..." He made a dismissive noise. "You don't have the killer instinct, honey."

She wanted to shoot him just for calling her "sweetheart" and "honey."

The commando's radio crackled, and a masculine voice shouted through the little speaker. "Battaglia, what's your status? There's no sign of the girl out here."

So, the Neanderthal had a name after all.

Grace caught a flash of movement as Battaglia reached up to press a button on his radio. He spoke in a tone sharpened by arrogance and tinged with cruel amusement. "I got a sign of the girl right here in front of me."

"You've got her?" the other voice asked.

"Affirmative."

"Take her inside. We'll meet you there." Static crackled. "And you'd better not lose her this time, Battaglia."

"She's going nowhere, sir."

The Neanderthal made a sweeping gesture with his left hand. "Let's go, sweet cheeks."

Grace gritted her teeth. "You first."

"No." He shifted his right hand, giving her a glimpse of his weapon's outline. "You first, or I blast a hole in your shoulder. It won't kill you, but it'll make you a lot more cooperative."

Well, she wanted inside the facility. He was giving her what she wanted.

So why did she have a cold lump in her stomach?

Turning to her right, she trudged along the wall of the building. Battaglia followed her, she knew, though she didn't glance back to make sure. His footfalls clomped slightly out of sync with hers. The building seemed interminable, cloaked in darkness, without any windows or doors. After a few minutes that felt like hours, Battaglia ordered her to stop where a rectangular depression in the wall suggested a doorway.

Crossing in front of her, Battaglia found a keypad next to the doorway and punched in the code. A mechanism chunked. He reached for what she assumed was a doorknob, twisted it, and thrust the door inward.

Muted yellow light poured out of the opening. It stung her eyes like the midday sun.

Squinting, she saw Battaglia remove his helmet. The light cast a flattering glow on his features, lending his skin a golden hue that complemented his dark-brown hair. He had a thin mustache that softened the angular planes of his face, but his squinty eyes and heavy brow hinted at the caveman within. He smirked, like the Neanderthal she knew he was.

"Ladies first," he said, gesturing with his gun for her to enter the building. He slipped his other hand into his pocket.

Now that he'd opened the door for her, she didn't need him anymore.

As if he'd read her mind, he lunged at her. Instead of grabbing for her gun, he threw his arms around her in a bear hug, crushing her to his chest. The gun was still in her hand, smashed between them. She struggled, but his muscle-bound body contained her like a cage. She couldn't shake free of him, couldn't move her arms, and couldn't get leverage with her legs.

Trapped.

No. She had one chance.

Battaglia clenched her tighter.

She couldn't catch her breath. Wriggling her fingers, she hooked one around the trigger of her gun.

"Time to say goodnight," he murmured.

Out of the corner of her eye, she saw his left hand slide up her shoulder, raising a syringe to her neck.

She pulled the trigger.

Battaglia jerked.

At first, she wasn't sure which one of them she'd hit. Then Battaglia stumbled backward, releasing his hold on her. The gun tumbled from his grasp. She still held her gun. A glance at her body revealed no blood or anything else to indicate a wound.

Battaglia stood there paralyzed, his body shaking, his face red.

She'd expected him to look pale and weak.

Instead, he looked thoroughly enraged. "You shot my foot, you—"

Grace fired at the keypad beside the door. As the shot exploded, the keypad shattered into bits.

Battaglia roared.

She swiped his gun from the ground and bolted through the doorway. Spinning around, she slammed the door shut. The lock chunked. She didn't wait to find out if Battaglia could force the door open manually. Clutching both guns, she ran.

The corridor dead-ended at another one. The new corridor went only left, so she skidded around the corner and took off in that direction. The passageway intersected with yet another, giving her three options—left, right, or straight ahead. She chose straight ahead. Where she was going, she didn't know. On and on she ran, deeper and deeper into the facility, past dozens of doors. She didn't try to open any of them because she knew what she needed did not wait inside any of those rooms. Instinct drove her onward, without reason but not without purpose.

To find the puppet master. That was her purpose. To track down JT, aka Jackson Tennant, and repay him for everything he'd done to her and her family—after she got the truth out of him.

David had asked her what she intended to do once she got inside the facility. At the time, she couldn't answer him. Finally, she knew what must be done. What *she* must do. Which villain she must confront. The destination was clear, if not the path, but something inside her knew where to go. She trusted that instinct.

Grace careened around a corner.

And smacked face-first into another human being.

Chapter Twenty-Five

HER BODY SLAMMED INTO HIS, HER EYES LEVEL WITH THE MAN'S nose. She recognized that nose. She recognized the warm solidity of his body and the scent of him that enveloped her. Resting her hands on his chest, she felt the knit fabric of his gray T-shirt. Joy swelled inside her as she tilted her head up to look at him, and a single breathless word issued from her lips.

"David."

He bent his head to meet her gaze, his eyes wider than usual. Though his lips parted, no sound came out.

It seemed ridiculous given the circumstances, but she felt her mouth curve into a smile. She wanted to kiss him, hug him, giggle uncontrollably, kiss him again.

But instead, she grinned at him like an idiot. "How did you find me?"

"I didn't. I was looking for Sean, but I'm too weak to find him psychically, so I have to search the old-fashioned way." He screwed up his mouth. "It's incredibly frustrating."

"Yeah, being normal sucks, doesn't it?"

His frown melted into a slight smile as he slipped his arms around her. "You have never been normal."

She couldn't help it. She had to rise onto her tiptoes and kiss him. He reciprocated, pulling her snugly against his body, and she looped her arms around his neck. Her right hand clasped her gun while her left gripped the strap of Battaglia's huge weapon.

When the kiss ended, Grace stepped away from David. Arms at his sides, he arched an eyebrow at her.

"I have to find JT," she said.

He flinched as if she'd slapped him in the face. "No."

"Yes. And you can either help me or get out of my way."

"He'll hurt you."

She noticed he didn't say JT would kill her. The lunatic probably wouldn't, at least not right away, not until he got from her whatever it was he wanted. Power, she assumed. What form that power might take, she hadn't figured out yet.

From down the corridor she'd just left, footfalls echoed. The noise drew nearer with each percussive step.

"Oh great," she said. "It must be Battaglia."

David's lip curled, and his jaw tensed. "Battaglia is chasing you?"

She nodded. "You know him?"

Although David said nothing, she saw the answer in the tightening of his features. He knew, and clearly despised, the muscle-bound commando.

David snatched Battaglia's gun from her and seized her hand as he took off down the corridor, dragging her with him. His longer legs moved him faster than hers could propel her, forcing Grace to sprint at full speed. The footsteps behind them were drowned out by the clapping of their own shoes on the smooth flooring. In her dreams, the corridors were lit by small bulbs along the floor. Tonight, however, bright daytime lighting spilled out of bulbs recessed in the ceiling.

Battaglia was unarmed, which gave them an advantage—unless the Neanderthal had another gun hidden on his person. It could've been tucked inside his jacket or strapped to his ankle. She should've shot him again when she had the chance, but she didn't like shooting anyone unless it was unavoidable. Shutting the door on Battaglia had slowed him down, at least.

With no warning, David stopped.

She barreled into his backside, knocking herself backward but hardly disturbing his balance. As she regained her footing, coming up beside him, he thrust an arm out to keep her back. He focused on the intersection twenty feet ahead of them. She heard nothing and saw nothing.

He tilted his head as if listening.

She wanted to ask what was going on, but the tension in his body and the intensity of his concentration made her hesitate.

The clomping of Battaglia's footfalls had ceased.

She glanced over her shoulder. No one there.

Damn, this was no good. No good at all.

David swung his head left and right as if searching for something. An escape hatch, maybe. A doorway. A window. Anything.

A cold finger trailed down her spine. She spun around, half expecting to see Battaglia right behind her with his hand stretched out to her. Nobody was there. She stared down the corridor, her back to David.

Battaglia strode out of the adjoining corridor. He raised a semiautomatic handgun, sighting it on her.

She held her gun trained on him.

David cursed under his breath.

She chanced a look backward, leaning a little sideways to peer around David's shoulder.

About twenty feet away, standing at the junction of two corridors, stood Waldron and a pack of armed guards. The men wore their black outfits, minus the helmets.

They could try shooting their way out of this quandary. Waldron's men wielded enough firepower to win the battle, however, and she or David or both of them might die or suffer a debilitating injury. She couldn't risk David's life. Besides, she wanted to meet JT. She'd intended to burst into his office—or his bedroom, or whatever—unannounced and fully armed. The universe had other plans.

She tossed her gun onto the floor. The clack as it hit the linoleum reverberated through the corridor.

David jerked his head to glance back at her. "What are you doing?"

Settling a hand on his arm, she exerted a gentle pressure. "Put the gun down. It's pointless."

His face contorted in a mixture of panic and anguish. She wanted to comfort him, but she had no comfort to give. Physically, she felt okay. Her psychic faculties, as David called them, still felt a little fuzzy and weak. David had said he was experiencing a power outage of his own. Forced to rely on everyday means of defeating their foes, they had little chance of succeeding given the current situation.

Seeming to reach the same conclusion, David flung Battaglia's gun toward Waldron. The weapon smacked onto the floor ten feet from the man and skittered across the surface, coming to a stop inches from Waldron's shoes.

"Good dog," Waldron said.

He motioned to the guards and Battaglia. Two of the men with Waldron marched forward to grab David by the arms. One guard brought out a zip tie, a nylon strap thingy equipped with a ratcheting mechanism that both secured and tightened the tie. The guard gathered David's hands behind his back and strapped the zip tie around his wrists, ratcheting it until he couldn't separate his hands.

From the other direction, Battaglia strode up to Grace. He picked up her gun, tucking it inside his waistband, and took both her wrists in one of his huge, muscular hands. At least he'd immobilized her hands in front of her, not behind her back. With his free hand, he reached into his pocket to extract a zip tie. He wrapped the nylon strip around her wrists, cinching it tight. She winced as the tie dug into her flesh.

"Too tight?" Battaglia said in a tone of mock concern.

He slipped a finger under the zip tie and yanked hard, spinning her around to face the others.

She stumbled two steps forward until she managed to re-balance herself.

Waldron locked his gaze on her, smirking. "I believe you're late for an appointment with the president of the company."

Giving a flick of his finger, Waldron turned on his heels and started down the corridor. The guards took his cue, herding their prisoners down the corridor behind Waldron.

They were going to see JT. She felt a disorienting combination of relief, anxiety, and numbness. Whatever the outcome of their encounter, she knew one thing for certain.

The nightmare would end tonight.

———

THEIR CAPTORS HERDED THEM THROUGH THE COMPLEX, INTO AN EL-evator that barely held the entire group, out into another network of corridors, and finally to a door at the end of the hallway. An engraved sign posted beside the door announced, "Jackson Tennant, CEO."

A shiver swept up her spine, prickling every hair on her body. Was it fear or anticipation? A lot of both, she decided. JT was inside that door. Before he tortured and killed her, she wanted some answers from the creep. Since he seemed to need something from her, that would give her leverage. She hoped.

Waldron approached the door. He slid a card through a reader attached to the doorframe, and when the mechanism beeped its approval, he punched a series of numbers into the keypad mounted above the card reader. The door lock chunked. He twisted the knob, pushing the door inward.

Grace looked at David. His expression was unreadable. Back to stoic man, which she supposed was a good thing in these circumstances. She felt nothing close to stoic, though she prayed her demeanor gave away no hints to her inner turmoil.

Waldron entered the room first. David's guards urged him through the doorway next, followed by a couple more guards for good measure. Battaglia hauled Grace across the threshold after them.

The windowless room was smaller than she'd expected, maybe two hundred square feet. A good size office, for sure, but not megalomaniac big. A wood desk the size of a small boat hunkered near the far wall, its surface gleaming. A floor lamp in one corner bathed the room in golden light while a huge, overstuffed leather chair squatted behind the desk. In that chair sat a man not much older than Grace. She recognized him without introductions.

Jackson Tennant reclined in the chair with one arm draped on each arm of the chair. His head rested lazily against the chair's back as he gazed at her with half-closed eyes. The image of him from the *Time* magazine article flashed through her mind. His dark brown hair was a little shaggier these days, and he wore a tan polo shirt with gray slacks rather than the jeans and T-shirt he'd donned for the magazine spread. He looked thinner too, verging on emaciated. The surfer-dude tan he'd shown off for the press had long since faded into a pallor that lent him a ghostly aura.

"Gracie," the man said, drawing out her name as if he were savoring a piece of chocolate.

The sound of his voice triggered another shiver. Steadying herself, she looked straight into his eyes. "Hello, Jackie."

His eyes flew open. He clenched his hands into fists. "My name is JT. Only my parents called me Jackie, and they're dead now."

Something about the tone of his voice when he'd told her his parents were dead made her wonder if he'd played a role in their demises. Coming from this man, no amount of cruelty would surprise her. At least now she knew one button to push to get him royally ticked off, though she still hadn't a clue how she might use that information.

JT twisted his expression into a peevish look as he surveyed the mini army of guards congregating in his office. Glancing at Waldron, he waved a hand in a negligent gesture.

"Get them out of here, Waldo," JT said. "You and Batman can stay, but make these other goons disappear already. I want some privacy."

Grace felt her eyebrows scrunch, an unconscious manifestation of her puzzlement. Waldo? Batman? Okay, she assumed Waldo meant Waldron since JT was pouting in the direction of the older man. But who was Batman?

"The prisoners are dangerous," Waldron said. "We need the extra guards."

JT snorted out a laugh. "They ain't going anywhere, man. They're tied up and locked inside a totally secure facility. They're way helpless."

A muscle ticked in Waldron's jaw. He remained silent for several seconds while JT eyed him with casual disdain. The younger man twirled a silver pen in the air with two fingers.

Waldron blinked first.

Hissing out a breath, he whirled to face his men. He issued quiet but stern orders to the guards, who filed out the door one by one. They shut the door behind themselves, leaving only Waldron and Battaglia inside the room.

Batman. Battaglia. Oh brother, the lunatic with psychic powers liked to make up nicknames for everybody. What was he, twelve years old?

Yeah, a twelve-year-old with the keys to a nuclear missile silo.

Still twirling the pen, JT fixed his gaze on her.

She squared her shoulders. "Did you kill my parents?"

He laughed.

It wasn't the throaty laugh of a masculine CEO. It was the whispery snickering of a little boy who thought he'd squirreled away all the good candy without anybody realizing it.

Her entire body tensed. She resisted the urge to hurl herself across the desk and throttle the murderous twit. He thought what happened to her family was funny.

"What did you do?" she demanded.

He gave a careless shrug. "They lied to me. So I punished them."

In a voice almost too soft to hear, David said, "Easy."

At the sound of his voice, the knot inside her loosened a smidgen. She kept her gaze locked on JT, but she took a slow, calming breath. The creep wanted to make her squirm and thrash and claw at his eyes like a wild animal. She would not give him the satisfaction.

JT crossed his right leg over the left, tapping his right foot in the air.

Grace willed her body to relax. If he wanted her tense and angry, he'd be disappointed.

He sighed, shaking his head. "David thought he pulled one over on me, telling Chris-Chris and Mikey to steal Waldo's car. Everybody knows Waldo had it put in his contract that we would not under any circumstances plant tracking devices in his car or on his person." JT snickered. "On his person. I love that. It's so anal."

Grace kept her face impassive. The twerp would get no response from her.

JT waited for only a heartbeat before continuing. "When I got back from the wild goose chase your mommy sent me on, I had Batman here review the surveillance tapes from the parking level. Then I activated the secret tracking device in Waldo's car and—ta-da!—I had them."

The childish glee in his voice grated on her nerves. The anger boiled inside her, contained but not extinguished. No amount of meditation would quell the fury. She could hope for nothing more than to disguise her feelings.

JT's voice took on a mock-wistful tone. "It was so thoughtful of them to drive way out into the woods on a deserted road. Not a car in sight for miles. Not that it would've mattered if somebody had seen the crash, 'cause I made it look super authentic. Mikey lost control, nobody'll ever know why, and the car flipped. Over and over and over..." He smirked at her. "They were dead and rotting before anybody even knew they'd crashed."

The room whirled around her, like one of those tilting, spinning rides at a carnival. Snippets of memory rushed past her mind's eye. The car. The road. The deer. She fought back a tide of nausea as her knees buckled. The ringing in her ears drowned out JT's laughter. She collapsed to her hands and knees.

The memory hit her so hard she gasped.

And then the present vanished, and the past engulfed her.

The car. Her parents in the front, talking, their faces pinched with anxiety. She was in the backseat again, perched on the seat's edge, as if a wormhole had sucked her into its time-warping depths, depositing her in the past. Her past. Yet she could do nothing to change what she knew was coming. Her thoughts—the thoughts of the old her, the one who'd lived through this the first time—echoed in her mind.

How did I get here? Oh lord, I did it again.

She'd traveled somewhere, without meaning to, without even knowing how she'd done it. A sense of impending danger had come over her and, *wham*, she knew her parents were in trouble. Knew it was her fault. Waldron must've found out about her and gone after her parents to get to her.

Gotta do something. Gotta warn them.

She tried to pound her fists on the glass, but they passed right through it. Dammit, she had to manifest right now. Even in the best conditions, while safely contained in a laboratory with medical types keeping watch over her, traveling and manifesting took great concentration and energy. At this moment, with her heart pounding and adrenaline coursing through her body, she had no hope of accessing her higher-level powers. She'd only begun to understand what she could do when her parents had made her run off to Texas.

David. She needed him. But she couldn't concentrate enough to even locate him, much less connect with him.

A breeze wafted through the car.

Her skin tingled. Someone else is here.

A deer galloped out into the road. It halted on the centerline, eyes wide as it stared at the oncoming car.

Her father slammed on the brakes. Her mother cried out in surprise as the tires squealed.

The deer bolted into the trees alongside the road.

Dad let out a heavy sigh and accelerated the car.

Her parents thought the danger was past. She knew it wasn't.

The breeze inside the vehicle tickled Grace's cheeks. Strange that she could feel it when she had no physical body, only the ghostlike one she'd created, the one that was an illusion only she could see.

The other traveler chose not to reveal his or her presence. The draft flowing through the sealed car, rustling her mother's hair, offered the sole evidence of another consciousness in the vicinity. She knew what the breeze meant. She sensed the other traveler nearby, like a storm cloud crouching at the horizon, about to unleash lightning and hail and torrential rains.

And she could do nothing to stop it.

Dammit, she must do something. If she couldn't manifest, then at least she could let her parents see her.

Deep breaths. In and out. She focused all her energy on one thought.

See me.

Christine Powell turned her head and gasped. "Grace?"

Their gazes met. Her mother saw her. That meant she could hear Grace too.

"Mom," she said, "there's someone else—"

A force hit her with the kinetic energy of a meteorite. The door behind her flew open an instant before she sailed backward out of the car. Falling, her body was falling through the air. She smacked into the ground on her back, landing with a thud that hurt as much as if she'd had a physical body. For a moment she couldn't breathe or move. The thunderous flow of blood through her veins obliterated all other sounds. A psychically imagined body could feel as real as a flesh-and-blood one.

Pow!

The sickening crunch snapped her out of her stupor, and she scrambled to her knees on the asphalt.

A hundred feet down the road, the car slalomed off the pavement into the ditch. It flipped into the air, hit the ground upside down, and rolled over and over, spinning toward the line of trees.

Grace screamed.

The car slammed into the trees on its side, then toppled over upside down. The crunch-bang echoed through the still morning air. The silence that followed rang in her ears.

She staggered down the road, then broke into a full run. She should've been crying, should've been shaking, but all she felt was cold and numb. Thirty feet from the vehicle, she froze. Bile rose in her throat as she gaped at the bent, broken thing that had once been a car.

A gust of wind blustered over her.

It was him. She knew. Though he hid his identity, she recognized what he was. A sick man with too much power. He must be stopped.

She pulled all the energy she could muster from the crossroads and hurled it at him. The energy spun around him like an invisible spider web. Though he struggled against her, she used the energy to force him to appear.

He was a shadow figure. Dark, swirling, not quite human. His face was obscured.

In a raspy voice, he said, "You are mine."

The energy disintegrated, and the world went black.

Chapter Twenty-Six

ON HER HANDS AND KNEES, SHAKING ALL OVER, GRACE FOUGHT TO catch her breath. She remembered waking up in her house on that day, lying on the kitchen floor, with no memory of what had happened—no memory of the previous eight months. The amnesia had set in on that day seven months ago. Ever since then, she'd been oblivious of the truth about her family, herself, and the dangers that lurked just out of sight.

She had dreamed about the accident, but the dream had misled her. Faced with gaps in the story, her mind replaced what she couldn't recall with whatever seemed appropriate, but appropriate wasn't always correct. What she'd experienced a moment earlier had been a genuine memory, as real and vivid and accurate as the event itself. She knew it was right. She felt the truth of it.

The shaking had subsided. She pushed up onto her knees and finally rose to her feet to glare at JT. "You killed them. I was there, I saw it."

He rolled his eyes.

Since he'd already admitted, obliquely, to killing her parents, she hadn't expected much of a reaction. He felt no remorse. To him, their deaths were an inconvenience at worst.

"What do you want from me?" she asked.

He glanced down at his desktop, then back up at her.

She took a few steps closer to the desk.

Waldron shifted as if he were considering stopping her, but JT gave a single shake of his head that halted Waldron where he stood.

Grace bent forward to examine the desktop. A laptop computer occupied one corner, but another object had caught JT's attention. A calendar covered a rectangular section of the desktop, directly in front of JT, and atop that calendar sat an adhesive bandage stained with a dark-red substance.

Blood.

A sick feeling roiled in her belly. She recognized that bloodstained bandage. Sure, those things all looked the same, and blood tended to look the same too. Nevertheless, she felt certain the bandage lying on JT's desk belonged to her. The bloodstain had come from her. The dream she'd had days ago, the one where she got cut and woke up with a wound on her hand that vanished later. She'd saved the bloody bandage, feeling she might need or want proof that the dream had been, in some sense, real.

"You stole that from my house," she said.

"Actually," JT said, looking almost proud of himself, "Waldo got it for me. He didn't see its value, but I knew."

Straightening, she gulped down the lump that had formed in her throat. "You knew what?"

He smiled at her, and a chill spread through her veins. Planting his elbows on the desktop, he steepled his fingers to rest his chin on them. "I needed a link to you. A connection to help me find you since your folks did such a bang-up job of hiding you from me. It was so rude, ya know?"

"What do you mean a link?"

"Blood is the essence of life. We can't live without it." Glancing down at the bandage, he sighed. "Your blood linked me to you."

"How?"

He picked up the bandage, lifted it to his mouth, and licked the bloodstain.

Waldron made a disgusted noise.

Grace managed to restrain her revulsion.

JT dropped the bandage. "That's how."

She said nothing, did nothing, keeping her eyes focused on him. If he wanted a knee-jerk response, he'd have to try harder. Licking her dried blood was gross, but not enough to break her composure. The little creep seemed to relish goading people into lashing out at him—or maybe it was only her he enjoyed goading. Either way, she would not give him what he wanted. Ever.

"This amount of blood," JT said, "helped me find you, but it didn't have enough oomph to give me a real, blood-and-guts connection to you. I want more. I need more. And you will give it to me."

"I don't think so."

He chuckled. "You have no choice, Gracie. I want your power. I will have it."

She wanted to shuffle backward, get away from him, huddle next to David, anything except stand here face to face with the craziest loon she'd ever met. Her hands trembled a little. She clasped them to hide the tremors. And she did not move. Did not break eye contact. An instinct warned her that doing either would escalate the situation.

Pulling out a desk drawer, JT procured from its depths a large rubber band and a needle attached to a blood collection tube. He intended to draw blood from her. And do what with it? She prayed he wouldn't drink it because that would be entirely too disgusting.

He set the needle and rubber band on the desktop. "You see, I need a more intimate transfer of life energy. I need your blood in my veins."

She glanced over her shoulder at David. He looked alternately perplexed and annoyed. Beside him, Waldron grimaced as if sickened by the very thought of what JT proposed. Yeah, it was pretty icky. Not as icky as licking her dried blood, though.

"If our blood types don't match," she said to JT, "you could die from injecting my blood into your veins."

"I've already checked that. We're good to go."

Terrific. She could only hope that he'd checked wrong, and her blood would kill him after all.

Or she could end this farce right now.

But how? Three against two sounded like iffy odds. Well, she had goddamn psychic powers, didn't she? Using them tended to leave her exhausted beyond description and often suffering from a massive headache. If David had recovered enough to use his powers, then the odds would tip in their favor. They might escape before depleting their energy, psychically or physically.

It was the only chance they had.

Now, if she could let David know her plan...

He'd said mind reading was dangerous, and she had no desire to turn into a frothing-at-the-mouth lunatic. Maybe, though, she could transmit an idea to him. No mind reading. Just thought projection. She had manipulated a man into practically giving her a car, but she didn't want to influence David's mind. She simply wanted to let him know what she intended to do and what she wanted him to do in return.

Worth a shot.

She closed her eyes.

"Uh-uh-uh," JT said in a scolding tone. "Use your powers in any way and David gets splattered on the walls. Not the décor I had in mind, but it'll work."

She looked back at David.

Waldron held his gun to David's temple, his finger over the trigger.

Could she act faster than he could pull the trigger? She couldn't risk it. After all, she wasn't exactly an expert at this psychic stuff. *Dammit.*

Maybe she could do something, without JT noticing.

He hunched over his desk, fingering the rubber band. The pallor in his face had deepened, and his lips looked drained of color as well. From this angle, she saw that his cheeks were sunken.

"You look half dead already," she said.

Head bowed, he rolled his eyes up to stare at her. "I'm fine. I'll be fantastic once I have the Golden Power."

"I don't have it. You won't get anything useful from my blood."

He picked up the needle and walked around the desk, halting a couple of yards from her.

Now or never.

Without closing her eyes, she pictured Sean in her mind and stretched out tendrils of energy to search for him. She'd never tried this before, as far as she remembered. The tendrils snaked out in several directions, invisible to everyone but her—if she'd done it right.

JT nodded toward Battaglia. "You better hold her, Batman."

Grace ignored the clomping of Battaglia's boots as he came up beside her. She concentrated on the tendrils of energy, feeling for a hint of Sean's presence.

Battaglia grasped her bound hands and yanked her toward him. His other arm he looped around her shoulders, squeezing her tight against him. She tried not to react, but even distracted as she was by her search for Sean, she couldn't help flinching at Battaglia's embrace. He jerked her hands up, stretching her arms out to expose her inner arms.

JT rolled up her left shirt sleeve. He tied the rubber band around her upper arm.

Sean. There, she felt him. He wasn't far away. David had said neither he nor Sean could manifest, or affect the physical world, without her assistance. Since she felt less than able to offer such help right now, she'd have to go with another plan. Instead of drawing him to her, she sent a message down the tendril that led to Sean and prayed whatever she was doing would work. Hard to feel confident when she didn't understand how her powers worked.

JT found a vein inside her elbow. He lowered the needle toward her skin.

She gathered every particle of energy inside her, compacted it all into a stream of thought, and beamed it straight into the brain of one man.

"Wait," Waldron said.

JT frowned like a child who'd been told not to eat that delicious cake sitting right in front of him.

Waldron cleared his throat and nodded toward David. "I, uh, think I should take this one outside. He's probably thinking about trying something while we're all distracted by your phlebotomy experiment."

Waving the needle at Grace, JT said, "He's our insurance against *her* trying something."

"I'll keep my weapon aimed at his head. But let me take him into the corridor. If she tries anything, I can still shoot him, but he won't be able to see what's happening in here or do anything to help her."

JT's expression turned contemplative for a moment, then he shrugged. "Whatever. Do it your way, Waldo."

Though she couldn't turn to look back at them, what with Battaglia holding her in a snugly threatening embrace, she heard two sets of footfalls move away toward the corridor. The door opened and shut behind Waldron and David. She felt David's absence like the sunlight disappearing behind a cloud.

Sean was almost here. Time to let Waldo go.

Grace released him with a snap of power that surged back into her, melting into a faint sensation of static electricity. Neither JT nor Battaglia seemed to notice it.

She needed more power. Way more power.

David had explained that psychic abilities stemmed from a place, or maybe a state of mind, known as the crossroads. His explanation had left many questions unanswered. Still, if she could reach the crossroads again—as she'd done twice now, once accidentally and once on purpose—she might draw in enough power to do something meaningful.

JT ran a finger over her skin. "Where'd that stupid vein go?"

Keeping her eyes open, hoping she looked scared rather than absent from her mind, she let go of the invisible tether that bound her to the world around her. Her mind soared out of her body, up through a dark tunnel, and shot out into the vast blackness of open space. Star-like pinpoints of light winked into existence. They surrounded yet never touched her. She imagined throwing her arms open wide, welcoming in the power that burned everywhere in the void. It flowed into her, warm and soft and as natural as the blood in her veins. It belonged to her, and she to it. Ribbons of light unfurled from the darkness between the stars to draw variegated lines connecting them.

Networks of power.

One line glowed brighter than the others. When she focused on it, the white strip pulsed green and then blue. At one end, the line broke free of the star anchoring it and writhed across the void, stretching out into nothingness. A new light coursed down the line, turning it a shimmering gold.

The path beckoned her to follow it. She wanted to obey. The need almost overwhelmed her as she sensed the raw and unfathomable power the line promised her.

No. She couldn't go anywhere except back to the facility. Everything that mattered to her in the world depended on it.

The golden line beckoned.

She turned away from it. The loss flooded through her like grief but faded as quickly as it had come. The power she'd gathered from the crossroads burned inside her, a welcome fire to chase away the cold. She sank through the void, falling faster and faster the closer she got to the real world. This time, though, she softened the reentry in a way she couldn't understand but knew how to accomplish. Rather than slamming back into herself, she settled in gently.

"Ah," JT said, tapping her arm along the inside of her elbow. "There it is."

He'd located the vein again. Adjusting his grip on the needle, he prepared to pierce her skin.

"Experiment's over," she said.

He scrunched his lips, squinting up at her. "Not hardly."

Without even tensing a muscle, she flung JT and Battaglia away from her simultaneously. JT crashed into his desk and tumbled backward over it, end over end. Battaglia hit the wall so hard the door rattled in its frame. His eyes bulged, then fluttered shut as his body slid down the wall to crumple on the floor.

With a quick burst of power, she snapped the zip tie that bound her wrists.

A crashing sound erupted outside the door, muffled by the barrier.

That wasn't her. Sean must've arrived at last.

Grace whirled toward the doorway.

"Hang on," a voice croaked from behind her.

She hesitated. A scrabbling noise made her twist around to glance at the desk.

JT clung to it like a castaway with a life preserver. His hair was tousled, his mouth open as he gasped for breaths. The redness of exertion, and perhaps pain, colored his pale cheeks.

Why was she waiting? Not because he'd told her to. No, surely not. An intuition encouraged her to hear him out. She could always hurl him into the wall in a minute or two.

The notion struck her as exceedingly odd, yet true. At least for the moment. The power burning inside her had dimmed a touch, but how much longer she could retain it, she didn't know.

JT levered himself up and onto his feet, dragged his chair closer, and plopped down onto it.

Grace nabbed Battaglia's weapon from the floor near the unconscious guard and yanked her gun out of his waistband. Striding to the desk, she trained her weapon on JT.

He was breathing hard, his face speckled with crimson.

"I need to show you something," he said, pointing at the laptop computer that occupied one corner of the desktop.

She marched around the desk to stand beside his chair, careful to keep her gun aimed at his head, then she nodded toward the computer. "Go ahead."

He dragged the laptop computer across his desk toward him. Flipping up the computer's lid, he tapped keys. A window opened on-screen. It looked like a video feed, though the room it showed was cloaked in shadows. He tapped more keys, and on the other end of the feed, lights powered on inside the room. He was remotely controlling the lights and who knew what else.

"What are you doing?" she demanded, jamming the gun's muzzle into his temple.

He paused in his typing. "Turning on the lights so you can see. Don't worry, Gracie, I can't kill you with my computer." He threw her a sidelong glance. "Which doesn't mean I can't kill you at all."

"Shut up and get on with your show and tell."

He punched keys. The camera panned left and stopped, then zoomed in on a lump on the floor. Though a blanket covered the lump, a rounded shape stuck out from under it.

A human head. The lump was a person.

Grace swallowed. Her jaw tightened.

"Watch this," JT said, pointing at the screen.

Above the blanket-covered human lump, a newspaper was taped to the wall. JT zoomed in on the paper until she could read the date printed below the masthead. Today's date.

JT zoomed out again. "I have the guards change the newspaper every day. I knew this time would come, and you wouldn't believe it without proof."

"Believe what?"

He waved his finger at the screen. "About time the old fart woke up."

On the screen, the person swaddled in the blanket stirred, shoved the blanket off, and clambered into a sitting position. The man scratched his bald head and yawned, deepening the wrinkles on his face.

Oh God. It was her grandfather.

"This is a trick," she hissed. "My grandfather died in a plane crash."

JT smirked, no longer breathing hard. "I made it look that way. But I needed to know what he knew, so I held onto Edward. No matter how much I hurt him, though, he wouldn't tell me anything. It was sooo annoying."

She couldn't speak. If her grandfather was alive...

"Oh no," JT said, studying her expression, "I'm afraid your folks are dead, dead, dead. I lost my head when Chris-cross lied to me. She shouldn't have done that." He leaned back in the chair, folding his hands over his abdomen. "When I found out Edward was lying to me, that he wasn't in Washington lobbying for grants for the project but was plotting with a senator to shut me down... Well, I reined in my anger and came up with a better plan for him."

She thrust the gun in JT's face. "Where is he?"

The scumbag smiled at her. He *smiled*.

"Where?" she demanded.

"I'm not telling." His lips worked, and his body trembled as if he were trying not to giggle. "Until you give me what I want."

"My blood."

"Mm-hm."

She bumped the gun's muzzle into his forehead. "No way."

"Can't kill me, Gracie. Not if you want to find Gramps."

She glared at him, anger boiling inside her. Killing him sounded like a great idea. Though she was no murderer, and she had never wanted to kill anyone before, right now she needed to pull the trigger more than she needed to breathe.

But she couldn't. Not yet.

JT propped his left ankle atop his right knee. "I can tell from your cute little frustrated expression that you're finally catching on. You have no choice."

He emphasized the last two words as if she needed a reminder.

"You can't find him without me," JT said.

Acid churned in her stomach, and she felt a surge of queasy desperation. Until a realization flooded through her, as cold and stunning as a bucket of ice water dumped on her head. He was wrong. She didn't need him to tell her where to find her grandfather. She could do it alone—psychically.

David had said a traveler needed a connection to the other person in order to track them. Everything he'd done, everything she'd felt from and for him, told her that she already had the best connection of all.

Love.

It linked her to David, and her grandfather. She could find Edward McLean without any help from anyone, especially not Jackson Tennant.

She took a step back, snaked her left arm under her right to reach the desktop, and slammed the computer's lid shut.

The look of self-satisfaction on JT's face crumbled. His eyes widened as his mouth dropped open just enough to prove he understood that his advantage had snuffed out in the space of one second. He knew she'd figured out she didn't need him, though he still needed her. Almost in slow motion, his expression morphed through childish irritation into seething anger. Lips squeezed into a pout, he huffed out a breath through his nose.

"It won't work," he said, sounding less than convinced himself. "You're not strong enough to find him with your powers. Amnesia makes you weak. You don't remember how to do that stuff, which means you totally suck at it."

His tone had shifted into childish territory again, lending him the air of a little boy holding his breath until he got his way. He wouldn't get his way this time.

She stood there looking at him, her gun pointed at his head. A moment ago, she'd wanted to kill him. Now, she didn't know. Maybe she ought to kill him because he sure as hell wouldn't give up stalking and tormenting her until he got his way. But shooting an unarmed man, that made her gut twist.

The door burst open.

Grace didn't jump. Didn't even flinch. Somehow, in the back of her mind, she'd known the door would be thrust inward, and she'd known who would walk through the opening.

David stomped across the office to the desk. He paused for only a split second to glance at the unconscious guard slumped against the wall. Battaglia showed no signs of rousing anytime soon. Sean hovered outside the doorway in the corridor, clutching a handgun, while Waldron lay sprawled on the floor at Sean's feet in the direct path of the weapon's muzzle.

Her guys had disabled Waldron and commandeered the man's gun. Sean must've received her message after all. She hadn't been sure that had worked until right now.

Across the desk from her, David glowered at JT. Wow, he looked as ready to kill the murderous twit as she had felt moments earlier.

She tossed Battaglia's gun to him.

David caught it in one hand.

"Keep an eye on him," she said, nodding toward JT. "While I plan our road trip."

He arched his eyebrows but leveled the big gun at JT.

She wondered why the creep hadn't tried to attack her. Given his pallid skin and sunken cheeks, he probably lacked the strength to challenge her physically. Crazy though he was, he must've known his current limitations. That was why he had Waldron and Battaglia, his devoted minions.

Well, maybe not that devoted. She got the feeling Waldron disliked JT with an intensity that bordered on the murderous. Battaglia seemed to care mostly about his wants, which all seemed to revolve around violence.

A sickly mastermind. Minions with shaky allegiances. Perhaps the situation wasn't as hopeless as she'd thought.

An alarm buzzed.

The sound echoed down the corridor. Red lights along the floorboards began to pulse outside the office door. Inside the room, everything stayed the same. A recorded voice issued from speakers hidden somewhere in the room and the corridor.

"Emergency," the female voice declared. "All personnel should make their way to an approved evacuation route in a calm and orderly fashion. Emergency—"

The message repeated, then fell silent as the alarm continued to buzz in rhythm with the pulsing red lights.

JT chuckled. "Guess you didn't know about the cameras. They're everywhere. Plus, Waldo would've called for backup."

Eyes and ears everywhere, Sean had told her. And she'd completely forgotten. Why hadn't he reminded her?

She glanced at the kid in the hallway, holding a gun on the much-bigger Waldron. Sean glanced up at her as if he'd sensed her attention on him. His cheeks flushed, and he shrugged one shoulder.

No, she couldn't be mad at him. He'd done what she'd asked, without question or hesitation. If she remembered knowing him before, maybe she'd understand why he trusted her that much. Sean was too polite to toss her an I-told-you-so.

Not that any of them could've done much about the security cameras.

Grace squinted at JT. "What's with the emergency declaration? Are you that afraid of me?"

"Not hardly. I don't need help anymore, but I don't want any witnesses either."

She almost asked witnesses to what, but then decided the answer would only unnerve her. And she needed all the nerve she had.

"Give up," JT said, spreading his hands wide. "You can't win."

She marched around the desk, heading straight for Sean. The boy looked up in surprise. She reached out to pat his arm.

"You warned me," she said, "and I screwed up. I need your help again."

Sean bit his lip. "Okay."

"You know this facility inside and out, right?" When Sean gave a weak nod, she whispered, "Good, I need your expertise right now. Want to help me save the world?"

The boy's eyes bulged. He blinked and glanced down the corridor. As his eyes returned to normal, his face took on an expression she'd never seen on him before—at least so far as she recalled. He looked not quite smug, but full of mischievous confidence.

"Sure," he said.

Grace tapped her gun against her thigh. She had an idea. And she was positive David would hate it.

Oh well. He'd get over it.

Stepping over Waldron, she sidled up close to Sean and ducked her head to whisper to him. "I need you to tell me how to do something."

———

DAVID REFUSED TO GLANCE BACK AT THE DOORWAY. HE WANTED TO see what Grace was doing, wanted to hear what she and Sean were talking about, but he knew if he averted his attention from JT for one second, the bastard would take advantage of the lapse.

From somewhere out of sight, down an adjoining corridor, boots pounded out a cacophonous beat. Soon a battalion of guards would arrive.

Whatever Grace was up to, it couldn't be good.

Boots thudded closer.

JT leaned his head back against the chair, eyes half-closed. He looked far too comfortable with his situation.

Turning sideways to the desk, keeping the gun aimed at JT, David called out to Grace, "Get in here, both of you."

Grace pointed at Waldron. "What about him?"

"Forget Waldron. Get in here and shut the door. Lock it manually if you can."

At Grace's urging, Sean hustled into the office first. Grace followed close behind him and closed the solid metal door. She found the lock, engaging it with a faint click.

"What now?" she asked, walking up beside David.

"Not sure yet."

Though her expression betrayed nothing, he sensed her unease. Not with his powers. He felt it in the way two people who knew each other intimately, in the emotional sense, could discern the other person's feelings. Unease was warranted. Once the guards arrived, they'd find a way through the locked door. Ram it down. Blast a hole through it. Anything.

JT lounged in his big leather executive chair, hands dangling off the chair's arms, a relaxed half-smile curving his pale lips. Despite his deathly complexion, he seemed at ease and confident. He believed they had no way out of the office and that his lackeys would rescue him in short order.

David ground his teeth. He'd had enough of JT.

Grace settled a hand on his arm. "It's not worth it."

He strode around the desk to JT. "Yes, actually, I think it is."

David smacked the gun into JT's head.

The bastard grunted. As his eyes drifted shut, he slumped in the chair.

"Feel better?" Grace asked.

"Somewhat." He crossed in front of the desk again. To Sean, he said, "Do you know another way out of this room?"

The boy nodded. He pointed a finger toward the left rear corner of the office. "Hidden door over there. I've seen him use it when he doesn't want anybody to know what he's doing. There aren't any cameras in here. He sneaks out to a secret control room where he can spy on everybody in the facility."

Grace made a disgusted noise. "Of course he does."

Sean led David toward the secret door, which was well concealed given the fact that David saw nothing but blank wall in that spot. Peripherally, he noticed Grace was grabbing the bloodstained bandage from JT's desk before she hurried toward him. Knowing Grace, she couldn't stand the idea of the lunatic licking her blood off the bandage. When she got home, she'd probably burn the damn thing. Hell, he'd light the fire for her.

Stuffing the bandage in her pocket, she halted beside Sean.

David stood on Sean's opposite side. Close up like this, he noticed a slender crack in the wall that was practically invisible unless a person knew to look for it.

"Hang on," Sean said. "Forgot about the code."

Before David could ask what code, Sean darted over to the desk. He flipped open the laptop computer. Fingers hovering over the keyboard, he scrutinized the screen. His expression went blank.

"The video feed," Grace said in a voice so quiet he strained to make out the words. What video feed, he wanted to ask, but the question could wait.

The doorknob rattled. Voices murmured on the other side of the door.

David glanced at the door. "The code, Sean, hurry."

The boy kept staring at the screen.

A fist, or a similar blunt object, banged on the door. A hard male voice said, "Sir, are you in there?"

Bang. Another fist thump.

Sean blinked several times in quick succession. He switched his focus to the keyboard as he punched keys for letters and numbers.

JT had clearly taken no precautions against travelers spying on him in his own office. Overconfident as he appeared to be, he'd likely assumed he had all the travelers under control, drugged into near-comatose states or so beaten down by the experiments that they lacked the energy for extrasensory spying.

Mostly, JT was right. David clenched his hands into fists. Even he and Sean had trouble pushing through the drug-induced stupor.

Sean tapped one final key.

Inside the wall, a mechanism thunked. A door-size panel separated from the wall with a faint hiss, opening away from them on silent hinges. Lights came on automatically to dispel the blackness beyond the portal. The doorway revealed a passage that extended for maybe thirty feet, then made a ninety-degree turn to the left.

David motioned for Sean and Grace to enter the passage. They crossed the threshold single file, Sean leading the way.

Half turning, David looked at the laptop computer on JT's desk.

"Coming?" Grace asked.

"Yes." David raised the gun and fired three rounds into the laptop. Splinters of plastic and metal spewed from the computer. "I'm coming now."

He walked through the doorway toward Grace.

A swishing sound drew his attention back to the threshold.

The door shut with a dull thunk.

David hoped destroying the laptop would at least slow down JT's efforts to track them. He had a hunch the jackass kept the program that controlled the secret door on his computer and no other. David had bought the three of them time, though how much, he couldn't say.

"Where are we going?" he asked Grace.

"JT's private control room."

"To do what?"

She looked straight into his eyes and said, in a matter-of-fact tone, "To destroy the facility."

CHAPTER TWENTY-SEVEN

ARE YOU INSANE?" DAVID SEIZED HER ARM, DRAGGING HER TO A STOP. HE gaped at her, his eyes wide and locked on hers. "Say that again, in case I was having a stroke and didn't hear you correctly."

"You heard me," she said. "I'm going to destroy this facility."

He squeezed words out between his gritted teeth. "I repeat, are you insane?"

"Possibly."

"Destroy it," Sean said in a quiet, almost reverent tone. "Get rid of all their research, so maybe nobody can do to anyone else what they did to us."

"Exactly," Grace agreed.

She'd considered the possibility that a computer whiz like Jackson Tennant might've backed up the data off-site, but then she realized if he'd done that he wouldn't need the flash drive her grandfather had left for her. Maybe he viewed the research as too explosive to risk letting it outside the facility's computer system, even for backup purposes. JT clearly didn't like to share.

It made no difference either way. She must destroy this place even if it proved to be but one head of the hydra. They could chop off the other heads later, one by one. Destroying this facility was, she felt certain, vital to tearing apart JT's clandestine empire.

"We can't do this," David said. "There are human beings inside this facility."

"They're evacuating," Sean pointed out, "so we won't be hurting anybody."

"We have to be sure everyone's out."

Grace studied David's expression. He looked tired, harried, and vaguely annoyed, but no longer in shock over her plan.

She laid a hand on his cheek and said, "We will be sure."

His skin felt different. She couldn't quite describe how. He felt more... real.

Sean led them through the network of corridors with a confidence she'd never seen in him before. He knew exactly where he was going. And he knew freedom was no longer out of his grasp. She had an idea of what that felt like because, though she hadn't been physically held prisoner, her amnesia had boxed her in like a cage. Now she sensed the bars weakening.

No doors opened off the corridors. The emergency lights cast a pulsating red glow on the blank gray walls. They rounded another corner and there, at the end of a short corridor, stood a metal door that bore no markings and had no knob. A keypad affixed to the wall beside the door restricted access. Sean trotted up to the doorway, hesitating with his hand over the keypad.

Grace and David came up behind him. Just as she started to wonder whether he knew the password, Sean tapped a series of keys on the pad. A blooping sound heralded success, and the door swung inward with a thunk and a hiss.

They walked into a room measuring ten feet wide by ten feet long. A huge flat-screen TV occupied one wall, its screen divided into eight square sections that displayed rotating, full-color views from the security camera feeds. Beneath the TV sat a surprisingly modest metal desk equipped with a new-looking desktop computer, complete with a wide-screen monitor and a wireless mouse and keyboard. A nondescript office chair completed the room's furnishings.

Sean sat down on the office chair and began typing on the keyboard.

"What are you doing?" Grace asked.

"Checking the thermal sensors." His fingers tapped out a fast, irregular rhythm on the keyboard. "If anybody's left in the facility, we'll see them here."

An image appeared on the computer screen—shades of blue, red, green, and yellow.

Beside her, David pointed at the colorful blobs on the screen. "These are heat signatures given off by human bodies. The facility is equipped with infrared sensors that can detect them." David bent to squint at the screen. "Where is this, Sean?"

"JT's office, and the corridor outside it."

"Is there anyone else left inside the facility?"

Sean shook his head. "Just us and the nine people at JT's office."

"Six guards plus JT, Waldron, and Battaglia."

Grace knelt beside Sean, her eyes focused on the screen. "Can you bring up the camera feed from JT's office?"

"Told you, there isn't one." Sean hunched his shoulders. "JT likes his privacy."

"Of course he does." She gnawed the inside of her lip, staring at the colored blobs on the thermal sensor. "What about the cameras in the corridor? If the door to JT's office is open, maybe one of the outside cameras can see inside."

"Maybe," Sean said, as he set about punching keys and tapping the mouse button. The images on the big-screen TV changed. All but three of the feeds disappeared from the screen, and the remainder expanded to fill the space. The feeds offered three slightly different views of the corridor. The closest camera was posted above the door to JT's office, aimed out at the corridor. The next camera pointed toward the office at an angle. The third was at the end of the corridor furthest from the office, aimed straight at the office door. It was too far away to see much, though.

"Can you zoom in?" she asked. "With the camera at the end of the corridor."

Sean fiddled with the mouse, and the feed from the camera furthest from the office expanded to fill the entire TV screen. The guards milled around outside the office, but between their bodies, she spied the interior of the room. Battaglia was out of sight, probably to one side of the doorway. Waldron stood at the desk, his hands on the wooden surface, bent over as if conversing with JT. The man in charge lounged in his executive chair, gesticulating with his hands. Although she couldn't see their faces, their body language hinted at an intense and not entirely cordial discussion.

Waldron threw his hands up and spun away from the desk. He stalked out of the office, past the guards, and out of sight.

JT retrieved something from a desk drawer.

"Can you zoom in more?" she asked Sean.

He tapped a button on the keyboard.

The image pulled in tighter. It had enough resolution to show JT's face with only a little fuzziness. In his hand, he clasped a syringe filled with light-blue liquid.

"What is that?" she asked, not expecting a response.

David, now hunched over the desk, turned his gaze toward her. "It looks like the drug cocktail they used to give some of their test subjects, back when they were trying to find ways to enhance psychic abilities. They stopped using the concoction because it had nasty side effects. Several people died."

Her chest tightened as if a phantom hand clenched her heart. "Did they give you the cocktail?"

"Once." He straightened, stepping away from the desk. "I survived."

She almost made a sarcastic comment about stating the obvious. Something in the tone of his voice stopped her. Later, she might ask him what the drugs had done to him. She might ask a lot of questions about his time in the facility. For now, she posed a different question. "What is JT doing with those drugs?"

"I remember there was some discussion about using the drug cocktail to trigger latent abilities," David said. "The scientists had a theory that everyone has the potential for extrasensory faculties buried deep inside them. They theorized that if the drugs could enhance existing abilities, then maybe a higher dosage could also bring out latent abilities."

"A higher dosage? More than what killed people?"

"Not everyone died. Andrew survived multiple injections. So did Sean."

"Who would be willing to risk that?" She glanced at the TV screen, which showed JT lowering the needle to his arm. A lunatic would risk it, naturally, for the chance to gain untold power. She rose from her crouch and shook her head. "JT's been injecting himself. That's why he can only use his abilities to harass me sometimes, and that must be why he looks like a man who's not just knocking at death's door but standing on the threshold. The drugs are killing him."

"Not fast enough."

The anger in his voice made her look at him. He seemed tense, though not vengeful.

"He's killing himself," she said. "We don't have to do it for him."

David remained silent for a few seconds, then he took in a long breath and, as he let it out, turned to face her. "How do you intend to destroy the facility?"

"The armory." At his puzzled expression, she explained, "It's full of ammunition, which is essentially explosives. I'm going to find a way to set it off."

He pursed his lips and fisted his hands. "Set off an explosion?"

David had almost shouted those words.

She laid a hand on his arm. "Keep it down, will you?"

He managed a calmer voice when he said, "And how do you plan on detonating the ammunition?"

"Not sure yet."

"Well, as long as you have a plan."

Sean had switched back to displaying three camera feeds on the TV screen. The guards were jogging down the corridor away from JT's office.

"They're coming for us," David said. "We have to get out of this facility while we still can."

"I agree," Grace said.

He narrowed his gaze on her. "You're abandoning your plan that easily? I was prepared to argue my case—" His expression went blank for a second, then he closed his mouth and clenched his jaw so tightly he probably could've squeezed charcoal into diamonds between his teeth. "You're not abandoning anything, are you? The plan is to remote view the armory, spot a way to set off an explosion, and manifest to accomplish the task."

Oh, she wished he didn't know her quite so well. Everything would've gone much smoother if he hadn't figured it all out.

"Yes," she said, "that's the plan."

He motioned toward the door. "Let's go. You can do that from outside the facility."

"In a minute." Looking at Sean, she pointed at the big TV screen. "Show me the armory."

The boy complied, tapping keys until another feed replaced the images from the corridor outside JT's office. This feed showed a dimly lit room packed with metal boxes, racks of guns of all sizes, and shelves of Kevlar vests. She willed the image to burn itself into her mind until she felt certain she could recall it later.

Then she let David usher her out of the room. Sean pushed past them to take the lead, guiding them around corner after corner. Minutes passed as they wended their way through the network of passages, but finally, they reached a sturdy door identical to the one Battaglia had led her to after he captured her outside the facility.

Sean entered the code on the keypad, waited a few seconds, and entered a second code. The locking mechanism chunked. The door swung outward several inches.

David shoved the door open all the way. He tiptoed across the threshold into the blackness beyond the threshold. Fluorescent lights flickered on, illuminating a narrow passage carved out of the bedrock.

Grace followed David into the passage, with Sean trailing behind her. The kid paused long enough to shove the door closed again.

"If you knew the way out," she said, "why didn't you escape before now?"

"Couldn't get into JT's office. Anybody who wants in has to swipe their ID card and enter a passcode, but that's just for show. See, what nobody knows is that JT looks through the security camera to see who's there. Then he decides whether to let you in."

It made sense. JT was paranoid, secretive, and possibly the biggest control freak the world had ever seen. And he loved messing with people's heads.

They started down the passageway. It was narrow, so they half walked, half jogged single file through the rough-hewn tunnel. The air grew stuffy and thick. She felt cramped, like she couldn't get enough room or breathe enough oxygen. The sweat evaporating from her skin did nothing to cool her. David and Sean appeared unaffected by the conditions. She watched them pull farther and farther ahead of her, and though she tried to call out to them, her vocal cords emitted no sound. Her head felt heavy, her thoughts fuzzy. This was wrong, all wrong.

Pain stabbed through her head.

She cried out. As the sharp pain dissipated, a crackling sensation erupted inside her brain. She fell to her knees on the floor, clutching her head in her hands, willing the crackling pain to end. It kept going, like an electrical storm in her brain.

The pain vanished.

She sobbed with relief, but something was still off inside her, something that felt dark and alien and intrusive. She dropped her hands to rest them on her thighs. Her mind felt numb and disconnected from her body. Had she traveled without realizing it? Was she physically here? And where was she?

A hard object pressed against her right palm. She looked down at her hand where it rested on her thigh. She was gripping a knife. A shiny, curved blade. Long and wickedly sharp. The wooden handle pressed into her palm.

David ran up to her, dropping to his knees in front of her.

Kill him, do it now, you want to, so go ahead and do it.

She rammed the knife into his gut.

"No!"

The word burst out of her as an anguished howl. She tried to yank the knife out, but it refused to budge. Tears streamed down her cheeks, blurring her vision while she shouted wordless cries of rage and grief.

Hands grasped her shoulders, drawing her into an embrace that felt warm and strong and familiar.

"David?" she asked, though she knew it couldn't be him. *But God, please let it be him.*

"I'm here," he murmured in her ear. "What's wrong? What happened?"

He stroked her hair and rocked her gently in his arms. Her face was tucked against his neck, and the scent of him surrounded her. The feel of his body, so warm and real and alive, broke the spell. It had been a vision, terrifying and vivid, but not real. The thoughts had come from her mind, yet not her mind. Different. Colder. She could feel the other mind, the invader, touching her psyche. Grasping for a handhold. A way to control her. She'd almost given it to him.

"Grace?" David said, his voice tight with worry.

Sniffling, she wiped the tears from her eyes. "It was JT. He got into my head and made me see things. Maybe the physical proximity gave him more power, or maybe he injected himself with even more of that drug cocktail." She lifted her head to meet his gaze. "However he did it, that was much worse than the other times."

So many deaths, all my fault, I could have saved them all. But I didn't want to, I wanted them dead.

No. Those thoughts originated from JT, the creep who wanted her sanity for a keepsake. He'd have to fight for it. He'd have to kill her for it.

She looked down at her hands.

Her nails. Crusted with blood. Red liquid dribbling from her fingertips.

Do it, do it, DO IT!

The voice screamed inside her head, the voice that was not hers. She fought back with everything she had. The presence ripped free of her, like claws tearing flesh. White-hot pain sliced through her body from head to toe. Her stomach heaved, but she choked back the gorge. Coughing, clutching her abdomen, she bent forward.

David grasped her face, one hand on each cheek, and tilted her head up to his. He locked his gaze on hers, his forehead wrinkled, a frown gouging deep lines across his face. Her pulse beat like a bass drum in her head. Though his lips moved, she heard nothing but the drumbeat.

Look at me, he mouthed. Or maybe he'd spoken the words. The drumbeat inside her drowned out everything else. With an effort that almost hurt, she forced her eyes to focus on him.

A gentle warmth washed over her, into her, chasing away the chill left behind by JT's attack. The false images and alien thoughts faded away until they became wisps of memory. The drumbeat silenced as her heart rate normalized. Sweat trickled over her scalp, down her neck.

"I'm okay now," she said.

She felt David relax and watched the lines on his face smooth out as his frown melted into a more neutral expression.

He brushed a lock of hair from her face. "Is he gone?"

"Yeah. I pushed him out."

A ghost of a smile flickered on his face. "I know how that feels."

"I pushed him a little harder than I pushed you. He did *not* want to go."

"I hope he's in so much pain he's curled up in the fetal position under his desk."

The dark thread of anger in his voice was unmistakable. She didn't like hearing it. If David gave in to his anger, JT would win. She could never let that happen.

She slid a hand through his hair, kissed him softly, and whispered, "He can't hurt me again. I won't let him."

He looked less than convinced in the half second before he touched his lips to hers and stood up, lifting her with him. He clasped her hand. "Let's put as much distance between you and that bastard as we can."

Then he led her down the tunnel.

CHAPTER TWENTY-EIGHT

GRACE HURRIED DOWN THE CORRIDOR IN SEAN'S WAKE, PROPELLED onward by David's arm around her waist. Though she felt stronger with each step away from the facility, the aftereffects of JT's attack proved longer lasting than ever before. Evicting JT from her mind had drained her, for sure, yet the attack also left her with a curious side effect. Along with her physical strength, she felt something else building.

Her powers.

She might've thought she'd tapped into the Golden Power, unintentionally, except that she didn't feel omniscient. Far from it. She felt like a dinghy out on the open ocean where land was out of sight. Still, she sensed an unknown source replenishing her psychic energy, boosting her powers. It made no sense. Then again, since when had anything about her extrasensory abilities made sense?

Other questions seemed more pressing. While concentrating on the ground ahead of her, afraid she might trip if she glanced away, she asked David, "Why do things that happen in my mind feel so real? I believed I'd killed you. I could see and feel the blood on my hands." She thought of the bloody bandage, the sole physical evidence of the cut that had once slashed across her palm. "I dreamed once that I cut my hand and, when I woke up, my hand was bleeding. Then later, the cut was gone. It's crazy."

"Whatever happens to your metaphysical body," David said, "also happens to your physical body. It's because of your mind that your body functions. The two can never be fully separated. If your mind thinks your hand is injured, then your hand is injured. It's that simple."

Ahead of them, Sean halted. The tunnel had dead-ended at a door identical to the one that granted access to the escape route. This door, however, had no keypad or card reader. Instead, a large metal lever opened the door.

Sean tried to move the lever, with little success.

David released Grace and strode up to the door to help Sean. Together, the pair heaved the lever up to unlock the exit. The mechanism groaned. Sean and David panted from the effort, their faces contorted, their arm muscles flexing. When the lever finally clicked into its open position, the mechanism let out one final groan of metal on metal. The men adjusted their holds on the lever and pulled on it. The door swung inward inch by inch, its bottom edge scraping across the dirt floor.

They opened the door a couple of feet and, sweat dripping from their faces, gave up the battle. The gap offered just enough space for one person to squeeze through, into whatever lay beyond.

Darkness, she saw as she leaned sideways to peek out the doorway. A breeze wafted through the opening, carrying with it the indefinable yet distinct smell of the outdoors. The dry, chilly air tickled her skin.

David motioned for Sean to step aside. When the boy did, David sidled out the door. He vanished into the darkness outside. The soft crunching of his footfalls provided the sole evidence of his presence.

Seconds later, his footsteps drew nearer again. His silhouette filled the gap between the door and its frame. Light from inside the tunnel revealed his face.

"It's clear," he said, "for now. Let's go."

Sean exited next. Grace shuffled to the door, turned sideways, and slipped through the gap. The night air enveloped her in its chill. Tilting her head back, she saw the clear sky speckled with stars. To her left and right, she found dirt walls and, straight ahead, a steep grade inset with steps cut out of the earth itself. The steps led up to ground level.

David took her hand, helping her up the steps. Sean waited for them at the top, his body visible as a silhouette against the starry sky. Far in the distance, a coyote howled.

"Move," David said, his tone gentler than his word choice.

She let him pull her away from the steps, out across the depression that cradled the facility. A statement he'd made minutes ago bubbled to the surface of her mind, and she had to ask, "Are you sure nothing can separate the mind from the body?"

"One thing can," he said. "Death."

"So whatever happens to your mind happens to your body."

"The mind *is* the body."

"Whatever."

She tripped over a rock.

David caught her, and they resumed their brisk walking pace.

She shook her head. "It's like I went to bed one night and woke up in a parallel universe."

"Same universe. But now your eyes have adjusted, letting you see the things that hide in shadows."

The shadows of what, she almost asked, then decided maybe she didn't want that much clarity. Understanding. Truth. She had demanded them, damn the cost. She'd sacrificed everything for a truth that didn't ease her mind and that nobody else in the world would believe. Despite what she'd lost, she knew with stark certainty that she would, without hesitation or regret, do it all again. Her parents had given their lives willingly to protect her, to protect the world from enemies bent on attaining a kind of power no living thing should possess. If necessary, she would make the same sacrifice, because she hadn't quite given up everything yet. She had one gift left to give.

Her life.

JT had murdered her parents. He had faked her grandfather's death and now held him hostage. She must know why. She must understand.

The cut on her palm had vanished, taking with it the memory of the dream all those days ago. Would everything that had happened lately dissipate into the void of yesterday? Would she someday think of it all as a bad dream?

No. Nothing could erase the memory.

Grace twisted around to look back. There, maybe a quarter mile away, stood the facility. It looked different from the first time she'd spied it in the darkness. Then she realized why. The tunnel had led them out on the opposite side of the facility from where she'd entered.

The plan. In the chaos following JT's attack, she'd forgotten about her plan to destroy the facility. Right now seemed like a good time to implement it.

Grace wrenched her hand free of David's and stopped dead.

He stopped too and glanced back at her, though she couldn't see his face.

She knew what expression he wore even without seeing it. Annoyed. Confused. Worried. She likely wore the same look.

"No," David said.

"Yes." She planted her hands on her hips. "I have to do it."

"Fine. Then I'm going with you."

He wanted to travel with her. The idea shot a spark of excitement through her. Had they traveled together before? What had it felt like to share a psychic experience? She wanted to find out. Sharing such an experience with JT felt like the worst kind of torture. But sharing it with David...

His hand found hers in the darkness. He twined their fingers.

Boom.

The ground shook. As the echoes of the first explosion died away, a second detonation rocked the earth. The booming ricocheted off the walls of the depression. A third explosion went off at the nearest end of the facility.

The ground shook so hard Grace lost her balance, stumbling into David's arms. They held each other up as the tremors subsided and the cacophony faded into a silence that felt unnatural.

David's mouth brushed across her ear. "Did you..."

"No. You?"

"Definitely not."

She peered into the darkness, which she would've sworn had gotten darker, but discerned nothing. A cloud of what she took for dust blocked out part of the sky. As the cloud thinned, flames emerged from where the facility's black shape had squatted.

"Who did it?" she wondered aloud. Then the answer struck her. "JT. It must've been."

"But why?" David asked.

"Because he's a spoiled brat who didn't get his way."

David tightened his hand around hers. Without a word, he turned and broke into a jog, hauling her with him. She had to run to keep up with him.

A sensation rippled through her. Indescribable. Unpleasant.

He's watching.

She froze. David nearly yanked her shoulder out of its socket before realizing she'd stopped. Halting, he half turned to glance back at her. His fingers still grasped hers, though barely.

"We're not alone," she said.

"Damn straight you aren't."

The voice was not David's or Sean's. The words, and the tone of the voice, rattled a shiver down her spine. Off to the left, a shape separated from the darkness. The shape drew closer until it resolved into a human silhouette that halted a dozen feet away. Although she couldn't make out any facial features, she knew who it was.

JT sniggered. "Gotcha."

David launched himself across the distance to JT, tackling the other man.

Except he didn't. He couldn't. David sailed right through JT—not past him, but actually *through* him—landing with a thud and a grunt.

"Oh, sorry," JT said with mock chagrin. "Shoulda warned you. I'm not really here."

Grace couldn't speak or move. She watched as David levered his body up off the ground, hopped to his feet, and turned to face the apparition of JT.

For he was a ghost, essentially. Not the ghost of a dead man. The ghost of a living soul.

"One more thing," JT said, his tone a little too smug. "I may not be here, but my peeps are."

Her vocal cords unfroze just enough to utter two words. "Your what?"

"My peeps. My guys." He waved an arm in an expansive gesture. "They've got you surrounded."

Lights flared on all around them.

Grace flinched and squinted, throwing an arm up to shield her eyes. Her vision adjusted fast enough that she saw the beams emanated from lantern flashlights, of the multi-million-candlepower variety, and the lights were held by black-suited commandos. Six of them. The guards who'd stayed behind when the facility was evacuated.

Shit.

"Let's get down to business," JT said. "Where's my flash drive?"

Chapter Twenty-Nine

GRACE STARED AT THE ILLUSION OF JT, WISHING IT WAS NOTHING BUT a hallucination. She knew better. The mechanics of psychic phenomena still confused her, but she'd learned from firsthand experience that something unreal could exert very real forces and cause genuine damage.

As she tilted one hip to adjust her stance, a hard lump pressed into her belly. Her gun. She'd tucked it inside her waistband during their flight through the tunnel. Even if she managed to pull it out unnoticed, she had little confidence that she could cause enough damage to matter, at least not before several large and heavily armed men tackled her.

"Do you think I'm dumb enough to bring the flash drive here?" she asked.

Although she might not have been the smartest person on the planet, she'd at least had the brains to mail the flash drive to herself at her Texas address. It was relatively safe, for the time being.

"Give me my flash drive," JT said, "or my guys will kill your guys. And they'll start with your boyfriend."

"Maybe you shouldn't have blown up your only other copy of your research."

"What makes you think it was my only other copy?"

"Because if you had another copy, you wouldn't be pestering me about the flash drive."

"Good point." The apparition of JT shrugged. "Might as well tell you. You won't live long enough to tell anyone else." He let out an annoyed sigh. "Edward didn't just make a copy of all the research, he also completely erased it from the facility's computers in the process. And he did such a good job we couldn't recover anything from the servers."

Well, at least one part of the nightmare finally made sense. JT and his minions had gone to deadly lengths to obtain the flash drive because it contained the only copy of the facility's research. She doubted one little flash drive could hold the entirety of that research, but it must contain the crucial bits needed to bring down JT, his cohorts, and possibly his whole empire. She'd had the key to his destruction in her pocket all this time.

One of them needed to travel to wherever JT was hiding and stop this madness at the source. Unfortunately, that plan had two problems. First, David couldn't manifest without her help, and second, her strength had returned but not to the point where she felt capable of manifesting for any meaningful length of time. For those two reasons, she'd ruled out stopping the physical JT. She must stop the astral JT instead. Despite the drugs, he must've lacked the ability to manifest.

JT seemed to have no powers, or only weak powers, without the drugs. That might mean they had a chance. She needed no drugs to access her psychic abilities and yet using them drained her quicker than slashing her wrists. From her past encounters with JT, she suspected his drug-induced powers drained him even faster. On top of that, he was dying. She knew what she had to do, but she wasn't sure how to do it.

Though David had gotten up off the ground after his spill, he lingered behind JT, twenty feet from Grace and Sean. She stared intently at David until he rotated his eyes toward her.

As if he could read her thoughts, David mouthed, "No."

She didn't dare make any response. If JT decided she and David were conspiring against him, she couldn't predict the madman's response.

"Give me the flash drive," JT said. His voice had taken on a petulant tone. "I'll count to ten and if you haven't given it to me by then, your boyfriend dies."

The commandos had spread out to form a circle around them. Because there were only six of them, that meant they stood widely spaced around the three prisoners and the apparition of JT. Two of the commandos held their weapons trained on David. One kept his eye on Sean while a full three commandos had Grace in their sights.

In a different situation, attracting the attention of three brawny men might boost her ego. Right now, it made her entire body tense.

She pulled her attention away from the three big weapons aimed at her and locked her gaze on the apparition of JT. He was, naturally, smirking at her.

"I bet I can find you," she said.

The smirk melted into a pinched expression.

She pointed toward the heavens. "You know, through the crossroads."

His eyes widened for an instant, but then the pinched look evaporated. "You wouldn't. Not with sweet David's life on the line."

He made the word sweet sound like a hideous insult. To him, it probably was.

She closed her eyes and let her mind float up, hovering a dozen feet above her body. As she gazed down at her physical form, a feeling coursed through her, one she could only describe as a psychic shiver.

JT glared at her physical self as he clenched his hands into fists. "Come back or he dies. You have five seconds. Four, three..."

She hurled out a blast of energy that manifested as a hurricane-force wind. The gust spiraled out from her position, flipping the commandos off their feet one by one and flinging them backward through the air. By the time the spiraling gust hit David and Sean, they were flat on the ground, facedown in the sand. The commandos were slower to react—too slow. They sailed a good fifty feet and hit the ground hard enough to knock the sense out of them if not render them unconscious. After circling their prey, the commandos had set down their lantern flashlights. Now, those lights sat on the ground unattended, forming a triangle around the three former prisoners and the madman who wasn't there.

The apparition of JT roared with animalistic rage. "Waldron! Battaglia!"

A hundred feet away, just over the lip of the depression, a monster snarled.

No, not a monster. It was the mechanical snarling of a vehicle engine as it revved to scale an incline. A pair of headlights popped into view as the vehicle, still invisible in the darkness, hurtled over the summit and down the slope toward them.

She had her gun, but she couldn't shoot JT's apparition, and shooting the approaching vehicle would do no good. She'd still have the men inside it to deal with.

Grace sank back into her body, opened her eyes, and shouted, "David, help me!"

As he sprang to his feet, David glanced at the vehicle and then at her.

She nodded.

Though his body hadn't moved, she felt him near her. His presence surrounded her, and she opened herself up to him in a way she couldn't have imagined until last night. She let him into her mind. Their combined powers surged through her, warm and sweet and crackling with energy. In unison, they switched their gazes to the onrushing vehicle.

The black SUV flipped into the air. It smacked into the ground upside down with a crunching thud. The windshield turned opaque as the safety glass cracked.

David's knees buckled, but he didn't collapse. He hung there like a marionette, arms and legs limp as if an unseen force clutched his neck. His face reddened as he struggled to breathe.

Ten feet away from David, the apparition of JT held up one arm with his fingers curled in a strangulation gesture. JT shook his hand, and David jerked in response.

Grace resisted the urge to lunge forward to help David, because if she moved, her muscles might give out completely. Ice-cold exhaustion flooded through her. The ground looked so inviting that it took all her strength to stay upright rather than dropping to the sand, curling up in a ball, and letting herself fall into the abyss of sleep.

JT shook David again.

The choked sound that grunted out of David yanked her out of her stupor. She sucked in a couple of deep breaths, swallowing enough oxygen to rouse her brain and body.

"The flash drive," JT said. "Or I snap his neck."

"It's not here, but I can tell you where to find it."

"Nice try." JT squeezed his astral hand, and David gurgled from the increased pressure. "Like mother, like daughter. I'm not falling for that one again."

Pounding noises erupted from the upside-down SUV.

Grace darted her eyes toward the vehicle. Someone had kicked out the gummy, crackled sheet that had once been the windshield. A pair of legs hung out the opening.

Waldron slid out onto the sand. He looked disheveled, his face streaked with what might've been blood, but he also looked enraged.

Grace focused on JT again. "Don't you want my power? Isn't that what you came for?"

A wild look swept over his features. His grip on David loosened a little. She could tell because David's chest rose and fell as he drew in as much air as he could.

"You think you're stronger than me, right?" She spread her palms in an invitation. "So come and get it. Come and take my power."

Without letting go of David, JT turned the remainder of his psychic energy on her. She experienced it like a rip current dragging her mind down and down into a swirling emptiness. Gathering every iota of energy she had left, she clawed her way out of the invisible vortex. It hurt like hell. She gritted her teeth, clenched her hands, and gasped from the effort. Still, she held on. Couldn't say how. Didn't know if she could keep it up for long.

David crumpled to the ground. Panting and wheezing, he pushed up onto all fours.

JT had lost his grip.

The sucking sensation lessened, and she pulled her mind free of it.

The JT apparition bellowed.

She squinted at him. He looked less solid now, though not quite transparent.

Over at the SUV, Battaglia had crawled out of the space where the windshield had been. He straightened and tried to walk but staggered a few steps instead. His face was not merely streaked with blood but coated with it. As he stumbled away from the vehicle, falling to his knees in the sand, another figure rolled through the punched-out windshield.

It was JT. The real one.

The lantern flashlights cast a pallid glow on everyone, but JT looked so pale he could've doubled for Casper the ghost. He crawled away from the vehicle, and Waldron had to help him stand because Battaglia was having mobility problems of his own. Saddled with propping up his boss, Waldron could do little more than glare at Grace. JT was muttering to Waldron, and based on the look on the other man's face, she guessed JT was issuing orders that the bigger, stronger man did not want to follow. The duo trudged away from the SUV toward Grace, David, and Sean. The boy still lay on the ground, covering his head with his hands.

The JT apparition stood motionless and dead.

His physical body went slack in Waldron's arms, forcing the other man to support the dead weight by hugging JT to him as he continued slogging through the sand.

The JT apparition came to life and fixed a hateful scowl on Grace. Both of his faces, the real and the projected, shared the same deathly pallor.

"Why haven't you taken my power?" she asked with a scornful tone. "That's right, you're about as strong as a Chihuahua that thinks it's a Great Dane."

He struck out at her psychically. She felt the hit like a blow to the gut, though not as strong a blow as she'd expected. Wincing, she shook her head.

"Is that all you got?" she asked. "You're nothing but a weak little twerp with delusions of omnipotence."

He lashed out again, in a different way, falling back on the same trick he'd used in the tunnel. She saw herself pulling the gun out of her waistband, raising it in front of her to take aim at David, and finally pulling the trigger. Unlike the first time JT had tried this trick, the effect was like a ghost image rather than a vivid hallucination. While she watched the semi-transparent vision of her hand perform the actions, she also saw her solid and real hand remain at her side. Meanwhile, JT completely lost his grip on David, who sat back on his heels gasping. JT was getting weaker.

Waldron seemed to recognize what was happening. He halted, and his entire demeanor changed from annoyed and strained to something darker and far more determined. He let go of JT's limp, vacant body. JT crumpled to the ground.

Reaching inside his jacket, Waldron brought out his gun. He swung it up toward Grace.

David launched himself across the space between him and Waldron, at first running, then flinging his body through the air to tackle the other man. Limbs flailed, and grunts echoed.

Grace yanked the gun out of her waistband and took two steps toward the battling men.

Something smacked her in the chest with the force of a boot kick. It felt real, and it sent her staggering backward a few steps. Yet she knew the force that had struck her was psychic, not physical. JT's last gasp, in telekinetic terms. She kicked back at him with a force exponentially greater than what he'd lobbed at her, and his apparition shattered and vanished.

His limp body, no longer vacant, stirred.

She had bigger problems.

Waldron had flipped David onto his stomach. Jamming one knee into David's spine, pinning him to the sand, Waldron settled the muzzle of his gun on the back of David's skull.

Grace curled her finger around the trigger of her gun as she targeted Waldron's back.

Arms clamped around her from behind, pinning hers to her body and squeezing so hard she couldn't breathe. The gun tumbled from her grasp. The arms that restrained her lifted until only her tiptoes touched the ground. She gasped for air, flailing her legs at her assailant, but her ears began to ring and darkness began to close in around her.

"Quit fighting," Battaglia snarled into her ear, "and I'll let you breathe."

She couldn't match his strength, anyway. So she stopped fighting.

He loosened his grip enough to let her breathe. The ringing quieted, and the darkness receded, giving her a clear view of David and Waldron.

"Now," Battaglia said, "you get to watch your boyfriend die."

CHAPTER THIRTY

GRACE LOOKED AROUND, SEARCHING FOR THE OTHER COMMAN-dos. While some of them lay prone and unmoving where they'd land-ed, others had begun to stir. Now, if she could just put them all to sleep the way David had done to her…

She didn't know how, and David couldn't help her. She sensed his diminished psychic energy. He looked awfully diminished on the physical level too.

Only one idea came to her. It was a bad one, she knew.

Waldron glanced over his shoulder to flash her an evil smile. Then he returned his attention to David, his body tensed, and she knew she was out of time.

So she did it.

A gust of hurricane strength blasted outward from a central point be-tween her and Waldron. Battaglia flipped over backward, dragging her with him into a somersault. The momentum spun her out of Battaglia's grasp. She heard men screaming and bodies cracking as they hit the ground. Oh God, how many people had she injured? Or killed?

No time to think about that. No time to think, period.

The instant she stopped rolling, she sprang to her feet and ran back to-ward where David and Waldron had been. They were gone. She spotted her gun, though, and snatched it up as she continued running.

Sean lay exactly where he had before. She stopped to crouch beside him and felt for a pulse in his neck. It surged under her fingers, strong and regu-lar. She saw no blood or obvious injuries. There was nothing more she could do for him right now.

Rising, she turned in a circle to study her surroundings. The lantern flash-lights had rolled away and cast wedges of light in three different directions, leaving deep patches of darkness in between. She spotted a couple of the commandos, probably a hundred feet away, lying motionless on the ground. The wind blast must've thrown the other four even farther away, out of sight.

The screams. The crunching.

Her gorge rose in her throat. She gulped it down. Given the lighting conditions, the fact that she couldn't see the other commandos didn't mean the wind had flung them so far that they now lay in crumpled in broken heaps far in the distance.

Battaglia had come to rest a good fifty feet away, sprawled on his back, at the edge of one of the lantern beams.

She marched to the nearest lantern, plucked it off the ground, and swept the beam over the landscape.

There. She backtracked with the light. It flashed over a man-shaped lump on the sand. Not David. He'd been wearing a T-shirt and jeans. The man-lump was Waldron.

David and JT were nowhere in sight.

Too many bad guys, too many dangers. *Dammit.* If she had a way to disable Waldron and Battaglia, then at least she would have gotten rid of two threats.

Battaglia carried zip ties, which he used like handcuffs.

As much as she did not want to get within grappling distance of Battaglia, she sprinted across the distance to him and knelt beside the unconscious muscleman. He looked no less intimidating in this condition. Nevertheless, she rifled through his pockets until she discovered a clump of zip ties held together with a rubber band. She secured one of the ties around each of his ankles and connected the two with a third tie, forming a tight shackle. Next, she rolled him over onto his stomach and bound his hands behind his back with a single zip tie.

Satisfied that Battaglia couldn't chase after, she trotted over to Waldron and bound him in the same fashion. Tracking down every one of the six commandos so she could tie them up would take too much time. Besides, judging by the two she could see, the commandos seemed out of commission.

She had to find David. Traipsing through the darkness in search of him, even armed with a lantern light, left her more vulnerable than she liked. JT was out there too after all. The last time she'd seen him he'd seemed incapable of walking, much less attacking her, but she couldn't count on it. He might have another syringe in his pocket, chock-full of power-inducing drugs.

To find David remotely, she had one option. It left her vulnerable, possibly more so than marching off into the night. But she had no choice. It was the fastest method.

She launched her mind up into the crossroads, fast as a rocket. The void enveloped her, welcomed her. Two stars glimmered brighter than the rest. One was David. The other, she knew, was JT. The stars hung close together. Maybe that meant David and JT were close together in the physical world. She couldn't follow both paths, but try as she might, she couldn't feel which one led to David. Her mind was getting tired. She was getting tired. Her time was running out, and she had to make a choice, albeit a blind one.

Down she went, plummeting faster and faster.

Then it stopped. Her astral self stood behind the overturned SUV. The indirect glow from the lantern light, the one she still held in her physical hand way over there, painted an eerie half-light over the area. An arm's length from her, JT crouched under the rear tire with his back against the vehicle.

Wrong choice.

She wanted to fly out of there, to the crossroads, to take the other path and find David. Something tethered her here. The energy was draining out of her slowly but surely. How long she had, she didn't know. When her energy was gone, she would have no chance of finding David this way. And given how weak her body felt, finding him the old-fashioned way might not be an option anymore either.

JT moaned. His eyes were bloodshot. Deep shadows around his eyes gave them a sunken look. His hands trembled as he wiped a rivulet of sweat from his temple. He could neither see nor sense her, she realized. His hand fell to the ground, and then his entire body went limp. Though his lungs still pumped labored breaths, his eyes stared at nothing.

She started to leave, but the tether tugged at her again. No, not a tether. More like a beacon. A signal that pulsed in her soul. She followed it around the end of the vehicle and froze.

David lay there, on his stomach facedown in the sand, with one arm pinned beneath him and the other flung out to the side. A dark liquid dribbled from the back of his head.

No.

She raced toward him, falling to her knees at his side. When she stretched out a hand to touch him, it passed right through his flesh. This was no good. How could she make sure he was still alive when she couldn't touch him? How could she help him?

Dammit, she needed energy. And she needed it now. Right this second.

Was he breathing? She leaned close to his face but couldn't tell through the pounding of her heart.

Now, now, now. She needed energy now.

Heat rushed through her. She felt woozy for a second as the world around her blurred and swirled. The motion stopped with a suddenness that shocked her. She knelt there for a few seconds, unable to think, then she dropped her hands to the ground and curled her fingers into loose fists, scooping up handfuls of cool sand. Goosebumps prickled her arms in response to a breeze.

Her heart thudded. She glanced down at her goosebumpy flesh. Lifting her hands, she turned them so she could examine the fistfuls of sand contained in her palms. What the… She dumped the sand and patted her arms, her hips, her thighs. They all felt real. Warm. Solid. Somehow, without even realizing it or meaning for it to happen, she had manifested. The question of how flitted through her mind, but the answer hardly mattered.

She settled her hands on David's back. Contact. He felt warm and firm, yet soft, in a manly way. When she pressed her fingers to his neck, a pulse throbbed against her skin. With great care, she palpated the wound on his head, parting the hair to get a better look. A scratch. It was only a scratch, one that bled a lot because of its location on the scalp. She let out the breath she'd been holding. He was alive and, unless he had another injury where she couldn't see it, his wounds seemed minor.

Grace laid a hand on his shoulder and shook it gently.

He moaned.

She took hold of him with both hands and, inch by inch, turned him over onto his back. Sand clung to his face. She wiped it away.

He made a little noise, halfway between a groan and a word.

Pain tore through her back. A scream lodged in her throat, choked off by the searing agony as her back arched. Her muscles went rigid and then gave out. She collapsed sideways.

A shadow draped over her as JT rose from his crouch behind her. He towered over her, his expression concealed by darkness, a bloody knife clutched in his hand.

He giggled with manic glee.

Pain. Hot and sharp and wet. It wasn't real. This body wasn't real.

It felt more real than any pain she'd ever felt before.

The mind is the body, David had said. Whatever happens to your meta-physical body, also happens to your physical body.

She had to get out of this manifested form. Now.

JT raised the knife over his head. He plunged the blade down toward her chest.

Go, go, go. Her manifested body disintegrated with a pop. Like a hot-air balloon cut loose from its moorings, her astral form drifted upward.

JT waved the knife through the air where she had been, his expression wild and confused.

She floated ten feet above the scene.

And then she flew. At breakneck speed, she zipped through the crossroads and pitched downward to descend so quickly that the shift hit her like a physical force. Spinning. Falling. The pressure of speed wrung her like a wet towel. But it was nothing compared to the soul-crunching impact of returning to her body.

Her knees buckled. She fell forward, throwing her hands out to brace herself. Although she recognized her surroundings, they lurched and twisted around her as if she stood on the deck of a fishing trawler during a category five hurricane. Nausea swelled inside her, and she nearly vomited. Sweat ran down her face to dribble over her neck and chest, chilling her skin.

The spinning sensation decelerated. Bent over, held up by her trembling arms, she sucked in breath after breath and willed her senses to calm.

David. He was unconscious and alone with JT.

Who had a knife.

She felt a twinge in her back. It was nothing compared to what she'd felt a moment earlier when JT had stabbed her other self. But she had a horrible feeling that within moments the damage to her psychically generated body would catch up with her real body. She must help David before that happened.

A hard object lay beneath her right hand. She glanced down, feeling a bitter smile curve her lips, and clenched her hand around the grip of her gun.

THROUGH SHEER FORCE OF WILL, DAVID PEELED HIS EYELIDS APART. IT felt like a Herculean effort. Everything was blurry. He blinked until his vision cleared.

JT stood over him wielding a bloody knife.

David felt his body awakening, though not fast enough.

JT raised the knife high and thrust it downward.

A shot boomed.

JT jerked, dropped the knife, and toppled onto David. The knife plunged tip first into the sand inches from David's neck. JT's lifeless body lay draped over his torso, and a dark stain had spread outward from the gunshot wound in JT's back.

David shoved the dead man off himself. He scrambled to his knees and then pushed up onto his feet. He spotted his savior twenty feet away, past the front bumper of the SUV. David smiled as Grace gradually lowered her gun.

Then she collapsed.

He bolted past the vehicle and straight to her. As he cradled her in his arms, he felt the warm wetness soaking into the back of her shirt. *Shit.* Lifting her carefully, he carried her across the open expanse to where Sean lay unconscious. He settled Grace down on the ground beside the boy.

Sean could heal her. If David could wake him. The kid was alive, he could tell that much.

David grasped Sean by the shoulders and shook.

The boy's head lolled.

David slapped Sean's face.

The kid's eyelids fluttered, opened for a split second, and drifted shut again.

A sensation of static electricity washed over David. He recognized the feeling of psychic energy pulsing and crackling in the air. Letting go of Sean, he turned to Grace.

The energy. The rising power.

It was coming from *her*.

Chapter Thirty-One

Everything around her seemed remote and detached, as if she sat inside a hermetically sealed capsule ten miles away, watching the scene through a telescope. As her eyelids drifted closed, she glimpsed David's anguished expression. It triggered no emotion in her. She couldn't feel anything, either physically or emotionally. She was a free-floating spirit.

She was dying. The realization came to her, but still, she felt nothing.

Her mind, her spirit, floated through a multicolored mist. Without form. Without attachment. Without anything that had made her human, that had made her… her.

Something tugged at her. It held her in place, though she wanted to float higher and farther. A feeling pierced the numbness, pricking her like a needle. She tried to pull away from the tether, but it refused to let her go. *He* refused to let her go. David was speaking to her, and though she couldn't hear his words, she felt them tugging at her, felt him begging her not to leave. She couldn't do this. She couldn't go. As good as it felt to float away, she had to fight it.

Energy surged through her like a bone-jarring shiver. In its wake trailed a tingling warmth that scoured away the numbness. Pain struck her hard, convulsing every muscle in her body, and then it faded away. A new feeling coursed through her very essence, a sensation of clear and infinite knowledge. It burned brightly for an instant, only to vanish as quickly as it had overcome her.

She opened her eyes.

David, kneeling beside her, stared down at her with an expression of unbridled awe. A few feet away, Sean had sat up and now gazed at her with an identical expression.

Grace pushed up onto her elbows. What the hell was wrong with them?

The back of her shirt felt wet and sticky. Blood, she realized, and her heart skipped a beat. Oh yeah, she remembered now. She'd been stabbed in the back, and not metaphorically. She felt fine now. Strong and healthy and right.

David leaned forward, bracing himself with one hand. He ducked his head over her shoulder to peer down at her backside. Straightening, he gazed at her with a more subdued, but still awestruck, expression on his face.

"You healed yourself," he said in a breathless voice.

"Huh." It was all she could think of to say.

David glanced at Sean, who looked quite well now, and then swiveled his head to take in the panorama around them.

As she pushed up into a sitting position, Grace followed his gaze. In the distance, the commandos had begun to rouse. They sat or crouched, scratching their heads and palpating formerly injured body parts.

Formerly injured. Why had she thought that? They couldn't have magically healed.

But she had.

The truth sliced through her on a sharp chill.

David met her gaze and nodded. "That's right. You healed yourself and Sean and me. You healed everyone."

"Everyone?" The word came out as a squeaky whisper. She gathered up the tattered remnants of her composure and cleared her throat. "How did I do that?"

David shrugged.

"I thought you knew everything about this psychic stuff," she said. "If you don't know, then I haven't got a clue either."

His lips twisted into a partial frown. He stared at the ground.

David knew something or thought he did. She slid closer to him, and her hand bumped into her gun, which lay on the ground beside her. Clambering to her knees, she sat back on her heels. Their faces were inches apart.

"Tell me," she said.

He sighed and lifted his head to look at her. "You won't like it."

She planted her hands on her hips. "Tell me anyway."

"I think you tapped into the Golden Power."

She must've looked as startled as she felt because his expression softened.

He grasped her shoulders. "Think about it. How else could you have healed not only yourself but everyone in the vicinity? Sean can only heal others, not himself, and only when he's in intimate proximity to them." He smiled. "You healed everyone."

She stretched out her hand to run it through his hair, feeling for the scratch that had bled so copiously moments earlier. It was gone.

Wow.

She brushed her fingers across his cheek and let them settle on his lips. "Just don't ask me to do it again. I have no idea how I did it in the first place."

He smiled against her fingers.

She let her hand fall away from his lips.

"What did it feel like?" he asked. "Tapping into that power."

Clear and infinite knowledge. Oh yes, she remembered that feeling with crystal clarity. The certainty. The completeness. The power. Whatever she'd tapped into had given her more than infinite knowledge. It had given her infinite power, at least for a moment. If JT had succeeded…

But he hadn't. And all of JT's research, contained on the flash drive, belonged to her now. She would destroy it as soon as she got home. The threat was over.

No. The thought zinged through her.

She grabbed the gun, leaped to her feet, and fired twice.

Twenty feet away, Waldron had just raised his weapon and trained it on David. Instead of exacting his revenge, however, he slumped onto the sand, dead. She'd shot him twice in the chest. He'd raised only his head and one arm to take aim. From her vantage point, David had blocked her view of Waldron. She hadn't seen him lifting his gun. She hadn't heard it either because he'd made no sound. Some fragment of the infinite knowledge she'd touched had stayed with her and warned her of Waldron's attack.

At least, that was her theory.

She marched past David and straight to Waldron.

His eyes were open and blank, devoid of life. A small pocket knife lay open on the ground beside his body. He must've managed to get it out of his pocket—the back one, she presumed—and cut himself free of the zip ties. She and David had been a little distracted by her almost dying and then healing herself and everyone in the vicinity. For all she knew, she'd inadvertently healed Waldron too, giving him the ability to make his attempt on David's life. If Waldron had succeeded, she had no doubt she would've been next.

I healed everyone.

A chill whispered over her neck, raising the hairs.

She sprinted toward Battaglia. He was still bound, though he writhed on the ground in a vain effort to tear free of his restraints.

He spotted the gun in her hand. His face blanched, and he stopped wriggling.

She tapped the gun against her thigh.

"Please," Battaglia whined. "Don't kill me. I was just doing my job."

She had no intention of killing a helpless man, but he probably assumed everyone was as nasty as he was. Given his current state of groveling, however, he possessed neither the ruthless determination of Xavier Waldron nor the maniacal drive of Jackson Tennant.

David came up beside her. He glanced at her gun and then at Battaglia.

The trussed-up commando whimpered.

Shaking his head, David grunted in disgust. "He's not worth a bullet. He's a coward underneath it all."

"I know." Grace tucked the gun inside her waistband. "We should go before his buddies snap out of their confusion and come for him."

"How do you suggest we get out of here?"

"In the car."

He stared at her. After a couple of seconds, he slowly turned to look in the direction of the overturned SUV.

Except it wasn't overturned anymore.

The SUV sat upright, tires on the sand. The top was a little banged up, the windshield was missing, and the other windows were cracked. But she knew—she just *knew*—the vehicle would hold together long enough to get them out of here.

"You did that?" David asked, in a surprisingly calm tone.

She shrugged.

Though she didn't remember doing it and hadn't consciously known she'd done it, some part of her had known. When David had asked how they would get out of here, the answer popped into her brain.

Without a word, David took her hand and led her to the SUV. Sean trailed along behind them. They had to crawl through the windshield to get inside the vehicle. Sean went first, wriggling between the front seats to get into the back, and David took the driver's seat, leaving Grace as the passenger. When David saw there were no keys in the ignition, he started to ask a question. Grace cut him off with a wave of her hand, although she hadn't intended the gesture to silence him. Instead, she had, without thinking about it, waved her hand in the direction of the car's engine.

It grumbled to life.

David said nothing. He simply shifted the car into drive, executed a U-turn, and headed up the slope and over the rim of the depression onto the flat desert floor.

"Which way?" he asked.

She pointed, and he followed her directions without hesitation.

The lingering knowledge and energy from whatever source she'd tapped into was beginning to drain away. She felt it. Oh well. It had been borrowed power, anyway. But even as the power boost faded, a fragment of knowledge stuck with her. It glistened like a diamond in her mind.

"Where should we go?" David asked.

"I know where my grandfather is," she answered. "We're going to get him."

Chapter Thirty-Two

THE CLUNKY, BEAT-UP SUV SOMEHOW MADE IT BACK INTO TOWN. They rented a nondescript sedan and headed out of Reston in the direction Grace indicated. David drove. She hunched in the passenger seat, stiff as a crash-test dummy, fighting desperately to hold on to the knowledge of her grandfather's whereabouts. With each passing moment, she felt the information slipping away from her.

She leaned sideways to glance at the speedometer. It read sixty-five miles per hour.

"Drive faster," she hissed.

He floored the accelerator. The car lurched forward, and she watched the speedometer surge upward.

Without looking at David, she murmured, "Thank you."

"You're welcome."

She chanced a sideways glance at him and caught his amused expression. "What's so funny?"

"Nothing."

"Hmm." She spotted a T-intersection up ahead. "Turn left."

David braked with caution and veered left onto a paved road with two narrow lanes and virtually no shoulder. They'd left Reston a couple of hours earlier, abandoning civilization to drive deep into a wilderness populated with towering pine trees and little else. Though they passed the occasional overgrown two-track driveway, they saw no other signs of human occupation.

Yet David followed her instructions without question.

She relaxed her death grip on the edges of her seat and glanced sideways at David. "Are you always going to do whatever I say?"

He chuckled.

She supposed that substituted for a response. She supposed she knew the answer to the question, anyway. Until today, David had done almost nothing that she told him to do. He was following her orders now because he recognized that she'd acquired some astonishing, if temporary, knowledge they needed right now. She shouldn't count on him bending to her will on an everyday basis. Not that she would want him to. Life would get pretty boring if he always acquiesced to her.

The paved road petered out into gravel. Grace instructed David to make two more turns onto two-track roads that got bumpier and bumpier. Just when she began to seriously consider duct-taping her teeth together, the trees opened out into a little clearing. The two-track dead-ended at a rough-looking cabin nestled amid the trees. The windows were boarded up. A generator hunkered alongside the cabin, apparently powered by a nearby propane tank.

David parked the car near the cabin's front door. Grace leaped out and hurried a few yards away, bending her head back to stare up at the trees. There, high above, a small satellite dish sat mounted to the top of a tree.

Inside the car, Sean pushed the rear passenger door open and started to get out.

David, standing halfway out of the car, leaned his head back inside to whisper something to Sean. The boy nodded and climbed into the backseat again. David strode toward Grace.

"Well?" he said.

"The windows and doors are electrified," she told him. "Do you know how to turn off a generator?"

"Yes. You're sure there's no backup power source?"

"Positive."

David marched toward the generator. Within a few minutes, he accomplished his task and returned to her side.

The cabin looked the same. No lights had been visible before, thanks to the boarded-up windows.

"Guards?" David asked.

She shook her head. "A male nurse with a gun. He would've seen us coming, but I, um… convinced him otherwise."

David's eyebrows rose. "From a distance?"

She gave him a sheepish smile. "Uh-huh."

He seemed both impressed, and a little mystified. She felt mystified too. When she'd manipulated someone's mind before, it had taken an enormous amount of concentration and willpower. Today, the same task had taken almost no effort, and she accomplished it from quite a distance without even thinking about it. She simply knew it needed to be done and did it. Of course, the level of thought projection required was swiftly eroding the last of her enhanced power. Soon the last drop would slip away from her—along with the vast, eerie knowledge she'd obtained.

David strode up to the front door, twisted the knob, and thrust it inward.

A thirtyish man dressed in a flannel shirt and blue jeans leaped up from his chair. He didn't even think to reach for the gun strapped to his hip. Grace made sure of that. The final effort triggered a sharp, though not intense, pain behind her eyes.

Rushing forward, David grabbed the nurse's gun and forced the man to sit down again. The nurse glared at David with a mixture of confusion, anger, and fear. David stared back at the man with such intensity that the other guy squirmed in his seat.

Then, as if someone had flipped a switch inside his brain, the nurse slumped against the wall and his eyelids drifted shut. He was asleep. And, Grace knew, someone *had* essentially flipped a switch in the man's brain. It hadn't been her, though. David had taken care of the task. He'd put the man to sleep, just like he'd done to her once.

Grace stepped across the threshold into the cabin. They stood inside a narrow entryway that dead-ended to the right, but to the left, it opened into a dimly lit room. She could see a sliver of the space beyond. David led the way, swinging rightward into the room. Grace hustled a few feet into the room and froze.

Nestled against the far wall, covered with a blanket, lay a human-shaped lump. The bald man beneath the blanket sat up, yawned, and smiled at her.

"Grandpa," she whispered, afraid to say the word too loudly for fear she would wake up from this dream. But it wasn't a dream. She knew that with a certainty that came not from her brush with the Golden Power, but from her heart and soul.

Tears stung her eyes and rolled down her cheeks.

Edward McLean looked reasonably well, though a little disheveled and in need of a shave.

David hurried over to Edward and helped the older man to his feet.

Grace ran toward them. She flung her arms around her grandfather and hugged him fiercely. When she stepped back, he reached out to pat her shoulder.

"I gather it's over," he said. "JT is—"

"Gone," Grace said.

"And the flash drive?"

"I mailed it to myself, to keep it away from JT and his goons. But once I get it, I'm going to destroy it."

David cleared his throat. "Maybe you shouldn't."

She glanced at him sideways. "Excuse me? People died for that damn thing. It needs to be thrown into an erupting volcano so no one else can get their hands on JT's research. It's too dangerous."

"David's right," her grandfather said. "You shouldn't destroy it. JT established multiple research sites around the world, which means he may have been holding more innocent people hostage."

"And there's Tesler," David said. "He escaped. Meaning he's free to torture those others."

"The information on the flash drive is our only means of finding them and Tesler." Sighing, Edward ran a hand over his bald head. "It was our research—mine, Christine's, and Mark's—that helped JT find, capture, and terrorize these people. It's my responsibility to set things right."

"You didn't know what would happen," Grace said. "And you didn't willingly hand over your research to JT and his minions."

"It doesn't matter. I still have to fix this."

She bit her lip, and in a matter of two seconds, she made up her mind. A quick look at David told her he'd guessed what she was thinking, and he agreed wholeheartedly.

"Okay, then," she said, squaring her shoulders and lifting her chin. "David and I will help you. After all, you'll need a couple of psychic weirdos on your side."

"I prefer extrasensory perceptives," David said with a wry smile.

She made an oh-please face. "You made that up, didn't you?"

"Maybe."

"Well," Edward said, "I'd prefer granddaughter and grandson-in-law."

He shoved a hand into his pants pocket and brought out a sparkly object, which he proffered to Grace.

She took the item, rotating it between her fingers. The object was a gold ring capped with a small diamond.

Her grandfather winked at her. "I've been holding on to that for you."

Grace closed her hand around the ring, shielding it inside her palm. "Can we get out of here please?"

David led them out of the murky room and down the short entryway.

At the threshold, Grace hesitated. She glanced back at the nurse slumped in his chair.

"What about him?" she asked.

"He'll wake up in a little while," David said. "When I was shutting down the generator, I saw his car parked out back. He'll be fine."

"Maybe we should call the cops and get these bastards arrested."

"We can't explain anything that happened," David said. "No one would believe it, and we have no evidence to support our claims."

"The facility…"

"JT may be dead, but his company is still alive. Even if they didn't know what he was up to out in the desert, I'm sure they'll come up with a reasonable explanation for everything. Corporations love to obscure the truth and subvert the law."

She frowned. The pain behind her eyes was growing into a headache.

David took her hand and squeezed it. "We stopped a homicidal madman. I'd say that's a pretty good day's work." He nodded toward her grandfather, who now stood beside the car. "And we saved a very important life."

She felt the frown relaxing into a smile. He was right.

David led her toward the car. Halfway there, she tugged his hand to stop him.

He turned toward her, his brow furrowed.

She held the ring out to him.

He took it and, bowing his head, muttered, "You don't want it anymore."

"No, that's not it." She grinned. "I love you too."

His head jerked up. He gaped at her for a few seconds, then his lips parted in a grin as joyful as the one she wore.

She held out her left hand.

He slipped the ring onto her finger.

Grace gulped against a tightness in her throat. "What if I never get my memory back? I can't even remember how we met—"

"I can tell you anything you want to know." He touched her cheek. "And we can make new memories."

She opened her mouth to protest, but she didn't get the chance. He pulled her into his arms and kissed her with a passion and enthusiasm that burned out all her anxiety and melted away her headache.

They got in the car and drove away. In the rearview mirror, the forest swallowed up the little cabin. Everything it represented dwindled along with it. The past receded into the distance as the road ahead became clearer, brighter, and smoother. She was no longer speeding headlong into darkness. Now, she rode into the light. Into the future. Into the unknown.

And for the first time in her life, that didn't bother her at all.

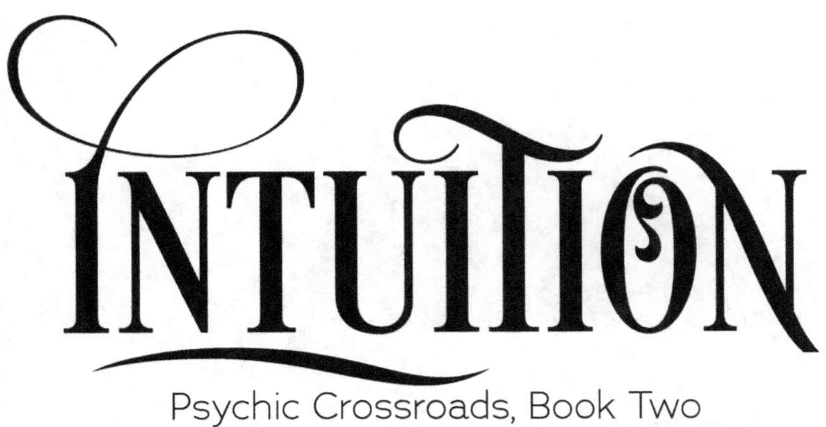

INTUITION
Psychic Crossroads, Book Two

CHAPTER ONE

GRACE POWELL SLAMMED THE FRONT DOOR, AND THE COOL AIR INside the house expunged the sultry October heat that clung to her skin. She stalked across the living room, down the hall, and into the bedroom. As she fumbled for the light switch, her fingers slipped off the plastic. *Dammit.* No one but David Ransom detonated her temper like this. At last, she flicked the switch, and light flooded the room. The bed stood empty, the sheets crumpled at the foot.

They'd fled the house in a near panic, racing from their home to the Cincinnati airport with tires screeching, all because of a thirty-second phone call David had received at one a.m. Another tip from a questionable source. Another threadbare clue in his quest for vengeance. Another search that yanked him away from Grace, away from their home, their life.

The emptiness of the bed tore at her heart like tiny claws, sharp and hot. Fresh tears pricked her eyes, and she gnawed her lip to stave off the downpour. *No crying.*

She fingered her engagement ring. A tear sneaked out of her eye to roll down her cheek, painting a hot trail on her skin. *No crying, dammit.*

Grace resisted the impulse to tap into their telepathic bond and check on her fiancé. It was an invasion, one she understood all too well, but how else could she know David was all right? She had to trust their latent connection, however faint, to warn her. If he stumbled into trouble, though, what could she do from here, over a thousand miles away?

Her heart clenched. Losing her parents had ripped her world asunder. She could not lose David too. Her head told her she wouldn't, yet the fear chilled her down to the essence of her being.

She trudged into the bedroom, kicking off her shoes. The lonely tear crept into her mouth, infecting her tongue with a salty tang. She tugged the cell phone out of her jeans pocket and tossed it onto the bedside table. Her muscles, stiff and sore, begged for a rest, so she collapsed onto the mattress on her back. Her gaze hit the ceiling where little acoustic balls clung to the paint, stuck there against their will. *I know the feeling.*

When they'd reached the security checkpoint at the airport, she'd longed to plead with David to stay. Instead, she cranked her lips into a smile, pecked a kiss on his cheek, and all but shoved him through the gate. Her stomach wrenched into knots as she recalled that moment when he strolled into the main terminal. When he paused to glance back, she prayed he would change his mind. But he simply waved, then strode out of sight.

Grace rolled onto her side. Her nose bumped into David's pillow. She drew in a long breath and let the spiciness of his aftershave flood her senses, along with another scent—a subtle, masculine smell unique to David. It was indescribable and delicious. Warmth suffused her, seeping into her heart and mind, smoldering in parts of her that ached for him. She inhaled another draft of his scent, her body responding as if he were there, caressing her. He might drive her nuts at times, but…

Oh, the way he kissed. Her lips tingled from the memory of it.

A chill whispered over her skin. Every hair on her body stiffened. Her sixth sense burst out of its slumber, clanging alarm bells in her psyche. *Someone is here.*

She bolted upright and whipped her head left and right. Nobody there. She swung her legs off the bed and pushed up onto her feet, nabbing her .357 Magnum revolver from the bedside table. A chill trickled down her spine. Eyes watched. Invisible, ethereal, but real. She turned toward the doorway. Nothing lurked there.

Why couldn't she pin down the source of the sensation? Her paranormal radar was blanked out as if overwhelmed by input.

Psychic energy crackled through her. *Behind you.* She whirled around, thrusting the gun up, clamping it in both hands, and confronted—

The lamp.

Hell. She'd let her unease blossom into paranoia. Nobody hunted her anymore. Probably. Tesler wouldn't find her here.

Her cell phone buzzed. A text message had arrived.

David. She snatched up the phone, tapping the screen until the message popped up. As she scanned the words, a shiver rattled through her.

"Come to me," it said, "I can help you. 1325 Meroz Road."

She didn't recognize the phone number the message came from, and no name was given. Oh sure, she'd rush right out to the address texted to her by an anonymous whackjob.

The phone buzzed again. Another text message: "Your lip is bleeding."

Her lip? She dabbed a finger on her mouth. It came away wet. Blood stained her skin. How did the texter know she'd bitten her lip? Without moving, she searched the shadows for a figure, a camera, something to explain this, though she knew she'd find nothing. A thick curtain shielded the window. The person sending the messages could either see through solid objects or had another means of viewing her. Extrasensory means.

The phone tumbled from her hand, clattering on the floor.

No, she was jumping to conclusions. An intruder must've stolen into the house. With the revolver in hand, she sprinted out of the bedroom, down the hallway, through the kitchen, and into the living room. Vacant. All vacant. She rushed back to the bedroom and dug through the closet, scoured the dresser, even dropped onto her belly to investigate the space under the bed. No cameras. No stealthy intruders. Not a damn thing. Which left her with one unthinkable possibility.

Maybe she should call the police.

What for? They couldn't help her with this kind of problem.

"You belong with me."

She jumped. Her head smacked into the bed frame. She clutched the gun tighter. Where had the voice come from?

No, no, no, not again. Nausea swelled in her stomach, bile rising high in her throat. The voice did not originate in this room, or from outside. The source was much, much closer. Someone had rammed the words into her mind.

A psychic intruder had just hacked her brain.

Grace crawled out from under the bed. She pushed up onto her knees, set the revolver on the carpet beside her knee, and grabbed her phone off the floor. Her heart implored her to call David, but her head warned against it. What if the psychic intruder had bugged the phones? She shuddered. An invisible stalker needed no bugs or cameras to track her every movement. He might spy on her anytime, anywhere.

Grabbing the edge of the mattress, she heaved herself up and onto the bed. Her eyes stung. Her lip throbbed from chewing it. She yearned to lie down and drift to sleep. As if she could sleep now.

Her phone buzzed.

She lifted her hand. On the screen, a message appeared. "Come to me when you're ready. No pressure. Last message, promise. Good night."

Grace gulped. The rock in her throat stayed put.

Good night? Sure, she'd sleep. Like a freaking baby—if the baby had guzzled a pint of tequila. Unfortunately, she didn't drink, never had. Thanks to her new "friend," however, she craved a big, tall glass of anything alcoholic, to soak her fears in the vaunted bliss of drunkenness. Maybe then she could pretend nothing happened.

David needs to know. Given her past, he'd want to hear about an intruder hacking into her mind. She punched the button to call up his cell number, but then froze. He was in the air right now, on his way to Utah. Did the airlines let passengers use cell phones in flight? Better stick to the one means she knew would work.

Ohhh, David wouldn't like this.

Screw it. He ought to know.

Grace slapped the phone down on the table. She slumped onto the bed on her back, folded her hands over her belly, and shut her eyes. Tension tugged her muscles taut. Thoughts swirled in her brain. If she couldn't block out the anxiety, she'd never tap into her powers. Drawing in a deep breath, she let it out bit by bit. *Relax. Picture the target.*

David. His face glimmered in her mind as if lit by heaven's own glow.

Her mind snapped free from her body. She floated in nothingness for a second, and then whoosh. She rocketed up through a dark tunnel into a field of blackness dotted with stars. Her mind drew lines between the lights, sketching out the connections between places and events and psyches in the crossroads, the ethereal source of all psychic power. A white line stretched out toward a pinpoint far away. The star pulsed. David. She'd found him.

Grace hurtled toward him through the darkness into the light, smashing through it into another tunnel. Psychic gravity hauled her downward, closer and closer to her destination. To David's mind. His presence cascaded over her, through her, penetrating deeper with each second, overwhelming her with warmth and love and belonging.

She tumbled out into the world. Shapes blurred into each other. Up, down, her senses struggled to separate the two. Precious seconds ticked by until her mind acclimated to the change. It shouldn't have hit her so hard. Something was different this time, but she couldn't deduce what.

Solid earth supported her feet. Though she lacked a physical form, her mind conjured an image of her body that behaved like the real thing. She turned in a circle, inspecting her surroundings. Trees loomed overhead. Green moss squished under her feet. The sun blazed behind the treetops, its rays puncturing the shadows below. This made no sense. She'd watched David walk into the terminal. He should've been in the air, not down here in the woods. Down where? She'd figure that out later. First, she must find David.

She stopped. Her heart thudded. A dozen feet away, David crouched in front of a thick pine tree. Facing away. Hands bound behind his back. Ankles bound too. Head tipped up. Grace zeroed in on the object of David's attention. A man, engulfed in shadows. His face obscured.

She tiptoed closer. Still couldn't see.

The stranger swung his arm up. His hand. He clutched something. A shiny metal object. He hoisted it higher. *Shit.* A knife.

"David!"

Her cry ricocheted off the trees. He didn't react. She charged forward.

And whacked into an invisible wall. Pain exploded through her, and she staggered backward. What the hell?

The stranger drove the knife downward, plunging the blade into David's chest. He gurgled. The stranger tore the knife out and raised it high. Blood drenched the blade, but he jammed it downward again. David convulsed and crumpled to the ground.

Grace screamed.

She flung her arms out to David, but the barrier hurled them back. She toppled over, scrambled to her feet. The stranger ripped the knife out and braced for another blow. Grace flailed for the knife. Her fingers smacked into the barrier, and pain racked her joints as she attacked the barrier with every ounce of psychic energy in her, pounding on it with both hands. It shattered with a whoosh of air that bowled her over backward. She scrambled to her feet, rushing toward David, and grappled for the knife. Her hand sailed right through it.

No body, dammit. No hands. No hope.

Like hell.

The stranger stabbed David again. A red stain erupted on his shirt. The blows wrenched Grace's astral body as if the knife shredded her own flesh. The slickness of his blood oozed over her skin, and his life spewed out of her as if it were her own.

No, no, no. I won't lose him too.

The assailant tossed his knife aside.

Manifest now, dammit. Construct a body. Nothing happened. She staggered forward, gasping, tears cascading down her cheeks. They stung like the real thing, and her chest ached from the pain of her hammering heart. She must manifest a physical form *right now*.

But she couldn't.

She pumped every ounce of psychic energy she had into the task, draining her metaphysical power lower than ever before. Her head throbbed. Everything twirled around her. The tether between her and David unraveled.

"No."

The word whispered out of her. Faint. Distant. Every bit of energy inside her vaporized.

The stranger waltzed into the light.

Grace peeled her gaze away from David and stared at the assailant. The sunlight glistened on the bald spot atop his head. A breeze ruffled his gray hair, and his freckled face warped into a smirk. Recognition jolted through her. She knew this man.

Karl Tesler.

He was the scientist David had hunted for six months. The man who captured and tortured psychics. The object of David's obsession, and the reason he fled to Utah.

Tesler surveyed the area. A cold draft whispered over her in the wake of his gaze. Goosebumps prickled her skin. He couldn't see her. Could he?

The scientist sneered down at David, his dark eyes narrowed and burning with amber fire. He fingered the blood stain on David's shirt, then lifted his hand to his face to sniff the blood—and grinned.

Grace clenched her fists, gritting her teeth. "Tesler, you bastard. You'll pay for this, I swear it. You'll pay."

Anger boiled inside her. Scorching. Swelling. Obliterating reason. Propelling her to do something. Anything.

She could do *nothing*.

He would pay for this. Somehow, some way, she would summon the strength to rip his heart out.

The tether snapped.

Her mind crashed back into her body, ramming into it with a force that punched the breath out of her. A vice bore down on her head, the pain so intense she nearly vomited. She jerked upright, still on the bed. A salty flavor drenched her mouth. *Tick, tick, tick.* Dampness pasted her clammy shirt to her chest. *Tick, tick.* Sobs twisted her gut as tears dripped off her chin to plop onto her shirt, ticking like a countdown timer. One thought consumed her.

David was dead.

CHAPTER TWO

THE SUN HAD LONG SINCE BREACHED THE HORIZON BY THE TIME DAVID smacked the car door shut and leaped up the front steps of their home, two at a time. The morning light glared in his eyes as he grabbed for the knob. It slipped in his damp palm.

What would he find inside the house? Was he too late?

He wiped his hand on his jeans and seized the knob.

The front door swung open, releasing a blast of cool air from inside the house that chilled the sweat on his face. Grace hunched in the doorway, her bleary gaze aimed at him.

He staggered backward half a step, the air trapped in his lungs. She was *okay*. Freaked out, but alive. He hauled in a breath, shoving aside his own anxiety, and moved toward her.

Grace's hazel eyes widened. Her face blanched. "You're alive."

"Obviously." He tilted his head, baffled by the way she stared at him like he'd hopped off a unicorn's back. "Are you all right? I sensed… something."

More than something. A tidal wave of fear and anger had battered him with such power that he'd nearly tumbled off the hard, plastic chair in the Denver International Airport, where he'd been waiting for a connecting flight. He recognized in a heartbeat the source of the icy burst of sensations. Grace. He'd sprinted to the ticket desk, his pulse racing, seized by a wild panic that hammered one thought into his brain over and over.

Grace is dying.

Yet she wasn't. No blood, no bruises—unless her clothes masked them. Other than her bloodshot eyes, nothing betrayed the terror that had coursed down their connection and skewered his heart. He touched his fingertips to her cheek. Warm. Smooth. Undamaged. The electrical charge of adrenaline that had buttressed him on the flight home flooded out of him. The world seemed to rock briefly. He sucked in a breath, jerked his hand away from her face, and willed his mind to settle.

Grace launched her body at him, sailing through the doorway and straight into him. He caught her in both arms. She hoisted herself up to wrap her arms around his neck, her feet dangling several inches off the ground. He tugged her against him, gripping her sides to press her closer. She flinched and gasped.

He snatched his arms away. "What did I do? Are you hurt?"

She bent her head back and laughed, her voice as melodic as the chiming of tiny bells. "I'm fine. Your fingers were digging into my ribs, dummy."

"Oh. Sorry."

She tucked her head under his chin. He nuzzled her neck, breathing in the clean scent of her. He beat back the urge to scoop her into his arms and whisk her away to some deserted island, a safe place where they could pretend the past year had never happened. He would stir her memories, the ones buried under eight months of amnesia, and then let her tender caresses and fiery kisses scour away his secrets. His nightmares. His past.

Never let her find out.

She clinched him so tight it blew the air out of his lungs. Had she read his mind? Sweet heaven, he prayed she hadn't. He could not stomach watching another person dive headfirst into psychosis, splintered by the ax-like power of mind reading. Watching the madness shatter Grace…

That would kill him.

Her arms squeezed him harder. He smothered the instinct to push her away and gasped through gritted teeth, "What's wrong?"

She let go, dropped onto her feet, and frowned at him. "You were dead. I saw it happen."

"Clearly not." He thumped his chest. "Still here."

Her gaze drilled into his with the heat of a laser beam, incinerating his every thought. The morning sun glittered on the green specks in her pale-brown irises, tiny jewels swimming in a pool of molten toffee. God, she was perfect. From her slender, round-tipped nose to her graceful, narrow feet and even her flawless little toes that wriggled on the concrete.

When she hugged him again, more gently, her auburn hair tickled his chin. The sweet, tropical scent of her shampoo sparked off a surge of intoxicating hormones that swamped his senses, evoking images that only intensified the desire. The shadows of palm trees swaying over a sun-blanketed beach, while they sipped virgin daiquiris from coconut shells. Grace draped across a towel, her bikini revealing acres of creamy, soft skin. The hollow of her hips. The flat plane of her stomach. The swell of her ample breasts. The delicate curve of her neck. His lips burned with the hunger to taste her small, full lips.

She pushed away from him. "Are you thinking about sex?"

"Not specifically." True, his fantasy had screeched to a halt a second too soon for that. But if he'd had more time…

Damn. He was an ass.

"You are thinking about it." She shook her head. Waves of hair splashed around her face. "I thought you died. I watched it happen. And all you can do is fantasize about sex?"

The meaning of her words crashed into him, cold as a liquid-nitrogen downpour, dousing the bonfire she'd lit inside him. She watched him die? Impossible. Yet Grace would not lie. Not about this. And she'd suffered too much, battled through too many losses, to crack jokes about death.

He grasped her shoulders. *Careful. Protect, don't suffocate, remember?* He loosened his grip, uncurling his fingers. "What are you talking about? I didn't die. You could not have seen it happen."

She folded her arms over her chest, thrusting her breasts upward.

He struggled to concentrate, to rip his gaze away from the sight. Dammit, why did she have to be so… breathtaking.

Grace took one step back. "I saw Tesler murder you. It was real."

His thoughts snapped into focus. The heat of desire sluiced out of him, displaced by a sharp chill. "What exactly did you see?"

She scowled, glancing around. "Maybe we shouldn't talk about this. Someone might hear."

"You think the house is bugged?"

"No, not the way you mean."

She slumped her shoulders, one hand rubbing her arm. A cold suspicion itched in his gut. Something wasn't right here. Maybe whatever she'd experienced had triggered the terror that swamped him. Their connection was potent. If his ordeal had stemmed from her, then he marveled at her composure.

He grasped her shoulders, bending his knees to level their gazes. "Tell me what happened while I was gone. Everything."

—

LIE DOWN, GRACE. NOW." DAVID POINTED AT THE BED. HE'D ALREADY folded the quilt at the foot and pulled back the blanket and sheet.

She rolled her eyes. "I need to build a psychic firewall to keep out hackers. You said so. I don't have time for a nap."

He stared into her bloodshot eyes, rimmed with dark circles, and willed her to obey him. He held out no hope she would unless he convinced her of the need for sleep. Commanding her to do anything never worked. Like the dolt he obviously was, he kept repeating the same mistake. Time for a new tactic.

"Please." He cupped her face in his hands. "Please lie down and at least try to sleep. You're exhausted." Which was his fault. A knot pulled taut inside him, but he trained all his focus on her. "I'm begging you."

She gazed at him, impassive, for two heartbeats. Then she laughed, her beautiful mouth splitting into a grin. "Really, David. I've dreamed about you begging me to do all sorts of things, but napping wasn't one of them."

Just like that, everything besides the two of them evaporated. He dropped his hands to her arms and skated them down until he found her fingers, entwining them with his. He said softly, "What have you dreamed about?"

The slight pallor in her cheeks gave way to a delicate blush, and she fixated her gaze on his chest.

He lifted one of her hands to feather a kiss across her knuckles. "You can tell me. I'd like to know."

She aimed her hazel eyes at him. "You're psychic, you figure it out."

"I can't read your mind." He tugged her into his arms, ducking his head close to hers. She smelled wonderful and felt even better. "Sometimes I wish I could hear your thoughts."

"Ditto." Eyes half-closed, she drew in a slow breath. "You want to know my fantasies, but you won't tell me yours."

"Mine are boring." A beach, palm trees, the scent of wild, exotic flowers on the breeze. And her, gloriously naked, while he explored every inch of her soft skin. That was his fantasy. He ought to tell her, if he expected her to confide in him, but shackles wrought from elastic iron restrained him, stretching taut yet unbreakable. He shouldn't have instigated this line of conversation. He fought the urge to strip both their clothes off and act out his fantasy right here, right now, screw the beach.

She traced a fingertip over the neckline of his T-shirt. "You're many things, David, but never boring."

"I'm not sure that's a compliment."

Her arms snaked up to encircle his neck, her fingers massaging the nape. "I'm not sleepy, but I'd be happy to lie down for you."

Her tongue slipped out to moisten her lower lip.

Every nerve in his body screamed for him to kiss her. When she smiled, slow and sexy, his chest tightened. "Are you trying to seduce me?"

"Yes."

The hunger smoldered inside him, relentless and inescapable. He stroked his hands up and down her back, closed his eyes, and reveled in her aura. *Love her, show her, let it all go*. But he must hold back, despite his selfish desires. Her powers had grown day by day, a fact he sensed even while she denied the truth. The last time they'd made love, the act had affected them both on a metaphysical level. Their telepathic bond, nearly destroyed by her amnesia and his secrets, had strengthened in that moment, fueled by the love they conveyed with their bodies. If he touched her again, he had no idea what it might do to her powers. Bind her to him? Forever?

The thought coursed a thrill through him, and he nuzzled her cheek, hungry for contact. If he told her about his suspicions, she'd vow she didn't care what happened. He knew her too well to expect any other reaction. He could not let her risk it. After what he'd done already, things he could never tell her, he didn't deserve even the latent connection they shared. He'd betrayed her—unwillingly, but that was no excuse. He should've been stronger, fought harder.

Sacrificed his life for her.

Grace raised onto tiptoes and nipped his chin. "Is my evil plan working?"

Her hips wriggled against him, exciting parts of him he was desperately struggling to calm down. Hell yes, it was working. "I can't remember you ever doing this before."

"What? Seducing you?" Her voice had gone sultry, whispery, irresistible.

"Yes, that." He growled the words. "Please stop."

"Why?"

"Because—" While she raked her nails up the back of his scalp, he battled to retain his wits, but her exquisite torment wore him down second by second. "We can't do this. You're exhausted."

She was worn out from more than their late-night escapade, he knew that. She worked too hard to support them both. He clenched his jaw. What if she got sick from perpetual exhaustion, all because of his failures? "Former psychic research subject" didn't fit well on a resume, and he had no other explanation for where he'd been for the past two and a half years. Besides, he had to focus on Tesler. For Grace. He prayed one day she'd understand why.

Excuses. Pathetic, half-assed excuses.

Grace tugged his head down, her lips closing in on his.

He summoned every ounce of self-control he possessed, took hold of her arms, and pushed her away.

She winced.

His fingers sprang open on instinct. "Did I hurt you?"

A heavy sigh deflated her. "Not physically."

But he had hurt her. *Dammit.* How long could he keep doing this to her before he bled dry her willingness to forgive him? Maybe he should end this and set her free. He couldn't.

Because he was a selfish bastard.

"I'm sorry." It was all he could manage to say.

"Yeah, I know." Her defeated tone scraped at his heart. "I am tired all of a sudden."

She scuffled to the bed and climbed onto it to lie on her side, hands clasped to her chest, knees bent. He crawled from the foot of the bed up to lie beside her, face to face. She looked so tired, so fragile, that he wanted to wrap his arms around her. After the way he'd just rejected her, he doubted she'd appreciate the gesture.

A big yawn overtook her.

Though glazed with fatigue, her gaze sharpened on him. "Why do you think Tesler hasn't come after me again? It's been six months."

The question he'd dreaded. The one he had no answer for. Although he harbored suspicions, he must not share them with her. She suffered enough anxiety without piling on more that might well be unfounded. Instead, he reminded her of things she already knew, praying to distract her tired mind. "That's why we moved from Texas to Ohio and rented a house under false names, to hide you from Tesler."

"Then why do you keep looking for him? Isn't that kind of like wrestling an alligator? Sooner or later, it'll turn around and bite you in the ass."

He flipped onto his back, staring at the ceiling. "Go to sleep, Grace."

"But—"

"We have more pressing concerns. And you need rest in order to deal with them."

"Fine." The word blew out on a deep sigh. "I can't relax like this, with you way over there."

Six or eight inches separated them, but he knew what she meant. He'd withdrawn. With good reason, he thought. But he owed her a little solace.

He rolled toward her, wriggling closer until their noses touched. With one hand, he tugged the sheet and blanket over them both. She moaned, a contented sound, her eyelids drifting shut.

She murmured to him as if she were half asleep. "I love you."

"I love you too." He kissed her forehead. "Rest. I'll be here."

"Mmm…"

And then she fell asleep. He watched her body go slack, her breathing shallower. But more than that, he sensed her mind sinking into a deeper, more tranquil place. He brushed the hair from her eyes, trailing a fingertip down her cheek, his touch so light she didn't stir.

He would never let Tesler harm her. Never.

Edward McLean, her grandfather, swore the fake IDs he'd provided them with would shield them from Tesler—for a while. How long, no one could say.

Grace believed his quest was for vengeance, against the man who'd destroyed his life. He let her believe it. To protect her, he must deceive her.

As he studied her face, counting the lashes on her eyes, weariness settled over him. No, he could not sleep. Not here, with her. He always waited until she drifted off, then headed into the living room to sleep on the sofa. Since he woke before her every day, he'd sneak back into bed before she roused. All to keep the truth from her. Yet another secret, wedged between them.

His lids grew heavy. He fought the slumber as long as possible, but finally, it swallowed him.

A whimpering noise woke him.

Grace was gone. He sat up, searching the darkened room for signs of her. Dark? Had they slept the whole day? Unease crawled over his skin. The shadows were too black, too oily. "Grace? Where are you?"

Whimpering. Coming from… everywhere.

His heart thumped hard and fast. He leaped off the bed and spun in a circle, but still saw no one.

She was dead. He'd hallucinated coming home, talking to her, holding her.

No. He was in their bedroom. Head gripped in his hands, he fought to wring comprehension from his brain. He had returned, which meant—

"Is this what you're looking for?" Tesler's voice echoed from within the darkness creeping in around the bed.

David froze.

Grace stumbled out of the shadows, tears rolling down her cheeks. Tesler emerged after her, one hand clamped on the back of her neck, the other wielding a gun jammed into her temple.

"Well?" Tesler said. "Is this what you want?"

The scientist hurled the gun at David.

He caught it, uncertain why. The object lay heavy and cold in his palm, unfurling a frost that leeched into him, infecting his entire body. *This isn't right, this isn't right.*

"Go on," Tesler taunted. "You know you want to."

Grace let out a sharp sob. "How could you do it? I trusted you."

Tesler shoved her toward him. "I destroyed her mind, but you murdered her soul. Finish the job."

David's hand lifted, his finger curled around the trigger. He couldn't control his body, couldn't stop this.

The gunshot exploded.

Chapter Three

GRACE JOLTED AWAKE. BESIDE HER, DAVID THRASHED ON HIS BACK, HIS arms pinned to the mattress as if something held him down. His distress tore into her psyche. It sliced, and it scoured her raw from the inside out.

She jostled him. "David, wake up."

His eyes flew open. They darted from side to side, in search of phantoms spawned from his own fears and guilt. She understood his pain, but not its source, because he refused to tell her.

David shoved a trembling hand through his golden hair, gasping, sweat streaming down his face. His gaze swung sideways toward her, and he grimaced. "I woke you. I'm sorry."

"Stop apologizing and start explaining. Let me help you."

"I don't know what you mean." He mopped the sweat from his forehead with his T-shirt. "It was a bad dream caused by bad memories. A singular event. End of story."

"Uh-huh." The man honestly had no clue. Well, it was time to give him one. "I know you haven't slept in our bed for months, until this little cat nap. And I know about your nightmares."

His body went rigid. His expression blanked.

She tucked her hands under her cheek, depressing the pillow. "Come on, David. What part of telepathic bond do you not get?"

He cleared his throat.

She poked him with her knee. "I can feel when you leave the room, and no matter how far away you run, I can also feel when you're having a nightmare. The same way you felt my panic."

David settled a hand on her hip, squeezing. "I didn't realize you felt it when I leave. I should've guessed." He pulled his hand away. "I am sorry."

His head rotated toward her, those gorgeous eyes focusing on her.

She stretched, draped one leg over his, and combed her hand through his hair. He was unharmed and oh-so-alive, which meant her vision of his death had been a mistake, it must've been. If he wouldn't talk, then she'd settle for nonverbal communication. "I'm feeling refreshed. How about you?"

"No, Grace."

"What?" She let her hand fall to his cheek, her thumb brushing the corner of his mouth.

He bolted upright and patted her hip. "Time to get up. We have work to do."

When will you stop running away? She knew the answer. Not until he got his revenge. She wanted Tesler to pay too, but not at the expense of her relationship with David.

Flopping onto her back, she groaned. "What now?"

"You need to build a wall in your mind."

"May I please pee first?"

"I suppose I'll allow it." A slight smirk slanted his lips. He ripped the blankets away, and cool air wisped over her skin. "You do that, and I'll make us breakfast."

She watched him rise, that muscular body unfurling. The sinews in his back flexed under his shirt as he stretched and yawned. He believed she was oblivious. Yes, she *was* oblivious of many things, hindered by amnesia. Yet she knew he was keeping secrets from her, most likely in the foolish male belief that ignorance equaled protection.

A few months ago, she'd caught him using her computer in the middle of the night. No big deal, she'd thought. But the sight of him had stopped her—the bulging eyes, the parted lips, the blankness beyond his usual stoicism, and the way his hands gripped his thighs. She'd hesitated in the doorway between the hall and the living room, her gaze glued to David, where he hunched in the recliner with her laptop balanced on his knees. The second he noticed her, he'd clapped the laptop's lid shut along with his emotions.

When she'd asked what was wrong, he dismissed the whole incident by saying he'd "stayed up too late trolling the Internet."

Yeah, right.

David strode around the bed, offering his hands to her.

She let him help her up but frowned at him. "What happened to your urgent lead? You know, the one that made us rush to the airport in the middle of the freaking night."

"I told Sean to wait for me and we'll check it out later."

"At one o'clock this morning, it was deathly important."

"Things change." He slapped her bottom. "Go. I'll meet you in the kitchen."

She started for the door but paused on the threshold to glance back. "What changed? What's more critical than your mission to find Tesler?"

Though his expression had shuttered, his eyes burned into hers. In a voice low and steady, he said, "You should know the answer."

He pushed past her, stalking down the hallway toward the kitchen.

———

GRACE SAT CROSS-LEGGED ON THE BED, HANDS ON HER KNEES, EYES closed. A touch danced across her skin, exciting places deep within her. Softening tension. Wiping away fear. She peeked out between her lashes. David perched on the bed's edge, angled toward her, hands resting on the comforter. His gaze trailed across her flesh like a physical touch. He could caress her without moving a finger. That knowledge shot fierce arcs of desire through her.

But when he did explore her body with those hands…

"Concentrate," David said.

Right. She was supposed to be doing that. He slid his gaze over her again, drinking in every inch of her, his sapphire-blue eyes gleaming. *Oh lord.* Her body melted, and she slanted toward him as if he commanded the response from her. The lamplight burnished his short blond hair, transmuting it into twenty-four-carat gold. He sat straight, shoulders square, like a warrior angel meditating before a battle.

David frowned, the expression carving lines into his features. "You're not even trying. Building a psychic firewall won't be easy, so you have to concentrate."

"It's hard to focus when I keep thinking about—" *You kissing me.*

He closed his hand around hers. "I didn't die."

An image punched through her mind. The knife slashing down into his chest. The blood. David sprawled on the ground. She shuddered and wrapped her arms around herself, pining for the warmth, but the frost inside her resisted it. "Tesler stabbed you. I watched it happen, and there wasn't a damn thing I could do."

"It must've been a dream."

"I was awake. And unless you're implying I've gone psychotic, I did not hallucinate it."

"You aren't insane."

He rubbed her arms, his touch banishing some of the chill. A breeze from the air conditioner wafted over her, though, and the frost inside thickened, sweeping through her from her scalp to her toes. David wrapped his arms around her, and his warmth enveloped her. She rested her head on his chest, relishing his heat. *Thump-thump. Thump-thump.* His heart ticked like clockwork.

"Maybe what you saw was real," he said, "but it hasn't happened yet."

"Huh?"

He enfolded her hand in his, massaging the sensitive flesh of her palm with his thumb. "You might've had a vision of the future."

"I don't have premonitions."

"Your powers must've grown."

"What if I don't want them to?"

He shrugged. "Can't fight it. Your brush with the Golden Power might've altered your psychic makeup."

"Great," she muttered.

His lips curved into a smile. "Your powers are the strongest I've ever seen. Who knows what new abilities you might develop."

She'd implored the universe to grant her amnesia about her brush with the Golden Power and yet the memory plagued her to this day. Biting into immeasurable power. Sipping from limitless knowledge. A piece of her buried deep hungered to feast once more.

Never again.

She scooted backward, drawing out a distance between them. "Maybe it was a premonition. In which case, you need to stay home."

"Can't."

"Why?"

"You know why." He traced his index finger down her blouse and over the center of her bra, stopping at the rectangular plastic object tucked inside it. She stroked her tongue across her lower lip, overcome by the notion she could taste him in the air, and her body bent toward him just a little. With his fingertip, he pinned the object to her breastbone. "Still safeguarding our treasure?"

The husky tone of his voice excited her skin, like sparks crackling over her. *Damn him.* He was doing this to her on purpose. The flicker of irritation couldn't overwhelm her hormones.

"Yes, your blasted flash drive is safe and sound." She dived a hand down her blouse, grasped the one-inch-long device, and yanked it out. "You can have the stupid thing."

David folded his fingers around hers, enclosing the flash drive in their hands. His gaze bored into hers with an intensity that fluttered her stomach. A blush fired up in her cheeks, so hot her face must've glowed.

He nodded at their joined hands. "Maybe I should keep this."

The flash drive contained all the research data from Project Outreach, the psychic research initiative her parents and grandfather had run. When a deranged man had bought out ALI, the company that funded the research, her world plummeted into a blood-soaked nightmare. Her parents were murdered. She'd believed her grandfather also died. And a door in her mind slammed shut then, blocking out every memory she had of those events—and of David.

Until he found her again six months ago. They'd reforged their bond, psychic and emotional, but she would've risked her sanity, her life, to regain the rest.

As for the flash drive...

She shook her head. "It's safer with me."

He stared at her for so long she wondered if he'd gone catatonic. Then he dropped her hand, slanting his head. His concern radiated through the air, swirling around her, and anxiety stabbed through her. When he ran off again, she'd have to cope with her psychic intruder alone. Why did she put up with his self-imposed mission to stop Tesler?

A dull ache tugged at her heart. She put up with it because she loved him too much to give up on him without a teeth-grinding, heart-ripping, soul-wrenching fight.

She rolled her shoulders back, shimmying to get a better position. "I need to build a psychic firewall. Before you leave."

He plucked the flash drive from her hand and dropped it down her blouse. It plunked back into her bra. "Then you need to concentrate. And relax."

She settled her hands onto her knees. Closed her eyes. Exhaled. "Where did the crossroads come from?"

"I don't know. Nobody does."

She opened one eye. "How does it work?"

"You know how. You've accessed it."

She drummed her fingers.

He studied her, his face impassive, his posture straight but casual.

"Yeah, but what is it?" she asked. "What's the crossroads made of? Who created it? Why does it work?"

"Like a real crossroads, the sort that carries cars, the metaphysical crossroads acts as a junction. It has many more connecting lines than any physical crossroads has, but the principle is similar."

"But how—"

"For Christ's sake, Grace, I don't know."

His lips had twisted into a frown, and he hissed a breath out his nostrils. Though his strength and composure reassured her, once in a while she craved a taste of the passion simmering below. A kiss would've sated her better, but an annoyed outburst would suffice.

He shook his head, fighting back a smile. "You did that on purpose."

She laughed. "Yep."

He patted her knee. "Back to work."

Grace shut her eyes.

David's voice, calm and gentle, guided her. "Relax and let go of everything."

She relinquished her hold on thoughts, on sensations, on everything. Her body lightened as if floating above the bed's covers.

"Focus," David said. "Think about building a wall."

"Right, a wall. What does that mean?"

"Whatever you think it means."

"Could you be less specific?"

He squeezed her knee. "I don't even know if this can be done. But you need to try."

Letting out a long breath, she unwound her muscles one by one. Her mind drifted into blankness, hovering there. She slithered through the dark tunnel and out into the crossroads. Stars glimmered, yet none beckoned her.

She had no wish to travel anywhere. Strength, power, she coveted those things. The crossroads could slake her thirst.

Vibrations bristled her astral body. She unlocked her mental gates, throwing them wide. The energy cascaded into her, bolstering her powers, chilling her down to the core of her psyche. *Enough.* She'd harvested sufficient energy from the crossroads.

Gathering the new power she'd absorbed, she imagined its glow encompassing her, solidifying, transmuting into bricks that constructed a circular wall. Holes in her psychic structure filled in, imbuing her mind with a new strength.

A ray of warmth prodded the chill inside her. David. Calling her home. She dived through the tunnel. Pressure constricted her mind, stuffing it back into her body.

Claws clamped onto her, wrenching her back out into the crossroads. Sticky, dark power fused to her astral skin.

She grappled with the force restraining her. Its talons dug into her psyche. Her head swam. Pain lanced her eyes. *Let me go.*

"Come back to me."

David's voice reverberated in the chasm. She latched onto it, her life preserver, and kicked at the restraint. The talons slipped, loosening. She plummeted into her body, and her eyes flew open.

Blackness drowned her vision. *Oh no, please no.*

Hands seized her. David's energy poured through her, scalding away the frost.

She hugged their connection and dragged herself up it like climbing a rope. The restraining talons tore at her. She funneled David's warmth into her, firing it at the force that held her. The talons popped free.

She vaulted out into the light, gasping for breath, sucking in blessed oxygen. David stared at her, his wide eyes searching hers, his hands fastened on her shoulders. Why was he so far away? She squinted as if peering through a telescope at an object miles in the distance. His touch anchored her, yet her mind still hovered. Numb. Remote. Separate from everything physical, even the hammering of her own heart.

David shook her. "Come back, Grace. Please, whatever it is, shake it off."

His voice, riddled with tension, chopped through the invisible fog. His words shepherded her out of limbo and back into reality. Air tickled her skin, cool and dry. Humming vibrated her eardrums. The AC had just kicked on. She wiggled her trembling fingers, the nails scraping across her cotton sweatpants.

She blinked once, twice. The world shifted into focus.

David covered her hands with one of his. The heat of his skin bled into her. Warm. Alive. Normal. She hadn't been dragged into a nether-world.

He grasped her face in his free hand. "What the hell happened?"

"I—I don't know. Something grabbed me, it was alive, it... wanted me."

He plowed his fingers into her hair to tilt her head up, bringing their gazes into alignment. "Are you okay?"

"I think so. Yes." She forced a smile. "Whatever it was, it's over."

His eyes narrowed, and his lips compressed.

"David, I'm fine, I swear."

If she told him about the talons, and the oily energy, he'd realize it might be connected to the Golden Power. She was tainted, forever. How could he want her if he knew? Then again, if he accepted it, he'd worry about her, about what was happening to her. The distraction, in the middle of his quest for Tesler, might get him killed.

She drew his hand out of her hair, feathering a kiss over his palm. "I get anxious about using my powers, you know that. Probably all this was. Anxiety."

His shoulders slumped a little, his lips relaxed, and he nodded. "Okay. We'll chalk it up to stress affecting your powers—for the moment. Did you at least try building a firewall?"

"Yes." She rolled her shoulders back and straightened. "I'm not sure what I did, but I think it worked."

"Good."

David's phone chirped. He wrestled it out of his pocket.

Grace leaned forward to read the caller ID, spotting a name she knew. Sean Vandenbrook. David's sort-of protégé.

He gave her a little shove. "Stop snooping. I have to take this."

"You know what he wants."

"Uh-huh." Tapping the touch screen, he grunted a greeting. His expression blanked. "I'm on my way. Don't move until I get there."

David jammed the phone back in his pocket.

She clasped her hands on her lap, quelling the lingering tremors. "You're leaving."

"Yes," he said. "I ordered him not to, but Sean traced the lead we got earlier today and he thinks he found another of Tesler's facilities in Montana. If I don't get there quickly, he'll go in alone."

She sighed, her shoulders deflating. He was right, but she still itched to throttle him, to burst into tears, to scream, to implore him to stay. Instead, she spoke in an even tone that demanded all her self-control to achieve. "Sean's even more obsessed with finding Tesler than you are. He could get himself killed."

The teenager needed adult supervision. Sometimes she thought David did too. Both he and Sean pursued every lead, no matter how lame, to track down Tesler. How many times had they stumbled home with bruises and cuts? She'd lost count. There was nothing she could say to stop them. Right now, she could've strangled the pair of them, one with each hand.

She anchored her hands on her hips. "Besides, even when you're here, you're not really here. I get more attention from the mailman."

"Grace, don't do that."

"What?"

"Don't retreat into your fortress of sarcasm."

The anger boiled off in an instant, dissipating into the air. He was right, again, and she hated herself for being such a bitch. "I'm sorry, I don't mean to do it. Stuff sort of bubbles out of me. You better head out, help Sean. I can call Grandpa if I need anything."

David scrunched his eyebrows, the only crack in his unreadable expression. "Are you sure you don't mind if I go?"

Of course she minded, dammit. But what else could she say? She'd deal with it. Like a mature adult.

Rats. She hated being a grown-up.

"Sean needs a rational adult to rein him in," she said. "I insist you go."

He nodded and then strode out of the bedroom. She pursued him down the hallway to the front door. A stoic mask cloaked his face, revealing nothing but those glittering eyes.

She bit her lip. "Remember, just because Sean can heal you doesn't mean you can take crazy risks. I expect you to come home in one piece. Don't make me have to rescue you again."

His features tensed, darkened by a reaction that baffled her. What had she said?

"I'll be careful," David said. He spun away and grasped the doorknob. "Are you sure you're okay with this?"

"Yes." The word burned on her tongue, but she had to say it. He needed to hear it.

He yanked the door open.

Humid air whispered over her, cloying and hot. Her socked feet slid across the wood floor, heavy and stiff, unwilling to let her lift them even while she closed the distance to David. Her hand lighted on his arm, and she soaked in the heady warmth of him. Her fingers caressed the firm ripples of his muscular body, tracing the lines up his arms and onto his back. Before he left, she yearned to etch him into her memory.

Fear crunched her heart in its icy fist. The vision. Tesler. Blood slicking her hands. Pain searing her chest. His pain. His blood.

He might not come home this time. *Remember.*

She explored him with both hands, relishing the contrast between hard muscle and tender flesh. As the fabric of his shirt rasped across her palm, a shiver vibrated through her. Even through the barrier, his heat spread into her palms. It poured into her body, dousing the tension, snuffing out the fear.

"Go," she murmured. "I'll be okay, and Sean needs you more than I do right now."

His body tensed. His muscles undulated, igniting a tingle in her hands. It unfurled through her body in a blistering, aching wave that tightened something deep inside her. *Oh God.* She gnawed her lip, battling the urge to drag him into the house. Slam the door. Jam the deadbolt. Fall on her knees and plead with him to stay here, with her.

David whirled around and crushed her against him.

His kiss consumed her in a fiery torrent that scorched away reason and doubt. Her body wilted against him as his lips sparked firecracker explosions inside her. Every ounce of his passion and anguish rushed through her mind and body, a gift of sensation that stole the breath from her. The world gyrated around her. A delicious ache washed through her body. Her legs quivered, on the verge of buckling. Heat flushed her skin, her chest heaved with every breath. *Oh David.*

He pushed her away and stomped out the door.

Chapter Four

The door banged shut. Grace sagged against the wood, tears streaming from her eyes. Sobs shook her body from head to toe. Her legs quivered, and breaths gasped out of her, spiking pains through her chest. She'd done what she must. She'd let him go. As the psychic gift David had granted her sluiced out, a deep chill numbed her heart and mind. The sizzle of living energy that had sparked between them fizzled out. Their connection crackled inside her, yet an emptiness cleaved her soul.

She sank to the floor, knees bent in front of her, back against the door. If he survived his quest, he would come back to her. Either way, she prayed she'd done the right thing.

Her head thunked into the wood as her eyelids drifted shut. So hard to force them open again. Why bother? Everything she'd fought for was yanked away from her. David. Her parents. At least David was alive.

For how long?

She hugged her knees, letting her head fall forward onto them. Life offered her two choices. Cower here bawling and wallowing in self-pity, or hoist her ass up off the floor and charge back into the fray.

Her body whimpered for a rest. Her eyes burned with fatigue. Her mind tumbled into a web of half-complete thoughts that tangled around her. Lying here, she might shut out the world. Disregard the drama. Relinquish control.

Get up, dammit. In all her life—at least the part of it she remembered—not once had she resigned control. Would she give up now? Weep and moan and bitch?

Hell no.

She jumped up, wiped the tears away, and tromped across the living room to her corner office. How could she help David? At this moment, she had no clue. Getting back to work, earning a little money to support them both, that would bolster her morale. And lord, did she need a boost.

Pangs sliced into her eyes. A vise cinched tight across her forehead. She slumped onto her desk chair, massaging her temples. Pain throbbed behind her eyes, spreading through her brow and down into her jaw. She snatched up a box of breath mints and popped one into her mouth. The soothing flavor of peppermint trickled down her throat, and still, her stomach churned.

The sunlight beaming in through the windows speared into her brain.

Damn. She should've known better than to tap into her powers twice in one day. The crossroads had leveled its penalty in the form of a migraine.

Shutting her eyes, she rubbed them with the heels of her hands.

Lights pulsed behind her lids. The room tilted and twirled.

She stumbled down the hallway and into the bedroom. Her stomach heaved. She bolted for the bathroom and collapsed in front of the toilet, draping her arms over the bowl. Seconds ticked by as she clung to the toilet seat. The sourness of bile tainted her mouth.

An engine rumbled outside, growing louder.

The nausea relented. She leaned back, inhaling long breaths of cool air. The chemical scent of toilet-bowl cleaner assaulted her senses. *Yuck.*

The rumbling ceased.

She kneaded the knot in her neck, but still, the migraine pulsated through her skull. She slapped both hands on the sink's lip and levered her body off the floor. Light glanced off the mirror, straight into her brain. She ducked her head. To avoid the brightness, yes. But mostly to avoid glimpsing her face in the mirror. Good thing David had left. Every woman dreaded being seen with red eyes and pale lips. And she couldn't forget the gonna-vomit-any-second look on her face.

The doorbell buzzed.

Wonderful. A visitor.

She splashed water on her face, pinched her cheeks for a little color, and trotted to the front door, ducking into the bedroom along the way to snag her revolver. The doorbell rang again. She peeked through the peephole. A gray-haired man stared back at her.

Who the hell?

Holding the gun in her right hand, behind her back, she swung the door open to the limit of the security chain and pasted on a generic smile. "May I help you?"

The man met her gaze head-on, with an expression of detached interest on his clean-shaven face. "Ms. Powell, my name is Roland Wickham. I've come on behalf of Gabriel Amador."

He spoke with an English accent, his words enunciated with precision.

Bracing her hand on the door, she eyed the man's polo shirt and khaki pants. "I don't know any Gabriel Amador."

"Yes, well, you may not recognize the name. But you've had contact with him." Wickham clasped his hands behind his back, rocking forward on his toes. "Quite recently. And in a rather… unusual manner."

Grace stared at him, her jaw slackening. Her tongue probably stuck out too, but she didn't care. Unusual manner. What the blazes was this guy talking about?

Wickham screwed his mouth into an uncomfortable expression. "Gabriel understands why you ignored his text messages, and why you're blocking his communications altogether. He asked me to call on you in the old-fashioned manner."

"I haven't blocked any texts or phone calls."

"Not telephone calls. You've blocked his… metaphysical contact."

A shiver tickled her spine. He meant the brain hacking. This man's employer—or friend, or whatever—was taking credit for the psychic assault that robbed her of any security she'd scraped together over the last six months. Gabriel Amador had hacked her mind. And now he dispatched this polite Englishman to smooth out her feathers. Did he honestly believe this would placate her? *He must be insane.*

Amador might've taken credit for the attack, but she had no way of knowing whether he actually was the psychic intruder, or how much he knew about paranormal powers. Better play it safe.

She locked her gaze on Wickham's green eyes. "I don't know what you mean."

"I believe you do." He inched toward her, stopping near enough that she tensed, but far enough away that she could bang the door shut in his face, if necessary. In a flat whisper, he said, "Gabriel understands your predicament. He's been there before. Give him a chance to explain, and I'm certain you will realize why he intruded on your privacy."

Grace dropped her hand to the doorknob. Intruded on her privacy? Was he joking? The psychic assault had torn through her innate defenses, exposing her innermost self. No permission. No warning. *Wham.* And her world imploded.

She adjusted her grip on the revolver behind her back. "Why didn't your pal pay me a visit himself?"

"He believed an intermediary would prove more helpful in easing your concerns. It's his way."

"Sure, sending his lackey fosters lots of trust."

With a curt nod, Wickham stepped back. "You have an open invitation to visit Gabriel's home, at the address he provided to you. I assure you he wants to help."

She rolled her shoulders back, lifting her chin. "Tell Mr. Amador he can take a flying leap off a very tall cliff. And I hope he lands face-first in a pile of cactus on top of a fire ant mound."

"I'm sure that will amuse him."

She grunted. "I'm thrilled."

Wickham extended a hand.

Grace shoved her free hand into her pants pocket.

"If you change your mind," Wickham said, withdrawing his hand, "our door is always open."

He rotated on his heels and marched down the concrete path to the driveway.

She poked her head out to watch the man as he tromped to the silver Jeep Cherokee parked in the driveway. She waited until the vehicle disappeared down the street, and then she shut the door. *Click.* The lock engaged. She clutched the gun to her stomach, its cold weight a mild comfort. Locks and deadbolts, even the revolver, couldn't protect her from telepathic spies.

Amador had resorted to sending his minion to deliver his message. If he was the psychic intruder, then her mental firewall worked. Nobody could break in.

Thank you, David.

Her pulse quickened. Had David arrived in Montana yet? No, he couldn't have. He'd just left. Their link assured her he was alive and un-harmed, for now. She itched to tap into her powers and remote view him, to see for herself nothing had happened to him. The impulse throbbed inside her. *Do it. You'll feel better.* No, she must not invade David's privacy the way Amador crashed through hers. When David uncovered another lead or stumbled onto Tesler's facility, he'd call her. *Patience.*

Crap. She'd never been good at that.

If she tracked down Tesler, then David would come home. But how might she locate the scientist? She sometimes employed her remote viewing, sort of a combination between astral projection and GPS-like tracking, to check on David, but she couldn't use it on anyone else. Without an intimate connection to the other party, her psychic GPS failed. No one she knew or had read about possessed the ability to locate another person simply by thinking about them.

There must be another way. She'd find it, dammit.

Back at her desk, she struggled to concentrate on work. Her latest client, who'd promised his self-help book would be "easy-peasy" to design, had way-laid her yesterday by insisting on adding complicated tables and charts. Green tea and chocolate sustained her for fifteen minutes or so, but then she flagged, cradling her forehead in both hands, elbows on the desktop.

The doorbell buzzed.

She heaved her body off the chair and trundled to the door, pulling it open with the security chain in place.

A bald man smiled at her, his hazel eyes sparkling a slightly darker hue than hers.

Grinning, she unhooked the chain and swung the door wide.

Edward McLean spread his arms in invitation, and she flew into her grandfather's embrace. He smelled of Old Spice and black coffee. His hand patted her hair, and the tension cramping her muscles, her heart, eased a bit. She ushered him into the living room and parked her butt on the sofa, slouching into the cushions. He sat in the recliner. David's chair.

She tore her attention from the chair's chocolate-brown fabric, evading the memories it evoked, and focused on her grandfather's face. "David called you."

"From the airport, yes. He's concerned. We both are."

"I'm fine." She folded her arms over her chest. "I don't need a babysitter."

He propped one ankle atop the other knee and clasped his hands over his belly. "You had a premonition."

"It's nothing, I'm okay."

With a sharp shake of his head, he frowned at her. "Grace, you have to stop downplaying these things. You had a terrifying experience, believed David was dead for hours, and you never called me."

She grunted. "Wake you up at an ungodly hour to tell you… What? I had a panic attack after a bad dream?"

"It was no dream, we all know that. And you do not panic. Not without extreme provocation."

The air rushed out of her as a loud sigh, and she flopped her head back against the sofa. "I have to do something. David will get himself killed if I don't—" She thumped her fists on her thighs. "Gah! I can't just sit here pretending life goes on as normal. Nothing about my life is normal."

Edward rose and shuffled to her, perching on the coffee table. His hands wrapped her fists. She flinched at the sudden warmth, unaware of how cold her hands were.

His eyebrows wrinkled, lifting into a V over his nose. "David told me about your visitor."

Her head snapped up. "What?"

David couldn't know about Wickham's visit. Could he?

"Yes," her grandfather said. "The mental assault must've been disturbing, more than you're willing to let on."

Ohhh, *that* visitor.

She shrugged. "It won't happen again." She wrested a hand free of his and tapped her temple with one finger. "Like a fortress."

"I heard. But the text messages—"

"Were creepy, yeah." She sat forward, laying her hand over his. "Frankly, there's not a damn thing you can do to protect me from telepathic stalkers. So please, trust me to handle this my way."

"Grace, I know you're strong and capable. David and I are simply trying to—"

"Protect me. I got the message." She stood and stomped to the window that overlooked the front yard and driveway. "I appreciate the sentiment, and I love you both for it, but honestly, I can take care of myself."

"You asked me to trust you." He came up beside her, hands in his pants pockets, eyeing her sideways. "But you won't trust us—me and David. Why?"

She leaned against the window frame and scrutinized a tiny crack in the glass. "I'm sorry. Please believe me, I'm trying, but I got used to handling things myself when I had amnesia and you guys were in California."

He bowed his head, shoulders sagging. "We shouldn't have left you alone in Texas. Keeping you in the dark was my idea, not David's. If you need someone to blame, it's me, Grace." Despair crept into his voice when he said, "I failed Christine. I can't bear to fail you too, Grace."

She threw her arms around him. In a tone as fierce as her hug, she told him, "Mom wouldn't blame you. I don't blame you. Please don't worry about me." She pulled away, blinking back stray tears, and straightened. "I'll be okay."

Whether he believed her or not, she couldn't say, but his mood brightened a bit, and by the time he departed, she thought he was moderately convinced she wouldn't die today. The best either of them could hope for these days. As she watched his car roll down the street, she shut and locked the front door.

Two visitors in one day. She preferred the second one. Roland Wickham had been polite but unforthcoming.

A thought bubbled to the surface of her brain. Gabriel Amador had contacted her at the exact time when Sean and David caught another lead on Tesler and his new undertaking. Coincidence? Reason said yes, but the gnawing in her gut warned her no. Once again, outside forces conspired to corner her. In this go-round, she refused to twiddle her thumbs and wait for David to guide her. If he chose to run off in search of his demons, then she would grab hold of the reins in her own life. David might find answers, or this "mission" might derail like all the others.

They needed outside support. *She* needed support.

Wickham had told her Amador wanted to help. Could she trust either man?

Hell no.

Her vision replayed in her mind. David on his knees. Tesler wielding a knife. Blood. Agony.

No, no, no. She must do everything in her power to prevent the premonition from coming true. But how? She lacked the one tool she needed. Information.

It granted power, right? Well then, she better steal some. Or wheedle it out of Amador.

A cold fist clenched around her heart. *Bad idea, this is a very bad idea.* She'd exhausted her options over the last six months. Maybe her vision wouldn't happen, but she refused to wait and see. Time to risk a new tactic.

Amador schemed to use her, though for what, she had no clue. Why not use him right back?

David would kill her for this. And for a psychic, that meant he didn't even have to come home to do it.

You've got to end this once and for all.

Time to investigate on her own.

CHAPTER FIVE

A CHILL WIND SIZZLED THROUGH THE TREETOPS AS DAVID CROUCHED behind a jack pine for shelter. He shoved his hands in his jacket pockets. Despite his clothing, olive-green camouflage, he preferred to hide behind the tree while scouting the location. He must enact every precaution, not just for himself, but for Grace too.

He never should've left her.

Stop thinking about it. You're here now, focus on that.

He exercised caution for someone else besides Grace. He did it for Sean.

The teenage boy crouched behind another tree, an arm's length from David. At seventeen, Sean fancied himself a man, yet David had trouble thinking of him as anything other than the cowering boy he'd met while interned at the facility in California's remote Mojave Desert. Tesler and his cronies at ALI had exulted in tormenting anyone with paranormal powers, whatever their age. The memory of his first encounter with Sean replayed in his mind—the boy curled up in the fetal position on his bed, a blanket lumped on top of him, cocooning him from head to toe. That had been less than a year ago.

Today, Sean crouched behind a tree dressed in camouflage, his red hair shaved into a buzz cut and his expression stern, the portrait of a commando wannabe. Sean might've shed his outward fear, but David sensed it lurking underneath, like a pond cloaked in ice.

The wind gusted, shaking the trees.

Panic flashed across Sean's face, blanching his fair skin. His freckles stood out against the pallor, like stars in reverse. Sean locked his green eyes on David for a second. Then the boy shrugged, twisted his mouth into an annoyed expression, and swung his gaze back to the object of their investigation.

David leaned sideways to peer around the tree. There, about a hundred feet away inside a clearing, hunkered a metal shed about ten feet square and eight feet tall. High above, a satellite dish clung to the trunk of a towering tree, mounted near the top. Nothing else hinted at the presence of anything more sinister than squirrels. Still, he and Sean needed to keep an eye out for the wildlife, as well as security personnel. If this was the new facility, then it would have security, of the covert kind.

David glanced at Sean. The boy pointed at his eyes with two fingers and then shut his lids. It was a signal they had developed. It meant one of them should remote view the location in question. Sean opened his eyes and pointed one finger at his chest.

David shook his head. He indicated his own chest.

Sean slumped his shoulders and rolled his eyes, his way of saying, "I'm not a baby anymore, you overprotective dork."

David supposed teenagers didn't say "dork" anymore. Whatever the derogatory phrase associated with it, the expression conveyed petulance. Sean wanted to take a more active role in their investigations, but David clung to his overprotective instinct. Besides, he was better at RV'ing than Sean was.

And the boy knew it. That was part of the sentiment behind the eye-rolling.

Closing his eyes, David let his mind go blank. He soared up into the crossroads, hunting for the path that would lead him into the facility, if the metal shed concealed a facility. A star in the crossroads pulsed, and he latched on to it, letting it pull him ever downward, spiraling through a dark tunnel.

He hurtled out into the real world.

Light blinded him. He winced and flung up a hand to shield his eyes. Though no one else could see him, and he had no physical body when remote viewing, he always envisioned himself in a physical form. So far as he knew, all travelers experienced it this way. The human mind, even when disconnected from its body, fought to make sense of its surroundings. That was his theory, at least.

He stood in a corridor. The glare of white lights swallowed details. With every second that ticked past, his vision acclimated to the light. After a moment that felt like forever, but must've eaten up no more than thirty seconds, he discerned more of his surroundings.

The brilliant glow emanated from bulbs recessed into the ceiling. He shuffled down the corridor, past closed doors set into the walls at regular intervals. White paint coated everything except the floor. Even the door-knobs were white. His phantom shoes traveled over the pale-gray linoleum in silence. He spotted no markings on the first two doors. As he strode deeper into the facility, he watched for signs of life, or at least an actual sign to clue him in to what function this place served.

The doors did bear markings, he realized, though none that made sense to him. Alongside each door, at waist level, raised figures—dots, lines, and squares—designated each door with a unique code. It looked like Morse code or a strange kind of Braille. He reached out to finger the markings, but of course, with no physical body, he couldn't touch them. His fingers met emptiness.

The ventilation system hissed overhead. He crept down the hall, glancing at each doorway he passed, spotting nothing that might alert him to this building's purpose. Another facility? Another hellhole where Tesler tortured psychics? He clenched his jaw, grinding his teeth. He must thwart the scientist, whatever the cost. Tesler must never get his claws into Grace or Sean or anyone else.

David rubbed his forehead. He'd essentially left Sean alone outside this building. The boy longed to expand his powers. Would he attempt more advanced feats of psychic ability while David was distracted in here? He hoped he'd taught Sean better than that, but the boy's impulse to grab more power was strong. A couple of weeks ago, he'd told David, "I want to manifest. That would be so cool."

"You can't."

"Why not?"

David had shrugged. "You're not Grace."

"But I'm strong too. Why can't I manifest like she does? Why can't you?"

"Because we are nowhere near as strong as Grace is." He'd laid a hand on Sean's shoulder. "We can't manifest without her help. Accept it."

Naturally, Sean balked at the suggestion. The truth was irrefutable, though. David knew of no other travelers who could manifest. He'd heard rumors, but nothing concrete. As far as he knew, Grace alone possessed the ability to manifest a physical body, for herself or others.

A thwapping reverberated down the corridor, from around a corner twenty feet ahead. David froze. The noise grew louder and louder, nearer and nearer. He backed up, staying close to the wall, and locked his gaze on the corner. *Thwap, thwap.*

Murmuring. Nearby. Getting closer. The thwapping sharpened into *clomp, clomp, clomp.*

Two men dressed in white lab coats traipsed into view. They paused at the intersection.

David hesitated twenty feet away. He pressed his body into the wall, a human pancake on a vertical skillet. He knew the men couldn't see him, since he had no physical body, but the instinct to conceal himself tugged too hard. He'd given up trying to rationalize the urge a long time ago.

"I know what the boss wants," the older of the two men said. He ran a hand through his rim of gray hair and over his bald crown. "It's a bad idea."

"We do what he tells us," the younger man said, "no matter what we think of it. That's called doing our jobs, Yellen."

"Even JT couldn't contain her. How the hell are we supposed to?"

The younger man shook his head, tousling his shoulder-length chestnut hair. "We do whatever we have to do."

Yellen snorted. "That's easy for you to say, Evans. You won't be involved in the containment process. If she lashes out, I'll die, but you'll be safe and sound in your office."

"She won't lash out. The boss will keep her under control."

Her. She. A double-edged blade of fear and realization sliced through David. They couldn't mean…

No, God, please.

"I don't like this induction program," Yellen said. The crow's feet around his eyes deepened as he tensed his features. "Don't care if Jackson Tennant himself dreamed it up, he was a lunatic after all."

"The boss isn't." Evans adjusted his black-rimmed glasses with one finger. "If he wants the girl, then we help him get her. If his methods don't work, then we use our well-tested induction procedures to bring her in. It's our job."

Yellen's shoulders deflated, accentuating his flabby physique. He scowled at his fit colleague. "I know. But I heard she blew up our best facility."

"JT did that, not the woman."

"Well, whoever did it, we still haven't recovered from the loss of data and materials. Besides, I don't care to be blown to smithereens, not even in the pursuit of knowledge and scientific advancement."

Evans snickered. "You think that's why we're doing all this? Scientific advancement?"

"Why else?"

"Power, man. Power." Evans leaned closer to Yellen, as if sharing a secret. "Whoever controls these freaks and their powers has the potential to control the world. If we do what the boss wants, then he might let us share in the spoils, get it?"

Yellen harrumphed.

The younger man sighed. "We do what the boss wants. Nothing more, nothing less."

The older man studied the floor for a couple of seconds. Then he raised his head and nodded. "You're right. We execute our duties, no matter what. Doesn't mean I have to like it."

"Induction works, dude."

Yellen jerked his head in a curt nod and grimaced.

Evans lifted his angular chin. "One way or another, either willingly or by force, we will bring in Grace Powell."

David jerked as if Evans had punched him in the gut. Pressure that originated deep inside him pulverized his heart. This was what he'd feared for six months, the impetus for his obsession, and yet he hadn't believed, deep down, that it could happen. Until now.

His insides crystallized into ice. His heart thudded in his chest, and although he knew it wasn't a real heart, the pounding ached no less than the genuine article. This must end. Today. This instant.

But first, he had to warn Grace.

Anguish tunneled straight through his heart into his soul. He collapsed to his knees, the imagined bones hitting the floor in silence. How could he have abandoned her, knowing about her vision and the telepathic intruder? What if the brain hacker obeyed Tesler's orders? This was all his fault.

So save her, jackass.

He snapped upright. Last time, she'd rescued him from a facility much like this one. But this time around, he would rescue her. He'd strap on his macho and gun down anyone who got in his way. No one would hurt Grace. No one.

Holding his position inside the facility, he stretched out his powers to connect with Grace. To contact anyone else, he'd have to retreat into the crossroads. With Grace, he required nothing more than to think of her. To fully contact her, to ascertain her whereabouts and communicate with her, he must strengthen the connection. Feed power into it. Widen the pathway.

A shock jolted through him. Everything around him spun. His mind whirled out of control. Pain, sharp and hot, gored him on a metaphysical level. His lock on the facility frayed. He struggled to link with Grace, but the shock walloped him again. His RV grip on the facility disintegrated. His mind shot upward, through the tunnel, into the crossroads. He twirled and twirled, like a top set loose on a smooth table. Lights blurred around him. He couldn't latch on to one light, couldn't grasp any connection that might guide him out of here. Every time he flailed for a hold, his mind pitched backward as if it bounced off—

A wall.

Shit. Grace had built a psychic barrier so strong nothing could ram through it, not even him.

His mind tumbled out of the crossroads, spiraling downward. He punched back into his body. For precious seconds, he struggled to breathe, to see, to untangle the sensory input overwhelming his brain. The surroundings blurred and mingled. His head pounded, his chest ached, and his head throbbed. Cradling his head in his hands, he forced his lungs to draw in deep breaths. Grace endured headaches after using her powers. He didn't. The amount of energy demanded by traveling drained him, yes, but it triggered no pain.

Until today.

The world around him coalesced into recognizable shapes. Trees. Bushes. Grass. The stench of sweat permeated the air. A breeze chilled his chest through his damp shirt. Between his fingers, he glimpsed Sean staring at him. Eyes wide. Face pale. Lips parted. David's stress must've shown on his face. He worked to erase the pained expression. He must've succeeded, because the color returned to Sean's face, though he still gaped as if David had grown a pair of horns. Just to make sure, David palpated his head. No horns.

Sean whispered, "You looked like you were dying."

"I'm fine," David said in an equally soft voice.

He did feel better. The pounding in his head had dissipated, although intense fatigue blanketed him. Sweat dribbled down his temples. He swiped it away with the back of his hand.

Grace's firewall blocked him, and yet, before leaving the house, he'd gifted her with his emotions in a last-ditch effort to reinforce their connection, even as he recognized the need to temper it, for her sake. She'd built her new psychic defenses before that. Their link wasn't severed, merely dampened. Maybe he could get through if he calculated it just right and—

No time to think about it.

Grace was in danger. Tesler's minions had zeroed their sights in on her. They would storm the house and capture her, if they hadn't already.

His throat tightened. He clenched his hands into fists, the nails digging into his palms. Pain sparked in his flesh. To warn Grace, he'd have to resort to old-fashioned, purely physical means.

He dug out his phone. A text message wouldn't do. She might not heed his warning unless she heard it from him directly. But if this facility boasted the kind of security he'd encountered at the Mojave Desert location, then the system might detect voices outside. He couldn't risk talking loud enough for Grace to hear him over the phone. But he must warn her.

Screw it. If a security squad lassoed him, so be it.

David caught Sean's attention by waving his hand. Then he risked speaking in a louder, though still hushed, voice. "Get out of here. I'll meet you at the car."

Sean shook his head.

David mouthed, "Go."

Sean glared at him for a second, but then rose into a semi-crouch and trotted back the way they'd come. His footfalls whisked against the grass and dirt, barely audible. David prayed no one else heard Sean's movements.

He tapped the phone's touch screen, dialing a programmed number.

Sean's silhouette vanished from sight. His footsteps faded into silence. With any luck, the boy had reached a safe distance.

The call transferred to Grace's voicemail. Her cheery voice instructed him to leave a message at the tone. His gut churned. Acid soured his tongue. How soon would she retrieve her messages? *Dammit.* He'd assumed he could catch her and deliver the news as close to face-to-face as possible.

A long beep rattled his eardrums. He had a minute, maybe two, to convince her before the blasted voicemail cut him off.

"Grace, it's me," he said. "Please listen carefully. Tesler's men are coming for you. Do not stay at home. Do not use your cell after this. Hang up, ditch the phone, and get the hell out of there. Your psychic firewall is—"

Click. The line went dead.

A low battery warning flashed on the screen.

David jumped to his feet. He must get home. As fast as possible.

Sean stumbled out of the woods straight ahead of David. The boy scowled, his shoulders slumped. "I'm sorry. I tried to get away."

"Away from what?" David eyed Sean through slitted eyes. The boy held his hands behind his back. David slouched forward, knees bent. "What's wrong? Are you injured?"

Two figures traipsed out of the trees behind Sean. The burly men wielded semiautomatic handguns, both trained on Sean. A third man emerged from the woods to David's left. The newcomer targeted his weapon at David. All three men wore camouflage outfits with military-style boots and two-way radios clipped to their belts.

The closest man, the one fixated on David, said, "You're coming with us."

David attempted to look confused. "We were just out for a hike. Didn't mean to cause any trouble."

The man shook his head, an unfriendly smile on his lips. "We aren't that stupid. And besides, we know who you are. David Ransom and Sean Vandenbrook. Ain't facial recognition software awesome?"

David exhaled a long sigh. What energy he had left flooded out of him. He must've talked too loudly, or for too long, on the phone with Grace's voicemail. And he'd gotten Sean wrapped up in his mess.

"Take me," David said, "but let the boy go. I'm the one you want."

"Nice offer," the stranger said. "But I don't think so."

The man shoved a hand into his jacket pocket, pulling out a nylon zip tie.

David surveyed the area for an escape route. He spied more human-shaped figures in the woods, encircling them like wolves homing in on their prey. David grabbed for his gun, berthed in a shoulder holster under his jacket.

One of the men behind Sean jammed his gun into the boy's temple.

The other man, the only one who'd spoken so far, told David, "Make it easier on both of you. Don't fight."

He couldn't fight, not with so many of them versus him and Sean. In any other situation, he might've tapped into his powers to barge his way out of this mess. Since he'd emptied his energy reserves in the failed effort to contact Grace, he had nothing left to fight them with.

At least Grace would know of the danger to her. Getting captured was worth any torment that might follow if it meant Grace would be safe.

David dropped his gun.

Tesler had won this round.

CHAPTER SIX

OWN A HALLWAY THE TWO OF THEM MARCHED, SINGLE FILE, WITH Roland Wickham leading the way. Grace stared at the back of his head since closed doors barred her view of the rooms on either side of the hall. Though Gabriel Amador had invited her to his home, clearly he did not care to expose all his secrets to her. Thoughts of what might lie beyond the doors bounced around in her brain, tickling her curiosity.

Wickham halted at a door and knocked. A voice inside invited them to enter, and Wickham swung the door wide, motioning for her to go inside.

She hesitated.

A thirty-minute drive down increasingly desolate roads, followed by a tooth-jarring trip up a long, two-track driveway, delivered her to this house. She'd opted to come here. Yet a quiet voice in the back of her mind warned her against it even now. Maybe it was David's voice, borne of memories.

Wickham waved his hand again.

She faced the room and swallowed. *Just do it, coward.*

Grasping her purse strap, she inched across the threshold.

The musky smell of leather washed over her, mixed with a lightly floral aroma. The combination peaked her senses.

The door clicked shut behind her.

Across the room, on the opposite side of a massive wooden desk, a man lounged in a leather executive chair. Gabriel Amador waved toward one of two leather chairs, smaller than his, positioned on this side of the room. Grace took a step and froze. She chewed her lip. Amador had probably hacked into her mind, for pity's sake. And what, he expected her to just sit down and strike up a conversation?

She scuffled backward a step, snaking her hand behind her back to grasp the doorknob. When she twisted, the knob turned. A coil of tension slackened inside her. Not locked in, at least. She dipped her fingers into her purse just far enough to touch the cold metal of her .357 revolver. The weapon granted her a modicum of security, but only that much.

Heaven almighty, when David found out about this, he'd chain her to the sofa to keep her at home. She knew she shouldn't have come here, but she couldn't sit at home watching chick flicks while David and Sean gambled their lives on a frantic search for a boogeyman. Her psychic wall blocked out everyone except David, as far as she knew, but she still needed to confront *her* boogeyman.

Amador flicked on a lamp. Sun-bright light glanced off the white walls, piercing her eyes. The remnants of her migraine throbbed behind her temples. She squinted and threw a hand up to shield her gaze.

"I won't harm you," Amador said, his voice seasoned with a light accent. "Take a seat, please."

Grace glanced at the nearest chair. Pursed her lips. Tapped her toe. Good or bad, crazy or sane, whatever his motivations, Gabriel Amador was a stranger to her. She thought. At times like this, amnesia really sucked. She might've met Amador last year and not remember it.

"If you mean no harm," she said, "then why did you hack into my brain and scare the holy living shit out of me?"

"I apologize for that, truly. But hacking seems an exaggerated description. A telepathic intrusion was the most expedient way to test your reaction."

Intrusion. He made it sound almost genteel.

She tilted her head, squinting at him. "Test my reaction to what?"

He shrugged one shoulder. "Me. Those things that we share in common. Our special connection."

Yeah, she'd heard this spiel before. From the only other person who ever hacked her brain. A man who believed he shared a "special connection" with her. *You are mine, golden girl,* he'd proclaimed. JT had battered his way into her mind, thrusting those words inside. Never again would she allow an assault like that.

She swallowed hard. "We don't have a connection, special or otherwise. Having the same powers doesn't make us soul mates."

Amador leaned forward to rest his elbows on the desktop. His expression faded into something inscrutable, halfway between curiosity and annoyance. He steepled his fingers and propped his chin on them. "I am not Jackson Tennant. I have no delusions that you and I share a psychic bond or that your blood will grant me your powers."

Jackson Tennant. The name blustered through her mind like a hurricane wind, propelling the memories of six months ago to the forefront. Acid rose in her throat. It tainted her tongue with a sour, almost metallic taste. Like blood. But the tang rose from her memories, not her stomach. Snapshots flashed in her mind, bits of memories she'd regained six months ago.

A car flipping end over end. A sickening crunch. Steam hissing. A voice wailing.

Gabriel Amador lowered his hands. His eyes widened a touch. "I'm sorry. I reminded you of something terrible, didn't I? Something Tennant did to you." He stood halfway, pointing to the chair. "Please sit. You look pale."

Was that concern in his voice? She dropped her arms to her sides. And for reasons she couldn't comprehend, words tumbled out of her mouth. Maybe she needed to say them, to sweep the memories away again. "JT murdered my parents. He caused the car accident that killed them and then—" She snapped her jaw shut and sucked in a deep breath. "Can we talk about something else?"

"Of course. My apologies for dredging up bad memories. I know how painful that can be."

The tight coil inside her unwound a little more. *Crap.* She did not want to like him. She shouldn't like him. He'd stalked and terrified her. Right now, though, she needed answers from him.

What had Wickham told her? *Gabriel understands your predicament. He's been there before.* Been where? She needed to know. Amador might have information that would help her. With Tesler's goons on her trail, she must take risks to survive. She needed to do this. She *could* do this. Alone.

Squaring her shoulders, she strode to the chair and settled her butt onto the cushioned seat. Perched on the edge, she plunked her purse onto her lap. Hands folded over the bag, she locked her gaze on Amador's dark-chocolate eyes.

He smiled, flashing neon-white teeth lined up in perfect rows. His cinnamon skin darkened a shade in the brilliance of his dental work. Oh yeah, no way those were natural teeth. "I've anticipated this meeting more than you know."

"How flattering." There she went again, mouthing off when she really wanted to cry or scream or bolt for the door. David called it her fortress of sarcasm. Not complimentary, but so true she winced even thinking about it. Today, she could use a fortress.

Amador folded his hands on his lap. "I do apologize for my intrusive methods. I hope you can forgive me."

"Forgive you?" She arched her eyebrows. "How about you try convincing me not to shoot you."

"Oh, you won't shoot me."

The utter certainty in his tone bristled her temper. She bit back a smart retort and instead asked, "How can you be so sure?"

"You avoid violence and do harm only when absolutely necessary."

"You don't know me. Maybe I'm a ruthless killer."

He chuckled. The accompanying smile tightened the crow's feet around his eyes and the lines around his mouth. A faint scar on his cheek danced. She couldn't blame him for laughing. Her statement sounded ludicrous even to her. Grace Powell, assassin for hire. Yeah, right.

"You are far too refined to be a murderer," Amador said. He rocked in his chair, aiming a faint smirk at her. "I am so pleased you've accepted my invitation. And may I say you are even more beautiful than I imagined. Quite stunning, actually."

She stared at him, her lips twisted into a half scowl. Flirting? Was he serious? If she threatened to stab him, maybe he'd propose marriage.

If David had spoken the same compliments, she would've blushed. Here, now, with this man, no such heat bloomed in her cheeks. Her stomach grumbled, but she doubted that had anything to do with Amador's flirtation. Something about him scraped at her nerves. She trusted her intuition, and it warned her to take care in dealing with Amador. She pulled her purse snug against her body. The hard lump of her gun pressed into her flesh.

"I'm here," she said. "So can we cut the crap and get down to business?"

"I do enjoy your directness. It's refreshing and immensely appealing."

She doubted her fiancé would agree. *David, where are you?* "I'm not trying to appeal to you, Mr. Amador. You're the one who invited me here. Time to prove I should stay."

"Of course."

"You claimed you could help me. What exactly did you mean?"

With one finger, he traced swirling lines on the smooth desktop. "I can help you understand your psychic abilities and use them to better effect. I know you suffer from debilitating migraines anytime you use your powers for more than a bit of remote reconnaissance. I can teach you how to set your powers free, so you will no longer suffer because of them."

She clenched her fists around her gun's outline. How the blazes did he know so much about her? Would he have risked insanity merely to read her mind and gain tidbits of knowledge about her?

Risk insanity? He must've tipped that boat a long time ago. No sane person would burrow into her mind, rummage around a bit, and then invite her over for a cozy chat.

Grace drummed her fingers on her purse, on the gun hidden beneath the vinyl. "Your offer sounds great. What's the catch?"

His brown eyes targeted her gaze, like a radar-guided missile zeroing in on its target. "You will need to drop whatever psychic shield you've erected."

"Mmm... no. What else have you got?"

A frown flickered across Amador's features, evaporating in the space of a heartbeat. "If you allow me to help you with your powers, then I will use all the money and influence at my disposal to help you find Karl Tesler."

Her heart skipped a beat. "Who?"

"Dr. Karl Tesler. The scientist David is searching for as we speak."

"I have no idea who that is."

He burrowed a hand through his black hair. "Please, Grace, I know you're lying. It's time we told each other the truth. I am not your enemy."

Right. Not her enemy. He was her new best friend. With fangs, venom, and a rattling tail.

Searing pain skewered her heart. She gasped. The pain spiked through her again, deeper, tearing into muscle and sinew. She clutched the chair's arms, panting, whimpering. *Jesus, no.* Tentacles of power lashed at her.

The agony dissolved into a yawning emptiness that ached in her heart.

She knew this ache. Not physical pain. A psychic shock. And it radiated to her through a connection so intimate, so alive, that it smacked into her with physical force. She squeezed her eyes shut as a silent sob wrenched her body.

David was hurt. Screaming. Bleeding. Dying.

Behind the ache, an oily energy roiled. Its tentacles flailed, striving for purchase.

This was not from David. Someone, or something, was laying siege to her defenses. Her fears tricked her into believing the agony originated with David.

Boiling agony scorched her veins. Blades ripped her flesh.

She toppled forward.

Amador snared her in his muscular arms.

And she passed out.

Chapter Seven

THE GUARD SHOVED DAVID THROUGH THE DOORWAY INTO A SHADowed room. The guards wore no name tags, and so he had no idea what to call them. "Assholes" came to mind, but he figured they wouldn't appreciate that.

David rubbed his shoulder, where the cretin had punched him when he protested at being separated from Sean. Another bruise on his forearm was blossoming a nice shade of plum. That one he received for blinking, or maybe breathing. The guard hadn't specified.

He scuffled deeper into the room. His shoes scraped across the concrete floor. At a dozen feet wide and long, at most, the space pressed in around him. It reeked of sweat and blood and fear. A single bulb recessed into the ceiling spilled flickering light into the center of the room, but the sickly glow petered out before reaching the corners. A narrow wedge of brighter light from the corridor sliced through the gloom. David squinted. He still couldn't make out much besides the square shape of the prison cell.

And that's what it was. No bed, no chairs, nothing to provide a modicum of comfort. He kicked his toe into the bare concrete, catching it in a pit.

The guard kicked the door shut.

A locking mechanism chunked into position. David trudged further into the room. Halfway across the space, he stopped. A humanlike shape huddled in the far corner, masked in shadows and motionless as a boulder.

He had a cellmate.

The man's ebony skin blended into the gloom. Indirect light glimmered off his clean-shaven scalp. When he lifted his head to gaze at David, the whites of the man's eyes almost glowed. A trick of the dim light, David knew. Still, the sight of the pure white of the man's eyes, with inky disks at their centers, made David hesitate.

At the Mojave Desert facility, the scientists had locked him in a cell outfitted like a hospital room, without the windows. His captors kept the door sealed at all times and, toward the end, they sedated him into unconsciousness. Here in Montana, without JT at the helm, Tesler clearly had adopted a new tactic for imprisoning psychics, something closer to the way prisons operated. At least the guard removed the zip tie from his wrists before dumping him into the cell.

A spasm wrenched his entire body. Electric shocks ripped his flesh.

He staggered into the wall, gasping, his chest racked with pains. His spine contorted as if a wire threaded through it was yanked taut. Sweat rolled down his temples, and blackness dotted his vision. He slumped against the concrete wall.

This pain. He'd endured it earlier today. It came from Grace.

Her firewall prevented him from contacting her directly, anyway. He must try the indirect route, via emotion.

Grace had teased him into an outburst earlier because she recognized his worst weakness. The inability to express his feelings. The irony of emotions being his only psychic path to her might've given him a laugh under other circumstances. But at this moment, afflicted with her suffering, he found no humor in it.

"Are you ill?"

David jumped away from the wall. He'd forgotten about his cellmate.

His new friend sat unmoving, turning only his spooky eyes to keep track of David. The man did not watch with wide eyes, however, but with a curious gaze. His mouth held a neutral position, not a smile but not a frown either. With his back to the wall, angled into the corner, he had his knees bent in front of him and his forearms resting on his knees with his hands dangling. The man appeared relaxed, yet David sensed a tension beneath the surface, coiled within the man's core like a serpent that might spring out to attack at any moment.

If his cellmate morphed into a werewolf, even that wouldn't stop him from what he needed to do.

"I'm fine," he muttered, to satisfy the other man.

Then he fixated his gaze on the far wall, unleashed his mind from his body, and soared up into the crossroads. No traveling this time. He dragged in as much energy as he could withstand, consolidated every drop of passion and longing and adoration for Grace he possessed, and fired the missile down at her wall.

The projectile splintered.

White-hot shards punctured his mind, and he slapped his palms on the wall, swallowing a cry. Force wasn't the way, he should've remembered it from the first time he tried to contact her after she raised her defenses. When he'd shared himself with her before leaving the house, it had been more subtle, more intimate. The fact she'd been in his arms then, completely open to him in body and mind, must've eased the way.

He tried again. This time, he avoided the crossroads and stayed in his body. Instead of attacking her wall, he concentrated on sending her another gift, wrapped in the intensity of his love and concern for her. A single message, conveyed in emotion.

I'm okay.

It slid through, he felt it. Her fear, her pain, it melted away in the heat of his message. She was asleep, he sensed, yet she relaxed out of the torment.

"You don't look fine," his cellmate said, and now David realized the man had an accent.

David pulled himself up straight and forced a smile. "I'm good. Why should you care? We're strangers."

"The smell of decaying flesh bothers me. I'd prefer you don't die until the guards return."

"I'll keep that in mind."

David shuffled into the corner opposite the man. He seated himself at a forty-five-degree angle to the room, mimicking his cellmate's position. David stretched one leg out in front of him and bent the other so he could rest one arm atop his knee. The other arm he let hang down, with his hand on his thigh. He too could feign relaxation.

David nodded at his new friend. "I've never had a roommate before. Not sure what the etiquette is." He leaned his head back against the wall. "My name is David Ransom. What's yours?"

The man stared at him for several seconds, the whites of his eyes gleaming. Then he let out a small sigh. "I am Nkosi Uba."

"Where are you from?"

"South Africa. Johannesburg, originally."

"I'm from Wisconsin." The words tasted strange. He hadn't spoken of his home in years. Though he'd told Grace about his childhood, those conversations happened during the eight months she no longer remembered. So essentially, he hadn't mentioned his home to anyone in a very long time.

Nkosi studied him in silence.

"Wisconsin is in the United States," David said. "It's north of—"

"I know where it is."

David shifted position, his pants scritching on the concrete floor as he moved out of the corner to lean against the flat wall. "How long have you been a guest in this luxurious resort?"

A trace of a smile played across Nkosi's face, but it faded swiftly. "I have been here for two months. I know this only because my watch tells me the date. Otherwise, I would have no answer for your question."

"They don't mind cruel and unusual punishment at these places. I imagine you haven't seen the outdoors in two months either."

"I have not, except for a blade of grass that fell off of a guard's boot."

David grunted. "I'm sure they believe that counts as seeing the out-doors."

Nkosi watched David intently, as if measuring up the man before him, and David wasn't quite sure if Nkosi liked the result.

"If they have sent you," Nkosi said, "to befriend me in hopes I will give them what they want, then you may inform them it will not work."

"Why would my befriending you get them what they want?"

"It is their way. It didn't work the four times previously, and it will not work this time either. If they burn you, I will not give in. If they slowly cut off your hand, still I will not give in. If they—"

"I get the idea." David felt a lump hardening in his stomach, like a meal he'd eaten too fast. He knew Tesler salivated at the prospect of tor-turing psychics, but this was the first he'd heard of burning or cutting off hands. Tesler favored cleaner methods that involved no messy fluids, other than tears. Seeing people cry and listening to them beg for mercy, that was Tesler's pleasure.

"Does your arm hurt?" Nkosi asked.

"What?"

Nkosi waved at David's left arm. "You've been rubbing it as if it hurts."

David glanced down and saw he was rubbing his arm. Old habits, he supposed. The bruise might have healed, but the memory lingered. He'd been strapped to a less-pleasant version of a dentist chair, veins combusting with a novel mixture of drugs meant to boost psychic powers and render the subject compliant. Tesler hunched before him, expressionless except for the glittering in his dark eyes.

"Who is Janet Austen?" Tesler demanded.

He slanted over David with one hand on each arm of the chair, pinning his already restrained arms to it. The pressure of Tesler's grasp triggered a dull aching in his arms that spread down into his hands. David winced, but said nothing.

Tesler pressed down harder. David gritted his jaw so hard he thought his teeth might shatter. He would never tell this man what he wanted to know. Never.

"I know it's an alias," Tesler said. "Tell me Janet Austen's real name and the pain will stop."

Grace. Her name flitted through his mind, soft as a breeze. Beautiful Grace. Sweet Grace. His gut wrenched. He couldn't betray her even when his own life depended on it.

"Have it your way." Tesler stepped back, releasing the pressure on David's arms. A sigh rushed out of him unbidden, like the release of air when a vacu-um-sealed container was torn open.

Tesler nodded to one of the guards posted near the door. The man strode over to David's chair and unhooked a billy club from his belt, which he of-fered to Tesler. The scientist took the club, slapping it on his palm.

"Tell me," Tesler said.

David shook his head.

Tesler slammed the club down on David's forearm. He stifled a cry as pain shot through his arm, into his hand, convulsing the tendons. The agony seared his muscles, rushing through his body in a wave that annihilated his thoughts. His ears rang. Darkness licked at the edges of his vision.

Kill me. The thought came from nowhere, it seemed. He didn't want to die, and yet he did not want to betray Grace, not even accidentally.

Tesler studied David with a look of detached interest. He might as well have been observing a baboon in a cage.

"I don't know who she is," David said.

Tesler pursed his lips, thumping the club on his palm. After a couple of seconds, he shrugged and tossed the club to the guard. "Ah well, perhaps the drugs will work better. You may have masochistic tendencies, after all."

Then the scientist had left the room.

"How did it happen?" Nkosi's voice broke David out of the past. "Your arm. How did you injure it?"

"Wrestling with a snake."

Grace compared his mission with wrestling an alligator. She was right, his foolishness had whipped around to bite him in the ass.

He scrubbed a hand over his face, but the stain of guilt was embedded too deep to wipe off so easily. If Tesler captured Grace, he'd get answers from her no matter what it took. If she denied him, he might even overcome his aversion to messes and unlock fresh, more agonizing methods of convincing her to cooperate.

All because of me.

"Now you seem angry," Nkosi said. "You must have troublesome memories."

"Troublesome." David laughed, though not with amusement. To his own ears, the laughter sounded harsh and bitter. "You could say that."

Nkosi's eyes narrowed. His lips flattened.

Metaphysical energy tickled at his brain. He winced. Nkosi was attempting to touch his mind without his consent. Only Grace had permission to poke him this way, though from her, it came through with subtle, nearly sensual tenderness. He batted away the mental feather irritating him.

Of course, if Nkosi resolved to get inside David's head, he could batter down the gates without much effort. Every human mind boasted a built-in barrier, not quite a wall, but more of a curtain. Grace's firewall, erected with conscious purpose, blocked out everything. The natural curtain impeded curious travelers. Anyone with a serious interest in mind reading could rip away the veil with little expenditure of energy.

Nkosi prodded him once more.

"Are you sure you want to do that?" David asked. "Maybe you enjoy the occasional psychotic break, but I prefer sanity."

"The risk is only to me."

"I still don't want you ransacking my brain." David relaxed against the wall. "Besides, I don't care to have a lunatic for a roommate. I'd rather not have to clean up after you when you lose control of your bowels."

Nkosi arched an eyebrow. "I thought it was speculation that mind reading caused such dire side effects. You've seen the results before?"

"Yes." David met Nkosi's gaze. "Trust me, you don't want to risk it."

Nkosi squinted for a couple of seconds, then nodded. "I have decided to trust you."

"Thanks." David supposed he should feel grateful, but he hadn't decided yet whether he trusted Nkosi. The man might be a plant, using the very techniques he claimed their captors used on him with his previous cellmates. David couldn't know for sure.

He sighed and said, "So you're from South Africa. I had no idea the induction program had gone global."

"Induction?" Nkosi's confusion seemed genuine.

David still had to play it safe. "How did you get here?"

The other man shrugged. "I was backpacking with my brother when men raided our camp. They wore black clothing and helmets that covered their faces. These men attacked while we slept, and by the time we knew what was happening, they had already tied us up. Once they determined our identities, they shot my brother in the head."

David jerked his head up and stared at Nkosi. The man stretched his fingers out, then clenched them. His upper lip curled in disgust.

"He was of no value to them," Nkosi said. "They wanted me, not my brother. I watched him die before they injected me with something that put me to sleep. I woke up in a place much like this, but in Siberia. I didn't know where I was at first, and only later discovered how far they had taken me from my home. Then two months ago, they shut down the Siberian facility and brought me here." Nkosi shut his eyes. "They killed everyone at the old facility—except for me. I don't understand why I lived when so many others died."

Nkosi's pain seemed real enough that David felt like a heel for doubting the man. Still, he must doubt. He must be suspicious, of everyone. He knew of just one person in the entire world who he trusted with no reservations or doubts.

Grace.

He had to get out of this place and get back to her.

David studied his cellmate for a moment. Nkosi had opened his eyes, but he stared down at the floor. His shoulders drooped. He did not move, except for the rising and falling of his chest as he breathed.

"Tell me," David said, "why do our hosts want you so badly?"

"They want me to give them something, but I don't understand what it is."

"What do they say to you?"

"They speak of Golden Power and transference of psychic energies. They force me to watch as they torture my cellmates, all the time demanding I help them acquire this Golden Power they crave. Only when my cellmate dies do they relent."

David knew he had to ask one question, even at the risk of exposing the depth of his suspicion. "Why do they torture your cellmates and not you?"

"They tried in Siberia. It did not work." Nkosi gave him a weary look. "I am not stronger than other men. I simply do not know what they want me to tell them. They used several means to encourage me to cooperate, but I could not. If I had the information, I would've given it to them. Believe me. I am not a superman."

The shame in his voice and on his face triggered a wave of sympathy in David. He knew what it felt like to struggle against Tesler's methods. In his case, however, he would die before talking. If he broke, Grace would be the one to suffer for his weakness.

Nkosi had endured the torture not out of moral conviction or love for another, but simply because he knew nothing about the Golden Power. Assuming he told the truth. Assuming he hadn't cracked. If David believed the man's tale, Nkosi let his cellmates die because he had nothing to give his captors, no way to save the others' lives.

If David believed him. If he could trust anything or anyone in this place.

Nkosi had just tried to sneak into his mind after all.

The other man twisted around to lean sideways against the wall. A beam of weak light flashed over his head and neck, revealing a network of thin scars that slashed across his throat. In a tired voice, he said, "They always leave us alone for a few hours, then they return to begin the questioning."

David glanced at the door. A few hours. He must get out of here before then. Under no circumstances would he betray Grace again, wittingly or not. But if he died…

He would not leave her alone. Some way, somehow, he must get back to her.

—

GRACE ROUSED IN STAGES. FIRST, THE COOLNESS OF THE AIR-CONDItioned environment kissed her skin. She wiggled her fingers, and her nails scritched across the chair's leather. Next, she tasted sour acid and sniffed spicy cologne. Finally, she parted her eyelids and blinked away the bleariness. Dim lighting eased her vision out of sleep, into awareness.

Amador crouched in front of her, his face creased with lines of worry. "Are you feeling better? What can I do?"

She recalled the suffering, the soul-rending certainty David was dying. Then, after she passed out, a warm serenity flowed into her, carrying with it reassurance and… love. The kind she luxuriated in whenever David drew her into his arms. Real, pure love.

David had penetrated her psychic fortress. For a few long seconds, she wondered how he'd done it. But of course, he accomplished the same feat earlier today, when he poured his emotions into her with an all-consuming kiss hotter than any they'd shared before. Though her firewall must've prevented him from traveling to her, it permitted him empathic communication.

"You are smiling," Amador said. "The pain is gone, then?"

She touched her lips, which were slanting upward. David's phantom embrace lingered around her, and a ghost of his lips tantalized hers. She cleared her throat. "Uh, yes. No pain."

"Are you injured or ill?"

"Neither. It wasn't physical pain." But it sure as hell shredded her insides like the real thing. "I'm fine, I swear."

Amador eyed her for a moment, lips tight, and then settled a hand on her knee. "You do look less pale than before you passed out. Perhaps I should call Wickham and have him fetch a doctor anyway. To be certain."

"No-no, I'm fine." She noticed he hadn't carried her to a bed or a sofa to make her comfortable, or waved smelling salts to awaken her, or dabbed a cool cloth on her forehead. So far as she could tell, he'd knelt there staring at her until she revived on her own. *Creepy.*

Without getting up, he grabbed the phone off his desk and dialed a number—an extension within the house, most likely, since he dialed just three digits. "Wickham, please bring some juice and a small snack for our guest. She's feeling peaked."

He hung up, plunking the phone back into its cradle. His attention centered on her once again.

She fidgeted, the solace David imbued her with diminishing. He might've communicated his okay-ness to her, but she needed confirmation. She dug her phone out of her purse, flipped it open, and frowned.

"Is something wrong?" Amador asked.

"No signal. I need to call David." An edge of panic sharpened her voice. *Damn.* She hated sounding weak in front of Amador, but she couldn't help it.

He snatched the receiver from his desk, offering it to her. "Please use my phone. I insist."

Of course he'd insist. He probably recorded every phone call made from his home, or at least the ones made by guests. He could've jammed cell signals too.

She must hear David's voice.

Her shoulders hunched as she accepted the phone. "Thanks."

Amador nodded. He did not back away to grant her privacy.

After dialing the number for David's cell, she clutched the phone to her ear. One ring. Two. Three. She drummed her fingers on her thigh. Four rings. Five. Six. His voicemail picked up the call. She hung up and dialed her own cell to retrieve any messages. One voicemail awaited her, time-stamped twenty minutes ago. Her fingers trembled as David's anxious voice spoke to her from the past. The tension in his tone infected her, and she gripped the phone tighter. Her frantic mind processed his words in snippets.

Tesler. Coming for you. Get out. Your psychic firewall is—

The message cut off. Ringing deafened her. Numbness tingled down her scalp, into her face. She hauled in a breath, and then another. The ringing and numbness faded, but a frozen ball of panic congealed in her gut.

Her psychic firewall was what? Working great? About to collapse?

She redialed David's number and got his voicemail again. "David, please call me as soon as you get this. I heard your message and—" Amador was scrutinizing her, no doubt paying rapt attention to her words. She performed a quick mental edit of what she wanted to say. "I think we should discuss the possibility before taking any action. I'm away from home, so call my cell. Love you, honey. Bye."

The last part she'd added for Amador's benefit. His hand still warmed her knee with a discomfiting familiarity. A niggling at the back of her mind compelled her to remind him she was taken.

She started to hand him the phone but froze. *Grandpa.* He was clueless about the danger. "May I make another call?"

"As many as you like."

And he'd observe and eavesdrop on every single call. Stifling a grumble, she dialed her grandfather's number. He answered on the second ring.

"Grace, I'm glad you—"

"Hi, it's Grace Powell. I'm afraid we'll have to cancel our meeting for this evening. Something's come up."

A pause. A gruff sigh. "You're in trouble. And you're not alone."

"Uh-huh. I'm sorry I have to flake out on you. The house is being fumigated, so I don't think we'll want to be in there for a few days at least."

"Fumigated?" He repeated the word slowly as if puzzling out her meaning. "You mean it may be bugged."

"Worse than that. Some kind of black fungus is invading the place."

"Black—Holy heaven, Grace. Are you talking about Tesler's commandos?"

"Yep. Don't put off your vacation on my account. We can catch up next week."

He said nothing for a few seconds. "I will not leave town without you. Tell me where you are, and I'll come get you."

"No." She nearly shouted the word, and Amador's mouth quirked in confused amusement. "I mean, uh…" She floundered for a way to convince him without Amador catching on. Oh screw it. "Please do as I ask. Please."

"Grace..."

"*Please.*" She made no effort to conceal her pleading tone. "I promise I'll make our next meeting."

"All right. I'll go to our backup location. But if I don't hear from you by morning... I don't know. I'll find you somehow."

"Thank you." She disconnected the call. He would be safe, which gave her one less worry to gnaw at her gut.

Passing the phone back to Amador, she scooted sideways in the chair. Her butt had started to ache despite the cushioned seat. Though she'd fainted moments ago, energy pulsed back into her, on both a physical and psychic level. Her connection to David hummed in the background, easing some of her tension.

Amador's hand caressed her knee.

She gripped the arms of the chair. "Tell me how you know about Tesler."

Amador observed her for a moment, eyes half-closed. Then he bent forward, resting his elbows on his knees. "I know of Tesler because I've met him. I spent time at a facility in Siberia where Tesler detained a number of travelers. It was not an enjoyable time."

Grace couldn't decide whether to believe him or not. The tightening of his features, the slight frown on his lips, the hunching of his shoulders, those things suggested the memory distressed him. Yet she didn't know him well enough to distinguish between real pain and great acting.

"The Siberian facility is shut down," Amador told her. "I managed to escape before the guards murdered me, as they did all the others."

Time for a strategic revelation on her part. At least she hoped it was strategic, and not plain stupid. At some point, she had to reveal a little to test his knowledge.

"I have some of JT's files," she said, "from the Mojave Desert facility in California. They name the travelers held at all the sites. Your name is not on that list, Mr. Amador."

"My friends call me Biel."

"We're not friends."

"Not yet."

He spoke with such complete certainty about the promise of their future friendship that she almost laughed. Almost. His certainty also struck her as arrogance, a trait she never trusted in anyone. "Whatever. The point is, your name appears nowhere in the database of travelers' names."

"I adopted a pseudonym, as you did." He arched an eyebrow. "Unless your true name is Janet Austen. I hope not, though, because Grace describes you far better."

"How do you know about Janet Austen?"

"I also have some files that once belonged to JT."

"Where did you get them?"

Dark glee colored his smirk. "I stole them. From the Siberian facility."

Liar. The word flared in her mind, but she struggled to keep her expression neutral. She guarded the sole copy of JT's private files on Project Outreach, on the flash drive tucked into her bra. JT had told her it was the one and only copy, and she believed him—considering the number of people he'd murdered in his zeal to reclaim the flash drive from her. Even a psycho wouldn't waste that kind of energy on a task unless it was vital. When JT had blown up his own facility, that act had also destroyed the computer system and those precious files. Amador could not have the same information.

Unless someone else, like Tesler, secretly copied JT's files.

Amador's extensive knowledge about her chilled her entire body, from her skin straight down to her core. He knew things JT hadn't known about, as far as she knew.

"Please," Amador said, "I speak the truth. You must believe me."

"You've been spying on me," she said. "In my bedroom. You RV'd me in my private space, and that tends to annoy me. So no, I don't have to do anything for you. Especially not believe you."

"I have already apologized. I did not realize you were alone in your bedroom until after the excursion began."

The hairs on the back of her neck stiffened. In Project Outreach, the scientists called the RV sessions excursions. Something about Amador's use of the term bothered her, an indefinable off-ness she couldn't describe.

"Will you trust me?" he asked.

She tapped her fingernails on her purse in a fast rhythm. Trust Amador? No way. But if she wanted to learn how much he knew, and what he really wanted, she had to take a few risks.

Lips pursed, she zeroed in on his dark eyes. "I'm not letting down my psychic wall just yet. First, you need to prove to me you're on the level." Snowballs and brimstone popped to mind. She kept the analogy to herself. "Show me everything you have on JT, his companies, Tesler, the facilities, everything."

"Of course."

He retreated around the desk, flipped open his laptop, and tapped keys on the keyboard. The tickety-ticking of the keys was the only sound in the room, except for the thundering of her pulse in her ears. Nobody else could hear that, though. She hoped.

After a moment, Amador spun the laptop around to face her. "Here it is. Everything I have on anything remotely related to Project Outreach. You may view it here, or I can copy it onto a DVD for you."

"How about I take a peek right now and you give me that DVD to take home."

He nodded. "I'll have Wickham prepare it for you before you leave."

"Thank you." She scooted her chair closer to the desk. Eyes on the screen, she asked, "What pseudonym did you use?"

"John Mendoza."

"Who knew your real name?"

"Only Jackson Tennant. He hungered for psychic power and strived to harvest the abilities of travelers. And he harbored a bizarre fixation with blood."

A shiver ran down her spine as a memory replayed in her mind. JT grasping a syringe. About to suck the blood from her veins forcibly. His expression wild. His desire for power palpable. He had honestly believed that by injecting himself with the blood of a psychic, he could acquire that person's abilities. Well, at least one part of Amador's story matched up with what she knew.

If he had JT's files, though, he might've learned about the blood thing that way. She hadn't read all of JT's files, since they were extensive, which meant the notes on his blood theory might await her somewhere deep inside the data. Amador might've found it first.

"I'm acquainted with JT's obsession," she admitted.

"He gave up on many travelers when he realized the blood types were incompatible. He never gave up on you, though, did he?"

"No." She clenched her jaw. "Not until I made him give up."

"Yes," Amador said, his tone contemplative. "You killed him, didn't you?"

She froze, her fingers over the keyboard. Without looking up, she asked, "How do you know that?"

"Postcognition."

She snapped her head up to squint at him. "Post what?"

"Postcognition. I'm sure you know that precognition allows one to see future events. Postcognition is a term my captors used to describe an aspect of remote viewing that allows one to see past events. It doesn't always work, and it can be quite difficult to control. My only successful attempt occurred when I tried to replay JT's death. I know you shot him."

"Why would you want to replay his death?"

"To know that he was truly gone." He offered her his hand, palm up. "And to thank the person who rid this world of a vile human being."

She glanced at his hand, knowing he wanted her to take it. She didn't move.

He curled his fingers shut. "You may not trust me yet, but know this. I admire you—your strength and determination, your loyalty to those you love, and your incredible psychic talents."

She focused on the computer screen, double-clicking to open a database file.

"I can help you get him back," Amador said in a soft voice. "If that is what you truly want."

Head bowed, she turned her eyes to glance at him. "Get who back?"

"David. Your beloved." Amador leaned over the desk, placing his head inches from hers. He smelled of the outdoors, fresh and clean and masculine. "Together, we can find Tesler and stop him. Then David will have no reason to abandon you anymore."

"My relationship with David is none of your business." She drummed her fingernails on the desktop. Through gritted teeth, she said, "How the hell do you know so much about me, anyway?"

He shrugged. "The files. And my remote reconnaissance of you and your associates. I needed to know as much as possible about you before I risked exposing myself to you."

She grunted. Yeah, his rationale made sense. She didn't like it, and sure as hell didn't trust him. At the moment, however, she needed him to think she might.

Forcing herself to relax, she said, "Thank you for sharing your information with me. But my relationship with David is off-limits."

"As you wish. Nevertheless, I will help you find Tesler." He glanced down at her left hand and the diamond ring on the third finger. "But in the process, you will learn things about your beloved that you may not like. Do you still wish to proceed?"

"Yes."

Amador settled back into his chair. "Then we shall find Tesler. I hope you are as prepared for the truth as you believe."

"I am."

Was she prepared? No clue. She had to proceed. For her, there was no choice anymore. To save David, she must risk losing him. To save the world from Tesler and his cohorts, she must risk everything—including her own life.

Tesler was coming. For her. Now.

CHAPTER EIGHT

G OOSEBUMPS PRICKLED HER SKIN. TESLER. SHE'D NEVER MET THE man, yet she knew from David's reaction to the very mention of Tesler's name the scientist was a sociopath at best. He tortured people in the name of science. What Tesler practiced bore no resemblance to real science. It was a dark perversion of a scientific experiment.

Why had David called her on the phone? In emergencies, he relied on their telepathic line, not the cell phone network.

David's final words echoed in her mind. *Your psychic firewall is—*

Her throat tightened, and her mouth went dry. She knew why he used the phone, and what he'd been about to say in his message. Her psychic wall, the one he encouraged her to build, must've blocked him from contacting her. No one, not even David, could breach her defenses.

She must lower the barrier.

No, she couldn't. Not with Gabriel Amador scratching at the wall. He wanted in too, and she had no intention of admitting him. But David...

He hadn't asked her to lower the wall. He must not want her to, or else he would've said so. Unless the message cut off before he got the chance.

Dammit. For the time being, she must keep the barrier intact.

Where could she hide? Where would Tesler and his goons not think to look for her?

Her foot tapped the floor in a frenzied rhythm. This wouldn't be the first time she'd gone on the lam, but no. She refused to flee and cower in some dank hideout. Going home wasn't an option either. Even she wasn't pigheaded enough to waltz right into an ambush.

She pushed up off the chair, muttering a rapid string of curses under her breath. "If you'll give me that DVD, I should be on my way."

"Of course." Amador rose to his full height, a good six inches taller than she was. "You are welcome to stay the night here, of course. I have spacious guest quarters."

"Thank you, Mr. Amador, but I have to be going." *Where to, dummy?*

"You will never assent to calling me Biel, will you?"

"It's doubtful." Realizing the statement sounded rude, and wary of poking a dragon, she added, "Sorry. It's just that I don't know you."

"Not yet. But you will." Again, his utter certainty rankled. He picked up the phone on his desk, punched buttons, and waited for the other party to answer. "Yes, Wickham, please bring the DVD for Ms. Powell. She is ready to leave us. No, forget the snack. She has urgent business to attend to."

As he hung up the phone, she said, "Thank you for sharing your information with me."

"It is a pleasure." He extended a hand to her, and she settled her palm into his. He brushed a light kiss across the back of her hand. *Weird.* He did not release her hand when he spoke. "We will see each other again very soon, Grace. I look forward to it."

His hand was warm and soft, like the skin of a man who rarely deigned to perform manual labor. His gaze, locked on hers, sent an odd shiver through her. Not desire, like with David. Not fear either. Something else she couldn't place.

"Who are you?" she asked.

He laid his other hand atop hers. "Gabriel Ricardo Amador, president and founder of Catalan Enterprises." He encased her hand in his strong fingers. "And your friend, I hope."

"I need to go, but I may have questions later."

"Naturally. Call or stop by anytime. Wickham will provide you with a number where you can reach me." He lifted her hand to his lips again, his flesh skimming over hers. "I am at your service, always."

He freed her hand. She stepped out into the hallway, shutting the door.

Wickham rounded a corner ahead of her. He held a DVD, sheathed in a hard plastic case. Grace met him halfway, accepting the disk from him with a thank-you and a smile. He pointed out the business card tucked inside the DVD case, assuring her she could reach "Biel" at any time if she called the number on the card. Then he escorted her back to the front door, smiling and wishing her a good day as he opened the door for her. When the door closed behind her, she let out the breath she'd been holding.

She still had no idea what to think about Amador. Maybe it didn't matter, since she planned on avoiding him whenever possible. Contact only when necessary to glean more info from him. Simple. Clean.

Then why did razor-wire butterflies flap in her stomach?

First up, she needed to compare the information on his disk with the data on the flash drive. Viewing the DVD's contents on her own computer seemed ill-advised. Sure, Amador presented himself as an amiable, if cautious, fellow. But she couldn't risk contaminating her computer or the flash drive, if Amador's disk turned out to contain a virus or worm.

She pressed two fingers to the valley between her breasts, pinning the flash drive to her sternum. David thought it was silly to keep the flash drive there. Today, with her home compromised, she was damn happy about her paranoia. Before she could consider viewing Amador's DVD, she had to accomplish another feat.

Track down a safe place to stay while evading Tesler's goons. Piece of cake.

Steel-reinforced concrete cake. And all she had to cut it with was a plastic knife. Well then, she'd forge herself a new blade. *No more running.*

She marched to her car, each step buoyed by a renewed purpose.

G RACE DROVE TO THE BANK AND WITHDREW THE ENTIRE BALANCE of her checking account. A visit to an electronics store netted her a new laptop, since she'd left her computer at home, and a clean cell phone, prepaid and untraceable to her. She stowed the Pontiac in a covered parking structure downtown, and then hitched a ride in a taxi, heading for an old house on the outskirts of town. A nice old lady sold her a beat-up, though well-maintained, Dodge Ram pickup. With her purse at her side, and the revolver berthed inside it, she drove along the interstate in search of a motel.

Maybe David was wrong about her developing a new ability, because if she could see the future, then she would've brought her computer with her. Then again, maybe not, since it might've been bugged or hacked or something. If she'd foreseen this trouble, she most definitely would not have let David run off to Montana.

Her vision of Tesler murdering him had been real, but for the vision to be true, she must've developed precognitive abilities. Maybe using her new power required a deliberate effort. Nice theory, except the first time she'd stumbled onto her precognition without any intent to do so. She rubbed her neck, squinting in the sunlight streaming through the windshield. She couldn't test the boundaries of her abilities right now. Too much risk. Too much unknown.

What if Gabriel Amador was stalking her again?

Calm down, you're safe. Her psychic barrier thwarted everyone, including David. If he couldn't break through, despite their telepathic bond, then Amador sure as hell couldn't tap into her brain.

Her thoughts circled back around to the dark presence clawing at her when she built her firewall, and the freakish incident earlier, when for the second time in one day, she'd believed David was in mortal jeopardy. Something—whether a human mind or a presence beyond her comprehension, she didn't know—still wielded the strength to manipulate her mind, with more vigor than any psychic mentioned by David or in JT's files.

David found a way into her mind through their emotional union. Six months ago, JT forced a link with her by injecting himself with enough drugs to boost his latent powers into the stratosphere. What if another someone discovered a new way to tap into her brain? A method too strong for her firewall to withstand?

She had to shove the possibility aside and keep moving.

The Ram carried her to a motel thirty miles outside of town, a dingy place with ten rooms and a heavily tattooed clerk with rings in his nose and lower lip. He wore a T-shirt that looked like a souvenir from a heavy-metal rock festival. A name tag pinned to his T-shirt identified him as Tag. She almost laughed, but suppressed it for the sake of politeness.

"Is that your real name?" she asked, in as un-sarcastic a tone as she could muster.

"Yeah," he said, with a Chicago accent. "It's actually Taggert, but I go by Tag most of the time. Specially when I'm at work. It makes the customers wonder."

"About what?"

"Whether I'm too high on drugs to remember my own name."

And then he smiled. A wide, welcoming smile that she couldn't help but reciprocate.

Tag chuckled. "I ain't, by the way. High, that is."

He tapped a small round button pinned to his shirt. She hadn't noticed it before, and she leaned forward a little to read it. The button, rusty and scratched, featured the slogan "Just say no."

"I got this when I was a kid," Tag said. "Kept it ever since. A motto to live by."

"It sure is."

He sighed. "You didn't come here for my anti-drugs lecture, though. What can I do ya for?"

"A room."

"Just you?"

"Yes." Just her. Alone. On the run.

Life sucked. Life as a fugitive amnesiac sucked like a Godzilla-size vacuum cleaner.

He nodded and turned to the PC on the counter. "Name?"

"What?"

"Your name. I need to enter it into the computer."

"Oh." She hesitated, wringing her brain for an alias. "Christine Marcus."

Combining her parents' first names was all she could think of at the moment. Tag seemed satisfied and pecked at the computer keys with both index fingers.

Five minutes later, he handed her the key to Room 8, and she walked out of the office. Room 8 lay at the far end of the one-story building, on the side facing the road. At least that meant she'd have a clear view of the office and the parking lot, to keep watch for any suspicious characters. These days, she didn't know exactly how to differentiate suspicious types from regular people. The clerk, Tag, had seemed threatening until he spoke and smiled. Gabriel Amador seemed friendly and upstanding, yet he kept secrets and spied on her. Damn, she really wished the bad guys would wear black hats so she could tell them apart from everyone else. It was rude of them to blend in so cunningly.

Inside the room, she shut the door and moseyed over to the bed, dropping her purse and her new computer on the table situated beside the double bed. The outside of the motel looked dingy. Here, though, she found a clean room with the usual amenities.

She returned to the bed, flopping onto it with all the delicacy of a dog jumping into a pond. Her eyes were gritty, her tongue cottony. A heaviness overwhelmed her as if she'd gained fifty pounds in the past hour. Her brain ached from the pressure of thinking. She needed a plan. She needed information too. She needed help, dammit, but instead, she got more trouble. Would Tesler himself show up to bag-and-tag her, or would he send his goons?

A memory snapped into focus in her mind. A man in a black outfit reminiscent of military fatigues. His head shielded by a black, full-face helmet. A large gun in his hand, aimed at her. The sound of his sneering laugh echoed in her mind.

The man had been called Battaglia. He neglected to share his first name when he captured her during her attempt to break into the Mojave Desert facility. He'd treated her like an animal. To Battaglia, psychics were nothing more than freaks of nature, not human beings, just wild beasts in need of putting down, or at least containing. Battaglia was nasty, but nowhere near as bad as Tesler because, underneath the bravado, Battaglia was a coward. She remembered his choked voice when he begged her not to shoot him. Since he'd been tied up at the time, and no longer a threat to her, she let him live. His commando buddies must've rescued him later on, after she and David fled the ruins of the facility.

Battaglia was still alive. Had he stuck with Tesler? Would he show up to hunt her down?

She wiped her slick palms on her pants. Sucking in a deep breath, she shut her eyes and exhaled slowly. No more fear. She must not let Battaglia or Tesler spiral her into a full-blown panic over the mere possibility of running into either of them. She'd stopped them before. She could do it again.

This time for good.

Rubbing her eyes, she yawned and stretched. She dragged her new computer off the bedside table, down onto the mattress beside her. The brief look she'd gotten at the files earlier, while Amador kept an eye on her, revealed nothing she didn't already know from the data on the flash drive. She popped Amador's DVD into the computer's disk drive and browsed the list of files it contained. The data was organized into dozens of folders, each of which contained multiple subfolders. She clicked on a folder called "Profiles." Within it, she found subfolders identified with abbreviations that she recognized. They were codes for the various types of psychic abilities—RV for remote viewing, AP for astral projection, TK for telekinesis, and on and on. The list included abbreviations she'd never seen before, like PRC and PTC. The letters TP undoubtedly referred to thought projection, and MR must indicate mind reading. Despite the dangers of mind reading, the scientists employed at ALI after the takeover by JT and his minions had coerced some psychics into attempting to use the ability.

The abbreviation on one folder stopped her: "GP."

She'd seen the abbreviation before. At the time, she hadn't understood what it meant. Since then, she'd learned the letters GP referred to the Golden Power.

Biting her lip, overcome by a dark sense of dread, she opened the GP folder. It contained two files, each labeled with a name. The first file was called "Janet Austen." Finding her alias listed in these files didn't surprise her. The second file was called "John Mendoza." Okay, so the name Amador claimed was his alias appeared in these files. He could've altered the data, though, to make her think he spent time in an ALI facility, or John Mendoza might not be his alias after all, but rather the name of another man interned at the Siberian facility. This proved nothing.

She opened the Mendoza file. It gave his basic description in bullet points—height, weight, hair color, eye color—and listed his psychic abilities as "high level." His powers included remote viewing and astral projection. That meant he could spy on anyone he liked and project an image of himself to whoever he liked as well. Manifestation was not listed as one of his gifts, but then she hadn't yet seen that ability listed as a separate power in any of the ALI files. Creating a physical body while astral projecting involved, from what David had told her, a combination of other abilities, including thought projection and telekinesis. Maybe ALI hadn't considered that to be a separate power. In common terms, astral projection was manifesting. In reality, however, manifesting a physical form required a massive amount of psychic energy as well as a connection with another person who could serve as a kind of conduit for the process. David could manifest only with Grace's help. Their combined powers made it possible.

And he'd assured her no one else possessed the ability.

She searched her brain for the memory of what David told her when he explained psychic abilities to her six months ago. She'd learned a little more on her own, by experimenting with her own powers, but his lessons still formed the basis of everything she knew about paranormal abilities. The truth, according to David. She trusted him, and yet she wondered sometimes if he'd disclosed everything to her. Amnesia surely affected their relationship, but he might have other reasons for holding back with her. More immediate reasons. Things he kept to himself because…

What? He didn't trust her? No way. What else might explain his reticence? She must figure out the reason. She couldn't accept that the man she'd admitted into her life and her heart—not once, but twice—didn't trust her. Their faith in each other had saved their lives.

She browsed the remainder of Amador's profile. Nothing of much interest there. A listing of excursions he'd taken under Tesler's direction, or that of another scientist. During an excursion, a traveler remote viewed a target location to demonstrate the extent of his or her powers, while the scientists measured their accuracy in describing the target. Her perusal of the files on the flash drive hadn't yet turned up a description of Tesler's methodology. Grace didn't know the specifics of how the experiments worked. She ought to find out. To do that, she would need to ask David or Sean.

Or Gabriel Amador.

She closed Amador's profile, if indeed the profile belonged to him. He might've been Amador, or he might've been a child. The data left her to assume Mendoza and Amador were the same person.

Next, she opened her own file. A knot tightened in her stomach as she looked at the profile. No photo in this file either. She hadn't actually expected to see one since her parents had done everything they could to shield her from Tesler and JT. The profile described Janet Austen in the vaguest terms, though it included her height, weight, eye color, and hair color. Strangely, it gave her hair color as blonde and her eye color as blue. The height and weight were correct. Had she worn a wig? Or bleached her hair blonde? She would've noticed the roots growing out even after she dyed it auburn again because matching her natural hair color precisely would've proved difficult and time-consuming. She must've worn a wig and colored contact lenses. Why? To confuse anyone trying to find her, she guessed. Hiding her weight and height would've proved next to impossible, but masking her hair and eye color wouldn't take much effort.

It had taken JT a good while to track her down. Her parents took every precaution to hide her from him. In the end, they died for her.

Tears burned in her eyes. Her throat constricted, and her breath shuddered with a silent sob. Crying would not help. Neither would guilt.

The tears rolled down her face anyway.

"Dammit," she hissed, and swiped the tears away with her fingers. She hated crying. It solved nothing and accomplished nothing except to make her eyes red and scratchy and puffy.

Her parents sacrificed their lives to preserve hers. If she hadn't gone to the Mojave Desert facility, if she'd stayed home, they might still be alive.

Six months ago, when David had found her again, he explained how she'd visited the facility while on vacation, to see what her parents did there. They received permission to show her everything, and on a lark, she participated in a test to determine psychic aptitude. The results had shocked everyone, he said, because they demonstrated she not only had psychic abilities, but they were "off the charts."

Her parents shielded her with a false name, but her file remained in ALI's records, and that was how JT learned about her. Why didn't they delete her file? They couldn't have guessed what horrors would ensue. No one could have. They kept her file because it was part of their research.

The text on the screen blurred, her eyes too weary to focus. She rubbed her neck, rolled her head in a circle, and gave her body an invigorating shake. No time for sleeping.

She backtracked through the DVD's folders, located a file that looked promising, and double-clicked to open it. The file was a report of a meeting between Tesler and JT, written by the scientist. Tesler outlined every boring detail of the meeting, from their decision to repaint one of the conference rooms to their disagreement over what type of ballpoint pens to buy. Toward the end of the report, she spotted something that grabbed her attention.

"JT insists it is my fault," Tesler wrote, "that the boy won't cooperate. He believes if the boy knows the truth, then he will stop fighting us. I assured JT it won't work, and I have no intention of ever acknowledging the mewling mutant. The child has no discipline, no self-awareness, and worst of all, no spine. No one will ever know he is my grandson."

Grace froze, her fingers hovering over the keyboard. Grandson? She had trouble visualizing Tesler with a family of any kind. Was the "boy" sadistic like his grandfather, or merely an innocent victim of his own genetic lineage? Even the worst parents on earth could raise a decent child, through no doing of their own. Or maybe the kid's mother or father fled from Tesler.

Either way, this changed things. She didn't know how yet, but it had to. Tesler's grandson had psychic abilities. Maybe that explained why the man seemed hell-bent on tormenting psychics in order to capture their powers. She couldn't quite figure out how his tactics related to his grandson, but she sure as hell wanted to find out.

Tesler's notes called his grandson "the boy," without giving any details about the kid's age. The term boy might refer to a five-year-old or a nearly full-grown teenager.

Or even a man. To a sixtyish cretin like Tesler, even a man in his twenties might seem like a boy in comparison to himself. Without knowing the identity of Tesler's grandson, she had no way of knowing whether she'd met him or not.

Amador claimed if she kept on her current path, she'd learn things about David she wouldn't like. Had he meant this? Would she find out David was Tesler's grandson? No, he couldn't be. The idea was ridiculous. She knew David better than anyone else in her life.

Did she really? She knew he kept secrets from her.

Not this one. He could not have any familial ties with Tesler, the man who tortured him for months. Until she identified Tesler's grandson, however, she lacked anything close to certainty, about anything.

The truth might await her on the DVD.

She clicked on a folder designated "AP" for astral projection. It was one of David's main powers.

There it was. A file labeled "David Ransom."

A shiver swept down her spine, and she hesitated with her finger over the enter key. She needed to know. She feared what she might find. The truth usually came with strings attached—in the form of razor wire.

Suck it up, woman.

She hit the enter key. The file opened on-screen.

At the top of the document, she saw a photo of David. He looked serious, as usual. Serious and beautiful, in a masculine way. A warrior with the face of an angel. Below the photo appeared the same kind of bullet points she'd seen in the other profiles, and below that, the list of his psychic abilities. Astral projection, thought projection, remote viewing. She scrolled down to see more of the document. A single line of text, printed in large red letters, rolled into view.

Her heart thudded. Fear exploded through her, cold and sharp, like a thousand microscopic blades tearing through her flesh from the inside out. No. She wouldn't believe it. *No, no, no.*

The line read, "ALERT: Extreme caution advised, subject has killed before."

Her ears rang. The room whirled around her. With a start, she realized she'd stopped breathing. As she hauled in long, slow breaths, she scrolled down to the next line of text in the file. Her breath caught in her throat, and a single word burst out of her. "No."

The document said, "During his stay at this facility, David Ransom murdered another traveler in cold blood."

CHAPTER NINE

GRACE HUNCHED ON THE BED, HANDS GRASPING THE LAPTOP, HER gaze nailed to the screen. David's profile contained no further information about the traveler his captors asserted he had killed. She'd spent the better part of an hour scouring through the records on the DVD in search of details, but found none.

He must've killed the other traveler in self-defense or to save an innocent life. He was no murderer. Hell, she'd killed men before. Gunshots fired by her hand snuffed out the lives of Jackson Tennant and his right-hand man, Xavier Waldron. Not that she celebrated the fact. Not that she didn't occasionally suffer a twinge of guilt. But overall, she knew she'd done what had to be done. Both men were evil, and she didn't apply the term lightly. Together with Tesler, JT and Waldron conspired to abduct, torture, and murder countless human beings simply because they displayed psychic abilities. Their deaths improved the world just a bit.

She knew why she'd taken lives. Now she needed to understand why David had. To find out, she must ask him. Would he answer? Would he bare his secrets to her at last? Despite his secrets, despite his collusion in concealing the truth from her last year, she trusted him with her heart, her life, her very soul. He'd seen her through a horrific time in her life, and he had opened up to her when she needed him to the most.

Please, David, do it for me again.

Why did this revelation about David appear nowhere in JT's personal data collection? Had Amador faked the file to upset her? With his agenda a big freaking question mark, she lacked the vital information necessary to decide. Vetting electronic data, especially the stolen kind, was not her forte.

The keys clacked beneath her fingers as she executed another search of the DVD. It coughed up no more information about John Mendoza. Combing through every file on the disk might take days, and she had a creeping feeling she didn't have that long.

Before she took any further action, though, she had to talk to David.

Snapping the laptop's lid shut, she slid the computer across the quilt, out of her way. Sitting cross-legged, she rested her palms on her knees and closed her eyes. Ghost images of the computer screen danced behind her eyelids for a few seconds. She took slow, deep breaths as she urged her body to relax and her mind to clear of all thoughts and worries. It was harder than it sounded. Thoughts ricocheted in her mind, gouging out bits of her self-control.

David killed someone.

Tesler is coming for me. Is David safe?

I have to do something.

Should I trust Amador?

Can I trust my own powers?

Lord almighty, she'd never get anywhere this way. The chaos in her mind threatened to drive her bonkers. She sucked in the deepest breath she could, held it for two seconds, and released the air slowly as she concentrated on counting out the seconds. Her shoulders relaxed. Her jaw loosened. The rest of her muscles followed suit, the tension melting out of them as she let go of more than the air. She let go of everything. Everyone.

Her physical body retreated from her awareness. Darkness replaced the light seeping in through her eyelids. She floated in the blackest night, alone, at peace.

With a swift determination, she soared through the crossroads to a pulsing star that was David and tumbled out into a twilit world.

For a few seconds, she wavered there, blind and numb from the trip. Then she spotted David. Seated on the floor, wedged into the corner of the room. Body slumped. Eyes closed. Mouth twisted into a frown. And he wasn't alone.

Another man sat in the opposite corner. His eyes were open. He stared at David without expression.

Grace looked around. Concrete walls and floor. No furniture. No windows. It was a prison cell.

She hurried to David, kneeling beside him. "Hey."

Though she knew the other man could neither see nor hear her, she still found herself whispering. David did not move or respond in any way. With her psychic wall in place, she couldn't feel him the way she usually did. The connection trickled through her instead of flowing like a stream. Being so disconnected from him gave her a strange queasiness.

She said a little louder, "David, it's me. I'm here."

He cracked one eye open to peek at her. "I know."

"So why are you ignoring me?"

The other man said, "What do you know?"

David pushed into a more upright posture. To the other man, he said, "I don't suppose you'd agree to plug your ears and close your eyes for a few minutes."

"Why?"

David scrunched his lips and huffed a breath out through his nostrils. He was thinking, she knew—thinking and annoyed. She recognized the signs. He must not fully trust his new friend.

He closed his eyes for a second and then looked at the other man. "Someone is here to see me."

"Ahhhh," the man said. "I understand. I will do as you ask."

The stranger jammed a finger into each ear and shut his eyes.

Grace studied David. The stoic mask slipped over his features.

"I'll do most of the talking," she said. "I need to ask you a question."

"Fine."

"Well, several questions, actually."

"Get on with it, please."

His flinty tone stopped her for a second. "Are you okay?"

"Yes." The syllable hissed snake-like, rife with impatience.

His state of okay-ness wasn't the main question plaguing her. She ached to ask the real question, but every time she formed the words in her head, her stomach twisted into knots.

"Go on," David said. "Whatever it is, ask it."

"Okay." She clamped her hands over her knees. "Have you ever killed anyone?"

His expression went blank. "Why would you ask me?"

"I—I came across a file that said you're dangerous because you killed someone at the Mojave Desert facility."

"Where did this file come from?"

"The man who lives at 1325 Meroz Road. Gabriel Amador."

He stared into her eyes with such intensity that she wanted to look away, but recognized she mustn't. "Your telepathic stalker."

"Right."

"And you went to his house? Alone?" Hisses and growls punctuated the words. "Are you insane?"

"Possibly." Anger flared inside her, but she clamped a lid over it and lifted her chin. "I didn't have much choice, since you took off on another mission."

"Didn't you get my message? Tesler wants you."

"I'm staying at a motel, and I ditched my old phone and car. I'm safe."

"For the moment."

She slumped, resting her hands on her thighs. "Amador offered to help me. He says he was a prisoner at another facility, in Siberia. I get the feeling he hates Tesler as much as you do." She dug her nails into her knees. "Amador said I'd learn things about you I wouldn't like."

David clenched his jaw. "Naturally, you believe everything your stalker tells you."

"No, of course not." She practically spat the words at him. "I am not an idiot, you know. That's why I'm asking you if it's true or not. Did you kill someone?"

"You shouldn't have to ask."

"Which is not an answer." Since he glared at her without speaking, she said, "We're engaged to be married, David. You say you love me. But you won't let me in on whatever secrets you're holding in. Why are you so afraid to confide in me?"

"You haven't been eager to do the same."

"I have amnesia. Hello, stress alert. What's your excuse?"

He slumped deeper into the corner.

She longed to reach for him, to draw him closer. How had they spiraled so far away from each other? She trusted this man more than she'd trusted anyone else in her life. He was right, though. She withheld certain facts from him, just as he held back from her.

Amador might be aiming to drive a wedge between them. He needn't bother. They were fashioning their own wedge.

David raised a hand as if to touch her face but then, realizing he couldn't, he dropped his hand to his thigh. His eyes glimmered less blue somehow, less vibrant, as if the color had drained away along with his anger.

"You're right," he said. "I have no excuse for the things I've done to you. I've put you in danger over and over, without intending to, but intentions are meaningless. I betrayed your trust."

"No, you haven't. Why would you say such a thing?"

"Because I—" He shook his head with a vehemence that ruffled his hair. "You have no idea what I've done, and it doesn't matter anymore."

His guilt and misery overwhelmed her, escalating her own. A tear dribbled down her cheek into the corner of her mouth. Bitter salt oozed over her tongue. She scuttled toward him and fell to her knees. "Please, David. Tell me what you think you did. If you hurt someone, I'm sure it was self-defense—"

"Don't." His brow furrowed, and his mouth twisted into an agonized expression. The look flitted across his face, vanishing within seconds as the old stoicism cloaked him.

And David the warrior angel returns.

She sank back onto her heels. David the distant angel. Unknowable, unreachable, untouchable.

Footfalls pounded in the corridor outside the room.

"Leave," David said. "Right away."

A command, not a request. She planted a hand on her thigh and bent forward. "I will not. I can help you escape."

"No." He snapped his back straight. "You'll only get in the way."

"Excuse me?"

"Go away."

The footsteps ceased outside the door.

She gaped at him. The anger in his voice. The stoic mask on his face.

Of course. Why hadn't she noticed earlier?

"You're lying," she said. "I can feel it, David. You're pushing me away out of fear. But of what?"

His eyes turned toward her, though he didn't face her. "For once in your life, could you not be so goddamn stubborn? Curse me, hit me, yell at me. But don't be understanding. I'm breaking up with you, Grace."

She inched nearer. If she'd had a genuine body, her kneecaps would've bumped his thighs. With her face a breath away from his, she waited until he grudgingly met her gaze. "I don't believe you. And I will not allow you to break up with me. We have to fight for each other, not run away."

"This isn't the time or the place to discuss it."

"I agree." Weakness rippled through her as her psychic energy dwindled. She wished like hell she could grab him by the arms. Throttle some sense into him. Instead, she glared into his gleaming blue eyes. "This conversation is not over."

She released the tether between their minds. As the crossroads dragged her back into the tunnel, she swore he mumbled, "Forgive me."

Then she was gone.

DAVID BLINKED AT THE EMPTY SPACE WHERE GRACE HAD BEEN A second earlier. He couldn't get the image of her out of his mind. The solitary tear dribbling down her cheek. The confused expression that morphed into sorrow, and finally, mutated into exasperation.

He'd expected tears. Dreaded them, yes, while knowing they must come. But frustration? It made no sense. Why didn't she rail at him?

Because she knew he was lying.

He cracked his fist into the floor. Pain shot through his hand, up his wrist, and straight into his forearm. He winced, grunting. He deserved the pain. After what he'd done to Grace, he deserved far worse than this. She'd loved him when no one else would. She trusted him. And how did he repay her faith? With a string of betrayals.

Nothing had unfolded the way he'd planned. Someday, maybe she'd understand and forgive him.

We have to fight for each other, she'd urged him, not run away.

Fight for her? He'd crawl naked through a jungle of poison thorns to revel in her warmth again. If he could guarantee her well-being. Which he'd destroyed in the first place.

Why couldn't she let him break up with her? He hadn't fought her refusal with much vigor. He let her have her way because...

He shoved both hands into his hair. He gave in because he didn't want to end their relationship. She was his weakness and his strength. He needed her. She had no use for him, though she would deny it. His incompetence forced her to track him down, and her very presence here jeopardized her safety.

If anyone realized he could communicate with her psychically, then Tesler would manipulate their connection to get to her. He didn't know how. He couldn't risk finding out. The wall she'd constructed around her mind ought to shield her from the worst of it. If Tesler tortured him, she might sense it but not experience it the way she would without the barrier. At this moment, he was glad of that. She must keep away from him until he escaped from this facility. Any attempt at contact endangered her. As much as he burned to see her—to hear her voice and feel her, psychically and physically—it was out of the question.

He was right back where he started two years ago. Alone.

"Has your woman left?" Nkosi asked.

David glanced sideways at the man. "What?"

"I assume you were talking with your woman, from the way you were so protective of her."

"You listened in?"

"No. I meant the way you ordered me not to listen or watch. That was protective."

"Oh." The explanation was quasi-plausible. And since David could use the help of a coconspirator to get out of here, he may as well give Nkosi the benefit of the doubt.

He would never, under any circumstances, admit to communicating with Grace.

"No worries," Nkosi said. "I don't expect you to confirm what I believe. She must be quite something for you to shield her so."

A mechanism thunked. The door swung inward.

Karl Tesler walked into the cell.

David stood up. Nkosi stayed on the floor.

Tesler halted just inside the doorway. He glanced from David to Nkosi and back again. A smirk tugged at the corners of Tesler's mouth. "Welcome home, David."

"You can torture me all you want," David said, "but I won't tell you anything."

"Torture you? No, I won't do that." Tesler swept one arm through the air to point at Nkosi. "I'll torture him."

David envisioned death rays shooting out of his eyes to scorch holes through Tesler's chest. Wouldn't do any good. The man had no heart. He probably wasn't even human.

Nkosi pushed up off the floor, favoring sore muscles, and rose to his full height, a good three inches taller than David. "Don't worry, my friend. Neither one of us will give this... person what he seeks."

Tesler made a sound somewhere between a growl and a chuckle. "Such bravery—and camaraderie. We'll see how long it lasts once we get you into the fun house."

Two guards trundled into the room. Both held stun guns at the ready. One guard herded Nkosi out of the cell and down the hallway out of sight. The other waved his stun gun at David, gesturing for him to exit the cell. David complied. There was no point in arguing, at least until he'd figured out a plan of escape.

As David walked past Tesler, the scientist murmured, "How is your golden girl?"

David stopped. He narrowed his eyes and glared straight into Tesler's. "You will never get your hands on her. She's tougher and smarter than you or any of your thugs."

Tesler smiled like a wolf baring his teeth before pouncing on his prey. "We'll see about that."

"JT failed, and so will you."

Tesler tsked. "Jackson Tennant was ill-prepared and stark-raving mad. I have a clarity of purpose he never found. And I have a plan that doesn't revolve around a harebrained hypothesis that blood contains the essence of psychic powers. I plan on extracting them directly from the source."

A chill ran through David because he suspected he knew the answer before he asked. "What source would that be?"

"The human brain, dear boy. The human brain."

David couldn't muster a response. His every thought centered on Grace and a terrible image of Tesler drilling into her skull to tap into the source of her power. A sharp pain in his chest blossomed, until it devoured his entire body, tearing through muscles. *God no.* He would never, never, never allow the image to become reality. Whatever the price to spare her, he'd pay it without hesitation.

Tesler chuckled again. "Do you know what the greatest prize of all is?"

David ground his teeth.

"The brain of a traveler with the Golden Power," Tesler said. "The pretty pink brain of your darling girl."

If he had to die for Grace, then he was dragging this bastard down with him.

CHAPTER TEN

GRACE LAY MOTIONLESS ON THE BED FOR SEVERAL MINUTES. NIGHT had fallen, and the harsh glow of sodium-vapor lights leaked in between the curtains from the parking lot outside. A horn blared out on the interstate. The draft from the air conditioner rustled her hair.

David had said awful things to her. Although she realized he'd spoken out of fear, his words hurt anyway. One day soon, he would explain himself. What happened then…

She thrust the question aside. Drained in body and mind, she could spare no energy on fretting over the future. David could have his way, for the time being. She'd leave him alone.

But not for long.

Gabriel Amador had offered to help her, and she might have to accept his offer. First, though, she wanted a little more information about the man. Since the DVD provided nothing of value, she must search elsewhere.

She called the front desk.

Tag answered on the first ring. "How can I help you, Ms. Marcus?"

"Uh—" He was calling *her* Ms. Marcus, she realized just in time, before she told him he must've confused her with someone else. She almost forgot her own alias. "Does the motel have Wi-Fi access?"

"Sorry, no. We're still living in the Dark Ages here." He paused for a second, then said, "You could use the office computer if you want. It's got DSL."

"Won't you get in trouble for letting me use it?"

"Nah," he said, his tone utterly dismissive of the possibility. "Nobody'll find out, but even if they did, they wouldn't care. This dog's leash is pretty loose, ya know. Come on down and I'll set you up."

"Thank you. I really appreciate this."

"Ain't nothing."

She hung up, grabbed her purse, and headed for the motel's lobby. The big neon sign at the edge of the parking lot declared "Stay-A-Night Motel—Vacancy." As the lobby's door swung shut behind her, Tag greeted her with a big smile and a sweeping gesture meant as an invitation for her to come around behind the desk. She returned his smile, ducking behind the desk. When she reached the computer, she saw he already had a web browser open on-screen.

"Have at it," he told her.

"Thanks."

She watched Tag pick up a pile of unopened mail and carry it to the far end of the desk, about six feet away from her. The computer monitor stood at an angle on the desk which meant he couldn't see the screen from his position. Still, she must assume the computer had some kind of tracking software on it that let Tag's employers keep tabs on his activity—a keystroke logger or similar application. Maybe she was being paranoid again, but paranoia seemed prudent when she had Tesler's goons on her trail.

Okay. She'd keep this brief and vague.

Navigating to a search engine, she typed in two words: Gabriel Amador. The search results came up with links to Facebook pages and Twitter accounts for various individuals named Gabriel Amador. None of them matched the man she'd met. She tried Gabriel Ricardo Amador, with no better luck. Next, she typed in "Catalan Enterprises." The top results had nothing to do with Amador's company but were instead links to informational pages about the Catalan people of northern Spain. She scrolled down to see more results.

Eureka.

She clicked on a link for "Catalan Enterprises: Venture Capital, Investment Services, and More." The website loaded in a few seconds. She skimmed the text on the home page, learning the company provided seed money for new businesses, ran an online stock-trading service, and owned a number of banks and other financial institutions around the world. The company was, predictably, based in the Catalonia region of Spain. She browsed the rest of the site but found no mention of Gabriel Amador. The site didn't name any of the company's officers or the board of directors, and it supplied nothing more exciting than gobbledygook-filled explanations of how venture capital worked and how to apply for it.

Maybe that was the point. Amador gave her his company's name because he knew it would lead her nowhere.

"You feel that?" Tag asked.

She glanced up at him. He surveyed the small lobby which consisted of a coffee table and three chairs situated in front of the desk. He held an envelope in one hand, and a letter opener in the other, as if he'd frozen in the middle of slicing open the letter.

Grace shut her eyes, letting her paranormal senses kick in. She felt something too, though it was vague. The nape of her neck tingled.

Her pulse shifted into overdrive. *Someone's watching.* She scanned the room, trying to listen through the pounding of her own heart. No use. She couldn't hear anything else. The sharp scent of Tag's coffee wafted into her nostrils, and she could almost taste the bitter brew.

"What was it?" she asked Tag.

He shrugged. "Weird feeling. Like a ghost walked through me or something."

A ghost. She'd never heard of a traveler walking through someone, but she didn't know everything about psychic abilities. Since travelers didn't have physical bodies, they could walk through solid objects—people too, she imagined. She hadn't tried it herself, though she'd seen David walk through walls. But walking through human beings? The thought of it made her queasy. Sure, in her astral form she was essentially a ghost, but still…

Walking through walls and people? *Ew.*

She surfed back to the search engine and typed in John Mendoza. A boatload of results popped up, and though she tried to sort through them for relevant information, she got bogged down by the myriad John Mendozas in cyberspace. Everyone had a digital footprint these days. Everyone except Gabriel Amador.

Out of curiosity, she searched for David Ransom. The results numbered in the millions. A listing for a yellow-pages website announced "268 David Ransoms in the United States." *Oh jeez.* Seriously? One David Ransom was all she could handle. Hundreds of them running around out there sounded like an awful lot of stoic, pigheaded men.

A ridiculous image unrolled in her mind. Hundreds of tiny Davids trotting around on a map of the United States. One little Grace struggling to herd them all with her lasso.

She couldn't help the chuckle that tumbled from her lips.

"No fair," Tag said. "You gotta share the funny emails."

"Oh, it's not an email. I had a weird thought, that's all."

Movement flashed in her peripheral vision. She glanced at Tag, but he held the same position as before, having moved only his head to look at her. The movement she'd spied seemed quicker than he would've moved his head. She must've imagined it. Or else it was a bird.

"Something wrong?" Tag asked.

"I thought—no-no, it's fine."

Tag shrugged and went back to sorting the mail.

Grace stared out the glass doors of the lobby. A few cars occupied spaces in the parking lot, scattered along the length of the motel. Although the establishment sat next to the interstate, it lay on a side road at the end of an off-ramp. She couldn't see the traffic whizzing by on the interstate. The occasional car exited the off-ramp, driving past the motel.

The movement she swore she'd seen had come from closer. Much closer.

If she could sense other travelers, then maybe she could sense normal people too.

Beyond the glass doors, the glow of the streetlights tinged everything with a jaundiced yellow. Focused on the light outside, and the beat-up cars bathed in it, she relaxed and cleansed her mind of thoughts. The crossroads tugged at her, but she resisted. Instead, she expanded her mind to sweep the vicinity like radar. Nothing. Nothing. She hit a blip when she scanned over Tag. Then nothing. Nothing. Nothing.

Blip.

She jerked. Was the blip a person? She locked onto the signal—a feeling really, impossible to define but definitely there—and aimed her remote-viewing sense at it. The wall barred her view, of course. She was psychic, for crying out loud. Walls didn't matter to her. She itched to shut her eyes, to block out all other stimuli, but she couldn't afford to limit her natural vision. A voice in the back of her mind warned this might be a trap, set by a traveler in league with Tesler or Amador, or both. She must keep her natural vision available even as she switched over to remote viewing. Sure, piece of cake.

You can do this. Concentrate.

The walls faded into semi-transparency as she tracked the blip back to its source. Her inner vision zoomed in on the target, flying through the ghost image of the wall. She panned left, toward the junction of the lobby wall and the rest of the motel that jutted out from the office and lobby section. There, in the shadows cast by the overhanging roof, she caught sight of a figure crouched against the wall. The person wore black military-style fatigues, black boots, black gloves, and a black full-face helmet. He had a radio clipped to his belt and gripped a big automatic weapon in both hands.

Her heart thudded in her chest. She swallowed against the lump in her throat as a wave of cold dread crested over her. A commando. The black-suited man was an ALI goon.

They were here.

She pulled back from the commando and resumed scanning the vicinity. Nothing. Nothing. *Blip.* Nothing. *Blip, blip, blip.* This time, she had no trouble peering through the walls to identify the blips. Four more commandos had spread out along the outside of the building. As she followed the contours of the structure, she found two more commandos inside a plain white van parked behind the lobby.

Oh shit.

How in the hell had they found her? She'd ditched her credit cards, her car, everything except her cash, her new computer, and her purse with the gun inside it. Even as she watched the commandos with her remote vision, she reached for her purse to pat the hard outline of the .357 revolver inside. Sliding her hand into the bag, she curled her fingers around the gun's grip.

"You okay?"

Tag's concerned voice broke her concentration. The walls snapped back into view. Her head spun a little. As she grasped the edge of the desk for support, she realized she'd stopped breathing. No wonder she was woozy. She sucked in a couple of deep breaths and, steadier now, pushed away from the desk.

Out of the corner of her eye, she noticed Tag taking a step toward her.

She held up a hand to stop him. "Um, I can't explain this, but some very bad people are trying to kidnap me. They're in the parking lot. I imagine they're about to storm in here and take me by force. I don't want you to get hurt."

"I can handle myself."

His expression had turned hard, and suddenly he reminded her of a hitman in one of those mafia movies Hollywood loved to make. He probably could handle himself. But against seven armed commandos?

Dammit. She hadn't intended for Tag to get caught in the middle of her nightmare. She didn't want him to suffer or die because of her, and yet she could not let Tesler capture her. Remaining free offered the sole hope of stopping the mad scientist.

"There's a back way out," Tag said, hooking a thumb toward the door behind her.

"Bad guys have a van out back."

Tag frowned, working his lips as if thinking hard. Finally, he said, "Take the side door. It opens off the back of the office, onto the sidewalk on the far side of the building."

"Okay. Thanks."

"I'll keep 'em occupied while you beat it."

He waved toward the office door.

She tugged her purse tight against her, the bulk of her gun jostling inside it. If she let this man cover for her while she fled, Tesler's minions would hurt him—or worse, if he failed to cooperate to their satisfaction. Tag's blood would stain her hands too.

No more deaths because of her. *Stand and fight.*

Trouble was, Tag wouldn't back down. Despite meeting him a few hours ago, she understood a basic truth about him, about men of his ilk, the noble warriors. They fought for what was right, without fail. She knew this because she loved just such a man.

David wouldn't abandon her in these circumstances. Neither would Tag.

Unless she urged him into it.

When she'd set out on a cross-country odyssey to free David from the California facility, he'd knocked her unconscious to slow down her progress, in the vain belief she might give up when she woke. Fat chance. If she could replicate his technique, then she might keep Tag out of harm's way without hurting him.

Much later, she'd asked David how he gave her a psychic mickey. He'd told her, "With a small, controlled burst of telepathic energy empowered by my fervent need for you to sleep. The subject must be willing on some level to succumb. That's how thought projection works. Desire coupled with power."

But if she employed too much power, she could damage Tag's mind.

Did Tag want to submit to her will? She'd given in to David because, though it chagrined her to admit it, deep down she liked surrendering to him. A little bit. On occasion.

Tag was a stranger. This might not work at all on him.

She'd once tricked an old man into believing a twenty-dollar bill was five thousand bucks. Putting a guy to sleep should be easy.

Tag urged her toward the door with a large, but gentle, hand on her arm.

Another door, behind him, caught her attention. "What's that?"

He looked where she pointed. "Closet."

Three, two, one...

With her gaze glued to his, she summoned a ball of psychic energy and blew it into Tag. His eyes widened. She beamed a fervent wish into his mind. *Get in the closet, sit down, sleep.* She repeated the command over and over until she felt his will softening.

He shuffled to the closet, swung the door open, and tromped inside. She kept up her inner chant, afraid he might snap out of it if she stopped. He sat cross-legged on the floor of the closet, leaned against the wall, and promptly fell asleep.

Thank heavens.

She kicked the closet door shut. The latch clicked into place.

A quick telepathic pass confirmed he was undamaged. If she interpreted things right.

She whipped the revolver out of her purse and peeked into the office. A door on the left must open onto the rear area. Another door led out the back of the office. The stale smell of dust drifted out of the air-conditioning vents. She wiped her clammy hands on her pants.

Tag had told her to take the side door. She hustled over to check it was unlocked, then retreated to the lobby, closing the office door.

From her position behind the reception desk, she reached out again with her psychic senses. The walls turned semi-transparent once more. It was strange, peering through the ghost image of the walls, seeing through solid matter but knowing she couldn't walk through it, not in her corporeal state. She spotted the commandos outside the lobby doors. As she observed them, they surged forward and headed straight for the doors, storming through them with guns raised. The doors banged open, and the commandos' boots thundered across the floor.

Her vision reeled back to the normal, and the seven helmeted, armed men arrayed in front of the desk. She held the revolver muzzle down, her arm slack, the weapon hidden behind the desk. Her finger hovered over the trigger, separated from it by millimeters of air.

One commando, apparently the leader, detached from the group to approach the desk.

"Grace Powell." He sounded far too pleased with himself. "Gotcha, sweetheart."

A glacier hardened in her chest, expanding to scour out her soul. That voice. The way he said "sweetheart" with a slight snarl. *Holy shit.* She swallowed hard and said, "Battaglia."

He removed his helmet and tucked it under his arm. The sneer was familiar too, and it triggered a flashback of him tackling her, threatening to stab a syringe into her neck. Her trigger finger itched to pull.

Six bullets. Seven men. Bad odds, even for a crack shot. Which she wasn't.

Battaglia sniggered. "I'm tickled pink you remember me, honey. Maybe this time you'll show me why so many guys are after your sweet little ass."

"Tesler wants me undamaged." She hoped.

"Yeah," Battaglia said, his leering gaze traveling down to her breasts and back up to her face. "But I can do lotsa things without causing permanent harm."

A legion of phantom insects skittered over her skin as she muttered, "You're just as crazy as JT."

"What was that, sweetheart? Didn't quite catch it."

She raised her voice. "Go to hell, you sick son of a bitch."

His guffaw echoed in the small space. He slashed one hand through the air, gesturing toward her. "Cuff her, boys."

Oh hell no.

She must lead them away from the motel, away from Tag. How long he'd slumber, she couldn't gauge. If Battaglia decided to check the closet…

No one else would die for her.

Raising her gun, directing it at Battaglia, she aimed a nasty smile at him. "I wouldn't do that if I were you."

Battaglia shook his head and sighed heavily. "You really are a dumb bitch."

"So come and get me."

She bolted into the office, thwacked the door shut, and locked it.

The knob jiggled.

Battaglia bellowed, "Unlock it or I'll blow it open."

With her inner radar, she did a quick check of the motel's vicinity. The two commandos in the van had not moved, and no others had shown up to join the operation. She withdrew her psychic senses, snapping the walls back into solid form, and ran for the door at the back of the office. Twisting the knob, she flung the door inward and fled outside. Her footfalls clapped on the sidewalk and echoed off the building as she tore down the pathway, past the closed doors and curtained windows of the motel rooms. No one so much as peeked out between the curtains.

The air whooshed over her. A gust of wind snatched up gravel and dirt, flinging it into her face. Grit stung her eyes, pebbles pinged her skin, and the earthy taste of dirt infiltrated her mouth. Her leg muscles burned hotter and hotter with every step she took, screaming for a rest. She pushed her body to run faster.

A gunshot boomed behind her, inside the motel office. Voices shouted, but she couldn't make out the words. The rushing of her own blood in her ears, the huffing of her breaths, and the smacking of her footsteps obscured the words of the commandos.

Just short of the end of the building, she swerved left to race across the parking lot toward the scrubby woods beyond it. The sickly light from the parking lot streetlights petered out at the edge of the woods. Her heart pounded so hard and fast it made her head swim, but she couldn't stop. Her feet left the pavement, landing on dry, rock-hard ground and parched grass. She kept running.

The shouting drew closer. She glanced back.

Commandos streamed out of the office.

Run. The thought spurred her body into more speed. In the instant she refocused her attention on the woods ahead, a shot detonated behind her. A projectile sliced across her arm, setting off a scorching pain that lanced through her, knocking her off balance. She stumbled, nearly fell, and caught herself a second before she hit the dirt. Her arm burned, but she refused to look at it. Not now. Not yet.

She pushed her legs to pump harder. Muscles cramped in protest. She ignored the pain, the sweat stinging her eyes, and the scrambling and thumping of boot-clad feet behind her. Another gunshot boomed. She ducked into the trees. Bark exploded from the tree she'd just passed. On and on she raced, panting so hard her chest ached, fighting for each breath.

Her toe caught on a tree root. She tripped, sailing face-first onto the ground. Her body struck the earth with such force it knocked the sense out of her. She couldn't breathe. Couldn't move. Couldn't think.

Branches cracked. Dry grass rustled. Boots clomped.

They were coming.

Snap out of it.

She sucked in a breath, pushed onto her knees, and glanced over her shoulder. Black silhouettes, distant but moving closer each second, headed straight for her. No time. She must do something. The only thing she could think of would come at a hefty cost.

No choice.

She disengaged from her physical body. Her mind soared upward, a balloon cut loose in the wind. Her mind flew into the dark tunnel, up and up. Bursting out into the crossroads, she halted with an abruptness that would've snapped her neck if she had a body. Pain radiated from the base of her skull, down into her neck. Floating there, she extended all her psychic faculties and reaped as much juice as she could from the energy matrix around her. The stars pulsed and swelled. Power, searing and molten, cascaded into her.

She plummeted downward, bursting out into the world and back into her body with a suddenness that stunned her. Every nerve in her body twanged, the psychic pain as sharp and real as the throbbing in her neck and the stinging in her arm. She focused her newly acquired power on one objective.

Destroy the commandos.

Wind erupted in front of her. In a wall of gyrating current as strong as a hurricane, the wind swept away from her toward the commandos. The gale uprooted small trees, drawing them into its eddies. Chunks of dirt and rocks twirled up from the ground, whirling on the currents of the wind.

The commandos ran straight into the maelstrom.

Someone shouted, "Jesus Christ!"

Male voices screamed in pain as rocks and airborne trees socked them. Still the wind spun, traveling forward at breakneck speed. The maelstrom hefted the commandos off the ground and hurled them through the air. Their bodies smacked down with wet thuds.

Nausea swelled inside her. She choked back the bile rising in her throat, tasting the bitter acid.

The screams ended.

She released the air. Saplings, rocks, and dirt rained down onto the ground. As the ruckus settled into silence, she bent forward and vomited.

Wiping her mouth on her shirt, she finally looked at her arm. Blood trickled over her elbow and down her forearm. It originated from a wound on her upper arm, a couple of inches below the shoulder. It looked like a deep scrape. A bullet must've grazed her. The wound still smarted, and she dabbed at it with her fingertip. Pain shot out from the wound. She gasped.

Her stomach hurt. Her head pounded as if a metal spike had been shoved straight up her spine into her skull. Every muscle trembled. She struggled to stand, but her knees buckled. She flopped onto her butt on the ground. Tears spilled down her cheeks, driven by sobs that racked her body, triggering sharp pains in so many places she lost count.

Hot shards pierced the backs of her eyes. The first signs of a migraine.

Shit. Considering how much power she'd funneled through her mind and body, she wouldn't have much time to get to safety before the migraine disabled her. She rose onto all fours.

Her right hand crunched an object.

With two fingers, she picked it up. Her cell phone. Demolished by a large and heavy booted foot.

Tossing it aside, she stashed her gun in her purse and crawled through the debris from her whirlwind. When she discovered the first body, she halted. The commando lay motionless, eyes wide and dead. She checked his neck for a pulse anyway. Nothing. She noticed the radio clipped to his belt, but that wouldn't help her. Not unless she wanted to chat with the buddies of the men she'd killed.

She bowed her head. She'd killed… how many men?

Don't think about it. They would've killed you in a heartbeat.

With trembling hands, she searched the man's jacket pockets for something, anything, that might help her. What dragged on like hours, but probably had been seconds, ticked by before her unsteady fingers closed around a hard object in the man's hip pocket. She jiggled the thing until it popped free of the pocket.

A cell phone.

Relief flooded through her. Tears flowed anew, streaking down her cheeks as she dug in her purse for the card Roland Wickham had given her. Finding it, she held the card up to read the text. Tears fogged her vision. She sniffled and wiped them away. In the few seconds before new tears emerged, she read the number on the card and dialed it. The phone rang once, twice, three times.

"Hello?"

She almost burst into sobs again at the sound of Gabriel Amador's voice. Her own voice rasped when she said, "It's Grace. I need your help."

"What happened?"

"I'll explain later. I'm pinned down behind the Stay-A-Night Motel, just off the interstate."

"I know where it is. Stay out of sight until I arrive."

"Okay." Despite her best efforts not to, she sniffled.

"Hold on, Grace," Amador said, his tone authoritative. "I am on my way."

He hung up.

She dropped the phone. He hadn't even asked what she meant by pinned down. He didn't seem surprised at all that she needed help. In fact, she could've sworn she detected a note of triumph in his voice—faint, but there. Probably her paranoia rearing its head again.

Either way, help was coming. If she could evade the remaining commandos until then.

A twig cracked.

She pulled the gun out of her purse. Hold them off, that was all she had to do.

For how long?

CHAPTER ELEVEN

GRACE CLAMBERED AWAY FROM THE BODY AS FAST AS SHE DARED move, and as fast as she could manage, taking the dead man's phone with her. Despite worrying about the commandos' ability to track their buddy's phone, she decided the benefit of keeping it with her outweighed the risk. At least she hoped it did.

The pulsating in her head strengthened with each passing minute. She started out waddling on all fours, but when her arms crumpled, she resorted to belly-crawling. The parched earth, cracked and jagged, clawed at her flesh. Her injury impelled her to adopt a limping belly-crawl that favored her wounded arm. The effort of hauling her body over the uneven terrain while hampered by a blinding headache, a wounded arm, and spry commandos on her tail drained her beyond exhaustion. She longed to collapse under a nice shady tree. She didn't dare stop for even one second, for fear she might never rouse herself again.

So far, she'd kept ahead of the commandos. Maybe they got distracted by the bodies of their comrades. The memory of their lifeless forms jolted her, yet she was fresh out of guilt. *They* shot *her*.

In the wake of her own deadly action, she realized one fact. If David had killed anyone, he must've done it in self-defense. She knew him, and she understood through far too much experience that sometimes a person was provoked into taking another's life. Her gut still churned from the desperation of choosing between her survival and the innate inhibition against killing.

Most people operated under that inhibition. Some did not. They were the ones who compelled people like her and David to enact deadly measures.

Please, David, just tell me the truth.

She prayed he heard her plea, even through the wall blocking off her mind.

The phone in her pocket vibrated.

Catching her breath, she paused to pull out the appropriated phone and glanced down at its screen. The number on the caller ID was familiar. She pressed the button to take the call but didn't dare say hello.

"Don't speak," Amador said. "I am at the motel. Leave this line open and I will track you."

Oh great. If he could track the phone, then her pursuers might be closing in on her too.

As if he'd read her mind, Amador said, "I don't think Tesler's men are tracking the phone. They seem to be setting up a perimeter to begin an organized hunt for you."

Could he read her mind? David swore trying to read minds led to insanity, but he might be wrong about that. Amador could've thought of the same thing at the same time she did by coincidence. Whichever it was, the answer hardly mattered right now.

"I have your signal," Amador said, in a hushed voice. "Hold on, Grace. I will mute my phone and come for you. Do not hang up."

The line seemed to go dead. He must've muted the call on his end.

She huddled there, on her belly, propped up with one arm and gripping the cell phone in one hand, her gun in the other. As she tilted her head to listen, she also scanned the woods with her eyes—her physical eyes. All her psychic senses were hollow, emptied of power. She could do little more than lie there, squinting from the migraine pain and struggling not to vomit again.

She yearned to curl up in a ball and sleep for days.

Would her psychic barrier stay in place if she slept? She hadn't taken so much as a nap since building the mental barrier, unless passing out earlier counted as rest. It felt like days had elapsed since she sat on the bed with David, both of them trying to figure out how she might erect a psychic firewall. She checked the display on the dead man's phone. It gave the time as 11:02 PM. She flipped the phone facedown in her palm to hide the glow from its display.

Even the fragile moonglow hurt her eyes.

Her eyelids threatened to close. With a gargantuan effort of will, she kept them open.

David, I need you.

He wouldn't come. He couldn't. Besides being held hostage at the Montana facility, he most likely couldn't track her down because of her psychic wall. Lowering the barrier would let him reach her, but it might also let in enemies. Soon she might not be able to fend off sleep any longer, and her psychic wall might become a moot point.

Rustling. Behind her.

She rolled onto her back, raising her gun.

Gabriel Amador stepped out from behind a bush.

She nearly keeled over right then, out of sheer relief. Her arm fell to the ground, and the gun tumbled from her fingers. White lights flickered in her vision, a signal her migraine had worsened. The pain swallowed her head, fractured her mind, and vacuumed every last ounce of strength from her body. She tried to push up onto her elbows, but her arms gave out. She toppled to the ground.

Amador crouched beside her. He plucked her gun from the dirt, shoving it into her purse. Her tight throat strangled the words she tried to speak. So tired. Sleep beckoned to her, though she battled against it. Keeping her eyelids open got harder and harder. They drooped half-closed. She peeked through her lashes, her gaze intersecting with Amador's.

His expression was pinched.

She tried one more time to speak but eked out nothing better than a moan.

And then, like a hero in a movie, Gabriel Amador scooped her up into his arms and lugged her out of the woods. David had carried her this way once, in a similar situation. In his arms, she'd enjoyed safety and warmth. Cradled in the arms of Gabriel Amador, she suffered an odd mixture of relief and tension.

The pain and exhaustion brought on by her migraine overpowered everything else. By the time they reached Amador's vehicle, an enormous SUV, she gave up the fight.

Her lids fluttered shut as she sank into a deep slumber.

———

DAVID SCUFFLED TO A STOP A FEW FEET INSIDE THE DOORWAY OF THE twenty-foot-square room. Fluorescent lights recessed into the ceiling cast quivering light onto the white walls and concrete floor. The far wall housed a two-way mirror that would, undoubtedly, allow Tesler's fans and cohorts to observe his sessions with travelers. Nkosi staggered in behind David, coming up on his left, an arm's length away. Armed sentries guarded them, one to Nkosi's left and one to David's right. Both their gazes were riveted to the sight in the middle of the room.

A metal chair hunkered there, padded with meager cushioning. The seat resembled a dentist's chair, though without the cozy atmosphere. In the chair—strapped down with restraints around his wrists, ankles, and forehead—huddled Sean Vandenbrook.

The boy's green eyes glittered with anger. He lifted his chin high, his lips compressed.

David tipped his head to Sean, and the boy almost smiled. In the past six months, Sean had labored to become a man, bolstering his body and mind through sheer force of will. To Sean, achieving manhood meant never crying or showing weakness. David tried to explain showing emotion didn't make a man weak, but it sounded hypocritical coming from him. He didn't exactly excel at sharing his feelings.

Which explained why Grace was angry with him.

He flashed back to his last conversation with her when he'd told her to leave because she'd only get in his way. On the surface, she'd been frustrated, but underneath she nursed a wound he had inflicted. Even now, her anguish congealed as a hard lump in his chest. He'd wanted to drag her into his arms, kiss her senseless, and vow to never leave her again. That was selfishness talking. Being with him brought her more pain, more danger, more of everything bad. The worst things in the world trailed behind him wherever he went. Grace deserved better. Maybe if he told her...

No. He had revealed the whole truth once and look what happened. Her parents were murdered, and her grandfather was imprisoned. David should've stayed away from Grace after that, but he'd given in to his need to be with her. Not this time. From here on, he safeguarded her above everything else.

He wouldn't burden her with the truth.

Please, David, just tell me.

Grace's voice murmured into his psyche, subtle as a breeze. He must've imagined it. His desire to confess everything to her led him to fantasize she was begging him to do exactly that. The psychic wall she'd built prevented him from touching her mind. But she could contact him, so maybe...

Wishful thinking.

David, I need you.

This time he knew it was her, without a shred of doubt. Her pain and fear walloped him in the gut. He breathed hard as if someone really had punched him. He tried to contact Grace without leaving his body, but the barrier knocked him back.

With less force this time. Her wall had thinned.

It signified either of two things. One, Grace had decided to let down her psychic defenses in order to contact him. Or two, she was sick or injured and couldn't maintain the wall any longer. Neither option neutralized the acid churning in his gut. He fisted his hands at his sides. If he tried to travel to her, through the crossroads, his body would be undefended. Tesler might notice his vacant expression, and punish him, or worse, he might punish Nkosi or Sean. David would not let that happen.

Damn Tesler. Damn himself for getting captured. He could either go to Grace and help her as she'd practically begged him to or stay here to protect Nkosi and Sean.

Shit, shit, shit.

He stretched out his psychic senses, gently, staying rooted in his body. Using this method, he couldn't see or speak to Grace, or determine her exact circumstances and condition. But he could get an inkling. As he snaked out his paranormal senses, feeling for Grace, he kept an eye on the room around him. Tesler had yet to arrive. David knew the bastard would come eventually once he thought they'd accrued enough anxiety to feed his hunger.

Grace. There. Her fiery aura sparkled in the cold void. Her barrier had weakened, though not disintegrated. It pushed back against him, with the gentle compulsion of one magnet repelling another when their opposite poles faced each other. He discerned enough to tell Grace was alive, not badly injured, and felt safe enough to sleep. He also detected another presence nearby, the vacant sensation of a non-paranormal human.

The door to David's right opened. He withdrew his psychic faculties, returning all his attention to the room around him.

Tesler strolled through the door, shutting it behind him with a sharp click.

David watched the scientist stroll to the chair that restrained Sean. Tesler patted the boy's arm in a gesture that seemed threatening rather than comforting, and then he confronted Nkosi and David.

"I will discover what you know," Tesler said. "The only choice is how I do it."

Nkosi watched Tesler without expression.

David bit his tongue to keep from uttering a sarcastic reply. He wanted to bash in the heads of the guards and Tesler. Smash his way out of here using all his psychic faculties. But what then? He didn't have Grace's power. Simply getting out of this room would probably drain him. To escape the facility demanded greater energy than what he, Nkosi, and Sean could muster combined.

A muscle in his jaw twitched, and he stifled a growl. He'd needed Grace to break him out of the Mojave Desert facility.

"Here's your choice," Tesler said. He waved at Nkosi, and then at Sean. "Which one of them do I torture to death first?"

David clenched his teeth and hissed. "None of us will talk. You're wasting your time."

"Oh really? I disagree. Your darling girl is nearly in my grasp as we speak. So perhaps you'd rather I wait until she arrives and torture her for the information I seek."

"You're lying. You don't have Grace." He'd noticed another presence near her, a non-paranormal human. Could Tesler have captured her already?

A bead of sweat trickled down his temple.

Tesler clucked his tongue, wagging a finger. "Cling to that notion as long as you like, dear boy. Moments ago, my men surrounded her. She has no place to hide."

If Tesler was telling the truth, then everything David had fought for was lost.

No, not yet. He still had a chance to save her. She was asleep or unconscious, injured, and exhausted, both physically and psychically.

David threw a sideways look at Nkosi. He deliberately spoke in a monotone. "I'm sorry. I have to sacrifice you to keep Tesler from getting what he wants."

"I understand," Nkosi replied, his voice filled with a level of certainty and understanding that surprised David. He hadn't expected the man to accept his fate so easily. Nkosi nodded at David and then looked at Tesler. "I will be the first."

"Excellent," Tesler said, almost crowing.

He thought he'd won. And in a way, he had. But David would make sure no one—not Tesler, not Amador, not anyone—would get their hands on Grace. Saving her might kill him. It might also cost Nkosi and Sean their lives. He hoped they understood the necessity of this. He couldn't explain, because he couldn't connect with them telepathically, the way he could with Grace. He might inject a thought into their minds, but even doing that wouldn't guarantee they'd get the message. Thought projection relied on the power of suggestion rather than the power of will. He couldn't force them to accept the thoughts he inserted into their minds. To coerce them into hearing the thoughts required far more energy than he dared expend.

Tesler glanced over his shoulder at the two-way mirror. He gave a quick nod before turning back to face Nkosi and David.

The door opened, and a technician entered the room pushing a cart loaded with tools. Sharp, nasty-looking implements. Syringes filled with liquid. Shiny needles. And, of course, a baseball bat.

David flexed his fingers slowly, then curled them into his palm, the nails scraping flesh. All three of them would, in turn, suffer and die to protect the rest of the world from Tesler and his cohorts. Sean, at least, recognized they also sacrificed themselves to protect Grace. And he would've volunteered for the pain because he cared for her too.

The technician parked the cart near Tesler and left the room. The door clicked shut.

Deep in the walls, something buzzed. The noise was familiar, yet he had no idea what it meant.

No time to wonder. He must go now.

Keeping his eyes open, David cut his mind free of the shackles that bound it to his body. He rocketed upward.

And crashed headlong into a barricade. Hot currents tore through him. He pushed against the impediment, but it stung him harder, hotter, sharper. The pain lanced his mind and sliced into his body. His muscles convulsed.

His mind crashed back into his body. Ten thousand volts of agony arced through him, and he doubled over from the force of it. What the hell was this? His muscles convulsed again, driving him to his knees, contorting his back. A million electrified needles stabbed deep into flesh and sinew. He let out a strangled cry. His entire body curled up as if the muscles had shrunk. He collapsed onto his side, coiled in the fetal position, and rode out the last wrenching wave.

He'd hit a wicked barrier. Not Grace's wall. This obstacle was designed to kill, or at the very least immobilize. Besides, he hadn't even gotten into the tunnel that preceded the crossroads. He got nowhere near Grace.

Tesler walked closer to look down at David with a faint, unpleasant smile on his lips.

David couldn't speak this time. He could do nothing more than scowl at the man.

"Ah," Tesler said, sounding pleased, "I see you've met my new toy. Can't have you skipping off to help your darling girl, now can we?"

From behind Tesler, where David couldn't see, he heard Nkosi say, "What have you done to him?"

Tesler chuckled. "I made a cage for your minds. The engineers who designed it call it an electromagnetic containment field." Tesler sneered, like a tiger admiring its wounded prey. "You see, we discovered quite by accident that EM fields of the right strength and frequency inhibit psychic abilities. Of course, we are risking cellular damage, but I think it's an equitable price to pay for the power you can help us achieve."

With his arms for support, David tried to sit up. His arms shook but held, for now.

He hissed out three words. "We'll fight you."

Tesler shrugged. "Go ahead and try. Inside this room, you are as vulnerable as any normal human being."

David felt weak and vulnerable. He felt... normal.

Tesler strode back to the chair and the cart beside it. He selected a syringe, tapping it to remove bubbles.

"Hmm," Tesler said, "I believe David should go first."

"No," Nkosi said, taking a step toward Tesler. "I am first. You said we choose, and we did."

The two guards grabbed hold of Nkosi's arms, hauling him backward toward the wall. They pinned him there, each keeping one hand clamped on one of Nkosi's arms while in their other hands they grasped their guns.

David's arms gave out. He collapsed onto his back on the floor.

"No," David said, meeting Tesler's gaze. "I'm first. I always have been."

Tesler walked toward David, kneeled beside him, and lowered the syringe to his arm. David winced as the needle pierced his skin. He would die in this room. The realization hit him as the liquid from the syringe heated his veins. He would die, and Grace would fall into Tesler's hands.

He prayed the man had lied. He prayed for more than that, though. *Please, God, spare Grace.*

CHAPTER TWELVE

G RACE SHIFTED HER ARM BUT KEPT HER EYES CLOSED. SOMETHING cool and smooth brushed her skin. She tried to roll over, but her nose smacked into a barrier, one that yielded under the pressure from her body. She inhaled a musty scent. Not a bed. Not *her* bed, for sure. A chill shimmied down her spine. Where was she?

She pried her lids apart. A brown, shiny surface filled her vision. Her face was pressed into a leather backrest. She pushed up into a sitting position. *Crunch.* She slid her legs over the sofa's edge, planting her shoes on the floor. *Crunch.* Nothing under her feet. She scooted forward. *Crunch.* The leather protested yet again.

Leather. Metal. Wood. Oh hell, she knew where she was. She'd called him, so of course, he had rushed out to rescue her. *Crap.* She'd needed rescuing? Oh yeah. Men with guns. Hunting her. Pain. Blood. Screams. Not hers, though. Theirs. She shuddered.

Gabriel Amador had saved her. She must be in his home.

The flash drive. She slapped her shirt, right over the breastbone. The flash drive cut into her skin. *Thank God.* Amador hadn't stolen it.

He might've borrowed it, though, while she was asleep. *Cripes.* She couldn't worry about everything. Anxiety over David ate up enough of her brainpower.

The weight of fatigue still blanketed her, almost suffocating in its intensity. Yawning, she peered into the near darkness. A lamp on the desk chased away the shadows, but its glow petered out after a few feet. She rubbed her neck. *Wake up.* Her head ached, though not with the throbbing pain of a migraine. No, her nap had obliterated the worst of the headache.

Her stomach growled. The ache of hunger battled with butterflies in her gut, creating a queasy mixture. Every muscle in her body screamed for more rest. Heaving her body off the sofa, she shuffled over to the desk.

The scent of leather and dust wafted over her. She inhaled a deep breath, and another scent, spicy and earthy, infiltrated her senses, erasing the scent memory of gun powder, damp earth, sweat, and blood. A shiver rattled through her. This place smelled like Gabriel Amador.

She brushed her palm across the slick wood. Polished to a brilliant shine, the surface glimmered in the ambient light. The laptop computer was gone. The phone stood upright in its base. Chewing the inside of her lip, she stared at the receiver. She ought to call the cops. Or her grandfather. Someone. Her arm trembled slightly as she stretched it out toward the phone.

Pow.

She gripped the desk. Her pulse roared in her ears.

Pow, pow, pow.

Panic knifed through her. The explosions had issued from somewhere outside. She rushed to the French doors. *Pow.* She peeked out between the curtains. There, maybe a hundred feet from the house, Roland Wickham stood with legs spread, arms raised in front of him. Black earmuffs protected his ears. He grasped a gun in both hands, homing in on a target mounted on a metal post. *Pow.* His hands jerked a hair as he fired the weapon.

Target practice? He was a butler or something, she'd thought. Maybe his job involved a lot more than opening and closing doors.

Click.

She spun around just as the door swung open.

Gabriel Amador strode into the room and flicked a switch on the wall.

Light burst from the desk lamp. She struggled not to squint. Her stomach flip-flopped.

Amador left the door ajar as he crossed the threshold, halting several paces beyond it. Muscles flexed beneath his gray slacks and long-sleeve dress shirt. The pinstriped white fabric hugged his torso. Two open buttons at the top let the collar drape outward, revealing cinnamon skin sprinkled with dark hairs. His brown loafers glistened with a high-wattage sheen. One of his hands dangled casually at his side. The other dipped into his pants pocket.

"You look better," he pronounced, aiming a genial smile at her. "That must have been a terrible migraine."

"Yes, it was." She leaned her buttocks on the desk, clamping her fingers on its edge. "Um, thanks for coming to—" The words *rescue me* popped into her head, but she dismissed them. "—help me out. I had a little trouble with Tesler's men."

"So I gathered. You may stay as long as you wish. I promise you will be safe here."

His vow bristled, like a stiff hairbrush grated across her nerves. She frowned at him, folding her arms over her chest. "You can't promise that. I don't even know how Tesler's men tracked me down. They might find me here too."

"No," he said, in his tone of absolute certainty. The tone that ticked her off big time. Then he added, "I have taken precautions against all varieties of surveillance."

"All varieties? Come on, there must be some type of surveillance you haven't thought to guard against."

He shrugged, his smile mutating into a smirk. Did he actually think he'd guarded his home against all possible surveillance technologies? And what about the non-technological kind?

"If a traveler attempts to breach this house," Amador said, "I will know. I will sense it. Would you not sense it as well?"

Once again, she had the skin-prickling feeling that he'd read her mind. Yet he didn't look frothing-at-the-mouth insane. Maybe he simply had excellent intuition.

"Yeah," she said, trying to sound more certain than she was, "I'd sense it if another traveler came on the scene."

"Of course."

A quivering spread from her knees into her calves and thighs. She glanced around the room. Her purse lay on the floor by the sofa, a few feet from Amador but farther from her. He watched her with a noncommittal expression, though his eyes darted to follow her gaze when she looked at the purse. With the jelly squiggling in her legs, she doubted she could run over there to grab her purse before he snatched it away.

Sighing, she lowered herself into the nearest chair. The same damn chair she'd sat in the day before. Or earlier today. Whenever the hell it was. Time had twisted into a Mobius strip, with no end and no beginning, everything turning in on itself.

Yesterday. She met Amador yesterday.

She rubbed her arm. The fabric of her shirt was crusty. Realization tingled over her skin. Her gaze flew to the spot on her arm and the blood dried onto her shirt sleeve. She shoved up the fabric to expose—

Unmarked flesh.

Amador chuckled, a light, airy sound. "Ah yes. I bandaged your wound in the car, but when I checked it later, it was gone. You healed yourself, no?"

A sick feeling sloshed in her stomach. She'd healed her own injuries before, six months ago, but hoped it was a fluke. *Nope.*

He plucked her purse from the floor, hooking one finger under the strap. Then he approached her and held the purse out as if he wanted her to take it.

Her mouth fell open a bit.

"Yes," he said, "I know you have a firearm in your purse."

"I have a concealed carry license."

He gave her a tiny smile. "I don't mind that you have a pistol, Grace. Why do you think I'm offering it to you willingly?"

She looked at the purse, dangling from his grasp at her chest level. The purse swayed a little as he adjusted his grip. She lifted her hand, fingers outstretched to take hold of the strap. At the last second, she pulled her hand away.

"Why do you hesitate?" he asked, thrusting the purse closer to her. "This is an act of trust, Grace. Take the purse, and you will feel safer because you have your pistol. I'm trusting you not to shoot me although, of course, you will be quite able to do so if you wish."

Well, when he put it that way...

She nabbed the purse. Cradling it on her lap, the gun's hardness under her palms, she regarded Amador. "Thank you."

He gave a dismissive wave of his free hand. "As I told you yesterday, I don't believe you would shoot me. I may not know you well, but I can see that you aren't a murderer."

A lump hardened in her throat. She ducked her head to stare at her hands. A murderer. That's what she was, though Amador had no way of knowing it.

Withdrawing his hand from his pocket, Amador dropped to one knee in front of her. His gaze landed on her with a palpable weight that commanded her attention, and a shiver swept through her, lifting the hairs at the nape of her neck. She did not flinch or avert her eyes from his.

"I killed a man today," she said, her voice flat. "Six months ago, I shot and killed both Jackson Tennant and Xavier Waldron. This evening, I killed at least one other man, maybe more. So you see, I am a killer."

Amador's brows knit together. "I saw a dead man in the forest when I came for you. He had a gun and was likely the one who shot you." He shook his head. "You defended your life against men who would have done grievous injury to you."

"I know." She leaned back, though she didn't break eye contact. "I said I'm a killer, not a murderer. You shouldn't be so cocksure I won't shoot you if I feel the tiniest bit threatened."

"Of that, I have no doubt. But I mean you no harm." Amador lowered his left hand leisurely onto hers. His flesh scalded her skin. She hadn't realized how cold her hands were. He slipped his right hand into his pants pocket, hesitating there, and then pulled it out to rest it on top of her free hand. Almost in slow motion, he coiled his fingers around hers. All the while, his eyes tracked hers, and she discovered she couldn't divert her attention. Those dark eyes trapped her. When he began to trace circles on her palms with his fingertips, the touch triggered a warm tingling in her hands that spread, inch by inch, up her arms and into the rest of her body.

He raised one hand to brush his knuckles across her cheek. "You are no killer, Grace. Tennant and Waldron deserved to die, and they left you no choice but to take their lives in self-defense. I saw it through postcognition, remember? I know."

"Right. I forgot." She should've shaken his hands off, but her muscles had liquefied. Her voice came out dreamy too. What was wrong with her? "I appreciate the reassurance, but it's not necessary, Mr. Amador."

"Biel."

"Huh?"

"Please call me Biel." His fingers kept sketching circles on her palm. With his other hand, he cupped her cheek. "I am on your side, Grace. I would never abandon you."

Like David had. Although Amador refrained from saying the words, she knew what he meant.

Amador stroked her cheek with his fingertips. "If you will allow me, I would take care of you."

His caress made the tension in her unwind and scattered her thoughts. Was this man manipulating her psychically? This morning, she would've thought it impossible. Tonight, she'd lost her unerring faith in her firewall.

It should've been David comforting her. If he sensed her anguish, he would've come to check on her. The fact he hadn't pointed to one of three things—he couldn't feel her anymore, he was unable to come to her, or he didn't want to come to her. He had ordered her to go away and proclaimed she got in his way. The memory of his words, and the hardness in his voice, conjured a pain in her chest that made her wince and suck in a shallow breath. Her heart had calcified, cold and brittle and no longer capable of beating.

David had been terrified, though of what, she couldn't figure out. His callous actions, his harsh words, they stemmed from his fear. If only he'd talk to her...

Unlike David, Amador had no trouble expressing his feelings. He also hadn't dismissed her with all the tenderness of a cat throwing up a hairball.

Gabriel Amador was attractive. And attentive. And he rescued her when she needed it.

He ran his fingers down her cheek.

She cringed inside. However attractive and attentive he was, Amador harbored a secret agenda.

And she loved David. No one else tempted her.

She tensed her hands, preparing to yank them free of his.

Amador released her hands and rose. Towering over her, he combed his fingers through her hair. "Even if you cannot or will not trust me, I will help you in any way I can. That is my vow to you."

She nodded. "I appreciate that."

He turned and headed for the doorway.

"Thank you again," she said. It galled her to need his help, but she did. So she opted for a strategic concession. "I'm very grateful to you... Biel."

He froze mid-step, and for a couple of seconds, he neither moved nor spoke. Then he twisted around to face her and flashed the first genuine smile she'd witnessed on his lips. "No, Grace, thank you. Together, we can accomplish incredible things."

"I'm sure you're right."

"Come, you must be hungry." He gestured toward the door. "I will have Wickham prepare something for you."

He waited for her to stand and then headed out the door. She trailed after him, walking slower than usual. At least she wasn't limping. Amador bounded down the hallway with a light step. He maintained a discreet, but distinct, gap between them. The prisoner led to the execution.

No. He would not harm her.

Yet.

"How long was I asleep?" she asked.

"All night."

A modicum of relief filtered through her. When she'd peeked out the French doors at Wickham, she had caught sight of the morning sun halfway over the horizon and worried she'd slept for days. All night was bad, but better than days. She couldn't afford any lost time, not with David held captive and Tesler on her trail.

Amador veered right, into a dining room.

When he pulled out a chair for her, she eased into it. The table gleamed in the ever-brightening daylight filtering through the windows. She rested her hands on the wood. Cool. Slick. Dark.

Smiling, Amador seated himself opposite her. He folded his hands on the tabletop, interlocking his fingers. "I am so pleased to have you here, Grace."

Unease trickled through her. Befriending Amador might prove her best chance of survival, yet it burned her soul like a betrayal.

David.

Circumstances winnowed her choices down to bad and worse.

Amador sneaked a hand across the table, slipping it over hers. Warmth tingled through her hand and wrist. It seeped up her arm, throughout her body, and into every crevice of her soul. The urge to yank her hand away flared white-hot inside her. What the hell was happening to her? The wrongness of it screamed in her head, frantic yet indistinct, like a voice from another room. If he was doing something to her, influencing her psychically...

But how could he? Her psychic wall blocked everything. Even David.

She couldn't be sure of that.

Gotta play along. Find out what this creep knows. She resisted gritting her teeth, exhaled slowly to relax her muscles, and aimed a tentative smile at him.

And then the heat swallowed her whole.

"I'll get that breakfast for you," Amador said.

"Huh?" His words vibrated her eardrums, but their meaning failed to register. Quicksand sucked at her thoughts, hauling her downward into oblivion.

Amador patted her hand and ambled out of the room.

Her heart thudded. Cold sweat broke out on her forehead. Conscious but numb, immobilized and breathless, she wrestled for control of her own mind.

And realized she'd already lost.

———

THE GUARD PITCHED DAVID INTO THE CELL. HIS BODY HIT THE FLOOR with a dull thud, his chin smacking into the concrete. Pangs radiated through his jaw. The pain failed to register as more than a background ache, driven aside by the fire searing his veins. The fire ignited by the drugs.

David struggled to push up into a sitting position. His arms collapsed under him. He whumped back onto the floor and groaned. What the hell had Tesler injected into him? Not JT's formula, for sure. Every cell in his body burned and throbbed. His muscles sagged like wet rags clinging to his bones. And Christ, how his bones ached.

The stench of sweat and blood permeated his clothes, his hair, his skin. He rolled onto his side. His head spun, fast as a tornado. His gorge rose in his throat, but he gulped it back. No vomiting. No passing out. Signs of weakness would please Tesler and embolden him to switch to phase two. David knew all too well how Tesler's methods progressed. First, drugs. Second...

Physical pain.

He clenched his jaw until the whirling subsided. His head rested on the floor. His shoulder, slumped beneath him, forced his head to lie at an angle. Discomfort tugged at his neck muscles. He raised his head, grimacing from the effort, and surveyed the damage.

Sweat soaked the fabric under his arms. Dots of blood spattered his T-shirt. Whose blood? He palpated his scalp, neck, arms. No injuries. He lifted the collar of his shirt to peek inside it at his chest. No wounds there, either. He inhaled, and the metallic scent of blood filled his nostrils. With one finger, he explored his nose. Dried blood caked around his nostrils. What kind of drug caused bleeding from the nose?

Maybe it hadn't been the drugs. He'd fought damn hard to break through the electromagnetic barrier blocking him from contacting Grace. His mind bounced off it with enough force to wrench his physical body. The power of the EM blockade might've overtaxed his brain, triggering a nosebleed. He'd seen similar things happen to other psychics. Never before had he experienced this kind of side effect.

If anyone could breach the barrier, it would be Grace.

Her face hovered before his mind's eye. Her auburn hair glowing in the sunlight. Her hazel eyes sparkling. A glorious smile enlivening her features. If Tesler got his hands on her, the tactics he'd used on David, Sean, and Nkosi would pale compared to his plans for Grace. Tesler's voice reverberated in David's head.

Do you know what the greatest prize of all is? The pretty pink brain of your darling girl.

David ground his teeth. The grating noise vibrated through his skull. Tension rippled through his body, tightening muscles that screamed in protest, and he choked back a gasp. *Please stay away, Grace.*

Trouble was, he knew her better than that. She would come for him. She would risk her own life to rescue him. Her stubborn determination, her willingness to endanger herself for others, those were two of the countless reasons he loved her.

But dammit, he should've been the one rescuing her. What kind of man couldn't manage to safeguard his most precious treasure, the woman he loved? Somewhere between his imprisonment at the Mojave Desert facility and his obsession with hunting down Tesler, he'd lost sight of what mattered most.

Grace.

Was it too late to rectify his mistakes? Could she ever forgive him? Only one way to find out. He must escape from this place. He needed to free Nkosi, Sean, and any other hostages. And then he must track down Grace before she barreled into this facility to find him. He would save her this time—from her own reckless, if well-intentioned, actions.

God, he loved her. More than anything in this world or the next. If he must make the ultimate sacrifice for her, he'd do it without hesitation. He would die for her.

The door burst inward, banging into the wall.

David thrust himself up off the floor. Seated there, he glowered at the man standing in the doorway.

"Nap time is over," Tesler said. "Time to play twenty thousand questions. I believe you remember the consequences for refusing to answer."

"Torture me all you want. I won't tell you a damn thing."

Tesler sniggered. "You don't have to." He hopped closer, bending over to meet David's gaze. "I'd venture to guess that Sean knows everything you do, or close enough to everything. I'll torture *you* until *he* cracks."

The scientist flicked his wrist. Two guards tromped into the room, seized David's arms, and dragged him out of the cell. As they rounded a corner, heading down a different corridor than before, David racked his brain to formulate a plan. No way to RV the facility to plot out an escape route. He'd have to rely on his mundane senses and his intellect. His limbs refused to acknowledge his commands, instead hanging limp.

Half dragging, half carrying him, the guards tossed David through an open doorway into a room much like the previous one where Tesler had administered the drugs. But this room contained three chairs. Sean and Nkosi sat strapped into two of the chairs. The middle one stood empty. Waiting. For David.

Two men in white lab coats hauled David into the chair. Yellen and Evans, the men he'd watched when he RV'd the facility, secured the straps around his wrists, ankles, and forehead. Evans buckled the chest restraint.

A long table nestled against one wall held devices of torture. Scalpels. Things with serrated edges and sharp pincers. A wooden paddle with holes in it. And that damn baseball bat.

Yellen scuffled toward the doorway. "Must I watch this, Dr. Tesler?"

"If you can't stomach it, then wait in the corridor."

Yellen rushed outside.

Tesler strolled into the room. He picked up the bat, thumping it on his palm.

Sean whimpered.

David glanced at him sideways. Tears streamed from the boy's puffy, red eyes. His face was pale and gaunt. On the other side of David, Nkosi sat with chin lifted, jaw set, eyes clear and fixed on Tesler. A gash cut a red line across his cheek, and a clump of bruises purpled his neck.

David glared at Tesler, willing the man to burst into flames. Even if his psychic faculties had been at peak levels, he'd never possessed the power of pyrokinesis. Too bad. The bastard deserved to burn, if not in hell, then here on earth.

Tesler raised the bat. His eyes focused on David, but he spoke to Sean. "Tell me, son, where is Grace Powell?"

Sean sniffled. His voice emerged as a trembling whisper. "No."

"Then you leave me no choice."

Tesler swung the bat at David.

Chapter Thirteen

GRACE WOLFED DOWN THE LAST BITE OF HER BREAKFAST. OMELET, toast, and sausages, with orange juice on the side. No point in starving herself. She'd need all the strength she could muster to accomplish her goals, which included getting the hell out of this house ASAP. That moment of possibility wouldn't arrive until she had milked Amador for everything she could—information, tricks of the ESP trade, and anything else she could think of.

When Wickham had brought the food, she suffered a bout of panic. What if her breakfast was poisoned? Or drugged? But then she flashed back to her reaction when Amador touched her, and she knew. He required no drugs or poison to control her. Regardless of whether she'd finally toppled over to the dark side, her mental state provided him with all the leverage he needed, without chemical assistance.

Unless he'd drugged her while she was unconscious.

She had no clue what was going on anymore. With herself. With David. With any of this. She no longer enjoyed the luxury of choosing her allies. Amador had selected her, and Tesler's men drove her into Amador's corner.

Her hunger sated, she leaned back and endeavored to seem relaxed, despite the tension crackling inside her. Amador lounged in a chair on the opposite side of the wooden table. He had also eaten, though food remnants littered his plate. Her plate was empty. Eggs had never tasted so good before.

Amador pushed his chair back and stood. "Please excuse me. I must attend to some business. It won't take long, though, and I believe we should talk afterward."

"Okay." *Whatever.* She had no plans to flee yet since she had nowhere to go.

"Wait here for me." He ambled out of the room.

The door lock engaged with a click.

Guest or prisoner? Question answered.

Well, at least he hadn't laid his hands on her again. Yet.

A shiver skittered down her spine. Amador's skin on hers had infected her with an eerie warmth and a disturbing slackness. The first time she met Amador, he had kissed her hand, and she felt nothing. This morning, similar contact knocked her off balance and nearly thrust her into a tailspin. Worst of all, the one person she could've talked to about this was incommunicado.

She missed David, so badly.

Was he still alive? Their connection buzzed between them, albeit with far less strength than usual. She tugged on the link. Nothing. No reciprocal pull from his end.

Leaning her head back against the chair, she closed her eyes and tugged harder. Zippo. No tautening of the link. No glowy warmth from their constant, low-grade connection. No sense of his physical or mental state, good or bad. Their bond persisted, but David seemed unable or unwilling to tap into it. Even if he'd stopped caring about her, which she'd believe on the day the sky turned pink, he would've permitted their link to pulse back to her a signal of his status. Injured, safe. Alive, dead.

The connection fed her zilch. This was bad. Very bad.

A chill sparked in her gut, blossoming outward into her entire body. The hairs on her arms and neck stiffened. Goosebumps pebbled her skin. A bitter taste oozed over her tongue, the sourness of bile rising in her throat. A tugging, wrenching pressure tore through her gut. Not physical pain. It originated from her soul.

David, what have we done to each other?

She needed to ascertain why they'd lost contact. She thought of one reason, but pushed it away, unwilling to let it linger in her mind. It couldn't be. He wasn't—

No. His death would've wrenched her inside out. He was alive, somewhere.

Her hands clenched the chair's arms. She worked on releasing the tension in her body and mind with slow, deep breaths. It took far longer than she would've liked, but at last, numbness drove out the world around her. She barreled into the crossroads and scanned the stars around her. Not a single star reacted to her presence.

An icy chill, transmitted throughout her body, mutated into a subzero shiver.

He wasn't dead. She refused to believe it. Until she witnessed his body, lifeless and bloody, she would never believe it.

Come on, David, show me the way.

An echo of power rippled through the crossroads to caress her mind. She latched onto the intimate feel of the familiar energy, scaling up it inch by inch.

A force hurled her away.

She plummeted back into her body. Unable to slow the descent, she hit so hard her body convulsed. Her jaw clamped tight, and pains shot through her head.

A hand enveloped hers. A finger massaged her palm, tracing ever-widening circles in her flesh. Warmth infected her skin, and then her muscles. The tingling swelled and expanded through her body. Her mind switched into a new mode, a cross between total relaxation and pure alertness.

Her eyelids flew open. Slumped in the chair, she jerked upright. Her heart pounded. She gaped at the man kneeling before her.

Gabriel Amador caught her gaze with a serene expression. His finger drew circles on her palm, sending out pulses of heat that intensified the tingling in her body and melted her brain. She couldn't hold on to a thought. Couldn't shake the connection unfurling between them, a tether that cinched tighter each second. This was wrong. The tether slithered deeper into her, alien and cold.

The impulse to jerk free of him flared inside her, but her muscles ignored her commands. Her voice came out breathless. "What are you doing to me?"

"Helping you to relax."

Run. This instant. Go, run, get away.

Go where? Her inner voice offered no answer. She was trapped. The realization whipped her out of the fog, into the harshness of her new reality. Trapped.

No, goddammit. She'd escape if she had to claw her way through the house's foundation to do it—after she mined Amador for what she needed.

Gritting her teeth while feigning nonchalance demanded a serious effort. Either her efforts paid off, or Amador simply didn't care she was deceiving him. "Are you relaxing me by psychic means?"

His lips tightened into a frown. "No, Grace. I am not employing any psychic powers. This is a purely mundane method." He reached for her hand. When she clasped it to her belly, he sighed. "No one can breach your psychic barrier. Yes?"

She shrugged. "As far as I know."

Amador's frown morphed into a knowing smile.

The urge to gnaw on her lip itched inside her. She resisted. Although she was far from reassured, letting Amador glimpse her unease struck her as an incredibly dumb idea. *Pet the dragon, don't pinch his scales.* "You're right. I'm sorry."

He rubbed his palm over the back of her hand.

She bit the inside of her cheek, an action hidden from his view. "I'm ready. For whatever ideas you have about my powers."

"Excellent." He released her hand. "My first suggestion may sound extreme, but please consider it carefully before refusing."

Nothing good ever followed a statement like that. But she told him, "I will."

"I would like to administer a serum."

Panic surged through her, jolting her pulse into overdrive. Her knuckles ached from gripping the chair's arms.

Amador laid a hand on her arm. "Please, don't be afraid. It's a drug my company has been working on. The serum is designed to foster a sense of calm and relaxation that will, I hope, enhance a person's psychic abilities."

A hard shiver rushed through her. "Is this JT's formula?"

He shook his head. "I wouldn't do that to you. His formula was barbaric and inhumane. My company strives for safe, gentle formulations."

"Your company? I thought you ran a venture capital thing."

"I do. Through a shell company I own other interests, including a pharmaceutical research firm."

He sounded reasonable. Even lunatics could pull that off sometimes.

At least the heat in her body had dissipated. She felt almost normal again.

Frowning, she eyed Amador. "Is this what you meant when you said you could help me with my powers? That you'd give me drugs?"

"No. I thought it couldn't hurt, though."

As much as she loathed admitting it, she needed help. *His* help. If he could do what he claimed. Her firewall blocked his psychic intrusions, but if he could teach her a few tricks then maybe, just maybe, she'd shed the migraines. For good.

Her feet wiggled, urging her to escape this place.

Rebelling against every fiber of her being, she said, "If you have some other, non-pharmaceutical way to help me use my powers without getting horribly sick from it, then I'm listening."

He opened his mouth to speak.

"No drugs," she said. "That's my rule, and it is nonnegotiable."

"I understand. We'll employ other means. What psychic task may I assist you with first?"

He uttered the phrase in a tone reminiscent of a customer-service guy answering a phone call.

She brushed aside the mild humor of that. "I need to find David. Fast."

Amador nodded. "Let's get started."

He dragged a chair closer to her.

She prayed he could help her because if he couldn't... No. David was alive, and she would find him.

"Close your eyes," Amador said. He clasped her hand in his. As the warmth infiltrated her body, spiraling her into oblivion, he told her, "Free your mind from thoughts. Hear only my voice. Feel my touch. Let it anchor you on your flight into the crossroads. Do not try. Simply be."

Thoughts fled. The weight of her own body, the firmness of the chair beneath her, the scent of leather, the ticking of a clock, everything drifted away from her until she floated in a void, numb and disconnected. Two things penetrated the emptiness.

Amador's skin pressed to hers. And his voice, deep and soft.

"Are you there?" he asked.

"Not yet." Her voice murmured from a distant galaxy.

His skin stroked hers.

She soared, like a cloud in the wind, up through the dark tunnel. No pressure. No struggle. She glided out into the crossroads.

"Yes," Amador said. "You are there, aren't you? Don't think. Don't fight. Let your mind do your will of its own volition."

A vague thought reared its head. His instructions made no sense. Her mind *was* her will. To effect her will, she must think.

"No," he murmured. "You are trying to implement your desires, aren't you? Stop. Empty your mind. *Feel* what you wish."

His hand. Warm. Smooth. Real. She relaxed into his touch, letting her mind go vacant. She floated there, among the glittering stars, overcome by a seductive sense of belonging. This place knew her. It hungered for her. And she for it. The energy of the crossroads, of its hidden reaches, tantalized her with the promise of boundless power.

"That's right," Amador said in a throaty whisper. "You understand now."

A star beckoned her. A connection. A human mind.

David.

Grace rocketed toward the light, through it, beyond it. Wild energy excited her psychic senses. She drank it in, her mind swimming, as the thirst for more burned inside her.

The tunnel expelled her into a gray fog, whirling her downward.

She smashed headfirst into a granite wall.

Agony stripped her nerves raw. Lightning gored her astral body. Psychic energy spewed out of her, sucked her dry, and cast her aside. She smacked into the wall.

And screamed.

CHAPTER FOURTEEN

THE REAL WORLD BESIEGED HER AT ONCE, A LANDSLIDE OF INPUT THAT overwhelmed her senses and contorted her body. She bellowed, hugged her knees to her chest, and buried her face against her thighs. Wheezing, she rocked in the chair.

How would she track down David without their link?

I lost him.

Not yet she hadn't.

A hand caressed her hair. For a second, she imagined it was David. Then reality collided with her fantasy, shattering the illusion. She shook free of Amador's hand and lifted her head just far enough to peek at him over her knees. Tears blurred her vision, though they no longer streamed down her cheeks. She swiped at her eyes, sniffling.

Amador touched his fingertips to her cheek, then pulled them away. Concern tightened his features, and his lips parted in an unformed question.

"I'm fine," she said, though she felt nothing close to fine. Her eyes burned. White lights danced in her vision. Sharp pains crackled in her head, slowly coalescing into a throb that lurched her stomach. A migraine. *Dammit.* She could not afford this, not with David a hostage somewhere in Montana. If he was in Montana. She had no clue, really. Tesler might've transferred him elsewhere. Despite the wild uncertainty about everything else, she could not deny one fact. Tesler would pummel David until he cracked and exposed both their secrets.

He'll die first. She might've become an outsider in David's life, but she understood one basic truth about him.

He was noble.

Amador leaned closer, his face pinched, as if he were in pain too. "What happened? Are you all right? Please tell me what I can do."

Nothing, she almost said. But the truth was, he could do something for her. As much as she despised asking him, she must. Desperation was a snarling bitch.

"I need to find David before Tesler kills him." She slid her feet onto the floor and sat up. Muscles in her neck stretched. Hot pain spiked up her neck into the base of her skull, and she winced, swallowing a gasp. "The psychic method of tracking him down did not work. I need another way. Do you have any suggestions?"

The tension smoothed out of Amador. He hopped up and gave a quick nod. "I may have a way. If you will be all right by yourself, I'll see what I can do."

"I'll survive."

She'd lived alone for so long, even after David barged back into her life. What did a few more minutes matter? Besides, she needed a break. His voice stabbed into her brain, each word a red-hot, acid-tipped needle. The sound of her own breathing hurt her ears.

"Can you provide any clues as to David's whereabouts?" Amador asked.

"Montana. That's it, I'm sorry."

"It will be enough." He marched to the door, then hesitated on the threshold. "You may not believe this, but I wish no harm to David. And I will do everything in my power to locate him."

She didn't know whether to believe him or not. "I appreciate that."

He studied her over his shoulder, lips scrunched in concentration. "If your goal is to eliminate your migraines, then you must uncover the reason for them. I suspect you are hindering your powers, unconsciously, for some reason. Root out the reason, and you will free yourself—and your mind."

"You may be right."

"Try to rest. And I will search for David."

She forced her lips to form a weak smile. "Thank you, Biel."

He flashed her a quick, tight smile. And then he left.

The door clicked shut.

Free her powers. Free herself. Sounded great, but how the hell was she supposed to do it?

Root out the reason. Amador had a point. Although he knew nothing of her motivations, he sensed she throttled back her abilities. Until he spoke the words, she'd pretended not to realize the truth. She must acknowledge her fears, and sort them out.

To save David.

To save herself.

At full power, with no migraines to saddle her, she might just save the whole damn world.

She buried her face in her hands. Pangs ricocheted in her head as her gut roiled with nausea. Too weak to stand, she curled up in the chair, rested her head on her knees, and shut her eyes.

Some savior she was.

DAVID SQUINTED TO SEE THROUGH A BLOOD-TINGED HAZE. HIS head lolled to the side, too heavy to hold up any longer. Everything throbbed or burned, from his scalp down to his toes. Tesler stood before him, legs spread in a confident stance, tapping the baseball bat on his palm.

"Shall we go again?" Tesler asked. "Or is one of you ready to talk?"

Spitting out blood, David hoisted his head upright. Pain lanced up his neck straight into his skull. He gritted his teeth. "Nobody wants to talk to you, Tesler. Your conversation skills leave something to be desired."

The scientist harrumphed. "We'll see how you feel when I start in on Sean."

David wanted to look at Sean, mostly to assure himself, but feared his beaten and bloodied appearance would terrify the boy more than Tesler had already. Sean was okay. In the past six months, he toughened up more than any boy his age should have to, but everyone had their limits.

At least no physical harm had come to Sean—yet. David had served himself up as Tesler's punching bag. Or batting practice. The bastard packed a mean swing.

Unease trickled into him, the sensation strange and... external. He focused on the discomfort, struggling to name it. To trace its source. The unease burgeoned inside him, like a leaky balloon filled with ice-cold water, slowly disgorging its contents into him. The chill sharpened and mushroomed out. Fear knifed into his heart.

Grace.

The sensation crumbled away as quickly as it had bloomed. His connection to Grace dwindled back to a whisper, one he could discern only if he concentrated all his psychic energy on the task. Had she broken through the EM screen for a second? *No, Grace, don't.* Could she even hear him? Or feel him? Conflicting desires warred within him. The need to sense her, to feel her, to know she was all right. And the lightning-bright fear that she would reach out to him. Connect with him. Share his experience.

Suffer his torture.

Tesler pointed the bat toward Nkosi. "Perhaps you care more for your new friend." He strode one step closer to Nkosi, raised the bat, and sneered. "Well, David? Shall we try this one on for size?"

David's nails rasped on the metal as he gripped the arms of his chair. A lacework of pain burst out from his knuckles to spread into his wrists. He choked down a gasp, denying the agony its outlet. Tesler would never see him grimace or hear him cry out. Never.

"No?" The scientist ambled past David, to Sean. He spun on his heels, facing the boy. Sean muffled a whimper. Tesler waggled the bat in the boy's face. "Will you tell me now, son?" He glanced at David, then back to Sean. "Or must I beat you to hurt your savior?"

"If you need to feel like a man," David hissed, "then make your statement on me. I'm the one you despise. I'm the one who ruined the plans you and JT cooked up together."

Tesler chuckled, his eyes gleaming with pleasure. "It was your darling girl who laid waste to those plans, not you."

He stepped in front of David, straddling the chair, and leaned forward to grind David's left wrist beneath his hand. Agony ripped through David's hand and arm, but he quashed it with gritted teeth.

Tesler smirked. "You are a worthless specimen undeserving of being called a man. Your lover had to rescue you how many times? Perhaps she only stays with you out of pity."

The truth in his words stung like a smack to the face. David fought not to wince. Grace had saved him. Repeatedly. He wasn't much of a man. He couldn't argue with Tesler on that point.

Did Grace pity him?

Of course not. She loved him. Her passion and affection nourished him during his worst moments. And yet, a sliver of doubt lodged itself in his psyche. Tesler had jammed the sliver in there. He knew this. But he could not silence the voice whispering into his brain.

How could she love you when you can't even protect her?

If he couldn't shield her from Tesler, then what good was he? Escape no longer seemed like a viable option. As long as he lived, he posed a threat to Grace. Tesler had been right about that too. He was leverage.

Protecting Grace meant saving her from her misplaced, pigheaded loyalty to him. He had one choice left. If he died, she wouldn't need to search for him.

At last, he had a plan. Stop Tesler. Save Sean and Nkosi.

Sacrifice himself for Grace.

Tesler poised the bat for a swing, zeroing in on Sean.

He froze. His brow furrowed, and his mouth warped into an expression of… Was that anguish?

Stunned, David could only stare.

Tesler let out a frustrated growl. He tossed the bat aside. It clattered on the concrete, spun across the room, and bumped into the wall.

This madman never held back his torture. And yet, he just had.

With a flick of his wrist, Tesler summoned a guard to his side. He snatched the semiautomatic handgun from the holster on the guard's hip. A snarled command sent the guard scuttling back to the doorway.

Tesler leveled the gun at David. "Last chance. Where is Grace Powell?"

David raised his chin. "Go to hell."

"No," Tesler said, his expression turning to mock gravity. "I won't be the one to make that journey tonight."

A gunshot cracked through the room.

Chapter Fifteen

G RACE TWISTED THE KNOB, SURPRISED WHEN IT ROTATED IN HER hand. Amador had left the door unlocked this time. *Hmm.* Forgetfulness, or purpose?

She eased the door open a couple of inches, peering into the empty hallway. Somewhere in another room, a grandfather clock chimed. A cool draft filtered through the opening, tickling her bare arms. She must go out there. Sitting in the dining room, alone, with the door shut was triggering her latent claustrophobia. A squirmy itch in her brain compelled her to action.

Maybe the closed door had nothing to do with it. She might feel trapped because, well, she was. Tesler's men had cornered her. She escaped only because she wielded her powers, and because Amador rode to her rescue.

He was no knight.

Now David she could envision galloping up on a white horse, armor glistening in the sun, those blue eyes gleaming with the fire of purpose. Even in a T-shirt and jeans, he was sexy as hell. Dressed up like a knight, he'd sweep her off her feet literally and carry her away on his steed.

Oh brother. She ought to be formulating a plan to save David, not fantasizing about playing dress-up with him.

Pulling the door wide, she tromped out into the hallway. Her head swung left and right as she debated the choices. *Pick one, for crying out loud.*

She swerved right, heading deeper into the house, away from the front door. The hallway housed six doors, three on each side, spaced at staggered intervals. Straight ahead, the corridor dead-ended at a blank wall. She veered toward the first door on the left, tried the knob, and found it locked. Back and forth she moved, testing each door. Left. Right. Left. A bizarre urge to goose-step cropped up in her brain, but she shook it off. All the doors were locked, except the one leading into Amador's office. She'd already seen that room, though. Since his computer no longer sat on the desktop, the office held nothing else of interest to her. She ducked inside just long enough to try the file cabinet drawers.

Locked, of course.

At the end of the hall, she hesitated. To her right, a short corridor led into the kitchen. She saw, through the open doorway, a refrigerator and gas range. To her left, a stairway descended into darkness.

A lot of houses had basements, but she had to wonder what a man like Amador did with his subterranean space. A wine cellar, maybe. Or a place to hide things he wanted no one else to see.

Grace tiptoed to the stairs. Half a dozen steps penetrated the shadows congregating at the base of the stairway. There, half masked by the gloom, stood a windowless metal door. She gulped against the tightening in her throat. Her breaths came shallow and fast. Why should a door frighten her? It wasn't the door itself. Her psychic senses crackled with the cold awareness of danger.

You've got to see what's in there.

She sidled down one step. Held her breath. Listened. Sidled down another step.

Thump.

The noise originated on the other side of the door.

A shiver skittered down her spine. Her attention telescoped down until her vision encompassed one object—the door.

She halted at the base of the stairs. Tilting her head, she opened her mouth a little, focusing on sounds. The hiss of the AC. The beating of her heart. The distant rumble of an airliner passing by overhead. And something else. Something familiar, yet alien. Muffled by the door.

She inched closer, settling her ear against the chilled metal.

Whimpering. She heard an animal whimpering, inside the room beyond the door. The pitiful sound escalated in volume, crescendoing with a sharp cry.

Every hair on her body stiffened.

Not an animal whimpering. A human being.

One instinct urged her to flee. Another warned her she'd better uncover the truth before it lashed out of the shadows to sink its teeth into her neck. Whatever Amador concealed in the basement, it involved a human being in pain.

She wrapped her hand around the doorknob and, with deliberate slowness, twisted. The knob refused to budge.

Behind the door, footfalls clapped on a hard floor.

Her heart thudded. She spun around and clambered up the steps. Her foot slipped. She flailed for a handhold, and her palms met slick, painted walls, sliding down the surface. Her toe, balanced on the edge of the step, flipped out from under her. An "ow" burst from her lips as her chin smacked into the concrete step. Agony shot through her jaw. White lights exploded in her vision.

The door lock chunked. The knob swiveled. The latch clicked. And the door swung wide open.

Prone on the steps, she twisted to face her enemy. Pain sparked in her neck. Wincing, panting, she gaped at the figure looming over her.

Gabriel Amador frowned. "What do you think you are doing, Grace?"

"Um…" Questions fired up in her mind, but the dark tension rippling through Amador warned her not to ask what she really wanted to know. "You said I could look around the house. I tripped on the stairs."

"No." He shook his head, his expression regretful. "You heard the girl's pain. You likely sensed it too. I should've guessed you would." He knelt before her, laying a hand on her shoulder. "But I wish you weren't quite so curious, or so determined. I had hoped to keep this away from you."

Terror ripped through her like hot lava, searing her down to her core. Her voice constricted to a hoarse whisper. "Keep what away from me?"

He stepped aside revealing the doorway and what lay beyond.

Inside the dark, windowless room, a single overhead bulb drove a wedge of brilliant white light down on a teenage girl huddled on a wooden chair. Ropes bound her ankles. Her hands were behind the chair, suggesting ropes secured her arms too. A red liquid dribbled down her face from her scalp, dripping onto her white tank top.

It was blood.

The girl lolled her head to the side and back. The light streaked across her face where a purple bruise surrounded her swollen eye. The good eye, dark and bloodshot, fixed on Grace. A sob erupted from the girl.

Grace's gut clenched. *My savior is a psychopath.*

She couldn't move. Her thoughts reeled and bounced off each other, like pinballs in a machine. The world tilted and rocked. The acrid taste of bile infiltrated her mouth as she choked back her gorge.

Someone had to stop this man.

Why me? her inner voice asked.

"Please," the raven-haired girl implored. "Please help me."

The pain radiating from the girl's tone stung Grace. She took a shaky breath.

Why me? Because nobody's riding to the rescue this time. She heaved herself off the stairs, onto her feet. Squaring her shoulders, she gritted her teeth. *It's me or no one.*

The terror ended right here, right now. Time to fight, with every ounce of courage and psychic power inside her. For the girl. For David. For everyone.

She whirled on Amador. "Let her go."

"I'm afraid I can't. If you'll allow me to explain—"

With a burst of psychic energy, Grace flung him backward into the wall.

He hit with a thud and a crack. His body slid down the wall, his knees buckling. Slumped on the floor, he shook his head. "I'm sorry, Grace."

She bolted into the room, straight to the girl. Fingers trembling, she wrestled with the knots binding the girl's feet.

"Wickham," Amador shouted, "push the button."

She hesitated in the middle of her struggle.

Inside the walls, a mechanism buzzed.

She spun around. From his position inches outside the threshold, Amador blocked the doorway with his body.

The buzzing echoed in the concrete room, hushed but menacing, like a horde of wasps holed up in the walls.

Grace balled up her power and slung it at Amador.

The energy ricocheted back to her, slugging her in the chest. She toppled over backward. Her skull whacked into the floor. Lightning bolts slashed in her vision as roiling pain hauled her toward an ever-darkening abyss.

Amador towered over her, his expression something like sorrow. "I didn't want to do this, Grace, but you've left me no choice."

She clawed her way out of the abyss, back into consciousness. Her head throbbed, her entire body ached, and the room seemed poised on the head of a spinning top.

Crouching beside her, Amador jabbed a sharp object into her neck. His voice murmured into her ear. "I need you, Grace. I've come too far to turn back, and my plans will fail without your power. It pains me to say this, but I cannot let you go." He pressed his lips to her forehead. "Rest. I will explain all of this when you wake."

She tumbled down and down, into the abyss of unconsciousness.

DAVID STRAINED TO OPEN HIS EYES. HIS EARS HAD STOPPED RINGing, and the muffling effect of the gunshot had subsided. His body had grown strangely numb. A bad sign.

His eyelids parted no more than a sliver. He peeked out through a bleary haze.

Tesler stood ramrod straight, hands balled into fists, shoulders hunched. Rage ignited redness in his face. The gun, smoking faintly, wobbled in his fist. He dropped his hand to his side.

David pried his lids further apart. Moving only his eyes, he surveyed the damage. No gunshot wound. Not on his body. He flinched. Not on *his* body.

He rolled his eyes to the side, catching a glimpse of Sean. The boy's lower lip quivered, but he appeared unharmed. David glanced in the other direction, toward Nkosi. A red stain had blossomed on his shoulder, soaking through his shirt.

Nkosi managed a tight, pained smile. "I will survive. Believe me, I've had far worse injuries." He glanced at Tesler, and his lip curled. "There will be retribution for this."

David tried to lift his head, but it felt as heavy as an iron bowling ball. His arms and legs seemed glued to the chair. His eyelids drooped, and he longed to let them drift closed, easing him into a deep slumber.

No, dammit, don't give in.

He breathed in and out slowly. A little of the fog cleared, though traces of it lurked around the edges, ready to swallow him.

Tesler stomped his foot. The concussion reverberated through the concrete room.

Nkosi flinched. Sean gasped.

"Wake up," Tesler said. "I'm through playing games with the three of you. Someone will tell me how to find Grace or—" He trained the gun on Sean's head. "—I pull the trigger. You have until the count of ten." He curled his finger around the trigger. "One, two—"

David floundered for a plan. His notion of escaping had sounded good, but he'd failed to come up with a viable, concrete scheme to realize his goal. His psychic energy was drained. Worse, he was disconnected and fuzzy-headed, numb and sleepy. He recognized the danger of giving in to the exhaustion but resisting got harder and harder every second.

Tesler counted down. "Four, five, six—"

Nkosi muttered words in another language. Maybe he was praying.

Sean had ceased trembling. He stared straight ahead without expression.

David drew in one more deep breath, and then he released the last thread of hope. "I'm sorry. I thought we could beat this, but we can't. Whatever happens, we must never give in to Tesler. Never."

Nkosi nodded. "Never."

When Sean spoke, his voice was stronger than his demeanor. "Never."

Tesler swung the gun to his right and fired.

Nkosi slumped. Blood oozed from a wound on his chest, right over his heart. The life disappeared from his eyes.

The EM field constrained David to this room, so he couldn't access the crossroads. Despite that, he'd managed to separate from his body when he tried to contact Grace—and rammed into the EM barrier. But still, he had used his powers in a small way. Any bit was better than nothing.

Targeting his gun on Sean, Tesler locked gazes with David. "One down, two to go. Whether you tell me what I want to know or not, I will hunt down your beloved. And when I find her..." He jerked the gun as if he'd fired a shot. "Bang. She will die. Her brain is all I need, after all."

I'll rip your heart out, you bastard. Anger and grief blasted through David, sharp and hot and electric, fueling his powers, re-energizing his body. Adrenaline heightened his normal senses and kick-started his thoughts. The boost wouldn't last, he knew. The fury amping up his energy, both physical and psychic, might grant him one last attempt.

Save Sean.

He pummeled Tesler with a telekinetic blast that flung him through the air backward. The scientist bounced off the wall, rolling across the floor. The gun skidded toward Sean's chair.

The EM field zapped into David. Pain coruscated through his head, but he focused all his residual energy on one final task.

Sean's restraints popped open.

The boy's eyes bulged. He whipped his head toward David.

"Go," David said, his voice hushed and raspy.

The boy leaped up, snatching the gun from the floor.

Drained, in every way possible, David let his head fall back onto the chair.

The guard threw a wide-eyed glance at David, then at Sean. The man bolted out the door. His footsteps beat out a frantic rhythm as he fled down the corridor.

Crumpled on the floor, Tesler moaned.

Sean hesitated in the doorway. Gnawing his lip, he cast a questioning look at David. "I can't leave you."

"Yes, you can." Mustering his last reserve of strength, David infused his next words with the finality they demanded. "I'm a lost cause, Sean. Grace is the only one who can stop this nightmare. Find her. *Run*."

Sean ran.

Tesler pushed up onto all fours. Glasses askew, he puffed out an angry breath.

David relinquished his hold on… everything. As he sank ever deeper into nothingness, Tesler spewed a parting shot.

"You are a pitiful failure. Your darling girl will suffer unspeakable pain for days until the moment I finally terminate her miserable life."

Goodbye, Grace. Please forgive me.

CHAPTER SIXTEEN

GRACE PERCHED ON THE EDGE OF THE COT, HER FEET PLANTED ON THE concrete floor of the basement room. Since waking up several minutes ago, she'd sat here immobile, her thoughts muddled by the sedative hangover. How long had she been unconscious? What had Amador done to her during that time?

Where was the dark-haired girl?

The wooden chair was gone, the girl too. Besides Grace and the cot, nothing else occupied the room. The overhead light sliced a circle out of the darkness. The white glow petered out before reaching her toes. Her cot, wedged into the corner of the room, creaked when she adjusted her position.

Her gaze was drawn to the center of the lighted circle. There, a dark stain had spread across the floor.

The heavy scent of blood permeated the room.

Had Amador killed the girl? Grace shuddered. She'd been a fool to come here alone, hunted by Tesler's goons. Amador could easily hand her over to the mad scientist.

Unless she agreed to whatever plans he had in mind for her.

His words replayed in her mind, searing her soul. *I need you*, he'd said, *I've come too far to turn back, and my plans will fail without your power.* Of course. Like every other nutjob out there, he coveted her psychic talents. His offer to aid her was a trick, to gain her trust. She should've seen this coming, should've steered clear of Amador. Instead, she let him guide her metaphysical endeavors, took his advice about her powers, and… believed him when he urged her to stop being afraid. His assistance had been a ruse, and she fell for it out of a reckless compulsion to liberate her mind from the shackles of amnesia and post-traveling migraines. She was as obsessed with her own quest as David was with his.

She should've listened to him.

The door pivoted inward.

Amador traipsed straight to her, carrying a tray of food. He deposited the tray at her feet. Crouching before her, he laid a hand on her knee. "How do you feel?"

His expression revealed nothing. His hand warmed her skin through her jeans when he squeezed a little, his mouth crooking into a ghost of a smile.

She resisted the impulse to slug him.

"I'm fine," she said. "Where's the girl?"

"Gone."

Her gorge surged up into her throat. She clutched the cot's edge.

Amador huffed out a breath, and his face scrunched with annoyance. "The girl is not dead. She needed a break, so I transferred her to a room where she may sleep for a time. I have no desire to kill her."

She grunted.

He shook his head. "I am not your enemy, Grace."

Words tumbled out of her mouth, despite her efforts to contain them. "Great, you won't kill her. But torture is acceptable? And how about drugging me? That's okay too, right? I thought you were sincere about wanting to stop Tesler, but you're just as bad as he is."

His head drooped. He lunged both hands up to clasp them at the base of his neck as he puffed out sharp breaths and rocked on his toes.

She reached out to touch his shoulder, then yanked her hand away. Why the hell should she want to comfort him?

An ache started in her forehead, this time from annoyance and drugs, rather than power usage. She stuffed her hands under her thighs. "What have you done to me?"

He lifted his head a smidgen, enough to meet her gaze. "You were terribly upset. I sedated you for your protection."

"Uh-huh." Arguing the validity of his claim seemed irrelevant right now. "I meant before that. Every time you…" She bit her lip. Saying too much afforded him an advantage, but she must know the answer. *Risk everything to save the world, right?* "Every time you touch me, I get confused and I feel weirdly limp. I don't feel like myself, and it's freaking me out."

He studied her for so long she wondered if time had skidded to a halt. Finally, he planted his hands on her knees and said, "You are correct. I administered an experimental serum designed to encourage compliance. I hoped it would relax you and help you overcome the fear of your own powers."

"How did you give it to me? In the food?"

Grimacing, he turned one hand over. "The serum works best when absorbed through the skin." He dived his hand into his pocket and brought out a small glass vial, holding it between his thumb and forefinger. "I place a small amount of this on my fingers, then I… touch you."

He tipped the vial, and the pale-yellow liquid sloshed inside it.

"If you had it on your skin," she said, "how come it didn't affect you?"

Amador replaced the vial in his pocket. "I gave myself a counteracting agent. It does not last long, but I didn't need much time." He returned his hand to her knee. "I regret the serum was necessary."

"I said no drugs."

"After I'd given you the serum."

"You drugged me again after that."

He exhaled a long, exasperated sigh. "That was for your own good, Grace."

"Bullshit." She sprang off the cot, jumped to the side, and flattened her back against the wall. The door looked so far away. "What the hell do you want from me?"

"Cooperation."

She barked out a derisive laugh. "This is how you think you'll get my cooperation? You're insane."

"Please understand. My priority, my sole purpose in life, is to end the horrific reign of Karl Tesler." He inched closer, but when she gave him a warning look, he backed off. "I need you fighting at my side, at full strength, not hobbled by migraines."

"Cut the crap. You've been manipulating me from the beginning, and I want to know why. What exactly do you expect me to do for you?"

"Fight. In ways I cannot."

She flexed her fingers against the cold wall. Her gaze flicked to the door, then back to him. A hard pit bounced around in her stomach, set off by a slithering suspicion she knew what he wanted from her. "No."

"Think about it." He strode toward her, grasping her shoulders in his big hands. "It is the only way to defeat Tesler. You are the one person in all the world capable of handling this task."

"I said no."

He squeezed her flesh and let go, squeezed and let go, in a gentle rhythm probably meant to lull her. Instead, it pissed her off. Oblivious, he kept up the rhythm, his fingers massaging deeper with each squeeze. "You must make use of your greatest gift. You must employ the Golden Power."

She glanced at the door and then down at his hands that restrained her. The sedative's aftereffects, coupled with dizzying fear, weakened her in every way. The last time she accessed her innate powers, a force had snapped her mind in two. The Golden Power was far more dangerous.

Why had her powers failed her?

She'd crashed into a barrier, like the one she had constructed to barricade her mind. Had the psychic firewall gone haywire?

No. The instant before her powers imploded, Amador shouted for Wickham to "push the button." Then the buzzing started. And her powers went kablooey.

When she tried to contact David, her mind had struck a similar blockade.

Her fingers curled slightly, and she tapped them on the wall. "You put up some kind of psychic dampening field, didn't you?"

Shuffling backward, he lowered his gaze to the floor. "You left me no choice."

"There's always a choice, and you made yours." Anger simmered inside her, but a solitary spike of ice punched through it. Not the cold of fear. The pacifying influence of reason. *Listen to his words. What is he really saying?* His statements replayed in her mind in rapid succession.

I need you. My plan will fail without your power. He referred to more than the Golden Power, which wasn't hers, but borrowed energy. *I spent time in a Siberian facility.* He carefully avoided calling himself a traveler or a prisoner. And when she chastised him for RV'ing her in her bedroom, his response had, once again, been carefully phrased. *I did not realize you were alone in your bedroom until after the excursion began.* Why not say "after I traveled to you" or "after my excursion began"? He was distancing himself from the action, misleading without lying outright.

The truth rippled through her in a chilling wave. Of course. She'd gotten everything wrong. Confronted with Amador's claims, and so intent on unmasking her psychic stalker, she hadn't bothered to consider another possibility. He was lying, yes. But about more than his motives or the fact he'd imprisoned and tortured a young woman.

She pushed away from the wall, narrowing the gap between them, and stabbed a finger into his chest. "You don't have any psychic powers, do you?"

His body jerked. Lifting his eyes to hers, he winced. "No. I do not."

A horrifying thought surfaced, and she prayed it was not true. But she knew it was. "That's why you abducted the girl. She has psychic abilities, and you tormented her, probably with drugs, until she broke down and agreed to do your bidding. You made her stalk me with RV. You made her assault my mind. That poor girl was your psychic puppet." Grace jabbed her finger harder into his chest. She recognized the folly of her anger, of letting it show, but the fury flamed too hot and wild to contain it. "You are a monster, just like Tesler."

Amador shook his head violently. His mouth hung open, his lower lip trembling. "No. Grace, no, please understand—"

"Shut up." Spittle sprayed from her lips. Her stomach roiled, and her thoughts whirled. Terror and rage melted into one swirling, scorching mass in her gut. This man conspired to torment her by enslaving and brainwashing a child. He was a monster. The impulse to throttle Amador mushroomed inside her, made her body go rigid, and consumed common sense. Through clenched teeth, she snarled, "Turn off the goddamn dampening field, or whatever the hell it is. Shut it down. *Now.*" She stomped one step closer, her face inches from him. Her breaths huffed in his face, reflecting onto hers. "Do it, or I will rip you apart molecule by molecule. You know I can. You've seen what I'm capable of. Remember the woods, and those commandos I eliminated without lifting a finger?"

The shame and anguish on his face converged into an indefinable expression. He stared at her for several seconds. Then, his features contorted, and a single tear rolled down each cheek. "I am sorry, Grace. I never intended to—I believed we could—" He hauled in a long breath, exhaling slowly. The pained look washed out of his face, replaced by the impassivity she'd witnessed on him before. "I had no choice, believe me. I needed you alone, and there was no other way to draw you out. Your affection for David is too strong."

Her hand twitched, anxious to slap him.

Get a grip. She watched him for a moment while she collected her wits. It took some time since her wits had scattered to the four winds. The fury dwindled to a bed of coals, radiating heat without setting fire to the landscape. Sweat sheathed her forehead, and she wiped it away with the back of her hand. "Most people introduce themselves with a handshake, not a mental assault."

"We are not most people."

"I am nothing like you." She took a breath, but her stance remained rigid. "You don't know me. We met yesterday. I appreciate how you lent a hand last night, but if you try to keep me here against my will, I'll find a way to escape. Or I'll die trying."

He raised an unsteady hand and let it hover near her cheek. "I have no wish to harm you. As long as you are under my roof, Tesler will not touch you. You have my word."

She snorted. "This from the man who swore he could help me with my psychic abilities."

"I did try to help you, no? I may not have abilities myself, but I have experience in counseling those who do."

"Is that what you call what you did to that girl? Counseling?" His lips parted, but she cut in before he could respond. "You lied about having powers. You used an innocent child to spy on me. Pardon me if I have trouble trusting your word."

He nodded in resignation. Bending over the cot, he began to fluff the pillow with a deliberate gentleness, so intent on his task that his lips pursed. "There is more you should know. If you are to trust me, then I must reveal everything to you. I see that now."

Grace caught sight of the doorway out of the corner of her eye. She edged sideways toward it. "Fine. Tell me."

"It's about Tesler." He smoothed the wrinkles out of the pillowcase. "I placed a tracking device on the DVD I gave you. Tesler's men found you at the motel because I alerted them to your location."

His admission stopped her in her tracks. Suddenly paralyzed, she watched him peripherally. "But you took me away from Tesler's men. You gave me shelter. Why would you do that if you called in the goons?"

He ran his hands over the sheet covering the cot, straightening it with a light touch. "I needed to isolate you, to drive you to me. I knew you would escape Tesler's men. And with David away, you would have nowhere to go." He straightened, turning to face her. "It was a gamble. I hoped you would call on me for help. If not, then I had plans to stumble upon you wherever you decided to hide."

"That's a pretty crappy plan." She shuffled toward the door, one inch at a time. Her shoes scraped across the floor. The walls buzzed faintly. Her pulse beat fast, and she fought to remember to breathe. "I didn't have the DVD with me anymore. You had no way to track me then."

"Cari did." He raked a hand through his dark curls. "The girl. She could've tracked you."

Wonderful. He'd conscripted a child to be his psychic GPS tracker. She tried not to think about what he'd done to the girl, but images flashed in her mind. Drug injections. Physical torture. Amador had a bizarre idea of what constituted noble behavior.

She must get out of here—with the girl.

The dampening field, or whatever it was, seemed confined to this room. If she got past the doorway…

Grace bolted for it.

Wickham leaped in front of the doorway.

She halted so abruptly her feet slipped. Her arms flailed. Her body tumbled backward.

And she stumbled straight into Amador's embrace.

His hands gripped her under her arms, suspending her fall. He eased her onto her feet and let go.

Breathing hard, she tugged her shirt hem down to cover her midriff. Wickham had planted himself just outside the doorway, jaw set, arms crossed over his chest. He must've jumped out from alongside the door, outside the room.

A memory unreeled in her mind. Wickham firing a handgun. Hitting the target with each shot. His deadly accuracy suggested he was more than a butler. He was Amador's enforcer.

The scent of Amador's cologne, spicy and musky, lingered on her skin and clothes, even in her hair. If she ever hoped to get out of this house, she needed a real plan.

"Please, Grace," Amador said. "Allow me to finish explaining."

"Apparently, I have no choice." She angled sideways to both men, keeping watch on them peripherally. "If you want to have any hope of earning my trust, then you need to make a show of good faith."

"In what way?" Amador asked.

"Shut down the dampening field. Or whatever it is you're using to block my powers."

"It is an electromagnetic field."

She braced her hands on her hips. "Turn it off."

Amador strode up to the wall, plucked a small remote-control device out of his pocket, and punched a button on it. A rectangular section of wall sunk inward, sliding out of the way to expose a doorway. Beyond the threshold, she spotted electronic equipment.

He entered the room, leaned over a console, and tapped keys on a keyboard.

The buzzing fizzled out.

Her powers bloomed inside her. Energized. Alive. Ready.

Agony slammed into her. She gasped, staggering backward. The pain ruptured her from the inside, blistering hot, razor-sharp, driven deeper and deeper each second. A strangled cry escaped her.

David.

Another surge battered her. She crumpled to her knees, weeping, overwhelmed by sheer terror. Her connection to David pulsed with pain and anguish. And guilt. Its gravity towed her down into an obsidian whirlpool. His last thought blasted through her mind.

Please forgive me, Grace.

Dammit, he did not get to abandon her again. Not like this. Not forever.

She launched up into the crossroads, barreling through the darkness toward a single blindingly bright star. Her mind crashed into the light. Dived down the tunnel. Exploded out into the world. She collided with the barrier, but her mind bounced back, reeling toward the crossroads.

No.

With every iota of energy left, she latched onto David's location. If she couldn't reach him directly, maybe she could anchor herself to the facility. The EM field surrounding David shoved her away. She clawed at it and scrabbled around the edges of the barrier. Trapped in the pitch dark, she couldn't make out shapes.

But she heard voices. Indistinct. Nearby.

Zeroing in on the sound, she catapulted toward it—and vaulted out into a control room.

An alarm screeched. Technicians banged their fingertips on keyboards at computer workstations, their movements furious and panicked. Two men in white coats stood behind the techs, arguing in loud, angry voices. The workstations faced a window that filled the wall's entire width and half its height.

"Where the hell did he go?" someone shouted.

Grace trotted to the glass. Please, God, let David be alive.

The window overlooked a larger room constructed from bare concrete. In the center of the room, three chairs hunkered. One was empty. The other two held human beings, though all she could see was the tops of their heads. A dark, bald scalp belonged to no one she recognized, at least not from the crown of his head. But the instant her gaze fell on the other head, covered with blond locks, her gut twisted and her head swayed with internal motion. She'd recognize that head anywhere, whether she could see his face or not. She'd run her hands through that hair and kissed the top of that head.

David.

Neither of the men stirred. Dread burrowed deep into her and crystallized into spikes that punctured her soul, shattering hope.

He wasn't dead. She would not believe it until she touched him.

But how? The walls and windows vibrated, evidence of the EM field's existence. Her mind pulsed with pains triggered by her link to David. Despite the barrier between them, part of her reached out to him constantly. She'd relied on that bond far more than she realized. She'd counted on it to always be there. Even now, her mind sought his—and bounced off the EM field.

An invisible vise bore down on her forehead. Starbursts flashed in her vision. How much time did she have before the migraine snapped the tether grounding her to this place?

Not enough.

She rushed to the nearest technician, a young man with dark eyes and tawny skin. Computer-code gibberish unfurled on his monitor as his fingertips fluttered over the keyboard. Sweat dribbled down his temple. His tongue protruded between his clamped teeth, and his breaths puffed fast and sharp.

One of the white-coated men barked, "Where's Dr. Tesler?"

Grace's attention snapped to the speaker. A name tag sewn onto his jacket declared the older man was "Dr. Yellen."

"Don't know," the young tech in front of Grace said, panic constricting his voice into a whine. "I lost track of him when he ran out into the corridor."

"In which direction?"

The tech shrugged and flapped his head from side to side, emitting tiny gasps of confusion and desperation.

"Dammit," Yellen said, "somebody find Sean Vandenbrook."

Sean had escaped. Good. But David…

Drawn by an inevitable need, her gaze veered to the concrete room. Tentacles of ice coiled around her heart.

Focus. She bent close to the tech's ear—and hesitated. The first time she'd exploited this aspect of her powers, the guilt over what she'd done haunted her for months. Using it again, on the motel clerk, had made her queasy. Regret lurked inside her still, an amorphous tumor on her soul. She'd had no choice those other times, and she had no other options at this moment either.

And so she gathered her courage, stifled her conscience, and adopted the most commanding whisper she could muster. "Destroy the EM field. Hurry, before it explodes and everyone dies."

The tech went still, from his furious fingers to his panting breaths. His eyes were aimed straight ahead, but unfocused.

She had no clue whether EM fields could explode, but that hardly mattered. Shutting off the field might not be good enough. Someone else could flip the switch to turn it back on. She needed the barrier gone. Permanently.

"Do it," she commanded, using her astral voice to inject her wishes into his brain. "Destroy the EM field. Save everyone."

His eyelids fluttered.

"Hurry," she insisted. "It's going to blow any second. You can feel the pressure building. Dismantle the field."

The tech's eyes closed.

She'd done this before without really trying. But today, when she needed her powers at full throttle, when lives depended on her ability to—

The man's eyes flew open. His fingers descended on the keyboard, typing with such speed and ferocity she expected the keys to smash apart.

The buzzing ceased. The pressure in her head let up a smidgen.

It had worked. A frenzied laugh bubbled out of her but died in an instant.

Giving the tech an imaginary pat on the shoulder, she told him, "Good work, but shut off the blasted alarm."

Keys clicked. The alarm silenced.

Yellen scampered to the tech, leaning over his shoulder. "What the hell did you do? Saints in heaven, Toby, you disabled the EM field."

Looking dazed, Toby muttered, "I did?"

"It'll take hours to get it back online, if we can do it at all."

The bickering of the men and the clacking of computer keys faded into the background. The world around her dimmed, like a TV screen with the brightness cranked down to the lowest setting. Something inside her dimmed too.

Her connection to David.

It hadn't died, not yet. But it had weakened into a thread, frail and tattered, ready to disintegrate at the slightest pressure.

Faster than a clock tick, she shot into the concrete room to stand before him. A sob tore out of her, rupturing the tomb-deep silence of the concrete vault.

No one could hear her, not even David. He no longer heard or saw or felt anything. Restraints pinned his limp body to the chair. Blood oozed from his nostrils and lips. His head sagged onto his shoulder.

And his eyes. Another sob jarred her body. His eyes were glazed and vacant.

Her knees folded under her, striking the floor.

David had sacrificed his own life to defend hers. Despite lacking any knowledge of what transpired here, she recognized what he had done for her. The truth of it ruptured her heart, smothered her breaths, and pumped the life out of her.

He had died for her.

"No!"

Her cry reverberated in the room. She scrambled to her feet. They had not conquered amnesia and psychopaths, clawing their way back to each other, for everything to end this way. The universe owed her a debt. It had ripped her parents away from her, stripped her most precious memories of David, and thrown her into a flaming pool of psychic trauma and unending danger. She was supposed to keep fighting alone? Like hell.

The universe would pay up. Now.

She rocketed into the crossroads. Hurled out tendrils of her power. Latched onto the limit of the crossroads. Tunneled into it. She split a hole through the fabric of the metaphysical plane, propelling her mind beyond the limits of psychic faculties, straight into the essence of the universe.

She seized the Golden Power.

And gorged on it.

CHAPTER SEVENTEEN

ENERGY SURGED THROUGH DAVID AS HIS EYELIDS FLUTTERED OPEN, vanquishing the remnants of pain that pinched his body. Brilliant light drenched him. He squinted and squirmed in his restraints. Something was off.

The truth roared back to him in a surround-sound memory of gut-wrenching proportions. Gunshots. Blood. Torment. And a blessed numbness right before the world spiraled away from him, replaced by nothingness.

He had died.

The realization chilled him from the inside out. Cold certainty burgeoned in his heart, spreading outward, freezing his veins. Nkosi was dead too. But Sean, thank God, had gotten away. He would find a hole to slip through and flee the facility. The boy knew how to sneak around places like this.

Warmth trickled into David, the blood pumping through his body once again. He still couldn't see much, his vision blurred by the shock of the bright light and… whatever had revived him. The energy flowing through him simmered with a familiar flavor. Sweet. Sharpened by electric pulses. It tingled on his skin and saturated him to his core. His mood lightened, buoyed by an external source, as a cocktail of relief and bittersweet bliss flooded into him.

Grace.

Her love infused his entire being, borne on the energy she funneled into him. She had resurrected him. Which meant only one thing.

The Golden Power.

Jesus, no. She shouldn't have risked it. Not for him, or anyone.

He sensed her nearby, her presence radiating over him like sunlight. The facility had gone eerily quiet. The hairs all over his body stiffened. The wrongness he detected a moment ago lingered in the air, almost palpable. He blinked furiously until his vision cleared and he glimpsed *her*.

Grace stood several feet from his chair. A breeze he could not feel stirred her dark-auburn hair so that it billowed around her face in a silky curtain. Her fair skin seemed to glow from within. Her eyes, focused on him, glimmered with a golden light, the hazel irises bright as faceted jewels. A cool smile curved her lips.

She looked… stunning. He gulped against a lump in his throat. A ghost of desire flitted through him, but it fizzled out the instant she spoke. Her voice echoed from a distant void. "How do you feel?"

"Normal." He stared at her. He couldn't help it. She was beautiful beyond words, ethereal, and more remote than the stars. "Are you all right?"

"Yes." She flicked one finger, and his restraints evaporated. "But we should go. I trapped the scientists and security guards in another corridor. They'll find a way out soon."

Someone moaned. David jerked his head left, toward the noise. Nkosi's chest rose and fell. His eyes drifted open, at first unfocused, then zeroing in on David.

Nkosi sat forward, scratching his head. "I thought I was shot, but I must've hallucinated it."

"No," David said, his tone calmer than the emotions churning inside him. "You died. We both did."

Nkosi cocked his head, his gaze traveling to Grace. "This must be the darling girl Tesler mentioned. The one you spoke with in our cell?"

"Yeah." David waved a hand toward Grace, though he kept his gaze nailed to Nkosi. The energy spinning out from her licked at his psychic senses and bristled an intuition buried deep. "She, uh, saved us. Long story."

"I believe you." Nkosi's eyebrows arched as another wave of power gusted over Grace and her hair fanned out around her. Nkosi threw a sidelong look at David. "The story must be quite interesting."

The man wanted to know, but he wouldn't press. David appreciated that. He hopped out of the chair and inched toward Grace, struggling to ignore the cold fist clenching his heart.

Her luminous eyes rotated toward him, and a shiver sidled down his spine.

An arm's length from her, he halted. "What happened, Grace?"

She blinked in slow motion.

That fist choked his heart. She was lost in another place, somewhere between the here and now and the crossroads. The last time she'd exercised her powers, to build her psychic firewall, an unknown force attacked her, intent on dragging her into the abyss. Could he coax her back this time?

Did she want him to?

Yes, dammit, of course she did. He raised a trembling hand toward her face, but she backed away. "Grace, talk to me. Please."

"I'm still in Ohio. At Amador's house." She turned away from him and glided toward the door. "I'll explain everything later."

As he trailed her out of the room, a memory replayed in his mind. Six months ago, when he'd tracked Grace down in Texas, she demanded answers from him. And he'd promised to explain later. Standing on the other side of that statement today, he finally understood why it infuriated her back then. Starved for answers and suffused with dread, he needed her to talk to him. Yet she refused, with a coolness that terrified him.

With Nkosi close behind, David let Grace lead him down the maze of corridors. She strode around corners, through doorways, and down more corridors with a purpose and certainty beyond anything he'd witnessed in her before now. Grace always possessed an inner strength, more than even she realized, but this was different. The tendrils of her power snaked out around her, invisible, yet palpable to him. Slippery, viscous tongues of energy. They swirled around him, but never touched his psyche.

She was shielding him. From her power.

Hope burgeoned within him. If she maintained enough control to steer her energy away from him, then he still had a chance to drag her back from the void and free her from the Golden Power.

Once, he'd encouraged her to utilize the power. What a fool he'd been. Grace feared it, and now he understood why. He prayed it wasn't too late.

Grace halted before a set of massive steel doors. She raised a hand. "Stay back."

David scuffled backward a few yards, thrusting out an arm to block Nkosi from proceeding further.

She swept both hands up, palms to the ceiling, and threw her head back.

The doors groaned.

Energy assailed her. The outskirts of it sideswiped David, knocking him off balance. He stumbled backward. Nkosi seized his arm. David righted himself and gaped at Grace.

White light pulsed out of her in glittering curtains.

"What do you see?" Nkosi asked.

David tore his gaze away from Grace long enough to frown at Nkosi. "Don't you see it? White energy coming out of her. It's everywhere."

"I see nothing." Nkosi fisted his hand and rubbed his thumb over the knuckles, his mouth tight.

The light kissed David's flesh, filled his psyche, caressed his power. Dizziness crashed over him, reeling him backward. If not for Nkosi's hand on his arm, he would've tumbled to the floor. Passion and adoration streamed into him, tainted with desperation. The sheer magnitude of the power overwhelmed his psychic senses, and pains shot through his head. His knees buckled, striking the floor hard. Nkosi hefted him to his feet.

David's voice emerged in a strangled whisper. "I have to stop her."

"Perhaps I—"

"No. Has to be me."

Nkosi nodded.

Hunched over, David staggered toward Grace. The energy ripped into him with ferocious force. His hand trembled as he stretched it out to grasp her shoulder. Scorching desire bolted out of her into him, and his knees threatened to crumple again.

The steel doors burst open.

Beyond them, crimson bulbs lit a tunnel carved out of the earth.

The light extinguished. The power pouring out of Grace dwindled from a raging torrent to a forceful stream. The pressure on David released with a near-physical rebound. The pain in his head faded. A trickle of desire wended its way through him, a faint tickle compared to the heat that had incinerated him seconds earlier. How she could think of sex while channeling the ultimate source of psychic energy baffled him. Questions bounced in his brain, but he ignored all except one.

He tugged her shoulder. "Are you still with me, Grace?"

She turned toward him inch by inch. Her eyes glowed with less intensity, more like the luminescence brought on by harnessing normal psychic abilities.

Normal. He never dreamed he'd use that word to describe psychic faculties.

"I'm here," she said, and relief flooded into him at the sound—the normal sound—of her voice. Her gaze latched onto his. "Why are you sweating?"

David swiped at his face. His hand came away damp. The sweat oozing from his pores hadn't registered before. Her energy had consumed his every thought and swamped his senses. Grasping her shoulders, he searched her burning hazel eyes for some sign she'd come back to him.

Then it hit him. His hands gripped her flesh. *Physical contact.*

"You manifested," he said, unable to quell the shock in his voice, "and you're not curled up in a ball, riding out a migraine." In fact, she glowed with a preternatural vitality. He tugged her closer, desperate to spur a reaction from her. He got nothing. "Grace?"

"Yes, I manifested. So what? It's easy." Her breezy tone set his nerves on edge, but she charged ahead. "I have to get you three out of here quickly. The distraction I arranged won't keep Tesler or his men busy for much longer."

"Where are we going?"

"Somewhere safe. Trust me."

He trusted her without reservation. But with the Golden Power influencing her, he didn't know if he should.

She spun away from him, toward the steel doors.

"Wait," he said, seizing her hand. She glanced back. "Us three? It's only me and Nkosi."

A knowing smile curved her lips. "Just wait. I sent him directions."

"Who?"

Bang.

David whirled around. A ceiling panel had popped out, clattering to the floor. A pair of sneaker-clad feet dangled through the opening. Sean plopped onto the corridor floor, knees bent.

"Him," Grace said, and she marched out the doors. "I retrieved Sean for you."

Stunned and immobile, David watched her backside retreat from him. No psychic he'd ever encountered commanded enough power and control to perform two tasks at once, much less three. From what Grace told him, though, he suspected she had. Locating and directing Sean. Setting up a distraction for Tesler and his minions. Freeing David and Nkosi. And she resurrected them too.

Make that *four* tasks at once.

Sean trotted past him. Casting a glance over his shoulder, he said, "Why do you look like your best friend died? We're escaping."

David tried to speak. Nothing came out.

Nkosi hurried after Sean and Grace. "We must go, David."

An eerie sensation prickled the skin at the base of his neck. Grace had amassed more psychic power than anyone should command. If he hadn't run out on her for the umpteenth time, she would never have needed to tap into the limitless power she'd feared for six months. The energy boost empowered her, for sure. But it also altered her on a fundamental level.

It was his fault. He must cleanse her of this... infestation. Whatever happened, he would not give up on her without a fight. He'd rather die—again.

His top priority had always been, and always would be, her. From this moment forward, he must prove that fact to her. He'd save her, dammit, whether she liked it or not.

Squaring his shoulders, he took off down the tunnel.

It dead-ended at a much smaller set of double doors, constructed from steel and buttressed with concrete. The doors hung ajar, their edges warped. Grace must've unlocked both sets of doors at once, employing the limitless energy granted to her by the Golden Power. A frigid current trickled through his veins. *Five* tasks at once. *Holy heaven.*

They pushed the deformed doors aside and clambered out into the night. Grace guided them onward, with a purpose and conviction that did nothing to alleviate his unease. She knew precisely where to go—down to the inch, he realized. Left at this tree, right at the next one, straight down a gentle grade and across a clearing. Their breaths condensed in the chilled air. He should've checked the weather forecast before waltzing out here on his half-assed mission. Nothing except his desperate quest had stuck in his brain, not even Grace's warnings and her silent pleas for his help. He was such a fool. And a total ass.

Goosebumps riddled his arms, but try as he might, he couldn't dismiss them as a side effect of frosty air on his bare arms. The fabric of his T-shirt protected him somewhat but left his arms exposed, since the guards had confiscated his jacket. Nkosi wore a long-sleeve T-shirt, and Sean had opted for the ultra-cool layered look with a long-sleeve shirt underneath his short-sleeve tee, granting him more protection than David had without his jacket. Both Sean and Nkosi rubbed their arms off and on, but neither shivered noticeably. David's teeth had begun to chatter, so he clamped his jaw tight. But as with his goosebumps, his clenched teeth stemmed from more than an attempt to ward off the outward chill. Another, deeper cold infiltrated his being.

And it centered on Grace.

He lost track of the minutes as they, with David in front, trailed Grace through the woods. East, west, north, south, he gave up trying to sort out the directions. Despite the gloom of night, pierced by only the occasional shaft of pale moonlight, their guide had no trouble navigating. The longer they trekked, the less David noticed the cold. His goosebumps disappeared, but the hairs at the nape of his neck remained stiff. Sweat beaded on his brow. The air chilled it within seconds, drawing the cold across his brow like a damp washcloth.

They broke out of the trees, heading down a hill into a clearing. A log cabin hunkered at the hill's base, near the other side of the clearing. The house was dark, more a shadow in the night than a beacon of hope and safety. Since Grace brought them here, though, he'd trust she knew what she was doing, even if he couldn't grasp the logic of it. They should've run as far as possible. Then again, how far would they get before Tesler's men caught up? This cabin must offer security, or else Grace would never have led them here.

At the cabin, they halted. A dirt two-track drew a line through the moon-lightened field, terminating at the roofed porch of the cabin. A stack of cut firewood, partially covered by a brown tarp, occupied one end of the porch. David saw no vehicles, no lights, no signs of habitation. Given the weeds and grass dotting the two-track, he surmised no one had visited the cabin in months, maybe longer.

Grace, positioned a few feet from the porch steps, waved a hand toward the front door. "You can hide here until morning. By then I'll have a plan to extract you."

Nkosi eyed the cabin with raised eyebrows. "Won't our enemies track us here?"

"No." Grace sounded far too certain, which scraped a steel file down David's spine. "I've obliterated our tracks and planted false clues to lead Tesler's men away from here. I've also permanently disabled the facility's electronics, as well as the mobile devices of everyone there tonight."

"Cool," Sean said, his tone rife with teenage wonder. "Can you teach me how to do that?"

David laid a hand on the boy's arm, urging him toward the cabin, and flashed Nkosi a look he hoped conveyed the import of his words. "You two go inside. I need to talk to Grace."

Sean balked, in typical rebellious-boy fashion, but Nkosi grasped his upper arm and, with a gentle hand, guided him up the steps and across the porch. At the front door, he paused. "Perhaps we should gather some wood first?"

Grace shook her head. "There's enough inside to start a fire and keep it going for tonight. There's also a generator, but it's out of gas."

Nkosi gave a curt nod and twisted the doorknob. It turned in his hand, unlocked. He did not comment on the open door, despite the curious twitch of his lips. Easing the door ajar, he entered first, with Sean close behind. Once the door clicked shut, David strode toward Grace, until inches separated them.

The whites of her eyes glistened in the moon's glow. Her expression conveyed such innocence and sweetness that, for a few ecstatic seconds, he forgot all about her shocking power and the dread coiling in his gut with each new feat she accomplished. In that fleeting moment, he gazed into the eyes of the only woman he'd ever loved. His true better half. His soul mate.

Then her psychic energy pulsed into him, electrified by the Golden Power, and shattered his serenity. Her love still warmed him, transferred into him by her telepathy, but the old chill resurfaced with a sharpness that scraped his nerves raw.

"You unlocked the door," he said.

"That's right." The disturbing calmness in her voice had faded, but not vanished. "I took care of everything. You'll be safe tonight."

He cradled her face in his hands. "You do these things without even a hint of discomfort. No migraine. No anxiety. Nothing." He ducked his head close to hers, their breaths mingling. "It's the Golden Power doing this to you. But why aren't you afraid of it anymore?"

"Because I understand it now. It's a part of me, always has been, and I've accepted that."

The woman he knew would never accept it. "It's changing you. I can feel it."

She shrugged.

"Please, Grace, listen to me." He stroked her cheeks with his thumbs, marveling at how she felt so warm and normal on the outside when oily darkness roiled within her. "You have to let it go. Stop channeling the Golden Power before it changes you forever." His nose bumped hers, and his lips grazed her mouth. "Come back to me. Please."

"I am here."

No, she wasn't. Not fully. Her body brushed against his, her skin heated under his hands, but the part of her he cherished most lay smothered beneath her newfound power. Words failed to crack the granite-hard wall of psychic energy shielding her mind, her heart, her soul. *No, dammit.* He wouldn't surrender this battle.

He claimed her mouth in a possessive kiss as he thrust his hands into her hair, grasping the back of her head, slanting it up to press his lips harder into hers. Her soft lips opened for him. He forged deep inside, lost in the silky sweetness of her mouth, the answering strokes of her tongue. Her body arched into him. He glided one hand down to splay his fingers across the small of her back and yanked her snug against him. She rasped her nails up and down his chest. They scratched over his T-shirt, a rough tease on his flesh.

The world dropped away. They plunged into a private pocket of reality where the only sounds were their frantic breaths and hungry moans, and the only sensation was the rubbing of their bodies against each other and the hot, slick dance of their tongues. The passion blazing between them disintegrated guilt and fear and inhibition. The darkness fled from their psychic link, conquered by a scorching desire and a fierce love.

He felt *her.*

The essence of this woman. Beautiful, supple, sweet as honey, but underpinned by strength and vitality. Joy blossomed within him, its petals fashioned from her, drawn open by the radiance of their indestructible bond.

They peeled their lips apart, so slowly he swore he tasted every cell in her skin. Their chests heaved in unison, her breasts mounded against him. Condensation billowed out from their mouths, but the cold barely registered on his skin.

"David. Wow." She murmured the syllables against his mouth, her eyes half-closed. "I had no idea you could kiss like that." She raked her nails down his chest to the waistband of his pants. "Do it again."

Words caught in his throat, constricted into a groan.

She rocked her hips into him.

Hunger coursed through him, arousing every part of his body. He fought the impulse to sweep her into his arms, carry her into the cabin, and drop her onto the first padded surface he found so he could make love to her all night.

The moonlight burnished her golden eyes and ignited the emerald flecks. He wanted to capture her bottom lip between his teeth to suckle her flesh.

She ran her tongue over her swollen lips, curving them into a shy smile. "Thank you."

"For what?" At least she seemed normal, but he couldn't shake the sensation of impending doom.

Her smile turned bittersweet. "You saved me."

His heart thudded, and relief rushed through him, flushing out the desire. Well, most of it.

"I was lost," she said, "and you found me. I gave in to the Golden Power but..."

Tears trickled down her cheeks. She veered her gaze down to the ground. Her shoulders slumped, bowing forward, and he knew, the way no one else would have, that she was trying to curl up in a ball while upright, to disappear into herself. What she'd done, absorbing the ultimate psychic power, had left her ashamed. The link between them hinted at it, but his intimate knowledge of her confirmed it.

His heart ached for her, his arms too. He enfolded her in his embrace and tucked her head under his chin. While he reassured her with his words, promises he wasn't sure he could keep but he'd damn well try, she relaxed into him. Even knowing this wasn't her real body, but a manifestation created by a process neither one of them fully understood, he still relished the warmth and softness of her body against his. Her hair smelled of coconut and vanilla, from the conditioner she used. How on earth a manifested body could smell like anything amazed him, and he briefly wondered whether his manifestations gave off any scents.

He caressed her hair, rewarded by her nuzzling his neck. "Why did you seek out the Golden Power?"

She lifted her head to squint at him. When she spoke her voice conveyed great patience and a hint of disbelief. "I did it for you. I came to find you and—" Her voice faltered. She raised a trembling hand to his face, etching a line down his cheek with one fingertip. "You were dead. I had to do something."

He shut his eyes, shocked by his own stupidity. Of course she'd done it for him. He remembered dying, recalled the pain and then the numbness, and he should've understood the moment he awakened. Reviving him from the dead, as well as resurrecting Nkosi and all the other incredible things she'd done, demanded a steep cost. To acquire that much psychic energy, she had no choice but to plug into the source she'd feared since the day six months ago when she first stumbled onto it.

Back then, she'd inadvertently harnessed it. Today, she sought it out and welcomed it into her mind, her body, her soul. Could she expunge it on her own? Could anything rid her of its influence? He wanted to believe his passionate kiss, his total commitment to her, expelled it. He'd seen too much in the past few years to delude himself.

She was back. She was his again. For how long?

He rested his forehead on hers and scrutinized her gaze for any remnants of the otherness he witnessed earlier. All he saw was her. "I'm sorry. I should've listened to you and stayed home. If I had, none of this would've happened."

"Sean would've charged headfirst into danger, and into Tesler's hands. Neither of us could live with ourselves if we let that happen."

"It's my fault. I..." He had no clue what to say, how to explain, how to rectify the mess he made.

She kissed him, a sweet and lingering touch imbued with sorrow, affection, need, and hope. He hadn't imagined the last one could've survived after her ordeals. And yet the hope flowed down their connection, a gleaming, unbreakable thread.

"I'll see you again," she said, "soon. Wait for me."

"Wait where? Here?"

"Yes." She backed away from him, her face glowing with tenderness. "The last time we talked, I told you the conversation wasn't over. It still isn't. So don't go dying on me again, at least until we've finished our talk."

"I'll try." He could promise no more, and she knew it. "Be careful. Please."

She nodded. "I love you."

Her manifested body winked out of existence as her mind retreated from him.

Gone.

Wind gusted over him, blowing grit into his eyes. He blinked it away and stared at the spot where she'd been a heartbeat ago. "I love you too."

CHAPTER EIGHTEEN

GRACE GLIDED BACK INTO HER BODY, NO PAIN, NO PRESSURE, JUST A gentle slide back into herself. David's final words, a warning to be careful, replayed in her mind, bouncing off the empty spaces inside her, the holes left behind by his absence. Their connection resonated in the background, but without direct contact, it diminished to a distant echo. She sensed his presence in the world, nothing more.

An ache sprouted in her chest, deep and spiritual, rather than physical. The ache built into a heart-rending throb, tearing her hard-won composure to shreds. *I miss you, David, I'm coming for you soon so please wait for me, please.* Would he hear her promise and her plea? No. Not with their connection reduced to a trickle. But she'd done all she could for him.

A weariness blanketed her, with almost suffocating pressure. She sank to her knees, then reality burst into her mind, sharp and bright and agonizing in its abruptness. The basement. In Amador's house. She slumped on the concrete floor, shoulders hunched, pangs webbing out through her knees from their collision with the hard surface. Amador knelt before her with his lips parted, his wide eyes fixed on her, face warped by panicked emotions she preferred not to decipher.

He stretched out a tentative hand to touch her arm, but pulled it back at the last instant, hovering his hand a few inches from her. "Are you… unharmed?"

She made a rude noise. "Yeah sure, I'm great. You suppressed my powers with your EM doohickey, drugged me into unconsciousness, held me against my will, and led Tesler straight to me. Your concern is touching. Thanks a bunch."

Amador flinched and lowered his hand. "I understand you hate me, and you should, but I have done these things to protect you, in my own way." He bowed his head, draping a hand across each knee. "You may leave this place whenever you wish. No one will stop you. However, Tesler's men are still hunting for you and I cannot call them off."

"I figured." She sat back on her heels and sighed. "I need to get to Montana, fast."

His head popped up, and his eyes were bright with curiosity. "You found David?"

"Yes." She'd keep the details to herself, though his desire to know crackled in the air. The Golden Power might've deserted her, thank heavens, but it deposited a trace of its energy within her, something she could neither erase nor explain. Amador's emotions slipped inside her, wending their way past her defenses and into her psychic essence. His need and desperation scratched at her, but she suffered no confusion over whose emotions were whose. "Can you provide transportation?"

"Of course. It is the least I can do, to make up for... what I've done."

Sorrow burned. Regret pinched. She shoved aside the invasive feelings, and the urge to chastise him for daring to suggest he might make amends so easily. It'd take a hell of a lot more than a ride to Montana. "I'd appreciate that."

He rose, towering above her. "I'll have Wickham arrange for my jet to take you wherever you need. You may leave within the hour."

With that, he strode toward the door.

"Wait." She heaved her body up off the floor, against the wishes of gravity and exhaustion. "I want to see the girl. Cari."

A muscle in his jaw twitched. His hands clenched, then slackened. Squeezing his lips into a tight smile, he said, "Of course. Follow me."

She marched out the door behind him, up the concrete steps, and down the hallway to a closed door on the left. He dug a key ring out of his pocket, jangling the keys as he selected the appropriate one. The grandfather clock she'd heard earlier bonged from somewhere nearby, muted by the walls. Amador shoved the key into the door's lock with a chunk.

Then he hesitated, casting her a sidelong look.

Her newfound heightened intuition kicked in, warning her with a tingle on her skin. He didn't want her to see the girl, which she'd already known, but now she realized why. She clamped her jaw tight against the anger burning inside her and balled her hands into fists, but the inferno blasted away her self-control.

"She's broken," Grace said, squeezing the words out between her teeth. "You pushed her so hard for so long she snapped. I've met others that's happened to. But they were tortured by Tesler and JT." She stomped one pace closer to him. Her hot breaths ricocheted off his cheek. "You did this to her. Admit it."

His expression fell. His lower lip trembled, and moisture glistened in his eyes. "She is damaged, but not insane. I admit I abused this girl for my purposes, and I have no excuse for it except to say I had no notion my tactics would harm her so terribly."

"But even after you knew, you kept on using her." The words fired from her lips, harsher than she'd ever heard her own voice sound. Grace shut her eyes, sucked in a deep breath, and exhaled slowly. *This isn't me, it's the Golden Power, it's not me.* Despite believing, praying, she'd shaken off the Golden Power's hold on her, the truth gnawed at her gut. *It's still inside me.*

She heard the click as Amador unlocked the door and opened her eyes. He pushed the door inward, stepped across the threshold, and moved aside, motioning for her to enter.

I'm not me anymore. The thought ricocheted in her brain, louder and louder with every concussive burst of repetition. How long would the Golden Power influence her? Did it control her even now, in ways she hadn't grasped yet? Questions flared in her mind, but above all the others, a single fear lanced her heart.

Can David love me like this? Can anyone?

Amador stared at her, his face blank. "If you still wish to see the girl..."

Grace stalked past him into the small bedroom. Cari lay on her back on the four-poster bed, hands folded over her belly, eyes shut. Her chest rose and fell in a gentle rhythm. Her dark hair fanned out over the white pillowcase, the strands draped over her shoulders. Grace perched on the bed's edge, alongside the girl's hips.

Cari peeked out between her lashes. Her body went rigid. A pallor lightened her cinnamon skin, and her lips too.

Waves of anxiety rolled out of Cari, crashing into Grace. She gripped the bed's edge to steady herself against the onslaught. What had Amador done to this girl?

Grace settled a hand on Cari's arm. "I'm getting you out of here. You'll be safe."

Amador scuffled into her peripheral vision. "Grace—"

She flashed him a scowl.

He clapped his mouth shut.

"Cari is coming with me," Grace told him. Then she looked back at the girl, offering her a consoling smile. "You've been in my mind, watched me, experienced who I am. You know I won't hurt you, and I'm not with him." A hint of fiery anger singed the last phrase. That wasn't the Golden Power. This anger steamed straight from her own heart. "Will you trust me?"

Cari swallowed, hard. Her wide eyes flicked to Amador, triggering a massive breaker of panic, but then she switched her attention back to Grace. Cari bit her lip and nodded. "I know you won't hurt me."

A mild Southern accent lent her sweet voice a melodic quality. Grace imagined Cari singing, her voice as glorious as a choir of angels. How in hell could Amador torture a lovely girl like Cari and yet claim to be nothing like Tesler? His motives, though noble to his mind, were twisted and cold.

No, not cold. Hot with desire—for power, and for something else she had yet to puzzle out. His emotions tangled up in an ever-expanding mass, confusing her attempts to sort out what he felt, much less what he craved deep inside. A shiver frosted her nerves. Maybe she didn't want to know his innermost desires.

Hopping off the bed, she held a hand out to Cari.

The girl grasped it fiercely. Once Grace helped her stand, Cari said, "I want to go home. Please. I want to see my mom and dad."

The plea in her tone made Grace's heart ache for this girl in a way she couldn't describe, gripped by a frantic desire to rescue her from Amador and shield her from Tesler. She slipped an arm around Cari's shoulders.

Amador hunched at the foot of the bed, impassive.

"We're taking her home," Grace said. "And then I'm taking your jet to Montana." She hugged the girl a little tighter. "I suggest you stay the hell away from both of us."

"I will arrange everything. Please wait in the living room." His shoes scuffed across the floor as he exited the room. Without looking back, he said, "I know you can never forgive me, but I hope one day you will come to understand my actions."

He disappeared down the hall.

Cari buried her head against the hollow of Grace's shoulder and wept, her body quivering with each sob.

Damn him. Amador must pay for his crimes. She must make certain of it.

But first… David.

CHAPTER NINETEEN

W ASHED IN THE SULFUROUS GLOW OF THE STREETLIGHTS, THE front door of the stucco cottage swung shut behind Cari. Grace gulped down the lump in her throat and rubbed out the tears stinging her eyes. Amador had sworn Tesler knew nothing about Cari, and he'd assigned three men from his private security force to watch over her. The girl was safe.

As safe as any psychic could be with Tesler on the loose.

The big black SUV pulled away from the curb. Hands gripped on the steering wheel, Amador fixed his blank stare on the street before them. The headlights pierced the false twilight of the streetlights, punching a path into the night. Amador had insisted on driving her to the airport, and she'd been too exhausted to argue.

"Floor it," she said, refusing to dampen the acid in her tone. "No dillydallying just to keep me around longer. I'm not interested in whatever wacko scheme you've cooked up."

His fingers clenched tighter around the wheel, but his voice remained eerily calm. "I know I've destroyed any chance I had of gaining your trust, but I hold out hope you will assist me, once you understand the purpose behind my actions."

She snorted, not minding in the least that she sounded like a dog rooting through garbage. "You're delusional. I've had it up to here with your machinations."

"I understand you, Grace. We've both suffered at the hands of JT and Tesler."

"And how precisely have you suffered?"

His shoulders flagged, and his expression did too. When he spoke, his voice flattened into a monotone. "I saw a photo of you, read your file, and I knew I had to have you as my ally. So I tried to trick you into helping me. I'm so sorry, Grace, so very sorry for what I've done to you and to Cari. I don't ask forgiveness. I simply need you to understand."

"Then explain." She slanted her head, studying him. "Start by telling me why you lied about having psychic abilities."

"It wasn't a complete fabrication. Though it was my son, Evander, who possessed those talents." Amador's features cinched tight, then slackened. "He was twelve when Tesler took him, tortured him, and finally, when he no longer offered anything of value, slit his throat."

She stared at Amador, unable to glean anything from his face or tone of voice. Tesler had murdered a child? The man knew no limits.

Amador dropped one hand to his thigh, the fingers tensing into claws that scraped on his slacks and routed the flesh beneath. "I altered the data on the DVD I gave you. I changed Evander's name to John Mendoza."

"Why?"

He yanked the wheel, swerving onto another street.

She clutched her arm rest to prevent herself from flying into his lap. Well, at least his bad driving staved off the weariness mounting inside her.

He said nothing for several more seconds, and then he hissed out another breath. "I suppose I wanted to erase the memories by erasing Evander's name from the records. It did not work."

The things he and Wickham had told her before rushed through her mind anew, and this time she grasped the true meaning.

Gabriel understands your predicament, Wickham had told her, *he's been there before.* And Amador spoke of *those things that we share in common, our special connection.* When he had compelled her to share the pain of her parents' deaths, he'd apologized for dredging up her bad memories. *I know how painful that can be,* he'd assured her.

The empathic aftereffect of joining with the Golden Power was waning, yet his grief rolled off him onto her, weakening with each wave.

He'd lied to her, over and over, and she wouldn't condone his behavior. But confronted with a truth she had never expected, she needed to reevaluate him. Just a little.

Amador veered the car around another corner. The tires squealed. The odor of burned rubber wafted in through the vents. "Grace, please, I need your help to stop Tesler. I couldn't save my son. At least let me play some small part in destroying the man who took Evander's life."

The anguish in his voice tugged at her heart, which was stupid. Why should she sympathize with Amador, a man as dangerous as Tesler? But she couldn't help it. Memories of her parents flickered in her mind. Her gut twisted, and her throat constricted. "I'm sorry about your son, really I am. But that's no excuse for what you've done."

"I tell you this not as an excuse, but merely an explanation."

"Save it. I'm not interested." Except a part of her was, for reasons too confusing to examine, out of fear he might lure her into forgetting his abuse of

Cari. Maybe he'd injected her with more of the anti-willpower drug, or maybe she'd lost her mind. Or else her intuition was speaking to her again. Urging her to, if not trust him, at least understand his mindset. *Know your enemy, right?*

A yawn overtook her, and she shook herself to cast off the fatigue, but to no avail. Her eyelids had morphed into lead aprons, drifting ever downward.

Images streaked through her mind, half dream, half memory. David standing rigid as a statue in front of her as she bid him goodbye. His blond hair glowing in the moonlight. The stoic expression on his face. Nothing revealed, nothing shared. Her warrior angel.

David. In the woods. With Tesler hot on his trail. Just like in her vision.

She jerked awake. Her heart hammered, her breaths gasped, and she gripped the cushioned arms of her chair so tightly her knuckles ached. A cone of lamplight enveloped her. A padded seat cradled her buttocks, and the chair's back supported her head and neck with equal cushiness. As she uncurled her fingers from the chair's arms, the velvety fabric caressed her skin. She dragged in a deep breath, letting it out in one long, ragged sigh. Her pulse slowed, though it still raced.

Where the hell was she?

Not in the car. She blinked away the bleariness of sleep, rotating her head back and forth to absorb her surroundings. She sat in a chair bolted to the floor, beside a small window. Outside, she spied clouds scudding by in the milky glow of the moon. A jet engine whined, muted by the insulation of the aircraft.

She must be in Amador's jet.

Her suspicion solidified into certainty when Gabriel Amador strode out of a curtained doorway to her left and took a seat in the chair across from her. He cupped a bottle of water in one hand. A small table, fashioned from what looked like polished cherry wood, separated them. She straightened, smoothed her shirt, and tucked a stray lock of hair behind her ear. Her heart no longer raced, but anxiety rippled through her like an electrical current.

"Why are you here?" she said. "I told you to stay away from me."

Sitting ramrod straight in his chair, he studied her without expression.

Why did men love to give her the stoic treatment?

"You were in no condition to travel alone," he said. "I couldn't wake you, and I will not abandon you on this plane without knowing you will awaken at some point."

"You could've called a doctor."

He shrugged one shoulder. "No physician can heal psychic wounds. Whatever you did to save David, it drained you with devastating effect." He offered the water bottle to her. "Drink this. You should replenish your fluids."

She stared at the bottle, her anxiety surging. Drugged? *Ah, hell.* If he wanted to drug her, he could've done it while she was unconscious. And her mouth was dry. Snatching the bottle from him, she unscrewed the cap and swigged several mouthfuls.

"Thank you. For the water, and for the ride." She watched a slender cloud slip past the window. "Where are we headed?"

"You said Montana, so I instructed the pilot to chart a course for a private airstrip owned by a trusted ally. It's located near Bozeman."

"Close enough." She didn't understand how she knew David's location, and she couldn't recite the coordinates, but she sensed his whereabouts. She'd given up understanding what the Golden Power did to her. At least for now. Once she had David back, and Tesler was dealt with, she'd examine her brushes with limitless power.

Brushes? Maybe that word applied to the first instance. This time, however, she had succumbed to the power completely.

The old anxiety buzzed in her veins, electrifying her skin. The sour taste of acid infiltrated her mouth. She gulped down another mouthful of water, but the acrid flavor lingered. For David, she would risk anything. Even if it creeped her out big time and made her long for a nice dark corner to hide in.

No hiding. With David in the woods, like in her vision, the premonition still might come true. Tesler sought David, and he would stop at nothing to capture him and use him for leverage, to draw her into the open. It might work too. She knew it. Confronted with a choice to save herself or David, she'd choose him.

Amador leaned forward, bracing his elbows on his knees. Hands clasped, he fixed his dark eyes on her. The lamplight ignited paler specks in his irises she'd never noticed before. Dark caramel dribbled onto coffee, that's what his eyes resembled. A silly image, but somehow it suited him.

"How long was I out?" she asked.

"Two hours. We've nearly reached Bozeman."

Her stomach sank as the jet pitched into a descent. She sipped the water, but her insides refused to calm. "When we land, I go alone. You stay here."

"Please, Grace, allow me to help you." He scooted forward to the edge of his seat and eased a hand down onto her knee. "I wish no harm to David. I will do whatever I can to protect you both."

What about Sean? And David's new friend? She bit back the questions, unwilling to reveal any more just yet. Then again, if she intended for all of them to flee on Amador's jet, he'd find out soon enough.

She grumbled out a sigh. "David isn't alone. He has two others with him."

"They are also welcome on my jet." He swept his arm through the air in an expansive gesture. "As you can see, I have plenty of room."

She counted the empty seats aligned in rows and the pair flanking a sofa. A dozen chairs. Yeah, he had room all right.

Goosebumps cropped up on her arms as the hairs on her neck stiffened. Amador's attention, riveted to her, triggered a physical response.

She folded her hands on her lap. "Why did you drug me?"

He sagged into his seat, closing his eyes as he shook his head. "It was a terrible mistake. I'm sorry." He raked a hand through his hair, mussing it. "I hoped the serum would help you with your powers, yes, but mostly I wanted to make you more receptive." He covered his eyes with his hand. "To me."

"You were trying to seduce me?"

"No." He pulled himself up and met her gaze. "I needed you to believe me, to help me. The serum seemed my best option to make that happen. Time is running out, Grace. For all of us."

His words penetrated her soul like pins and needles jabbed into her core. "What do you mean time is running out?"

He exhaled, and his shoulders slumped again. "Tesler. He plans to capture you and mine your brain for the secrets to psychic power. He already knows how to shatter minds and bend them to his control. Once he has what he needs from you…" Amador grasped his knees. "He will create an army of psychics who obey his will and his will alone. The Golden Power will make it possible."

The world lurched around her, though the jet stayed level. She gripped the arms of her seat, hanging on until the spinning ceased. An army of brainwashed psychics. Tesler in command. Her breaths quickened, her pulse too. Heartbeats thundered in her ears, raged through her veins, and scorched out her thoughts. She'd seen what Tesler's methods did to psychics. Andrew Haley, coerced into reading minds, catapulted straight into insanity. And her own brushes with the Golden Power tainted her with a sourness she could not shake. If Tesler mined her for answers, unlocking the secrets of imbuing anyone with psychic abilities and controlling those subjects, then he could rule the world. Literally. Plant a damn jeweled crown on his head and make everyone genuflect before their master.

Hell no.

Grace shot to her feet, hands clenched at her sides. "We have to stop him."

Amador rubbed his forehead. "It will not be easy. He'll fight and claw and destroy anything that gets in his way. Even you aren't strong enough to stop him." Amador eyed her, his lips compressed. "Unless…"

"I use the Golden Power again."

"Yes."

A shudder racked her body, knocking her off-kilter. She dropped back onto her seat. Though she'd vowed never to use the Golden Power again, her sabotage of Tesler's facility wouldn't slow him down for long. He'd hunt down David. Punish him. Leverage him.

And she'd cave in to Tesler's demands.

Which left her one option.

Tap into the ultimate power, no matter the cost. If it meant insanity, fine. If it molded her into something else, something both more and less than herself, then she'd swallow the consequences whole. Even if it choked her.

She glared out the window, into a night as thick and suffocating as a drenched wool blanket. "I'll do it. To stop Tesler, I will tap into the Golden Power."

And if it mutated her into a monster, heaven help the rest of the world. She squeezed her eyes shut and beamed a message out to David, praying he'd receive it.

Kill me, David. If it comes down to me or the world, kill me.

CHAPTER TWENTY

DAVID JOLTED AWAKE. THE BACK OF HIS HEAD SMACKED INTO THE wall, radiating pains through his skull. The hammering of his heart shattered the quiet inside the cabin, though only inside his head. *Dammit.* He'd fallen asleep, despite his promise to Sean and Nkosi that he'd keep watch while they slept.

Burning wood crackled in the stone fireplace a dozen feet away. Tongues of flame licked at the air and spilled flickering light into the living room, drowning out the pale moonglow beyond the windows above his head. Nkosi dozed on the sofa. Sean, curled up in an overstuffed armchair, watched David through half-closed lids.

Kill me, a voice begged him inside his mind. *Kill me, David.*

He jerked forward, palms on his outstretched legs, nails digging in. Grace was calling to him. Her energy coursed down their connection, her words a despondent plea. Why the hell would she ask him to kill her?

Amador.

David ground his teeth. The bastard must've hurt Grace. Tortured her. Driven her to the brink of insanity. For no other reason would she beg to die.

With a flourish of power, he reached out to Grace. Her life essence burned like a fireball, blazing into him, around him, through him. He gasped and pulled back from the link, from her. The withdrawal carved out a hollow space nothing could fill except for her—with him, for real this time, not as a manifested entity of shocking power, but as the sweet and passionate woman he cherished.

He snaked out a tendril of energy, testing the waters. *Grace, are you all right?* Her love beamed into him—incandescent, gentle, endless— wringing tears from his eyes. Tears? God almighty, he had never cried before. Never. But bathed in her reverence, he could not stem the flow, because beneath the love simmered a darker energy that clawed for control of Grace. The Golden Power squatted within her, a ghost of limitless power, and it craved more.

Let it go, Grace, please let it go.

"What's the matter?"

Sean's voice, tight with anxiety, shattered the connection, yanking David back to the here and now. Gasping for breaths, he swiped at his eyes. Sean did not need to see him weeping. Aside from the macho reasons for hiding his tears, he knew the sight of them would ratchet up Sean's anxiety.

David cleared his throat and straightened. "I'm fine. Go back to sleep."

Sean slid off the chair and crawled across the bare wood floor to David—crawled because he'd admonished Sean to keep a low profile in the vicinity of the windows. "I can take over so you can rest."

"No thanks." As if he could take a nap knowing Grace was in trouble. Maybe not physical danger, but the psychic variety might prove equally dangerous. The knowledge of her state, of the threat lurking in her own mind, grated on his last nerve. "I'd rather sit up a little longer."

"Me too." Sean scooted backward into the wall. "Can't sleep. Keep thinking about... stuff."

David eyed him sideways. "Tesler won't find us yet. Grace made sure of that. She'll come for us before any bad guys track us down."

"Yeah..." Sean drew his knees to his chest and folded his arms over them. "That's what I keep thinking about. Grace."

"What do you mean?"

"Her power. She's... scary strong." Sean flinched, as if in expectation of a slap. "I like her, you know I do, she's really cool."

But he was afraid of her. Who wouldn't be? David propped one elbow on his bent knee and cradled his forehead in his palm. "I know she was different the last time we saw her, but she's still the same old Grace." He prayed he wasn't lying. "She needs a little time to recover from using the Golden Power, that's all."

Sean stiffened. "She used it? Again? I thought she hated it. Why would she use it knowing what it does to her?"

David sighed, a long and wistful breath. Sean knew nothing about what had gone down in the room with Tesler. About the deaths. About Grace's appearance. He scratched his scalp, his forehead still braced on his palm. "She had to do it to save my life." Which made all of this his fault. He must right the wrong before Grace lost her humanity, her sanity, to the ultimate power. "Tesler killed me and Nkosi. Grace brought us both back."

Sean's mouth rounded into an O, his eyes widening. "Whoa. I didn't know she could pull that off, even with the Golden Power."

"Yes, you do." David lifted his head to look at Sean. "She did it six months ago."

"Noooo, that was way different. We were injured, not dead."

The last thread of David's hope snapped. Sean was right. Grace had gone too far this time, too deep into the psychic realm. How on earth could he bring her back?

An ember of hope hid beneath the ashes. Earlier tonight, he'd coaxed her back from the depths. He could do it again.

How many times would his failures push her to take measures no one should have to resort to? He'd let her down in so many ways. Taking off on Tesler hunts. Abandoning her. Refusing to answer her questions. Ignoring her fears because it suited his needs, his quest for… What? Protecting Grace, yes. If he was man enough to admit the whole truth, though, he had another reason for his obsession with Tesler. He sought redemption.

Did he deserve it? His betrayal loomed between them, a monolithic impediment, one she knew nothing about because he was terrified to tell her.

Sean coughed and rubbed his neck. "You know, since my mom died, you guys are like my family." He fiddled with his shoelace. "So try not to get killed, okay?"

David leaned his head against the wall. "I won't let anything happen to you or Grace."

"Wish I could heal the dead. Can't even heal myself. Is the Golden Power really so awful?"

"You don't want it. Trust me."

Energy rushed through him, hot and sweet and oh-so-familiar. She was here.

David leaped up, tore the cabin door open, and barreled out into the night, toward the one thing in this world that mattered more to him than his own life.

Grace.

———

SHE SPOTTED THE CABIN UP AHEAD, THROUGH A SCREEN OF TREES. HER heartbeat quickened, and her skin tingled with awareness. *David.* Their connection swung wide open, her mind welcoming his without reservation. The energy of him flooded into her, stealing her breath. She stumbled.

Amador seized her arm, steadying her.

She jerked free of him. "Thanks. But remember, the only reason you're here is because I need backup in case Tesler's men find us." She tapped the grip of the handgun strapped to his belt. "You sure you've got the stomach for shooting somebody?"

He bristled. "Yes. If you can do it, so can I."

"It's not a contest. Shooting people is… unpleasant." Memories flashed through her mind, sharp and blinding, but she cast them aside. "If it comes down to us or them, I need to know you can do whatever it takes."

Amador nodded. "I can. I will."

His expression gave away nothing, and a thought flitted through her brain. *Maybe he likes hurting people.* He had tortured an innocent girl. Yet harming a helpless child was far different from firing on well-armed, well-trained muscle men. Would he cower in the face of real danger?

She'd let Amador tag along strictly because she realized he planned on trailing behind her if she rejected his offer to accompany her. Men. Psychotic or sane, they all had macho streaks laced with pigheadedness.

"Shall we continue?" Amador asked.

"Yes." She faced toward the clearing, and the cabin nestled on the opposite side. "When we get there, you do not speak or do anything unless I say so. Got it?"

"Of course." He grunted. "David will not be pleased to see me."

So naturally, Amador sounded smugly satisfied with himself for the future irritation he'd inflict on David.

Grace marched out into the clearing.

The cabin door banged open, the sound echoing off the trees. A figure rocketed outside, headed straight for them. Her heart pounded. Tears spilled down her cheeks.

She bolted toward David.

He swept her up into an embrace so tight it squeezed the breath out of her. She flung her arms around him, burying her face against his neck. Her feet dangled in midair, but she cared about nothing except losing herself in the feel of his hard, warm body. Life surged through his veins, down their psychic link, pouring into her. She sealed her mouth over his, thrusting her fingers into his hair while his hands stroked her back. She savored the spicy taste of him, the delicious friction of his mouth on hers, the unique and irresistible scent of him.

"Oh man," Sean hollered, "you guys need a room so bad."

His taunt barely registered through the fog of desire. David had kissed her hours ago, in her manifested form, but this...

No comparison.

He set her down. His flavor infused her mouth, and she licked her lips. Though she yearned for more, she sensed his mood had shifted.

His hands settled on her hips. "I'd like to finish that conversation we started yesterday."

"Oh, you mean when you tried to dump me?"

He shifted his gaze to the ground. His mouth twisted into a grimace. "Yes. I mean that conversation. You said it wasn't over, and I realized you were right."

"Great. Let's talk on the plane."

"No. We need to talk now. Alone. Please."

Ominous, she thought, but since Amador didn't need to hear her misgivings, she said, "Sure. Give me a minute, though, okay?" She nodded toward her companion. "I need to have a chat with Amador first."

David's mouth compressed. "Why?"

"Because I'm trusting him with our lives, and I need to make sure he knows how angry I'll be if he screws us over. His jet is our ride home."

"I've got a better idea." His lips quirked in a near smile. "Let's tie him up, steal his jet, and chuck him out over the mountains."

"Ha-ha." She skimmed her fingers over his cheek. "Trust me. I can handle Amador."

"Is that supposed to make me feel better?"

"No, it's a statement of fact." She prayed it was a fact and not a self-inflicted delusion. "Wait here."

She turned away from him.

A shiver of knowledge rattled through her.

She whirled on David, seized fistfuls of his shirt, and hauled him toward her. The force of her hold bent him over, his face inches from hers. His fear coursed into her, stronger now thanks to the physical contact. Her jaw trembled. Tears burned in her eyes, tightening her lids.

His face blanched. He knew she knew.

"I can feel it," she said, her voice strained and rough. "Your fear, your anger, your absolute conviction that you're about to do the right thing. Did you think you could hide it from me?"

"No." Emotion roughened his voice too, though his expression was unreadable. "No, I—that's why I wanted to talk to you alone. To explain."

"Explain what?" She tugged him closer. Spittle sprayed his face when she spoke. "That you're abandoning me?"

"I'm not. I wouldn't."

Anxiety rippled through her from all around, not just from David, but from their friends too. Everyone worried when Mom and Dad fought. And weird as it was, that's what she and David had become. The parents of this dysfunctional family.

She released his shirt. Dragged in a long breath. Straightened her blouse. Then she cleansed her face of all emotion and locked her gaze on David's, firing every shred of her anger and terror and adoration into him down their link. His eyes widened a hair, just enough to expose the fact her message had hit him, loud and clear.

"You're not coming with us," she said, careful to speak in a hushed tone, so no one else would hear. "You're staying, to fight Tesler."

"I have to." He matched her soft voice, his face as empty of feeling as hers must've been.

She wasn't calm, not on the inside, but it felt like someone had poured concrete over her to contain her emotions.

"Grace, I'm sorry. I have to stay."

"Okay then."

She tromped toward Amador. David's gaze tracked her, pinned to her back like a ray of concentrated sunlight heating her flesh. She focused on

Amador, and his self-satisfied expression. The bastard enjoyed seeing her and David argue.

"I need you to listen," she told Amador. "Agree with everything I say and mean it. Then I'm going to ask you a few questions, which you will answer without hesitation—and you'll tell me the truth." She barred her arms over her chest. "Do you understand?"

"Yes."

"Good. You're taking Sean and this other guy away from here on your plane. David and I are staying." He opened his mouth, but she raised one palm to silence him. "No questions, no arguments. I speak, you agree. Understand?"

"I do. And yes, of course, I will take your friends to a safe location. I know of one—"

"Uh-uh. You're taking them to my grandfather."

His brow arched. "Edward McLean?"

"He'll protect them." She recited her grandfather's cell number. He was at their backup location—their emergency hideout, an old farmhouse in Kansas, purchased under a false name with cash. Grandpa would take care of them, but he wouldn't trust Amador, a stranger. "Have Sean make the call and do whatever my grandfather says. Got it?"

He nodded. His lips moved as if he wanted to speak.

She dangled her arms at her sides, trying to look nonthreatening. If he needed to tell her something, she probably ought to hear it. "What is it?"

"You should know the entire story. About me." He ducked his head, shoulders quivering. "My wife. She couldn't handle Evander's death. She—" His words were choked off as he jerked his head up, his gaze intent on hers and gleaming with tears about to spill forth. Yet his voice emerged in a hardened tone. "She cut her wrists while I was away on business. After that I..." He clutched Grace's hands, lifting them to his face. His breaths flared over her skin. "I lost my mind, Grace, which I imagine is no surprise to you."

"It's not too late to come back from it."

"For me, I fear it is. Vengeance has eroded my soul."

Vengeance. She gulped back a swell of nausea. Amador was obsessed with the same goal as David—with the same target, Karl Tesler—and his compulsion had toppled him over the edge. If David couldn't relinquish his quest, would he tumble off the same cliff?

Amador and David were different men, with different temperaments. David could survive what had destroyed Amador.

The lunatic in question pressed the backs of her hands to his cheeks, shut his eyes, and sighed. A tear trickled down his face, oozing onto her skin. "I long to be as good as you, as strong and compassionate. But I'm weak." He nuzzled her palm. "Please try to understand. What I've done, I believed these were right things. You've shown me I was wrong."

"You need to understand something too." She took one step toward him, cupping his face in her hands, forcing him to meet her eyes. "I can help you, Biel, if you'll let me. You can reclaim your life."

He shook his head, pulling away from her hands. "No. I've gone too far. After my wife's death, I poured all my wealth and connections into hunting down Tesler. But when I found him, he took me prisoner simply to keep me from reporting what I had uncovered about him." He averted his gaze. "I stole files from the Siberian facility, and that's how I learned of you. I prayed your powers could bring Tesler's world crashing down on his head."

"They still might." She glanced over her shoulder at Sean, Nkosi, and David, whose gaze drilled into her though he watched without expression. Her attention glued to David, she told Amador, "Take Sean and Nkosi."

"You know the other man?"

"Huh?"

"Nkosi. You must know him, since you spoke his name, but he looks at you as if he's not met you before."

"I haven't met him."

"Then how do you know his name?"

The Golden Power. That was how she knew. Tiny blades dug into her heart, nicking and scraping at her soul. "Just do as I say. Please."

"You have my word." He fidgeted, his gaze darting left and right, up and down. Finally, he drew two objects out of his pocket and held his hand to her, palm up. "These may be of some use to you."

A glass vial rested on his palm. It contained pale-yellow liquid.

"The serum you gave me," she said.

"Yes."

She took the vial and poked the other object with her little finger. It looked like a pen with no writing tip and a little button on one end. "What's this?"

"An auto-injector. It holds the counteracting agent. There is a single dose left, and it will last fifteen minutes at most."

"Thanks." The serum might prove useful, somehow. She palmed the auto-injector along with the vial and slipped them into her pocket. "Time to go our separate ways."

"Where will you go?"

David's energy infused her, warm and sweet and spiced with desire. Every iota of her being called out to him. The barest smile curved her lips. "Where I belong."

Grace watched Nkosi and Sean stride off into the woods with Amador. Then she let David take her hand, leading her into the cabin. A fire crackled in the hearth. She inhaled the musty scent of dust and stale air, but the earthy aroma of burning wood overpowered the other smells. David tugged her toward the sofa, an overstuffed number with flower-print fabric. She sank into the cushions beside him.

He scooted away.

"What is wrong with you?" she asked. What if he said he couldn't stand the taint of the Golden Power that lingered in her? What would she do then? What could she do? Wringing her hands, she bit her lip and waited.

The distance between them measured in inches, but it gaped like a vast canyon. She swore she could hear her words echoing back to her. *Do not cry.* An emotion she couldn't puzzle out darkened his expression. She yearned to smooth the lines from his forehead with her fingertips, to brush away the tightening of his lips, to caress the tension out of his shoulders.

He slipped a hand over hers, his arm stretched across the gap between them. "It's not you, Grace. You're... perfect." He sucked in a ragged breath. "But I have to tell you the truth, and you won't like it. I don't expect forgiveness, I won't ask for it, but you need to know the truth."

His voice had quieted to a whisper, his tone bleak and fraught with pain. When he raised his chin, revealing his face, his expression unleashed a torrent of sympathy inside her. Never had she seen him so anguished, so defeated, so repentant. She lifted a hand, desperate to touch him, but pulled it back. Her hands trembled. She tried to rip her gaze away from his, but the connection between them imprisoned her. Their psychic link. It smoldered within them, between them.

His fingers tightened on hers. "You asked if it's true. If I killed someone."

Everything inside her froze. She stared at her fingers, at his laid atop them, at the creases of his knuckles. Oh God, oh God, she'd changed her mind. She did not want to know. David would not commit cold-blooded murder, but what if he'd been forced to kill in defense of himself or another? She could handle that. But what if Tesler had pumped David full of drugs and coerced him into murdering someone? *Suck it up and be here for him, like he's done for you.* Yeah, she could do that. She must do it.

David retracted his hand. In a voice devoid of emotion, he said, "It's true. I am a killer."

"I—"

He pressed two fingers to her lips. "Shhh. Let me finish."

She swallowed, nodded, and tried to smile but failed miserably.

"It was self-defense," he said, refusing to look at her. "Another traveler broke into my room and tried to coerce me into telling him who Janet Austen was. He thought if he found you, and delivered you to JT, then he'd be released unharmed." David withdrew his fingers. Stiff and impassive, he stared into the shadows past her shoulder. "He gave me no choice, tried to strangle me. I grabbed a lamp and hit him over the head. End of story."

She reached for his hand.

He yanked it away.

"David." She slumped against the sofa, deflated inside and out. "It wasn't your fault. Why would you push me away because of that? I don't get it."

"I was answering your question. But that's not the reason I…" He rubbed his hands on his pants as if struggling to cleanse them. "Listen to me. Amador was right. There is something I've done, something unforgivable."

"You don't know what I can forgive."

His eyes had gone glassy, his demeanor so remote she wondered if he'd dispatched his mind to another world. A psychic knew how to literally let his mind wander. She lifted a hand to touch him but drew it back. Foreboding weighed down on her so heavily that it immobilized her.

Then he turned his gaze on her, and she saw the yawning distance in his eyes, their color somehow faded. He spoke with a detachment that chilled her. "You've wanted to know how JT found you. Who told him your real name. Who's responsible for the torment he inflicted on you, and that Tesler wants to continue inflicting on you. You need to know who to blame, right?"

She hesitated. "Yes."

But she wasn't sure at all she wanted to know. Her skin crawled. Her throat went dry. She could not tear her gaze from his, though, or stop herself from hearing what he told her next.

"It was me. I told Tesler who you were and exactly where to find you." He shut his eyes for a second, then opened them again. "I betrayed you, Grace. I am responsible for the hell your life has become. All the people who died because they got in the way of JT capturing you, I'm the one who set him loose on them."

She shook her head, unable to comprehend.

His mouth twisted into a sad, sardonic smile. "Can you forgive me now?"

Chapter Twenty-One

DAVID CRINGED THE SECOND HE UTTERED THE WORDS. HE FLATTENED his hands on his thighs, then dropped them to the cushions and dug his nails into the padding. He couldn't breathe, didn't dare glance at her. Adrenaline pumped through his veins, electrifying his nerves, scouring away thoughts. The impulse to drag her into his arms swelled and crashed against his willpower. *Don't touch her, don't do it, let her process this.*

How could she process it? He'd just confessed to betraying her in the worst way and ruining her life. No one could forgive that.

Grace's hand crept across the sofa toward him, her fingers crawling ever nearer. When the tips bumped his hand, she slid her fingers over his skin. He tried to pull away, but she clamped her hand firmer around his. The warmth of her flesh leeched into his skin as her scent wafted over him, and the urge to plunge into her tempting mouth, to bury his pain and fear in her kiss, exploded inside him.

He would not do it. Not unless she gave him a sign she wanted the contact.

She was holding his hand. Wasn't that a sign? It might be pity, nothing more.

When she spoke, her tone was hushed. "I don't believe it. I will *never* believe it."

"You have to."

"No, I don't."

Her thumb caressed his palm, and he longed to accept her reassurance, but he couldn't. Her love pulsed down their connection, warm and gentle and fueled by empathy. A piece of her burrowed into him, overpowering the shame and guilt. He could not let her do this. He could not let her forgive him.

"Go on," she said. "Tell me everything."

Once she knew, she'd hate him. She must. He deserved it.

"I wasn't strong enough then," he told her. "I—I didn't expect what they did to me. The drugs made it hard to focus, and then they'd start in with the cutting and the beating. I could deal with pain, but the chemicals… They messed with my head. I fought as long as I could. It wasn't enough." He slung his head back against the sofa. A tightness in his throat roughened his voice. "I made a horrible mistake, and I wound up giving Tesler and JT exactly what they wanted. You."

Her hand went stiff, but only for an instant. She drew his hand to her chest and clasped it between her breasts while he focused on the carpeting, obsessed with a loop of loose thread.

She kissed his fingertips one by one.

He squeezed his eyes shut. She was so much stronger than he was, so much better, and he loved her with a passion he'd never known before. He would do anything to protect her. Well, not quite anything. Her parents had died to shield her from JT and Tesler. And what did he do? He cracked.

She nuzzled his hand, guiding his fingertips over her mouth. He felt his body lean toward her as his lids opened of their own volition and his head slid across the cushion, ever closer to her shoulder. God, he needed her touch, her kiss, her supple flesh. To lose himself in her. To scrub away the stain inside him. But it wasn't right. He couldn't accept comfort from her after what he'd done.

"It's okay," she said.

"No." He yanked his hand away, straightened, and riveted his gaze to the knob on the front door. "It will never be okay. I should've let them kill me. That's what I swore I'd do, to save you. But I was too damn weak."

A gust of wind buffeted the cabin. Wood creaked. A tree branch grated across one of the windows.

Grace wriggled her butt, jostling the cushions and him. "I don't understand. You've only been acting weird for a couple months. Before that, everything was good, relatively speaking."

"I must've repressed the memory. I had no idea until—" He sank his forehead into his palms. "Until I found the video. Irrefutable proof that I—"

"Wait a minute."

Her voice had taken on the suspicious, no-nonsense tone he knew so well. It usually made him smile. Tonight, he couldn't bear to hear it. Though he raised his head, he watched her peripherally.

She folded her arms over her breasts and studied him with squinted eyes. "The night I found you in the living room, staring at the computer like it was sucking the life out of you. That's when you stumbled onto this so-called evidence."

"It's not so-called. The video is ireffu—"

"Baloney. Videos can be doctored or faked altogether." She silenced his protest before he could voice it, by flashing him a sharp look. "Tell me exactly what you saw. I want the blow by blow."

"Grace."

"Don't *Grace* me. Describe the video, in detail, just the facts."

He heaved himself off the sofa, stalked to the window, and glared out at the darkness. "The file was damaged, I think. There was too much static at the beginning to see or hear what was happening. But then the picture cleared, and I saw... me. Strapped to the old dentist's chair. Tesler was hovering over me, the way he does, gloating about how he'd finally broken me. He thanked me for giving him Janet Austen." He squeezed his eyes shut, ducking his head. "He said JT would be very pleased with me."

He spat the last phrase, but the sourness of it coated his tongue.

From the rustling behind him, he knew she was getting up off the sofa. Her footfalls were light and quiet, almost imperceptible. Her arms encircled his chest, her warm, soft body flush against his back. Her cheek rested on his shoulder, her hair tickling the nape of his neck.

"You don't know what you saw," she murmured. "The file was corrupted, possibly tampered with. If you were drugged, Tesler might've been lying to trick you into exposing me."

"No one else knew your real name."

"Grandpa did."

"He wouldn't betray you."

She kissed his neck, her lips a delicate flutter on his skin. "Neither would you. There has to be another explanation. I will not accept that either one of you led JT to me."

The conviction in her tone buoyed him a little, for a heartbeat, or maybe two. He yearned to believe it.

She set her chin on his shoulder. "This is why you wanted the flash drive. To, what, delete the incriminating evidence?"

"I tried to delete it when I found the video. Didn't work. I'm not as good with computers as you are."

"Then why did you want the flash drive?"

"I don't know." His hands moved on their own to cover hers. "All of a sudden, getting the thing away from you seemed vitally important."

"Guilt makes you irrational. But you have nothing to feel guilty about. Understand?"

"The video—"

"Is crap." She entwined her fingers with his. "I know you. No matter what Tesler did, you wouldn't tell him squat. You'd die first."

He'd always assumed he would. The evidence suggested otherwise.

"Even if you did this," she said, her breaths hot on his skin, "I would understand. Tesler tortured you. Drugged you. I won't let you push me away because—"

"Stop." He wrestled out of her embrace and avoided her tender gaze. "Don't do it. Don't forgive me."

"Or what? You'll dump me again?" She made a soft sound, almost a laugh. "You tried that already. I'm not so easy to get rid of."

"I know." He should've walked out the door, but his feet seemed nailed to the floor. "You can't trust me anymore."

"Of course I can." She moved in front of him to take hold of his shirt and shake him. "Get this through your thick skull, David. I trust you. Whatever you think you've done, it changes nothing. I will never give up on us."

He stared at her, blank in mind and spirit, desperate to believe but unable to accept it.

"Never." She shook him harder. "Not even when we're dead."

"Don't talk about dying. If anything happened to you…"

She looped her arms around his neck, hands linked at his nape. Her fingers traced delicate circles on his scalp and ruffled his hair. His muscles relaxed, even as her body pressed into him. She splayed her fingers through his hair and gently urged him to slant his head toward hers. He obeyed, as always a slave to her tenderness.

Her hazel eyes were alive with passion, the emotional kind. It filtered into him through his pores from her skin, through his parted lips from her breaths that flavored his tongue. Sweet. Electric. More powerful than anything in the universe, it eclipsed even the Golden Power.

"I love you," she said. "No conditions. No qualifications. And I fight for what I love, fight with everything I've got until there's nothing left in me. You should know this by now. You know *me*."

He did. And that was what terrified him. Grace Powell would never give up because she loved him. Her passion flowed out of her whenever their eyes met, whenever their fingers brushed or their lips tasted each other. He'd struggled for so long to restrain his ardor, his devotion to her, his need to unite with her in every possible way. She owned his heart, his mind, and his soul.

At last, he understood what he must do. His mistake had been to shut her out in a vain attempt to divorce their minds and sever, or at least weaken, their connection. Why had he ever believed that would protect her? The solution was right in front of him, entwined with him, caressing him and gazing into his eyes with the gleam of pure love in those beautiful golden irises.

He hugged her tight. "I will never leave you again. We're in this together, until the end." He let his lips skim over hers, and the intoxicating sweetness of her teased his senses. "No more running. I'm with you, forever."

She smiled against his mouth. "I'm with you, David. Forever."

His feet, once rooted in place, lightened, along with the rest of him, until he was sure he must've floated up off the floor with her secure in his arms.

She canted her head, stroking her fingertips down his cheek. The movement of her head streaked firelight across her eyes, making the shadows beneath them stand out against her creamy skin.

He grasped her hands and pulled them down to his chest. "When did you last eat?"

Chewing her lip, she considered the question. "Not sure."

"Grace, 'not sure' is too long." He glanced around the cabin. "I wonder if there's any food around here."

"Bottled water and canned goods in the pantry." She nodded toward a doorway at the far side of the living room. "Through there."

"How..."

She hunched her shoulders. "Limitless knowledge."

Understanding bloomed in his mind and heart. The information she'd gained from the Golden Power persisted inside her.

Not for long. He knew how to save her from ever again having to tangle with the ultimate power source, and the answer was ridiculously simple.

All he had to do was love her.

With passion, purpose, and absolute conviction.

CHAPTER TWENTY-TWO

GRACE SAT AT THE KITCHEN TABLE IN A STRANGER'S HOUSE, WHICH she'd appropriated without permission, and scooped up the last forkful of baked beans purloined from the pantry. The rustle of pine needles on the roof, stirred by the wind, lulled her senses. The low purr of the cordless electric can opener lured her attention to the man busily liberating a second batch of canned peaches. *Her* man.

She couldn't recall thinking of him that way before, but tonight she embraced the term. Her man. He was hers, after all, bonded to her by a ring and a telepathic connection. And love. Deep, unfaltering love.

The beany scent wafting up from her fork made her wrinkle her nose. Her stomach protested at the idea of accepting more food, particularly beans. It wasn't a very romantic dinner, what with gas-inducing dishes and eating straight from the cans.

"I'm full," she said.

He half-turned to frown at her. "Fruit has electrolytes or something, stuff you need after overtaxing your powers and your body."

"I'm regular taxed, not over." She waggled her fork. "I'm finishing the beans, and that's it. I'll barf if you make me eat any more peaches."

"Gr—" He'd been about to *Grace* her, but thought better of it. *Smart man.* Instead, he set down the can opener and plucked up a peach slice. Juice dribbled onto the counter. He tossed the slice into his mouth, chewing with vigor.

She wrinkled her nose again when he tipped the can toward her.

One corner of his mouth dimpled downward.

He was anxious, she realized then. About her health and their relationship. About their inevitable confrontation with Tesler. About the future, if they lived long enough to have one.

So she rolled her eyes, shoved the beans in her mouth, and forked a peach slice.

David turned away, absorbed by the task of replacing the can opener precisely where he'd found it, in a holder affixed to the wall. His actions afforded her the chance to admire him in secret. With his back to her, he didn't know she was ogling his tight ass, the way his muscles rippled under his weekend-warrior outfit. Damn, he looked hot in camo.

Done with the can opener, he nabbed a container of disinfectant wipes and set about cleaning up the juice he'd drizzled on the counter.

She thrust the peach slice into her mouth and munched with more ferocity than necessary. The crisp efficiency of his movements as he swept a soft, damp cloth over the smooth counter awakened her body more than she would've expected. She was exhausted. But suddenly, her skin tingled with anticipation and she squeezed her thighs together to squelch a dull throb in her most intimate places.

Oh, to be that countertop, bathed by his deft hands.

Grace averted her eyes to her plate and chewed harder. The owner of this cabin clearly adored beans—the pantry was stocked full of them—as well as canned corn, sliced peaches, and ravioli. Her first meal in more hours than her weary brain could calculate consisted of these items. David had insisted she eat all of it, and just to be more stubborn, he gobbled up his own servings of the odd feast.

She hadn't wanted to eat anything, despite the grumbling in her stomach. Questions battered her mind. How long would her confusion tactics deter Tesler? Was the facility still in the dark, or had her permanent disabling of their systems turned out to be not so permanent? Had Tesler already dispatched commandos to hunt them? What could she and David do to save themselves?

Run. That was their sole option.

Swallowing her food, she dropped her fork onto the table with a clack. They couldn't run. Tesler would hunt them wherever they hid. This ended one way—with a battle, bloodshed, pain, and death.

They must ensure the death was Tesler's.

David snatched up her fork and the empty can of beans, pecked a kiss on her forehead, and strode back to the counter. Damp cloth. Strong hands. Swirling motions of his powerful fingers.

He tossed the used wipes in the trash and took a seat opposite her, one arm draped on the table, one ankle braced atop the other knee. A slight smile relaxed his mouth, and his entire expression. Since his pronouncement he would never leave her again, his demeanor had altered so much her head spun from the shock of it. Tense, distant David morphed into relaxed, determined David. It was like he'd reached some important decision.

His anxiety hadn't completely fled. He'd needed to clean up, after all. But otherwise, he was... different.

Maybe this was the man he'd been before, during those months she still couldn't remember. Whatever the reason for his change, it did things to her. Subtle, sensual things.

He stretched his hand out to lace his fingers with hers.

She had to test this, to make sure he wasn't glossing over his issues for her benefit. The heat of his hand spread into her, though, melting away doubt.

Dammit. She snapped her spine straight and zeroed her gaze in on his, on those gleaming blue eyes. "Do you still believe you betrayed me?"

He flinched, just a tad. His fingers loosened their grip on hers, only for a second, then clinched her tighter. "I did, Grace. We both have to accept it."

She let out a long sigh. "No, David, I'm not convinced we do. I think I can prove whether the video is accurate."

"How? There's no computer here. You can't access the flash drive." His gaze flew to her breasts, right where the device in question lay nestled between them. His lips curved into a hungry slant.

Desire thrummed inside her.

Snap out of it. Her self-admonishment broke the spell, and the idea she'd hatched a little while ago resurfaced in her hormone-drenched brain. "Amador mentioned a power called postcognition. According to him, some people can view past events as if they were there at the time it happened. Kind of like psychic time travel."

His lips pursed. His fingers dug into her palm. "You and Amador have gotten close, I gather."

The acid in his tone burned her, but she wouldn't relent this time. "I barely know him, and no, I do not trust him." She wrapped his hand in both of hers. "This might not work. I mean, for all I know, Amador's full of shit."

David snorted.

She pinched his hand, rewarded by his playful smile. "I'm going to try it. Postcognition."

One of his brows lifted. "Do you have any idea how it works?"

"No. Do you?"

He shook his head. "First I've heard of it."

She shrugged. "I didn't know how to use the Golden Power either, but I did." She leaned forward, her grip on his hand firm. "If the video is real, and you did this, it wasn't your fault. Nothing changes between us. But if you didn't do it, don't you want to know?"

He rubbed his neck and shifted in his seat, grimacing. She massaged the back of his hand with her thumb. When she was about to speak, to reassure him, he abruptly bent forward and his expression switched back into relaxed assurance, as if he'd reaffirmed his mysterious decision.

"All right," he said. "Do it."

"Close your eyes and remember the video."

One corner of his mouth lifted. "Thought you had no idea how to do this."

"I don't, but I have a plan." She gave his hand a light slap. "Shut up and do what I say."

"Yes, ma'am." With his free hand, he saluted her.

She restrained a grin, stifled a laugh, and forced herself to concentrate on the task ahead.

David closed his eyes.

Grace raised her hands before her as if praying, with his hand sandwiched between them. "Try not to freak out at what I'm going to do. Okay?"

"I don't freak out." He cracked one eyelid to peek at her. "I can handle whatever you can."

"This is not a test of your machismo." She rested her chin on their joined hands, her lips grazing his knuckles. "I'm about to throw open the floodgates."

"What are you talking about?"

"Between our minds. I'm going to open the psychic floodgates. I don't know what will happen."

His eyes locked on her with unnerving intensity. "You think I'm holding back with you."

"Aren't you?"

He wiggled his fingers to tickle her lips. "Not anymore."

Something in his tone convinced her he meant it, which shot a bolt of heat lightning through her entire body. David unbridled? She couldn't remember a time when he didn't hold back. Hell, she couldn't remember a time when *she* didn't either.

His jewel eyes glimmered from inside, with the secret fire only a traveler sustained. He was unleashing his powers even now. The tendrils licked at her psyche in an almost sensual way.

"Go ahead," he told her, in a husky tone. "My mind is yours."

Somehow, he turned the statement into an erotic challenge.

He shut his eyes, his expression serene, and spoke in a calm voice. "Whatever you do, Grace, make sure you keep that firewall up."

"Okay." Suddenly, her heart was pounding. She drew in several deep breaths to steady herself, closed her eyes, and knocked down the barriers shielding her mind, her soul, from him—though she kept the firewall intact. These were private floodgates in a channel connecting the two of them, and no one else. Her psychic intruder couldn't sneak in, she knew it, without understanding how she knew. The truth of it resonated inside her.

The essence of David flowed in as she poured all of herself back into him. No hiding anymore. If he could let loose, in mind and spirit, then so could she. Part of her had longed for this, dreamed of it even, the day when they might come together without fears or doubts. This was it.

Their link unfurled, an iridescent thread of blue in the darkness. She took hold and let it draw her in, to a place buried deep in his memory.

Static. Voices.

Pain bit down on her. She wrestled free of it, undeterred from her goal. *Help me see, David.*

White light exploded around her. She tumbled headlong into the brilliance, toward the voices and the static. Without warning, she burst out into the world.

Into the past.

David LIES IN A CHAIR, STRAPPED DOWN, SLUMPED, EYES OPEN BUT vacant. The drugs have immobilized him, in body and mind. A bruise, dark purple and blue, covers one entire forearm, and blood trickles from a gash on his head. She senses him there, but too weak to form coherent thoughts. When she reaches out to his mind, her powers bounce back from it. This is the past. She can't communicate with him.

Yet even here, their connection binds them. It's how she's found him. David in the present guided her. David in the past anchors her.

Tesler slouches a few feet from the chair, at David's feet. He holds a syringe in one hand, turning it over and over between his fingers. The syringe is empty. He stares at David, his expression cool, detached.

Behind him, another man waits. He touches his face, eyes wide. "Dr. Tesler? Is he..."

"Alive." Tesler's tone is cool too. "Though perhaps I should terminate him. He's of no use to me anymore."

"Terminate?" The other man pushes up his glasses, clearing his throat. "Uh, is that really necessary?"

Tesler whirls on his colleague. His lip curls as he spits words. "It is if I say so."

"Yes, Dr. Tesler."

"Perhaps he can still be of some use..." Tesler glances over his shoulder at David, who blinks slowly, his jaw slack.

Tesler marches past his colleague, and with a flick of his hand, orders the other man to follow him. She follows too, a ghost in this event. Tesler storms out into the corridor, down the passage, to another door marked as an excursion suite. He flings the door inward. It bangs into the wall.

Inside the room, a startled technician jerks his head up to gape at Tesler. "Sir—"

"Has he told you anything yet?" Tesler says as he barges into the room.

"Nothing, sir."

She freezes. God in heaven.

There, bound to a chair, sits Sean. He's weeping, sobbing, his face streaked with blood that runs from wounds hidden by his hair. Raw, red burns blister his arms.

Detached. She must remain detached. This happened last year. It's horrible, but it's over, and Sean is fine now. She just saw him, walking off with Amador and Nkosi.

She must stay focused.

"What about Ransom?" the tech asks.

Tesler hurls the empty syringe into the wall. "He's with her now, I know it. Yet he resists all my attempts to wring the information out of him. I gave him a stimulant to pull him back from the excursion, but he resists that too." Tesler cocks his head, focusing in on Sean. "Perhaps this mewling mutant can be of assistance."

David is traveling. That's why she sensed a vacancy in him, what she mistook for an effect of the drugs.

He's with her, the her from this moment in time.

Tesler waves the tech away and turns to his colleague. "Get me the serum, Yellen."

The other man shoves his hands in the pockets of his lab coat. "Which serum?"

"The only one there is!" Tesler snarls. "Fetch me Jackson Tennant's personal formula."

"But we're not supposed to use that anymore."

"Bring it here!" Tesler's voice booms off the walls, a deafening assault on her astral eardrums. "And spice it up with a bit of thiopental sodium."

Truth serum? Of course. To encourage Sean to cooperate. The monster thought of everything.

Yellen trots out of the room.

Tesler moves to stand beside Sean. He rests his hands on the chair's arm, no more than an inch from the kid's arm. His gaze drops to the floor, his brows gathered tight.

Head bowed, he speaks in a hushed voice. "She loved you."

Sean is too lost in his agony and terror to hear, to comprehend. Tears sting her eyes just watching his features contort with each sob.

Tesler's hand floats up, toward Sean's face.

He yanks it away. Lips drawn in a pucker, he scowls at Sean. "I did love her once. You may not believe it, but I did. So very much. I wish this could be another way..." He steps back, squares his shoulders, and the icy expression overtakes him again. His voice is equally chilled. "But there is no other way to deal with your kind. I need Janet Austen, and you will give her to me."

Footsteps clap in the corridor.

Yellen scampers into the room and hands Tesler a syringe. "The serum, sir."

Tesler snatches the syringe from Yellen's fingers and lowers it to Sean's arm. He hesitates, his brows pinched again.

With an annoyed sigh, he stabs the needle into Sean's arm, depressing the plunger.

The kid flinches, but tears choke his voice. Sean convulses. His eyes bulge. He sucks in one wheezing breath, then his body slumps in the chair. His eyelids flutter, and his face settles into a dazed look.

Tesler bends near Sean's face. "Now, track David Ransom."

"Can't..." Sean's voice is slightly slurred. "Not my power."

"I just gave you more power than a weakling like you deserves. Track David Ransom."

Sean moans.

Tesler slaps him across the face.

The kid jerks.

"Do it," Tesler hisses. "That's an order."

She feels the shift as Sean departs his body, like a change in a ship's ballast. He's gone for minutes, and all she can do is glare at Tesler. She itches to slug him, throttle him, strap him to an evil dentist chair and pump mind-scorching drugs into his veins.

Sean rouses, his head rolling from side to side. His glassy eyes gaze toward the ceiling.

Tesler grabs the kid's chin and wrenches his head. "Who is she?"

Sean clamps his teeth shut.

"You. Will. Tell. Me." Tesler smacks Sean so hard that his head snaps back and his mouth pops open. "Who is Janet Austen?"

"She... ahhh..."

"Tell me!" Tesler seizes Sean's shoulders and rattles him viciously.

His jaw quivers as tears stream down his cheeks. She sees him battling the drugs, but he can't break free of them. A sharp sob racks him. "Grace Powell."

A sickening grin splits Tesler's mouth. His eyes sparkle with dark glee. To Yellen, he says, "Make sure the boy remembers nothing."

The other man nods.

Tesler sprints out of the room. She flies after him, unbound by physical laws, a spirit in pursuit of a madman. Tesler races into the room where David still sits tied to the chair, though now his eyes are open, if bleary. He glances around as if he doesn't recognize the surroundings.

Tesler stops in front of him and claps his hands. "You, dear boy, have given me exactly what I wanted." Bouncing on his toes, he inclines toward David. "I broke you at last. JT will be quite pleased with this development—and with you, for finally acquiescing."

David stares blankly at Tesler.

The scientist plants his hands on the chair's arms and bends over David, their eyes level. "You gave her to me. Grace Powell is ours."

David shakes his head, slowly at first, then with ever-increasing ferocity. His hands grip the chair with such tension they tremble. He stills his head, and for a moment, his face becomes a stony mask. Then his jaw clenches, muscles twitching, and he sears Tesler with a look of pure hatred.

Tesler rises and casually places one hand in his pocket. "After all your suffering to protect her, you are the one who handed her to us. Waldron is already on his way to her. Thank you, David. JT's plan was floundering, but you saved it."

She feels the moment David gives up. Mechanisms click and whir in his psyche, realigning memories, altering perception. He chooses to forget, and this event recedes into the safe little box his mind manufactures for it.

Tesler begins to hum a cheerful tune and, spinning on his heels, prances out of the room.

David's head droops.

She knows. She understands. This is how they found her.

And this is the true torture inflicted on David.

Tesler will pay. She'll throttle him with her own hands, wring his filthy neck until his eyes pop out of his skull.

He must die.

Chapter Twenty-Three

AVID'S BACK ACHED FROM HOLDING THIS POSITION—BENT FORWARD, arm outstretched, one hand on the far side of the table—but he did not budge. Not one of his limbs would move an inch until she came back to him.

Her eyes flitted behind her closed lids. REM sleep? No, she wasn't asleep. Her mind had disconnected from her body to travel not elsewhere, but else*when*. Was it even possible? He disbelieved anything Amador told her, and yet…

There was still too much he didn't know about psychic faculties. Especially with Grace. She'd resurrected him from death, for pity's sake. *Death.*

Sean had been right. Her use of healing was different this time. Everything about her powers had altered, escalated, mutated. He winced at his own thought. Mutated? Grace was no sideshow freak. She was beautiful, sweet, intelligent, compassionate, and powerful beyond comprehension.

Did he fear her?

Never. He might worry about the changes in her psychic makeup, but he would never, could never, fear her.

His arm cramped. He bit down on the pain and held still.

Grace muttered, her words indecipherable. Her eyes popped open.

David nearly collapsed from relief. The tension slackened out of him.

A grim, knowing smile stretched her lips. She clutched his hand to her chest as if his flesh moored her mind to the present. He watched her, careful to conceal his abject relief and enduring concern.

"You're back," he said, his tone guarded. "Everything okay?"

"Fine. How long was I gone?" She sounded calm, unfazed.

He didn't believe it for one second.

With his arm pinned to her, he could shrug only one shoulder. "You were gone a minute or two, I guess."

"You didn't experience it with me?"

"No."

She kissed his fingers, one by one. "I saw what really happened."

He ducked his head, shoulders flagging. Once, he would've sacrificed anything to know the truth, but now he wanted to slap his hands over his ears and pretend none of this mattered. Except it did. If he had endangered her, and he saw no other explanation for the video, then how could she trust him? She might've sworn it made no difference, but that was before she traveled back in time to uncover the facts. After witnessing the event in person...

"David, look at me." She waited until he complied, and though he ironed his expression into a placid sheet, he feared his eyes disclosed his sorrow. She rested her chin on his knuckles. "Listen to me. Tesler tried to convince you after the fact that you gave him my name. But it's a lie. The leak didn't come from you. No matter how hard he pushed, you refused to give me up."

Speech, movement, thought, he'd lost his mastery of all those things. So he huddled in silence, unwilling to look away from her, unable to respond.

"It wasn't you, David. That's what matters."

He narrowed his gaze on her. "Who was it? Who exposed you?"

She gave him that world-weary smile again. His fury, contained on the physical plane, must've bristled her metaphysical senses, but she simply pressed his hand to her cheek.

He ground his teeth. "I want to know. I demand to know."

She let go of his hand.

No anger? She hated it when he ordered her to do anything, which he rarely bothered to do because she ignored his commands, anyway. For her to make no snide retort, it set his gut to churning.

He fisted both hands on the tabletop. "Tell me."

"You may think you want to know," she said, "but it won't make you feel any better. For once, let something go. Let this go."

He pounded his fists on the wood. "Whoever it is, I'm going to track them down and punish—"

"It was Sean."

The statement doused his fury in a heartbeat, and ice rushed down his veins in its wake. He jerked backward, making his chair rock. The front legs thumped down again.

"Tesler made him do it," she said. "He gave Sean JT's formula, plus truth serum. Then he ordered him to find you because he was sure you'd come to me. The trick worked. Sean learned who I am, and he couldn't help spilling the news to Tesler. The poor kid was drugged out of his head."

David propped his elbows on the table and dropped his head into his hands. "I know what that's like. They gave me JT's wonder serum once. It's like having hydrochloric acid injected into your veins, and then the world turns into a fun house and your powers get amped up so high it's unbearable. Feels like your skin's peeling off, your brain's dissolving, and at the same time, you can do anything. There's a compulsion to do more, more, more. But it rips you apart from the inside out."

Dammit, why Sean? Why did Tesler have to drag a teenage boy into this nightmare?

It's my fault. And yes, it was. If he'd cracked, then Tesler would've left Sean alone. He wished he could claim he would've done things differently if given the chance, but he knew that was a lie. To protect Grace, he would sacrifice anything, anyone.

Once, he might've thought that made him a monster, like Tesler. No more. The woman he loved, his only family in this world, should come before everything else, even his friends, the world, his own life. His one regret was that it took him so damn long to figure that out.

He raised his head a little to peer at her from between his fingers. His hands muffled his voice. "We can't tell Sean."

"I know." She rubbed her arms.

"You're cold." He jumped up from the chair and held out his hand. "Come on. We need to get you back by the fire."

Without protest, she accepted his hand and allowed him to shepherd her to the living room, to the sofa he'd angled toward the fireplace earlier. At his behest, she plopped down on the cushions. He settled in beside her, one arm across the sofa's back, behind her shoulders. She rested her head in the crook of his shoulder.

The familiarity, the intimacy, of the action and the moment uncoiled a spring deep inside him, relieving a pressure he'd lived with for far too long. The pressure of a secret. The horror of what he believed he'd done. Grace proved he hadn't betrayed her. Though he worried for Sean, the boy seemed unaware of his actions. Ignorance really could be, well, if not bliss then at least a kind of sanctuary.

Grace's head sprang up. Her eyes flew wide, and her mouth slipped open.

He turned her face toward him and searched her eyes for some clue. Their pale-brown depths revealed nothing. "What's wrong? Are you feeling sick?"

"No." She leaned into his touch. "It's not me I'm worried about."

"Tell me. Please.'

"It's Sean." She shut her eyes. "I think he's Tesler's grandson."

———

G RACE SHIMMIED AWAY FROM DAVID. SHE PERCHED ON THE SOFA'S edge, hands gripping the cushions, and fought the urge to look at him.

"I'm sorry," she said. "It's awful, but it makes sense."

While cocooned in David's arms, her thoughts had wandered back to her postcognition experience. Something Tesler had said bothered her. She'd replayed the incident as best she could with her mind so worn out. After Tesler went to Sean, he complained about David resisting his efforts to control him. Then he decided to use Sean instead, and he referred to Sean by an insulting term instead of his name.

"Tesler called Sean a mewling mutant," she explained to David. "I suddenly remembered that, and then I remembered where I'd heard the term before."

David huffed. "Tesler thinks all psychics are scum."

"Shut up and listen." She risked a glance then, and his wry smile pinched her heart. "Sorry. But please, let me finish."

One arm on the sofa's back, his posture relaxed and casual, he looked like a normal guy having a normal conversation with his normal fiancée. If only.

"In the files on Amador's DVD," she said, "I read a report written by Tesler. He mentioned a boy, his grandson, who he would not acknowledge because the kid had psychic abilities. He called his grandson a mewling mutant."

"That doesn't mean anything."

"I think it does." She straightened her spine and rotated toward him, her body twisted at the hips. "Tesler has freckles, like Sean. His hair's gray these days, but it might've been red once, like Sean's. During my postcognition episode, Tesler seemed almost regretful about the need to torture Sean with JT's formula. Then he said the strangest thing."

David's brows rose, then scrunched together. "What did he say?"

"He told Sean, 'She loved you.' And later, 'I loved her once.' I think he was talking about his daughter, Sean's mother."

Much as she'd flailed for another explanation, the facts had bobbed up from the depths over and over, like apples in a barrel of water. Poisoned apples.

"I'm not saying Sean is in league with Tesler," she told David, "at least not willingly. But Amador says Tesler wants to create an army of psychics he can control. Maybe Sean was his first test subject."

"You think he's brainwashed." His tone was flat, and he remained perfectly motionless. Though he'd clamped down on his emotions, threads of them tantalized her mind. He was silent for a few seconds, then he said, "I can't swear he's not. All those months at the Mojave Desert facility, it wasn't Tesler who worked Sean over. It was always his underlings. And lately, I have seen Tesler go easy on Sean, though I didn't understand what I was seeing at first. After what you've told me... I think Tesler might care about Sean, in his own twisted way."

"He didn't torture Sean, did he? When he—" The memory strangled her voice, but she cleared her throat and forged ahead. "When he killed you. He could've hurt Sean to make him talk, but he didn't. I think, on some level, Tesler regrets forcing Sean to out me."

"You may be right. But if Sean is brainwashed, there's nothing we can do about that right now." He leaned forward, his head close to hers. He pressed his warm, strong hand to her back and roamed it over her flesh, separated from his by only the cloth of her shirt. "I want to talk about you. Ever since you showed up here, you've been distant."

"I threw myself into your arms. That's not distant."

His fingertips splayed over her shoulder. "We can feel each other, re-member? Even with your firewall, I can tell when something's wrong. You're uneasy, about more than Tesler and how we're going to stop him."

She cocked her head. "We? I thought this was your lone-wolf quest for vengeance."

"I shouldn't have let you keep thinking my missions were about revenge. I was afraid to tell you the truth when I thought I'd betrayed you. I was a selfish prick."

"David, you don't have to explain. After seeing what Tesler did to you and Sean, I understand why you're hell-bent on destroying him."

"No. You don't." With both hands, he grasped her upper arms, and his thumbs massaged in slow, delicate strokes. His voice was quiet and fervent. "This was never about my vengeance. It's always been about you. Pro-tecting you from Tesler. Making sure he can't get his hands on you and turn you into his test subject. I could not stand by and let you be tortured, or worse." He dragged her into his chest, his grip firm, his expression deter-mined and heated. His lips grazed hers with each syllable he spoke. "I would rather die than lose you."

His hot mouth slanted over hers. Hard. Hungry. She tried to catch her breath, but his lips devoured the air.

When he tore his mouth away from hers, he stared straight into her eyes. "Can't you understand? Everything is about you."

The quest for Tesler. Leaving her for days at a time. Risking his life to track down the new facility. He'd done it all for her. He had died for her.

She shut her eyes and rested her cheek against his. Life heated his flesh. The spicy male scent of him surrounded her. She ran her palms up and down his chest, her breasts skimming his muscles with each shift of her arms. Alive. He was *alive*.

Death couldn't keep her from him. Nothing could.

Her lips trembled against his cheek. "Don't die for me anymore. Live for me. Live *with* me. Stay with me."

"There's nothing I want more."

Cheek to cheek, they held still in silence. The fire crackled. The wind buffeted the cabin, creaking its frame.

"Tell me the rest," he said.

"I don't know what you mean."

He took hold of her hair and gently tugged it until her head fell back and their gazes intersected. "Tell me what you're afraid of. And don't say

Tesler. I know there's more." His fingers combed through her hair, his touch light and stimulating. "I won't hold back anymore with you. So do the same for me. Let me in, Grace."

Yes, she did hold back. How could she not?

After criticizing him for keeping her at a distance, now she was pushing him away. And pulling him in closer. Push, pull. Push, pull. No wonder he was frustrated with her, but if he knew... If she revealed all...

The truth didn't matter anymore. She understood what must be done. He'd wanted to save her, but the time had come for her to save him. Again.

He'd hate it. Well, screw his male pride. She'd save his ass a thousand times and never apologize for it.

"Listen to me, David." She bracketed his face with her hands. "You were right all along. Tesler must be stopped, for good this time, and the whole network of facilities has to be shut down. But you can't do that. Only I can."

His hand in her hair froze.

"I have to do this," she said. "I'll tap into the Golden Power and destroy this facility, destroy the remnants of JT's empire and every scrap of Tesler's research."

"No, Grace. I won't let you."

She skated her lips over his, aching for a deep, wanton kiss that would erase her fears and doubts. This wasn't the time for it. If she gave in to the need, she might never stop. "Only I can do this. You have to leave me here, go someplace safe. Promise me you will."

"I won't leave." His fingers tightened on her scalp. "You wouldn't leave me here. Don't expect me to do it to you."

Tears pooled in her eyes, hot and stinging. "David, please, do this for me. I don't want you to see me like that again."

He squinted at her, the expression etching faint lines around his eyes. "Like what?"

"The—the Golden Power. What it did to me last time, when I broke you out of the facility." She bowed her head, and his hand slid down her neck. "Please, I'm begging you, go. This time will be worse. This time, the Golden Power will take me." It had tried before, when she'd gathered the energy necessary to build her psychic firewall. When she accessed the Golden Power again, to save David, it nearly consumed her. "I can't fight it anymore, David. I can't come back from it."

"Yes, you can. You will. I won't let it have you."

The determination in his tone broke the dam, and tears flooded out of her on hiccupping sobs.

He pulled her onto his lap, rocking her in his powerful, tender arms, enveloping her in his heat and strength. She sagged into him, her face buried against his neck. A chill had seeped into her the more she considered what she must do, but his body cradling hers eradicated the cold. His warmth suffused her from her skin down to the core of her being as their link swung wide open, funneling all his love and need into her, heightening her desires until she knew nothing but him, with her, around her, in her soul.

The tears dried up, and a spark ignited, kindling a fire deep inside.

She skated a hand up to his shoulder. "Let me go, David. I have to do this."

"No." He drew her tighter against him, his embrace unrelenting. His chest rose and fell against her breasts. "You don't have to do it alone. And you don't need the Golden Power."

"But a piece of it is still inside me. I can't get rid of it."

He stroked her arm in lazy, provocative circles. "I believe you about Tesler's plans. Earlier, when you broadened our link, I felt the truth of what you said and I felt the Golden Power too, but it's weak. We can sever it from you. Permanently."

"What do you mean 'we'?"

His hand on her arm stilled. He hooked a finger under her chin and, with delicate pressure, persuaded her to lift her head. She moved her hand off his shoulder, up to his neck, and dipped her fingertips into his silky hair. His eyes seemed to glow with an inner fire. She longed to dive into the blaze.

Lightning split the darkness. Thunder shattered the stillness, vibrating the walls and floor.

She jumped and yelped.

David just sat there, unmoving, as if the bomb-like boom hadn't registered in his brain. David the warrior angel. Always calm, always in control. Once it had bothered her, a little, but tonight she gleaned strength from his calm. Besides, he'd exposed his fears to her and shared a part of himself no one else saw. Here, in this moment, she adored the warrior in him.

He rubbed his thumb over her lips. "We can do this together, Grace. Expunge the Golden Power from you and defeat Tesler."

"How?"

"Join our powers."

Chapter Twenty-Four

GRACE FELT HER JAW DROP A SMIDGEN AS SHE GAZED AT DAVID, dumbfounded by his suggestion. Yet liquid heat burgeoned inside her, sizzling in her veins and warming her from the inside out. "Join our powers?"

"Yes." David slipped his thumb between her lips and teeth to tease her tongue. The salty flavor of his skin shot a bolt of desire through her, but she marshaled all her self-control to focus on his words as he said, "I don't know exactly how it'll work, or if we can reverse it. I'm willing to take the risk."

"But I'm tainted. The Golden Power—"

"Is not controlling you." He thrust his hand into her hair, tipping her head back, and lowered his mouth enticingly close to hers. "You are the best person I've ever known. Nothing can corrupt you. Trust me on this, I know you better than anyone, better than I know myself. You are a part of me, Grace, in a way no other human being could possibly understand." His lips claimed hers, stoking her passion to such fiery heights that her head spun. When he withdrew, his mouth lingered a hair's breadth from hers. "Be with me forever. Join your powers with mine, bond with me on the metaphysical plane, give in to what we've both wanted since the day we met."

Breathless, she couldn't wrench her gaze away from his.

He combed his fingers through her hair, trailing them over her scalp. "Each other. Nothing else. That's what we both want. I won't hold back from you anymore, and I will make you my only priority. Will you join with me?"

"Yes." She traced her fingers over the muscles of his chest. "I want you, only you, in every way."

His lips tightened against hers, parted by a smile that crinkled the skin around his eyes. Joy swelled in her heart, and passion blazed deep within. His eyes glittered with love and hunger and a joy rivaling hers. It was hers, in a way. Their bond already blended their emotions. To deepen the connection, to merge her psychic energy with his…

Oh God, it would be incredible.

And yet, doubt pecked at her. Weak at first, but stronger and stronger the more she contemplated their joining. A lump in her throat impeded the words she needed to say, but she shoved them out anyway. "Do you think I've changed? Since the amnesia, I mean."

"You are different."

She nodded and wiped at the damn tears welling in her eyes. *Different.* His words provoked an ache in her chest.

Lightning flashed once, twice, three times. Rolling booms rattled the windows. Hail bombarded the roof, rumbling like a stampeding herd of cattle.

David flattened her palm over his heart. "Being different isn't bad."

"Oh, thanks. I feel all better." She winced, realizing she'd retreated into the fortress of sarcasm again. "I'm sorry."

"For what?"

"Being sarcastic. I know you hate that."

"I don't hate it. Never did." He cupped her cheek in his hand. "But I don't want you to hide behind sarcasm because you're afraid to tell me how you really feel."

His eyes blazed even brighter somehow, like pools of sapphire flame. His inner warmth flowed into her, igniting a new fire that dissolved the cold ball of fear and anger lodged in her heart. Everything inside her melted, from her muscles right down to her soul, and her body quivered with need. She craved him with an intensity that should've terrified her. But it didn't. Not anymore.

"What if," she said, "I've changed too much and I can't remember what we had before. You might get sick of it and leave me."

He grasped her waist and eased her over to straddle his lap. His hands glided up her back and tugged her into him. "One, I asked you to marry me. Two, I'm asking you to join with me on a metaphysical level. What about those two proposals makes you think I have any desire to leave you?"

"Nothing, I guess." She squirmed, suddenly aware of his hard body underneath her. Two needs warred within her—the urge to rip his shirt off, and the panicked impulse to run. "I'm poisoned by the Golden Power. How can you still want me?"

"You're not poisoned." He pulled her closer, her breasts mashed against his chest. The taut peaks tingled, and she burned to tear off her bra to relieve the delicious pressure. "I want you for the same reasons I always have. You're wonderful, beautiful, sexy as hell, and I love you more than life itself."

"Oh. Is that all?" A giggle bubbled out of her. "I, um, think you've gotten me drunk."

He smirked. "On what?"

"You. I mean, your psychic energy and, well, other things." His hunger for her crashed into her again and again, an exquisite torment. "I can feel your passion."

She gulped in air but couldn't get enough.

His smirk broke into a sexy grin, and he chuckled. "I told you I'm not holding back anymore. And I can feel your passion too." His hands drifted up to her shoulders, and his voice roughened. "What should we do about that?"

The weight of her ardor bore down on her, shortening her breaths, flaming over her skin. His eyes transfixed her until she felt herself spiraling down into their depths, but instead of recoiling, she reveled in the sensation. *Join with me*, he'd offered. And oh, did she want to.

His lips explored hers tenderly, savoring her taste just as she savored his. Her body yielded to the ravenous fire, and everything else in the universe vanished from her perception as they plunged into a pocket world of their own.

David scooped her up and carried her into the bedroom. With one flick of his wrist, he whisked aside the plastic sheet covering the bed. It crumpled to the floor. He swept back the quilt, revealing silky, cream-colored sheets.

She ripped her gaze away from his just long enough to take in the hungry slant of his lips. There was no one else for her, only this gorgeous, passionate, courageous man who stood by her no matter what. She'd already gifted him with her heart. Tonight, she would relinquish all of herself to him.

He peeled her clothes off layer by layer, caressing and kissing every inch of her before tearing off his own clothes. When he laid her down on the mattress, his body hovering over her, she raked her fingers up and down his muscled chest, around to his back, dancing her fingertips up the ridge of his spine. He ducked his head close to hers and murmured two words that ignited a bonfire inside her.

"Be mine."

She was his forever, willingly, in every way imaginable.

He claimed her body then, writhing with her, their moans as entangled as their bodies, every breath a promise and every movement a fulfillment. She arched into him, and he cradled her with one arm, stroking and kneading, driving her wild and yet soothing her fears, chasing out the remnants of the Golden Power, leaving nothing behind but the sweetness and power of their minds and bodies united. The pleasure broke over her in wave after exquisite wave, drowned her yet awakened her, scoured out shame and filled her to bursting with a rapturous love. She clung to him until the last swell engulfed her and his own release pulsed within her.

Joined. At last. Hers forever.

The ecstasy of that realization unleashed another burst of pleasure, more powerful than any other, intensified by his hands roving her body and his lips exciting her skin. The doors of her mind blew open, obliterating a wall she hadn't known existed. Memories flared, brilliant and fleeting, vivid and uncatchable.

David smiling. David laughing. Their first kiss. The nights they'd spent entwined in each other, delighting in every sensation. David sharing his secrets. She'd reciprocated, trusting him more than she'd trusted anyone in her entire life. Their deep connection, forged from a shared destiny. Her powers emerging. David patiently teaching her to use them. David loving her. Needing her. Drawing out of her an openness and passion too long denied her.

She floated back to the present, her memories reconstituted, whole again because this man loved her. And with all her being, she loved him in return.

David rolled onto his back, taking her with him. She sprawled over his body, exhausted in the most wonderful way, satisfied beyond measure. He caressed her hair, pecked a kiss on top of her head, and snuggled her against him. With her ear on his chest, she listened to the pounding of his heart as it slowed one beat at a time. She inhaled the smell of his sweat, mingled with the unmistakable scent of him—heady, earthy, masculine.

With one finger, she etched circles on his chest. "I remember."

"What do you remember?"

"Everything."

He froze, his heartbeats accelerating.

She turned her face into his chest and smiled against his skin, too overwhelmed by the revelation of recovering her past to do anything, even look into the eyes of the man she cherished. "It all came flooding back to me. How we met, what we did together, the things we talked about." She tucked her arm around his waist, snuggling into him. "I remember us."

His heart thudded beneath her ear. His chest heaved.

Grace raised her head then and beheld her warrior angel's expression—the tears threatening to overflow, the lopsided grin, the wonder glittering in his eyes. Never had she witnessed this David crying, and yet he teetered on the verge of doing just that.

She feathered her fingers over his cheek. "It's okay. You don't have to worry about me anymore. I'm me again, completely. No more crazy amnesia girl."

He exhaled a long sigh and blinked away the moisture in his eyes. "I'm not worried, Grace. I'm happy."

"Me too. And by the way, you were right. You can strip the Golden Power out of me. You just did it."

His hand skipped down her back to cup her bottom. "That's not all I stripped."

Steam rushed through her at the memory of his hands deftly removing her clothes, his fingers grazing her flesh, his eyes worshiping her curves. "I wish we could stay like this all day, but I don't think Tesler will sit still much longer. Sooner or later, they'll finagle a way to get their systems back online. They've probably got backups, you know."

"I checked right before you arrived. They weren't quite there yet, but I'll check again."

She considered offering to do it herself. Then again, she supposed she ought to let him do something occasionally.

His eyes went distant as his expression blanked. Though his arms held her, she sensed the vacancy inside, left behind by his mind's departure.

Grace tapped one fingernail on her chin and counted the seconds, the pace of her taps accelerating as she passed twenty, then thirty.

Come back to me.

David blinked, drew in a deep breath, and tightened his hold on her. His eyes, bright and mesmerizing once again, fixed on her. "They're still working on it. Won't be long, though."

They both understood what they must do. As much as she loathed breaking away from him, as much as she craved his touch and his kiss, she uncoupled her body from his and rose to a seated position. The absence of his heat chilled her skin. His scent faded, yet the energy pulsing between them filled the void. She would never be without him again, not really, even if continents separated them. Their connection had always granted her a taste of him in his absence, but their newfound bond, forged in their love-making, bequeathed her more than a sampling. He smoldered inside her like the missing part of her soul restored.

And they hadn't joined their powers yet.

David sat up and took her hands. "It's time."

"I'm ready."

CHAPTER TWENTY-FIVE

AVID TIPPED HIS HEAD FROM SIDE TO SIDE AND SCRUTINIZED HER face, determined to ferret out any traces of misgivings in her expression. He found only love and certainty there, but a frozen seed had taken root in his chest. Did she fully understand what merging meant? Did he understand?

To hell with the consequences. Nothing bad could come of letting Grace in, whether that meant into his heart or his mind. She knew his darkest secrets, and he'd vowed to share everything with her from this moment forward. If she perceived his emotions more keenly after the joining, if her psychic GPS expanded into a live television feed from his brain to hers, he was fine with it. Hell, he'd relish every minute. To be with Grace, he'd surrender his privacy and his mind to her.

But should he expect her to do the same?

He coughed, scratching his ear. "Are you sure? We've shared a telepathic bond, but this will be so much more. As far as I know, nobody's done this before. Once we merge our powers, I don't know if it can ever be undone."

"The Golden Power is gone, and I'll never tap into it again. I promise."

His heart sank. If it took the rest of his life, he'd convince her she wasn't corrupted.

Capturing her hand, he fluttered a kiss across her knuckles. "I'm not worried about that. But are you sure you want to shackle yourself to me permanently?"

"You make it sound so romantic." The worry wrinkling her forehead encouraged him to trace his fingers across the skin as if he might smooth out her fears. Her eyes shuttered, and she inclined toward him just enough to rouse his thirst for those soft, pink lips. Through their connection, he experienced the subtle shift as tenderness displaced worry. The lines on her forehead disappeared. She gazed up at him, and her lips quirked in a sly half-smile. "I want to do this. Besides, I'm pretty sure we already started the process."

"That was our bodies merging, not our minds."

"I meant when you helped me shed the Golden Power. We did it together." She rolled her shoulders back and gave a quick nod. "I'm ready, David. Stop stalling."

"Right. Let's do it."

He twined his fingers with hers, letting their linked hands drop. Each of their wrists rested on their respective knees, with their fingers bridging the gap.

Their gazes collided.

Power snapped taut between them. Energy surged through the bond, scorching and seeking, ricocheting from her into him and back again, over and over. Dizziness hurled his mind off balance, but he clutched her hands, her power, for support. Fevered lust swelled deep inside, a voracious need so profound that he gasped. Her eyes rolled shut, her head lolling backward, mouth open, cheeks flushed with desire.

"Look at me," he rasped, breathing hard from the intensity of his desire for her. "Look at me, Grace. *Now.*"

She obeyed. Her hazel eyes flamed with psychic energy and rapacious hunger.

Her powers poured into him. He drove his own powers back toward her in a feedback loop that pumped in and out of him while the essence of her consumed him, transformed him with her sweetness and passion, invigorated him with her laughter and courage. A love more reverent than anyone deserved penetrated him to the core. Her love. His love.

Their love.

His mind settled, the energy dwindling from a torrent to a gentle stream. The ecstasy of melding with her lingered and stimulated his entire body. God, he wanted her. Right now, right here, for hours and hours, damn the rest of the world. He ached to taste her, arouse her, and worship her in the most carnal ways.

Her lips curved into a sensual smile. "I know what you're thinking."

"Don't need psychic powers to know that."

Her arousal vibrated into him, supercharging his own. He sucked in a breath. She was doing it on purpose. "Better stop that, unless you want me to ravish you again."

"Maybe I do."

He chuckled. "I know you do. What I should've said was, we don't have time for me to ravish you again."

She feigned a pout. "You're no fun."

"When this is over," he said, sliding a hand up her thigh, "you have my word I'll make love to you nonstop until you beg me to quit."

A blush rose in her cheeks, though not from embarrassment, from the heat of passion. She was dazzling in her amorous glow, and delicious enough to eat. Maybe just an appetizer...

He jumped off the bed. "Get dressed. It's time to end Tesler's reign of terror."

———

GRACE CROUCHED BEHIND A TREE, EYES CLOSED. THE TRANQUIL warmth of David's energy suffused her mind and soul, rejuvenating her powers. Her mind soared above the forest to scout the vicinity, and she swooped down low to check out every vague signature of life, determined to rout out Tesler's men before they swarmed her and David. Never before had she been able to detect life-forms this way. Since their merging, though, she discovered she could scent them out, for lack of a better term, with her psychic faculties. Her mind interpreted each scent as a flickering dot in the woods.

Remote viewing had transformed into something more.

A flicker below her brightened. She dived toward it. The single signature separated into multiple lights, a dozen at least. She struggled to differentiate them, to count her enemies. Too many. Heaven above, how would she and David get past them without hurting anyone?

Relax, Grace.

David's voice resounded in her head. No longer did they need spoken words to communicate. His thoughts, his emotions, translated into phrases in her head—more than just words, but his voice speaking them. The intimacy of the contact shuddered a thrill through her. At the same time, it unsettled her. She knew he couldn't read her mind, and his words and emotions reached her only when he chose to share them. Right now, he beamed comfort to her in a soothing wash, like lowering her body into a warm bubble bath.

We can do this, he told her.

Can't hurt anyone, she said.

Except for Tesler.

Cold dribbled into her. *David...*

Relax, no one gets hurt unless they try to hurt us.

Okay.

Grace winced at the sting of his anger, so strong and hot that he couldn't hold it back completely. Still, she knew—despite his loathing for Tesler, his vow to destroy the man—that he would keep his promise to her. No violence without provocation.

She marked out a path to the congregation of commandos, and then she opened her eyes. Adapted to the night, they revealed her surroundings in shades of shadow and pale light. The first rays of the sun trickled over the horizon, spilling out across the sky, squelched by the heaviness of the receding night. To her left, the silhouette of David hunched behind a bush. His eyes fluttered open, exposing the burning blue of his eyes, aflame with the power of his mind.

His hand found hers and squeezed. *Ready?*

No, she would never be ready for war. Tesler had eliminated every alternative.

She nodded.

David scuttled closer, clasping both her hands. She focused on his eyes and let her mind sink into him, embracing the potency of his gifts, granting him unfettered access to hers. His essence swirled inside her, slow and gentle, yet ardent. Her body flashed back to the moments in the cabin when his passion had consumed her with the same sizzling tenderness. His heart and mind, like his body, stimulated her from the tips of her toes to the hair follicles on her head, and way down into the most secret parts of her. She exhaled a shaky breath, and somehow her knees, despite resting on the ground, weakened at the memory of his skin, his mouth, and his hands on her.

She shoved aside the thoughts and commanded herself to focus.

As one, they disunited from their bodies and rose through the crossroads, then out again to materialize in front of the commandos.

The men froze, eyes wide. A few gasped. One by one, they jerked their guns up to target Grace and David.

"You can shoot," David said, his tone low and dangerous, "but you won't hit us."

A figure moved out of the center of the throng to halt a few yards away. "Can't stay away from me, can ya, sweetheart?"

Her heart thudded, and her mouth went dry. "Battaglia."

A wriggling itch crawled over her skin. The arrogant slant of his lips, the oily eyes fixed on her, the massive shoulders hunching as if in anticipation of his next tangle with her... His every gesture awakened a seed of anxiety. It swelled and multiplied until she battled for control of her jackhammering heart.

A wave of empathy from David enveloped her like an invisible hug. The panic dissolved under his telepathic ministrations. *Thank you, my hero.*

Peripherally, she glimpsed his lips twitching into a brief smile. *You're welcome, my heroine.*

She chanced a fleeting look at him. Heroine? She was no savior. He must've been joking, except she'd felt the fervent intent of his message.

"You're astral projecting," Battaglia said, careful in his enunciation of the words. "I know all about you freaks. But we're not scared of you. We won't stop until we find your bodies and blow enough holes in them to shred you to pieces."

Grace latched onto David's calm energy. The bite of anger tainted it, but she'd take whatever she could glean from him. Calm and angry. Only

David managed to hold both in his heart at the same time. She fed a bit of herself into him, praying to assuage his demons for a little longer.

They were in the woods. The fact had not escaped her notice. The vision she'd endured, of Tesler murdering David, had unfolded in a forest identical to this one.

I won't let it happen.

David glanced at her sideways. His question hovered between them.

Oh damn. He'd sensed her state of mind and guessed what she was thinking. He longed to ask if she was okay but couldn't waste any mental fuel on transposing his feelings into words she might hear in her mind, or vice versa. Remote viewing this location demanded every ounce of psychic energy they both possessed, as they combined astral projection, telekinesis, and thought projection into a cohesive image of themselves standing before the commandos.

Battaglia sniggered. "Don't have a plan, do ya? Stupid freaks."

She swiveled her head toward David. His eyes met hers, and the fire in them sparked with a power that crackled between them. *Now.*

They fired their entire arsenal at the commandos, the combined energy of all their powers, consolidated and electrified, fortified beyond anything either of them could accomplish alone.

The commandos twitched. Their eyes rolled back in their heads.

More.

Grace culled all she could from David and dragged in energy from the crossroads. *Not the Golden Power, don't go there,* her own mind warned her. She veered away from the pathway to the ultimate source of psychic power. However much she'd managed to devour from the crossroads, she hauled back down with her.

David stumbled, his eyes bulging.

The power surging between them exploded tenfold. She hurled it at the commandos.

And they crumpled to the ground, unconscious.

The power sluiced out of David, straight through her mind and out into the ether. He vanished, yanked back to his body.

Her mind whirled. Blackness swamped her vision. She slammed back into her body and tumbled sideways. Her head smacked into the ground, bursting stars in her vision as pain wrenched her body, and she curled into a ball, whimpering like an injured animal.

Heroine, my ass. She tried to gulp down the whimpers, to unsnarl her limbs, but she had no control.

David gathered her in his arms. His firm body encased her, yet no heat or comfort leeched into her from him. He rocked her and murmured consoling phrases, but they bounced off her brain, incomprehensible. Shooting stars twirled around her, and she fought to regain her bearings. Up, down. Real, not real. What had she done?

"Not the Golden Power," she croaked.

"I know." David smoothed hair from her face. "It's okay. This is normal power drain. Just relax."

"Normal?" She zeroed in on his eyes, no longer flaming but gleaming in the pastel shades of sunrise. The spinning lessened, and the earth below them rolled out into a flat surface again. "It's not normal. I've never felt like that before."

"You don't have a migraine."

He announced it with authority as if he knew this to be true. Of course he knew. Her feelings, emotional and physical, bled into him. She could restrain the flow somewhat, but in her current state, she lacked the energy.

And he was right. No migraine. For the first time in months, using her powers had not set off an excruciating, nausea-inducing headache.

She twisted out of his arms, her butt plopping onto the ground. "Why don't I have a migraine?"

He smiled. "Because your powers aren't blocked anymore. Whatever happened to free up your memories, it freed your powers too."

When he'd made love to her, that's what had done it.

His smile transformed into a suggestive smirk that instigated a tingling deep inside her. He wrapped an arm around her waist to nudge her closer. "We both know what freed you up."

"Don't get full of yourself. I think it was more than your... prowess that did the trick."

"I know. It was love."

Oh yes. The truth of the statement resonated in her. She loved him more than even she comprehended, and he loved her the same way. Their commitment to each other had shattered the wall in her mind.

David jumped to his feet, hoisting her up with him. "Let's finish this."

A chill whispered over her skin. The worst part was yet to come. "It took everything we both had to knock out those guards. How in hell are we going to breach the facility?"

"We don't need the Golden Power."

"But we barely managed phase one of our brilliant plan."

"Shh." He took her face in his hands and brushed his lips across hers. "We can do this. If you stop being afraid of your powers."

"I'm not. We merged, and I feel great about that." True. But that old worm of doubt, though skinnier than before, writhed in her gut whenever she accessed her powers. The memory of the Golden Power inside her, poisoning everything she was or could be, roused the worm to lash its tail.

"You don't need more power." His nose bumped hers, their eyes close enough the heat from his eyes would've burned her if it were real flames. "Stop being afraid. Let it go. You are wonderful and sweet, the best person I've ever known, and you would never hurt anyone if you had another choice. The Golden Power doesn't own you. No one and nothing does." He moved his hand behind her head, cupping it, slanting it up toward his face. "You belong to me, remember?"

"You said nobody owns me."

"I don't own you. I love you. We belong to each other, now more than ever. Right?"

The mere thought of belonging to him, with him, made her breaths quicken. "But how can we break into the facility, just us, no energy boost from—"

His mouth devoured hers in a kiss so full of passion that it erased every doubt, cleansed her soul, flared so hot inside her that she melted into him. He withdrew, head angled to the side. "Do you trust me?"

"Yes."

"Then trust what I'm about to say, don't ask questions, and follow my lead. Okay?" When she nodded, he dropped his hands to her shoulders. "You and I can do this. We will do this. If we get in there and Tesler has fixed his EM field, then we'll deal with that. You are the strongest psychic I've ever heard of, and together we are unstoppable." He took hold of her hands and laced his fingers with hers. "Let's go end this."

They sprinted through the woods, away from the slumbering commandos, to a spot they'd identified earlier. A shallow ravine shielded them from anyone prowling the woods. Grace sat down at the base of the ravine, her back to the steep wall. David settled in beside her.

Ready? He didn't have to say it. She heard him anyway.

Nodding, she slipped her hand into his. He laced his fingers with hers and gripped her hand.

They sped through the crossroads and back down into the facility, touching down in a corridor bathed in white light from the bulbs recessed in the ceiling. A map of the facility floated in her mind, etched with red lines marking a path. It led in the opposite direction.

Without a word, they both whirled around.

A shadow descended out of the ceiling, dark as the void of space, featureless and human-shaped, a silhouette throbbing with black energy. White disks glittered within its ill-defined eye sockets.

Invisible power snaked out to her, coiling itself around her astral body. She clutched David's hand, but her fingers sailed right through him. *No bodies.* Without manifesting, she couldn't connect with him. The tendrils of power constricted around her like a straitjacket manufactured from psychic energy as ghostly fists pounded at her firewall, to no avail.

David stood immobile, his face blank.

The power collared her throat. "David!"

He stared straight ahead.

She grappled with the thing constraining her, helpless to break free. The thundering of her pulse drowned out her own cries. "David, what's wrong with you?"

His eyes rolled to the side, his focus fixated on her. Fear and anguish steamrolled through her. His fear. His anguish.

The dark power strangled her.

She gurgled, wrestled against her invisible restraints, but gained not one inch. This force, it could touch her, affect her, as if both she and it had manifested physical forms. But she hadn't.

Had she?

The tendrils from the shadow-thing bound her, but her legs were free of it. She stomped her boot on the floor. Pain webbed out through her foot. What the hell was going on? She hadn't wanted to manifest, hadn't tried to, and yet something had forged a physical body for her.

A shiver jolted her entire body. The truth socked her in the gut, and she struggled for breath. The shadow-thing had compelled her to manifest. When its power had entangled itself around her, its will had become real. The thing wanted her in a body, in a tangible, crunchable form.

David, can you hear me?

His eyes never wavered from hers, but he did not respond.

She squeaked out the words. "David, fight it."

The shadow-thing slithered down the corridor toward them. Its amorphous body coalesced into arms and legs and a torso, all corded with thick muscles. The oily surface of its form solidified into dark skin. The eyes flamed as white as the hottest fire, and the bulbs in the ceiling cast glistening rays on the man's bald head and nude figure.

Every hair on her body stiffened, electrified by the recognition careening through her.

The shadow-thing. It was… Nkosi.

He halted a few feet from her. A smile of vicious portent warped his face. "At last, I have what I craved."

Nkosi's fingertips traced the line of her jaw, and though she struggled against the tendrils binding her, they tightened and sharpened. She gritted her teeth, refusing to gasp, repressing the agony that sliced into her flesh and pierced down to her soul.

His smile widened. "The golden girl is mine."

Golden girl. She ground her teeth hard, fending off the memory of the last time someone had called her golden girl. Jackson Tennant's voice echoed in the recesses of her mind, but she slammed the door on it.

Nkosi scraped a nail across her cheek. A streak of pain singed her flesh in its wake. "You don't yet understand, but I will explain. First, however, I must sever you from him." Nkosi threw a blazing glare at David. "His power corrupts yours. I crave your pure, unadulterated energy. It will feed us both and make us one in a way his puny powers could not accomplish."

The energy wafting out of him enveloped her, and she gagged at the acrid taste of it. No, not again. She recognized the taste and the greasy energy seeping into her. She'd suffered this invasion before. Yet it couldn't be. It just couldn't.

"You are beginning to see," Nkosi told her. He seized her chin, forcing her to meet his gaze. The white-hot coals of his eyes seared her mind. "You feel it. But perhaps your lover does not yet comprehend the truth."

David, oh God, David, please break free.

Nkosi aimed a devious grin at David. "I am not this weak human you know as Nkosi. He died long ago when I consumed his essence and replaced it with my own. Psychic powers are more than energy. They are living things inhabiting human bodies." He ducked his head close to hers, and his lips grated over her mouth, his breath hot and fetid. "Tell him."

"No." A choked rasp, nothing more.

"Fine. I will do it." The creature in Nkosi's body hauled her across the floor, until her body pierced the astral image of David, their eyes almost converging. The shadow-thing said, "I am the Golden Power. And your girl belongs to me now."

Energy exploded, rupturing her link to David. Agony wrenched and contorted her body. Power cracked through her. The last thread of her connection to David snapped.

She screamed.

CHAPTER TWENTY-SIX

OWER TORE THROUGH DAVID. GRACE SCREAMED AS HE WAS hurled back into his body, far from the facility and Nkosi. And Grace.

He staggered backward and hit the ground with a thud that echoed through his body and set his nerves on fire. His head pounded. White lights popped in his vision. His muscles twitched and burned. He clambered onto his hands and knees, panting, but when he tried to move, to crawl even one inch, agony contorted him from head to toe.

Grace.

Her scream ripped through his mind, replayed over and over. She'd pleaded with him for help, not with her voice, but with the tormented look on her face and the terror radiating out of her into him. Severing their link had torn her away, stranding him out here in the woods, blind to her anguish, powerless to save her.

"Man, are you okay?"

Sean's voice pierced the haze of agony and anguish. David blinked until his vision shifted back into the physical plane and the blurry shapes around him coalesced into bushes and trees, grass and moss—and Sean and Gabriel Amador.

"What are you doing here?" David tried to scramble to his feet, but his legs gave out. "You were supposed to be on your way to Edward."

"Yeah." Sean jammed his hands in his pants pockets. "We changed the plan."

"Dammit, Sean, you shouldn't be here."

The kid rolled his eyes and scrunched his mouth. "We know what's going down, and no, I wasn't gonna run off in Gabriel's plane. It's a Gulfstream, which is really cool, sure. But you're family."

David clenched his jaw. He understood Sean's decision, even admired him a little for it, but fury ripped through him at the sight of Amador's face, pinched and pale. Grace wouldn't have resorted to the Golden Power if Amador hadn't pushed her, tormented her, scared her into actions she'd sworn never to take again. The bastard had coerced her. *Scared* her. *Tormented* her.

David lunged at Amador. His hands closed around the man's throat.

Sean seized his arm and pulled. "No-no-no! What are you doing? Stop it, he helped us."

David squeezed.

Amador spluttered and choked, eyes bulging.

"Cut it out, he saved you." Sean clawed at David's hands, desperate to pry them free. "He stopped the guards from taking you when you were in transit."

Fingers hard as a vice around Amador's throat, David snarled. "What did you do to Grace? Where is she? Tell me, Amador, or I'll snap your neck right here."

Amador gurgled.

Sean punched David in the side. The blow knocked him off balance, and his hands popped free of Amador's throat. Sean socked him again. David tumbled sideways and whumped to the ground. Pain ricocheted through his ribs and torso. He grunted, rolling onto his back.

"Jeez, you dumb-ass." Sean loomed over David, his mouth twisted into a sardonic expression. "Let people explain before you go all psycho-killer dude on us. You're a real shithead sometimes, you know?"

David pushed up onto his elbows. Sean had never sworn at him before.

Sean plopped onto his buttocks on the ground, knees bent before him. "I know you're freaky protective of Grace, but come on. Get a grip, man. We're trying to help you."

David raised an eyebrow.

The boy snorted. "Don't gimme that look. You're the one being an asshole."

"So now you're friends with the dick who held Grace hostage?"

"No. But he did save your dumb-ass life." Sean screwed up his face and slanted his head sideways to study David. "Did the Golden Power make you stark-raving bonkers or what?"

David heaved his aching body into a sitting position, his legs outstretched, torso braced upright by his shaky arms. Sean had been scared—that David might die, that he might return from his "transit" mentally injured or insane, that the only two people he trusted would be stripped from his life. Of course the boy cursed at David. He was terrified.

"I'm okay," David said, assuming a placating tone. "I'm sorry I lost it there. You don't know what happened in the facility. Nkosi is—"

"A total psycho." Sean's lips warped into a mirthless smile. "We know that already. He convinced us to come back for you guys, but when we found you in that ravine, he tried to slit your throat." Sean nodded toward

Amador, who slumped against a tree massaging his throat. "If it weren't for him, you'd be a meat sack lying in a blood puddle."

Teenage boys had such a way with words. David felt a grim smile overtake his mouth. Had he been like that once? It seemed so long ago and far away. He couldn't remember.

His shoulders folding in, Sean hugged his knees. "We lost her, David."

Blades of ice gutted him and rammed straight up into his heart. *God, please no, not Grace.* His throat cinched tight around the words he needed to speak, but he forced them out one syllable at a time. "What happened?"

"Nkosi and his Nazi pals took her. We tried to fight, but…" Tears glistened in Sean's eyes. "They were too strong, and I'd spent all my energy on saving you. There wasn't enough left."

Saving you. David considered the phrase for several seconds and understanding flared as bright as the sun in his mind. "Nkosi did slit my throat. You had to use your healing power on me."

Sean chewed his lip and nodded.

David narrowed his gaze on Amador. "What did you do, whimper and whine? Why didn't you employ the Golden Power?"

"I—" Amador slouched lower, his pallor deepening, his eyes wild with fear. "Please forgive me, I lied to Grace. I have no psychic abilities."

The rage erupted inside him, but David doused it with a single thought. *Grace is in danger.* He hoisted himself off the ground and offered his hand to Amador. The other man eyed him warily but clasped his hand and accepted a boost in getting to his feet. Amador dropped his hands to his sides, fingers working.

David wiped his hands on his pants. "No forgiveness. I won't kill you, and that's the best offer you'll get."

Amador nodded. "I understand."

Sean scrambled to his feet. "They must've taken Grace back to the facility. How are we gonna rescue her? I'm wiped, and you must be too. We're powerless."

David's nails burrowed into his palm as he fisted his hand tight. He was not powerless. Even without Grace's energy bolstering his, he claimed enough psychic power to do… something. Anything. What?

Save her.

He could do this. He must do it. They shared a connection stronger than telepathy, a bond fortified by passion and commitment—and love. The kind that spawned legends. The kind no amount of distance could weaken. He latched onto that love now, wrapping it around himself like a blanket.

Warmth shimmered inside him, sweet and familiar. It trickled into every crevice of his being. It scoured away the darkness, the fear, the pain, and shrank the distance between them to nothing. The sensation of nearness, of Grace's presence skimming his flesh, flowered inside him. He knew this feeling. But it couldn't be. He'd endured the wrenching pain when Nkosi shattered his connection to Grace, and he'd suffered the aching emptiness left behind. Yet the gentle weight blanketed him, and her warmth filled him, suffused him, altered him, empowered him.

How did he know Nkosi had broken their link? Because the monster told him, that's how. What if the thing that called itself Nkosi had deceived him? He was clutching at phantoms of hope, he knew it, yet the hazy echo of sunlight inside him evoked one thing and one thing only.

Grace.

He threw his head back and laughed.

Exuberance bubbled out of him, dispersing into the air, and he felt sure Sean and Amador must think he'd gone insane. Daylight streamed in through the treetops to bathe him in streaks of gentle radiance. Light, dark. Grace, Nkosi. Human potential versus unspeakable power. The battle had begun. But evil would not win the day because he and Grace wielded the greatest power in the universe. Their love.

David slapped Sean's arm. "Let's go get her the old-fashioned way."

The boy's expression brightened. "With guns and fists?"

"Hmm. We can manage the fists, but as for the guns…"

Sean reached behind his back and yanked out a semiautomatic gun similar to an AK-47, with a long, curved magazine. He reached back again and brought out a much smaller handgun. Offering both to David, he grinned. "Will this work?"

"It'll do." David took the bigger gun, testing its weight. He could handle this. Checking the magazine, he discovered a full complement of ammo. Oh yeah. He could definitely handle this. "Let's get moving."

He called up the mental map of the facility and its environs that he'd compiled before traveling to the facility. The route stretched out before him. With Sean in tow, he strode off into the woods.

Amador toddled up beside him. "I am going with you. This is partly my fault, and I must rectify it."

"Partly?" David halted, struggling to rein in the anger. He fixed his glare on Amador. "I don't have time to talk about your guilt, or how much I hate you and how much you'll suffer if anything happens to Grace. Get out of my sight before I demonstrate for you."

Amador straightened and lifted his chin. "I will come with you."

If he had a rope, he'd tie the bastard to a tree and let the wild animals take care of things. But he didn't have time to argue. "Fine. Just do what I say and keep the hell out of my way. Got it?"

"Yes."

They marched onward. David pushed them to a faster pace until sweat dribbled down their faces and their breaths huffed. Still, he pushed harder, accelerating into a jog, then a run. He hurtled through the woods with a clock ticking in his mind, each second eating away at Grace's life.

Nkosi claimed to be the Golden Power. Was it even possible? Maybe Nkosi had tapped into the ultimate source of psychic energy, but it drove him insane, to the point where he believed he'd become the Golden Power. Andrew Haley lost his mind after trying to read someone else's. Who knew what damage the Golden Power might wreak on a mind too flawed or feeble to handle the influx of energy.

Whatever Nkosi was or was not, he wielded enough power to trample almost anyone who tangled with him. Grace might prove the exception.

Not might. She would.

David stopped to lean against a tree, catching his breath. Sean and Amador did the same. He would help Grace defeat Nkosi. Their link persevered, but Nkosi must've shut the door on it. The thing about doors was, they could be kicked in.

He shut his eyes. Focused on Grace. Latched onto the remnants of their connection. The ribbon of energy joining them led him straight back to her. He couldn't see or hear or touch her, yet the soft, glowing essence of her swelled inside him.

David?

Not a word. Not a thought. A sensation of her mind seeking his, questing for contact.

He had one chance before his psychic energy was spent.

I'm coming, Grace.

With an effort that twisted his gut and seared his brain, he pulled in all the energy left inside him and flung it at the door segregating their minds.

And then he kicked it in.

———

GRACE'S EYES SPRANG OPEN. HER HEART THUDDED, HER BREATHS gasped, and sweat dribbled down her temples to drip, drip, drip onto the table beneath her. A table? She tried to sit up, but restraints pinned her down at the forehead, wrists, and ankles. Her manifested body was tied down?

Yeah, here she was, strapped to a table. She shot out a burst of psychic energy, intending to crumble her manifestation. The energy ricocheted back to her core. The body Nkosi had stuffed her into retained its form. Trapped in a manifested body and trapped in this room.

As her vision shifted into focus, she caught sight of her surroundings.

Goosebumps erupted up and down her arms.

She lay on a metal table in a square room with concrete floors, a mirror on one wall, and a single door. The dimness of emergency lights spilled over her and permitted shadows to creep in at the corners of the room. The mirror must've been two-way, to allow scientists to observe the goings-on in here. She could see the mirror out the corner of her eye, her prone form reflected in its surface. Did someone watch from the other side?

Her skin prickled. Tesler might be there, studying her from the safety of a hidden room. Or worse, Nkosi might lie in wait behind the glass.

Nkosi.

Grace shuddered. The power he'd exhibited when he controlled her and David simultaneously. The ease with which he fractured their link. Maybe he was the Golden Power as he claimed. She had no other explanation for what he could do.

Heat rippled over her skin. She drew in a ragged breath. *David.* The sensation evoked him, but Nkosi had separated them on the psychic and physical planes. It couldn't be him.

Liquid summer flowed through her mind, into her veins, infusing her soul with a deep longing for what she'd lost. No. She hadn't lost David. He was here, inside her, with her always.

The door to the room banged open.

Grace flinched.

Nkosi stomped through the doorway. He slammed his fists down on the table between her feet. Rage deformed his face and seethed in his eyes.

She tried to cringe, to pull away from him, but the restraints held her in place.

Nkosi took hold of her ankles, his nails digging into her flesh. "You can't be communicating with him. I broke your bond. You are mine."

He knew. He'd detected it the instant she reconnected with David, though the link had lasted only a few seconds.

She clenched her hands and her jaw. "I am not yours."

"You are. You should be." He yanked her legs. The restraints gouged her, and she bit back a cry. "I severed the link. I severed it, I did, I took you away from him, and yet—" He threw his hands up and let out a feral bellow. "How can you still be with him? I am the Golden Power and I commanded you to be mine."

He was insane. Period.

Nkosi moved around to the head of the table. He ran the backs of his fingers across her cheek and gazed down at her with reverence. "You are the key to my liberation."

"From what?"

"The crossroads." He settled a hand on the strap over her forehead. "It keeps trying to pull me back, to confine me in my little corner of the psychic matrix. I don't want to be a prisoner anymore. Your power will free me." His thumb stroked her brow. "This is your destiny, Grace. Only you can access my energy. We are one."

"Oh great. Another psycho who's in love with me."

He gave a low, menacing chuckle. "I'm not interested in your body or your personality. It's your power I crave."

"My power's inside me, which means you need me too."

"I have no use for you." He lowered his face to hers. "I need your brain."

Every nerve seemed to sensitize at once, the air on her skin abruptly sharp, like a thousand needles nicking her flesh. Her brain? How did he intend to…

Realization iced through her. He'd cut it out of her.

But how could he slice out her brain? She was in a manifested form, not her genuine body.

Wasn't she?

Oh shit. For a long moment, she forgot to breathe. Tingling started in her face, paralyzed her lips, and spread out into her limbs. She forced herself to take slow, deep breaths until the tingling faded. Then she spoke with deliberate care. "How did you find my body?"

Nkosi leered at her. "Heat signatures. We used infrared technology to pinpoint your location."

Heat signatures. Infrared technology. Why did someone who claimed to be the incarnation of the Golden Power need infrared to find her? The Golden Power granted limitless knowledge. An omniscient being should not need technology.

"Once we captured you," Nkosi said, "it was simply a matter of eliminating the others."

Others? The meaning of his words burrowed into her and crawled under her skin. Three faces flashed in her mind—Sean, Amador, and David. If any of them had died because of her…

David was alive. His energy reached out to her even now. But Sean and Amador, if they'd suffered because of her arrogance, her blind belief that she and David could conquer the world together, then she'd never forgive herself. Too many people had died for her. People she loved.

No more.

"I give you one more chance," Nkosi said, "to grant me your power willingly. Otherwise, I'll be forced to wrest it from you by whatever means necessary."

"Screw you."

He straightened, aiming a curt nod at the mirror. "We do this your way, doctor."

Footsteps clapped in the corridor, approaching the doorway. A figure waltzed into the room, his gray hair tousled and his white coat dotted with stains. A scrape slashed across his left cheek.

Tesler halted at her feet. His mouth twisted into a vile smirk. "We meet at last."

"Screw you too." If she'd held onto any shred of her wits, she might've cobbled together a better comeback. But her wits had scattered into the ether.

Get them back, idiot.

Nkosi and Tesler exchanged a look she couldn't decipher. Glee, maybe. Or hungry lust for power—of the psychic variety for Nkosi, and of another type for Tesler. What the scientist really wanted, deep down, eluded her. He despised psychic abilities and viewed travelers as freaks, yet he sought the power he believed resided in her brain. Amador claimed Tesler dreamed of controlling an army of puppet psychics. But his endgame struck her as far more complex than the old world-domination gambit.

"Bring in the tools," Tesler called out to the mirror. Then he spoke to Nkosi. "When this is over, I'll have what I wanted, what you promised me. Correct?"

Nkosi nodded.

Grace squirmed in her restraints. No weak links she might exploit. Her bonds were leather and metal, not chain.

The emergency lights lent the room a haunted-house vibe. She squinted at Tesler. "How long will the backup generator last? I know your computer systems are fried, so the generator gives you light and ventilation, but not much more."

He stared at her, blank.

"What have you got left?" she asked. "A couple hours?"

"Shut up." He rattled her ankle restraints. "You're the one tethered to a table, about to be split open."

He had a point. She was helpless.

Like hell.

She commanded more psychic power than anyone else Tesler or her parents or David had ever seen. But she lay there like a salmon caught on a lure. Flopping. Suffocating. Nkosi had commandeered her psychic faculties, right? That's why she was helpless.

No. She'd lost control of her abilities for one reason, and it had nothing to do with the strength of Nkosi's will. He hadn't defeated her. She was helpless because she'd given up. She would never free her mind and body as long as she feared her own powers. David was right.

It was time to stop being afraid.

David beckoned her, his voice a whisper in the darkness.

Let him in.

So she did. Without understanding how, she flung the doors of her mind open, and he rushed in like a hot wind blustering through her. The exhilaration of melding with him again swept into the depths of her being, and she couldn't contain the laughter that bubbled out of her. *Oh, David.* Nkosi had disrupted their connection, but he hadn't broken it.

David's love cascaded into her. No one could sever this bond. No one.

Tesler stabbed a needle into her arm, and the world spiraled into emptiness. His voice growled from far away.

"Hand me the saw."

CHAPTER TWENTY-SEVEN

DAVID CROUCHED AMONG THE TREES, THE FINGERS OF ONE HAND resting on the ground. In his other hand, he grasped the big gun Sean had given him. His eyes were locked on the structure thirty feet ahead. The metal shed that concealed the underground facility.

Grace was in there. Alone.

His fingers tightened around the gun's grip. Metal dug into him, and his knuckles ached from the effort. This was his fault. He'd suggested Grace join her powers with his, and he had talked her into a joint traveling session that put them both at risk. How could he have been so stupid? Of course their psychic journey into the facility had left their bodies vulnerable and exposed. Of course Tesler and Nkosi had taken advantage of the opening to capture Grace. Of course he'd failed her again.

One night of amazing sex had drained the blood from his brain and rendered him useless.

A rustling to his left drew his attention to Sean, who huddled an arm's length away. The boy's eyebrows lifted. Waiting for David to formulate a plan. So he could screw up and get them all killed. No wonder Grace had to rescue him all the time. He was incompetent.

Fingers lighted on his shoulder. He threw a sideways glare at Amador. The other man withdrew his hand but still knelt too close to David. The bastard had no sense of boundaries.

Amador bent his head close to David. "What is our plan?"

Good question. "Rescue Grace."

"That's a goal, not a plan."

The acid boiling in David's gut swelled up into his throat. He hissed a breath out his nostrils, narrowing his gaze on Amador. "Unless you have a brilliant idea, shut the hell up."

In the sulfurous glow from the floodlight on the shed, Amador's self-satisfied expression transformed into a devilish gleam. Or maybe David just really, really hated the man.

The doors of his mind flew open. He swayed on the balls of his feet and sank his fingers into the ground. Energy poured into him in a sweet, steamy torrent that inundated his psyche, his heart, his soul, and…

His libido.

Memories of sensations flashed through him. Grace's body beneath his, warm and supple. Her breasts mashed into his chest. Her panting breaths heating his skin. Her fingers clutching his shoulders, raking down his back.

"Are you okay, man?"

"Fine," he growled, though he dared not look at Sean. The naked hunger overpowering him would expose itself on his face for sure. He battled with his willpower, but the memories kept pummeling him.

"You don't look fine," Sean said. "I've never seen anybody look like that. It's—" He repressed a laugh that came out as a series of snorts punctuated by a hiccup. "Are you seriously thinking about what I think you're thinking about?"

David shoved a hand through his hair and focused all his attention on the shed. And on structuring a plan. And most of all, on quashing his out-of-control libido. He ignored Sean's question, because he'd vowed never to lie to the boy and telling the truth was out of the question.

The desire burned off quickly, reduced to glowing embers. The smoke left behind clouded his mind for a moment, but as the psychic air cleared, a familiar and wonderful presence rained down on him. *Grace*. Their minds had reconnected, bolstering their bond and reinforcing their joined powers. Nkosi hadn't torn her away from him forever. She'd found a way back. *Yes*.

And suddenly, he knew how to save her.

"I have an idea," he said to Sean. "Do you have enough energy to RV the facility and locate Grace?"

"Yeah, I think so."

"Good. What I'm about to do may knock me unconscious, or kill me." He clapped a hand on Sean's shoulder and squeezed. "I'm relying on you to free her."

The boy's face blanched, but then he rolled back his shoulders, straightened his spine, and set his jaw. "I won't let you down."

"I know you won't." David switched his attention to Amador and fought back the urge to slug him. "You're going with Sean."

"But I have no powers."

"You have a gun—and a brain, allegedly. That's enough." He glared at Amador until the other man cringed ever so slightly. "If anything happens to Grace, I'm blaming you. If I die, I'll come back from the grave to haunt you for the rest of your pathetic life. Understand?"

"Yes."

"Don't forget it." David handed Sean the big gun. "You might need this."

Sean accepted it without comment, though his lips twitched downward and drew together in the middle.

David aimed his gaze at the metal-shed facade. Gathering in all the power he dared from Grace, and tapping into the crossroads for an added boost, he fired everything he had at the facility. But not at the shed. Not at the structure beneath it. He shot a wave of psychic fire into the air within the building and watched it race through the corridors, smacking each person it met with a burst of energy so intense it shut down their minds. One by one, like flesh-and-blood dominoes, every human being in the facility fell to the floor, unconscious.

The wave shot back into him in a feedback loop that fried his nerves. Agony scoured him from the inside out, contracting his muscles, and he swallowed a cry, desperate not to give away their position. But there was no one left awake in the facility to hear it. As the feedback convulsed his body, wrenched his gut, and exploded in his brain, he glimpsed Sean and Amador dashing toward the shed. Grace would be okay. He hadn't failed her this time. With his last ounce of mental acuity, he prayed she would forgive him for abandoning her again.

Then he collapsed into blackness.

———

GUNFIRE SHOCKED GRACE BACK TO WAKEFULNESS. THE BRIGHT lights above her, where she lay strapped to the metal table, stung her eyes, and she winced. More gunshots detonated in the corridor, louder, closer. Her heart raced, though not because of the melee outside this room. Adrenaline burned in her veins, consuming her breaths, because of what she saw inches from her face.

Tesler poised a scalpel above her head. Its blade glistened as he turned it from side to side, his lips pursed, his eyes blurry behind his glasses. His gaze lowered to hers, and his eyes sprang wide. "How are you awake?"

Hell if she knew.

But she did know. David's power, hot and anxious, lingered inside her. He had joined with her again. His will had jostled her awake just in time. But what could she do? Tesler had her restrained, and though whatever drug he'd given her had waned, its aftereffects made her fuzzy in the head.

Stop whining. Start acting.

Nkosi stepped out from behind Tesler. He grasped a saw in one hand. "Are you ready for this yet?"

"No," Tesler snapped. "I have to peel back the scalp first."

A gunshot exploded.

"Shut the door," Tesler hissed, and Nkosi waved a hand. The door banged shut.

Grace shifted in her restraints, hunting for a weakness. "Who's out there?"

Please let it be David.

"I don't know," Tesler said. "Our surveillance cameras are still offline, thanks to whatever you did to them."

She'd done more damage than she'd realized. Celebrating her success seemed a bit premature, though.

It must've been David out there. Who else would shoot up the place to reach her? Sean might, especially if David instructed him to, and Amador... Well, he might. If it benefited him in some way. Or if his guilt proved stronger than she'd estimated.

Tesler laid a hand on her head. "Perhaps I should shave the scalp, though we're in a bit of a rush. It would make for a cleaner—"

Nkosi clobbered the table with his trembling fist. The concussive waves rattled her bones. "Quit talking and just do it, Tesler. No more stalling."

The scientist *was* stalling. Why?

Grace fidgeted some more, but the bindings held. This was the wrong tactic. She lacked the physical strength to snap her bonds, but she wielded another kind of strength too.

Tesler lowered the scalpel toward her head, then hesitated. His lips parted as if he wanted to speak. His dark eyes bored into her, and he mouthed words that she swore were—

Help me. That's what he'd mouthed. Tesler was begging for her help?

The world had just flipped upside down and inside out.

No time to consider the change. She relaxed onto the table, letting every muscle slacken and soften. The release of tension freed her mind. Energy from David plowed into her with tsunami force, and she funneled all of it into the straps pinning her down. The metal buckles split apart. The leather bands sailed across the room to bounce off the walls and splat onto the floor.

She leaped up and flung her legs over the table's edge. Her boots clapped down on the floor. She snatched the scalpel from Tesler's hand, spun toward Nkosi, and rammed the blade into his chest.

He shimmered and vanished.

A manifested body. *Shit, shit, shit.*

Grace whirled on Tesler, seizing his shirt, and raised the scalpel to the hollow of his throat.

His Adam's apple bobbed. The whites of his eyes gleamed in the murky light.

She thrust her face close to his, and spittle peppered him as she spoke. "Where is he? Nkosi is hiding somewhere. Is he in this facility?"

"I—I don't know. I had no idea he was manifesting."

From the shock on his face, she figured he was telling the truth. She needed more answers from Tesler, but another volley of gunfire boomed in the corridor, so close her eardrums vibrated.

The door burst inward.

Sean Vandenbrook leveled a huge semiautomatic gun at her. His mouth dropped open, his eyes bulging, and he lowered the gun to his side. "Grace. Are you okay?"

"Yes. What's going on out there? Where's David?"

"Me and Gabriel came to get you. Everybody's asleep out there except us, but we had to blow a bunch of doors open with bullets." He glanced over his shoulder, and Amador shuffled up behind him, his clothes disheveled and his face darkened by shadows of exhaustion. Sean faced her again but kept his focus on the metal table in front of her.

A chill rippled through her. "Where's David?"

"He, um, stayed outside." Sean meandered into the room, to the table. "He said what he had to do might knock him out or…"

Kill him. That's what Sean couldn't say. David had drawn on both his power and hers to accomplish some feat that rendered everyone in the facility unconscious. It must've required a huge effort and exacted an unknown toll. He wasn't gone. No, no, no, she refused to accept that.

Besides, his presence flickered inside her. His energy. His life.

Tesler shifted, grunting as the scalpel pinched his flesh.

"Wait a minute," Grace said, eying Sean. "If David knocked everybody out, then why are Tesler and I still awake?"

Sean shrugged.

Footsteps clomped in the corridor, and a figure pushed past Amador to stride into the room. "Because I excluded this room to keep you awake."

Her knees buckled at the sight of David. The scalpel tumbled from her grasp, clacking on the floor. She barreled into him, flung her arms around his neck, and lavished him with kiss after torrid kiss. When she let him catch his breath, he brushed his knuckles across her cheek.

"Don't," Sean snapped.

She twisted her head around to see Tesler bent over scrabbling for the scalpel, and Sean targeting his gun on the scientist's head. Tesler stood up, hands raised.

Grace stunned David with one more molten kiss, then turned toward Tesler. David's body buttressed her from behind, his hands on her upper arms, his muscular frame hard against her backside. She asked Tesler, "Nkosi isn't the embodiment of the Golden Power, is he?"

"No. But he is infested with it."

"How?"

Tesler gritted his teeth, curled his lip, and gazed longingly at the scalpel on the floor.

She shook her head. "You begged me to help you. And I did. Now you're in our custody. Don't you think cooperating might benefit you at this particular moment?"

David tensed against her. His fingers tightened on her arm for a second but loosened when she reached up to close her hand over his.

Groaning, Tesler rolled his eyes. "If it will keep me from having to watch the two of you nuzzling each other, I'll tell you anything you want to know."

"Then spill." She leaned into David just to annoy Tesler, and as if he'd read her mind, David circled his arms around her waist to link his fingers over her belly. She reveled in the warmth of him, the vitality resonating from him into her.

"After JT destroyed the California facility," Tesler said, "and you escaped with David and Sean, I sent another traveler to find you."

"Nkosi was that traveler," Grace said.

"He couldn't track you, but in the process of trying to, he encountered something unexpected. When you rejected the Golden Power, it was released into this physical plane, orphaned from its home in the metaphysical realm. It was adrift."

"I didn't set the Golden Power free. A piece of it stayed inside me."

"A piece, yes. But the bulk of it roamed free, like a toxic cloud floating across the ocean on the jet stream. That cloud met Nkosi. He wasn't as strong as you." Tesler glowered at her. "It swallowed him whole. Well, his mind anyway. You are to blame for his condition. You made him what he is."

David lunged toward Tesler but froze mere feet from the man. His voice was harsh and rife with pent-up contempt. "Bullshit. Grace has never hurt anyone." David jabbed a finger into Tesler's chest, and the scientist grimaced. "You created this problem, with your experiments and your insane quest to control psychic abilities. You're even worse than JT was. If anyone is to blame for Nkosi, it's you."

Tesler lifted one shoulder, his expression blasé. "He's your problem now."

A bolt of white-hot rage shot down their connection. Grace clutched her stomach, the breath vacuumed out of her. She stumbled backward a step.

The muscles in David's arms went taut, his whole body tensed for a fight.

She raced to his side and grasped his arm.

Hard as a marble statue, he moved only his eyes to look at her. His hands hung suspended between him and Tesler, the fingers clawing at the air, sinews rigid and ready to strike. He itched to strangle the scientist. His black hatred seethed inside her too and whipped a frigid current through her soul.

This wasn't him. David did not want to hurt anyone.

But Tesler blamed her for Nkosi's condition. David had withstood unspeakable abuse from this man, but he would not stand for anyone, especially Tesler, harming her in any way. He understood the guilt would gnaw away at her if she were responsible, and she understood he would go to any lengths to shield her from it.

"Let it go," she murmured to him, stroking his arm with her fingertips. "He's not worth it. And we don't know whether to believe him or not, anyway."

"He's blaming you."

"I don't care." She flattened her palm on his cheek and rotated his head toward her. Those blue eyes glowed with a secret fire, and she dived into their depths, welcomed him into her at the deepest level, accepting his fear, his anger, his wrath, and most of all his commitment to her. "You have nothing to prove to me, David. You saved me. I'd be missing a jarful of brain cells if you hadn't attacked the facility."

The fire in his eyes softened, and his body followed suit.

She pulled him to her. "*You* saved *me*."

A smile trembled on his lips, strengthening with each passing second, bolstered by the love she pumped into him. He accepted all that she offered him, which was everything.

"How sweet."

The accented voice rumbled behind her.

David stiffened, his face hardening. Grace confronted the man who loomed between them and the concrete wall.

Nkosi chuckled. "You have renewed your love, but I have something far more impressive. Tesler's crowning achievement, at my beck and call. I will return for you, Grace, and the entirety of your power will be mine."

The image of him snuffed out.

Grace scuffled backward until David's body halted her. She looked at Tesler. "What did he mean by your crowning achievement?"

His lips curved into a rueful smile. "I figured out how to transfer psychic abilities into subjects of my choosing. None of them are as strong as you or even David, but they have enough juice to do considerable damage out in the world. They were chosen based on their malleability and programmed to respond to specific visual and auditory cues."

"You brainwashed them."

"To put it crudely, yes." He glowered at the spot where Nkosi had been a moment earlier. "He stole my army."

Amador's intel had been spot-on. Damn.

"What will he do with this army?" she asked.

"The man is insane and infected with a power beyond imagining. Now he commands a small army of psychics programmed to do his bidding." Tesler barked out a hollow laugh. "What do you think he'll do, start a knitting circle?"

Words fled from her mind, dragging all her thoughts with them.

"He wants your power, and he'll stop at nothing to get it." Tesler's lips tightened into a grim smile. "He'll destroy the world to get to you."

David tugged her against him. "How do we stop Nkosi?"

Tesler shook his head. "You can't. Nothing can stop him."

"We will." David dug a zip tie out of his pocket. "I stole this off one of the sleeping beauties. I think it's about time you experienced the delight of being a prisoner."

The acid in his tone scraped at Grace's nerves. She understood his anger, shared it in part, but she doubted she could ever grasp the extent of what Tesler had inflicted on him and the others at the Mojave Desert facility.

David skirted around her, grabbed Tesler's wrists, and secured the nylon band of the zip tie around them. As he ratcheted the tie tighter, the nylon pinched Tesler's flesh, and he winced.

She settled a hand on David's arm. "Easy."

His gaze traveled to hers, sharpened by an angry glint. The hairs on the back of her neck bristled. She swallowed, curling her fingers around his arm. He exhaled a long breath that deflated his shoulders and quenched the searing heat in his eyes. With a swift jerk of the zip tie, he herded Tesler toward the door.

As she trailed behind them, an odd niggling started up in her gut. What would David do if he got Tesler alone? Her vision from two days ago flashed through her mind. David on his knees. Tesler slashing a knife down at his chest. Blood. Death.

It won't come true. We've changed things, haven't we?

That might've been wishful thinking. For the moment, she decided to believe it, but stay vigilant anyway.

Sean and Amador brought up the rear of their little procession as they tramped out of the facility. They departed via the elevator and up through the metal shed, nothing more than a husk to cover up what lay beneath. The trek through the woods, to the vehicle Amador had acquired—rented or stolen, she didn't care anymore—consumed more minutes than her frayed nerves could handle. By the time they parked on the airport runway alongside Amador's jet, she was wringing her hands and chewing the inside of her bottom lip.

David handed his prisoner over to Sean and Amador, who steered Tesler in the direction of the jet's airstairs. Their footfalls created only the barest sound on the asphalt. David positioned himself in front of her and hovered his hands near her forearms without making contact as if he feared touching her. The sun, dimmed by a thin layer of clouds, cast shadows on his eyes but could not hide the tension on his face.

"What's wrong?" he asked. "It's more than what Tesler said about Nkosi."

"Yeah." She hunched her shoulders. "I saw Tesler murder you. And now he's with us."

"Would you rather I kill him?"

Her head snapped back, in sync with the massive thud of her heart. The matter-of-fact way he'd suggested murdering someone...

David drew her closer, their bodies inches apart. "I wouldn't kill him unless he tried to hurt one of us. You know that, or you should." His thumbs rubbed her flesh in vigorous circles. She must've flinched, because he looked chagrined for a split second, then let up on the pressure, the movements mellower and almost sensual. "Don't you know I'm not a cold-blooded killer?"

Less a question than a plea. "I don't know anything anymore."

"Yes, you do." He tucked her into his embrace with his forehead resting on hers. His breaths tickled her skin. "You're blocking our connection, or at least trying not to feel it. Aren't you?" When she gave a tiny nod, he sighed. "Why? What are you afraid of? Is it me?"

"No." She meant it too. "I'm worried about what you might do to Tesler if you get the chance. He—he tortured you. For months. I know you're not a killer, but if Tesler starts taunting you and there's nobody else around..."

"You think I'll kill him."

"I..." She focused on his eyes and the familiar fire there. "I'm not sure. But I don't want you to do it. You'll regret it for the rest of your life, and I couldn't stand to feel that happening to you. So yes, I'm blocking our link."

He shut his eyes, and his hands roved over her back, comforting rather than arousing. She looped her arms around his waist and leaned into him.

"You know me," he said. "You know I would never murder anyone in cold blood. But you're scared, I get it, because Nkosi is out there with an army and Tesler planted a seed of doubt. He made you think what happened to Nkosi might be your fault. Let it go, Grace. Embrace our connection. Invite me into your soul again and I swear you won't regret it."

He was already there, inside her. She'd tried to ignore it, to box it up in a corner of her psyche, but his passion and adoration refused to be contained. It surged through her, a firestorm blustering into every crevice of her being. His mouth descended over hers, and she surrendered to the kiss completely, granting him all of herself in the melding of their lips.

Stop being afraid.

His ardor, infused into every thrust of his tongue and slant of his mouth on hers, vanquished the tatters of her fear. The heat evaporated the cold. It suffused her from head to toe, inside and out, until nothing mattered except him.

"Watch out!"

Sean's scream ruptured their passion. David yanked his head up, his narrowed gaze flying to a spot behind her. His body went stiff.

She pulled out of his arms and spun around to look.

A hunter-green Jeep roared toward the fence that hemmed in the runway. It crashed into the barrier with a clanging *pow* and slashed a hole in the fence. The Jeep plowed through the opening, fishtailed, and rocketed straight toward her and David.

He seized her arm and dragged her toward the jet. "Into the plane. Hurry."

They bolted for the airstairs. Before they could clamber halfway up the steps, the Jeep blasted into the stairs.

The wheeled structure spun sideways. She lurched, flailed for a hand-hold, and sailed out into open air.

Chapter Twenty-Eight

AVID THWACKED INTO THE GROUND ON HIS SIDE. PAIN SHOT through his shoulder and hip, radiating out into the rest of his body. White lights punctured his vision. Behind the glare, he spotted a slender shape slumped on the ground. Auburn hair spilled over a pale face. She lay limp on her side, one leg bent across the other in an awkward pose.

"Grace!"

She did not move.

No, goddammit. He hoisted his torso off the ground and propped his weight up with one arm. Fresh agony wrung his muscles and rooted him in place. He stared at Grace where she lay motionless on the asphalt, near the front wheel of the jet. He saw no blood. That was good, wasn't it?

Go get her, you raging idiot.

His body screamed when he shifted his weight, but he gritted his teeth and heaved himself off the ground.

"You okay?" Sean called from the open door of the jet.

"Yes."

"Engines won't start."

"What?" David's head snapped up. "What happened to the engines?"

"I think somebody fried them."

A psychic somebody. Nkosi's army had begun the siege.

From further down the runway, an engine roared. He stumbled leftward until he could peer around the stairs. The Jeep was back, and it tore across the tarmac straight at Grace.

Damn the pain. He bolted for her and collapsed to his knees beside her slack form. When he carefully pressed a finger into her neck, her heartbeat pulsed strong and steady against it. He palpated her head and neck in a cautious exploration but discovered no open wounds, just a small bump on her head. Her lips fluttered on a muffled moan.

He sank back on his heels, one hand on his forehead. The heaviness of dread whooshed away, and he teetered from the release. She'd be okay. *Thank you, God.*

The Jeep roared.

Lost in his worry for her, he'd completely forgotten about the maniac in the Jeep.

David scooped Grace into his arms and raced away in a direction perpendicular to the Jeep's line of travel. The airstairs had skidded too far from the jet's door, and he couldn't waste time wrestling the contraption back into position. The driver of the Jeep wouldn't sit idle for a timeout. David angled across the runway, toward the hole the Jeep had sliced into the fence. *Get Grace to safety.* The single goal drove him onward, despite the searing pain in his limbs, despite the throbbing in his skull. Up ahead, a gray metal hangar squatted in a wide, empty tract of land, its enormous doors shut. He sprinted for the smaller, human-size door at the building's corner.

The weight of Grace strained the muscles in his arms, but he clutched her to his chest, gasping and grunting. He wouldn't drop her. He would never let her go, no matter what.

The Jeep's engine snarled behind him.

Fixated on the door, he pumped his legs harder, faster, heedless of the pain and the black spots in his vision. *Save her, save her, save her.* Adrenaline spiked through his veins, sharpening his senses until he was certain he smelled the sun's heat. *Save her, save her.* The door swelled bigger and bigger in front of him.

A clanging crash erupted behind him.

He resisted the impulse to look. The Jeep had bashed into the fence again, the driver hell-bent on annihilating the precious cargo in David's arms.

Tires squealed.

At the hangar door, he shifted his hold on Grace just enough to seize the knob and wrenched it. Locked. *Dammit.*

He stumbled backward one step, pulled in a deep breath, and kicked the door as hard as he could. It burst inward, cracking into the wall and bouncing back. He shoved past the door, into the gloom of a deserted hallway, and gave the environs a cursory scan to verify nobody was around. Then he took off down the hall into the unknown.

A shaft of muted sunlight spilled out of a room to his left. He veered through the open doorway into a small office. A chair with a high back faced a metal desk. His legs burned, his chest ached, and his arms quivered around Grace. He dropped into the chair and cradled her limp, soft body in his arms.

She stirred a little, mumbling words he couldn't understand.

His heart leaped at the sound of her voice. She was alive and awake, sort of. Better sort of than not at all. He combed his fingers through her hair, sweeping it away from her face. A whispery moan escaped her parted lips. He skimmed his thumb across her mouth as she snuggled into him like they were napping in bed together.

If only. Instead, they were hiding out from a crazed individual controlled by an evil entity—or energy, or whatever the hell Nkosi was. He should go check on their pursuer, but that obligated him to leave her here.

His hands trembled as he tugged her closer, unwilling to break the contact yet.

The Jeep was still out there. So were Sean and Amador, and Tesler too. He must stop the assault. But he knew of only one way, and it required him to appropriate Grace's power without her consent. She couldn't consent because she was dazed or unconscious. He couldn't tell which. In either case, to stop the Jeep and its driver, he needed an influx of her power.

"I'm sorry," he whispered into her hair.

"Mmm."

Her mumbled noise might've signified consent, or maybe he was so desperate he'd grab onto anything he might interpret as permission. It didn't matter. He must do this.

Please understand.

David untethered his mind from his body and rushed into the crossroads where he commandeered all the energy he could. It wasn't enough. He tapped into his link to Grace and let her power fill in the gaps, until the psychic energy glowed inside him, ripe and ready. Then he plummeted back to the physical plane, steering his mind away from his body. He glimpsed himself slumped in the chair, and Grace cuddled against him.

It's all for you.

His mind flew out of the building.

The Jeep screeched to a halt mere feet from the door he'd kicked in moments earlier. The driver's door swung open. A man in camouflage fatigues jumped out, his boots thumping on the asphalt. His ashen skin, a contrast to his blue lips, shimmered with a glaze of sweat. Psychic energy roiled out of the man to lick at the air with invisible tongues. This man commanded metaphysical power, yes, but a weakened version of it. No match for David.

The man shuffled toward the door. In his right hand, he wielded a gun.

David hurled everything he had at the man. The intruder flipped backward and whacked into the ground on his back. His eyes rolled up in his head. Dead?

He hadn't meant to kill the man. He was a puppet, after all, tortured in ways even David couldn't fathom. But the man looked… No, not dead. David hurried toward the unmoving man, and for the first time, he cursed his inability to manifest. If he had a body, he could render first aid.

Energy infused him, sweet and rich and potent, like… Grace.

His feet touched down on the asphalt. Solid feet. On solid ground. He tested his weight, bending his knees and bouncing a little. Yes, this body was real. He'd manifested, without Grace's direct help.

Yet she had helped him. In her semi-conscious state, she recognized his need and channeled more of her power into him to launch him into a manifestation. She was amazing.

God, he loved her.

David crouched beside the prone man and checked for a pulse in his neck. It thumped against his finger, strong but irregular. The man's skin chilled him, the clamminess transferred onto his flesh. He'd seen a man in this condition before. When Jackson Tennant had pumped himself full of drugs to stimulate his latent psychic abilities, it left him sickly and pale as death, exactly like this man.

Nkosi's army had a flaw.

"Man, that's not fair. You can manifest without Grace's help now?"

David glanced up at Sean. The boy ducked through the gap in the fence to trot toward him. Amador escorted a bound Tesler in Sean's wake. David rose to greet them.

Sean's lips twisted into a teenage frown, rife with disgust at the injustice of just about everything. "Can Grace teach me to do that?"

"No."

"But you—"

"Still need her help to manifest, trust me."

The boy slouched, his mouth tightening into a half-hearted pout. "It's not fair."

He slapped Sean's arm. "Get used to unfairness. That's life."

The boy grumbled.

"Who knows," David said, "one day your powers might expand and you may find yourself manifesting all over the place."

His expression brightened. "You really think so?"

"Sure." David pointed at the fatigues-clad man on the ground. "Keep an eye on him. I have to get back to Grace."

"Sure, man. We got this."

David released his hold on this body, on this location. He spiraled back into his real body, and the weight of Grace resting against his chest anchored him to reality. He nuzzled her hair, drinking in the fresh scent of her. The eyes he cherished opened to focus on him, and he tumbled into those hazel irises.

She smiled with a lazy movement of her lips. "You rescued me again."

"Did I?" He traced his fingertip down her jawline, to the corner of her mouth.

"Yes, honey, you did."

He ran his finger over her lips. "Honey?"

She writhed, trying to sit up. Her buttocks ground into his lap, energizing parts of him that he didn't need to wake up right now.

He hopped to his feet, Grace in his arms, and deposited her on the floor.

She swayed a little, her smile going dreamy. "Would you prefer 'sweetie'?"

"Call me whatever you want." He slanted his mouth over hers, delving deep to savor the taste of her. "As long as you're all right, I don't even care if you call me dumb-ass."

She giggled. "Dumb-ass?"

"I've been hanging around with Sean too much." He cupped her bottom and tugged her into him. "But from here on out, I'm with you."

"Think you'll start talking like me?"

Another voice answered. "I sure hope not. That would be sooooo embarrassing."

David shook his head at Sean but felt his lips curl upward at the corners. Anyone could call him anything and he wouldn't care. As long as he had Grace, nothing else mattered.

And so, right there in front of Sean and Amador and Tesler, he ravished her with a kiss that would've made a sex therapist blush. Just because he could. His quest for vengeance seemed a dim memory, a lapse in judgment he vowed to never repeat. He knew exactly what he had to do to make things right.

He parted his lips from hers long enough to murmur, "Marry me. As soon as possible."

Her smile radiated into him. "Yes."

***

GRACE WRIGGLED, BUT INSTEAD OF LOOSENING HIS GRIP ON HER derriere, David squeezed lightly. She let out a sharp squeak. "David, really."

"Yeah, man," Sean said from behind her. "At least spring for a hotel room before you start mauling her. I'm not old enough to watch porn, at least until September. And I think you're wigging out our prisoner."

A volcanic blush raged in Grace's cheeks. What had gotten into David?

Without relinquishing her, he leaned to the side to frown at Sean. "I thought I told you three to stay outside."

"The puppet dude is out cold, and I mean way cold."

David's fingers dug into her buttocks. "Dead?"

"Nah, but I don't think he's waking up anytime soon. Besides, we locked him in his own Jeep."

The tension eased out of David, and he shifted his hands to her hips. Thank goodness. Maybe her cheeks would cool down without his hands all over her ass. If the rest of her half-melted body would follow suit, she might pretend her fiancé hadn't made out with and fondled her in front of a live audience. She ought to chastise him, but it had felt so good she couldn't muster enough annoyance.

Instead, she patted his cheek. "You saved my life for the second—or is it the third?—time in one day. Feel better?"

"I'll feel better when we take out Nkosi."

He damn well knew what she'd meant. Did he seriously want her to ask "do you feel more manly after rescuing the damsel in distress right here in front of our entourage"? She doubted that, so she let it go. "The guy outside looked half dead. Nkosi's army isn't exactly the Mongol hordes bearing down on us."

He arched a brow. "How do you know what the man outside looks like?"

Oops. She'd assumed he noticed her presence, but clearly not. "I, well, kind of hitchhiked with you on your little expedition through the crossroads." At his stunned expression, she hunched her shoulders. "I didn't mean to, honey, it sort of happened unconsciously."

Her use of the endearment *honey* dissolved the confusion from his face. "That's how you knew when I wanted to manifest and you shot me up with more of your power."

Sean sniggered. "You guys a couple of druggies or what? She's shooting you up?"

David sighed. "I didn't mean it like that."

Someone behind her cleared his throat. Amador's voice wafted into the room like a spicy, but chilly, breeze. "Perhaps we should concentrate on locating Nkosi. If we stop him, his army will be headless."

David gave a sarcastic laugh. "Headless?"

"Yes, like a snake with its head cut off. No?"

Grace nudged David with a finger in his side, the only spot on his body that wasn't lined with hard muscle. "Amador's right. We need to track down Nkosi."

"I know. But how?"

Here came the part she dreaded. The thing she'd avoided since her last psychic debacle, and the one task that, at the mere thought of it, hardened frost over her from the inside out. "There's only one way. He's too powerful for normal remote viewing to work." She clutched handfuls of his shirt, her fists balled on his chest. "I have to tap into the Gold—"

"No." He growled the word, but it was panic pinching his features. "You don't have to do that. We'll find another way."

"We don't have time." Willing her pulse to slow and her hands to uncurl, she lifted onto tiptoes to level their gazes. "This is the only way."

He pinned her against him with his muscular arms. His eyes, wide and wild, searched hers. His lips parted, but he did not speak.

She flattened her palms on his chest. "There's a catch, though. Since we're, um… bonded on a much deeper level now, I have no idea what this will do to you. The Golden Power might infect you too."

"I don't give a damn what it does to me. It's you I'm worried about."

His hold slackened a bit, and her heels hit the floor. She longed to bury her face in the hollow of his shoulder, but she must remain strong, now more than ever. Swiping the tears away with the back of her hand, she touched his cheek. "I know you're worried. The Golden Power corrupts me, and I—"

"Shut up."

She tried to push away, but he grasped her hips. "Excuse me?"

"I said shut up," he growled. "Nothing can corrupt you. I told you that before, and I haven't changed my mind. It's a fact."

"But you said you're concerned."

He held her face in both hands. "I worry because I know how much you hate using the Golden Power. But I still believe you are stronger than it is. If you can believe that, then there's nothing to worry about."

"David, I'm not that powerful." He grounded her, in mind and spirit, without a doubt. Was their bond truly strong enough to overcome this?

He kissed her, hard and quick. "Can you believe it? Can you believe *me*?"

She studied his eyes, and the truth rippled through her. "Yes. I believe."

"Then do it."

Sean trotted up beside them. "Whoa, are you serious? You're gonna use the Golden Power, right here?"

Grace looked at him. "Maybe you guys should wait outside after all."

The kid stared at her for several seconds, and she could practically hear him chewing on the problem, weighing the risks. But then he nodded, swiveled on his heels, and marched out the door, shouting, "Come on, Gabe, let's go."

In the doorway, Amador was scowling, but whether at Sean's nickname for him or at the prospect of being banished outdoors, she couldn't decide. Finally, he headed out the door.

Sean shouted, "Hey, where's Tesler?"

Amador poked his head inside the room just long enough to say, "Tesler has escaped. We will search for him."

"Wait for us," David said. "We'll worry about him later."

Alone again, she and David stood silent, face to face. There was nothing left to say. They both understood the stakes and had made the decision together.

He enfolded her in his arms, and she nestled her head on his shoulder, against his neck. The feel of his sturdy body against hers calmed the noise inside. She relaxed, shutting her eyes. Her mind shook free of her body and soared into the crossroads, then higher still, beyond the limits of normal psychic power and into the heart of the darkest energy.

She dived into the Golden Power.

Nkosi's voice vibrated in her mind. You've come home, Grace, and you will never leave me again.

Chapter Twenty-Nine

AVID SCUDDED ALONG IN GRACE'S WAKE, THE TAIL TO HER FLAMING comet, as they traveled through the crossroads together. With Grace, every barrier he'd believed existed crumbled into dust. He could neither see nor hear her voice, yet the glowing essence of her ferried him higher and higher into the star field that comprised the psychic crossroads.

A wall. Up ahead.

Pressure constricted his mind, stabbing pains through his metaphysical form. He struggled to draw back from the barrier, but Grace rocketed both of them toward it. They collided with the wall. If he'd had a voice, he would've screamed from the shock of impact.

The pressure vanished.

He hovered somewhere near Grace, bathed in the glow of her energy. Beyond her fire, darkness gaped its maw, hungry for the power it sniffed out in her. Alien thoughts bombarded him.

You've come home, Grace, and you will never leave me again.

Nkosi's astral voice. They must've breached the hideaway of the Golden Power.

He shouldn't have allowed Grace to do this. What kind of coward made his fiancée fight the ultimate battle alone? He was here, sure, but how could he aid her? Liberating her from the facility, and then from Nkosi's puppet man, had depleted his metaphysical reserves. She must feel that.

The darkness closed in around them.

Oily energy slithered through him, seeking cracks and holes in his psyche, avenues by which to sneak inside and break him apart bit by bit. The power would consume Grace. As for him…

It would annihilate him.

Maybe she's better off without me.

He didn't mean it, didn't believe it, but the fleeting thought split open a hairline fracture somewhere inside him. The Golden Power clawed at his soul, pried open the crack, wormed itself into the gap, into him. Slimy, viscous, and putrid, it crept inside.

If it took him, Grace would fall next.

A glistening, incandescent outpouring of love shot down the connection from Grace into him. His own words, the ones he'd admonished her with, echoed in his mind. *Stop being afraid.*

The time had come to take his own advice.

He threw open the gates of his heart and soul and embraced the essence of her. Hope and anguish. Passion and trust. An aching loneliness, at last quenched by his vow to value her above all else. *I won't let you down this time, Grace.* He would sacrifice his very soul for her.

And it was time to live up to the promise.

Summoning all the power he harbored inside himself, he lashed out at the invading entity that was the Golden Power. Slashing. Goring. Spraying black energy into the ether and lapping it up with a ravenous thirst.

Gorged on the ultimate power, he hesitated.

This time, Grace didn't need to taint herself. He'd absorbed the brunt of it for her. And the unbridled knowledge gushing into his mind bestowed on him the one ability he'd failed to master before. The power to deliver her from her darkest fears.

He knew where to find Nkosi.

A wave of anxiety streaked into him from Grace. She sensed the change in him. Her panic begged him to stop, but it was too late.

He raced toward Nkosi.

———

GRACE HURTLED AFTER DAVID, STILL BOUND TO HIM BY THE PSYCHIC tether of their connection. Her mind bucked and scraped across barriers she could neither see nor touch, but that scuffed her raw anyway. The stinging and constriction of repressed sobs wracked her astral body.

Stop, David, please.

What had he done? One second, the Golden Power was pawing at her, with Nkosi's thoughts injected into her mind. The next second, the pressure let go with dizzying abruptness, and a silence deeper than the vacuum of space deafened her. David's energy, once warm and comforting, devolved into a writhing, oily mass of—

No. It couldn't be.

She reached out to caress him with the psychic equivalent of fingers and plunged into the viscous morass. The amorphous thing smothered him, burrowing deeper with each second.

He had absorbed the Golden Power.

Why, why, why?

A sick feeling infiltrated her. She knew why. He'd done it for her.

To save her. To free her. But instead of unchaining her from the tainted lure of the Golden Power, he was dragging her down with him. She'd follow him into Hell, if necessary, but not at the expense of losing him. And she would lose him. Forever. He'd ingested too much of the supreme and insatiable power source, granting it unfettered access to another human body and mind.

This was her fault. He wouldn't have sunk to this level if she hadn't made him feel unworthy. Her nagging, her accusations, drove him to this.

She was going to save him, dammit.

Light exploded around her. She plummeted out into the world, whirling and whirling, without form or focus. David's energy—the warm, sharp energy of him and only him—shielded her from the onslaught. It calmed every nerve and anchored her to the world around them. His arms caught her as she struggled to sort out what she saw.

Trees towered all around them, sentinels that penned them inside a claustrophobic clearing. Green moss squished under her feet. The sun blazed behind the treetops, its rays puncturing the shadows below. A frozen sliver of realization pierced her heart. She'd visited this place before. This was where her vision had unfolded. David died here.

His fingers cinched tight, cutting into her flesh.

She hissed. "Ow."

His fingers dug in deeper.

Grace pulled out of his grasp. Her gaze swung up to his, and her heart stopped beating for an agonizing second.

His eyes. They flared a bright white, the pupils and irises overwhelmed by the terrifying glow that radiated from within. The brilliance expanded, inch by inch, to engulf his body in a sterile aura composed of raw power. The force of it battered her mind. If not for the psychic firewall she'd built, the Golden Power would be breaking through to pillage her mind. The energy roiling out of David scratched at her flesh, inciting a hard shiver.

Her skin. She felt it. His hands had grasped her.

They had manifested. *He* manufactured bodies for them both.

"No, David." The grief rending her heart bled through in her voice. She reached for him, but a wave of sickening power punched into her from him, and she yanked her hand away. "No. David, no, you have to let it go. Please, for us, scrub it out of you and come back to me."

His eyes flashed brighter, tiny stars about to go supernova. The power in him distended, hot and thick and vile, rising toward an outburst of galactic proportions.

She dived into the power envelope that barricaded him. It scorched her skin, scraped at her body and mind, desperate to drag her back into its clutches. *No, dammit, never again, you will never take me and you can't have David.* She seized his face with both hands. Energy seared her flesh and coiled around her wrists, like wires ratcheting tighter. Pain shot up her arms. She bit back a cry and pulled his face to hers.

"It can't have you." Her voice growled as if a feral animal possessed her. Yet it was her voice, her fury infusing her tone and hardening her resolve. "David, goddammit, you listen to me. The Golden Power can't take you unless you give in. Fight it. Scratch and scream and thrash until it lets go." She jerked his head down, their lips touching, her hands clamped to his face. "You're stronger than Nkosi. You can conquer this power and come back to me."

His lips twitched against hers. His body tensed. And in his eyes, a glimmer of blue broke through the screen of white-hot fire.

"That's it," she said, tears running down her cheeks. "That's it, keep fighting. You're mine, remember? Nothing else can claim you." With her next words, the fierceness of her voice reverberated in her soul. "You are mine."

The blue glittered and swelled, annihilating the white brilliance one spark at a time. The darkness seething into her from him weakened. Her heart pounded at the sight of blue fire overtaking the nuclear glow. What else could she say to rouse him, to drive out the alien power?

Nothing. Words were over.

The memory of what he'd done for her surged to the surface.

She crushed her mouth to his, delved her tongue inside, branding him as hers with each swipe and swirl. At first, he held still, his mouth open to her but his entire being oblivious to her wanton assault. Then, with devastating swiftness, the inhuman facade imploded and avid passion combusted between them, ricocheting up and down their connection until she couldn't distinguish his fervor from hers. The whiteness evaporated from his eyes, cast out by the blue bonfire in his irises. The blinding aura around him snuffed out. His arms clamped around her, and his tongue thrust deep into her mouth, demanding more while giving it in return. She let her eyelids shut and basked in the euphoria of their bodies fused.

Their manifestations disintegrated. As one, their minds soared back across the metaphysical distance to their bodies, uncoupling at the last second.

Sean slouched on the desk, perched on its edge. "Back already?"

David pushed away from her, his posture casual, yet with a coiled tension beneath the surface. "I know where Tesler is. Let's go."

His resolve, steel hard and impenetrable, brooked no argument. She would've tried anyway, but she knew it would do no good. The battle was imminent, and he would not be dissuaded from his goal.

Resigned, she let him lead her out to the Jeep.

GRACE EYED THE MASSIVE PINE TREE AND REPRESSED A SHUD-der. They'd arrived here, in the clearing where her vision had taken place, a few minutes ago. Sean and Amador had hung back to keep watch. No sign of Tesler or Nkosi. Those facts did nothing to disperse the chill that kept rushing through her every time she looked at the tree.

David kicked the pine's trunk. "He was here, I know it."

"Maybe you were wrong," she said. "We didn't see Tesler when we RV'd this place. You might've been, I don't know, channeling my vision."

"No. He was here."

She grasped his shoulders and turned him toward her. Angry lines carved into his features. Ordering him to chill out, or even begging him, wouldn't work. What else could she do?

Ka-chunk.

David scanned the forest. "I know that sound."

Yeah, she recognized the sound too. It was a round being chambered in a gun.

She stepped away from him and searched the shadows between the trees.

"You won't see them," said a voice colored by a familiar accent. "Not until I command them to reveal their presence."

Nkosi strode out of the trees.

Tesler lurched out behind him, eyes as wild as his gray hair, his cheeks splotched with red.

"Over there," Nkosi told Tesler, nodding toward a thick pine tree.

The world seemed to skid to a halt, and the air caught in her lungs. The tree. In her vision that was where Tesler had murdered David.

She clutched his hand. He was focused on Nkosi, his lips compressed, his eyes narrowed. She tugged his hand.

He turned his head, brows furrowed.

"Please get us out of here," she said. "This is where it happened."

His brows knit tighter.

"My vision." She wound her fingers through his and gripped him with all her strength. "This is where my premonition took place."

He didn't ask if she was sure. He didn't need to. Their link, no longer poisoned with the Golden Power, told him all he needed to know.

The wrinkles ironed out of his brow, and his expression went stoic. "We changed things. It won't happen the way you saw."

"Please, David. Let's get the hell out of here."

"No." He shook free of her hand. "Tesler and Nkosi must be stopped."

"David." The sharpness in her tone made everyone jerk their heads in her direction.

Nkosi chuckled. The sound chilled her to the core and reverberated off the trees. "A lover's tiff? I will gladly give you a moment to mend the rift before I rip the brains out of your heads."

David swelled taller somehow, his stance wide, every muscle tensed and ready for battle. His blond hair glistened in the sunshine, and his eyes glinted with a purpose she'd never witnessed before. Her warrior angel. Her hero.

At that moment, she loved him more than she'd imagined possible.

He hurled himself at Nkosi. A snarl ripped out of him as he tackled the other man and their bodies tumbled to the ground in a blur of motion. They rolled, kicked, clobbered, bellowed. Nkosi's eyes glared white. His lips peeled back, and his crooked teeth sank into David's shoulder. David rammed his knee into Nkosi's gut. The other man convulsed, his face contorted with pain.

David threw a glance at her. In an instant, she knew what he needed.

She poured all her energy into their connection, into him.

He drew his fists back and slugged them into Nkosi's chest. The power gushing through David transformed his fists into masses of energy, and even as his knuckles struck Nkosi's flesh, the energy punched straight to the heart of the other man's power.

Nkosi screamed.

A crack split the air. The power coruscating out of Nkosi shredded and dispersed into the void of the crossroads.

David flung his hands away.

Moaning, Nkosi rolled his head from side to side.

Each breath a wheeze, David clambered to his feet and stumbled backward.

"You fools," Nkosi said, his voice slurred. "Did you think it would be that simple?"

David tripped, flailing toward the ground. Grace hurried to catch him, her arms latching around him so fast he'd barely tipped over yet. He listed against her, and they both stared at the man sprawled on the ground.

Nkosi pushed up onto his elbows. "I was willing. I welcomed the Golden Power. It granted me untold potential, and I offered up my mind and soul to it. You—" He speared the air with a finger pointed at Grace. "You rejected it. I gave it form and purpose."

David trembled in her arms, too weak to move or speak. His body weighed down on her, but she gritted her teeth and held on. No way in hell she'd ever let go of him again.

Nkosi wrestled to his feet and wiped his hands on his pants. "You may have driven out the Golden Power, but I still have plenty of my own psychic energy. Yes, you are the strongest traveler my ally Tesler has ever seen, but I am almost as powerful as you."

"Maybe," she said, "and maybe not."

Nkosi massaged his jaw, one of the places where David had clouted him. "I volunteered for the project. Your parents were weak, unwilling to take the risks necessary for advancement. I was terribly pleased when Tesler came on board, and when he shared with me his vision for the project, I invited him to test his methods on me."

"You let him torture you?"

"Of course." Nkosi grinned with predatory lust. "How else could we discover if the technique would work?"

David stiffened against her, and she hugged him to her. "Technique? You aided in the torture of hundreds of psychics, not to mention the ones who died because of it. You're insane." She shook her head, unable to process the depth of his madness. "You've lost your big advantage. The Golden Power is gone."

"But I still have Digital Prognostics." He took one lithe step toward her. "I purchased JT's company after his demise, which means I own Tesler's files. I own the facilities scattered around the world. You stripped me of my greatest asset, but I hold more cards than you believe."

Like hell. They hadn't come this far, survived this much, to lose the final battle.

She must destroy all the files. There had to be a way. Without JT's secret files, which she still kept tucked inside her bra back in her real body, Nkosi would have nothing if she obliterated Tesler's data. The loss would terminate Nkosi's manic dreams.

But she had no idea how to destroy the data.

Nkosi knew how.

David pushed away from her, though his hand lingered on her back. "No."

"I thought you couldn't read my mind."

"Don't need to. I know you, Grace, and I know how you think. This is not the way to end things."

"I'm afraid it is. If I don't stop him here and now, the suffering will never end."

"Please don't do this. Please."

She kissed him, a light and tender expression of the immortal flame he'd lit inside her.

David's eyes, his beautiful soul, pleaded with her.

I'm sorry. His tiny flinch assured her he'd heard.

She confronted Nkosi. He bared his teeth in a nasty imitation of a smile. She balled her hands into fists, battling the urge to sock him in the gut. Instead, she marched up to him, nailed her gaze to his, and bashed through his mental ramparts.

He wailed. His eyes rolled back in his head. His mind fought her, pushed back, floundered for a weapon to fend her off.

She battered him with the last remnants of her psychic power. His mind splintered under her assault. A crack opened up, and she charged inside.

Not so powerful now, are you, Nkosi?

He whimpered, wailing again, and collapsed to his knees. His thoughts rushed into her, a swirling, seething mass of words and intentions, laced with panic and rage and engorged with a madness beyond comprehension.

Gunshots boomed around her.

David shouted her name.

None of it registered in her conscious mind. None of it mattered. She held a man's mind in her hands, and every thought he ever conceived slithered in her palms. She dived her fingers into the quicksand, digging, hunting, ripping, tearing.

"David, no!" Sean's voice. Distant. Unimportant.

Need, I need, yes, I need this.

She rifled through Nkosi's memories. Tossed each aside. Dug deeper. With one final thrust, she captured the information she coveted and ripped it from his mind without hesitation.

Far away, he shrieked.

A sharp pain jabbed into her neck. Weariness flooded through her, buckling her knees, and she toppled into the void.

Chapter Thirty

AVID RUSHED TO CATCH GRACE BEFORE SHE HIT THE GROUND. HIS heart jackhammered against his ribs, and the torrent of blood thundering behind his eardrums muffled all other sounds. He lugged her behind the big pine tree, cradling her limp body, with her feet dangling a few inches above the ground. Her head fell onto his chest and the silky strands of her hair feathered across his chin.

Amador and Sean circled the two of them, eyes on the woods, postures tense. Two of Nkosi's human puppets lay dead at the edge of the woods, both shot by Amador. David couldn't believe the man had swooped in to fend off their attackers. He did not want to feel obliged to like the lying son of a bitch.

Amador's gaze flicked to David. "How is she?"

Ah yes, of course. That explained why he'd stepped in—for Grace. For now, David had given up worrying about the man's intentions. "I don't know, she's out cold."

"Care for her. We will guard you."

"Thanks," David said, uttering the word slowly, unable to grasp that he not only thanked this man, but he meant it.

Amador nodded, his attention returning to the woods. Despite the bright sun overhead, a screen of trees cloaked them in false twilight. The gloom hid their attackers, but with any luck, it masked their exact whereabouts too.

David tipped Grace's head back to expose her face to him. He settled a hand on her shoulder and jostled her carefully. "Grace?"

She didn't move. Didn't speak. Didn't stir at all.

His chest constricted. He ran a hand over her forehead, the pale skin cold against his. When he dipped a finger to the pulse point on her neck, the beating of her heart pulsed in a slow but steady rhythm. Relief weakened his knees, but he sucked in a breath and clutched her tighter.

She was alive. For now, that was all he needed to know.

Behind him, inside the small clearing, Nkosi lay crumpled on the ground. His body depressed the thick moss. His eyes gaped wide and empty.

Dead. A chill shimmered through David. Grace had killed Nkosi, without intending to, and she would have no reason for guilt. Nkosi had attempted to kill all of them. He'd imprisoned innocent people and hollowed out their minds to reshape them to his will. How many lives had he taken? One was too many. Grace acted in defense of herself and countless others. When she woke, he'd convince her she did the right thing.

What if she doesn't wake up?

The thought shredded him like an electrical shock. She would wake up, she had to. Her heart still beat, and her psychic energy still crackled through him. She would come back to him. She must.

But he understood what she'd done and the cost it might exact. The look on her face right before she'd enacted her plan, a mixture of determination and intense regret, had conveyed her intentions to him. Their bond compelled him to experience a fraction of what she unleashed on Nkosi, of what she endured to accomplish the feat, and he knew. She'd exploited the one ability he'd made her swear never ever to attempt.

She read Nkosi's mind.

Worse, she tore it apart and rummaged through the fragments to unearth what she sought. David realized what she'd been searching for too, the key to bringing down the entire network of psychic research facilities. The vital piece of information that would serve as the nail she might drive into the coffin of Digital Prognostics, Tesler, and everything both had represented.

David touched her cheek, hunting for some sign of awareness on her face, but detected none. His heart ached with a desperation that burned him from the inside out. He could not lose her, would not stand for it. She owned his heart, his soul, every part of him that was worth anything. Before her, he'd been a zombie, not unlike Nkosi's puppets, devoid of passion or purpose. Grace brought him to life. He owed her more than he could ever repay.

Crunch.

David froze at the sound. It had come from the woods behind him. He bent sideways to peek around the massive tree, careful to keep Grace secure in his arms. Amador and Sean both trained their weapons on the area where the noise had originated. Even the birds no longer chirped, and the breeze had ceased its rustling.

The sharp crack of a twig breaking lanced the silence.

Among the trees, a shadow shifted.

"Who goes there?" Amador shouted.

"Give up," a strained voice replied. "Or die."

Sean sidled toward David, his back to the tree. He said under his breath, "Shouldn't we run or something?"

David shut his eyes and made a quick sweep of the vicinity with his RV senses. "We can't run. They've got us surrounded. At least a dozen people."

"Their master dude's dead. Why are they still doing what he told them?"

"I don't know."

Why? The question plagued David as he surveyed the forest for human-shaped silhouettes. Why hadn't the enslaved psychics abandoned their mission? With Nkosi dead, logic suggested they should stop. Instead, they pushed forward with unstoppable resolve.

And the puppets had guns. Ammo. Knives. He, Sean, and Amador had barely escaped when two of the zombie psychics assaulted them. With a dozen closing in around them...

Grace roused with a faint grumble.

He stared at her closed eyes, afraid to move, to bump her too much and push her back into unconsciousness. She shifted against him, her eyes darting behind the lids. He rubbed his thumb back and forth over her mouth, and at the feel of her warm, alive skin, his gaze flew heavenward. *Thank you.* Her eyes, though bleary, gazed up at him with trust and love. The sun illuminated the green flecks in her irises.

Her lips wriggled under his thumb, then stretched into a smile. He lowered her onto her feet but kept his arms around her until she stopped swaying.

"Are you okay?" he asked.

"Mm-hm." Her gaze rolled toward Nkosi. Her eyes went wide and her mouth fell open. She whipped her head toward David. "Is he..."

"Dead. Yes." David clasped her hands. "You did what you had to do."

"I know." She inhaled, straightened, and gave a sharp nod. "And I found what we need."

"What do you mean?"

"The computers at all the facilities around the world are linked through a secure network. If we destroy the mainframe, everything's wiped out."

Oh hell. Just when he'd given up global quests for justice. "Let's talk about that later. We need to figure out why Nkosi's puppets are still carrying out his orders."

She lifted her fingers to her throat, her gaze distant. After a few seconds, she glanced around as if hunting for something. "Do the puppets have guns?"

"Yes. And clearly plenty of ammo, plus knives."

She fingered the bark on the tree trunk. Her lips compressed, the corners pulled tight. Although she studied the tree, he had the distinct impression she was concentrating on a sight beyond the reach of normal vision. Her psychic senses expanded through him, around him, encompassing them both and fanning out.

Her expression hardened, and her nails scraped the bark. "Tesler."

David moved to enfold her in his arms, but she batted them away. His hands stayed poised near her arms because he didn't quite know what to do with them. "What about Tesler?"

Her hazel eyes glowed a soft, gorgeous green, lit by the otherworldly energy enlivening her mind. "He slipped away from us. He's hiding nearby, though. And he is the reason the puppets are still enslaved. They switched allegiances, and answer to him."

"How? Tesler has no powers."

She shook her head. "Somehow the Golden Power latched onto him too. I didn't notice it before because the energy is subtle and I was focused on Nkosi. Now..." Her expression slackened, as her mind receded from the physical world. Seconds elapsed, each tick of the clock an anvil pounding on his chest. At last, her eyes swam back into focus. "What's left of the Golden Power took refuge in Tesler. I don't understand how, and it doesn't really matter at the moment. To stop the assault, we have to stop Tesler."

Sean and Amador stared at Grace, their faces blank. Thanks to the power boost he'd gotten from merging with Grace, David felt the other men's wariness. About Grace? Or about the Golden Power taking over Tesler?

"Okay," he told Grace. "We go after Tesler. Sean and Amador can occupy the zombie army while you and I track down their new master."

Sean raised a hand, like a kid in a classroom asking for his turn to speak. "Uh, how do we find Tesler? I can't see him, even with RV."

"We can."

"Are you serious?"

David nodded.

The boy's brows lifted. "Wow. You guys are kinda awesome since you did whatever it was you did to each other last night."

Grace flashed a suggestive smirk at David, and he smirked right back. With great effort, he resisted the impulse to haul her into his arms for another super-heated kiss.

"Jeez, you guys." A blush fired up in Sean's cheeks, and he averted his eyes. "I didn't mean—I was talking about the thing where you joined powers or whatever."

Growling resonated in the air. Silhouettes bobbed among the trees.

The puppets were getting closer.

David stripped his attention away from Grace, which was damn difficult considering the way she licked her lower lip. "We'd better get moving. Tesler's minions are getting closer."

Sean scratched the back of his neck. "When you say moving, do you mean literally, or psychically?"

"Have you recovered enough to travel the astral way?"

"Yeah. I'm cool."

"Good. You distract the puppets while Grace and I deal with Tesler."

Amador cleared his throat. "Where does this plan leave me? I cannot... travel as you do."

David squinted at the man, measuring Amador up as best he could. Though pale, with dark patches under his eyes, he stood straight and gripped his weapon with determination. David suppressed a sigh. He might've misjudged the creep a little, but under no circumstances would he forgive what Amador had done to Grace or the young girl he kidnapped. Today, though, he needed the bastard's help.

And the task he had in mind was the only thing he'd trust Amador to do.

"I need you to stay here," David said, "with our bodies. Protect Grace at all costs."

She slapped the back of her hand on David's chest. "He means protect all of us."

"No." David stalked up to Amador and glared into the man's bloodshot eyes. "You protect *her*. Tesler wants Grace's brain, and it's your job to make sure none of his minions get anywhere near her." David leaned closer until his breaths reflected off Amador's face. "Protect Grace. That's your only job. Get it?"

"I understand."

"If you abandon her—"

"You will hunt me down, even after death, et cetera. I've listened to this speech before." Chin elevated, Amador gave him a self-satisfied smile. "I am the one who has never left her to suffer alone."

David swung his arm back, his hand fisted, ready to wallop Amador. But then he glimpsed Grace out of the corner of his eye, and the fury evaporated. He *had* abandoned her. Over and over. Amador was right.

He dropped his hand. "Just take care of her, all right?"

Amador inclined his head. "You have my word."

Right. As if that meant squat.

But he knew Amador would defend Grace.

With two long strides, David bridged the distance to Grace, towed her into him, and planted a quick, firm kiss on her mouth. "Let's go for a ride."

She looped her arms around his neck. "I'll go anywhere with you."

A weight slammed down on him, forcing out a strangled gasp. His head pounded, and a humming vibrated painfully through his skull.

Grace fell into him. The breath exploded out of her. She snared handfuls of his shirt as her eyelids pinched together, almost shut.

Sean doubled over, hands on his head. "Ah! What the hell?"

The pain subsided in seconds, but a pressure compressed his mind in its wake. Not a headache, not anything he could identify. An external pressure. Faint yet powerful.

David rubbed his temple but held onto Grace with his free arm. "What was that?"

Her head snapped up, her gaze intent on his. "Tesler. He just threw an EM shield up around us. We're not traveling anywhere."

"Shit." An EM field, like the one Tesler had employed in the lab. The one that prevented him from contacting Grace. "We're back to the Stone Age, then."

With a sly grin, Sean waggled his gun. "Not quite the Stone Age."

He tossed the big semiautomatic to David and whipped out of his waistband the smaller gun he'd used earlier.

Grace frowned. "Where's my gun?"

Amador reached under the back of his shirt and produced Grace's personal weapon, the .357 Magnum revolver. He lobbed it to her. "I took the liberty of salvaging that from your purse."

"Thanks." She flipped out the cylinder, and even David could see it contained only three rounds. "Please tell me you stole some ammo when you were rampaging through the facility."

"A few extra clips," David said. "That's all the guards had."

"Maybe we can still run," Sean offered.

A twig cracked. Foliage rustled.

Footfalls whomped. Hard. Fast. Homing in.

Before any of them could process it, a dozen mind-controlled men trudged out of the shadows in a circular formation, penning them in.

A second line of jaundiced and haggard men scuffled up behind the first circle. At least a dozen more minions now reinforced the first group.

Grace chewed her lip. "How many bullets have we got?"

David grasped his gun, eying Tesler's puppets. "Not enough."

CHAPTER THIRTY-ONE

GRACE HUDDLED AGAINST DAVID, HER GUN TARGETED AT THE ground. This was bad. So, so bad. When Nkosi had said he commanded an army, she'd assumed he was exaggerating. No such luck.

David's arm clamped down around her. The gun in his free hand was pointed at the ground.

Sean and Amador flanked them. Every single one of the men in her life looked grimly resolute.

They would fight. They would die.

She would live long enough to have her brain cut out.

A hard shudder jarred her. After everything she'd survived, after the arduous journey she and David crawled through to get back to each other, was this how it ended? Trapped. Helpless. Powerless.

A gunshot boomed.

Sean crumpled.

David and Grace rushed to him. A dark stain was spreading across Sean's left arm, near the shoulder.

"I'm okay," he croaked. "Hurts, but I'll live. Gimme a minute and I'll be good to go."

"Don't worry about that," David said.

Grace waved a hand at Amador. "Get down."

He dropped into a crouch near a tree.

A new sound emanated from the woods—the scraping of feet dragging across the ground. The shuffling of half-catatonic human beings. Tesler's army.

David thrust a hand into her hair. "We have to run, it's our only shot."

"It's too late." She surveyed the trees, counting the silhouettes that approached at a slow but relentless pace. "They're already here."

A voice shouted to them, a voice she knew all too well.

"Drop your weapons," Tesler said. "There's no hope of escape. If you surrender, Grace, I may spare your friends by granting them a quick, painless death. Otherwise, they will suffer along with you."

She would suffer either way. That's what he meant. She'd shoot herself in the head before surrendering to Tesler.

Men shambled out of the shadows to encircle them in an ever-narrowing line of armed and mindless soldiers.

"Shoot them!" David said.

Grace slapped a hand on his gun as he raised it. "Don't bother. There's another band in the woods behind these two groups, at least half a dozen more men. I can see them in my mind. We don't have nearly enough bullets to take them all out."

David's face twisted in anguish. Breathless noises sputtered out of him as if he couldn't quite form words.

Tears stung her eyes, but she blinked them away. In a voice so calm it surprised even her, she told him, "It's over, David."

Their powers were squelched. A small army surrounded them. Yeah, it was all over.

He nodded. The anguish had given way to a bleak resignation, which matched the cold certainty wending through her.

Then his head jerked back, and he squinted at her. "How could you see the men in the woods? The EM field…"

She shrugged. "I don't know. I just did."

His lips parted, and his eyes flared wide for a second. Then his angelic face lit up with understanding. "When Tesler had me strapped in back at the facility, the EM field kept me from contacting you. But I was able to use my powers at a low level, briefly."

She didn't dare think it. Didn't dare hope for it. "The field doesn't shut down our powers?"

"No, it dampens them." He smiled with such brilliant optimism she couldn't prevent her cheeks from dimpling with a matching smile. His hand lighted on her shoulder. "Since we combined ours, maybe we're strong enough to breach the field, or at least slip our fingers through it."

Please, yes, let it be true.

The crashing of footfalls snared their attention. Their heads swiveled toward the clearing in unison.

Karl Tesler stomped out into the open, his back straight, arms at his sides. A ghost of a smile lent him the look of a man supremely satisfied with himself.

His eyes glowed pale white.

Grace swallowed, stepped back, and bumped into David.

Tesler gestured to his minions. "Bring them here."

And so they were herded into the clearing, single file, and their weapons were confiscated. Two minions flanked each of them, one at either side. They halted in the center of the clearing, in a line. The dampening effect of the EM field stifled her as if she'd been locked inside a casket buried six feet under the earth. Could their combined powers overcome the field?

Tesler strolled past them, studying each in turn. His stare flickered unease through Grace, but she noticed a pallor beneath his skin and redness in his eyes.

When he reached David, the last in line, he halted. "Dear boy, did you honestly believe you could keep her from me? I've existed far longer than any human. I am everything."

David snorted. "You're nothing. Just a lunatic who's temporarily holding the remnants of the Golden Power."

"I am the Golden Power."

"Bullshit."

Grace pivoted on her heels to face Tesler. "I drove the power out of Nkosi, and a scrap of it took root in your mind. You are the host to a parasite, nothing more."

Tesler tossed his head. The minions at either side of David seized his arms to haul him toward the big pine tree they'd hidden behind moments earlier. One of the minions whipped a zip tie out of his pocket and bound David's wrists and ankles. Tesler sauntered past the trio, positioning himself between David and the tree, his back to the trunk.

A memory exploded in her mind, a fragment from her horrifying vision the other day. In the premonition, David knelt before Tesler, hands bound behind his back.

The vision was coming true.

Strangling a cry, she tried to run for David, but the men guarding her caught hold of her arms and locked her in place. Impotent, she quivered with repressed rage and terror. *No, no.* This was not happening.

Tesler extracted an object from his pocket. A knife. Long and glistening.

"A gunshot to the head is too clean and quick for you," he told David. "I want you to suffer, while your darling girl watches."

Sean bellowed and jumped, about to bolt for David. One of his captors grappled him to the ground and subdued him on his stomach with a knee in the back. Sean cursed and flailed, unable to break free.

Grace ransacked her brain for an answer. A plan. Some crazy scheme. Anything.

Nothing came to her. Nothing. The blood freezing in her veins crumbled all her thoughts.

Tesler raised the knife. His eyes bulged, his expression wild.

Her heart battered her chest, and her head whirled. No, no, do not pass out. You aren't a weakling. You are the most powerful psychic anyone in this clearing has ever seen. Don't just stand here.

She was powerful. Everyone said so. She'd proved it more than once.

David stared at her, not a hint of emotion on his face. But at the instant their gazes converged, she understood what he wanted her to do.

Shut down the EM generator.

Where was it? The field surrounded them, which suggested the generator was nearby, if not inside the field itself. She had no clue what the contraption looked like.

"I'm going to bleed you," Tesler hissed, "until you beg for mercy, and then I'll make you watch while I cut your beloved to ribbons. Only then will I slit your throat."

She was goddamn sick of listening to this deranged bastard.

As she squeezed her eyes shut, she sank into the depths of her mind, hunting for a spark of the energy she relied on to fuel her powers. Deeper and deeper she dived, searching, pawing, desperate to unearth—

A spark. Tiny but bright.

Its tentacles lashed out to her, eager to latch on and never let go.

Not this time.

She reeled back from the Golden Power. Scrap or not, it tempted her with an easy way out, but the price was too high. She sought out David's energy and gathered it to her heart. Without any conscious decision, she tossed out feelers to locate the EM generator. Its field burned red in the air, from her astral viewpoint, casting the world in a bloody haze.

There. She spotted a box, metal and equipped with a parabolic dish.

She condensed a ball of energy, took aim, and—

Wait. If she knocked out the EM generator, it would unchain the psychic powers of everyone inside the field. *Everyone.*

Including Tesler.

She had no idea whether the field caged the Golden Power, but she could not risk setting it free.

Besides, if Tesler's power was bridled, like hers, then she had a shot.

One shot only.

She opened her eyes. Tesler might be crazy, but he was cunning, especially with the limitless power corked up inside him.

Tesler stood motionless, cloaked in shadow, in front of David. Ambient light glanced off the knife's blade.

Some of the minions lacked weapons. Others held various types of handguns. The one nearest to her wore a semiautomatic pistol holstered on his hip, with a leather strap to keep the weapon berthed in its holster. She might grab for the gun of the man nearest her, but he was eying her as if expecting some kind of attack. She'd have to do this the other way.

When she tapped into David's energy, he blinked and one eyebrow ticked upward for a heartbeat, though his expression gave away nothing. The boost she received from him enlivened her mind and arced through her body, an electric tingle composed of his warmth and stolid nature. It grounded her. Braced her. Strengthened her.

Thank you, my warrior angel.

His lips ticked up then, at the corners, just a touch, before flattening out again. *Warrior angel?* She felt his question rather than sensing his thought. She'd explain that one later.

She used only her peripheral vision to spot their confiscated weapons piled up near a thin jack pine. Her .357 Magnum lay on top. Perfect.

Tesler hoisted the knife above his head. "Time to bleed!"

With a single burst of telekinetic energy, she whisked the gun up off the ground, spun it through the air to her, and clamped her fist around it as the weapon smacked into her palm.

The minion closest to her sucked in a sharp breath.

She slammed the butt of the gun into his head. He crumpled.

"Stop her!" Tesler shouted.

Grace fired one shot at the man restraining Sean, striking him in the leg. He cried out and slumped sideways. Sean seized the chance to snatch the man's gun from its holster and leap to his feet.

Amador broke away from his stunned guards and ran for the weapons pile.

The outer circle of psychic puppets edged inward.

She whirled on Tesler, swinging her gun up to target his chest.

Tesler slashed the knife downward.

Grace pulled the trigger.

The minions roared and swarmed toward them.

CHAPTER THIRTY-TWO

THE GUNSHOT THUNDERED IN THE CLEARING. ITS ECHOES BOUNCED OFF the trees in a cacophony that rattled David's eardrums. A red stain blossomed on Tesler's chest as he collapsed to his knees, out of breath, eyes wide.

The knife tumbled to the ground.

David's bindings snapped free, cut by a spurt of power from Grace. He couldn't control telekinetic energy the way she could, and they both knew it.

Tesler toppled forward just as David sprang to his feet.

In unison, Tesler's army stumbled, halted, and the life sluiced out of them with visible effect. Their shoulders wilted. Their heads drooped. Many of them foundered and thumped to the ground.

David raced toward Grace and swept her into his arms.

Gurgling, blood oozing from his mouth, Tesler crumpled.

David saw nothing except Grace. He clinched her tight, and she gripped him just as hard. Their lips found each other's at the same instant, hungry, plundering and being plundered in a brief kiss of such intensity it flared like a supernova, wiping out everything around them.

Not literally, of course.

When their lips parted, and he set her down, they could do nothing more than grin stupidly at each other.

"Uh…" Sean's hesitant query disrupted their afterglow.

David finally noticed Sean and Amador had collected all the weapons from the guards and bound them with their own zip ties. The man Grace had shot sported a bandanna tied around his wounded thigh.

After a quick peck on Grace's lips, David plucked up one of the minions' guns and turned to face Tesler. He lay still, eyes closed, body limp. Blood soaked his shirt.

Grace laced her fingers with David's. "Is he dead?"

"Not sure." He extricated his fingers from hers. "Wait here, I'll check."

He took one step.

She seized his arm. "Stop."

David paused, glancing back at her worried face. "What is it?"

"I... don't know." She gestured at the knife that rested inches from Tesler's unmoving hand. "It's too close, he could reach it. And I feel... energy or something, coming out of him." Her fingers sank into his flesh. "Please stay here, for now."

"I could shoot him in the head, and then we'd know for sure."

"I'm afraid that might release the energy again, like with Nkosi." Her gaze darted to Tesler, then settled on David. "Please stay away from him, just until I sort out what I'm sensing."

With a sharp nod, he stayed put.

But his trigger finger itched to blast a hole in the bastard's skull.

Sean and Amador stared into the woods.

"Grace could see other men in the woods," Amador said. "Perhaps the boy and I should see what happened to them."

"Boy?" Sean balked. "I'm seventeen, asswipe."

"It's a good idea," David said to Amador. "But take weapons."

Sean and Amador made their way toward the woods, where the puppet psychics lay motionless in varying degrees of awkwardness.

"Whoa," Sean said, with teenage awe. He bent over to swipe a weapon from one of the minions, a rifle with a pistol grip mounted on its underside and a curved magazine extending down from the stock. "Zombie dude has an AK-47. Sweet."

He swung the muzzle toward a thick tree and pulled the trigger. Rounds sprayed the trunk. Bark pattered on the grass.

Sean's awe morphed into wide-eyed glee. "Full auto. Wicked."

"Fully automatic weapons are illegal," David said.

Grace made an unladylike noise, which only made him want to kiss her again. "Nkosi picked weak-willed people with questionable morals for his army. You're surprised one of them flouts the law?"

He stuck his tongue out at her.

She drew her head back as if shocked.

Amador and Sean headed out into the forest, Sean toting his new treasure, Amador looking aggrieved for being saddled with a rebellious teen. Their footfalls receded into silence.

David brushed his palm across Grace's cheek. "I have to check on Tesler. It can't wait any longer. I'll tie him up." He nodded toward the unconscious minions. "See if one of them has another zip tie."

"David."

He squeezed her hand. "I know you're worried, but we have to secure him."

If we're not killing him. He kept the end of his sentence to himself. The only secured Tesler was a dead Tesler.

She sighed. "Okay. I'll stay here. But I am not searching for zip ties until you've got Tesler in hand. And take a gun. That is nonnegotiable."

They stood sideways to Tesler and the pine tree. To their left, branches bobbed slightly in the wind. The breeze fanned her hair out over her face, and David combed it back with his fingers.

"Deal." He feathered a kiss across her lips, then bent to nab a gun.

Movement flashed in his peripheral vision. He pivoted his head, overcome by a strange slowing of time as if his brain had downshifted. His thoughts lagged behind what he saw, delaying his actions.

Tesler snared the knife. Hefted his body into a crouch. Took the knife in a throwing hold. Bared his teeth.

And launched the knife at David.

Grace flung her body at him, shouting as she threw them both to the ground. The moss cushioned their fall, but they landed askew, her leg under his, their arms entangled.

Her .357 plunked down by his head.

Rational thought disintegrated.

David grabbed the revolver and, still tangled with Grace, swerved his arm to level the weapon at Tesler.

The scientist lunged.

David fired.

Karl Tesler whumped down in a lifeless heap. His eyes gaped, vacant.

This time, David did not wait for Grace's permission. He lifted them both to their feet and marched straight to Tesler. When he found no pulse, no breathing or signs of life at all, he turned to Grace. "He's dead."

"Good." She nailed her gaze to a sight beyond his shoulder.

"What is it?"

Before he could glance back, her mouth fell open on a cry of "no!"

A gunshot detonated.

She propelled her body into the gun's trajectory, behind his back.

He wheeled around.

The impact of the shot flung her backward into him. She gurgled, convulsed, her hands like talons on his arms. Then her whole body slumped, held up by his arms.

Another shot exploded. Then another.

He fell to his knees, cradling her. He touched her face, her neck, her arms, and—*shit.* Her stomach.

Blood. Too much blood.

With one trembling hand, he reached down to palpate the wound, but couldn't make himself touch it. His hand hovered over her abdomen. Rocking her in his arms, he ducked his head near hers. "Grace, no. Why did you do that?"

Her head lolled into his chest. A soft grunt issued from her, muffled by his shirt, and she winced. He stretched his hand out to caress her cheek but pulled it back at the last second.

"Are you shot?" Her voice was weak, shaky.

"No." It was a strangled word, dense with an anguish he couldn't contain. "You took the bullet. Why, Grace? Why? You could've used your powers to stop him."

Her voice was even weaker now, barely a whisper. "Didn't think."

Of course she hadn't. Their attacker allowed no time for thinking.

"There he is!" Sean's enraged voice barely registered in David's ears. "I'll get the scumbag."

The rat-a-tat of automatic gunfire. An infuriated scream. More shots. More yelling.

None of it mattered.

Grace's eyelids drifted half shut.

"Sean, get over here!" David splayed his hand over her cheek. She was cold. So damn cold. "Hold on, Grace. It'll be okay, I promise." He scraped his quivering lips across her forehead. "Don't leave me. I need you."

A torrent of love and anguish, fear and devotion, ripped through him down their connection. The link persevered, even as he felt her slipping away.

"Fight, Grace." His voice trembled with the conviction he mustered from deep within. "Fight for me. For us. Come back to me, please."

Her lids closed. The rise and fall of her chest ceased.

David punched his fist through the moss, straight down to the hard earth.

***

GRACE COULDN'T MOVE. SHE HEARD NOISES, DIMLY. VOICES? MAYbe. Her dwindling mental acuity turned everything into a radio show playing from a remote speaker. She succumbed to the numbness, to the blessed relief of spiraling down and down into infinity.

"No, goddammit! You do not get to leave me like this."

Was that David? Yes. Why was he screaming at her from so far away?

Drifting down. Weightless. Painless. A brilliant star beckoned to her, its light a promise of peace and fulfillment. She belonged...

With David.

The epiphany hurtled her out of the tunnel, away from the light. *It's not your time.* The statement filled her, awakened her, though it was not her own thought. The words emanated from the beautiful radiance, from the ever-receding star of eternity.

Her hearing returned first. She heard Sean, his voice desperate. "I'll try, oh jeez, I'll try. But if she's dead, I can't—"

"Do it anyway!" David this time. Angry. Terrified.

Physical sensation filtered back into her next. Her body shifted, coming to rest on a bumpy, firm surface. Hazily, she realized they'd laid her flat on her back. Damp moss tickled her nostrils. Voices chattered around her, but her brain couldn't decipher the meaning of their words. *Sleep now,* a voice inside urged.

Warmth penetrated her wound, spreading outward until it encompassed her whole body, tingling with an odd energy. The numbness gave way to a dull ache in her chest, a pain that dissipated second by second. The key to her mind twisted in the ignition, and the engine of her thoughts chugged back to life. The clean scent of earth and grass wafted over her.

She sneezed.

Whoops erupted around her.

Peeling her lids apart, she stared at the three men huddled around her. David crouched by her head, Amador alongside him near her hip, and Sean…

She rolled onto her side to look at him. He'd been kneeling on the side of her opposite David and Amador, with both hands suspended over her wound. The strange energy she'd sensed originated from him.

"Did you heal me?" she asked.

Looking a bit sheepish, he scrutinized a loose thread on his pants, picking at it. "Uh, yeah. David would've throttled me if I hadn't. But you kinda helped out."

"Helped out?"

"Yeah. I felt your power, like, adding to mine. It was cool."

Okay, she'd helped heal herself while she lay dying. *Weird.*

Sean scrubbed his face with one hand, yawning. Dark circles bruised the skin under his eyes, which were red and tinged with yellow.

"You're tapped out, aren't you?" She knew the signs of power drain.

"Pretty much."

She pushed up into a sitting position, with an assist from David, who immediately threw his arms around her and pulled her close, ensconced in his embrace. She hugged him back and then, on an impulse too strong to deny, she crushed her lips to his. He responded with abandon, their passion energizing their psychic bond until it sizzled. Her body did a little sizzling too.

"Gross," Sean whined, though it sounded less than sincere.

With great reluctance, she severed the kiss. "What about the minions?"

"They're unconscious, very weak." David's attention strayed past her, to the edge of the woods. "No sign of the Golden Power since Tesler died." He curled a lock of her hair around his finger, careful to avoid her gaze. "Do you feel it?"

The uncertainty in his voice made her hesitate. Did she feel the oily, alien energy? "No. It's gone—back to where it came from."

"Is it alive?" Sean asked. "Nkosi said it was, but if anybody would know, it'd be you."

Arms linked around David's neck, she craned hers to examine Sean. He watched her with a steady gaze. The kid honestly believed she was the expert on all things psychic.

"Nkosi was full of shit," she said. "The Golden Power is not a living thing. It's energy, pure and simple." She glimpsed the blood on her shirt and her heart skipped. "Who shot me? Did you get him?"

David slid his hands under her bottom to boost her up onto his lap. "It must've been one of the minions. You saw him. That's why you jumped in front of me, right?"

"Is it?" She ran through events in her mind, but cobwebs obscured her memories.

"Can't you remember?"

"It's all fuzzy." Grunting with the effort, she struggled to get up and plopped back down on David's lap. "A little woozy."

He rose and hoisted her up with him. "Can you stand?"

"Think so." When he set her on her feet, she found her legs weren't as wobbly as she'd feared. "So you didn't find the shooter?"

"We assumed he was one of the minions, and they're all out cold."

Sean thumped his new AK-47 against his hip. "I scared him away for sure."

"Did you see a body?" she asked. When Sean shrugged, she turned her attention to David. "You didn't check? RV the area, I mean."

He looked at her as if she'd spoken gibberish. "The EM field is still up."

Ah. Of course. She hadn't gotten a chance to tell them where to find the generator, and so they worked with limited powers.

She pointed across the clearing. "Generator's over there. Behind that tree."

Amador took off at a trot. He disappeared behind the tree and fired his gun once. She flinched—at the noise and the sudden influx of power.

"Woo-hoo!" Sean hopped up and down. "We're back."

She smiled at him and laughed.

Amador returned then, and the four of them trooped over to the nearest clump of limp psychic puppets. Men, she had to remind herself. They were men, not puppets or minions. It had been easier to think of them that way when Nkosi and then Tesler had controlled them, because they'd behaved like zombies. Now, as she studied two of the men, tendrils of empathy unwound inside her. Their lips and skin bore a deep pallor. Saliva drooled out of their open mouths. Their limbs lay in haphazard, awkward positions. Blood had dribbled out their ears, crusting on their skin.

She turned away, her throat tight. Mind control from someone channeling the Golden Power exacted a terrible toll on the victim, worse than she could've imagined. Would they ever wake up? Would they be normal if they did?

Once, she would've blamed herself for this. No more. Nkosi and Tesler, and JT before them, had embarked on a quest borne of sheer lunacy, determined to mine psychic power from her body. She never asked for this. She never encouraged their obsessions. They undertook vile experiments due solely to their arrogance and insanity.

"We have to take care of them," she said.

Amador, standing beside her, settled a hand on her shoulder. "I donate any of my resources you need to treat these poor men."

"Thank you." She patted his hand and did not miss David's tiny grimace when he saw her gesture. She sent a pulse of reassurance down their connection, plus a small hit of raw desire, a preview of things to come. And they would come very soon.

He grinned.

She still hadn't gotten used to him grinning like a… Well, like a normal, happy guy. But the sight awoke pleasant butterflies in her stomach.

Twigs cracked behind them. Brush scraped and rustled.

Grace and Amador whirled around in unison.

Battaglia roared out of the woods into the clearing. He swung up his huge gun, training it on Grace. "You won't cheat death twice, you freaks."

Grace yanked the gun out of Amador's hand and shot three times at Battaglia. His finger twitched reflexively over the trigger of his gun. The rounds flew wild, nicking trees and popping chunks of moss into the air.

He collapsed, dead.

David trotted to the body and checked. "He's gone."

She shoved the gun at Amador, who took it. "Battaglia shot me. I remember seeing him, about to shoot you, and I—Well, I won't apologize for what I did. I'd do it again."

David bowed his head. He stayed like that for so long she worried he was disgusted with her for taking out Battaglia.

Then his head came up, his eyes aglow, and she understood.

"It's over," he said. "I checked out the area and it's clear."

"The people in the facility?"

"Gone. They evacuated."

She nodded. "It's time to destroy the facility."

He walked to her, took her hands, and gave her an amused smile. "I'm beginning to think you're a pyromaniac. Blowing up facilities all over the place."

"Hey." She batted his chest with the back of her hand. "JT blew up the other one."

"Because he beat you to the punch. Your master plan was to torch the place."

She leaned into him, her hand on his chest. "You didn't have a better idea."

"It's okay." He pinched her butt. "Apparently, I'm attracted to pyromaniacs."

"This time is different. I know for a fact destroying this facility will erase every scrap of data related to Project Outreach. It'll finally be over."

"We'll be free." He bent his head toward hers, his lips aiming for her mouth.

Sean made a vomit-like yacking noise.

David pulled away without kissing her.

She could've strangled Sean.

The kid let out a melodramatic sigh. "Are we gonna blow stuff up or what? I want to get away from the creepy ex-puppet guys and the rotting corpses."

"Sure." She locked gazes with David. "Give us a minute."

She and David traveled to the facility, breaking away from their bodies as easily as they changed shoes. They didn't need words. Their minds, along with their powers, operated in perfect synchronization. Thank heavens for Tesler's paranoia, and his need to defend his facility at any cost. They located the right spot, an armory stacked high with boxes of ammo, and set off a spark.

They shot back into their bodies.

A deep boom rumbled in the distance. The earth shuddered.

Project Outreach had been terminated.

CHAPTER THIRTY-THREE

DAVID WOKE GRACE WITH A FEW GENTLE NUDGES AS THEY PULLED into the parking lot of the private airport near Bozeman, the same strip where they'd battled brainwashed, zombie-like men a few hours ago. A small building, almost a shack, hunkered alongside a control tower. A short distance away, sequestered from the other structures, loomed the hangar. He could just make out the ruined fence.

Amador led them to his jet. The airstairs had been restored to their rightful position, and their group trudged up and into the plane. David, the last in line, paused inside the portal where Amador waited to shut the door.

"About the bodies," he said. "Tesler and Nkosi."

The other man shrugged, his expression unconcerned. "I have already contacted Wickham about all of this."

Yes, David remembered Amador making a phone call during the drive back to the airport. He'd spoken in Spanish—or at least it had sounded like Spanish—most likely to prevent David or anyone else from eavesdropping.

"Wickham will arrange for the remains to be taken care of," Amador said.

Of course he would. "Taken care of" was probably a euphemism for "chucked into an incinerator." The lunatics deserved nothing better, anyway.

David despised relying on Amador to deal with the aftermath. Hell, he despised the man in general. But he had no choice in this case because he lacked the resources to clean up after his own mess. "What about the men they brainwashed and abused?"

"Wickham will have them sent to a private hospital I recently purchased. They will be well cared for, you have my word."

David bristled at the suggestion he should trust Amador's word, but Grace did, so he deferred to her judgment. Still, that didn't bar him from a little scornful suspicion. "You own a hospital? Awfully convenient. When did you buy it?"

The smug look on Amador's face had David's fist itching to connect with the bastard's jaw. "I purchased the hospital during my telephone discussion with Wickham in the car."

Jeez. The son of a bitch could buy an entire hospital in the space of one ten-minute conversation over the cell network. Rather than jealousy, as he might've expected, he experienced a bizarre twinge of appreciation. Wickham was doing the grunt work, but Amador orchestrated things. Both men had earned a little credit for their efforts.

David offered his hand to Amador. "Thank you. We'd be in a heap of trouble if you hadn't stepped in."

The other man accepted the handshake. "Do not thank me. This is the least I could do to begin to make amends."

Sean scuffled up beside Amador. "Whoa, dude, how are you gonna explain all those bodies to the cops?"

Amador arched an eyebrow. "There were only five corpses, including Tesler and Nkosi. The rest are alive. And my colleague Wickham has contacts at the FBI and CIA who understand the importance of glossing over any deaths related to ALI or Digital Prognostics."

Grace wandered up behind Amador. "Why would FBI agents help us cover up this mess?"

"Because they owe us, Wickham and I." His mouth twisted into a somber, yet slightly amused, smile. "We liberated them from facilities elsewhere in the world."

"They're psychics?"

"Oh yes. The FBI and CIA often hire individuals with extrasensory abilities, though they don't advertise for those positions." Amador sighed. "Wickham recommended them for the jobs. He was MI6 at one time and had fostered relationships with several individuals at those agencies."

David stared at the man, his mind sputtering in an attempt to process what he'd said. Gabriel Amador, who had abducted and tortured a teenage girl, had also rescued detainees from ALI facilities *and* gotten them jobs back home? The two types of behavior clashed. Didn't they? A person couldn't torment a young woman to the brink of insanity, then traipse off to be a hero.

"You don't believe it," Amador said, his gaze intent on David. "Do you, Mr. Ransom?"

"Might as well call me David," he said with a resigned sigh. "And no, I can't quite reconcile your supposed heroics with what you did to Grace or the way you treated that girl Cari."

Amador had the sense to bow his head, in imitation of shame if nothing else. He rubbed his neck. "Desperation makes the weak-willed do terrible things."

David analyzed the man's posture—stooped, head down, arms slack—but he wasn't ready yet to accept Amador's shame as genuine. "You're admitting to being weak."

"Yes." Amador's head lifted slightly, enough for him to turn his eyes toward Grace. "I do not ask forgiveness, but please believe me. I will do anything within my power to set right the grievous wrongs I've inflicted on you and others."

"Don't talk to her," David said. "You speak to me."

Grace gave him an exasperated look. "Cool down, cowboy. We're all on the same team, you know. We, all of us together, defeated Tesler, Nkosi, and a passel of mind-controlled, armed men."

Teeth grinding, David glared at Amador.

Grace sidled past Amador and slipped an arm around David's waist, snuggling against him. His body reacted the way it always did, without his consent, curling an arm around her shoulders and relaxing into her warmth and suppleness. The feel of her body against his comforted him more than he'd realized until this moment. Until he'd almost lost her.

But dammit, he wanted to be annoyed. At the man feigning regret. At the scumbag who drugged the woman he loved. He had a frigging right to be pissed.

Her hand slid across his belly, her fingers dancing over his shirt and exciting the flesh underneath. Her every action was directed at him, but she spoke to Amador. "David needs a little time to adjust and accept you're sincere. I'm sure you can understand that."

She injected the last sentence with a faint sternness, a directive for Amador to comply.

"Naturally," Amador said, his head raised to meet David's gaze, "I understand your need to see proof of my intentions. I will demonstrate with actions, not words. One day, I hope you'll see I wish to change." His attention shifted to Grace for a second, and a mysterious emotion flickered over his face. "Grace told me once it's not too late to come back from the madness I gave in to. Her compassion and conviction have persuaded me she is correct. From this day forward, I will commit myself to that recovery."

"How?" David asked.

"By signing myself into the same hospital where the men from Nkosi's army will be tended to." He shoved his hands in his pockets, then pulled them out, reaching up as if to touch his face. He retracted his hand. "There is a psychiatric unit. The doctors are excellent, or so Wickham assures me. I trust him implicitly."

Grace's smile was genuine, if muted. "Good luck, Biel. I hope you find your peace."

"You are far too generous a soul, Grace." Amador's lips curved up but faltered. "If I can achieve a fraction of your goodness…"

David almost smiled. Almost. "Don't set a goal you can't achieve. Nobody will ever be anywhere near as good as this woman." He gave her a quick squeeze. "She's a living, breathing miracle."

She poked him with her elbow and rolled her eyes. "Oh brother. If you lay it on any thicker, I might join Sean in barfing."

The boy snickered. David shot him a glance that shut him up.

Amador managed a sad smile. "No, Grace, David is right. You are a miracle, and I am blessed to have met you. I hope someday to become your friend." He cast a sideways look at David. "A friend to both of you."

"We'll see," David said.

Amador's expression changed subtly, into something akin to gratitude. He gestured toward the sofas and chairs in the cabin behind him. "Make yourselves at home. There is a galley stocked with food and beverages at the rear of the cabin. I will sit with the pilot. He is a good friend and ally."

"Thank you," Grace said.

As he watched Amador meander toward the cockpit, David wondered if the man was hiding out with the captain to give him, Grace, and Sean privacy—and a break from the man they barely trusted. Maybe Amador had some tact after all.

"Hey," David called out, just as Amador reached for the cockpit door handle. The man glanced back. "Good luck with your recovery."

It was the best sentiment he could offer honestly, and Amador knew it. Amador nodded and entered the cockpit. The door clicked shut.

Sean skipped down the aisle—yes, actually skipped, like the kid he denied being—and flopped down onto a cushy sofa a few rows down. Grace clasped David's hand, leading him past the teenager sprawled on a cream-colored sofa, and straight back to the last row. A sofa awaited them there, behind a quartet of chairs arranged around a rectangular table. A long, low table fronted the sofa. The chairs provided a sort of privacy screen, which, combined with the distance between them and Sean, made for a cozy nest.

"I figured," Grace said, "we'd want to be alone for a while."

Yes, yes, and hell yes. They'd won a vicious battle, against human enemies, but also against their own demons. She knew everything about him, and even when the evidence suggested he'd betrayed her, she never gave up on him. This woman fought for him, for their love, without hesitation. He worshiped her. He needed her. He craved her.

"Hungry?" she asked, and waved toward the galley. "Or thirsty? I can get us a drink or a quick bite."

"No thanks." He was starving, but not for food.

The pattering of footsteps drew their attention to the aisle and Sean padding toward them. He rolled his eyes as he moseyed by, on his way to the galley.

"Don't worry," he said. "I'm grabbing a drink. Then you guys can get back to drooling over each other."

He did indeed grab a can of Coke and hustle back to his makeshift bed. A pop and a fizz ensued, then the hushed whine of the engines was the only sound.

Grace moved around the table and eased her lithe body down onto the sofa, wriggling her lovely little butt to scoot backward. She cuddled into the cushioning with a soft, contented moan.

He settled in beside her, with those luscious curves tucked against him and her head on his shoulder. Her silky hair teased his chin. Ducking his head, he inhaled a long breath, entranced by the scent of her. Though tainted with a hint of blood and dirt, her hair still gave off the intoxicating aroma of coconuts. Surrounded by her, he let his thoughts travel back to his fantasy from days ago. Grace in a bikini, on a beach, sunning herself beside him. He'd rub lotion all over her body, starting with her shoulders and working his way down, inch by inch, tracing the elegant contour of her back, the curve of her hips, the perfect mounds of her bottom, and—

"Stop that."

He whipped his head up, startled. "Stop what?"

She tilted her head up, targeting her glorious eyes on him. "You're fantasizing about sex again, I know you are. I can feel you're getting… aroused." Her eyes flicked down, toward his crotch, and then back up. Amusement curled one corner of her luscious lips. "And I feel it with more than my psychic senses."

Right. His pants had grown tighter all of a sudden.

One of her delicate fingers poked into his side. "We can't do anything here, so don't go torturing yourself with erotic daydreams."

"Thinking about you is never torture." He nuzzled her ear and whispered, "You know, we're connected on a much deeper level these days. Maybe we could share a fantasy. I'd love to show you mine."

Her breath hitched. Excitement pumped into him from her, a thrill triggered by his suggestion. *She wants to share this with me.*

A thrill of his own fired through their link, straight into her.

Her sharp intake of breath made him ache in a way that would get him arrested if he acted on it in public. But after a second, she virtually purred her response. "David, I would love to share your fantasy. But can we do that?" A note of anxiety crept into her voice. "I mean, reading minds is bad news, trust me, I've got firsthand knowledge of it."

He'd expected that reaction. After everything she'd been through, extrasensory powers were a boogeyman under her bed. He knew this, but he also knew she possessed more than enough strength to overcome those fears. Her journey toward fearlessness had begun the moment she defeated Nkosi.

Stroking her cheek with one hand, he kissed her earlobe, tugged it between his lips, and suckled gently. Her faint moan turned him on even more. The salty-yet-sweet flavor of her skin whipped his need into a near frenzy. *Take it slow, don't rush her.*

Releasing her lobe, he let his lips tantalize her ear as he spoke. "This won't be reading minds. It'll be more like thought projection mixed with telepathy, and a dash of empathic energy for good measure." He skimmed his hand down her neck and paused with his fingertips at the hollow above her collarbone. "If we get really ambitious, we could astral project somewhere nice and manifest."

Her chest heaved with each breath. She dropped one hand to his thigh and raked it up his jeans until her fingers grazed his swelling erection.

He whisked his tongue across her lower lip.

She clutched his shirt. "That would take a lot of energy. We'd be... exhausted afterward."

"But it would be worth it."

"We'll be home soon. Maybe we should wait."

The light pressure of her fingernails through his shirt pushed him beyond longing, right into raw, hot lust. "Can't wait. I've got to have you *now.*"

"David, I... oh." She thrust a hand into his hair as he blew a gentle puff of air onto the tender skin below her ear. Arching her neck, she exposed her slender throat to him, and he trailed kisses down her neck. "David, we shouldn't... please... mmm." Her hand in his hair gripped harder. "Let's do it."

He ran the tip of his tongue back up her throat. "Are you sure?"

"Yes." She groaned the word and cupped his erection through his pants.

David tipped his head up. "A real kiss first."

"Please, yes."

He took her mouth, too famished for her to care how much noise they made. They groped and fondled, devoured and drank each other in, lost in the fervor of skin on skin. It wasn't enough. He needed all of her skin, bare and creamy, ripe for the taking.

They couldn't do that here.

But her lips, her tongue, her fingers...

The jet engines whined dully, but the noise receded, along with the rest of the world, out of the bubble their desire had fashioned around them. He pulled them both down to lie on the sofa, and she clung to him while he grasped her hips, dragging them into him over and over in a frantic, erotic rhythm. She abandoned herself to the kiss, her passion stripping away his control. Their minds touched, melded, whirled out of their bodies into the crossroads.

And still, he felt her slick lips on his, her hot hands on his back. Their minds spun through darkness made of living energy, thrusting out into pure sunshine. The connection to his body waned to a background hum, but their passion joined them as powerfully as ever.

They stood on a beach. Palm trees swayed in a gentle breeze, casting flickering shadows on the golden sand. Crystalline blue water lapped against the shore, and the aroma of exotic flowers whispered over them. No humans in sight. No animals either. Nothing except the two of them, separated by mere inches. Alone. Aroused.

Grace wore a bikini. When that fact finally penetrated his brain, he couldn't stop himself from smirking.

She glanced down at her attire, blushed, and bit her lip. A shy smile tugged at the corners of her mouth.

He was in pants and a khaki shirt, unbuttoned. Naked would've seemed more appropriate, but he'd let her choose his wardrobe—not with words, but with silent permission. She'd given him the same leave, to dress her. Or undress her. That delectable body curved in all the right places, the skimpy bikini more of an adornment than an outfit. Her creamy skin took on a slight flush in the sunlight.

She gazed up at him, her lips parted. "Shall we manifest?"

"Yes."

Psychic energy poured into him, coursed through his entire being, and swept back into her, then repeated in a cycle of exquisite highs and soothing lows. His mind came alive, buzzing with power.

The sun heated his face.

Grace wiggled her toes in the sand. "It worked."

"Of course it did." He hauled her into his arms for a deep kiss. "We're the two most powerful psychics around." He skated his hand up her side, molding his palm to her breast. "Let's see how good we really are at manifesting."

Sure, he'd made love to her while manifesting once before, but this time was different. The bond between them would alter their responses, he sensed that, but how intense it would get remained a mystery. One he intended to solve.

This instant.

Grace dragged her nails down his chest with feather-light pressure. When she reached the waistband of his pants, she raked her nails back up his skin. By the time her fingers hit his pecs, he was throbbing for her. The bikini he'd imagined for her, and manifested onto her body, featured strings for easy removal. He untied them one by one, and her bikini fluttered to the ground. His shirt and pants went next.

They lay on the sand, Grace stretched out beneath him, her skin glistening with tiny beads of sweat. The sight of her—nude, nipples hardened into peaks, her skin damp, her mouth open—stole his voice, his breath, and his thoughts. How could he ever have chosen hunting for a madman over staying with this woman?

A ghost of a frown tensed her features. "You've never been this adventurous before. And you've barely kissed me in the past two months until the other day." With a sharp and questioning look, she nailed him to an invisible wall. "Why go all late-night cable on me all of a sudden?"

"You know why." He lowered a knee between her thighs to ease them apart. "Enough talking."

"Maybe we shouldn't."

His body screamed for action, friction, the ecstasy of burying himself inside her. She crossed her arms over her chest in a gesture that normally indicated annoyance, but her fear trickled into him, tempering his desire. Unable to read her mind, he could only guess at what disturbed her. "Is this about the power merge? Do you think I only want you because I can feel your passion?"

One of her shoulders hunched in a tiny shrug. "You felt my passion before we joined our powers. Our connection was getting more intense even then, but now... Would you have ever wanted me this much if things had stayed the way they were before I got amnesia?"

"Yes." He almost growled the word, infusing it with all his certainty. "I love you. The longer we're together, the closer we get. It's natural and normal, although our relationship has extra oomph."

Amusement sparkled in her eyes and curved one corner of her mouth. "Oomph?"

"Exactly. Our powers are a bonus, not the source of our bond." He ducked his head to touch his lips to hers. "I love you because you're you, end of story."

"But you weren't like this before."

True. He'd been reserved in their lovemaking, afraid to embrace the hunger gnawing at him, desperate to come out and play. Fear of hurting her, scaring her, had restrained him. And, if he were totally honest, fear she wouldn't approve of his fantasies.

Yet she had. He'd offered her the key to his inner sanctum, and she had accepted it. Despite the countless mistakes he'd made, running after Tesler and keeping secrets from her. Despite everything. She never wavered in her commitment to their relationship.

Her love and trust had liberated him.

Elation rushed into him, sweet and warm and tasting like her. He felt the grin that split his lips. A wide, stupid grin borne of the unbridled joy consuming him.

The look on her face—a mixture of adoration, euphoria, and desire—took his breath away. She knew what he felt, though not what he thought. Crazy, silly thoughts that were unmanly in their gushy nature. He had to tell her. The words clamored to get out, and at last, he realized he didn't give a damn if he sounded like a moron.

"You freed me, Grace, you showed me unconditional, boundless love and I couldn't fight it anymore. I love you, I need you, I'm so sorry for the way I've treated you these past months. You're sweet and strong and beautiful and fragile. You make me laugh when I don't want to, you push me to do the hard things because it's right." He took a single, gasping breath. "You changed me. You—"

She sealed his lips with her fingers. "Shh. No need to gush, honey. I know how you feel because you've shown me."

"But all those months—"

"Yeah, I'll admit your standoffish behavior irritated me." Her fingers toyed with his lip, and he ached to suck those little digits. "But I love you, David, and love is never easy or neat. It's messy and difficult and sometimes painful. I'm in for the whole package, whatever happens."

"Me too," he said. Her fingers muffled his words, but she must've understood because she smiled. "Can we stop talking yet?"

She tugged his lip down with her fingertip. "Yes, enough telling. I'm in the mood for some showing."

He sucked her finger into his mouth, and her smile broadened. When he let her finger slide out, she slicked the wet tips over his chin, down his throat, onto his chest. He shimmied down her body inch by inch, relishing the salty tang of sweat, colored with the sweet, rich flavor of her, exploring her breasts, her belly, her hips. When he dipped his head between her thighs, she let out a surprised cry.

"Relax," he said, and peppered her inner thigh with kisses. "You wanted me to show you how much I adore you. So here I go."

And then he did. With all the single-minded focus he'd once reserved for his Tesler hunt, he demonstrated exactly how much he cherished her body, her heart, her soul, by tormenting her with pleasure and driving her wild with the need for release. She thrust a hand into his hair and writhed beneath him, beautiful, ardent, full of life and heat. Her heavy breathing escalated into pants and groans, as her hips bucked and her fingers clutched his hair, the nails scraping his scalp. His passion merged with hers, engulfed him, hardened him, consumed his every thought and fueled his every movement, revved up by the flavor of her desire and the feel of her slick heat against his mouth. Her shuddering climax hit hard, her back arched, her hips fastened down by his hands.

He exhaled a ragged breath against her flesh, and she shuddered again.

"Oh, David." His name emerged as a breathless moan.

Lifting his head, he gazed up at her, his breaths coming hard and fast. The afterglow flushed her cheeks, and her lips, swollen with desire, parted in a plea for a kiss. She was the most magnificent thing he'd ever laid eyes on—and she was his. Every molecule of her delectable body belonged to him and him alone, but more than that, she'd given him the gift of her trust and love.

Her mouth curved into a dazed, lopsided smile. "You've never done that before."

"I know." His grin must've looked wicked since that was how he felt. "I plan on doing a lot of things I've never done before, if my fiancée doesn't mind." He skated his mouth down her inner thigh, nipped her knee, and worked his way back up to her hip to kiss the hollow there. "Does my fiancée approve?"

She nodded and licked her lower lip. "Oh yes. I do, absolutely, no doubt, yes-yes-yes." She hooked one leg around him, rubbing her heel under the curve of his buttock. "I'm ready for whatever you have in mind."

With a naughty smile, she tugged her hand free of his hair to caress his cheek. The sunlight sparkled on the diamond in her engagement ring. Soon she would be his wife. His heart thudded. His wife. The phrase set off a torrent of emotions—happiness, adoration, satisfaction, and oh yes, lust. He drew her left leg up onto his shoulder, rose onto hands and knees, and fixed his gaze on hers. The psychic bond snapped tight between them, coursing her hunger into him, swirling it through his body and mind in an intoxicating mixture that drew a sigh out of him. "Do you feel that?"

"Mmm…" She dived her hands into the sand, fingers curled, and bowed her back. Her breasts heaved upward, the taut nipples grazing his skin. "All I want to feel is you."

For a moment, he gazed down at her in wonder. They lay on a beach, amid the shadow-dappled sand and the glittering sunshine. The tropical vista was stunning, but the breathtaking view beneath him captured all his focus.

He grasped her hips and sank inside her gradually until he'd filled her to the hilt. The exquisite torture of her velvety soft flesh enveloping him nearly pushed him over the edge.

Her fingers clutched his wrists. Her mouth fell open, and a single syllable escaped her lips. "Please."

"I would give up everything to be with you." He ground his hips into her. "Never doubt that again."

He slid out of her, sucked in a breath, and plowed into her glistening folds with one powerful thrust of his cock. He drove so deep the breath exploded out of him, and her hips rocked up to meet him. He plunged in over and over, desperate for her, for this, for everything her body promised and everything she surrendered to him, without hesitation or regret. The pressure mounted with every thrust, every thrash of her hips, every heave of her full breasts and their rigid, mouth-watering peaks. Her body clenched around him, ready to burst, and he lunged into her hard, blinded by need. She cried out as her release pulsed around him, and he exploded inside her, pumping until he was spent.

"Grace." Her name tumbled from his lips, a prayer and a thank-you. He flopped onto the sand beside her, sated more than ever before, and flung one arm around her to pull her close, her head nestled in the crook of his shoulder. "What should we do now?"

"You mean right this minute, or in the more general sense?"

"With our lives. What should we do?"

She traced circles on his chest with her finger. "I still have the flash drive with all of JT's research on it. That includes the location of every ALI facility on the planet and the names of all the people they kidnapped."

"Don't say what I think you're about to say."

"We have to track them down and help them." She lifted her head, those gorgeous eyes studying him. "Remember what Sean was like when you first met him? Terrified and beaten down. There may be others like him and Cari out there, people who need us."

He groaned. "I swore I'd give up insane quests."

"This isn't vengeance or a crazy attempt to protect me." She rolled on top of him, her hair spilling over his chest. "This is a meaningful quest. A good deed. Don't you want to help the powerless?" The weight of her on top of him, and the way she flitted her tongue over his skin, tempted him to do things he couldn't, not with their energy waning and their manifested bodies on the brink of dissipating. Mercilessly, she licked the corner of his mouth. "Say yes."

"To what?" He'd lost all memory of their conversation.

"Saving the world, one psychic at a time."

His mind blanked when she sucked his lip between her teeth and stroked her tongue over it. The second she released it, he sputtered, "Yes, let's save the world."

The craziest part was, he meant it.

"You know," she said, "I won't hold you to that promise. You made it under duress."

As she straddled him, his hips cradled between her shapely thighs, he moved his hands up them to chart their tempting contours. "We both know I would've agreed anyway. This is our destiny. I think it's time we embraced it."

The psychic fuel sustaining them fizzled out, vanishing their manifested forms. They zipped through the crossroads, too lost in each other to notice anything else. Stars streaked by, distant and unimportant, then retreated into the darkness.

The crossroads is never completely dark. Lights glitter there, innumerable beacons lighting the way to the unexplored, the undiscovered, the unknown.

Whether it was her thought or his hardly mattered because the words illuminated a truth he'd ignored until life had forced him to face it. Grace was his beacon. His anchor to the world, to life. She was a part of him, and he was a part of her. The destiny he'd fought for so long had found its fruition in her, and in their future together.

Before he knew it had happened, he was back in his real body, on the plane, with the hum of the jet engines in the background. His arms were still wound around Grace, her body snuggled into him with her face resting against his neck, warm air puffing out of her nostrils onto his skin.

"Wake up, you pervs."

David cracked one eye open.

Sean towered over them where they lay on the sofa, stretched across its length, entwined in each other in so many ways. The boy made a disgusted face. "We just landed in Cincinnati. If you guys can stop psychic sexting for a few minutes, maybe we can get off this plane and go home."

Cincinnati. They were home, almost.

Rousing Grace with a gentle shake, David sat up. "Psychic sexting? We weren't using our cell phones."

Sean snorted. "Maybe sexting isn't totally accurate. Point is, I don't need telepathy to know what you two were doing—and I mean *doing*—back here." He winced, frowning at the floor, and mumbled, "I heard some... uh... moans."

Grace bolted upright. Her hair lashed David's face. With a struggle that wrenched his mind too, she kept her expression neutral, though her embarrassment radiated into him. He laid a soothing hand on her back, drawing circles on her flesh. Her shoulders relaxed.

Oblivious, Sean did what every teenager excelled at. He spouted more blatant observations designed to knock adults off-kilter. "There was a kind of weird energy or something too. I felt it."

Grace's eyes bulged. She'd stopped breathing.

He gave Sean a stern look. "What are you talking about?"

The boy hunched his shoulders, jamming his hands into his pockets. "I think it was, ya know, related to your... activities."

Grace slammed a thought into his brain, and he gritted his teeth. *Please tell me he didn't feel what we were feeling? Is that even possible?* He heard her voice pleading the questions, and her anxiety knifed into him. Sliding his hand down to encircle her waist, he pulled her closer.

She pushed away and swung her feet onto the floor, then braced her elbows on her knees.

He ran a hand through his hair. "Sean, are you saying you sensed our emotions and physical responses?"

Grace lowered her head to cover it with her hands.

Sean pursed his lips, unable to meet David's gaze. "Maybe."

"Oh God." Grace groaned the words with a hint of a whine in her tone.

David cleared his throat. He reassembled his self-control, which had cracked and splintered at Sean's admission, and rose to face the boy. In the most matter-of-fact tone he could muster, he said, "You'll need to learn to control your new power. We'll help you."

"What new power?" Sean asked.

"Empathy. Sensing other people's feelings. It's a natural offshoot of healing."

"Cool!" The boy pumped his fists in the air. "I finally got a new power. This is so incredibly awesome." He aimed a sly look at Grace, who stayed hidden behind her hands. "Don't worry. I won't write any blog posts about your sex life."

Grace peeked at him between her fingers, then shut her eyes and uttered a pathetic, if melodramatic, noise.

David tore her hands away from her face and hauled her to her feet.

She scowled, though a bit half-heartedly. When he smiled, she compressed her mouth into an adorably miffed expression.

He pecked a kiss on those rosy lips. "Let's get married."

Puzzlement intensified her adorableness, and he had to restrain a powerful impulse to give her a no-holds-barred kiss. His lust must've revealed itself on his face, or in their psychic link, because a smile twitched at the corners of her mouth. "So far, David, we've gotten engaged twice. How many more times do I have to say yes?"

"I'm not asking you to agree to marry me. I'm suggesting we do it as soon as possible." He caught her chin between his thumb and forefinger. "We've waited long enough."

"Then let's do it."

He whooped and swept her up in his arms, whirling them both around and around. She laughed, the sound light and airy, full of joy.

Sean bounded down the aisle just as Amador emerged from the cockpit. He slugged Amador's arm and hollered, "I got a new power!"

Looking unimpressed, Amador sidestepped Sean to open the jet's door.

A few minutes later, David carried Grace off the plane, despite her stubborn protests, and to a waiting SUV driven by Roland Wickham. When their group arrived at the house he and Grace shared, he whisked her out of the car and into his arms again, kicked the car door shut, and without a word of goodbye marched up to the front door.

The last ribbons of sunset fluttered across the sky, and the perfume of roses drifted out of the bushes nestled against the house. He heard Sean exit the SUV behind them, saying goodbye to Amador and Wickham, then he jogged up the walkway in their wake.

"I'd pick you a rose," he told Grace, "but I won't risk you getting pricked by a thorn."

"Are you going to be this overprotective forever?"

"Yes." He realized with a stir of heat that she didn't look entirely displeased by the prospect.

Her annoyance reared up, however, when he insisted on carrying her through the front door. Her protests were weaker this time, but her smile was brilliant.

Once the door clapped shut, Sean wandered off to his room. David and Grace lingered at the door, arms around each other, unwilling to let go for one second. The topaz glow in her eyes entranced him and calmed him with the love she exuded from every pore and every neuron. If he gave off half the emotion she did, they were both wrecked.

Her fingers tickled the back of his neck, and he bent down for a kiss, a sweet and innocent one.

"You know," he said, "I used to wish I could lose myself in you. Today I realized I found myself in you, and I'll never forget the gift you gave me."

Then he carried her into the bedroom and laid her on the mattress. Not to ravish her again but to sleep. Lying in her arms all night was a treat he'd denied himself for months. No more. When she snuggled her soft body against his, he let go of wakefulness, succumbing to slumber.

That night, he slept better than he had in years.

Another gift from Grace.

Chapter Thirty-Four

THE AIR CONDITIONER HUMMED, AND A DOG BARKED OUTSIDE, BUT OTHerwise, the house had descended into silence. Grace clamped her hands together to stop her fingers from drumming on the tabletop. None of them had a clue what to say after she'd related what she learned from her dive into Nkosi's mind, because it shed a bizarre light on Sean's grandfather. She supposed this was what people called a pregnant pause.

This pause was having quadruplets.

David closed his big, muscular hand over both of hers. The knot in her gut loosened a smidgen. Seated beside her, in one of four wooden chairs positioned around the oblong kitchen table, he said nothing—but his mind spoke an encyclopedia's worth of words. She was still adjusting to their new, broader link.

Across the table from them, Sean slouched forward and planted his elbows on the wood. His forehead fell into his palms. Rubbing his skin, as if he might squash the information out of his brain, he pulled in a long, quivering breath and expelled it in a rush. Sean snapped straight, his back thumping into the chair. Jaw set, lip curled, he huffed a breath out through his nostrils.

"So," he said, his voice too calm, "Grandpa was a psycho. I can deal with it. Mom was right to get away from him."

Grace leaned forward. The table's edge pressed into her abdomen. "Listen, there's more."

He barked a single, harsh laugh. "No shit? Of course there's more to the Gramps-was-a-serial-killer-who-tortured-me story. That just wouldn't be awesome enough by itself."

"Actually," David said, "Tesler only hurt you one time, when he gave you JT's formula. Otherwise, he steered clear of—"

"The torture sessions? Yeah, it's too bad he missed out on all the really sweet stuff."

Grace stretched a hand out to Sean's, but he folded his arms over his chest. The kid had a ways to go before he'd accept physical affection.

She took David's hand instead, grateful for the warmth and comfort. "Sean, your grandfather made a deal with Nkosi. You see, Nkosi needed Tesler's help to figure out how to create and control psychic puppets. But he had to promise Tesler something in return."

His gaze fixated on the tabletop, he shifted in his seat. "What, he wanted some toddlers to experiment on?"

"No." She glanced down at David's fingers, curled around hers. "He wanted you."

The kid's head popped up then. His forehead crinkled as his brows knit together. "I don't get it. He hated psychics, and he said he'd never admit we're related, seeing as I'm a mewling mutant."

"He wanted Nkosi to excise your powers, make you a normal person, and then erase your memories of the last two years. It seems like he had plans to adopt you then."

"Seriously? Like I'd be a lost puppy he could rescue?" Sean shook his head as a scowl darkened his face. "Think I could cut out the DNA I got from him? Don't need that crap inside me."

"This may be hard to understand, but I think, in his warped way, he was trying to protect you."

Sean closed his eyes. When he opened them again, the scowl gave way to a look of solemn determination.

"Are you okay?" she asked. A dumb question, but she couldn't think of anything else to say.

"I'll deal." He pushed his chair back and stood. "Need some time to think, that's all."

He headed down the hallway to his bedroom. The door clicked shut.

The silence returned, but only for a moment.

David squeezed her hand. "He'll be fine. After everything he's been through, believe it or not, this is probably the easiest for him to handle."

"You know him better than I do." She knew Sean was a tough kid, though, and he'd have the two of them to guide him through this. Besides, she had another matter to discuss with David. "I remembered something else."

"I thought you recovered all your memories the other night."

She noted the manly satisfaction in his tone, prompted by the knowledge that their lovemaking had restored her Swiss-cheese brain to wholeness. Her body tingled at the recollection of that night, but she forced herself to concentrate. "I mean, I remembered how I forgot. How I developed amnesia."

His chair scraped on the vinyl flooring as he rotated it toward her. With an ease that sent a shiver of desire through her, he lifted her chair to turn it toward him so they faced each other sideways to the table. One glimpse of those fathomless blue eyes, and she developed a new kind of amnesia.

"Well?" he said.

"Huh?" His lips begged for a kiss, a nip, a—

"You were going to tell me how you got amnesia."

"Right. I was." She flattened her palms on her thighs and squared her shoulders. "I did it to myself."

"I don't understand."

"Neither did I, at first." The amnesia had set in on the day her parents were killed. Six months ago, thanks to JT's torments, she'd regained the memory of that day, when Jackson Tennant used his drug-induced psychic abilities to cause a car accident. She had sensed their peril and traveled to them, with RV, but had been helpless to save them.

David patted his leg. "Come over here."

She hopped over there, perching on his lap, and looped her arms around his neck. He hooked his arms around her waist, linking his hands over her hips. She loved this new-and-improved, uninhibited David. He lavished affection on her and grinned with unabashed joy. He could still be stoic, when necessary, but their night in the cabin had freed them both, in their own ways.

"After I saw my parents die," she told him, "I was so devastated and terrified, I lost control of my powers. While I was in the crossroads."

Silent, he watched her without expression.

"My mind got, well, sort of fractured." She dug around for a better way to explain it but came up empty. "The barrier around my memories was built from my fears and guilt. I couldn't save them. I'd lost you too, in a way, because you were imprisoned at the California facility." She squirmed on his lap, which encouraged him to tighten his hold on her. Part of her wanted to break free, run, hide. Mostly, though, she longed to stay right here forever. "I flipped out and caused my own amnesia. I'm not strong like you think, but I'm getting better."

He lifted a hand to her face, his fingers curving over her cheek. "You've always been strong, Grace. What you went through, it would make anyone flip out. You came back from it, stronger than ever, and that's what counts."

"I think you're a little biased."

His hand drifted down to her throat, his fingertips teasing her skin. "I'm thoroughly biased. And from here on out, you'll never have to suffer alone. I'll be with you, always. So if there are any more villains out there, we'll take them out together."

My warrior angel to the rescue.

His brows rose. "Explain this 'warrior angel' thing to me."

"It's silly."

Smirking, he trailed his hand down to the slope of her breast, his skin warm through the thin fabric of her shirt. "I like you silly. Giggling and jiggling."

"Excuse me? Jiggling?"

"When you laugh, your breasts jiggle." He sealed his hand around one mound. "Tell me."

She shrugged. "I started thinking of you as my warrior angel back when you were Mr. Stoic-and-Standoffish. You have the face of an angel, and you're very heroic, so warrior angel seemed appropriate."

"Stoic and standoffish? I guess I deserve that." He brushed his thumb over her nipple. Her breath hitched, and he did it again. "I like the heroic part."

"Me too."

She ground her bottom into his lap, fully aware of how it would affect him. He gritted his teeth and kneaded her breast with ferocious pressure. She smashed her mouth to his.

Footsteps clapped down the hallway.

"If Mom and Dad are gonna screw around, I need to go for a walk. Your happy-sappy horny feelings are wrecking my sulky mood."

They peeled their lips apart to stare at Sean.

He gave them a playfully exasperated shake of his head. "You guys are so weird."

David let go of her breast. "Sorry we're ruining your sulk."

"I wasn't really into it, anyway. I figure it like this. I never really knew my grandfather, and my mom was totally cool, so who cares if I shared some genes with a whackjob. I take after my mother." He hustled toward the door, swung it open, and glanced back. "Besides, I've got a new family."

He strode out the door, head high, a faint smile on his lips.

She stared at the door for a few seconds, but then it hit her. Sean was a tough kid. He was smart and resilient and not just a kid anymore. He was becoming a man.

And with a role model like David, he'd do just fine.

The man whose pants were straining at the crotch tapped a finger on her lips. "He's okay."

"I know."

"Good. Then we can move on to other business." He jumped up, hefting her with him and depositing her on her bare feet. "Let's fly to Vegas tomorrow and get married."

"Yes. Let's."

He threw his arms around her and kissed her with unadulterated passion, proving once and for all that he was no chaste angel.

But to her, he always would be her warrior angel.

EPILOGUE

Two Months Later

THE CORK BURST OUT OF THE CHAMPAGNE BOTTLE, CRACKING INTO the wall and plopping down on the fluffy pillow where David's head had rested a few moments ago. Champagne frothed out of the bottle onto Grace's naked body. She shivered from the sudden hit of cold and giggled from the tickly sensation of bubbles on her skin.

She gave him a sly grin. "You did that on purpose."

The bubbles foaming on her breasts captured his full attention and made his pupils expand into dark pools of desire. Her nipples pebbled from the chilled liquid, an invitation no man, not even a stoic warrior, could resist. At least she hoped so.

Bending his head, he licked the champagne off her skin. His deft tongue raced up the slope of her breast.

Her breaths quickened. "Honestly, David, I thought we'd use the glasses."

"So did I." He glanced up at the flutes on the bedside table. "This is more fun."

Grace lay sprawled on their new bed in their new house, on new sheets woven from silky Egyptian cotton. David had insisted on the highest thread count for their bedding after she'd made the mistake of oohing over the buttery smoothness of the silk sheets in the five-star hotel where they'd spent their wedding night. They couldn't afford silk, but Egyptian cotton did nicely.

Tonight, he subjected her to the sensual pleasure of soft sheets against her backside and hot, sweat-slicked male flesh mashed to her front side. The combination drove her batty with need and transformed her into a sex-crazed idiot.

"Stop that," David said in the low, throaty voice he assumed whenever she was nude, and sometimes when she wasn't. His tongue flicked over one nipple.

"Oh… stop what?"

"Feeling guilty about stripping me naked every chance you get."

Damn. There were times she wished he didn't share her feelings quite so much. "You're the one who stripped me this time, so it's your fault."

He closed his mouth around her hard peak and suckled gently. When he set her nipple free, he flashed her a sexy grin. "We're newlyweds. Everyone assumes we're ravishing each other on a daily basis." He chuckled, dissolving her willpower, if she'd had any left. "Or hourly, as needed."

"But we should be concentrating on Sean and Cari. They both have powers they can't fully control." She struggled to sound convincingly stern, but his talented tongue kept toying with her flesh. A woman had her limits. And this man knew exactly how to push her past them. Still, she had no intention of ending this conversational thread yet. "We also have defunct ALI facilities to check out and abused psychics to rehabilitate."

He exhaled with an exasperated grumble. "The poor orphan psychics can wait, and we've helped Sean and Cari plenty, every day, for two entire months. For the first time in weeks, we're alone in our own house. Tonight is for us." He blew a breath over her breast, eliciting a deep shiver in her. "It's our anniversary."

"Anniversaries are once a year."

"Grace, my eternal soul mate—"

"Cut the crap, David. This two-month celebration is just an excuse to goof off."

"I was thinking more about getting off."

The phone rang.

Grace fumbled to grab her cell off the bedside table. The instant her fingers closed around the phone, David snatched it away.

He frowned at the caller ID. "Wickham. I thought Brits were supposed to have impeccable manners, but he manages to call at the exact wrong moment every time. I think Amador's given him instructions to interrupt us."

"As if he could know when we're in the midst of things." She grabbed for the phone, but he swung his arm behind his back. "David, it could be important."

"Then he'll leave a message and we'll deal with it later." He rubbed his body against hers with delicious friction. "Even world-savers get a night off."

"But it'll just take a sec—"

He hurled the phone across the room. It bounced off the wall with a *thwack* and clattered to the floor. "Amador might be funding our new project, but that doesn't give his lackey the right to pester us ten times a day."

"He's only making sure we've got everything we need."

"At least Amador doesn't call you."

Because he knew David hated him like a cat hated a bath. Sequestered at the private hospital he'd bought, Amador had made no attempts to contact her in the last two months. She was fine with that and with David's insistence that she shouldn't visit Amador. She'd never intended to, anyway. She might sympathize with the trauma that drove him to madness, but she didn't know if she could ever forgive the horrible things he'd done in the name of vengeance.

David patted her thigh. "You're thinking about Amador, aren't you? That ends this instant."

"Yes, sir." Her thoughts circled back to their self-imposed mission of aiding the people who had been held captive by first JT, then Tesler and Nkosi, which led inevitably to more thoughts of Gabriel Amador. Here she was in bed with her new husband, and she kept thinking about a whackjob. "I'm trying not to, but my brain has other ideas."

"I can shut down your brain in a heartbeat."

Her body awakened at his words. Oh yes, he could do that. He'd proved it on numerous occasions.

With a flourish of his hand, he spritzed champagne along the length of her body. She willingly rewarded him with a long, husky moan. He cleaned up the liquid with his lips, his tongue, lapping up every drop with impressive focus and thoroughness. She arched into his ministrations. He nibbled her hip. She plunged a hand into his hair.

The light glittered on her diamond engagement ring and sparked on the gold of her wedding band. She was married. To him. At last.

She ought to tell him. He deserved to know. Well, maybe she could wait until after...

He abandoned his quest to cleanse her body of champagne, slithering up her body to settle down alongside her. "What's wrong?"

"Nothing." She'd slammed that opening shut. Why? She longed to tell him the news, but she worried about his reaction. It was stupid. Then again, they'd never had *that* talk.

"Tell me, Grace. My wife, the love of my life, my most splendiferous goddess."

She laughed. "Splendiferous is not a word."

"Yes, it is. Look it up in the dictionary—later." The contentment on his face faded into concern. "Are you okay? You said your doctor's appointment was nothing, just getting a refill on your allergy pills."

Yeah, she'd fibbed about that so he wouldn't get his hopes up or freak out. "Well, you see, that's not entirely accurate." She clasped her hands over her belly, tapping one finger. "We're having a baby."

His smile beamed into her with the heat and brilliance of a hundred suns. His elation spun through her mind and accelerated both their pulses. His mouth opened, then closed, then opened again as he finally rallied his voice. "Really? We're having—"

He gasped for air, too happy to breathe. She knew this because he fed his joy into her, and she accepted it with all her heart and soul.

The anxiety sluiced out of her. She stroked her fingers down his cheek to dance them over his lips. "Yes. Really. I'm about two months along."

"Two months?" She practically heard the cogs turning in his brain. Then realization sparked in his eyes. "The night in the cabin. When we merged our powers."

"Yep, I think so." A new kind of anxiety iced through her. "Do you think the process of merging our psychic energies will have any effect on our baby?"

"If it does…" He rolled on top of her. "It'll be a good effect. Nothing bad could come out of what happened between us that night."

He was right. She felt the truth of it deep inside, a glimmer of hope and faith she prayed would burgeon into a twinkling star in the form of their child.

David shut his eyes, his lips curving into a contented smile. He nuzzled her belly and painted kisses across her flesh, then raised his head to gaze at her with rapt adoration. "Our baby. This is…" He burst into laughter, startling a tiny cry from her. "This is the best day of my entire life."

"Just wait until our kid's born."

Their child, his and hers, another link bonding them on a new level, somehow more profound than even the psychic connection they shared. She focused on his sapphire eyes, letting herself dive into their gleaming pools, drowning in the passion and love she found there.

He swirled his palm over her skin, down to the sensitive skin at the apex of her thighs. "I hope our daughter is just like you."

"Daughter?" She raised her brows. "I thought I was the only one in this family who had premonitions."

"Let's call this intuition. It has to be a girl because I love you too much for this baby to be anything but another version of you."

"You think you love me enough to affect the DNA of our baby."

"Damn straight I do."

"Okay then, prove it." She wrapped her legs around his waist, pinning his arousal to the dampness between her thighs. "Show me how you did that."

His mouth found hers, and his tongue explored with delicate strokes. She tugged his head down to deepen the kiss.

When their mouths parted, she licked her lips. "You taste like champagne."

"Hmm… good idea."

He snagged the bottle and dumped the last of the champagne onto her chest. It splattered onto the sheets and fizzed on her breasts.

Then he showed her. Everything. And they both knew, with a certainty that resonated in their souls and empowered their psychic faculties, that their daughter would be perfect. Their life would be perfect. They'd have ups and downs, and sometimes they'd drive each other nuts, but when it really mattered, they would stick by each other through whatever lay ahead for them. Nothing would tear them apart again. She knew that.

Call it intuition.

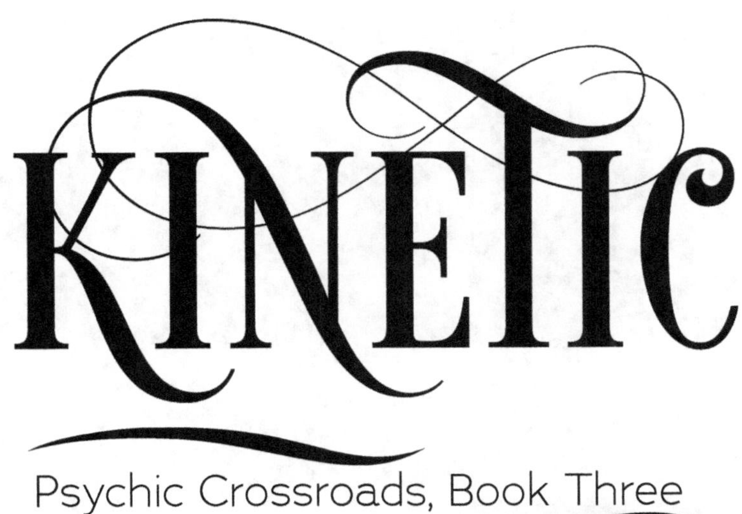

Psychic Crossroads, Book Three

Chapter One

HEAL, DAMMIT. SEAN VANDENBROOK COMMANDED HIS PSYCHIC powers to activate, but got a big zippo in response. He hunched over the table, one hand lying palm up beside his empty lunch plate, and ran a finger of the other hand along the seam of the cut he'd gotten this morning while slicing open a well-taped box. Too bad he couldn't get rid of the stupid cut. What was the point of having the power to heal if he couldn't fix his own injuries? Psychic powers totally sucked.

"Did you hear me, Sean?"

He glanced up from his hand.

David Ransom was staring at him with narrowed eyes the way he did when he was in surrogate-father mode. Like David was old enough to be his father. Annoying big brother, maybe. Not a father. Why the hell did Sean care what David thought about him, then? He shouldn't. He wouldn't. Not anymore.

Sean felt nothing these days, by design. Maybe psychic powers didn't *totally* suck after all.

He leaned back in the white-painted, wrought-iron chair that matched the legs of the mosaic-tile table. His black leather jacket was making him a little too warm, but he didn't want to take it off. Maybe the jacket was his armor. Maybe he needed armor these days.

Elsewhere in the outdoor cafe, people talked and laughed and munched on trendy sandwiches. Sean barely noticed them, and he sensed nothing from them. No pain. No fear. Not even joy. He sighed at the relief of not knowing what other people felt. His first public outing in a couple months was going okay except for David's pestering.

Never mind that niggling uneasiness in his gut. It meant nothing.

"I heard you," Sean said. "Just don't have anything to say about it."

"Grace is worried about you," David said, slanting forward on the other side of the table to study Sean. "What have you been doing for the past two months? You don't call us. We only talk to you if we call you, and then it's brief and uninformative. You skipped your college graduation. Even dyed your hair brown."

Sean instinctively ran a hand through his hair. He'd let it grow out a few inches, and yeah, he'd covered up his red hair with brown coloring. So what? "I can change my hair without your permission."

"You're sitting there like a robot, like nothing affects you. What's wrong?"

Sean hiked up one shoulder and let it fall again. "I'm fine. Busy, that's all."

"Too busy to see your niece? Abby asks for you all the time."

"Your kid's not my niece."

David frowned. "You're her honorary uncle."

Sean snorted. "Honorary uncle? That's not a thing."

"At the time, you thought it was 'wicked awesome.' A direct quote from you."

"Gimme a break." Sean rolled his eyes. "I was eighteen and stupid. Maybe I don't need an honorary family anymore. I'm a big boy now, and you are not my dad."

Blocking his empathic powers might've made him a little...testy. No choice. He had to keep his powers in check for the sake of everyone else in the world.

David sat back, one hand on the table, fingers tapping. He fixed his blue eyes on Sean, and the irises began to glow with a preternatural fire.

Sean sensed the prickling pressure of David's mind trying to tunnel into his own. He gave it a psychic swat.

Across the table, David winced.

"What are you doing?" Sean asked, his voice low and dark. "Trying to read my mind? Grace told you to never, ever, ever do that. Better listen to your wife. You wanna go bat-shit crazy?"

Mind reading was the biggest no-no in the world of psychic powers. Grace had done it once and swore she'd never try it again. She'd made David and Sean both swear they'd never do it either.

Why the hell was David attempting it?

"You've left me no choice," David said, almost as if he were answering Sean's thought-question. "We know something's wrong with you. This hard-as-nails, don't-give-a-damn-about-anything attitude is a cover for whatever's going on with you lately. What happened to the boy who loved his powers and loved his honorary niece?"

"He grew up and grew a pair. I can take care of myself. Don't need my wannabe daddy giving me a heart-to-heart."

David watched him for a few seconds, then braced his elbow on the table and let his forehead fall into his raised hand. The energy seemed to flood out of him, sagging his shoulders. He drew in a long breath and raised his head to pin Sean with his gaze. "We care about you. You're a part of our family, and we won't give up on you no matter how much you act like a knucklehead. Do you realize how your behavior hurts Grace?"

Her face flashed in Sean's mind. Grace, with hazel eyes and auburn hair. Grace, with that kind smile and teasing manner. She liked to tousle his hair, even now, like he was still a kid. She'd encouraged him to get his GED and go to college. She'd saved him from torture of the most literal, physical kind—and of the psychic variety. If not for her...

A pang stabbed through his chest.

No, no, no. His shields had slipped. He slammed them back into place, shutting out all the emotions inside and outside himself.

Blessed emptiness.

"Not trying to hurt anybody," Sean said. The exact opposite, in fact. "You're all better off without me around, trust me."

The unease he'd experienced since entering this cafe resurfaced, tugging on his metaphysical senses. Movement caught his eye, and he glanced at the courtyard archway, the entrance to the cafe a dozen feet away. A young woman stood there, shoulders bunched, tension evident on her face. She'd tied her raven hair back in a long ponytail, the locks glistening in the sunshine. The light also glinted in her eyes, igniting the lighter highlights in her deep-blue irises. She was beautiful.

And for the first time in two months, despite his shields, he felt something. A twinge of what he could only describe as...longing. A bizarre impulse to wrap her in his arms. She seemed so lost, almost afraid. Of what?

"Sean," David said, with an uncharacteristic sharpness to his tone.

Blinking rapidly, struggling to shake the...whatever the girl had incited in him, Sean returned his attention to David. "What?"

"I'm glad you're still interested in girls," David said, "but we were having a serious conversation. Why would you think we're better off without you?"

"Because—" His gaze inexorably traveled back to the girl. She was fidgeting and scratching her arms, exposed by the short-sleeve shirt she wore. Her jeans had trendy slashes in them that gaped open around her knees, complete with fashionable threads dangling from them.

The girl lowered one hand, her arm straight at her side, parallel to her body. She flexed her fingers.

"For Christ's sake, Sean, pay attention."

He flicked his gaze to David, but his focus was pulled back to the girl by an inexplicable sensation of impending danger. Sean's body went rigid. He stared at the girl, not blinking, not moving, racking his mind for the source of this dread.

"Grace thinks you're suppressing your powers," David said. "Is she right?"

"What if she is? It's my business, not yours."

"Sean, suppressing your powers is dangerous. Not to mention bad for your health, mental and physical."

"I'm fine."

Sean couldn't look away from the girl. She'd closed her eyes, her face pinched. The power of her anguish battered his shields, but only a trickle penetrated them. It was enough, though. Even a taste of her pain left a bitter tang in his mouth. He shouldn't care, goddammit, but something about her...

He jumped up. "Back in a minute."

Before David could protest, Sean stalked toward the girl, weaving his way around tables and chairs.

Eyes squeezed shut, the girl curled her fingers into her palm.

Sean reached her just as she snapped her fingers straight.

The building exploded.

CHAPTER TWO

THE FORCE OF THE DETONATION THREW SEAN INTO THE GIRL. THEY tumbled to the stone-paved floor of the entrance with her pinned beneath his body. Debris rained down around them, and something large whumped to the ground nearby, sending shock waves through the floor. Sharp fragments of debris clawed at his skin. Dust surged into his nostrils and mouth, making him hack and spit mud.

As the debris cloud settled, he made out shapes. His ears rang, though behind the noise, he detected muffled voices shouting and screaming.

Sean looked down at the girl.

Her blue eyes, enlarged by shock, stared up at him. Powdery debris turned her face a muddy, mottled shade of pale. Her entire body trembled. Her lips parted, and he could tell she was speaking, but the ringing in his ears drowned out her words. She pounded her little fists on his biceps, shouting loud enough he barely made out what she said.

"Get—off—me—can't—breathe!"

Sean rolled to the side, onto a sharp metal object. It stabbed into his hip. With a snarled curse that sounded far away even to his ears, he pushed up onto his knees. His chest heaved with every breath, his eyes burned, and cuts on his arms and face stung like the devil. He started to wipe at his face with his shirt but stopped when he realized the fabric was coated with dirt and spattered with blood. His blood? Her blood?

His heart thudded.

Not enough blood to suggest a major injury. He prayed neither of them had anything more serious than cuts. But the other people in the cafe…

The girl was struggling to get to her knees, hindered by the top of a table that had come loose from its legs and slid onto her feet. Sean grabbed the tile tabletop and heaved it off her. The thing crashed onto a pile of rubble, shooting up a plume of dust. He grasped the girl's hands and pulled her up with him as he clambered to his feet. His knees quivered. The rest of him seemed okay, but she was still shaking from head to toe.

He leaned in close, bent to level their gazes, and spoke in loud, precise syllables. "Are you okay?"

She nodded shakily. Her eyes remained wide, her pupils large. Her skin, what he could see of it through the dirt, looked ashen.

No, she didn't seem all right.

He frisked his hands over her body to check for obvious wounds but found none. When he closed his fingers around her wrist, feeling her pulse, it was fast and fluttery. She swayed a little, blinking slowly. Jeez, she needed a doctor. He took her upper arms in his hands to steady her.

Sirens ululated in the distance.

Or maybe they were close, he couldn't tell for sure. The ringing in his ears was lessening, but he hadn't regained normal hearing yet.

David.

The thought slammed through him, and his hands fell away from the girl. He swung his head around, zeroing in on the table where he and David had sat.

It was gone.

No. His heart pounded so hard it seemed like his ribs might crack from the pressure. He should never have left David. If he'd been hurt or worse—

The girl bolted.

Sean took a step to follow her but froze. She'd sprinted out the entrance and out of sight down the sidewalk. He had no time to worry about her, though, and had to hope the EMTs would find and help her.

He barreled across the remains of the cafe, vaulting over debris piles. He stopped once to help a woman who lay dazed amid the wreckage, but she needed aid he couldn't give. Since she wasn't bleeding too badly, he told her to wait for the EMTs and not move. Then he raced the last short distance to where the table should've been, the one where he'd left David.

A pile of bricks slumped where the table had stood.

One foot, covered by a brown sneaker, stuck out from beneath the pile.

No, God, no.

Sean seized one brick, tossed it aside, grabbed them two at a time and then three at a time. He hurled them away, praying he wasn't burying another victim he couldn't see. *Save David.* That single thought consumed him. He uncovered one of David's legs, then the other, and with agonizing slowness he freed the rest of the man who'd been like a brother and a surrogate father to him. His best friend.

David lay limp on his stomach, his arms and legs askew, his head bent to the side. His eyes were closed, his mouth open. Blood oozed from a wound on his head, etching red trails through the dirt on his skin.

Falling to his knees, Sean felt for a pulse in David's throat. Faint, but there.

The sirens had gone silent.

Sean glanced toward the entrance, what remained of it, and saw the pulsing lights of emergency vehicles. A fire truck had pulled up right in front.

"Help!" Sean hollered. "We've got injured people here."

While EMTs wended their way through the debris, Sean sat vigil beside David, unwilling to leave until he knew his friend would be found and treated.

The explosion. It replayed in his mind over and over. What had happened? Something caused this, someone caused this, but who and why?

Sean gritted his teeth. The girl. She'd done this. He had no idea how or why, but when she'd flicked her fingers, the whole place had erupted.

A psychic attack?

He didn't give a damn right now. Until he knew David was okay, nothing else mattered. If David died…

Sean would find that fucking girl and murder her.

KIRA MAGNUSSON STUMBLED AROUND THE CORNER ONTO ANOTHER street, avoiding the EMTs by running in the opposite direction. Maybe she needed medical attention, but she couldn't risk it. Nothing seemed to be broken, so she ought to heal okay—eventually. On the outside. Inside…

A memory seized her mind, a nightmare come to life. Choking. Gasping. Lungs burning. Crawling on her stomach across the floor, desperate to escape. She deserved what they'd done to her that day. Compared to the horror of what she'd just done in the cafe…

Her stomach lurched.

She doubled over and vomited on the sidewalk.

Oh God, what had she done? *What you had to do*, a voice whispered inside her. Had this been her only option? They'd said it would be a smoke bomb, not—not—this.

Her stomach heaved again.

She staggered into an alley, knowing she couldn't make it much farther. At least in an alley, no one would notice her. Everyone was distracted by the…disaster. She sagged into the wall of a building, its concrete blocks cold against the bare skin of her arms. The disaster? She'd caused it. What if someone had died? She couldn't think about that, not now. Tears burned in her eyes, but she sucked in a breath and tried to stave them off. *Stay strong, for Caleb.*

Her phone rang.

She jerked at the sound, then dug the phone out of her pocket. With trembling fingers, she answered the call—no name, no number on caller ID. But she knew who it was.

"Well done," the familiar, electronically altered voice said. She couldn't tell if the speaker was a man or a woman, but the voice had an odd lilt to it.

"You told me it would be a smoke bomb," she hissed into the phone, sounding far stronger than she felt. Her knees quivered, threatening to buckle. "If anyone died, I'll—"

"Do exactly what we say, nothing more and nothing less. If you wish for your brother to live."

She absently flicked her thumbnail against her forefinger. A tiny spark flashed on the pad of her finger. She clamped her hand into a fist. "Let me talk to Caleb."

A scuffling noise suggested the kidnapper was handing his phone to someone else. "Kira? Are you coming to get me?"

Kira choked back a sob, clutching her stomach with her free hand. "Soon, sweetie, I promise. You be strong for me, 'kay?"

"I don't like it here."

"Won't be long, I promise." Lying to her eight-year-old brother? She had no choice. Telling him the truth, that she had no clue when the kidnappers might release him, would only escalate his panic. "I love you, Caleb."

"Love you too, Kiki."

She swallowed another sob when he spoke his nickname for her. Caleb was in this mess because of her. If she'd been more careful…But how could she have been? She didn't know how these evil bastards found her, much less how they got Caleb three days ago, sometime between school ending in the afternoon and Kira arriving to pick him up. In a matter of minutes, they'd taken her brother. She'd gotten slowed down by traffic and showed up three minutes late. *Three minutes.*

More scuffling. The altered voice of the kidnapper growled in her ear. "I suggest you find a place to hide and await further instructions."

"No, dammit, I will not—"

"Do you wish for your brother to die?"

The hand over her belly fisted, twisting her shirt around her fingers. She didn't dare speak, her emotions too wild to be trusted.

"I didn't think so," the kidnapper said. "We will be in touch."

Click. The call ended.

Kira stuffed the phone in her pocket. Pulled in a deep breath. Shoved a hand through her hair, filthy with dirt and who-knew-what other substances. Caleb had no one else, not since their parents ran away to another continent. To get away from her. She could almost understand that, but abandoning Caleb was unforgivable.

He had no one else, which meant she had to save him.

By whatever means necessary? Her conscience prickled at the thought.

She pushed away from the wall and hurried to…anywhere but here.

CHAPTER THREE

Hospitals smelled like the aftermath of disaster and death as embodied by the odor of disinfectant used to clean up and cover up the catastrophes that brought people here. Sean hated the smell, hated the sterile colors and the hospital beds, hated sitting in a chair that barely fit his frame and made his tailbone hurt. The medical types had taken David into the ER, and though Grace had gone with him, they wouldn't let Sean accompany her. He wasn't family, not technically.

So, he slouched in an awful chair in the waiting room. And he waited. And waited.

Being in the hospital niggled at his memories, the ones he'd repressed for so long with so much effort. Now, the memories unreeled in his mind's eye. Screeching tires. The explosive bang of metal slamming into a wooden pole. Smoke. Flames. A blur of noise and movements, sirens and ambulances. When he'd finally had time to process the event, he was sitting in a chair like the one he occupied today. Just like then, his stomach churned and acid scorched up his chest into his throat. His muscles ached from the tension stretching them taut. His jaw ached too, thanks to his gritted teeth.

Someone entered the waiting room, but Sean noticed the figure only peripherally until a hand settled on his shoulder. He lifted his eyes to the newcomer.

Gabriel Amador gazed down at Sean with a tight smile.

Though his fingers crooked toward his palms, Sean maintained an outward calmness when he spoke to Amador. "Why are you here?"

"Grace called me," Amador said in his slightly accented voice. He skimmed his gaze over Sean, his brows tightening. "You are injured?"

"Some cuts, nothing major."

"You can relax," Amador said. "I am here to assist."

Oh how awesome, we're all saved. Sean kept the thought to himself.

Why on earth Grace trusted this man, Sean had no clue. Five years ago, Amador had drugged her and tried to convince her he had psychic powers when he had none, just to gain her cooperation in his nutjob scheme for revenge. He'd held a teenage girl hostage too. Grace had forgiven him, though, because Amador had a great sob story. His young son had been taken by Sean's grandfather, the wacko Karl Tesler, and tortured until he died. Then Amador's wife had committed suicide, broken by the loss. By Amador's own admission, he'd gone loony tunes after that.

Sean's nails dug into his palm. Good old gramps had tortured him too, but nobody caught Sean doing wacky things because of it.

Amador squeezed Sean's shoulder. "How is David?"

"Don't know yet."

The ER door swung open, and Grace shambled into the waiting room.

Sean jumped up, hands jammed in his jeans pockets, shoulders hunched beneath his leather jacket.

Amador hurried to her, clasping her in a quick hug.

Disgust slithered through Sean. He couldn't like Amador, no matter how "nice" the guy pretended to be. Cari, the girl Amador had abducted and abused, was one of Sean's closest friends.

Grace looked ashen and tired, dark circles under her eyes. She tried for a small smile, but her lips quivered, and the expression disintegrated.

"David?" Sean asked, his entire body as rigid as concrete, his feet heavy as concrete too. He awaited her response with his pulse racing and a coldness washing over him.

"He's alive," she said. "They put him in a medically induced coma, so his body can heal."

A coma? David must've been seriously injured, more even than Sean had realized when he pulled his friend out of the rubble. "How long—I mean, do they think he'll be okay?"

"The doctor says he's optimistic, but only time will tell." She hugged herself, rubbing her upper arms. "Abby's going home with her great-grandfather. I'll stay here until visiting hours are over."

Amador took her hand in his, a smarmily concerned look on his face. "What can I do?"

"Nothing. But thanks for coming."

Sean wanted to tell Grace to go home, get some rest, because she couldn't do anything for David right now. He couldn't form the words. Grace and David had the kind of relationship Sean had thought only existed in romance novels. Their love had saved their lives and the lives of countless others—and that was no metaphor. The psychic bond they shared imbued their love with real power, the kind that could save the world. Sean knew he couldn't hope to find anything even close to that.

"David's still in there," she said. "As long as I can feel him, there's hope."

"Of course there's hope," Sean said. He raised his hands, intending to hug her, but let them fall back down. She'd let Amador hug her, but did she want comforting from Sean? He decided to try expressing his support with words instead. "You and David are like…I don't know, like Cinderella and that prince guy. You're meant to be together. Nothing can get between the two of you, not even this."

"Cinderella?" Grace almost smiled, though it dissolved into a downward curve of her lips. "Our relationship has never been a fairy-tale romance. We survived two psychos who wanted to destroy us, not to mention my amnesia. Maybe this is how it ends."

"No way." Sean grasped her upper arms, bending his knees until he could look her in the eye. "You're freaking out right now, that's all. David will get better. He *will*."

"Yes," Amador interjected, "he will."

The urge to smack the man seized Sean, but he restrained himself. He hated the way Amador had insinuated himself into Grace's life over the past five years. Still, it was her choice whether to trust him.

She nodded weakly, unshed tears shimmering in her hazel eyes. Never one to let the tears roll or let life knock her down, she swiped them away with the back of her hand, then hauled in a breath and straightened. "We need to find out who did this and why. They need to pay."

A steely edge gave her voice a sharpness Sean had never heard before from Grace. Sure, she could be tough when necessary. But she had the kindest heart of anyone he'd ever known.

If she wanted vengeance, he would mete it out for her and for David.

For everyone who'd been caught in the explosion.

"Revenge will not help," Amador said. "You're upset, Grace. Make no decisions now. I'm certain the authorities will apprehend whoever is responsible."

Yeah, sure. Once again, Sean wanted to deck the guy.

The ER doors opened, and Edward McLean trudged out with four-year-old Abby Ransom in his arms. The little girl had her teeth clamped down on her lower lip, her eyes red and her cheeks stained with the tracks of tears now dried. Her great-grandfather carried the little girl over to Grace but kept Abby in his arms.

"I talked to my friend at the police department," Edward said. "There were no fatalities from the explosion, but fourteen people were hurt. David has the worst injuries."

Grace struggled to stay calm, Sean could see it, but the tears won out. She sagged against her grandfather, wrapping her arms around her daughter. No sobs, though. No, Grace wouldn't do that, not with her child right there. Sean knew tears must be streaming down her cheeks, yet from this angle, she seemed to be simply hugging her daughter.

Edward's lip curled in disgust—not for Grace's reaction, but for someone else entirely. "Who could've done this?"

Sean realized the older man wasn't asking a question. He was expressing what all of them felt. Fear. Frustration. Confusion. Anger.

Abby stuffed a thumb in her mouth, something the four-year-old hadn't done in a long time.

The coldness that had infiltrated Sean, once borne of fear and shock, transformed into a tight, iron-hard ball of dangerous resolve. Vengeance? Yeah, he could do that.

"Don't worry," Sean said, hands clenching into fists. "I will find out who did this, and I will make them pay for it."

Edward shook his head. "Sean, let the police handle this."

"Police? Screw them. They can't help with psychic attacks. I saw a girl right before the bomb went off. I think she caused the explosion."

"How?" Edward stared into empty space for several seconds, his lips tight. "My friend said the bomb consisted of two substances that are harmless when found alone, but when combined they're explosive. Each was held in its own glass container. There must've been a trigger to shatter the glass, but they haven't found the trigger itself yet or detected any evidence of how it worked."

Like a frigging cartoon character, Sean sensed a light bulb popping on above his head. No one else noticed his epiphany, of course, since it was contained inside himself. Suddenly, though, the facts of what he'd observed fit together to form a coherent picture.

The girl. The bomb.

She'd flicked her fingers and then—*boom*.

A trigger? Hell yeah, he knew what it was. The girl had used a psychic ability, maybe telekinesis, to shatter the glass containers and set off the bomb.

"Cops won't find a trigger," he said to Edward. "But I know exactly what it looks like."

Grace's head sprang up, her bleary eyes trained on him. "What are you talking about? You saw the bomb?"

"No." He flattened his lips into a line, recalling the anguish he'd sensed from the mystery girl. "The bomb was triggered by a psychic. And I'm beginning to think it was no coincidence the girl who set it off picked the day when David and I would be there."

"How could anyone have known," Edward said, "when the two of you would be there?"

Grace pushed away from her grandfather. "Psychics have a lot of ways to spy. I think Sean may be on to something here, but I can't leave David to go investigate." She glanced up at Edward. "And I need you to look after Abby."

"I'll get it done," Sean said. "Trust me, I will track down the girl and find out what the hell is going on, one way or another. All of us have pissed off plenty of bad guys over the years. The ones we know about are long dead, but they had facilities all over the world. Could be cronies who escaped. Either way, I'll root out the truth."

"This is a mistake," Amador said, his tone oddly sharp. "Grace, please do not encourage Sean. This is a reckless idea."

"Sean will be careful." Grace rushed forward to clasp Sean's face with both hands. "Don't do anything crazy. Promise me, Sean. I can't lose anyone I love, not again."

Grace didn't mean David, though all of them worried for his fate. Grace meant her parents who'd died at the hands of the lunatic Jackson Tennant seven years ago.

"I'll be careful," he assured her. "You won't lose anybody. Not David, not me, not anyone. We all will get through this safe and sound, you have my word."

He'd make sure nobody harmed his family, even if he had to take extreme measures to ensure it. After all, he'd promised he wouldn't get himself killed—not that he wouldn't take out the bad guys.

Sean understood Grace's fears of losing the people she loved. He feared for the same thing.

No one would die. No one except the scumbags who'd brought it on themselves.

Amador eyed Sean with a strange expression, almost curious, almost annoyed, but not really either one.

Well, the jerk had spent a good chunk of the past five years in a psychiatric clinic, off and on.

"I should get going," Sean said. "I know exactly where to start investigating."

The last place he'd seen the girl. The cafe.

***

THE STENCH OF SMOKE PERMEATED THE AIR, AND SLENDER TENDRILS OF it curled up from the blackened remnants of the cafe. The sallow glow of the streetlamps outside the entrance wall, which stood mostly intact, illuminated the smoke trails with a ghostly effect. Kira hunched in the entrance on the exact spot where she'd stood ten hours earlier. Though yellow police tape was strung across the entrance, she'd ducked under it. No one had been around to stop her since the cops seemed to have gone home for the night. She supposed they saw no need for guards. Only an idiot would sneak back into the scene of the crime she'd perpetrated.

Nighttime lent the devastation an eerie, almost otherworldly aura.

Cuts and bruises, that's all she had. But the victims in the cafe…

She fingered the strap of her little purse. The strap hung over one shoulder on a diagonal across her chest, the purse itself positioned over her hip. Inside the bag, she had chocolates and cigarettes. Her mouth watered, though not for candy. A smoke, that's what she needed. Even the toughest person would fall off the wagon in these circumstances. Who cared about wrecking six smoke-free months? She'd caused a catastrophe.

Biting down on her bottom lip, she tried not to think about cigarettes. But her thoughts came back to the bomb, the detonation, the screams. Carrying a pack of cigarettes in her purse to test her willpower had sounded like a good idea a month ago. Now, she craved a smoke so badly.

A chill skittered down her spine. She had done this. If anyone had died…

They said it was a smoke bomb. No excuse, and she knew it. For the rest of her life, she would live with the knowledge of what she'd done.

For years, she'd feared the possibility of anyone discovering she had powers, feared what the wrong people might do to her if they knew. Her nightmares had come true, more horrifying than she'd ever imagined.

"I knew you'd come back to admire your handiwork."

Kira jumped and spun around. Her heart thudded so hard she couldn't breathe for a second.

There, backlit by the streetlamps, hunkered a manlike silhouette. Shadows obscured his features. He seemed huge, like a demon straight out of Hell sent to drag her into the bowels of eternal torment.

The man surged forward to clamp his big hands around her arms. "Don't even think about running."

His voice snarled, like she'd always thought a demon's would.

"Who are you?" he demanded.

No voice. All she could do was gasp.

The demon spun them both until they stood sideways to the entrance, facing each other, his grip on her never easing up even the tiniest bit. His fingers pressed into her flesh, eliciting pains that webbed out into her shoulders.

And at last, she saw him.

The man who'd landed on top of her after the bomb went off.

His green eyes seemed luminescent in the spooky glow of the streetlamps. He must've been six feet tall, maybe a little more, with arms corded with muscles she could see even through the leather jacket he wore. His biceps bulged from the effort of holding her. His V-neck black T-shirt clung to his body, and so did his jeans, accentuating his every muscle.

This man could crush her with his bare hands.

"You detonated the bomb," he growled, "and I want to know why. Scratch that. You are going to tell me why if you want to keep all your limbs."

She started to scratch her thumbnail across her forefinger but tamped down the nervous instinct. Had he known someone who died here? Had she killed a human being?

No, God, no.

Kira didn't think about what she was doing. Panic gripped her in its icy talons, and she lashed out with all the power inside her, flinging it at the stranger.

He flew backward. With a thud and a grunt, he smacked down flat on his backside.

Run. The instinct propelled her. She barreled out the entrance, swerved left down the sidewalk, and—

Powerful arms latched around her torso and hauled her to a stop, her arms pinned to her body.

She yelped as the stranger hoisted her up, her feet dangling inches above the cement.

"You can talk here," he hissed into her ear, "or I can take you somewhere more private and find ways to motivate you to tell me what I want to know."

Was he threatening to abduct her? Like hell she'd let that happen.

"Don't," he said, and squeezed her so hard she couldn't breathe. Letting off the pressure just enough she could gulp in sweet oxygen, he told her, "I know you have powers, and I'm sure you want to use them on me again, but don't bother. Wherever you go, I'll find you. Someone I love is in a coma because of you."

What could she say? People had been injured—died, for all she knew—and maybe she deserved to be crushed to death by an avenging angel.

If she died, Caleb died too.

Kira marshaled all the energy she had left, tapping into her powers to the point of draining them, and willed his body to fly backward.

He jerked but held his ground. Held his grip on her too.

She was too weak to fight. Tears burned her eyes, but she refused to let them flow. Showing weakness in front of a man bent on exacting vengeance on her seemed like a really, really stupid idea.

"You've got a tell," he murmured into her ear.

"I've got a what?"

"A little movement you do right before you activate your powers. It gives away the game and gives me time to get ready for the attack." His lips were hot and dry against her ear. "You caught me off guard once. It won't happen again."

Wonderful. She had a tell, and he knew what it was. She didn't.

"I won't tell you anything," she said. "Either kill me or let me go."

"Nice try." He straightened, his arms still buckling her to his hard body. "But I'm not letting you out of my sight until I have all the answers I need."

Why oh why hadn't she bought a gun? A knife, even. Hell, a Taser would've done the trick. She'd never needed to defend herself until a few days ago, and by then it was too late.

She couldn't fight back against an invisible enemy.

The man grasped her wrists and yanked her hands behind her back, cuffing them in one of his hands. Something like hard plastic or nylon, a thin but strong cable of it, closed around her wrists. A zip tie? Her captor cinched it tight, though not so tight it would dig into her skin. Just snug enough to restrain her.

"I notice you're not screaming for help," he said, his strong hand holding onto the zip tie, his fingers between her wrists. "More proof you're guilty. Innocent people pray for help, fight to get away until they're bloody and beaten, scream for help until their throats are raw and they can't breathe."

The way he said those words, with a roughness and a slight break on the last syllable, she got the weirdest sensation trickling down her spine. He sounded like he knew people fought and screamed because he'd been in their shoes. He'd been a victim.

Oh no, she would not feel sorry for the man abducting her.

For all she knew, he was the world's greatest actor, conning her into empathizing with him as a means to break her will.

The stranger tugged on the zip tie. "Time to go."

He dropped a burlap sack over her head, plunging her into darkness.

She couldn't scream for help because she was guilty. She couldn't fight either because she was exhausted and powerless.

The stranger hauled her down the sidewalk. She tripped when they veered off the curb into the street. He kept her from falling down but dragged her onward until they halted, and she heard the distinctive sound of a car door opening. He shoved her into a bucket seat, shoved her feet inside too, and then strapped her in with the seatbelt. It pinned her to the seat with her hands bound behind her back, the strap at a diagonal across her chest. The lower portion of it banded her pelvis.

The door slammed shut.

Another door opened—the driver's door, she assumed—and slammed shut a moment later. The engine growled to life. The car shot forward, swerved right, rocketed ahead.

The momentum of each movement thrust her first backward into the seat, then sideways, and finally backward again. The zip tie dug into her wrists with sharp, stinging pain. She winced, gritting her teeth.

"Where are you taking me?" she asked.

"Not telling. Why do you think I put a hood over your head?" The car swung around a corner, and the engine roared as he floored the accelerator. "So you can't see where we're going."

Her wrists burned. A warm liquid oozed down from her wrists to her palms. Every wild movement of the vehicle shifted her position until the diagonal section of the seatbelt pinched her throat.

"Slow down," she said, her tone rife with a disquieting, almost pleading tone. "My wrists are getting rubbed raw, and the seatbelt is about to choke me."

Her captor let out a soft, harsh laugh. "This is a kidnapping, princess, not a spa vacation. You're probably lying, anyway. Criminals like to do that."

"Not lying," she grated between her clenched teeth. "Blood is running down my wrists. Look for yourself if you don't believe me."

Silence. Kira counted the seconds. One Mississippi, two Mississippi, three Mississippi.

The man in the driver's seat muttered, "Shit."

He swerved the car to the right, stopping with a suddenness that threw her forward. The seatbelt cut into her throat, choking her.

With a click, the seatbelt sprang free and withdrew into its housing with a *zzzt* sound.

The release of pressure made her haul in a deep breath, but that brought on a coughing fit.

He waited until she'd stopped coughing, then clasped her around the waist and angled her to the side. Large fingers felt around the zip tie. He muttered another oath. She heard him moving around, followed by the sharp sound of nylon snapping, and her wrists were free. Air wafted over them, making the scrapes sting and her eyes tear up from the pain. She gasped, partly from the pain, partly in relief.

Noises indicated he was rooting around in the backseat.

He wrapped a smooth rope around her wrists and cinched it tight enough to bind her without the rope cutting into her wrists. Once he'd knotted the rope, he secured the seatbelt around her again, leaving her hands free of the waist strap.

"There," he said. "You can't escape, but I don't have to listen to you whine about the zip tie anymore. No sneaky shit, understand? If you try to get away, I'll zip-tie you from head to toe. Besides, I turned on the safety locks which means you can't get out of the car. No sneaky—"

"I get it." What choice did she have? She leaned back into the seat, her bound hands in her lap. "The safety locks are only for the backseat, you know."

"Stop talking."

Considering that she had nowhere to go anyway, she complied with his orders. The rope irritated her raw skin, but that was the least of her worries. Blinded by the hood, she shut up and prayed this wasn't part of a plot devised by the people holding her brother. What they wanted her to do next, she had no idea. Their endgame remained a mystery too, one she needed to figure out but feared uncovering.

No way out.

CHAPTER FOUR

S EAN PARKED IN THE SPACE RIGHT IN FRONT OF THE DOOR TO THE motel room he'd rented earlier. Yeah, okay, he'd planned on kidnapping the girl. Goosebumps prickled his arms and raised the hairs on his skin. Kidnapping. He was a kidnapper. Christ, that made him almost as bad as Bomb Girl and her cohorts.

Almost. But not quite.

He hadn't killed anyone.

Not yet, a voice whispered in his head, *but you're awfully close to hurting this girl.* Anything to get what he needed from her. That's what he'd sworn to do, though he'd promised himself he wouldn't go too far. Trouble was, he didn't know what "too far" meant anymore. Every time he considered untying Bomb Girl, he flashed back to the explosion and the injured people—and David crumpled under a pile of rubble. David in the hospital, comatose. Grace crying. Little Abby crying.

Sean yanked the key out of the ignition. He twirled the keyring, and the metal keys jangled each time he caught them in his closed fingers, only to swing them around again and again.

"What are you doing?" Bomb Girl asked, shrinking away from him.

"Planning how to torture you." He cringed at his own voice. Was that him growling like a bastard bent on revenge? Well, he supposed he was. Only a bastard would tie up a girl and drag her off to a motel. And vengeance was what he craved. Retribution. Bad enough to lose his mom when he was fifteen and just coming to terms with his powers. Worse to find out the mad scientist who tortured him had been his grandfather. But he'd be damned if he'd lose his new family, the people who'd saved his life and taught him to understand and appreciate his psychic gifts.

David and Grace had no idea how whacked he'd gotten. His powers...He caught the keys, fisting his hand around them. His powers weren't gifts anymore.

Sean had already hurt one girl. So what if he hadn't meant to? He'd done it. If he could hurt an innocent girl, one he'd cared about, he could sure as hell do whatever it took to wring the truth out of the terrorist in the passenger seat.

"Listen up, Bomb Girl," he said, "you've got two choices here. Walk into the m—the room I'm taking you to, or I tie up your feet, gag you, and throw you over my shoulder to haul you in there."

"Gee, let me think." She bobbed her head side to side as if considering the options. "I'll walk, Un-incredible Hulk."

"I'm not green." He thrust the driver's door open. "I'm red, with horns and a forked tongue."

She scoffed.

He almost smiled at her defiance. She had spunk, a quality he liked in women.

Not that he liked her. The terrorist.

As he climbed out of the car, he said over his shoulder, "You sure talking back to your kidnapper is such a bright idea? Getting sassy won't earn you any leniency."

He shut the door before she could talk back some more. Striding around to the passenger door, he swung it open and bent down to unhook her seatbelt. She flinched. He stepped back.

"You wanted to walk," he said, "so get your butt out of the car."

Bomb Girl swung her legs out first, testing the ground's solidity with her toes before setting her feet flat on the pavement. She struggled to get up, hindered by her bound hands.

Watching her flounder made his throat tighten. When she bumped her head on the car's roof, he grimaced and took hold of her rope-tied hands to help her stand.

On her feet at last, she shook her hands free of his.

Sean rested a hand on her back to guide her to the motel-room door. He warned her about the curb, but she stumbled over it anyway. When she fell backward into him, he couldn't help noticing the firm roundness of her buttocks.

He held her to his body and hoisted her over the curb.

Naturally, she scrambled away from him—and nearly smacked into the wall.

With one hand on her arm, he halted her inches from disaster and re-directed her to the door. She sniffed, as if annoyed that she'd needed assistance. He felt a near smile tugging at his mouth again while he unlocked the door with the keycard.

Once he had her inside the room, with the door shut and locked, he pushed her down onto the bed. "Sit there."

He whisked the hood off her head, tossing it onto the table by the windows. Thick curtains blocked the view through the windows. He shed his leather jacket, draping it over a chair.

"No sneaky shit, remember?" he said as he dropped into the nearest chair and draped his arm over the table.

She speared him with her midnight-blue gaze. "Now what?"

He shrugged one shoulder. "You could tell me everything I want to know and save yourself a lot of trouble."

Save him from doing things he didn't really want to do.

Of course, she had to be contrary about it.

"I can't tell you anything," she said. "Might as well kill me."

"What kind of kidnapper offs his victim before getting what he wants?" Sean leaned back and propped one ankle on the other knee, feigning a casual attitude he didn't feel. His gut burned with acid, and his jaw ached with tension. "What's your name?"

She lifted her chin, those blue eyes shimmering in the harsh light from the bedside lamp.

He tapped a finger on the tabletop. "Guess I can keep calling you Bomb Girl."

"Whatever."

"Or I could come over there and search you for ID." Sean let his gaze wander over her body. Lush breasts. Narrow waist. Womanly hips. She had a body made for sin but a face worthy of an angel, with a small mouth and a perky little nose. The idea of frisking her made his blood heat up and his skin tighten.

She said nothing, just glowered at him and tossed her raven hair.

"All right," he said, and rose to stride toward her. "Body search it is."

He fought to ignore the excitement that rushed over his skin like an electrical current. What kind of creep got turned on by the girl he'd abducted? Well, she was a terrorist after all.

A beautiful, sexy one.

Sean gritted his teeth and slanted down until his face hovered in front of hers. The feminine scent of her surrounded him. Her eyes went large, and her lips parted. He tore open her tiny purse, the one she'd slung around her neck so it hung at a diagonal across her torso. Searching with one hand, he found no ID, just lipstick, a compact, a cell phone, a bag of candy, and a pack of cigarettes. Tossing the phone on the table, he settled his hands on her thighs, trying not to notice the soft curves of them, and slid his palms around her hips to her backside. When he found the hip pockets of her jeans, he thrust his hands into them.

Eureka.

He pulled out a thin, pink wallet.

Bomb Girl's mouth popped open on an irritated gasp. She clapped her jaw shut and glowered at him some more. Pissed because he'd found her wallet.

Or maybe because he'd kept his other hand in her hip pocket, pressed against her behind.

He withdrew that hand, straightened, and flipped open the wallet. He couldn't stop the triumphant laugh that chuckled out of him. "What kind of terrorist carries her ID with her when she's committing a heinous crime?"

A faint blush tinged her cheeks, and she averted her eyes.

The driver's license photo didn't do her justice, but at least it gave him a bit of information about the suspect seated in front of him.

"Nice to meet you," he said, "Kira Magnusson of Walnut Drive, Topeka, Kansas. A local girl, huh? Got a funny way of showing your community spirit."

She pursed her lips, glaring at the ugly carpeting for a change.

"I love having the upper hand," he said as he sat down at the table and slapped her wallet down on its surface. "I know a lot about you now, and you don't even know where you are."

She glanced around, her focus landing on the bedside table, then her lips kinked in a haughty, closed-mouth smile. "I know exactly where I am."

He gave a harsh laugh. "Yeah, you're my hostage in a motel room. But you have no clue—"

"We're in the Home Sweet Motel in Lawrence."

Sean froze. Slowly, he rotated his eyes until he spotted the telephone on the bedside table. It featured a big sticker emblazoned with the information she'd recited. "Crap."

"You suck at kidnapping."

He ran a hand over his face. "Yeah."

She studied him with measured interest. "What do you hope to gain from holding me hostage?"

"The truth." His voice had grown rough, and a pain gnawed at his gut. "That bomb put my best friend in a coma. I want to know why you blew up the cafe."

"I had no choice."

"Everybody has a choice."

Kira chewed on her lower lip, and her gaze turned assessing, like she was sizing him up.

"Fine," she sighed. "You want the truth? Some very bad people took my eight-year-old brother and threatened to kill him unless I do what they want."

Sean narrowed his gaze on her. "Let me get this straight. To save one kid, you blew up a whole building full of innocent people? Why didn't you call the cops?"

Kira stared down at her lap where she wrung her hands. "I tried, but they basically laughed at me because I couldn't say who these people are or where they're hiding. I had no proof they'd taken my brother. My parents are in Uganda, and I was supposed to take care of Caleb—"

Her voice choked off.

Sean hated the twinge of sympathy he experienced when he saw her anguished expression.

"They swore," she continued, "it was a smoke bomb, nothing more."

"Bad guys always tell the truth."

She shot him a hard look. "You should know, being a bad guy yourself."

"I'm not a villain." He squirmed in his seat. "And I never set off a bomb."

"Maybe you don't believe me, but I'm telling the truth." She inhaled a shaky breath. "They showed me what they'd do to Caleb if I refused to do what they wanted."

"They—hurt the kid?"

"No." She bowed her head, and her shoulders slumped. "They hurt me."

He clenched his fist, itching to punch something, anything. Why did she have to say that? He hated anyone who hurt kids or women, which explained why he hated himself these days.

"I couldn't let my brother suffer," she said, "because of me. I believed the device was a smoke bomb and no one would get hurt. This was the final test of my powers, they said. I'm guilty of being an idiot, but I am not a terrorist."

"How the hell did you set off the bomb? Can you use your telekinesis from a distance?"

Mouth tight, she flicked her thumb against her index finger, and a tiny spark ignited.

Telekinetic *and* she could make electricity? *Damn.*

As the spark fizzled out, she said, "I didn't know I could until three days ago when these people took my brother and ordered me to practice setting off the smoke bomb. They told me to get two glass bottles and place them inside a metal box with a gap between them, close the box, and break the glass with my powers. I had to do this repeatedly, moving the box farther away each time. When I could break the bottles while the box was in another room, they said I was ready for the final test."

"Detonating the bomb at the cafe."

"Yes." Her thumb raked across her finger again, setting off another, bigger spark that floated down to the floor as a miniature ball, sputtering out just as it touched down. "I've done everything they wanted."

"Where have your parents been this whole time?"

"Gone."

"Oh jeez, I'm sorry. When did they—"

"They're not dead." She caught her bottom lip between her teeth. "I don't want to talk about them. Like I said, I'm an idiot and maybe a coward. But I am no terrorist."

Should he believe her? He didn't trust his intuition right now because the battle between his anger and his need to squelch his emotions had him tied up in knots.

"Can't let you go," he said. "Not until I've got proof of what you're saying about your brother and these mysterious bad guys. If you help me find that proof, it'll go a long way to showing you're not evil."

"Fine, I'll cooperate." Kira lifted her bound hands to him. "Untie me. Please."

"Please?" Sean raised one brow. "Playing nice won't make me let you go. I still don't trust you."

"I know." She stood, hands held out to him. "The rope is rubbing on my wounds from the zip tie. I won't try to escape, you have my word. Please untie me."

He mulled the situation for a moment, fingers drumming on the tabletop.

Then he removed the rope.

THE SECOND THE ROPE FELL AWAY FROM HER WRISTS, KIRA BOLTED for the door. Two feet from it, she was yanked backward by a pair of powerful arms that snared her around the waist and hoisted her off her feet. Pinned to her captor's body, she flailed her feet but couldn't kick him. He'd pinned her arms too, and she couldn't reach any part of him to bite. *Trapped.*

Her heart hammered, her breaths came shallow and fast. Caleb needed her. She could not let this jackass waylay her. When the next call came…Would she obey their commands?

No choice.

The man restraining her in his vise-like embrace set her feet on the floor. His arms stayed belted around her. His lips scraped the shell of her ear as he hissed, "I'll cooperate, you said. I won't try to escape, you said. That one was a promise. I was nice, and you took advantage."

She swallowed hard. A cold sweat broke out on her forehead, and her palms grew clammy.

"Can't trust your word," he snarled. "You brought this on yourself."

He dragged her toward the TV stand near the foot of the bed. A black duffel bag slumped on the floor there, its zipper undone. He forced her to kneel with him, so he could dig items out of the bag. She couldn't see what he was doing, but she heard the rustling and felt his muscles flexing around her as he maintained his iron grip with one arm.

She ought to be able to wrestle free of him. He held her with one arm. But struggle as she might, she failed to gain any leeway. Holy cow, he was strong. He'd said she brought this on herself, but what exactly did he plan to do with her?

He leaned sideways, the heat of his body retreating, and pulled her hands together in front of her belly. While he held her wrists in one hand, with the other he wrapped something soft around them. Soft? She glanced down and saw he'd folded a length of fleece in half. Once he had the material around her wrists, he secured them with a zip tie again. The thick fleece protected her skin from the sharp edges of the nylon restraint.

Confusion made her brows draw together and her lips fall open a crack. Why would he bother cushioning the zip tie? The action implied he cared about her well-being. He wanted to spare her any additional pain? It made no sense.

He'd cut the first zip tie back in the car, when she'd complained it bit into her flesh. And he seemed more desperate than psychotic. What had he said about his best friend? She winced a little, her stomach lurching. He'd said the bomb put his friend in a coma. The bomb she'd set off. What had she done? Someone might've died. Maybe this guy had a point about her risking dozens of lives to save one little boy.

But he was her brother. She couldn't forsake him.

Her captor secured another zip tie around her ankles, cushioned with fleece.

"Did anyone die?" she asked, her throat constricting. "From the explosion. Did anyone—"

"No." The gruff reply rasped in her ear, because he'd slanted in again. His lips grazed her skin. "People got hurt, though, so don't go feeling better about yourself because nobody kicked the bucket."

People like his best friend.

Her gut twisted as if a fist had clamped around it. "I'm sorry. About your friend."

"If he dies, you die."

Despite the nastiness of his tone and his words, she had the oddest feeling he didn't mean them. Pain drove him, not rage. *Yeah, right.* Like she could know that from his voice. She'd never been empathic or had any mind-reading ability. She couldn't divine his emotions or intentions, and yet she sensed he...What? Meant her no real harm?

She couldn't know that. This prickly sensation, the way she sensed she understood him in some small way, it was probably the onset of Stockholm syndrome.

He swept her up in his brawny arms and dropped her onto the bed. Her body bounced a little, but her head landed on a pillow with a *whuft* sound. He scanned her body, his lips compressed, towering over her from his position beside the bed.

"You cold?" he asked.

Once again, he sounded gruff but evinced concern for her comfort. *Weird.*

"I'm fine," she said.

His fingers worked as if he were considering doing something with them. His gaze flitted around the room. "Better gag you."

A chill raced through her. "Please don't. I promise not to scream."

He flashed her a scowl. "Like I can take your word for anything."

"I'm sorry for lying." Hey, wait. Why was she apologizing to him? "But you kidnapped me. What did you expect? You're lucky I didn't nail you in the balls."

She swore his lips quirked the tiniest bit.

"Being feisty won't get you anywhere," he said. Then he hesitated, eying her with a strange expression. "Why didn't you hit me with your telekinetic powers?"

Goosebumps raised all over her arms. She wouldn't tell him she'd exhausted her psychic reserves. "What makes you think I have powers?"

He snickered, the sound rife with derision. "You got amnesia? We've been through this already. I know because you walloped me with your powers back at the scene of your crime."

"Excuse me for getting forgetful when I've been abducted."

"Or maybe you were hoping I'd forgotten."

The statement he'd made earlier about knowing she had powers actually had slipped her mind. Everything had unfolded so fast, with him hauling her away in his car, that she couldn't recall the exact sequence of events when he'd found her at the destroyed cafe.

"Most people," she said, aiming for an even tone despite her rapid pulse, "would dream up a so-called rational explanation for something like that. They wouldn't jump to 'she has psychic powers' like you did."

He lifted one shoulder in a half shrug. "I trust my perception."

What an odd way to phrase it, she thought. Rather than saying he trusted what he saw or what he felt, or even what he experienced, he'd said he trusted his perception.

A new wave of goosebumps erupted on her skin, lifting every fine hair. *Perception.* The meaning of that word finally struck her. "You have powers."

He jerked his head back, eyes flaring wide for a split second.

"I'm right," she told him, enjoying a spike of victorious pride. "What's your gift?"

Jaw clenched, he shot her a hot glare. "Shut the hell up."

What had she said that set him off? He hadn't gone all Terminator until she asked what his gift was.

She bit the inside of her lip but plowed ahead. "Why are you sensitive about discussing your powers?"

"I'm not." He tunneled his fingers into his hair, molding his hand to the back of his head. "Don't want to talk about this with you. Shut up or I'll gag you."

He spun away and stalked past the foot of the bed, then stalked back up the length of the bed. While he paced like a caged lion, she lay there bound but not gagged. Maybe she should've been grateful he hadn't silenced her with a sock in her mouth or a length of fleece tied tightly.

Fleece. She glanced at her hands. The fabric he'd padded the zip tie with prevented her raw wrists from hurting. Her abductor took care not to hurt her, yet he held her prisoner. He seemed desperate, and she knew his friend had been injured because of her. Considering the frantic actions she'd taken to save her brother, she had no right to criticize his behavior. She understood the panic induced by learning a loved one was endangered by a criminal act.

Her criminal act had harmed innocent people.

What he'd done had harmed no one, not even her.

Oh no-no-no, you will not empathize with the kidnapper.

She couldn't help empathizing a little, though she would not trust this man. No way. Never.

Her phone rang with the silly ringtone Caleb had picked for her. It was the theme song to some cartoon show.

The man pacing the length of the room whirled around to stomp toward her. He halted at the bedside near her hip. The phone rang a second and a third time. He snatched it up and frowned at the screen before tilting it toward her. "Unknown number? This your cohort?"

"It must be them, but they're not my cohorts." She tried to sit up but fell back onto the bed. "If I don't answer, they'll hurt my brother."

He waited for a fourth ring, then swiped the screen to answer and tapped the speaker-phone symbol. As he held the phone near her face, he mouthed, "No tricks."

She raised her head. "Hello?"

"It's time," said the altered voice she'd come to know too well. "I will text you the address. You know what to do."

"You said you'd let Caleb go if I did what you wanted. I set off the— bomb."

"No, child," the distorted voice said, "we told you we would release the boy once you completed your mission. This is phase two."

She opened her mouth but couldn't speak. Phase two? How many phases did this mission have? How many crimes would she have to commit to free her brother? How many innocent people would suffer this time?

Her skin crawled. She wanted to scratch her arms, but the zip tie constrained her. She would've settled for a smoke.

Neither smoking nor scratching could eradicate the burning itch in her soul.

"Please," she said, "let Caleb go. He's just a kid."

"Trigger the device," the caller said in an eerily calm voice. "You have until one-fifteen a.m."

Click. The call was terminated.

She tightened her trembling fingers around the phone.

It made a tinkly noise, indicating a new text message.

"They're sending the address," she said. "I have to—"

"You have to what?" Her captor bent low over her, his green eyes luminescent with the spooky glow of psychic powers ramping up. "You have to hurt some more people?"

"They have my brother." Tears pooled in her eyes, stinging and hot. "I don't want to do this, not again, but I have no choice."

"Don't you get it?" He slapped the phone onto the bedside table and punched his fists into the mattress at either side of her pillow. "They will never let him go."

Against her every hope, she knew he was right. She'd known it for a while, maybe all along, but couldn't make herself face up to the truth.

"The only way you save him," her captor said, "is if we track down those bastards."

"I don't know where they are." Tears poured from her eyes, streaming down the sides of her face to trickle into her ears. "Please believe me, I don't know."

He stared at her, his face unreadable, for so long her tears morphed into sobs. All the fear and anguish she'd repressed since the moment three days ago when those people took Caleb was unleashed in a torrent of scorching tears that flowed down her face to drizzle onto the pillow. Her body wrenched with each sob. The salty liquid dampened her hair. She couldn't see her abductor through the watery haze.

"Shit," he growled.

And then he shoved his arms under her torso and pulled her up—into his waiting embrace.

CHAPTER FIVE

S EAN INHALED THE SWEET FRAGRANCE OF HER HAIR, OR THE SHAM-
poo or whatever. It smelled feminine and delicate, the way she felt in
his arms. Kira's body sagged into him, and her face was buried against his
neck while she wept softly. He had his arms around her, cradling her soft
and curvy body against him.

Why the hell had he pulled her close like this?

Because she'd started crying. That was the simple answer, but the sim-
plicity was deceptive. The second he saw those tears and the anguished
look on her face, he'd been overwhelmed by the need to soothe and protect her. Protect the woman who'd nearly killed David? *Crazy.*

The shields he'd erected to contain his powers had cracked. He sensed
it. Like the sun peeking between the halves of closed drapes, he'd begun to
experience…things seeping in through the cracks. The sharp and bitter tang
of her fear. The hot and wrenching pain of her guilt and shame.

"Caleb," she moaned against his neck.

A cold spike stabbed into his chest, knocking the breath out of him. It
wasn't his pain, though. It was hers.

His empathic ability had surged to life again, with only a sliver of an
opening to sneak through. He wasn't really feeling bad for her, she was
making him feel this way. Her emotions had crept into him, poisoning his
psyche. Hell, maybe she did it on purpose. Other than her obvious telekinesis and that weird sparky thing, he had no idea what powers she might
wield against him.

He pushed her away.

Kira blinked at him slowly, confusion clouding her eyes.

Sean slammed his shields down again, reinforcing them with every
shred of psychic energy at his command.

Fresh tears rolled down her cheeks.

"Cut the tears," he said. "I'm not falling for your sob story. Everybody's got problems and past traumas. That's life, Bomb Girl."

His deliberate and snarling emphasis on the moniker made her cringe for half a second. But then she set her jaw and lifted her chin, those blue eyes catching fire. "Go to hell."

Sean gave a derisive laugh. "That's my home address, babe."

Kira bristled, her lips tightening into a slight pucker.

He'd pissed her off. Good. The last thing he needed was her getting under his skin again, literally, with whatever voodoo she had in her arsenal. No more cracks in the armor.

"What's your deal?" she asked. "You act like a creep most of the time, but then you care if these bindings hurt me."

Not anymore. He didn't care. He wouldn't care.

Emotions were weakness. Emotions were dangerous.

"Don't worry about my deal," he said. "Start worrying about how you'll convince me not to kill you along with your phone buddies."

Whether he *could* kill someone, he had no idea. In self-defense, for sure he could. But for vengeance?

An image flashed in his mind, of David in a hospital bed with needles and tubes stuck in him.

Yeah, he could kill someone.

But a woman? One who cried and swore she hadn't meant to blow up innocent people?

A thread of doubt wound through him. What if she was telling the truth? If someone had taken Abby and threatened to hurt her unless Sean did what they wanted, would he have said no? If they'd fed him the same story they fed Kira, about the device being a smoke bomb to test her powers, maybe he would have agreed. If he'd known it was a real bomb, maybe he still would've agreed. To save someone he loved, to save a kid...

Maybe he wasn't so different from Gabriel Amador. The man had committed terrible acts because losing his family had ripped him apart. Now Sean had kidnapped a woman for reasons not unlike Amador's.

Sean's gaze landed on Kira's wrists and the zip tie binding them. Why had he padded the tie this time? He shouldn't have cared if it rubbed her skin raw.

"I can't do what they want," Kira said, her tears finally subsiding, though her gaze had gone bleak. "But if I don't go to the address they texted me and set off another device, Caleb will die."

"You'd risk more lives for your brother?"

"No, I can't, I won't. But I have no way to find him and save him before the deadline." She sniffled, wiping her nose on her sleeve. "If I don't do this, they'll probably get someone else to set off the bomb. Caleb will die, I will die, and it won't save anyone."

Yeah, he'd figured as much. But still…

An idea burst in his mind like a firework in the sky. The flare of hope, he realized, however puny it might be. He had to try.

"There may be a way," he said, "to track down these creeps."

Kira perked up, though her eyes were bloodshot and puffy. "How? GPS or something?"

He slid off the bed and straightened. "Or something. I have to go talk to somebody."

She swung her legs off the bed. "Take me with you."

"Oh no," he said, shaking his head. "I don't trust you. After that little escape attempt earlier, I can't risk you getting another chance at it. You stay here, tied up and gagged."

Kira puckered her lips again. "Don't gag me. I won't scream."

"Yeah, sure, like you wouldn't try to run away either. If I could generate an EM field, I'd know for sure you can't use your powers on me. Even then, I wouldn't know you won't try to escape. You tricked me once."

"A what field?"

"Electromagnetic," he said with exaggerated precision. "Set to the right frequency, an EM field can dampen psychic powers."

"Oh."

He snagged a sock and another length of fleece from his bag, returning to the bed with the items. "I didn't do this, you did. If you hadn't broken your word, I wouldn't have to gag you."

Why was he explaining himself to her?

Her gaze darted to the fleece strip and then to his face. "Where'd you get these long, narrow pieces of soft fabric?"

"I had a girlfriend who liked to be tied up."

"You had a girlfriend? Was she the Unabomber's granddaughter?"

He balled up the sock, shoved it in her mouth, and secured it in place by tying the fleece around her head. He knotted the fabric at the back of her head.

She could get out of the room, even bound like this, if she really wanted to.

Another restraint ought to do the trick. He rushed back to his bag, dug out the rope he'd used to confine her earlier, and tied it to a rail in the headboard. Once he'd secured the other end to her zip tie, he nodded, satisfied.

"There," he said. "No more snarky comments from you, and you won't be sneaking out while I'm gone."

Her eyes narrowed, and he knew she was itching to snap a scathing retort.

But she couldn't. *Hah.*

As he strode out of the motel room, he wondered if he should have given Kira a drink of water before he gagged her. No, he decided, she'd forced him to do this by betraying his trust. An annoying little voice whispered in the back of his mind. *You kidnapped her, genius, what did you expect?*

No time to think about that. He needed a hand from someone he shouldn't be asking for help right now. He needed Grace—or more specifically, he needed her powers. He knew of no one else on earth who might have a snowball's chance of finding these terrorists.

Grace could do almost anything because she could tap into the greatest source of psychic energy in the universe. The Golden Power offered omnipotence, but it came at a hefty price. Last time, it had nearly killed her.

Sean stopped at the driver's door of the car, his fingers hovering over the handle.

Yeah, Kira was right about him. Only a cold-hearted bastard would ask a woman whose husband was in a coma to tap into a power that scared the hell out of her on a good day. Only a villain of the first order would bind and gag a woman, then leave her alone in a motel room. Kira seemed genuinely afraid and genuinely horrified by what her actions had caused.

He smacked his palm on the car's roof. He had become as narcissistic and rotten as Gabriel Amador. Would he wind up in a mental hospital too? Pushed over the edge by his own need for revenge?

That was no way to help Grace and David. After everything they'd done for him, they deserved so much better.

Sean spun around and stormed back into the room.

Kira jumped, her eyes wide.

He stalked to the bed and removed the gag.

She eyed him like he was a rabid wolf circling her.

Teeth gritted, he hissed a breath out his nostrils. Scaring girls had never been his goal. After what he'd done to Bree…God, he had so many sins to atone for that it might take his whole life and then some.

With a long sigh, he dropped his butt onto the bed's edge. "I'm sorry."

She started, her eyes flaring wide again. "You're sorry?"

"Yeah." He pulled out his pocket knife, turning it between his fingers. "I shouldn't have done this to you. I believe what you told me about your brother."

Her mouth opened, but she said nothing.

Flipping the knife open, he sliced the zip ties around her wrists and ankles.

She drew her knees up, massaging her wrists.

He heaved his body off the bed, scuffled to a chair, and collapsed onto it.

"You can go," he said, waving toward the door.

Sean dropped his face into his hands, elbows on his thighs. The weight of a hundred buildings seemed to have settled on top of him.

"I thought you had to talk to someone," Kira said.

He heard shuffling as she moved around on the bed. "Just go. I can't help you or anybody."

What had he thought he'd do? Save everybody. Punish the bad guys. Groaning, he ducked his head, his fingers plowing into his hair. How full of shit he'd been.

Delicate fingers closed around his wrists and tugged gently.

Sean lifted his head just enough to peek through his fingers at Kira. "What are you doing?"

"No idea." She tugged again, and he relented, letting her lower his hands to his knees. "But I think we should stick together. I can't do this alone, and neither can you."

He scrunched up his face. "Why the hell would you want to help me?"

"Because you're all I've got." She smiled bitterly. "Crazy, isn't it? The terrorist and the kidnapper joining forces."

Kira didn't mean it as a jab at him, he knew that. But the statement pierced his chest like a rusty nail. He had become a kidnapper.

"I'm sorry," he said again, helpless to think of anything better to say.

She sat back on her heels. "I'm sorry too. Your friend got badly hurt because of me."

"Because of them." He leaned back in the chair. "How long do you have to do the next thing for them?"

Kira snatched her phone off the bedside table and swiped her thumb over the screen. "Three hours. I'm supposed to go to this address and—" She swallowed hard, looking sick. "I'm supposed to set off another device."

"What kind of target is it?"

She bowed her head, shoulders caving in. "A movie theater."

At this time of night on a Friday, a theater would be packed.

They had to stop this, somehow.

***

KIRA SLAPPED THE PHONE DOWN ON THE TABLE. THREE HOURS. THE seconds drained away one by one, siphoning minutes and soon hours from their timeline. Their timeline? Well, it was theirs now. She needed help, and this guy was all she had.

She didn't even know his name.

The man in question slumped in his chair, eyes closed.

"Who are you?" she asked, wriggling around until she sat cross-legged on the floor.

He cracked one eyelid. "What?"

She drummed her fingers on her knees. "Who are you? What's your name? You know mine, but I have no idea what yours is. If we're joining forces, don't you think I should know what to call you?"

Both his eyes opened, and he peered at her with a blank expression. "Sean Vandenbrook."

Kira held out a hand to him. "Nice to meet you, Sean."

One of his brows quirked, along with one side of his mouth, but he took her hand. "Yeah, it's a monumental honor to meet you too."

His hand enveloped hers, big and warm and rough. She should've pulled away, but the contact fired an electric shiver through her. Sean. His name was Sean.

She let her gaze wander over his body, over the muscles partly concealed under his T-shirt and jeans. His biceps were thick and corded with muscles, his thighs strong and muscular. Though he had brown hair and tanned skin, she spotted a smattering of well-hidden freckles beneath the bronzing. His eyes were a striking green, and those lips...They were wide and thick, the kind of lips that could strip away a woman's inhibitions if she pressed her mouth to them.

Not that she would. He may have plucked her sympathy strings and stopped acting like a total dick, but she would not succumb to Stockholm syndrome.

Even if succumbing sounded kind of nice.

His gaze locked onto hers, the brilliant color of those eyes seeming to intensify and almost glow.

She cleared her throat, at last withdrawing her hand from his. "When you stormed out of here, it seemed like you had a plan. What happened?"

"I can't do it."

"Do what?"

He squirmed in his chair, his mouth crimping. "Nothing."

She barred her arms over her chest. "You can't do that. If we're working together, we've got to be honest with each other. Agreed?"

"There are things I can't tell you, and things I won't tell you. Deal with it."

The flinty edge had returned to his voice. A defense mechanism, she decided. Act like a prick to keep anybody from asking uncomfortable questions.

"Cut the crap," she said, "I'm onto your game. We'll both have to share things we don't really want to share if we have any shot at stopping a massacre. If you know someone who can help—"

"No." He jolted forward, glaring into her eyes. "I can't go there. She—"

He clamped his lips together as if he'd slipped up.

"So, it's a woman," Kira said. "The person who might help but you won't go there."

"Can't go there." His features had gone hard again, his voice too. "I've screwed up enough for one day, for one lifetime, and I will not hurt another woman. Especially not this one."

The way he talked about the woman, the tone of his voice and the look on his face, suggested he had intense feelings for her. "Is she your girl-friend? Sister? Mother?"

"None of the above. She's married to my best friend."

"Are you in love with her?" Kira knew she shouldn't ask, and honestly, she didn't care about the answer. Why had she asked, then? The words sprang from her mouth before she could stop them.

One corner of Sean's mouth twisted upward. "No. She saved my life more than once. Grace and David—" He flopped back in his chair, hissing a curse under his breath. The self-loathing on his face faded quickly, though, replaced by resignation. His shoulders slumped. "What the hell, huh? Might as well tell you about them since I blurted out their names. Grace and David gave me a home when I had nowhere to go, and they taught me how to control my powers and not be afraid of what I can do. I owe them everything."

Kira studied him for a moment as he lapsed into silence, seeming lost in his own thoughts, but she couldn't hold back her curiosity for long. They didn't have time to waste.

"Okay," she said, "they're obviously important to you. But why can't you ask Grace for help?"

He braced an elbow on the chair's arm, his hand raised, and rested his chin on his fisted fingers. His green eyes assessed her for a couple seconds before he spoke. "How much do you know about psychic abilities?"

"Not much. Just what I found on the internet." She shimmied backward until her back pressed against the bed. "Mostly conspiracy websites."

He rolled his eyes heavenward, shook his head once, and rolled his eyes back down to focus on her. "You know nothing, do you?"

She shrugged. "I'm telekinetic, I know that."

"Ever hear of the crossroads?"

Kira shook her head.

"Thought projection? Remote viewing?"

She shook her head again.

"Manifestation? The Golden Power?"

"No." She compressed her lips. "You can stop reciting the Dictionary of Psychic Stuff because I don't know about any of it."

He let out an irritated sigh. "Guess I'll have to explain everything to you, since you won't understand anything I say otherwise."

The condescending tone of his voice made her bristle. "Gee, I'm so sorry I didn't get my copy of the Psychic Powers Owner's Manual. Was there a club I should've joined? Freaks International, maybe?"

"We are not freaks." He shot forward, hands clamped on his knees, gaze nailed to hers and his irises glowing with a preternatural emerald fire. "None of us asked for these powers. The universe decided to play a sick joke on some people by stuffing crazy junk in our heads. You can call yourself a freak all you want, Bomb Girl, but don't ever call my family that."

She drew her head back, stunned by the vehemence of his outburst. Bomb Girl? He called her that when he was pissed at her—or maybe when he was scared. The rest of his outburst triggered more questions she probably shouldn't ask an unstable man, but she needed to know. After all, she had no choice but to hitch her fate to his.

"I didn't say anything about your family," Kira told him. "Do they have psychic powers too? I've wondered if these abilities have a genetic component, but my little brother doesn't have powers and neither do my parents."

The fire in his eyes dimmed a little, seeming to lessen along with his anger. His head drooped, leaving her to stare at his crown of dark hair. The roots looked lighter, slightly reddish.

"Grace and David," he said in a measured tone, "*are* my family. We may not be related by blood, but we've been through hell together. They are the only family I've got now."

"I'm sorry I used the word freaks. Didn't mean to insult your family." Kira clasped her hands on her lap. "I feel like a freak, and I guess that's what I meant."

His head tilted up, and those spooky eyes became riveted to her, but he said nothing.

She fidgeted, unsettled by the intensity of his gaze. "What happened to your birth family?"

"None of your business."

Bam. He'd slammed the book shut on that subject. Fine, she didn't really need to know, anyway. This guy was damaged goods, for sure, and she would not give in to her curiosity by pushing for answers that made no difference to her life.

She itched to know, sure, but she wouldn't ask.

"About those terms you mentioned," she said. "What do they mean?"

"You seriously have no idea about the crossroads?" He stared at her, his lips parted, for several seconds. Then he cocked his head. "When you use your powers, what do you see and feel?"

"I feel energy, kind of like electricity. Don't see anything."

He linked his hands, the intertwined fingers hanging loosely between his knees. "You aren't accessing the full potential of your powers. Not if you've never experienced the crossroads."

Kira bent forward a smidgen. "What is it?"

"A metaphysical place, sort of like another dimension of reality. The crossroads is a hub for psychic energy and for everything that is, was, or will be known." He leaned forward more, the force of his gaze almost mesmeric. "All the knowledge of the universe, all the psychic power in the universe, exists simultaneously in the crossroads. Once you access it, you'll realize the full magnitude of your abilities."

A tingle swept over her skin, lifting every tiny hair and raising goose-bumps. She had trouble catching her breath, so caught up in the hypnotic effect of his deep voice and those burning eyes that she couldn't rip her focus away from him.

"What else?" she asked. "How do I access this crossroads?"

"The how we'll get to in a minute," he said. "First, you need to know a few things about being psychic. Most of us have more than one ability. In fact, having only one is pretty much unheard of. You've probably got more than telekinesis, abilities you haven't discovered yet. Most of us can do remote viewing, also known as traveling. It's when you can visualize anyplace you want by just thinking about it. You feel like you're there, like you're a ghost observing everything, and you can have referred feelings like your body is really there and you can really touch, smell, and hear the world around you."

Kira couldn't move, transfixed by his words and what they meant for her. She might have the ability to travel to other places in her mind. *Cool.*

"The next step up from traveling," Sean said, "is manifesting. That's when you actually create a duplicate body while you're traveling. Don't get excited about it, though, because only the strongest psychics can manage it. Manifesting is rare, but not as rare as the Golden Power."

"Golden Power?" The name alone shivered a thrill through her. It sounded exotic and potent.

"Yeah, it's the ultimate psychic ability. It, uh..." He fidgeted, his face pinched. "Gives the person a kind of omniscience. If you could tap into the Golden Power, you'd get access to everything in the crossroads—all the power, all the knowledge, everything."

Holy cow, to know everything...*Imagine the power.* She swallowed hard, suddenly needing to know the answer to one vital question. "I'm guessing there's a serious downside, right?"

"There is." He rose and moved around the table to the window, using two fingers to part the curtains an inch, his attention on the view outside. "Grace is the only person who's ever tapped into the Golden Power, as far as anybody knows. It almost destroyed her. She's determined never to use it again because she's afraid she would lose herself to it. The Golden Power is not a living thing, but it can seem like it is, that's what she says. It's energy, plain and simple. But the power is so intense it feels like a living, breathing, ravenous energy that craves a conduit."

He let the curtains flutter shut.

Kira thought for a moment, then asked, "Did you plan on asking Grace to use the Golden Power to help us?"

Sean winced and hunched his shoulders. "Yeah. For about three minutes, I thought it was a good idea. Her husband is in a coma, and I was ready to push her to tap into a power she fears more than anything else in the world."

The crazy impulse to comfort him rocked Kira, and she wrapped her arms around herself. This man had kidnapped her, but she was beginning to understand why. He kept up a facade of arrogant disinterest, occasionally broken by his anger. Yet underneath the facade, she sensed a vulnerability that seemed to relate to the things he didn't want to talk about—his family and his powers.

"You were desperate," she said. "I did a horrible thing out of desperation, and people got hurt. You stopped yourself before you asked Grace to do anything that might've hurt her."

He turned his head toward her slowly, his expression unreadable. "Are you trying to make me feel better?"

The hard tone he'd spoken with most of the time had softened a little, his voice expressing a faint surprise at the idea she might've wanted to commiserate with him.

"I'm just pointing out," she said, "we have things in common."

He strode toward her, dropping into a crouch to glare into her eyes. "Don't feel sorry for me, Bomb Girl. I don't need your pity."

"Pardon me for acting like a human being. Wouldn't kill you to give it a try."

"It might, actually." He surged to his full height, towering over her. "Time to teach you how to access the crossroads."

Chapter Six

S EAN STARED DOWN AT KIRA, HIS FINGERS CURLING INTO HIS palms. What the hell was he doing? Offering to teach her about psychic abilities. Offering to help her find the terrorists who'd kidnapped her brother. Sure, both things dovetailed with what he wanted—revenge—but he didn't need this annoying person tagging along on his quest for justice.

Revenge. Justice. Which did he want? Vengeance had sounded awfully good right after the explosion, right after he'd seen David lying in a hospital bed comatose and Grace distraught over his condition. But would punishing the perpetrators make him feel better? Already, he'd abducted and tied up a girl.

His gaze flitted down to her wrists where red marks circled them.

Yeah, he'd done great so far. He'd hurt another woman, and he hadn't gotten one frigging inch closer to the real villains.

Kira huffed. "We don't have time for you to teach me anything. In less than three hours, either I set off a bomb or my brother dies. Either way, someone will get hurt."

She was right. And he had no idea what to do about it.

Her rosy lips tightened into a loose pucker, and her gaze sharpened on him. "Well, genius? What's your plan?"

"*My* plan?" He slanted toward her, looming over her in a way he hoped would intimidate her into not harassing him anymore. Yeah, sure, that had worked out great so far. "How about you come up with a clever way out of this mess you made?"

"I'm not Bruce Willis. I can't *Die Hard* my way out of this."

Sean canted his head, considering the strange girl in front of him. "You like action movies. Well, that figures, doesn't it? I mean, you blew up a building."

Kira flinched, and suddenly, he wished he hadn't reminded her of what she'd done. Again. Why did he keep feeling guilty about pointing out her actions? Studying her sapphire-blue eyes, he knew why he'd done it. He could still feel her emotions, just a little, and it messed with his head.

Why couldn't he block her out completely?

"Tell me about your powers," she said, her tone cool and calm, the opposite of her tempestuous emotions and the pain in her eyes.

"My powers?" Yeah, he was trying to avoid talking about this because then he'd have to explain that he was blocking his abilities. That would lead to needing to explain why. "I've got nothing that can help us."

She met his gaze head-on, her eyes simmering with a hint of the preternatural glow indicative of a psychic accessing her powers. He doubted she realized she was doing it since she seemed to know zip about psychic stuff.

"No evasions," she said. "If we're in this together, then we need to be honest with each other. What are your powers?"

Of course she was right. Of course she'd have to point that out to him. And of course he had no choice but to fess up.

He knew he should step away from her, but his body had become rooted to this spot. He couldn't make himself look away from her eyes, either. "Healing, mostly."

"You can heal injuries?" She shook her head. "Why haven't you fixed your best friend?"

The question sounded more confused than accusatory.

"I can't," he said. "I tried, but his injuries are too serious and I could kill myself trying to do it. Grace wouldn't let me, anyway. She says I need to conserve my energy in case I need it soon."

"Suppose that makes sense. I got tapped out setting off the bomb and trying to shake you off my tail." Kira folded her arms over her breasts, the fingers of one hand tapping on her arm. "You said it's rare for someone to have only one power. What else have you got?"

He fisted his hands, loosened them, fisted them again. "Empathy."

The annoying girl stared blankly at him for a second, then burst into laughter. "That's hilarious."

"In what way?" he said between his clenched teeth.

She reined in her amusement, though her lips stayed curved in a knowing smile. "You repress your emotions more than anyone I've ever met, and you're an empath. It's hilarious."

"You said that already." He leaned in closer, baring his teeth as he spoke. "It's not funny. You have no goddamn idea why I repress my feelings and throttle my powers."

Aw, jeez. Why had he said that? This woman pushed all his buttons like a wild toddler pounding her fists on the control panel of a nuclear missile silo.

Her eyes widened little by little as if understanding were dawning in her mind. Her mouth formed a little O. "That explains so much."

"No, it really doesn't." It probably did, but no way was he discussing any of this with her. "My powers can't help us. End of story."

"I don't think so." She watched him with that canny glint in her eyes that made him feel like she could expose all his secrets if she wanted to do it. "What else can you do?"

"Remote viewing, that's it."

"Have you tried to do anything else? Like maybe that thought-projection thing, or manifesting, or...whatever."

"Only Grace and David can manifest." Sean shoved his hands in his pockets, rocking back on his heels. "I've never tried thought projection. What I've got is bad enough."

"Bad?" She angled her head again, watching him with that disquieting interest like she could see straight into his soul. "Why would you call your powers bad?"

"Enough," he hissed. "Interrogation over. Neither one of us has the power to track down these bad guys."

"Maybe we could combine our powers. Is that possible?"

He froze, everything inside him going ice-cold. "Grace and David merged their powers, but she's an incredibly powerful psychic. Their emotional bond helped fuel the merging too because they're crazy in love." He waved a hand from himself to Kira and back again. "We don't even like each other."

Kira bit down on her lower lip. "Okay, no merging. If you can remote view a distant place, couldn't you track down a specific person that way?"

"I'm not that strong."

"Try. Please."

Sean grumbled because no way did he want to try this. It would require him to lower the shields he'd built up to contain his powers. Threads of ice slithered in his gut. Unleash his powers? *Bad, bad, bad idea.*

A memory exploded in his mind. Bree screaming. Beating him with her fists. Kicking and clawing and struggling to get away from him.

He'd sworn never to use his powers again, but if he didn't do it now...people would die.

"Fine," he said gruffly. "I'll try. But you have to go in the bathroom and shut the door."

"Is this a tornado drill?" she asked with a wry note in her voice.

"No, and it's not a joke either." Maybe the walls between them would prevent him from accidentally hurting Kira. It was the only thing he could think of to protect her. "Just do it, okay?"

She studied him for a moment, then nodded and trotted into the bathroom.

Once the door shut and the latch clicked into place, he began.

He closed his eyes, exhaling a slow, deep breath and letting it relax his muscles. He sank into his mind, floating within a black abyss, warm and free and untethered from his body. A force, like the gravity of a black hole, pulled him closer and closer to an unseen portal.

Whoosh.

He rocketed through a dark tunnel. Its confines squeezed him, but he couldn't turn back now. The crossroads had latched onto him, dragging him through the tunnel at breakneck speed and spitting him out into a field of glittering stars. Energy flowed into him, tingled through his astral body, reinvigorated him with its pure, untainted power. He had the odd sensation of inhaling a cleansing breath, though he had no physical body here.

Find the kid, he reminded himself.

A chill rippled through his psyche. How would he find Kira's brother? He had no idea what the kid looked like. Gah, he'd screwed up again.

Maybe not. He knew the kid's name. If he focused on the name, Caleb Magnusson, maybe that would be enough to guide him.

Sean concentrated all his will and intention on the name, repeating it in his mind over and over until the sounds no longer resembled words.

One star twinkled brighter than the rest. Was it the point that might lead him to Caleb?

More power, he needed more power.

A warning shiver racked his astral form. He brushed it aside and opened his mind to the power he knew lived in this place. The crossroads concealed it, but if he sought it with all his willpower, maybe he could tap into the ultimate source of psychic energy.

Something nudged him. Something cold and hard and inhuman.

Back away. Leave here now before it consumes you.

He couldn't. So many lives at stake...

The power reached for him, its fingers greasy and talon-sharp.

Sean launched back through the tunnel and the void, slamming into his body with a force that sent him staggering two steps backward. He stumbled into the table. It lifted up and thumped back onto the carpet.

The bathroom door swung open.

Kira raced out, heading straight for him. She stopped at the foot of the bed, her eyes large and her face pale. "What happened? Are you all right?"

"Yeah." Sean scrubbed a trembling hand over his face. "Bumped the table, that's all."

She shook her head slowly. "That's not what I mean. I felt something. It was dark and oily and…nothing I want to feel again."

He blinked rapidly. She couldn't have sensed the power he'd almost tapped into back in the crossroads. Could she?

"Was that the Golden Power?" she asked, her voice hushed.

"Not sure. Maybe." He leaned his butt against the table, his body weaker than it should've been considering the amount of energy he'd absorbed in the crossroads. "I'm not strong enough to access the Golden Power, though. It must've been something else."

"Or maybe you have more power than you realize."

"Doubtful." He gripped the table's edge and glared at the carpeting. "I couldn't find your brother."

Because he hadn't unleashed his powers, not all the way. He couldn't do it, so he'd failed. If he told Kira that, she'd push him to try harder and he couldn't do that either. Not after Bree.

Kira squared her shoulders. "Then we need a new plan."

"No problem, I've got one. Let's go to the cops."

She rolled her eyes. "We've been through this. The cops can't help us."

He glanced at the clock on the bedside table. "We don't have much time, anyway. There's only one thing we can do."

"And what's that?"

"Get all those people out of the movie theater." Sean held up a hand when she opened her mouth—to gripe, no doubt. "Listen, okay? We need to convince the people in the theater to get out, which means we have to give them a reason to think they're in danger."

"If we warn those people, Caleb will die."

"That's why we won't warn them. We'll give them a reason to leave on their own." He stepped closer to take her upper arms in his hands, and he tried really hard not to notice the warmth of her skin under his palms or the luminous blue of her eyes when they focused on him. "We start a fight."

Kira snorted. "You and I are going to start a brawl? That's a horrible idea."

"No, not like that. We use thought projection to convince somebody else to start a brawl."

She squinted at him. "And you can do this? You said you'd never tried thought projection."

"I haven't, but yeah, I should be able to do it."

"That's so comforting." She screwed up her mouth. "We don't need a brawl. Leave it to a guy to come up with a plan that revolves around fist fights."

He huffed out a breath and threw his hands up. "What do you suggest we do?"

"If you can make people believe whatever you want, then just make them all think they need to use the restroom."

"That's the dumbest idea I've ever heard."

Kira tapped her finger on his chest to emphasize each word. "No fist fight."

"Convincing everyone to take a bathroom break might not save them," he said. "What if the bathroom's right next to the theater? Or maybe the bomb's big enough to damage the whole building. We need everyone to go outside."

"Okay, so we could make them think the fire alarm went off. Or actually make it go off."

He made a frustrated noise, throwing up his hands and letting them fall slack again. "How do we do that? Can you affect electronics?"

She hunched her shoulders. "Don't know. I can make sparks, though. It's part of my telekinesis—I think."

"I really hope you're not suggesting we start a fire to get people away from the bomb."

"Do you have a better idea?" Before he could answer, she said, "No, you don't."

No, he didn't. But her idea still stank.

He couldn't think of anything better.

"Fine, have it your way," Sean grumbled. He grabbed his leather jacket and shrugged into it. "We go to the theater and convince everyone to take a piss at the same time."

"Then what? There's a bomb, we have no idea where it is, and they expect me to trigger it."

"For Christ's sake, this was your idea."

She wrapped her arms around herself. "I know, but I was thinking about evacuating the crowd, not what to do after that."

Awesome. Half of a half-assed plan, that's what they had.

With no other options, he added his own lame contribution to this lame idea.

"Once the people are safely out, we find the bomb and somehow neutralize it." He raised a hand to silence the protest he knew would come out of her mouth. "Don't ask me how. Not yet."

She rubbed her arms, goosebumps visible on her skin.

He took off his jacket and held it out for her to shrug into it. "You look cold."

She eyed the jacket like it might bite her but then accepted it. "Thank you."

Kira trailed him out the door and to the car. As he steered the vehicle out onto the highway, he considered the craziness level of this plan. High, for sure. But they had no choice. If he couldn't thought project those people into leaving the theater…if they couldn't find the bomb…

Everyone would die.

———

KIRA AND SEAN STOOD AT THE BACK OF THE THEATER, IN THE SHADows, while an action movie played on the grainy screen. The screeching tires and gunfire blaring from the speakers embedded in the walls grated on her nerves, but she knew Sean was right. They had no options except this insane one.

They had forty-two minutes left.

She looked at Sean and mouthed, "It's time."

He nodded, his expression grim, his lips flattened into a slash. His entire body had gone rigid, his shoulders bunched and a muscle ticking in his jaw. His green eyes had begun to glow faintly, but she had the oddest sensation of fear emanating from him. She wasn't empathic like he claimed to be. She couldn't detect his emotions in a psychic way, but maybe their shared pain and fear gave her insight of the normal kind. He didn't want to use his powers, for reasons he wouldn't share, reasons that made him anxious almost to the point of panic.

And yet he'd volunteered to do this. To save lives.

She folded her hand around his fisted one, gently pushing against his coiled fingers until he opened them in claw-like fashion. She slipped her fingers between his to grip his hand. He didn't move for a moment. Then his fingers loosened, though the rest of him remained stiff, and he clasped her hand in return.

He didn't look at her.

A few hours ago, she'd labeled him a creep and a kidnapper, thought of him as a cold-hearted criminal. Now, she was holding his hand, relying on him to save the lives of over a hundred innocent men, women, and children.

Yeah, her life had veered into Crazy Land.

Sean pulled in a deep breath and exhaled slowly. The tension eased a bit, making his shoulders slacken and his jaw muscle cease pulsing, though he kept his teeth gritted. He rolled his eyes to glance at her, gave a sharp nod, and returned his focus to the moviegoers.

It was time.

Kira clinched his hand tight, willing this to work, praying for it to work. With every fiber of her being, every shred of power she might have, she prayed.

Energy tingled through her palm, spreading out into her fingers and up her wrist into her arm. It coursed outward into her body, a stream of psychic power originating from their joined hands.

Holy heaven. Were they sharing their powers? Sean said that couldn't happen without an emotional connection, but maybe he didn't know everything.

Whatever it was, she didn't care as long as it helped them save lives.

Sean's eyes flared with green fire.

A chill shivered down her spine, raising the hairs all over her body.

In the middle of the theater, a man jumped to his feet, his head swinging left and right as he searched for something or someone.

Power tingled hotter and harder through her body, and her knees quivered.

Stay standing. Don't fall down. Stay standing.

While she locked her knees, the man in the audience thrust an arm out to jab his finger toward the man in the row behind him.

"You!" He shouted loud enough to be heard above the din from the movie. "You kicked my chair."

The other man leaped up and bellowed, "Sit down and shut up, you blockhead. The rest of us want to enjoy the movie."

The first man seized the shirt of the second man, hauling him over the seats, and pulled one fist back to wallop the guy.

What on earth was going on here? Sean had said he'd make people want to go to the bathroom, not start attacking each other. She glanced at him, but he'd squeezed his eyes shut, his mouth crimped, his whole face pinched.

She inched closer to him. "What are you doing? They're supposed to need a pee break, not start a riot."

"I'm trying to do that. Something's wrong, though." He squinted his face harder, his teeth gritted. "Can't make them stop this and do what I want. It's—can't—not working."

More power. More tingling. Her locked knees wobbled, her heart raced.

A woman screamed. Fists flew. And chaos erupted within the darkened theater.

"Dammit," Sean growled.

Other men joined the fight while more women screamed and shouted. A tough-looking woman charged into the fray to punch a wiry man. Children wailed.

The rest of the crowd stampeded.

Kira lost the capacity for breath, her heart pounding so hard and fast she could scarcely think.

Sean dragged her backward against the wall, against his body, her back to his front with his arms latched around her midsection.

People ran. They screamed. They shouted. The original fight seemed to have broken up, but now everyone barreled toward the exits. Bright light lanced the darkness when someone kicked open an emergency exit.

Footfalls pounded, drowning out the noises from the movie.

Kira squeezed her eyes shut, grateful for the security of Sean's arms encircling her. Somehow, she knew nothing would happen to her as long as he was there.

And yeah, she recognized the insanity of feeling safe with her kidnapper.

Former kidnapper.

Silence fell with such abruptness she thought she'd gone deaf. But then, she noticed the gunfire from the movie and the ragged huffing of Sean's breaths. They fluttered her hair as his chest heaved with labored inhalations. His hands, clamped over her belly, trembled the tiniest bit.

They stood there like that for a long moment before he released her, stepped back, and spoke.

"Your turn," he said. "Find the device."

"Did anyone get hurt in the panic?"

"Not that I could tell. I reached out with my empathic power a little bit but couldn't detect anyone suffering." He speared her with a sharp look. "Find the bomb. Before anybody decides to come back in here."

"What happened to our peaceful plan for a mass bathroom break?"

"Later. The bomb, now."

"I don't know how to find it."

He grasped her shoulders and bent his head to level their gazes. "Did you know exactly where the cafe bomb was?"

She shook her head.

"Right." He tightened his hold on her a smidgen. "You could set off a bomb in another room when you had no idea where it was. You can find this one, I know you can. Do what you did before, except instead of triggering the bomb, see its location."

His expression of faith in her abilities made her throat go thick. Since the day her powers had first emerged, nobody had trusted her with them. But this man did. Sean did.

Of course, he might've been saying whatever to make her try.

With his hands on her shoulders, anchoring her, she let his eyes transfix her with their shimmering emerald glow. She reached out with her powers, seeking the bomb, picturing a box with glass bottles inside it. A red trail formed in the air, but she knew this was no physical manifestation. The trail existed in her mind's eye. She'd never witnessed this phenomenon before, and yet she understood its purpose. The trail led to the bomb.

She sensed her mind detaching from her body, and she floated along the path delineated by the red trail. It drew her down the aisle between the theater seats, straight to the small stage that hosted the big screen on which the movie still played. The trail swerved right, around the edge of the stage, and then veered left.

It pierced a metal door.

Kira dived through the door to track the red path inside.

The trail dead-ended at a stack of metal shelves.

On the second shelf, a metal box sat in plain sight.

This looked like a storage room, filled with bags of popcorn kernels, containers of oil, and cannisters of soda syrup. The terrorists must've been certain no one would enter this room before the bomb detonated.

A chill skittered down her spine. They must've placed the bomb here moments before she and Sean arrived.

She zoomed back to her body. "It's in the storage room. Follow me."

They rushed down the aisle. She blew the storage-room door open with a telekinetic burst. They hesitated in front of the box on the shelf, exchanging glances, neither of them sure what to do now. She didn't need telepathy to realize he was as confused and scared as she was.

"We have to open it," he said. "I'll do it."

"Are you sure that's a good idea?"

"No." He felt along the seam where the lid met the box. "Can't find a latch or anything."

"Maybe they didn't bother with locking it up. I mean, they didn't bother hiding it."

"Good point." Gingerly, he lifted the lid with the tips of his fingers—and froze. "Oh hell."

She leaned in to peek inside the box.

Two thick glass vials lay nestled on a block of gray foam. Each vial held clear liquid. A thin red wire emerged from beneath the foam and snaked up to split in two, one end touching each of the vials, held in place with some kind of clear glue. A black rectangle with a shiny surface lay below the vials atop the foam.

"Something's not right," Sean said. "The first bomb had no evidence of a triggering mechanism, but this one has wires."

"Maybe—"

The black rectangle came to life. Green numbers counted down on the little screen. *Ten, nine, eight—*

"Run!" Sean hollered.

Seven, six, five—

He seized her hand, half dragging her out of the storage room. They bolted through the theater, up the sloping aisle toward the doors while green numbers flashed in her mind.

Four, three, two—

They burst through the swinging doors into the lobby.

A boom thundered inside the theater, shaking the walls and floor, and a cloud of dust and debris plumed out the open doors.

CHAPTER SEVEN

SEAN DIVED FOR THE FLOOR AND LANDED ON TOP OF KIRA FOR THE second time in twelve hours. Chunks of who-knew-what spattered his backside. He waited until the onslaught ended, until the rumbling subsided and the dust had cleared. Then he jumped up, hoisting her up with him.

Her eyes were big and glossy. Dirt crusted her hair.

Sean brushed the locks from her face. "You okay?"

His ears still rang, but he heard her say, "Not hurt."

"Good." He should've pushed her away, but a weird sensation in his chest made him hold still with her soft little body pressed against him. They could've both died, but he was more worried about whether his stunt had driven everyone out of the theater.

He should've checked before they fiddled with the bomb. He should've come up with a different plan. And what had gone wrong with his thought projection? He'd meant to make everyone leave in an orderly fashion, not start a freaking riot.

Another mistake. He couldn't seem to stop screwing up these days.

Kira peered around his shoulder at the dark and destroyed theater. In a halting voice, she asked, "Did everyone get out?"

"I think so." He prayed they had. Grace could've used her powers to check for any people hiding in the theater, but he hadn't even been able to track down Kira's brother. "I know my original idea was a brawl, but I swear I was trying to make people go to the restroom. Something got messed up. I couldn't control what was happening. Tried to send out a calming wave, but it was too late."

Jeez, that sounded idiotic. But he had tried to calm things down. Didn't work, naturally. He seemed incapable of doing anything lately except making things worse.

Kira pulled in a shaky breath, squared her shoulders, and looked up at him. "They all got out. I trust my intuition, and it's telling me we saved everyone."

"Thought you were telekinetic and nothing else."

"I've always had good intuition. Never thought of it as a psychic thing until now, until you explained that stuff to me." She glanced around as if only just realizing she was in his arms. Her brows crinkled. "Um…Why are you hugging me?"

Good question. He'd meant to support her until she regained her equilibrium, but she felt so nice against him he couldn't seem to make himself release her. Though he'd never been a big hugger, he'd liked to hold his girlfriends. But ever since Bree, he hadn't wanted anyone to touch him. His powers might've gone rogue again and gotten someone hurt.

Like they had a few minutes ago. Please let everyone be okay.

A chill rattled him down to his bones. What if he hurt Kira next time?

Clearing his throat, he backed away from her. "Sorry."

She puckered her lips, then took a deep breath and blew it out. "You're very confusing."

"I can live with that." He reached for her hand, intending to guide her out of the building, but then changed his mind and waved for her to follow him. "Let's get out of here before the cops show up. They'll have questions we can't answer."

As they pushed through the swinging glass doors and exited into the night, the cool air felt brittle on his skin. The parking-lot lights painted the scene in shades of sickly yellow. They hurried to the car, and just as they settled into their seats with Sean behind the wheel, Kira's phone rang.

She jerked, her hand flying to her chest.

"Better answer," he said.

Kira took a breath and exhaled it slowly, her lips forming a small O. Then she tugged the phone out of her purse and held it to her ear. Before she could speak, the caller started talking. Sean could hear the voice, tinny and indistinct.

"Okay," she said, and punched a button on the phone. "He's listening."

She must've meant him, Sean figured. But how could the bad guys know he was with her?

Psychic powers, numbskull.

That creepily altered voice emerged from the speaker, the words clipped with a funky cadence. "You betrayed us, Kira, and there must be consequences."

"The bomb went off," she said. "I did what you wanted."

"No, you evacuated the premises and searched for the device. We triggered it." A pause. "This was your mission, but you brought Sean Vandenbrook into it. We are not pleased."

Despite what the guy said—or the woman, he had no idea based on the distorted voice—it sounded like the person was kind of pleased with the situation.

Sean leaned over the center console. "Don't blame Kira. This was my fault. I made her take me along."

"Yes, we're aware of that," the voice said, with an oddly familiar tone that raised goosebumps on Sean's arms. Silence followed as seconds elapsed. "We've decided this is acceptable after all. Two of you will accomplish the next task faster. However, we know you chased the patrons out of the theater before the explosion. Therefore, we must exact punishment."

"No!" Kira shouted, jerking forward, her fingers clenching the phone. "Please don't hurt Caleb."

"Oh, he will remain unharmed—for now. Since Sean took it upon himself to become involved, the punishment will be his."

"Do whatever you want to me," Sean said. "I can take it."

"You misunderstand. We punish not you, but one you love."

His gut twisted, the pain visceral and real. "You bastard—"

"We will be in touch later with your next assignment."

The words "call ended" flashed on the phone's screen.

Sean yanked the key in the ignition, wrenched the gear shift lever into reverse, and floored the accelerator. The tires squealed as he swerved the car backward and to the left, then burned rubber out of the parking lot and onto the highway.

Peripherally, he saw Kira gripping the armrest and the center console. Her eyes had gone wide again.

"Who will they hurt?" she asked.

"Since they like hurting kids," he said, grinding the words out between his teeth, "I'm betting they'll try for Grace and David's daughter, Abby."

"Oh God."

"I'm not giving them the chance to hurt her."

The speedometer read seventy. He floored the gas pedal again, and the car shot forward, pinning them to their seats. Eighty, ninety. They flew over the asphalt.

He prayed they would get there in time. If they didn't...

Sean clamped his hands tighter around the wheel, his jaw throbbing from the pain of gritting his teeth. If they hurt Abby, he'd unleash his powers all the way this time. He'd hunt them down and show the scumbags the real meaning of pain.

———

TEN MINUTES LATER, THEY PULLED INTO THE DRIVEWAY OF A NONDEscript house in the suburbs. Kira peeled her hands off the armrest and center console, at last taking a good, deep breath. She guessed this drive would've taken twice as long, or longer, at normal speeds. Sean had driven like a genuine bat out of hell, like they were being pursued by flaming demons.

The fact his eyes had glowed softly during the whole trip only reinforced that imagery.

She'd never seen anyone so grimly determined, someone burning with an anger she couldn't comprehend. What had happened to him? She got the distinct impression he'd suffered way more than she could imagine.

As Sean shut off the engine, a porch light popped on. The interior of the house remained dark.

They climbed out of the car. Kira stopped at the front bumper, unsure of whether she should accompany Sean into the house. This was his family, not hers.

He cupped her elbow on his way toward the porch, urging her to follow. At the front door, they halted.

"Maybe I should wait in the car," she said.

"No." He swung his attention to her, and though the glow had subsided, the way his gaze bored into hers made her uneasy. "We stick together. Okay?"

She nodded.

A locking mechanism released with a click, and the door opened a couple feet. A bald man with a face etched with wrinkles peered out at them, at first seeming suspicious, but then he looked at Sean and relief flooded over him. A weary smile tugged at his mouth.

"Sean," the man said on a gusty sigh. "Thank goodness you're all right. I heard the news report a few minutes ago on the radio. Another explosion."

"Yeah," Sean said, "we were there. That's why we're here. Can we come in, Edward?"

The man blinked as if surprised. "Oh. Yes, of course."

He swung the door open wider, and Sean exerted slight pressure on Kira's elbow to lead her inside.

The house wasn't completely dark, she now saw. Blackout curtains shielded the windows. A low-wattage lamp situated on a table at the end of a sofa cast its warm, muted light into the room.

Edward, the bald man, glanced from Sean to Kira. He hiked up one eyebrow.

"Oh, uh…" Sean waved a hand toward her. "This is Kira Magnusson. She's helping me look for the scumbags who were responsible for both explosions."

She squelched the surprise that surged inside her. Mere hours ago, Sean had called her Bomb Girl and a terrorist. Now, he told this kindly looking man she was helping him hunt for the culprits.

Yep, her life had totally veered into Crazy Land.

"This is Edward McLean," Sean told her. "He's Grace's grandfather."

Kira offered her hand to the older man. "Nice to meet you, Mr. McLean."

He took her hand, sandwiching it between both of his. "Call me Edward. I'm glad to see Sean with a girl since he's been avoiding other people for two months."

She threw Sean a sidelong look. Months? Avoiding people? This guy kept a secret, for sure, but she hadn't thought he kept it from the people he said he loved.

He must've guessed what she was thinking, because his gaze slid away from hers and he scratched his neck.

"Where's Abby?" Sean asked.

"Sleeping in her room."

"Gotta check on her." Sean started for the hallway, but Edward grasped his arm. Sean's expression turned almost panicked. "Please, I have to check."

"I just looked in on her a minute ago. She's fine." Edward tugged Sean's arm until the younger man gave in and faced him again. "What's going on?"

Sean's expression hardened into steel. "Something bad."

SEAN CRACKED THE BEDROOM DOOR OPEN JUST ENOUGH TO PEEK in at the small body tucked under the covers. In the twilight within, Abby was a shadowy lump in the bed, though he could make out enough to tell she was sleeping. Safe. For now.

He shut the door gently and headed back to the living room. He'd checked on Abby twice in the past five minutes, but he still didn't feel secure about her safety.

Edward had switched on a second lamp and sat in the armchair across the coffee table from the sofa. Kira perched on the sofa's edge, hands clamped together over her lap, spine straight.

Sean settled onto the sofa a few feet from her and slouched back into the cushions. His body ached like he'd gone on an exercise binge, and a deep weariness penetrated him to the core. His mouth split open on a yawn that was loud and inappropriate.

Edward leaned back in his chair, one elbow on the puffy arm, his raised hand braced under his chin. "You've checked on Abby twice. I know you're worried about her, but no one will get into this house without our knowing. It has a state-of-the-art security system."

Sean drummed his fingers on his thigh. "We're dealing with nutjobs who use psychics to commit terrorist acts. Can't be sure any security system will be enough. Maybe you should call Grace again."

"Grace and David are fine."

His fingers drummed faster, harder. Sean couldn't stop them, couldn't stop his thoughts from whirling and colliding, couldn't make his stomach settle down either. *We punish not you,* the disembodied voice on the phone had said, *but one you love.* If not Grace, David, or Abby, then who? He didn't care about anyone but them and Edward.

A shiver sidled down his spine, raising the hairs all over his body. Could these bad guys, whoever they were, somehow hurt Edward? Losing her grandfather would destroy Grace. And Edward had become a kind of substitute grandfather to Sean, a replacement for the lunatic who had been his actual grandfather. Maybe Sean did love Edward, kind of. Being a guy, he would never say it out loud because guys didn't do that kind of thing.

The psycho on the phone couldn't have meant…

Sean shot upright, hands gripping his knees. "Edward, how do you feel?"

The older man smiled with the sort of calmness only a mature person with seven decades of life under his belt could pull off. "I'm fine. Your terrorists must have changed their minds, or else they were simply trying to unsettle you."

"Yeah, they've done a bang-up job of that."

"Terrorists want to incite fear, Sean. You can't believe everything they say."

"I know, but—" Sean rubbed his jaw, realizing he'd been gritting his teeth hard enough to trigger pain. "They said they'd punish me by hurting someone I, uh, care about."

A small smile tightened Edward's mouth. "Glad to know you care, but they can't get to me here."

"Psychically, they could."

Edward sighed. "If they have psychic powers themselves, or have others with them who do, why would they need you and Kira to perform their evil deeds for them? Why would they need a physical means to detonate the bomb in the theater?"

Sean shook his head, unable to come up with an answer.

Kira cleared her throat. "Um, what if they needed my specific powers? Maybe none of them have telekinesis, and they can't set off the bombs on their own."

"It's possible," Edward said. He tapped a finger on his chin as if considering the idea. "I suppose—"

He jerked. His eyes bulged, his mouth fell open, and he slapped a hand on his chest.

Sean's heart thudded, but he couldn't move. "What's wrong?"

The older man clutched at his chest, his fingers twisting in his shirt. He gasped.

"Edward!" Sean launched off the sofa and bolted for the armchair. On his knees beside Edward, he grasped the other man's wrist to feel his pulse. Fast. Thready. "Kira, call nine-one-one."

She fumbled with her phone. It tumbled to the floor.

While she cursed and snagged the phone, Edward lurched up and forward, half out of the chair.

"No," Sean said, grasping Edward's shoulders in his own shaking hands. "Sit down, don't try to move."

Edward collapsed to the floor.

Sean was paralyzed, in body and mind, unable to move or think.

Legs and arms bent at odd angles, Edward lay motionless on the carpet. His eyes were open and lifeless.

No, no, no. Not lifeless. Sean's heart pounded so hard and fast he could barely breathe. *Not losing anyone else, not now, not ever.*

A harsh noise erupted from Kira's phone, the sound of a busy signal.

She made a choked sound. "I can't get through to nine-one-one. System must be overloaded."

Gulping against the parched tightness of his throat, Sean scrambled closer to Edward. No sign of breathing. He felt for a pulse in Edward's wrist and his throat. Nothing. Panic ripped through Sean, freezing his muscles and his brain, freezing the blood in his veins.

Kira waddled toward him on her knees. She clamped a hand on his arm. "Can't you heal him?"

Her voice trembled, her hand too.

Wake up, he commanded himself. Wake up and fix this.

Sean carefully rolled Edward onto his back. He laid his palms on the man's chest, closed his eyes, and focused on the power. His mind soared out of his body toward the crossroads.

And slammed into a barrier.

He sucked in a heaving breath, knocked off kilter by the psychic momentum of his ejection from the crossroads. What was going on? He knew how to get there, how to access the energy contained in the metaphysical plane.

"I can't," he gasped. "I can't get to the crossroads."

Kira seized one of his hands, pressing her palm to his. "Let me help, like you helped me in the theater."

Could it work? He had to try.

Sean clasped her hand tighter, his other palm flat on Edward's chest over his heart. Eyes closed, Sean willed the power to come. He couldn't get to the crossroads, wouldn't attempt it after the last time when he'd been ejected. Instead, he took them both up the tunnel, almost to the crossroads, close enough the power inherent in that place sought them out like a magnet seeking metal. Energy poured into them, warm and tingling, energizing their powers like nothing he'd experienced before. In the theater, their joined hands had amplified their powers somehow, but without them traveling out of their bodies. Bound to each other as they floated in the ethereal tunnel, he let the energy stream into him until the flow dwindled into nothing.

He hummed with power.

As they flew back into their bodies, Sean opened his eyes and concentrated on the sight of his hand plastered to Edward's chest. He willed the energy crackling within him and Kira to flow into Edward, to repair the damage and restore vitality. The hairs on Sean's arm raised visibly as if an electrical current stirred them.

His hand. He stared at it, not blinking, not breathing. Must've been an optical illusion or something, but he swore—

"Your hand is glowing," Kira said, breathless, her large eyes glued to the sight.

And yeah, his hand was glowing. A faint white light emerged from his palm, seeping out around the edges. Power pulsated through their joined hands, through his body, down his other arm into his glowing hand.

Edward's chest heaved with a hoarse inhalation.

The energy fizzled out. Sean's hand no longer glowed. Frozen in place, his hand around Kira's and his palm on Edward's chest, Sean waited for…more.

Edward's breathing normalized. His eyelids fluttered open.

He glanced down at Sean's hand on his chest and then eyed Sean and Kira with curiosity. "What's going on here?"

"You died," Sean blurted out, seeming to have lost control over his brain-to-mouth filter. "I mean, it seemed like you did. Your heart stopped, and you weren't breathing, and I—we—"

Sean glanced helplessly at Kira.

Her lips curved into a sweet smile, aimed first at him, and then at Edward. "Sean healed you."

Edward sat up, as spry as ever, and patted Sean's arm. "Thank you."

"You're, uh, welcome," Sean mumbled. "You feel okay?"

Stretching, Edward drew in a long, deep breath. His lips formed a satisfied smile. "I feel excellent."

"Good," Sean said, because he couldn't think of anything else to say. He'd healed Edward with Kira's help. They'd saved someone's life together. Though the energy that had powered up his healing ability had faded, a tingling still energized every cell in Sean's body. He felt awake, alive, and...aware.

Abruptly, he noticed Kira's hand still latched onto his. The softness of her palm. The heat of her skin. The way her thumb traced circles on his flesh.

Her gaze swiveled to him, her blue eyes shimmering, almost glowing with residual energy.

Right there in front of Edward, without a thought for anything except the need that surged up inside him, Sean took hold of Kira's face and crushed his mouth to hers.

CHAPTER EIGHT

FOR A STUNNED MOMENT, KIRA WAS PARALYZED BY THE FEEL OF Sean's lips on hers. She gazed at his face so near to hers, gazed into his smoldering green eyes, while her pulse raced and a warmth blossomed in her chest. It spread outward on a tingling wave of sensation. Her body softened, her eyes drifted closed. His lips, warm and firm against hers, began to move over her skin, sweeping back and forth as his tongue teased the seam of her mouth.

She melted against him, against his firm chest, his big hands still bracketing her face.

When he withdrew his lips for a second, her lips parted like they had a mind of their own. He tunneled his fingers into her hair, pressing his mouth to hers once more, and slipped his tongue between her lips. Slick. Hot. Agile. He explored her mouth with leisurely sweeps of his tongue, his fingers massaging her scalp, his breaths tickling her skin.

Edward cleared his throat deliberately.

Kira and Sean froze at the same instant, their lips fused.

Sean ripped his mouth away from hers and jerked his hands away too, flinging them wide like he'd just realized he was touching a radioactive object.

"I don't mean to interrupt," Edward said, "but we do have urgent matters to discuss."

Jaw slack, face blank, Sean stared at Kira for a long moment before he pulled in a big breath and retreated into his hard facade, teeth gritted. He jumped to his feet. "Better check on Abby again."

He sprinted down the hall.

Edward eyed Kira with something akin to humor tinged with curiosity.

His attention made her squirm. She scrambled to her feet and offered him her hands. "Let me help you up."

"I'm old, not infirm." He rose without her assistance, brushing his clothes off with his hands. "But I appreciate the offer, dear. How long have you and Sean been dating?"

"Dating?" Her brain blanked, leaving her to flounder through an answer on her own. "We just met earlier tonight. Yesterday, I mean. Last night. What time is it?"

Edward smiled a touch. "Two-thirty?"

Where had the hours gone? Sucked into the void of desperation and panic, that's where.

She tried not to let Edward's keen gaze unsettle her, but it did anyway. The man wanted to know more about how she and Sean had met, she could tell that much. He didn't need to hear about how Sean kidnapped her and the strange truce they'd reached, not to mention their idiotic scheme to chase everyone out of the movie theater. If Sean wanted to share all that information with Edward, she wouldn't stop him. But she would not reveal it without his permission.

He'd *kissed* her.

The thought burst into her mind, setting off a replay of the sizzling heat she'd experienced when he took her mouth. Not only had she let him kiss her, she'd responded in kind. She'd liked it.

Stockholm syndrome, for sure.

Didn't matter right now. She had no option except to keep trusting Sean and keep working with him. No more power sharing, though. Absolutely none.

Sean tromped back into the living room. "Abby's fine."

Edward nodded, then settled down in the armchair again. "We should call Grace."

"I'll do it," Sean said, digging his phone out of his jeans pocket.

"Don't tell her what happened to me. Say you're checking in again, nothing more."

Sean nodded and dialed a number.

While he retreated to a far corner of the room, Kira perched on the sofa, her hands clamped over its front edge.

Edward observed her with even more interest than before, rubbing his chin with his thumb and forefinger. "You and Sean seem closer than two strangers who met earlier tonight."

She shrugged. "Things aren't always how they look. Besides, we've been through a lot together in the past few hours."

The forced intimacy of shared trauma made them seem closer than they were. That had to be the answer. Like Sean had said earlier, they didn't even like each other.

But lord, did he know how to kiss.

"Grace and David are okay," Sean said, approaching the sofa to take a seat on it a few feet from Kira. "He's still in a coma, but his condition is stable. Unchanged. Those bastards didn't get to Grace or David."

Edward flattened his lips, his attention diverting to the corner. "Sean, why do you talk as if the terrorists had something to do with my heart attack?"

"They must have." Sean leaned forward and braced his elbows on his knees. "They said someone I care about would be punished and then you almost died."

"It could've been a coincidence."

Sean huffed. "You had a complete physical two months ago, and your heart was fine."

Edward's expression turned pained, and his shoulders slumped.

"You don't want to believe it," Sean said, his tone gentler than Kira would've thought he was capable of sounding. "It's too scary, I get that. But somebody must've gotten to you. Did you run into anyone strange at the hospital? Maybe you got poisoned or something."

"Poisoned?" Edward rubbed his forehead. "I was in a public place, a hospital, for most of the day. I ran into dozens of strangers. But I've been here at home for more than eight hours, and I felt fine until moments ago. Poison seems unlikely."

"Yeah, it does," Sean said, scowling down at the carpet. "It had to be a psychic assault, but I've never heard of anybody having the power to kill remotely."

Kira wriggled in place, biting down on her lip before deciding to speak. "Sean, if you could heal Edward's heart, then why couldn't someone else make it stop beating? I'm sure you don't know everything there is to know about psychic powers."

Sean rotated his eyes to nail her with a hard look. "Never said I know everything. But if these terrorists have got people who can kill remotely, why would they need you and me to set off bombs for them?"

"Maybe the heart-stopping psychic can't affect multiple people at once."

He nailed his gaze to hers, his eyes faintly luminescent, his mouth tight.

She refused to break eye contact and give him the satisfaction of knowing he'd unnerved her, even though he had. The intensity of his gaze, the steely expression on his face, they reminded her of when he'd dragged her into his car. A chill raced over her skin at the memory. He'd been nicer since then, but she still didn't know whether trusting him was a good idea.

Especially when he glared at her like that.

But it was a defense mechanism. She'd recognized that hours ago. If he would talk to her, really talk to her, she might understand his motivations and his actions.

Sure, he'd rip open all his old wounds and show them to her anytime now.

"Maybe," she said, forcing her tone to remain level, "they don't need us to do these things. Maybe they have some reason to want us involved, to use us as scapegoats once they do whatever it is they're trying to accomplish."

"Scapegoats?" Edward said, scratching his chin. "I suppose that could be."

He sounded unconvinced, despite his assertion.

"Bull," Sean said. "There's something else going on here. Don't know what it is, but this is not about needing somebody to take the blame."

Kira raised her brows. "How do you know?"

He swerved his gaze away from her. "I feel it. Intuition."

"Okay," she said slowly. "Considering this is all about psychic abilities, I guess I have to accept your intuition as evidence. If these bad guys don't want us as patsies, what do you think they want?"

He shrugged.

Edward cleared his throat. "The only way you'll find out is by tracking down these terrorists. The two of you are the only ones who've had contact with them. Find these criminals. Stop them. I know you can do it."

"How?" Sean asked. "How do you know?"

"I may not have powers, but I do have a functioning brain, Sean. I know the facts of this case, and I know you." Edward glanced at Kira. "And this young lady seems as stubborn, determined, and intelligent as you are. I'd say you're a perfect match—as psychic detectives."

The twinkle in his eyes and the slight upward tick of his lips suggested he thought of them as a perfect match in other ways too.

And the idea made Kira's skin itch.

Yes, she found Sean attractive—and sexy, in an alpha-male sort of way that made her want to deck him—but she did not believe in soul mates or whatever Edward thought they might be.

"Go," Edward said. "Find these villains."

"What about you and Abby?" Sean asked. "And Grace and David too. We can't leave all of you alone. What if somebody tries to kill one of you again? I won't be here to heal you."

"Make them believe you're doing what they want, and we will be fine."

"You don't know that."

Edward blustered out a breath and slapped his hands on his thighs. "Go, Sean. Don't make me throw you out the door."

Sean tensed as if he wanted to complain, but Kira laid a hand on his arm.

"Let's go," she said. "He's right. Our best hope is to play along and keep trying to hunt down these bad guys."

He rubbed his nape. "I know."

Dragging in a breath, he surged to his feet.

Kira pushed up off the sofa too.

As Sean passed Edward's chair, he paused to gaze down at the older man. "Be careful."

"You too."

Kira trailed Sean out of the house.

———

OUTSIDE, THE SUN PEEKED OVER THE HORIZON, PAINTING THE SKY in shades of gold and pink. In the false twilight within the motel room, slumped in a chair by the window, Sean watched Kira sleeping on the bed. She lay on her side with one hand tucked under the pillow, her face slack and her eyes darting the way they did when someone dreamed. He hoped she was having nice dreams, but he kind of doubted it after the hell they'd been through last night.

He'd slept for a few hours, fitfully.

Yawning, he scrubbed a hand over his eyes. No way could he hope for more sleep, not now, not anytime soon.

A sigh whispered out of Kira between her parted lips.

Sean studied her sleeping form, noting her eyes had stopped fidgeting and her lips had curled into the barest of smiles. For a little while last night, while she slept, he'd considered the possibility she might've done something to Edward to cause his heart attack. Kira had been alone with Edward while Sean checked on Abby. She could've slipped him a poison or, hell, used her powers to try to kill him. If she could set off bombs with her telekinetic abilities, then maybe she could use them to squeeze Edward's heart until it seized up.

But Sean couldn't make himself believe it.

Yesterday, when he'd found Kira at the ravaged cafe, he would've believed her capable of any depraved act. Now...His stupid intuition kept niggling at him, encouraging him to trust her for reasons he couldn't understand.

Empathic abilities, moron. You've got 'em, remember?

He'd blocked his powers, shut them up in the deepest vault of his mind, but how could he be sure the seal hadn't cracked? When she wept over her brother, Sean had sworn he experienced her emotions, her pain, her fear. Maybe he couldn't contain his powers behind a mental shield as thoroughly as he'd thought. Maybe something of her got through the barrier.

She hadn't hurt Edward. Sean knew it on a visceral level, and he didn't have time to explore the reasons why.

His phone vibrated in his pocket. He'd set it to vibrate instead of ringing, so the noise wouldn't wake up Kira if someone called. He dug the phone out of his pocket, trotted into the bathroom, and shut the door while he muttered hello.

"Sean, I was concerned for you."

He bristled at the sound of Gabriel Amador's voice, but tried to keep his irritation out of his tone. Yeah, he always had great luck with that. "What do you want?"

"I heard of another bombing on the news this morning, and I was worried since you did leave to search for the culprits of the first attack." Amador paused, then added, "Where are you?"

"What do you want?" Sean repeated with more emphasis this time.

"Have you spoken to Grace this morning?"

"No. Why? Is something wrong with her or David?"

Amador said nothing for several seconds, the silence reverberating through Sean's soul and making his pulse quicken. If something had happened, Edward or Grace would've called Sean. Unless the terrorists had gotten to both of them.

"I'm afraid," Amador said, speaking slowly and with a grim tone that implied bad news ahead, "your mission of revenge is causing Grace distress. You are, after all, only a boy and ill-equipped for the task."

The way Amador had drawn out his answer, the way he'd started with "I'm afraid," it had triggered a stark panic that overtook Sean for the briefest moment that seemed like an eternity. Sean had the weirdest feeling the guy had done it on purpose to make him worry. To cause him stress. To hurt him. And the jibe about him being "only a boy" and "ill-equipped" struck him as weird too. Annoying, for sure, but weird. Even Amador wasn't normally that rude. Had the guy wanted to tick him off?

Sean had never liked Amador, but he'd never done anything to the guy. He couldn't imagine why Amador would want to hurt him or tick him off. He must've misread the man.

If Sean turned on his empathic ability, he might know for sure.

Too dangerous.

"Was that it?" Sean said. "Or did you have something else to say? I'm kinda busy."

"I will let you go now, with a bit of advice. Give up on finding the parties responsible for these attacks, Sean. Allow the authorities to handle this."

Amador hung up.

Sean stared at his own reflection in the bathroom mirror. He'd developed reddish stubble and reddish roots showed close to his scalp. Hints of the past. Reminders of his bloodline. Acid burned in his gut, but a coldness slithered in his chest.

He searched the bathroom for a razor but couldn't find one. This was a cheap motel, not the Hilton. The only amenities were a tiny bar of soap and plastic cups on the counter. He scratched his head, suddenly itchy on the outside and the inside. *Got to get rid of the red.* But he couldn't.

With his hands on the counter, he bowed his head. No way to erase the past.

After a moment, he shambled out of the bathroom and slumped into the chair again.

Kira stirred, made a little moany sighing noise, and rolled onto her back. Her lids fluttered open, and she focused her lustrous blue eyes on him.

"Good morning," he said.

"Morning." She pushed into a sitting position, wriggling backward to lean against the headboard. "Not sure it'll be a good one, though."

Sean crossed one ankle over his other knee. "Might as well start off optimistic."

Her brows shot up. "You're feeling optimistic? Mr. Gloom and Doom?"

"I have my moments." He folded his hands over his belly. "Sleep okay?"

"Well enough." She stretched and yawned. "What about you?"

"Good as I ever do these days."

She squinted at him, biting down on her lower lip. "You don't look rested. There are dark circles under your eyes."

He hissed out a sigh. "Forget about my sleep habits. We've got more important things to worry about. Like teaching you how to access the crossroads."

"Can we get some breakfast first?"

Sean's stomach grumbled at the mention of food. He couldn't remember the last time he'd eaten, and Kira probably hadn't grabbed a snack either. Leaving her while she slept so he could get some food hadn't seemed like a good idea.

Thinking about it had made him…uneasy.

"Now that you're up," he said, thrusting his body up and out of the chair, "I'll run over to the burger joint across the street. I saw they do breakfast too. Got any preferences?"

"Food. That's my preference."

She smiled, her lips sealed, her eyes sparkling in the muted lighting.

His chest tightened, his groin too. She looked so beautiful and innocent with her sleep-tousled hair and her rumpled clothes.

Sean coughed into his fist. "I'll be back as quick as I can."

Kira slid off the bed and stretched again, her breasts rising with her arms. "Think I'll freshen up."

He stared at her shapely ass while she sashayed into the bathroom. When she shut the door, he headed out.

Maybe he liked her ass and her breasts, and maybe he didn't think she was a cold-blooded killer, but he did not like her or have…feelings for her. No way.

As he strode across the street toward the burger joint, he tried to ignore the images that flickered in his mind. Kira sleeping. Kira smiling. Kira stretching her lithe body.

Not feeling a damn thing.

Chapter Nine

TWENTY MINUTES LATER, THEY'D POLISHED OFF THEIR BREAKFAST OF biscuits loaded with eggs, cheese, and bacon. He'd eaten three, while Kira managed one and a half. Sean had finished off the half she left, then swigged milk from a tiny carton. Kira had daintily drunk her milk throughout the meal, but only after complaining he'd bought low fat instead of whole milk.

"I thought women ate low fat all the time," he'd said. "Every girl I dated would've shrieked at me if I bought whole milk. Besides, the restaurant didn't have any."

"Maybe other girls are constantly dieting," Kira had told him, "but not me. I believe in eating what I want, not what's in fashion. I am not obsessed with having the perfect figure."

He'd eyed her up and down, admiring her curvy body. "You don't need to diet. Your figure is just fine."

She'd looked shocked for a second but then went back to consuming her meal like she hadn't eaten in weeks.

Now, she swallowed the last of her milk and plunked the empty carton on the table. She sat across from him, her legs tucked under her cross-legged style. Her hair was wet, since she'd showered while he got the food, but her clothes were still rumpled.

"We should go to your place," he said, "and get you fresh clothes."

"Later." She folded her hands on the tabletop. "First, I want to know more about you."

"Why?" Despite his casual posture, with one arm draped over the table and his legs stretched out with his ankles crossed, he felt tension rippling through his body, tightening every muscle.

"Because we're in this together," she said, "and I need to know who I'm dealing with."

He rapped his knuckles on the table. "I've got powers, you've got powers, we're both being blackmailed by anonymous psychos. Nothing else to know."

She sat back and barred her arms over her chest. "You're reining in your powers, aren't you? If that's the case, I need to know why. Your pent-up powers might bite us both in the ass."

"What makes you think I'm reining in my powers?" He was, big time, but he'd never told her that.

She made a derisive noise. "Please. I'm not stupid. You say you're an empath, but you act like you haven't experienced a genuine emotion in your entire life."

"I've got feelings." The statement came out harsher than he'd meant it to, almost a growl. He did not want to talk about this. Ever.

"Working together means trusting each other, which means understanding each other." She dropped her hands to her lap, and her expression softened. "I need to know, Sean. What happened to you? What happened to your real family?"

"Grace and David are my real family." Sean fidgeted in his chair. His stomach churned with acid that burned into his chest. His jaw ached, and he tried to stop gritting his teeth but couldn't make himself relax.

"I didn't mean to offend you," Kira said, her voice so gentle he felt like a bastard for snapping at her. "I'm sorry, Sean. But you have to realize I need to know what's going on with you. Like it or not, we are stuck with each other for the time being."

"Yeah, I know." He closed his fist around the empty milk carton and crushed it. "What makes you think anything happened to me?"

Delay. Denial. He'd go for any D-word that might keep him from having to talk about things he'd vowed never to talk about again.

"Things you've said," she told him. "You decided I was guilty because, in your words, innocent people pray for help and fight to get away until they're bloody and beaten. They scream for help until their throats are raw and they can't breathe. Those were your exact words."

He let go of the milk carton, giving it a little shove that sent it skittering across the table. "Let me guess. You've got a photographic memory."

"No, but the words of my kidnapper seemed important to remember."

Sean winced and snatched up the milk carton. Kidnapper. Yeah, that was him.

Kira angled her head, studying him with a keenness that made his skin crawl. "Edward said you've been avoiding other people for months. And you're sensitive about your powers, don't like to talk about them, much less use them. I had to go in the bathroom while you tried to access that crossroads thingy."

He pitched the crushed milk carton into the trash can behind Kira's chair. It flew past her head, and she cringed away from the projectile.

She shook her head. "Throwing things at me won't make me stop asking questions. Who made you scream for help until you couldn't breathe?"

Memories. They assailed his mind like nightmares, except these had been real moments in his life. Real terror. Real agony. Never talk about this again, he'd vowed. But Kira was too stubborn to let him get away with holding back, and she was right, they were stuck with each other. Dependent on each other, in a way. She needed to know, but he didn't know if he could speak the words. Relive the pain.

"It's okay," she said, her voice soft and full of compassion. "I won't tell anyone what you tell me. It'll be our secret, I promise."

Last night, she'd promised not to run away if he untied her—but she'd run anyway. So much had changed since then. He didn't want to trust her, but he had the weirdest feeling he could trust her. She'd suffered too, at the hands of these scumbag terrorists.

Sean braced his elbows on the table and cradled his forehead in his palms. "I don't remember my dad. My mom was all I ever had, and she died in a car wreck when I was fifteen. Her name was Sophie, which means wisdom, and it suited her. We had moved to California the year before because my mom got a job there. I was walking home from school one day when I saw her car come around the corner from the other direction, two blocks away. She was driving so fast the tires squealed. She kept going faster and faster. I stood there like my feet had gotten buried in concrete, watching, somehow knowing what was about to happen. She lost control and slammed into a utility pole. Died instantly."

"Oh, Sean." Kira stretched her hands across the table like she might touch him, only to pull them away. "I'm so sorry."

"Yeah, everybody was sorry." He couldn't meet Kira's gaze, instead focusing on the scratched tabletop. "I came into my powers when I was fifteen. My mom, she was amazing. She didn't get scared of my powers, she didn't freak out when I healed the old guy who lived next door to us. I freaked, but she told me I was special, and I should be proud of what I could do. Somehow, she found out about a research project in California at a place called ALI. They wanted to study psychic phenomena. My mom thought maybe they could help me cope with my powers. Edward McLean ran Project Outreach back then, and he gave my mom a job so we could afford to move."

Though he avoided her gaze, he sensed Kira's attention on him. It affected him like physical contact, like she'd laid her soft hands on him.

"Something happened at ALI, didn't it?" she asked.

"It was great at first. I met David and Grace there, and I got more comfortable with my healing power." He shifted in his seat, suddenly uncomfortable. "A year after we moved to California, my mom died. I was a mess, but David and Grace helped me through it. I moved into a suite at ALI since I had nowhere else to go. Six months earlier, a company called Digital Prognostics had bought ALI, but I didn't realize things were changing. I hadn't spent much time in the facility at that point. I mostly talked to Edward and Grace, plus her parents who were scientists like Edward. We would meet at the house where my mom and I lived. After Mom died, things got way worse."

Nausea swelled in his gut, his gorge surging high in his throat as he recalled those months after the accident. Edward and Grace's parents, Christine and Mark Powell, hadn't realized what was going on at first. Most of ALI's scientists were let go and replaced with people handpicked by Digital Prognostics, but the Powells and Edward were kept on as managers who had little involvement with the psychics living at the facility. The new scientists hid their increasingly invasive techniques from their supposed bosses, Grace's family. They realized the truth only when Karl Tesler came on board two months later, and everything went to hell in the most literal way.

Sean explained all of this to Kira in a voice devoid of emotion despite the pain and fear swirling inside him. He stopped short of delving into the torture, and Kira noticed his reticence.

"You can tell me what happened to you there," she said. "Please."

He palpated the partially healed cuts on his arm one by one, a reminder of the latest tragedy, the one that left David in a coma. His chest grew heavy, weighed down by memories of yesterday and other days much further in the past.

"Grace's parents died two months after that," he said. "Another car accident. This one was caused by Jackson Tennant, and it was not an accident at all. They'd discovered what the lead scientist, Tesler, and his buddies were up to and vowed to stop them. JT made sure they never could."

"JT?"

"That's what Jackson Tennant liked to be called."

"Do you think, um…" Kira squinted her face, clearly loath to ask her question.

"Spit it out."

She bit her upper lip. "Do you think JT or someone else at ALI might've caused your mom's accident?"

"I saw it happen. She lost control."

"How did JT cause the accident that killed Grace's parents?"

Sean scratched at one of his cuts. "He took a serum he'd concocted that brought out latent powers in people who didn't have them otherwise. It could also enhance existing powers, but he didn't have any without the serum. He traveled to the Powells, in the psychic sense, and used telekinesis to flip their car end over end."

"Well, if he could do that…"

Maybe he or someone in his cadre might've caused the accident that took Sean's mom away from him. The revelation rushed through him on a tide of tingling cold. If someone had killed his mom—

"No," he snarled. "It was an accident."

Kira raised her palms. "Okay, take it easy. I was just thinking out loud."

"Keep your thoughts to yourself." He scrubbed both palms over his face. "I'm sorry. I don't like to talk about the accident."

"I get that, I do." She hesitated before saying, "You haven't told me what Tesler and his cohorts did to you."

He had to tell her. She needed to know because everything that went down at ALI influenced him to this day. "When Tesler and Xavier Waldron took control of ALI, they stopped pretending it was a benevolent research facility. They turned Project Outreach into a nightmare. Torture was their favorite tool, and later, drugs came into the picture. I was—" Sean gulped but couldn't dislodge the scratchy, sharp rock in his throat. Maybe saying it out loud would be cathartic, but he doubted it. "They cut me. Burned me. Beat me. Whatever it took to make me do whatever they wanted. I remember the drugs more than the torture, though. It was like fire scorching my veins, melting my brain, and I'd convulse until my body throbbed with a kind of agony I can't describe."

He felt Kira's attention on him, sensed her compassion even through his mental shields. Staring down at the tabletop, at the scrapes in the fake-wood vinyl surface, gave him something to focus on besides the memories. Not that it helped much. He followed the jagged line of the deepest scratch. It reminded him of lightning.

"Oh God," Kira said. "That's—I can't even imagine what that was like for you."

No one could imagine it. No one who hadn't lived through it.

"I screamed," he said, "until my throat was scorched raw and I couldn't talk anymore. I cried until my eyes were swollen shut. I fought the restraints on the chair they strapped me to until my wrists were bloody." He lowered his hands, forcing himself to meet Kira's wide-eyed gaze. "But that wasn't the worst part. Torture seemed like a walk in the park compared to finding out the truth about my family."

She kept watching him, her big eyes locked onto his.

He sank down in his chair. "Karl Tesler was my grandfather."

CHAPTER TEN

"HE WAS WHAT?" KIRA ASKED, HER VOICE A BREATHLESS WHISPER. SHE couldn't believe what Sean had said, figured she must've misheard him. Her heart ached for him, for everything he'd been through, and she'd begun to understand why he behaved the way he had yesterday when they first met. She wasn't excusing him for kidnapping her, but his past gave her an idea of why he'd snapped.

Any victim of torture would suffer from PTSD. A man tortured by his own grandfather…She couldn't comprehend the damage that would do to a person's psyche.

"Karl Tesler," Sean said, sounding weary and angry at the same time, "was my grandfather. My mother's father. I knew she'd run away from home after her mom killed herself, but I had no idea her father had any involvement in psychic research. After Grace and David got hold of ALI's files, I found out some other stuff too. Like that my mom had known dear old Gramps wanted to experiment on me. He'd known I might have powers because my grandmother had them. My mom never did. She took me to ALI because she believed Christine and Mark Powell would keep me safe, and they helped her hide from her father, giving her a house owned by ALI and a job too. Tesler tracked her down right before she died. JT told him where we were. He knew because he owned ALI by that point. I don't know what my mom and Tesler talked about. All I know is she died a week later."

"And your father?"

"Told you, I never knew him. Never knew his name or anything. Mom never liked to talk about him."

"God, Sean. What you went through…" She had no words adequate to describe it or to express her sympathy. He probably wouldn't like sympathy, anyway. "Is this the reason you're afraid to use your powers? Because of being tortured?"

"No, that's why I don't trust people. Except for Grace and David and Edward." He squirmed in his chair, his face pinching. "I've been blocking my powers for two months. It's because—because something happened."

Kira studied his face, the bleakness in his eyes, and another statement he'd made came back to her. "You said once you would never hurt another woman. What did you mean by that?"

"Nothing."

"Sean—"

"Not talking about it. Understand?"

"I get that you don't want to," she said, "but you have to. Stuck together, remember? Anything that affects your powers and your psyche might get us both in trouble if you keep holding it all in. You need to tell me, please."

Sean levered his body out of the chair and wandered to the window, lifting the edge of the curtain away from the wall to peek outside. After a moment, he shambled to the bed and flumped onto it, feet on the floor, slumped forward to stare at the carpeting. "There was a girl. Bree Johnson. We'd been dating for three months and, uh, sleeping together. I decided to tell her about my powers, and she seemed cool with it. At first."

Kira didn't move, still cross-legged in her chair, afraid if she budged at all or said anything he might stop talking. Whatever he was about to say, she sensed it would be important.

He ran a hand over his face, but with his head downcast, she couldn't make out his expression. When he spoke, his voice was a monotone.

"One night," Sean said, "she told me she wanted to experience my powers. Said I shouldn't hold them back while we made love, she wanted to feel it. I warned her I'd never had empathic sex before, and I didn't know what might happen. She swore she could handle it, practically begged me to show her what I can do. We got naked and started kissing in bed. Things were progressing, and then…"

His shoulders bunched. He grasped his forehead in both hands but didn't speak.

Reluctantly, Kira pushed a little. "What, Sean? What happened with Bree?"

Forehead still in his hands, he continued in that unsettling monotone as if keeping a tight rein on his emotions deadened his voice. "At first, she liked it. The exchange of our emotions and sensations, it was intense, but she liked it. Suddenly, she got agitated. I thought she was getting, uh, more excited. Then she started pounding on my chest, shouting at me to stop. I did, but she was still freaked. Kept thrashing and screaming that she didn't want this and somehow I'd made her do it, but she didn't want it. I didn't get what she meant until she screamed I was raping her. I would never force a girl to—" His voice cracked, his hands trembled. "She jumped up and started grabbing her clothes to pull them on, but she was shaking so bad she kept dropping things. I tried to help her, but she just kept hitting me. I said I'm sorry, I didn't mean to hurt her, and besides, she'd wanted to feel my powers, hadn't she? I begged her to calm down and talk about this. She swore at me, punched me in the face, and told me—she said—"

He thrust his shaking hands into his hair, his head bowed so far it ducked between his knees.

Kira couldn't stop herself. She flew out of the chair to crouch before him, her hands on his knees. "Sean, what are you saying? What did she think you did to her?"

He sucked in a deep breath, and as it blustered out of him, he responded in that monotone voice. "Bree said after the way I'd just violated her mind she had no idea if she'd ever really liked me in the first place. Maybe I'd made her believe she did. After she left, I realized I couldn't swear I hadn't done what she said. I didn't mean to do it, but I might've accidentally used my empathic powers to force-feed her my feelings. I wanted her from the moment I saw her. I thought she liked me, but what if she never really had?"

"No, Sean, you wouldn't do that. Not even by accident."

"You don't know that, not for sure." He lifted his head, his gaze flinty, his upper lip twitching. "My grandfather was a monster. Maybe I am too."

Her throat had gone thick. She had no clue what to say to his revelations, but she could not believe he'd been able to influence a girl strongly enough to make her have sex with him when she didn't want to, when she didn't even like him. The girl had panicked when she experienced his empathic power. Most people would. Kira doubted Sean had told Bree about his horrific past, and so the girl hadn't realized she needed to be careful with him. She'd wounded him more deeply than ever.

Without any conscious intent, Kira took Sean's face in her hands. "Maybe you projected some of your feelings into her mind, but I don't believe you made her feel all of that. She must've liked you, must've been attracted to you. She panicked when she realized your powers are real. Hearing you tell her about them is different from feeling their direct effect. She wasn't strong enough to deal with it. Probably thought, subconsciously, psychic abilities couldn't be real."

"No. This was my fault."

She tugged his face down until their noses grazed each other. "Sean, you can't keep torturing yourself over something that was an accident."

"You don't know what you're talking about." He pushed her hands away. "Don't know what it's like to have the power to influence people's minds and not be able to control it."

"I don't know about that, you're right." She sat back on her heels. "But I know how it feels to have a power inside you that you can't control and don't understand."

He broke eye contact, rubbing his palms on his thighs.

She studied him for a moment, then said, "This is why you're repressing your powers. It's why you're afraid to go into the crossroads. You think you'll hurt someone else without meaning to."

Though he said nothing, he winced the tiniest bit.

"You can't live like this, Sean." She moved onto the bed beside him. "You have to forgive yourself."

"Can't. I'm a monster." He held up a hand to stay her response. "No point telling me I'm not. I kidnapped you, remember? I'm one screwed-up asshole."

"Yeah, you are," she said in a softly teasing tone. "But I'm beginning to understand why. You've been through hell for a lot of years, and that's bound to screw with your head."

He grunted, but his hard expression had relented somewhat.

"Thank you for telling me all of that," she said. "It couldn't have been easy, but I'm glad you shared this with me."

Although his head stayed aimed straight ahead, he rolled his eyes sideways to look at her. "How can you not want to run after what I just told you?"

"I'm not afraid of you."

He stared at her for several seconds, unmoving, unblinking. Then he squared his shoulders and aimed his bright green eyes at her. "You should be."

———

FOR THE REST OF THE MORNING, THEY DID MEANINGLESS THINGS THAT got them nowhere. Sean let Kira drive them to her house—her parents' house, she'd insisted on calling it—only because he had no idea where it was. After she'd changed into fresh clothes and packed an overnight bag, they headed to his apartment so he could do the same. After that, they returned to the motel. At Kira's urging, Sean tried again to get into the crossroads, but it didn't work any better this time. He was, according to her, too pent up with angst and self-loathing to make good use of his powers. He'd become useless.

Why had he told Kira about his mom? His grandfather?

I did love her once. The words slithered through his mind, an echo of a recurring dream he could never quite remember. Strapped to a chair, he recalled that part. A chair like an evil version of what dentists had in their offices. Red, raw wounds on his arms. Pain. Crying. *She loved you,* a voice would say. And then, *I did love her once.*

A nightmare, nothing more. It didn't mean a thing.

Kira offered to tell him her secrets since she'd encouraged him to spill all of his to her. Sean had told her to wait. His confessions had left him raw inside, emotionally spent. He needed a chance to regroup before she told him everything about her. Maybe he was a little afraid of what she'd say. She'd mentioned the bad guys hurt her to prove they could and would hurt her brother, though she hadn't given details. He couldn't bear to hear about it right now, not until the old wounds he'd just ripped open scabbed over again.

Selfish? Yeah, probably. He couldn't help that.

Back at the motel, he tried to teach her how to access the crossroads, but after an hour of instruction, she'd flopped onto her back on the bed and announced, "Your instruction technique bites."

"Sorry, I didn't sign up for the Psychic Teaching Skills class at college." He'd dropped onto the chair by the window. "Grace would be a lot better at this."

"Maybe your repression is affecting your ability to teach me about this stuff."

He'd slapped his palm down on the table, making it quake, and hissed, "Stop calling me repressed and pent up."

And of course, she'd rolled her eyes. "You really need to get laid."

Even now, forty-five minutes later after a silent lunch of burgers and fries, Sean still remembered the exact shade of pink her cheeks had turned when she realized what she'd blurted out. The color reminded him of the hydrangeas his mother had grown in their backyard when he was a kid. The flowers, normally white, took on a pale pink blush when the soil conditions were right. Kira's cheeks had looked like that, creamy underneath the faint blush of salmon pink.

He'd been a gentleman for once and not made a big deal about what she'd said, biting back a retort about whether she subconsciously wanted to help him out in the laying department.

Even if he wanted to, he couldn't touch her. Couldn't let her touch him. The risk of hurting her was too high. And still, he couldn't stop thinking about her curvy figure and those sweet little lips.

Perched on the edge of the bed, Sean slanted forward to rest his elbows on his thighs, hands draped over his knees. Six feet away, Kira sat ramrod straight in a chair by the window. With the thick drapes shut, the yellowish glow of the bedside lamp spilled across her features, accentuating her high cheekbones and her blue eyes, turned a deep shade of sapphire by the muted light. She stared at her purse where it slumped on the bedside table, her expression filled with morose longing.

She carried a pack of cigarettes in her purse, he knew. Because he'd rifled through her purse yesterday while she glared at him like daggers might shoot out of her eyes to stab him. When she'd been his hostage. When he'd been acting like a gigantic dick. *When did you stop being one?* his stupid brain asked. He told it to shut up.

Kira absently rubbed her wrists, and he caught sight of the faint red marks around them. He winced. He'd cinched the zip ties too tight yesterday. *Damn.* At least he'd untied her—eventually.

He shouldn't care. He didn't care. More to the point, he *couldn't* care anymore, since he'd locked down his empathic powers and his emotions. Besides, this girl had tried to blow his surrogate family to smithereens. He pinched the bridge of his nose between his fingers, squeezing his eyes shut. Trouble was, he believed Kira when she said she had no idea the device was an explosive, not just a smoke bomb. Her look of sheer horror right after the bomb went off...

Dammit. He did not care. Feeling for other people brought nothing but misery.

Whatever they'd shared earlier when he'd blabbed about his past, that didn't mean anything. Why had he told her all of that? Things he'd never told anyone. Okay, fine, he trusted her not to blow his head off with a gun or a bomb. But he would never trust himself with a woman. Never again. *Never.*

While he watched Kira, she watched her purse, bit her lower lip, and tapped her toes on the ancient carpeting. She heaved in a breath, and her shapely breasts lifted ever so slightly. Sean shifted his weight, his pants too tight all of a sudden.

Kira wound a lock of her raven hair around her middle finger, twirling it round and round while worrying her lip.

His body ached in ways he'd never experienced before. This woman stirred his desire. So what? He could want her without...feeling for her.

She let out a long, wistful sigh, her gaze fixed on her purse.

He stifled a chuckle. "Jonesing for a smoke?"

"What?" She whipped her head toward him. "Oh. No. I quit six months ago."

"You're staring at your purse like you want to rip it apart with your teeth to get to the cigarettes."

With a snort, she twisted her mouth into a half frown.

Sean leaned back, braced with his hands on the mattress, and gave her his best suggestive smile. "Go on, suck that smoke. I don't mind."

Kira rolled her eyes. "Is everything about sex with you?"

"I was talking about smokes. Maybe you're the one with sex on the brain."

She huffed, sprang to her feet, and marched to her purse to yank open the zipper. Her dainty fingers dug inside the bag until she snagged something, her face lighting up with satisfaction as she extricated the foil-wrapped object and held it up for him to see. For a blood-scorching second, he thought it was a condom. But no. She held up a candy, sheathed in red-and-gold foil.

"This is what I wanted," she told him, chin lifted. "Whenever I resist the craving for a cigarette, I let myself have one chocolate."

As she licked her rosy lips, gaze locked on the candy, she slowly peeled the foil wrapping open, exposing the dark, decadent square of chocolate nestled inside it. With her thumb and forefinger, she plucked up the treat and slid it between her moist lips. They puckered slightly when she drew on the confection, and a little moan of pleasure escaped her.

A bolt of hot lust shot through Sean. The breath caught in his throat. He jerked forward, his attention riveted to her lips, to the way they worked in rhythmic motions as she devoured the chocolate, her eyes almost closed. He cracked open the vault door in his psyche, admitting a taste of her emotions inside him. Warm. Satiated.

Her lids fluttered open. Her eyes had gone glossy, lit by a fire within. A thread of heated desire unfurled from her, through him, snaking deep inside to tease his body and his...heart.

Sean slammed the vault door shut. *Do. Not. Care.*

But he could want. Take. Savor. He pushed up off the bed and sauntered to her. She darted her tongue out to swipe away a smear of chocolate with one languid stroke. He imagined pressing his mouth to her throat, dragging his lips down, down, down until he nuzzled his face between her breasts.

He snatched the foil wrapper from her fingers. "I can think of better ways to satisfy a craving."

CHAPTER ELEVEN

"Satisfy a craving?" Kira struggled to keep her tone even, to not expose the fact she'd gone warm and liquid in the most intimate places. How could she want Sean? He was a jerk most of the time. So what if she'd learned the reasons why. So what if he'd revealed his vulnerable side enough to make her feel oddly protective of him. He was still a jerk.

A hot one with smoldering green eyes and a body that made her want to climb all over him.

Kira ripped the candy wrapper from his fingers. "I don't need to know your ideas, and I definitely do not need to satisfy anything. I'm fine, thanks."

Never in this lifetime or whatever came after would she ever tell him she hadn't been craving a smoke. She'd been craving him.

The chocolate hadn't helped. Its rich, dark flavor reminded her of him, of their kiss last night and the way he had tasted—like sin.

He leaned in, his voice deep and sensuous. "I think you need a hit right now, but not from a cigarette."

The candy wrapper fell from her fingers, fluttering to the carpet. Her pulse accelerated, and her skin tingled.

Sean skimmed his thumb over her lips. "I'm not the only one who needs to get laid."

Breath. Hard to catch. Hard to hold in her lungs. It emerged as little panting exhalations. He was so close, too close, his firm body within an inch of hers.

He slid his hand up her cheek, diving his fingers into her hair to cradle her nape.

She angled her head back into his hand, her lips parting without her permission.

"You smell good," he rumbled, his mouth a hair's breadth from hers. "Taste good too, the way I remember it. Need to taste you again to be sure." He brushed his lips over her mouth. "Bet you'll taste like chocolate now. Sweet, with a dark undercurrent."

No breath. No thoughts. A need burgeoned inside her, searing and intoxicating.

He pressed his lips to hers tenderly.

She sagged against the dresser, her knees buckling under the weight of this lust for him.

He flicked his tongue out to tease her mouth, and she moaned low in her throat. His hand in her hair gripped her a smidgen tighter, those big fingers encompassing her nape.

Those hands. On her body. She wanted it like she'd never wanted anything, not even a cigarette.

"Sweet," he murmured against her lips.

And then he took her mouth, mashing his lips to hers while he thrust his tongue inside. She met his lashes with her own, savoring the flavor of him, the taste she couldn't quite describe, the way it erased her inhibitions and liquefied her entire body. Only the dresser and his hand on her neck held her up—until he slipped his other arm around her waist to hug her to him. She gasped into his mouth at the feel of the hard bulge in his pants.

He jerked away from her as if an electric shock had jolted him. His eyes flared wide for a split second, then narrowed to slits while his mouth compressed into a line.

She folded her arms over her chest, doing her damnedest to pretend that kiss hadn't left her breathless and confused. When she could speak in a normal voice without risk of stammering or panting, she said, "Don't glare at me. You started it."

"I know." His features relaxed a bit so he no longer seemed pissed, but he fisted his hands and veered his gaze away from her. "Shouldn't've done that."

"Because you think you don't want to be touched, right?" She just stifled a derisive snort. "That's a load of crap. You're afraid, I get it. After what happened with that girl, I can't imagine how awful that must feel. But it's clear you do want to be touched."

He gritted his teeth, slinging a sideways glare at her. "Not by you."

A spike of…something jammed into her chest. Resentment? Disappointment? She wasn't sure, but she knew one thing for certain. Hoping for any kind of intimacy with this man was a setup for disaster. Maybe he was too damaged for her, or anyone, to fix him.

Trying to save a person who didn't want saving would be the dumbest idea ever.

She stuffed her hands in her jeans pockets. Sean didn't like being this way, that much was clear. Maybe he did need someone to…What? Smack him upside the head and throttle some sense into him? She doubted anything less would make an impact.

Not saving him. Not going there.

Her cell phone rang, muffled by her purse.

She jumped, and Sean whipped his head around to nail her purse with a hard glare like the bag had committed a heinous crime. Kira tore open the zipper and dug out her phone, answering it on the fifth ring. One more ring and it would've gone to voicemail.

Before she could say hello, an all-too-familiar altered voice resonated in her ear.

"Your next assignment," the voice said, "will require travel. Go to Great Falls, Montana. Once you've arrived, we will call again with more instructions. You have three hours before we will call again, and you had better be in Great Falls by then."

"Is this another explosive device?"

"Think bigger, child. Think much bigger."

Click. The call ended.

Sean raised one brow. "What is it this time?"

"Not sure." She dropped the phone into her purse. "We have to get to Great Falls, Montana. They say they'll know when we arrive and call with more instructions. We have three hours to get there."

He cursed under his breath. "Another bomb?"

"They said to think bigger." She rubbed her chest, right over her breastbone, but the slithery feeling inside wouldn't abate. "I have a really bad feeling about this."

Sean gave a derisive huff. "Worse than when they ordered you to set off two bombs?"

"Yes. Much worse."

His expression crumbled into a kind of shock she recognized all too well from glimpsing her own face in the mirror. Every time the terrorists called with a new mission, she wore that look. She felt it in her soul. The horror of being at the mercy of lunatics bent on terrorizing the world for incomprehensible reasons.

She looked at Sean. "How do you think they'll know when we get to Montana?"

"Could be tracking our phones, or tracking us psychically."

"They can do that?"

He shrugged. "If they've got a powerful psychic on their side."

Great. Villains who commanded powerful psychics. How could she and Sean defend against that kind of spying?

"Three hours isn't much time," Sean said. He lodged one hand on his hip and scratched his head with the other. "We can't drive there fast enough, and we can't rely on commercial air travel. Topeka doesn't have any flights, I'm sure, and Kansas City is fifty miles away. Plus, I doubt they'd have a direct flight to Great Falls."

"What do you suggest we do?"

"Borrow a private jet."

———

THEY FOUND AMADOR AT THE HOSPITAL, IN THE WAITING ROOM, SEATed beside Grace on a cheapo couch. He held her hand with a familiarity that bristled Sean's nerves, but he said nothing because Grace's husband was in a frigging coma. She needed support, and Sean hadn't been here to give it.

But he had an idea of how to fix things.

Grace glanced up at Sean when he and Kira walked into the waiting room. Her smile was bittersweet, and her eyes were red.

"Hey," Sean said, parking his butt on the squat table in front of her. "How are you doing?"

She lifted one shoulder in a weak shrug. "I can't help him. It stinks."

The resentment in her tone told him it way more than stank. The way her voice cracked a little told him she was fighting to stay calm and think positive.

Sean took hold of her free hand, the one not suffocated in Amador's palm. "I've got an idea about that. I want to heal David."

"No," she said slowly, biting her lip and shaking her head once, "We've been through this already. I can't let you try. Your powers have been off for a while now, and besides, healing David might drain you to the point of sickness. I won't let that happen."

The decisive edge in her voice told him the old Grace was still in there. The stubborn woman who'd traveled thousands of miles to rescue her soul mate, braving murderous bad guys and the harsh desert to get to him.

"Listen, Grace," Sean began.

Amador cut him off. "Grace has made her decision. Respect it."

Oh, Sean really wanted to deck the bastard. So what if the guy had no friends or family of his own anymore? Sean had sympathized for about six months before Amador's glom-on-iness started to grate. Even Roland Wickham, Amador's right-hand man, had gotten sick of it and taken off two years ago. Amador claimed Wickham left without notice, leaving only a note to explain he was homesick for England. *Yeah, right.* Wickham had no doubt gotten weary of holding his boss's scattered wits together with his bare hands. Like anybody could manage that for long. Amador was nutty, batty, and loony all rolled up in one big ball of crackers.

Instead of decking Amador, Sean wrested Grace's hand from the other man's hold and clasped both her hands in his. Focusing on Grace—and only on Grace, despite Amador's irritated noise and the way he glowered at Sean—he said, "I've got help now."

He nodded toward Kira, who'd hung back near the doorway.

Grace glanced a Kira, then swiveled her gaze back to Sean. "I don't understand. Who is she?"

Oh crap. He'd forgotten to introduce them.

"This is Kira Magnusson," Sean told Grace. "She's a friend. The terrorists kidnapped her brother and—" Telling Grace about Kira's Bomb-Girl activities didn't seem wise right now. "And they're blackmailing her into doing what they want. We're still not sure what they really want, ultimately, but they're determined to cause trouble and hurt people. Anyway, Kira's helping me look for them."

"Okay," Grace said, sounding confused.

"The point is," Sean said, "Kira gave me a psychic assist earlier, and I think together we can get David fixed up."

Kira gave him a confused look this time, which he noticed peripherally.

Sean grasped Grace's hands more firmly and looked straight into her eyes. "Let us try. Please."

Grace gnawed on her bottom lip for a moment, the sheen of burgeoning tears in her eyes. "Okay. But if you kill yourself doing this, I'll hunt you down in the crossroads and whup your hide."

"I know." He almost smiled at her vow of retribution. Releasing her hands, he squeezed her shoulder. "It'll work."

Grace left to find a nurse and ask about taking two friends into David's room in the ICU.

Kira sidled up to Sean and muttered, "What are you doing?"

"Saving a life."

"What if we can't?"

He'd asked himself the same question, but he refused to consider failure as a possible outcome. Negative thinking had interfered with his powers before, but he couldn't allow it to interfere today, not with David's life on the line. "If we can bring Edward back from the dead, we can heal David's injuries."

"I don't think it's the same thing. Edward must not have been really dead, not yet. His heart stopped, but he didn't have wounds." She laid a hand on Sean's upper arm. "David's injuries might be too severe."

"You don't know that," Sean snapped, realizing he sounded like a jerk but not caring. He would not leave David in a coma if he had even the remotest shot at fixing his best friend. "I'll do it by myself if you're scared to help."

"I am scared, but not for myself." She squeezed his arm gently. "Grace said this could kill you. And you aren't exactly operating on all thrusters with your powers, are you?"

"Don't worry about me," he said, his voice harsh like it belonged to somebody else.

Kira withdrew her hand, her lips cinched into a tight expression. "Have it your way."

She hadn't said whether she'd help him this time.

The three of them—Sean, Kira, and Amador—waited in awkward silence for Grace to return. Amador kept giving Sean weird looks, like the guy knew something or thought he knew something about Sean but wouldn't say so. Screw Amador. They had bigger problems than one nutty guy who wanted to get in Grace's pants even while her husband lay in a coma. Sean would've loved to punch Amador for the way he'd glommed onto Grace, clearly determined to take advantage of David's absence and Grace's weakness to make a play for her. Amador needed a good beat-down.

The guy had always had a thing for Grace.

But she was devoted to David, and that pissed off Amador.

Sean knew this, despite Amador doing a bang-up job of concealing his irritation. Maybe no one else would've noticed, but Sean did. Before he'd locked up his empathic abilities, he'd sensed Amador's true feelings—and it had given him a serious case of the creeps.

Could Amador have something to do with the terrorists?

No, that was crazy. Sure, Amador was crazy, but conspiring with terrorists...

Kira poked his arm and murmured, "What's wrong? You've got that storm-cloud look on your face again."

"What?" Sean glanced down at her, noticing the slight upward curve of her lips and the sparkle in her eyes. "Not in the mood for jokes."

"I wasn't making a joke." She stretched her lips into a closed-mouth smile. "Teasing you, sure. But not joking."

"Why are you teasing me about the fact you think I look mean or whatever?"

"Decided you need more teasing to loosen you up."

He stared at her for a moment, baffled by her inappropriate humor and charmed by it at the same time. She wasn't afraid of him. Even when he'd held her hostage, she hadn't acted terrified of him. She'd razzed him then too.

"You do seem upset," Kira told him, with no humor.

Sean took hold of her arm and guided her to the farthest corner of the waiting room. He bent his head closer to hers and said, "It's Amador. Something about him is…off." Sean sighed. "More than usual."

"I don't understand. He seems genuinely concerned."

"You don't know Gabriel Amador like I do." Sean glanced at the other man, who was watching them with an oddly calculating expression. Amador noticed Sean watching him and reverted to a bland expression. Sean turned back to Kira. "I'll explain later, but trust me, Amador is not someone you want to put your trust in."

"Grace seems to trust him."

"She's got blinders on where he's concerned. Never could figure out why. Maybe she feels sorry for him." At Kira's questioning look, Sean added, "Explain later. Okay?"

She nodded.

Grace walked into the waiting room, waving for Sean and Kira to follow.

Amador got up as if he intended to go with them.

"Stay here," Sean said, meaning to sound sharp this time.

The jackass looked to Grace, clearly hoping for permission from her, but she just shrugged. "This is a delicate operation. Sean's right, you should stay here."

Something flashed on Amador's face, but it passed too swiftly for Sean to identify it. The guy sat down.

Grace led Sean and Kira through double doors that swung open for them automatically and down a corridor to the ICU. They entered David's room where he lay on the bed as motionless as a corpse. Only the faint rise and fall of his chest suggested he was alive.

Sean's chest tightened with a pang behind his ribs.

David was pale, hooked up to multiple machines. Though breathing on his own, he languished in a limbo Sean couldn't comprehend. Would he hear them if they spoke? Would he understand what they were about to do? Or did he exist somewhere beyond his body, beyond this room? The crossroads, maybe?

Sean spoke to Grace. "You said he's in there, you can feel him. Did you go to the crossroads?"

Grace shook her head. "I can feel him through our innate connection. I tried to access the crossroads, but I'm too weak to get there."

Weak with grief and pain and fear and exhaustion.

Sean clasped her hand. "We're not losing him."

Grace squeezed his hand, then let go and clamped her hands under her arms. She backed up to the wall across from the foot of the bed.

Sean approached the side of the bed and gestured for Kira to come up beside him. When she did, he slipped his hand into her palm, his fingers laced with hers. As one, they closed their fingers around each other. A current zinged through him from their joined hands.

"You ready?" he asked.

She nodded. "Let's do this."

He spread his free hand on David's chest.

Energy flowed through him, through his palm, into David's body.

Nothing happened. He sensed the energy seeping into David, but it couldn't gain enough momentum to regenerate the cells, fizzling out before it reached the most damaged parts of him.

"Dammit," Sean hissed, even as he struggled to pull in more power, to no avail.

"What is it?" Kira asked in a rough whisper.

"It's not enough. David's injuries are too severe." Sean flung his hands up to cover his face, scrubbing as if he might clear his mind that way. Healing someone whose heart had stopped due to psychic manipulation was one thing, but repairing damage caused by a very real, very physical explosion proved something else altogether. And it didn't help he'd been suppressing his powers.

My fault. The thought burst in his mind. If David didn't recover, if he died, it would be Sean's fault. He held the power to fix this but couldn't make it happen because he'd repressed his gifts. Kira was right. He was repressed.

"What can we do?" Kira asked.

"Need more power," Sean said. "We have to get into the crossroads."

Chapter Twelve

He zeroed in on Kira's eyes, willing her shock and confusion to melt away. How could he expect her not to be stunned? He'd suggested doing the one thing he'd failed at yesterday and earlier today—accessing the crossroads to gather more psychic energy. He'd failed at teaching Kira to do it too. They had to try, though, because he would not run off to Montana while David lay comatose in a hospital, his spirit and his body withering away.

David had saved his life, literally and metaphorically. Sean owed him everything.

No backing out. Despite the cold knots cinching tight in his gut and the cold tension stiffening his body, he would make this happen. He would heal David. He had to.

His gaze flicked to Grace, where she hunched in the corner of the room, her haunted eyes locked on her husband's inert body.

Teeth gritted, Sean focused on David. He would fix this—for David, for Grace, and for Abby. Sean would heal David even if he had to drain every iota of energy in his body and his mind.

Even if it killed him.

"How do we do that?" Kira whispered. "I can't get there, and you said you couldn't either."

"I'm repressed, remember?" He twisted his lips in a sardonic smile. "But this is what we've got to do. Fear can be a great motivator."

"Then abject terror must be the key to accomplishing the impossible."

"Not impossible. We can do this if we both believe we can."

Her eyebrows rose a smidgen, and her lips kinked up at the corners. "You're expressing optimism? Wow, that's twice in one day."

"Don't get used to it." He clamped his hand around hers. "Follow my lead."

Kira nodded.

Sean closed his eyes—then cracked one eye open to peek at her, just to make sure she'd closed her eyes. She had, so he shut his own again. He drew in a slow, deep breath and released it gradually, willing his muscles to unwind. For Kira's benefit, he murmured, "Relax."

Her hand, enclosed in his, loosened the tiniest bit, and he sensed her relaxing into the moment, into the connection their joined hands provided. A modest current of power coursed between them, through their palms. They needed more.

Release the vault.

A frisson of anxiety slithered through him, but he'd made a vow, and he never reneged on a promise to the ones he loved. He took another deep breath and exhaled in a rush this time, shedding the anxiety like a wet dog shaking water off its body. Some of the fear lingered, until a sweet pulse of Kira-flavored energy flowed into him, triggering a memory of their kiss earlier, of her soft lips and the enticing if all-too-brief taste of her he'd enjoyed. Buoyed by the memory and the sensation of a sliver of her inside him, he let go of the fear.

The chain that had fettered his psyche crumbled away.

He soared out of his body with Kira tethered to him, flying through the dark tunnel toward a destination beyond the comprehension of the average human. They burst out into a field of stars peppered across an inky blackness. The sensation of chilled air on his skin was a phantom, he knew, his mind's way of making sense of his surroundings. Nothing physical existed here. And yet, he felt his hand around Kira's and her presence beside him. Phantoms, but he'd take them.

The stars glittered all around them, white pinpoints in the darkness.

He'd done it. He'd gotten them into the crossroads.

Something nipped at him, seeking, testing, an unseen force hungry for power.

No, not again. The same force had pushed him out last time, but he would not let it happen again. Drawing on the energy trickling into him from Kira, he shoved the hungry force away.

Free. Unfettered.

More than his astral body had broken free. For the first time in two months, he'd unleashed his powers.

And more than psychic energy pulsed down the link with Kira. He experienced her emotions, just the surface ones but enough to send a thrill racing through him. He'd really done it. He was liberated.

God, it felt good.

No time to revel in the freedom. He let his mind go blank as he floated with Kira amid the field of stars. He threw open the gates of his psyche, letting the energy inherent in the crossroads pour into him and into Kira through the connection of their hands. A sliver of fear sliced through her, he sensed it, but she let it go with a rush of heady exhilaration.

She'd never been to the crossroads before. Of course she'd be excited.

But her enthusiasm swirled through him laced with another kind of excitement. Desire. He struggled to ignore it because getting turned on wouldn't help them right now. The connection they'd forged to get this far mimicked genuine intimacy in many ways, but it wasn't intimacy. It was shared power. Shared lust. Nothing more.

When he'd absorbed enough energy, he shut off the spigot. Too much power was bad, Grace had warned him once upon a time. He trusted her assessment. Invigorated by the energy, he whisked Kira through the void of the tunnel.

He slammed back into his body with a sharp grunt.

Kira's gasp told him she'd returned too.

The power surged through them both, hot and urgent, desperate to serve a purpose.

Sean slapped his palm on David's chest. Sean's hand glowed around the edges as if the light emanated from his palm. He funneled everything he had into the act of healing, visualizing tissues and cells, commanding them to regenerate with a level of power he'd never achieved before. It scorched in his veins, ripped through his mind, sizzled on his skin even as goosebumps erupted up and down his body.

David's chest heaved once.

More energy. More. Targeting damaged cells. Rebuilding and reshaping the molecules.

Sean couldn't breathe, couldn't move, wouldn't stop the energy from performing its task. Never had he wielded so much power. Maybe the intensity of it should've unsettled him, but Kira's warm and calming aura centered him, steadied him, kept him sane.

The moment he sensed the last shred of damage had repaired itself, he yanked his hand away from David. Sean was breathing hard, his heart racing, his body alive with power. He glanced at Kira, and her eyes nearly undid him. Her pupils blown, she locked her gaze on him with her irises burning like rings of blue fire. Her lips had turned a darker pink, and a beautiful blush tinted her cheeks.

Desire. Hot. Hard. Unstoppable.

He battled against the urge to drag Kira into his arms and kiss her again like he had after healing Edward. The impulse raged stronger than before, thanks to the massive amount of energy they'd both ingested. He needed to devour her mouth, to run his hands all over her body, to meld with her in a very physical way. But he couldn't do that here in the ICU with Grace huddled in the corner and David lying unconscious on the bed.

David.

Sean ripped his hand away from Kira's, severing their link. He bent over the bed, scrutinizing David's face, searching for a sign of…anything.

David's eyes darted behind his lids. His chest rose and fell on deepening breaths. The pallor of his cheeks had given way to the faint pinkness of life.

He was alive, yes. But would he wake up?

A groan resonated in David's chest. His eyelids fluttered.

Sean stepped back, waving for Grace to come.

Just as she hurried to the bedside, David's eyes opened. He blinked rapidly, then focused his clear blue eyes on his wife—and smiled.

"Hi," he said, his voice a little hoarse.

Grace burst into tears of joy. Her trembling lips formed a lopsided smile. "Hi."

David lifted his head off the pillow, glancing around with a furrowed brow. "Why is everybody staring at me like I just came back from the dead?"

His wife flung her arms around him and kissed him—on the mouth, on the cheek, on the forehead, on the nose, anywhere she could.

Sean lodged his hands in his pants pockets. "You kinda did come back from the dead, man. You were in a coma."

David looked down at his body, the parts he could see with his wife plastered to him kissing his ear and his cheek. He raised one arm to gaze at the IV attached to it, his expression curious. Next, he took in the medical equipment around him, and the heart rate monitor measuring the beats.

Grace tore herself away from him long enough to perch her behind on the bed and seize his hands, kissing each of his knuckles in turn. Her tears had dwindled, but she still seemed vulnerable like she couldn't quite believe David was awake. She brushed her fingers over his cheek. "How do you feel?"

"Fine." He shrugged. "Like I never almost died and fell into a coma."

She kissed him full on the mouth, with tongue and everything.

Kira averted her gaze, her mouth warped with a mostly suppressed smile.

Sean looked away too, giving Grace and David a modicum of privacy. After a minute, though, he had to interrupt. Clearing his throat, he said, "Kira and I have to go."

"Kira?" David said, and he glanced at Sean's companion.

"It's a long story," Sean said. "Grace can explain. We're trying to find the bastards who made the bomb that—" *Almost killed you.* Sean's throat tightened. "The bomb at the cafe, and another one in a movie theater."

Kira waved to David. "I'm Kira Magnusson, by the way."

"Nice to meet you," David said cautiously, his confusion evident on his face. "Seems like I missed a lot."

Grace cupped his face with her palm. "I'll explain it, honey. But yeah, you missed a lot."

She gazed into his eyes, hers full of love.

Sean coughed. "I'll call you guys later, but we have to go now. Be careful. Those creeps are still out there and still want to do more havoc-wreaking."

"We'll watch our backs," David said. "You be careful too, Sean. You can't keep healing everybody without exacting a toll."

"I know." Sean rested a hand on Kira's back, guiding her toward the door. "See you guys later."

They'd see each other again if he and Kira stopped the bad guys. Otherwise…

He couldn't think about that right now.

In the waiting room, Amador was pacing with his hands linked behind his back. When he spotted Sean and Kira, he stopped moving, his expression expectant.

"David's awake," Sean said. "He's all fixed up."

Sean swore disappointment flashed across Amador's face, but he couldn't be sure. Maybe his dislike of the man made him see things that weren't there.

"I need a favor," Sean said, resisting the urge to grind his teeth. He hated asking Amador for anything, but they had to get to their destination fast. "We need to borrow your jet."

———

THE JET TOUCHED DOWN AT THE GREAT FALLS INTERNATIONAL AIR-port thirty minutes shy of the deadline laid down by the terrorists. Kira would've loved to admire the scenery, since she'd never visited Montana before, but they weren't tourists. They were marionettes for madmen.

When Sean had asked to borrow Gabriel Amador's jet, the man had agreed without hesitation. On the plane, Sean had expressed his surprise.

"First, he tells me not to get involved," Sean had said, scratching behind his ear, "and later he tells me I'm not equipped to handle the mission. Then, he gives us his jet without any bitching or insults. I'll never understand that guy."

"Maybe you should stop trying," Kira had told him.

Sean had only grunted.

Gabriel Amador had wanted to come with them—insisted on it, actually—but Sean talked him out of the idea by reminding him Grace would still need support. She could tell Sean hated encouraging Amador to hang around Grace, but it seemed like the only tactic that would convince the man not to tag along on this mission.

The puppet master pulling their strings wouldn't like that one bit.

Sean rented them a car using a credit card Amador had given him. The card had no limit. She'd noted the way Sean's mouth tightened when Amador gave him the credit card, but he'd accepted because they had no choice. Kira didn't have any money, and Sean seemed not to either. Thanks to Amador's financial assistance, they secured a car and a motel room.

They had just walked into the room when the phone on the bedside table rang.

Both of them froze, their gazes snapping to each other.

Sean moved to grab the phone.

Kira stayed his hand with her own. "I should answer."

He nodded and sat down on the bed.

Neither of them wondered how their enemy had gotten the phone number here. No point in wondering since the villains seemed to have vast resources at their disposal.

She picked up the phone. "We're here."

"We know," the eerily calm, distorted voice said. "You are in place for your next mission. We realize this one is more complex and will require more time to accomplish, so we're granting you eighteen hours to rest and recharge your powers. We need you both at full strength."

Complex? She clutched her belly with her free hand, exchanging tense looks with Sean. Though he couldn't hear the phone conversation, he must've sensed her mounting unease. A complex mission that required eighteen hours of psychic recharging beforehand? This sounded so much worse than the two explosive devices they'd forced her to detonate.

"I want to talk to my brother," she said. Maybe it was partly a delaying tactic since she dreaded hearing the details of what they would make her and Sean do next. Mostly, though, she needed to hear Caleb's voice to know he was all right.

"We will grant your request," the voice said.

A scuffling sound followed and then Caleb spoke through the phone, his voice not altered like the kidnapper's was. "Kiki?"

She choked back a sob of relief. "Yes, baby, it's me. Are you okay?"

"Yeah, I'm okay." He sounded tired and a little depressed, but otherwise normal. "I want to go home."

"I know. Soon, I promise."

More scuffling. The unknown voice returned, distorted as usual. "That's enough."

At least she knew Caleb was still alive. How long could she keep promising him they'd be reunited soon? She had no clue if she was lying about that since she had no clue what these madmen might do next.

"Your instructions," the voice said, "will be delivered later. After you have rested and are ready for the mission. Do not attempt to thwart our plans or locate us, or your brother will be punished."

Click. The call disconnected.

Kira slapped the phone back into its cradle, biting down on her bottom lip hard.

Sean leaped up, grasping her upper arms. "What did they say to you?"

"We're supposed to rest and recharge our powers for eighteen hours, then they'll call back with instructions for our next mission." She chewed her lip. "If we try to stop their plans or find them, they'll hurt Caleb."

Kira fought the tears burning in her eyes, refusing to let them roll down her cheeks, blinking furiously to keep them at bay.

"Your brother?" Sean asked.

"He's okay." She forced herself to stop gnawing her lip, squared her shoulders, and lifted her chin. "We have to find them. Stop them. They'll hurt Caleb anyway, I'm sure of it. They'll probably kill all of us once we've done all their insane missions for them."

"No more missions." Sean's voice was gruff, but his grip on her had eased. "We've got eighteen hours to hunt them down."

She considered the terrorist's words for a moment. "Isn't it odd they gave us eighteen hours with nothing to do? They must figure we'll try to find them since they told us not to. It doesn't make sense."

"None of it makes sense. We're dealing with whackjobs."

"I know, but even crazed terrorists have an agenda."

"Yeah, terrorizing lots of people. That's the agenda." Sean frisked his hands up and down her arms. "We'll find Caleb and rescue him."

"How?"

Sean guided her to the bed, and they both sat down. The mattress creaked. The room smelled of stale cigarettes and mold, but she couldn't complain about the accommodations. People on the run didn't have the luxury of…luxury.

"I'm all Caleb has," she said. "He's sure I'll come for him. But I can't risk more lives just to save my baby brother."

Sean studied her for a long moment, his expression unreadable. "Where are your parents?"

Kira blinked at him. "What?"

"Your parents. What happened to them? Your brother's been kidnapped, but nobody called the cops about it. Nobody calls you, either. You said your parents are gone, but they're not dead."

"They're alive as far as I know." She focused on her hands, which had begun to wring themselves on her lap. "I haven't seen or heard from them in sixteen months. They took off for Uganda on a humanitarian mission. They'd never been very civic-minded before, but they needed any excuse to get as far away from home as possible. As far away from me and Caleb as possible."

"Why?"

She clamped her hands together to still their wringing. "My powers emerged when I was seventeen. My parents adjusted to the reality of psychic abilities pretty well, I thought, better than I did. I was twenty when they abandoned me and Caleb, leaving nothing but a crappy little note as explanation. The day before, everything seemed fine. I still don't understand what happened. They just…left while we were asleep."

"Jesus. I'm sorry."

The tone of his voice made her look up at him. He sounded genuinely sickened by the idea of parents forsaking their children, and his expression matched his voice. He seemed stunned, like he couldn't quite comprehend how anyone could do such a thing.

"What was your mom like?" she asked. "You said she was okay with you having powers."

"She was. I mean, she worried about me, but she never made me feel like a freak." He gazed at the window, shielded by curtains, his gaze going distant. "Mom was awesome."

"You really never met your dad?"

With a groaning sigh, he aimed a warped smile at her. "No, I never met my dad. Don't even know his name or what he looked like. Mom never wanted to talk about him, so I figured he wasn't a nice guy. Whenever I asked about my dad, she'd change the subject. I didn't push."

Kira turned toward him slightly. She couldn't imagine not knowing who her parents were. They might've turned into jerks, but at least she knew where she'd come from. "Didn't you ever want to know about your dad?"

"Sure, but I gave that up after I met my sweet old granddad." Sean laughed without humor, the sound harsh and tinged with anger. "When my gramps turned out to be a psycho scientist bent on torturing me and digging the powers out of my head, I figured I was better off not opening any more cans of family worms. One slimy, spineless bastard in the family tree was enough."

"I can't imagine finding out you're related to someone as awful as that." She watched his face, though he'd gone stoic again, retreating behind a mask to escape the horrors of his past. *Can't blame him.* "You said before that Tesler was related to your mom, right?"

"He was my mom's father. She never talked about him, and I kind of thought he was dead. Mom probably hoped he was." Sean's expression darkened. "Now he's six feet under with the maggots, where he belongs."

She studied his eyes, their green irises shimmering in the light from the bedside lamp. After learning about his family, she understood why he preferred to put on an ironclad facade and lock up his emotions—and his powers. He'd shown her glimpses of the man beneath that facade, a complex person composed partly of a teenage boy who'd lost everything and suffered more than anyone should, and partly of the adult who struggled to move on while coping with the fact he'd inadvertently tormented someone. The girl, Bree, had torn open old wounds that had never quite healed.

Kira settled her hand over his where he'd crooked his fingers into his thigh. "You worry you're like your grandfather, don't you?"

He ground his teeth, a muscle popping in his jaw. "Karl Tesler was insane."

"You are nothing like him."

Sean grunted. "You've known me for less than two days. And I kidnapped you."

"I understand why now." She slipped her fingers under his palm, clasping his cold hand. "And I forgive you."

He stopped blinking, and his features went slack. "You can't."

"After everything you've been through," she said, sidling a little closer, "you've earned a few mistakes. Besides, your best friend had just been seriously injured in an explosion I caused. We've both made big mistakes. It's time to forgive ourselves and move forward."

"You were protecting your brother. I was—"

"Protecting your family." She raised her other hand to his cheek, his skin cool against her palm. "You are not a bad man."

Their gazes had become locked, and she couldn't have looked away if she'd wanted to. The connection between them, it was more than psychic powers or traumatic experiences. They shared a pain no one else could understand. The pain of doing terrible things in the name of sparing the ones they loved, sparing the world.

She skimmed her thumb across his lips. "We do these things so no one else has to, but that doesn't mean we have to punish ourselves. We deserve happiness too."

His breathing had grown labored. She fought to catch her breath too, entranced by the green of his eyes and the way his skin seemed to be warming under her touch. Dragging her fingers down his jaw, she realized he *was* getting warmer. A matching warmth blossomed inside her, spreading out into her entire body, settling low in her belly as a delicious pressure. Her hand floated down to his chest, her fingers exploring the muscles concealed under his shirt.

"You don't want this," he said, his voice a rough whisper. "Not with me."

"Don't wreck the moment, Romeo." She gave him a playful smile. "I'm trying to seduce you."

Sean choked on a breath. "We can't. My powers—"

"Everything will be fine. Trust me."

"You can't know—"

Kira took his face in her hands and scraped her lips over his. With their mouths in contact, she murmured, "Shut up."

His lips curled into a sexy smile. "Yes, ma'am."

Both his hands landed on her back, gliding up to cover her shoulder blades.

She sagged into him, one hand trapped between their chests, the other resting on his thigh. She squeezed his leg, relishing the firmness of his thick, powerful thigh.

He plowed both hands into her hair, caging her head. "No turning back now."

"Don't want to turn back."

A sound, half growl and half groan, reverberated in his chest and tickled the stiff peaks of her nipples, crushed to his body. She gasped, her mouth falling open.

He devoured her mouth in the deepest kiss she'd ever experienced.

No turning back.

CHAPTER THIRTEEN

WHEN KIRA HAD OPENED HER MOUTH, SEAN HADN'T BEEN ABLE to stop himself from taking advantage. He'd plunged inside with abandon, savoring the sweet flavor of her, loving the way she responded with the same reckless passion that had taken hold of him. Their tongues tangled and separated, teased and glided over each other. No kiss had ever been this good.

They shouldn't be doing this, no way, but he couldn't break away from her. Touching him, getting close to him when they had clothes on, those things endangered her enough. But doing this…In a few minutes, they'd be naked on this bed together. He knew it. The last time he'd had sex, he'd tormented an innocent woman. Not on purpose, but that didn't matter. His powers had hurt her. Bree had thought she understood what she was getting into with him, with his powers, but she'd known nothing.

Kira was different. She'd experienced his powers. More than that, she'd shared them in a way more intimate than sex. They'd forged a psychic bond.

She shoved her hands under his shirt, whisking her soft, warm palms up his chest to push his shirt up over his head. They tore their mouths apart, both gasping for breath. He tossed his shirt aside, not giving a damn where it landed. They ripped each other's clothes off, alternately kissing and groping, sometimes both at the same time, until they wound up naked and sprawled across the bed at a diagonal on top of the bedspread.

He pushed up on straight arms to gaze down at the woman underneath him. Kira was gorgeous. With her pink cheeks, swollen lips, and soft eyes, she looked like an angel with a naughty streak. She'd wanted to seduce him, and holy smokes, she'd done it. He let his gaze travel down her body so he could admire her perfect breasts and the taut nipples jutting up from them, her wide hips and the gentle curve of her waist.

"You're perfect," he whispered, his tone expressing the awe that swept through him when he drank in the sight of her nude body. She was perfect. And despite knowing what he'd done to Bree, she wanted to be with him. Here. Now.

She lighted her palms on his chest and skated them up to his shoulders. "I want you. Please."

God, he wanted her too. But his powers…

As if she'd heard his thoughts, Kira cupped his face and said, "I've felt your powers before. I can handle it."

Maybe she could read his mind. They were both psychics after all.

He pressed his lips to hers, then kissed a trail down her throat and between her breasts. He paused there to draw one nipple into his mouth, suckling and flicking his tongue over the stiff peak.

She gasped and tunneled the fingers of one hand into his hair.

The scent of her arousal teased his senses. He dragged his lips down her belly, circling his tongue inside her navel, and kept going down, down, down until the hairs at the juncture of her thighs tickled his chin.

A soft moan whispered out of her as she lifted her hips.

He slid his hands between her legs, one palm on the inside of each thigh, and eased her open for him. When he caught sight of her flesh, glistening and pink, his breaths grew ragged. *Perfect.*

"Sean," she moaned, clutching at his head. "Yes, please."

Taste her. He couldn't resist the urge. Without a thought for what might happen, he gave in to the desire for her. His mouth descended on her sweet, soft flesh, and with every throaty moan from her, his exploration grew fiercer. She tasted like heaven, like everything good in the universe, like…salvation. His salvation. He tormented her nub while she thrashed under him, kept tormenting her until her breaths came quick and sharp, then he thrust a finger inside her wet sheath. Then another finger. And another. She bucked and cried out, riding his fingers to the rhythm set by his mouth on her nub.

Her body went rigid.

A hoarse cry burst out of her as her back flattened into the mattress, her fingers dug into the covers, and her body pulsated around his fingers.

She went limp, panting, her cheeks ruddy.

He raised his head. The sight of her, so soft and willing, made his chest ache. He wanted her, yeah, but he wanted more than to get off. He wanted to share everything with her.

But his powers…A cold pit congealed in his gut. His every muscle seemed to transmute into brittle steel. He couldn't do this.

She pushed up on her elbows, gazing at him with complete understanding. "It's okay. If you're not ready for this, we can stop." Her luscious mouth curled into a sexy smile. "But I'm really hoping we don't."

"I don't want to hurt you."

"You won't." She stretched out one hand to caress his cheek. "I trust you."

He swallowed against the tightness in his throat, his mouth suddenly parched. "What if I can't control it?"

She went silent for a moment, her fingertips dancing along his jaw. "Do it on purpose. Open up your empathic powers. Try it before you get too caught up in things to think about controlling yourself."

"I don't—Are you sure you want me to do that?"

"Yes, I'm sure."

He stared at her, unable to comprehend that she wanted him to invade her psyche, to steal her emotions and inject his own into her. Bree had wailed and beat him, screamed he was a rapist, kicked and clawed and—

"I'm not her," Kira said. "Psychic stuff doesn't scare me. You don't scare me. Give it a try and see how it goes."

His chest seemed to have a weight bearing down on it even though he hovered above her on hands and knees. He couldn't pull in a full breath. She wanted this. She wanted him, powers and all.

"Okay," he said shakily. "But you have to promise to tell me if anything I do makes you uncomfortable."

"I promise." She painted a cross over her heart with one slender finger.

Sean summoned all his willpower to haul in a long, slow breath and release it bit by bit. He shut his eyes for a second, then forced himself to keep breathing in a regular rhythm. *Slow and easy. Just keep breathing.* He could do this without hurting Kira. She trusted him.

He opened the vault door a crack.

Warmth stole inside him from her, the supple and sultry heat of desire. This was the surface, though, and he needed to go deeper to know for sure she could handle it. Handle him.

He pushed the door open farther.

Emotions poured into him, so many he couldn't sort them out. Sympathy. Affection. Fear for the future, tempered by excitement about the present, this moment, here with him. He let his eyes drift shut, floating on the tide of sensations from her.

"All the way," she murmured. "Let go, Sean."

He shoved the door wide open.

Kira. Warm and strong, like a summer breeze, full of life and power. Sizzling currents of electric energy danced in the metaphysical space between them, borne from the psychic powerhouse contained within her. Everything about her turned him on, from her psychic abilities to her sarcasm and especially the way she understood him so thoroughly after two days like she'd been meant to be his and he was meant to be hers. Never before had he believed in fate, but this woman made him believe.

She whimpered.

His eyes shot open. He gaped at her, terrified she was suffering because of his emotions, forced into her in a torrent.

Eyes half closed, she worshiped him with her gaze, soft and heated. Her breasts rose and fell on heavy breaths. A rosy flush dusted her creamy skin. She slid her tongue out to moisten her lips, their pink color having turned a dusky shade of rose.

Not terrified. Aroused.

A pulse of lust ripped through him.

She whimpered again, her neck arching, her mouth falling open.

That sound, it had nothing to do with pain. It was all pleasure.

"I can feel it," she murmured, her voice throatier than he'd ever heard it. "I can feel you. What you want. What you need." She gasped, her back bowing. "I need it too."

He hadn't even touched her, and she seemed about to come.

But he had touched her. With his mind. With his emotions.

Her desire pulsated through him, hot and liquid, irresistible.

She spread her thighs, bending her knees just a little.

An invitation.

How many times had he fantasized about a woman wanting him this way? A heady rush swept through him until cold reality crashed down around him.

Sean dropped his head. "I don't have a condom."

Kira placed one finger under his chin and urged him to look up at her. "I'm on the pill. We can skip the condom this one time. And honestly, if you don't do something right now I'm going to lose my mind."

"Can't have that," he said with a smirk, though underneath the humor he experienced a pang of something else. Something way more intimate. It felt like tenderness.

She latched one leg around his hip, tugging lightly, all but begging him to take her.

And at that moment, every last shred of the fear vaporized.

He plunged into her fast and hard, driving deep inside her hot, slick sheath. He plowed in and out, lost to the sensation of her flesh around him and the drugging scent of her desire, the little noises she made that drove him wild, the vision of her breasts jostling with every inward stroke. She locked both legs around him, offering up her body for the taking. And he took her. With swift, strong thrusts that had her moaning and clutching at his shoulders. He pushed deeper, as deep as he could possibly go, desperate to meld with her in every way while their powers surged inside them, between them, an indescribable ebb and flow. He could no longer distinguish his powers from hers, his needs from hers, and that thought should've unnerved him. Instead, it amped up his lust until the world telescoped down to the two of them on this bed, bodies entwined, powers entwined, and he couldn't hold back anymore. He pounded into her with a relentless need, bouncing her body off the mattress with every wild thrust.

The bed creaked and thumped on the floor. Their bodies slapped together. The sounds they made filled the room, mingling until he couldn't tell which cries were hers and which were his. They had joined completely, as one in their pleasure and their powers.

Energy coursed through him. Tingling, electric energy.

She dug her nails into his shoulders, squeezing her eyes shut as her mouth opened wide on a cry of pure ecstasy. Her body clenched around him, wave after wave of her pleasure, and he lost it. He spilled himself inside her until he couldn't give any more, his shouts echoing in the room.

He collapsed onto the bed beside her, tugging her close, tucked under his arm. Their bodies were slicked with sweat, and the scent of sex permeated the room.

"Wow," she said between panting breaths. "That was…"

She shook her head as if she couldn't find a word to describe it.

"Yeah," he said, not even trying to describe the experience. "It was."

"I wish we could stay like this forever, cocooned in our own little world." She draped an arm over his chest, snuggling into him. "But we can't."

"No, we can't." He kissed the top of her head, inhaling the perfume of her shampoo mixed with the smell of sweat. "We have to find the terrorists."

"How?"

"In the crossroads."

KIRA DREW FIGURE-EIGHTS ON SEAN'S CHEST WITH HER INDEX FINger, loving the feel of his muscles and his smooth skin. This body had just taken her to the heights of pleasure, delivering more satisfaction than she'd ever known in her life. She wanted him to make love to her again, not remind her of the looming threat of unknown terrorist acts and the fact the world's fate rested in their hands.

Make love? She didn't love him. Not yet, anyway.

She gave herself a mental eye roll. Sure, that was the part of her thoughts she ought to ponder deeply right now. Sex. Not whatever horrible things the bad guys would make them do next.

He nuzzled her hair.

A pang ached in her chest, and she couldn't prevent herself from saying, "I like you, Sean."

With his face in her hair, his chuckle was somewhat muffled. "I like you too, Kira."

"Don't laugh. Yesterday, you said we don't like each other. So, I thought I should make it clear." She pressed her lips to his chest, then dragged them to his collarbone, peeking up at him through her lashes. "I like you now."

"Message received." Humor glinted in his eyes and twitched his lips, making him seem younger, not burdened by guilt and fear. "I've decided I'll put up with you."

She slapped his chest. "You can't take back saying you like me."

"Not taking it back." His expression turned serious, putting an end to their playful exchange. "I don't get what these terrorists want. They instigated two explosions and didn't take responsibility for them. Now, they want us to wait around for a day. It doesn't make sense."

"I told you that earlier." She kept a hand on his chest, unwilling to give up the physical connection yet. "What if they're not terrorists? What if they have some other purpose besides scaring everybody?"

He threaded his fingers through her hair, teasing her scalp. "Like what?"

"I don't know." She chewed on the inside of her cheek. "Maybe it's got more to do with us. Our powers."

"Your powers, you mean. They had no idea I'd be at the cafe."

"Are you sure?"

He combed her hair with his fingers. "Right after it happened, I thought maybe the attack was aimed at me and David. Doesn't make sense, though. Nobody could've known we'd be there. David showed up at my apartment that day and practically abducted me to that restaurant. His version of an intervention. He picked the cafe because he drove past it on his way to my place. None of it was planned."

"But we're dealing with psychics. One of them must've caused Edward's heart attack." She sat up, propped on one elbow. "Maybe they've got somebody who can see the future or track people like GPS."

"Maybe. The only way to find out is to find them—in the crossroads."

"Together? You and me?"

"No, I thought I'd get a dog to go with me." He tucked his hands under his head. "Yeah, with you. Unless it's too scary."

"The crossroads doesn't scare me. Lunatics with murky plans do." She shoved a hand through her hair, and her breasts jiggled, attracting Sean's attention. Though his lustful gaze triggered a new ache between her thighs, she told him, "We better get a move on if we're going to hunt down these crazies."

For the first time since they'd met, he hit her with a genuine smile. "I'd rather lie here and admire your tits, the way they wiggle when you move your arms, but you're right. We have to do this."

They got up and got dressed without saying a word to each other.

Sean patted her butt through her jeans. "Shame to cover up this body."

"Ticking clock, remember?"

"Yeah, thanks for the reminder. I almost forgot."

The sardonic tone in his voice assured her he hadn't forgotten anything.

She sat down on the bed, her feet on the floor, and Sean settled onto the mattress beside her. The lamplight caught his hair in a different way, highlighting the paler roots. She couldn't resist whisking her fingers through his hair to feel its sleekness against her skin, the way she had when he'd ducked his head between her legs earlier. But then those roots caught her attention again, and thoughts of being naked with him gave way to a question.

"Do you dye your hair?" she asked, spreading her fingers to expose the lighter roots. "Is your hair actually red?"

He flinched away from her touch. "Yeah, it's red. So what?"

"Why did you change the color?"

"Brown suits me better." He leaned in to graze his lips over her cheek. "The color of dirt, and you know how I like to get dirty."

Despite his sultry tone, she sensed the tension in him. He didn't want to talk about his hair color for some reason, but her intuition told her this topic was important.

She captured his face in her hands, spearing him with her gaze. "Why change your hair color?"

He scowled, but only for a moment before he sighed with a resignation that slackened his features. "My grandfather had red hair the same color as mine."

"This would be the grandfather who, um…"

Sean's lip curled. "The sweet old guy who tortured me for months and months. Yeah, I inherited my hair color from him. My mom had strawberry-blonde hair, but I inherited the full-on flame red from dear old Gramps."

That explained so much, more than she could comprehend right now.

He combed his fingers through her hair, so tenderly she couldn't help sighing with contentment.

"You said the kidnappers hurt you," he said. "But you've never seen them. What did they do?"

"Tossed a cannister of poison gas into my house. My parents' house, I mean. The cannister shattered a window and landed five feet from me, already spewing gas." She tried to stay relaxed, to let his touch keep her from tensing up at the memory, but it didn't work. "It burned my eyes, my throat, my lungs. I thought I was going to die, slowly suffocating from the gas. I'd been on the phone with the kidnappers, and somehow, I managed to hold on to the phone even while I was balled up on the floor choking and gasping. The same voice I always hear told me if I wanted to live I should swallow the pill hidden in the box under the table with the palm tree lamp on it. I belly-crawled to the table and found a plastic box. I took the pill inside it. Turned out it was the antidote to the gas. They said that was the kindest death they might give my brother if I don't follow their instructions."

Sean's hand in her hair went still. "Christ, Kira..."

"I don't want to dwell on it. They made their point, end of story."

He resumed brushing her hair with his fingers. "I admire your tenacity."

"Not tenacity. I have no choice but to keep going. For Caleb."

Sean fell silent for a moment, then asked, "What went down right before your parents took off? Anything unusual?"

This was turnabout. She'd quizzed him about his family, so he got to ask her similar questions. As much as she hated talking about it, she owed him reciprocation.

She rested her cheek on his shoulder, needing his warmth to banish the chill growing inside her. "There was something. A week earlier, I got into an argument with my parents about a boy I was dating. They'd seen him getting very cozy with another girl, but I didn't want to believe it. I got so upset I sent the barbecue grill flying across the backyard. Things escalated from there."

"Escalated?"

The way Sean kept stroking her hair helped her stay calm even while she related painful events she'd never confided to anyone before. "I confronted my boyfriend. He admitted to, in his words, getting it on with girls who knew how to make a guy feel good. He said there was nothing wrong with screwing around because one girl couldn't satisfy a real man like him. He needed lots of hotties to take care of his needs."

Sean's body tensed, and he pulled his hand away. "That guy sounds like a real prick."

"Dylan was," she admitted. "I got very upset again listening to him explain about his 'needs.' This time, I sent *him* flying—across the quad on campus. Other people saw it, but they started cheering because they thought it was a stunt for one of those TV prank shows. Dylan realized I'd done it. He was really shaken up, almost freaked out, and he screamed that he wished he'd never touched a freak like me."

"That dirtbag needed a beat-down," Sean said, his voice deceptively soft and calm, though tainted with a sliver of cold anger. "What happened with your parents?"

"Dylan called to tell them what a freak their daughter is." She cuddled closer to Sean, grateful for his warmth and tenderness as the memories chilled her. "They told me he's a jerk and I'm better off without him. Honestly, they seemed okay about it. Three days later, they vanished. Took off in the middle of the night and left a note on the refrigerator. The note said they needed to get away for a while to think about things, so they'd signed up to do humanitarian work in Uganda. Caleb never even got to say goodbye to them. When I told him they'd left, he didn't cry. Just hugged me so hard for so long I thought I'd pass out from lack of oxygen."

"That's all your parents said?" He wrapped his arms around her, tucking her head under his chin. "I can't understand how anybody could do that to their own kids."

"Not everyone is as accepting as your mom," Kira said. "My parents never believed in the paranormal until I came into my powers. Maybe the Dylan incident was too much for them, the proverbial last straw. The note they left said, 'Don't hate us, we never wanted this.' That was sixteen months ago. I had to drop out of college to get a job and take care of Caleb. Every day I pray social services won't come knocking on my door. Maybe I should've reported my parents abandoned us, but I was terrified they'd take Caleb away from me. What an awesome parent I turned out to be. My brother got kidnapped by lunatics."

"Stop blaming yourself." He turned their bodies so they faced each other, his hands bracing her upper arms. "You did the best you could. And there was nothing you could've done to protect your brother from these people. They've got resources and power you couldn't fight."

Tears slid down her cheeks. "What good is telekinesis if I can't use it to save my brother?"

He swiped her tears away with his thumbs. "You couldn't stop them from taking Caleb, but you're not powerless now. You and I can find them. We will find them. We'll shut down their big plans for terrorizing the world and rescue your brother."

"You're awfully sure we can do this."

"I'm dead sure." He kissed her softly. "It's time we paid another little visit to the crossroads."

CHAPTER FOURTEEN

SEAN AND KIRA LAY ON THE BED, ON THEIR BACKS WITH THEIR clothes on, eyes closed. He took hold of her hand, twining their fingers. Unease trickled through him, but he focused on her, on the connection between them and on what they needed to do.

"This is our anchor," he said, squeezing her hand and talking like he knew what the hell he was doing. He'd never gone into the crossroads with anyone except Kira, and he'd never had any luck tracking someone this way. Neither of them had. "Don't let go no matter what happens."

"Don't let go of your hand? Or don't let go psychically?"

"Uh…" Why did she have to ask questions he didn't know the answers to? Made him feel like a moron, though he knew she didn't mean it as an insult. She genuinely wanted to know, so he told her the truth. "I'm not sure. Both, I guess. Don't break the connection, that's the important thing."

"Okay. Got it." A hint of humor colored her voice when she added, "Probably."

"We're real superheroes, aren't we? Two psychics who've got no clue what the hell we're doing."

"You know more than I do about this stuff." She bumped her shoulder into his. "I'll follow your lead."

He grumbled. "Hope I don't lead you into a big honking mess."

"Sean, you really need to start trusting yourself."

"That's a tall order." Keeping his eyes closed, he lifted her hand to kiss it. "But I trust you."

"And I trust you, so by extension, you trust yourself."

He snorted a laugh. "That's some impressive whacked-out logic."

"Thank you."

Sean lowered their linked hands to the bed again and took a deep breath. "Time to do this. Focus on Caleb. You have a connection with him, so tap into that."

"I will."

He led the way, soaring up through the dark and desolate tunnel holding on to her in the physical and metaphysical sense. The real world receded like an image in a rearview mirror while they barreled closer and closer to their destination. They popped out into the crossroads. Black emptiness, glittering with the whitest stars imaginable. A blanket of pristine, flawless points of starlight. Hovering there, unable to speak to Kira because they had no vocal cords or spinal cords or any physical form, he did his damnedest to send her a pulse of encouragement. He sensed her bearing down on a single thought, a single destination, a single human being among billions.

Caleb.

Though he had no ears to hear it, he perceived her thought. A beacon in the abyss.

Nothing happened.

Sean concentrated on her, firing one idea straight into her mind. *Try harder.*

Her irritation came through loud and clear. She tried again, and this time, he sensed the call resonating through the crossroads.

A star flared bigger, brighter. It pulsated and shimmered, calling to them.

Their astral selves couldn't resist the call. They rocketed toward the star so fast the rest of the stars blurred into elongated shapes, and the speed of their travel ripped them through the tunnel out into a blinding brightness.

Before Sean had time for his astral eyes to adjust, sharp talons of psychic energy scrabbled for a hold in his mind. Seeking, digging, demanding. Someone in the vicinity had detected an intrusion but couldn't yet zero in on the source of the breach or its nature. He slammed his mental shields down hard—around Kira and himself. How he expanded the shields for her, he had no clue. He'd wanted to cover her, and the shield obliged.

He'd given up trying to understand this stuff a long time ago. When it came to psychic abilities, a person could understand only so much. The universe seemed content to keep the rest a secret.

Beside him, now an astral body invisible to everyone except Sean, Kira cast him a surprised glance.

Yeah, he was kind of shocked this had worked too.

They stood inside a windowless room with concrete walls and carpeted floors that, he felt sure, concealed more concrete. The ceiling was barrel shaped, the side walls curving up to it while the ends of the long, narrow room had flat walls. Everything was painted gray. Furniture of the utilitarian and totally uncomfortable variety littered the space, from metal chairs and tables to laminate cupboards and cardboard boxes. At the far end of the room, a wall partitioned off a smaller space beyond. The wall reached the ceiling but left gaps at either side like ceiling-height doorways without doors.

Up against the island wall, on the other side of a low table, a little boy huddled on a puffy couch that seemed out of place in the Spartan room. The kid had his knees drawn up to his chest, arms folded over them, and his face buried against his arms. His dark hair matched Kira's.

"Caleb," she breathed as if she couldn't believe they'd found him.

When she moved in the boy's direction, Sean stayed her with a hand on her arm. "He can't see you. And we came here for answers, not a reunion."

Her lips puckered, and her eyes narrowed.

"I'm a big, mean jerk," he said. "I know. But we need to scour this place for clues, and I have no idea how long we can hold on to this remote-viewing session. Besides, even if we could let Caleb see us, he might accidentally let on we're here. He's a kid, not a grown-up used to repressing his feelings." Sean twisted his mouth into a rueful smile. "Not like me, you know."

Kira gave him an empathetic smile that made his chest hurt.

On the couch, Caleb lifted his head and sighed. No tear tracks stained his cheeks, his color was good, and he seemed more bored than terrified. The kid dropped his feet so they dangled over the couch's edge and stretched his arm out to snatch a thin paperback book from the table. A pencil was stuck between the book's pages. Sitting back, Caleb flipped the book open to the page marked by the pencil.

The book's cover said, "Crossword Puzzles for Kids."

Caleb concentrated on the page, his fingers wrapped around the pencil.

Kira gazed at her brother with a melancholy expression, squashing her lips between her teeth. Her hand seemed to float up without her consciously realizing it like she wanted to touch her brother from afar. She glanced at her hand, her eyes flew wide for a heartbeat, and she lowered her hand as she faced Sean.

"He's okay," Sean told her. "Caleb's doing crossword puzzles, so I don't think he's in danger at the moment."

"You're right," she said, casting one last glance at her brother. "Let's dig through this place."

They explored the room from one end to the other, combing through everything they could see without needing to touch it. To interact with the environment would've required manifesting, and Sean had never done that on his own. Grace had helped him do it once or twice, but he'd never managed it without the assistance of her incredible powers.

None of the cupboards contained anything more illuminating than cans of beans and packages of ramen noodles. The cardboard boxes held paper plates and plastic cups along with plastic cutlery.

Kira gestured toward the area behind the island wall. Sean headed in that direction. They discovered a ten-foot-wide space with metal file cabinets lined up down the center.

Sean cursed under his breath when he discovered the file cabinets were locked.

Kira pointed a finger at the key lock. "I could pop that for you."

"No." He couldn't help staring at the cabinet like it was a bratwurst slathered with cheese. Not being able to access the files inside made the cabinet seem like the best food he couldn't have.

"Why not?" she asked. "One little flick and—"

"Don't." He tempered his tone with a lot of effort and explained, "Unless you can break into this thing without breaking the lock, we can't risk it. Can't have our enemies figuring out we paid them a visit."

"Oh." She folded her finger into her palm. "You're right."

Even if they manifested, they couldn't breach the cabinets without leaving behind evidence of their burgling.

Kira's mouth slid into a sly smile. "What if we poke our heads inside?"

"Poke our—huh?"

She nodded toward the file cabinet. "Poke our heads inside there. Take a peek. We don't have physical bodies right now, so why can't we just—" She mimed shoving her head into the cabinet. "You know."

He stared at her, totally bewildered. This girl had the weirdest brain of anyone he'd ever met. Damn if it wasn't the hottest thing ever.

"I've never tried that," he said. "Not sure if it's possible."

She tapped her lips together several times, making a faint popping sound. Then she hiked up her shoulders and let them fall again. "I'll give it a go."

"Kira, come on, this is nuts."

Flashing him a devilish smile, she thrust her head into the metal cabinet.

She went right through the barrier—which was no barrier at all to an astral-projecting, remote-viewing, badass psychic.

Despite the fact he had no physical body here, his dick ached with a burgeoning hunger for the bizarre, brilliant, and beautiful woman who had her head stuck inside a file cabinet.

Kira pulled her hands into the cabinet too.

He couldn't stop his lip from curling. It was too weird. He couldn't do that.

Oh what the hell.

Sean dived his head into the file cabinet at the opposite end from where Kira hunched with her head and arms inside it.

The interior was lighted.

He blinked slowly, sure he must've been hallucinating. *Nope.* A tiny ball of gently flickering fire hovered between their heads, bathing the interior in a soft light reminiscent of candlelight.

A hushed exclamation rushed out of him. "What the hell?"

Kira jumped, and her head disappeared above the cabinet for a second before she ducked inside again, aiming a half scowl, half smile at him. "You scared me."

"Sorry." He pointed at the tiny fireball. "What on earth is that?"

"A light," she said, like he'd asked what that thing was attached to her neck. "I couldn't see these papers in the dark."

"You made a light?" he said, not even trying to disguise his shock. When she nodded, he asked, "How'd you do that?"

"Kinetic energy." The unspoken *duh* in her voice matched her expression. "It's my thing, you know. You've seen me create sparks. I manipulated the kinetic energy of the air molecules to make them vibrate and—" She made a growling-grunting noise. "Really, I don't know how to explain it. I just do it. End of story."

Scientific explanations never took the paranormal into account. How could any psychic explain the use of their powers?

"Never mind," Sean said. "I couldn't give you a detailed explanation of how my powers work either."

Kira resumed rifling through the hanging file folders in the cabinet. The pink tip of her tongue poked out between her teeth. She looked so adorably focused on her task that he wanted to kiss her, but he couldn't have done it even if he'd tried. No bodies, no smooching.

Later, he'd kiss her good.

She looked up at him. "Why don't you search another cabinet instead of watching me?"

Busted. "Uh, yeah. Good idea, except I don't have a little fireball for a flashlight."

Giving him an exasperated look, she rasped her index finger across the pad of her thumb. A spark ignited, swelling into a ball of fire. It clung to her fingertip. She stretched out her astral finger, offering the fireball to him.

"What am I supposed to do with that?" he asked.

"Take it." She lunged her finger closer to him.

He raised one finger near hers, gingerly accepting the fireball when she tipped her finger to roll the ball onto the tip of his finger. No heat. No burn. He turned his finger left and right, admiring the tiny light. "Not sure how I can be holding this when I don't have a body."

Kira smiled. "It's magic."

Well, he supposed psychic stuff was magic, in a way.

Sean retreated from the cabinet, found another, and dived inside. With his miniature flame poised in the air, he searched the files but uncovered nothing more informative than a bill for propane. Maybe they had a stove or a furnace powered by propane, but the fact was irrelevant. He moved to a different cabinet with no better results. Boring accounting ledgers there, and he'd never taken accounting classes so he couldn't decipher the ledgers. He doubted they contained the solution to the mystery of who was behind the kidnapping of Kira's brother and the bomb they'd made her detonate. None of the documents included an address for the bunker property.

After browsing a third cabinet, he gave up.

Kira was hunched inside the last cabinet in the row.

He strode to her and shoved his head inside the cabinet. "Got anything?"

"Zilch." Sighing, she abandoned the hanging files and pulled out of the metal box with Sean right behind her. "Guess it was too much to hope they'd leave their manifesto lying around for us to find. These files seem to be from decades ago. I think this place was a bunker for a survivalist group, and these are their records. I've seen enough receipts for freeze-dried meals to know I never want to live in a bunker. I'll let the apocalypse take me, thank you very much."

Her gaze wandered across the length of the room to her brother on the couch. He was engrossed in his puzzles. A crease tightened between her brows, right above her nose.

She worried for her brother, he knew. The kid was okay for now, but the ordeal wasn't over yet. Sean wanted to hold her but couldn't.

"Maybe there are other rooms," he said. "Hidden doors. Something."

Kira compressed her lips, her eyes glistening with the sheen of newborn tears. "Couldn't I talk to Caleb? Let him know we found him and—" She bit down on her bottom lip. "Tell him he's not alone."

"Even if you could, we can't risk it. We talked about this, remember? He's just a kid, he might slip up and tip them off to the fact we were here. We'd lose our advantage."

Though she nodded, the tears in her eyes multiplied, threatening to spill out and roll down her cheeks.

He reached for her, but his hands passed right through her astral body. To see her brother but not be able to speak to or touch him must've been a gut-wrenching torment. He knew a lot about gut-wrenching anguish, and he would never have wished it on her. She deserved better than this. Her brother deserved a normal childhood, safe and happy with his family.

But all this psychic baloney had ripped the kid's family to shreds.

Sean stalked to the wall, examining every inch of it for hidden panels. Kira joined him, exploring the walls in the opposite direction to cover more ground faster.

"Wait," she said. "Think I found something."

He hurried to her, squinting at the straight line she indicated with her finger. The line stretched up the wall, made a ninety-degree turn, continued for three feet, and shot down again at another ninety-degree juncture.

A door.

Unfortunately, it had no handle.

He shook his head at his own dumbness. Like they needed a handle.

Kira studied him with a quizzical expression. "Why do you look like you just found the secret door to El Dorado?"

He smirked and strolled right through the closed door.

When she didn't follow, he poked his head out to say, "Hurry up, slow poke."

She stepped through behind him, and they turned around to find themselves inside a gloomy room occupied by banks of electronic equipment with flashing lights and steady, glowing lights. The electronic hum of the equipment merged with the whispery hum of the ventilation system. In the center of the room, a table hunkered next to a chair that resembled the ones found in every dentist's office, except this chair featured leather straps and metal shackles.

They'd walked into Sean's worst nightmare.

"What is it?" Kira asked. "You're white as a sheet. What is this room?"

He gritted his teeth, fisting his astral hands so tight pain lanced through them, which must've meant he was clenching his actual hands just as tightly back in the motel room. The sting of his nails piercing his skin couldn't tear his attention away from the chair.

"This," he said in a hard tone he hardly recognized as his voice, "is an isolation room. It's where they torture psychics."

CHAPTER FIFTEEN

KIRA GAVE THE ROOM A CURSORY INSPECTION, MOVING ONLY HER eyes. Then she returned her attention to Sean. The hardening of his features and the coldness of his voice belied the pallor of his skin. This room had shaken him deeply, and she wondered if she wanted to know what had been done to him in a room like this one. He'd mentioned being cut, beaten, and burned. She wanted to know the details, but she didn't know if she could handle the information. Her heart might break.

It already ached for him, for the boy who'd been tortured by his own grandfather and for the man who feared hurting innocent people even by accident. His fears ran deep, she understood that, but she would not push him to share more than he had so far.

She moved her hand as if to touch him, but of course, she couldn't. A pain tightened the back of her throat. She longed to pull him into her arms and soothe away his angst. Unable to do that, she strived to make her voice soothing and comforting. "We can leave this room. Right now. We might not learn anything in here, anyway."

His lower lip quivered ever so slightly, but he clamped his lips together, squeezing them into a pale slash. "No. We have to look around. This room is important."

To him, for sure. She recognized that the moment they'd walked inside the isolation room.

"Okay," she said. "We'll look around."

He nodded gravely, his expression still granite-hard but his eyes haunted.

They roamed around the room examining the banks of equipment and the computer monitors recessed into them. The computers had been logged out with a password login visible on the screens. No chance of perusing their computers, then. *Damn.*

She spotted a sticky note half-hidden under a computer keyboard and leaned closer to examine it. Someone had scrawled an address on the slip of paper. Her intuition urged her to remember that address, and she'd learned to trust her instincts.

Kira reached the end of the equipment banks and spotted a well-camouflaged door there. Turning away from it, she faced Sean and froze.

He lingered in front of the chair, the one with leather straps and metal shackles—like one or the other wouldn't have been enough. What had these evil people done in this room to make psychics fight so wildly they needed two types of restraints on one chair?

A shiver rattled down her spine. She probably didn't want to know.

Had Sean been strapped into a chair like this one?

No, she didn't dare think about that.

Kira moved alongside the chair, a few feet from Sean, who kept staring at the contraption.

Sean raised a hand, hovering it over one arm of the chair, above the straps and shackles. His fingers trembled so faintly she might not have noticed if she hadn't already become intimately acquainted with his strong, steady hands.

"What is it?" she asked.

He curled his fingers into his palms. "Nothing. There's nothing here to help us."

"Let's go, then," she said. "Look for other rooms."

"Yeah." His voice was hushed and uneven. "I've had enough of this room."

The door she'd discovered a moment ago burst inward.

A group of men dressed in black uniforms stormed inside, two of the men hauling another person between them. They had their hands under their prisoner's arms. The prisoner's legs dragged along the floor, scraping across the concrete. The man's head drooped and lolled, his face concealed. The uniformed men seemed not to see Kira and Sean.

Remote viewing, remember?

Sean gestured for her to follow him toward the door to the room where Caleb was being held. They stopped a few feet from the door and observed the goings-on inside the isolation room.

The uniformed men—guards, she decided, based on their outfits and the guns strapped to their hips—hoisted their prisoner to his feet, spun him around, and shoved him into the chair. One guard strapped the man in with the leather restraints. The other guard joined his friends where they'd lined up along the equipment banks.

Four guards in total, Kira noted. Four men to transport and restrain one man?

The prisoner blinked slowly as if coming out of a trance or fighting off the effects of drugs. Streaks of gray tinged his light-brown hair, and faint wrinkles stretched out from the corners of his eyes when he squinted. Gray-tinged stubble roughened his cheeks. Dark circles discolored the skin beneath his eyes. His pale-blue irises were glassy.

The man twitched his arm, seemingly a weak attempt to shake off the restraints.

"Oh no, Nathan," the guard at his side said. "You're not getting away this time."

A slender woman strolled through the door the guards had left open to halt in front of the chair. Dressed in a pant suit and utilitarian flats, she surveyed the prisoner with her cool, detached gaze. Her blonde hair was cut short with a few locks curling over the tops of her ears. Her dark eyes gave away nothing.

She might've been beautiful if not for the icy hardness of her stare.

"Yet another escape attempt," the woman said, shaking her head. "Really, Nathan, you should've learned by now you won't get away. After all these years, how can you hold out hope? I'd be impressed if it weren't so pathetic."

The prisoner, Nathan, squeezed his eyes shut and opened them wide. The action didn't clear his gaze or, apparently, his mind.

"He's high as a kite," the guard said. "Might as well be talking to the wind."

"Give him the antidote," the woman said.

"You sure, Dr. Ferrell? You know how he gets when he's wide awake."

Dr. Ferrell shot a piercing glare at the guard. "Do as I say, Watkins. Now."

Watkins nodded, pulled an autoinjector out of his pocket, and stabbed it into the prisoner's arm.

Nathan roused swiftly, his eyes clearing and his demeanor turning attentive. He sat up straight and glanced around the room as if assessing it for the first time—or just now realizing where he was. Recognition made his jaw tighten and his gaze narrow on the blonde doctor.

"Welcome back," Ferrell said. "You were out a long time this go-round. I doubt you remember all the things you told us."

"I told you nothing," Nathan said, his voice sharp and rough and deep. "No matter what drugs you force-feed me, I will never betray my family."

"Your family?" Ferrell said with a mirthless little laugh. "Your wife is dead. And you will never see your child again."

Nathan fisted his hands, his arm muscles bulging from the intensity of his grip. "I got away once. I can do it again."

"You escaped once, briefly, a decade ago. And that was under the inauspicious supervision of Karl Tesler." Ferrell swept her gaze over the guards arrayed along the wall. "I have much better—or rather, much less moral—employees than Tesler did. Give up the fantasy, Nathan. You will never get away from me."

The prisoner lifted his chin and glowered at her.

"Defiance," she said in a mock-wistful tone. "It's charming, but it will do no good. I'm giving you one last chance to tell me what I want to know."

"Kill me. I don't care."

"You misunderstand." Ferrell sauntered up to the chair, stopping alongside it and resting her hands atop his arms. "I won't kill you. I'll kill more innocent people, and I'll keep killing them until you cooperate." She leaned in, her face inches from Nathan's, and snarled, "Give me the boy."

Nathan faced straight ahead.

"Have it your way." Ferrell raised one arm, flicked her wrist, and walked out of the room with the guards in tow. As she pulled the door shut, she said, "Enjoy solitary confinement."

The door chunked closed, indicating a powerful lock had engaged.

And then the lights went out.

Sean's voice murmured close to Kira. "Let's get out of here."

"We should help him escape."

"No. It's way too complicated, and we have a deadline. Remember?"

She turned and stepped through the darkness, through the wall, into the room where Caleb sat on the puffy sofa. He had a tablet computer in his hands now, his gaze riveted to the screen. Cartoon noises emerged from the tablet's speakers. Caleb smiled at whatever the characters on-screen were doing.

At least he wasn't suffering. She had to take solace in that.

I'll get you back, baby, whatever it takes.

What if "whatever" entailed detonating more bombs?

It wouldn't go that far. She and Sean would stop this madness before anyone else got hurt.

A wave of dizziness set her head to rocking and rolling.

"What is it?" Sean said, his voice tight with concern.

"Suddenly feel…weak."

"Power drain. We've been traveling too long. Time to get back to the motel."

Though her stomach churned at the thought of leaving Caleb alone here, she knew he was right.

Sean stepped in front of her, and together, they fled through the crossroads to slip back into their bodies. Kira stared numbly at the ceiling with its swirling pattern of plaster and dirty spots here and there. It took a minute for her brain to adjust to the change from remote-viewed world to real world. Her body felt heavy, her mouth cottony. She pushed up onto her elbows.

Beside her, Sean stretched and yawned. "Long excursion."

"What?" She sat up and studied him, surprised to find him looking so relaxed and almost refreshed. "I'm ready for a nap, and you look fresh as a daisy."

"I've had powers longer than you have. Traveling's kind of second nature."

"So, I'll get better at it? Stop feeling wiped out when I come back from—what did you call it?—an excursion."

He levered up into a sitting position, legs stretched out before him. "Yeah, you will."

Kira rubbed her arms, struck by a sudden chill. "Caleb's all alone with those people. That woman doctor, what if she's hurting Caleb the way she hurt that man, Nathan?"

Sean spread a hand on her back and caressed it in big, slow circles. "Relax, Caleb's okay. I took a little peek through my shields and felt it. He's scared, and he misses you, but nobody's hurt him."

"A peek? Through your shields? What are you talking about?"

"It's how I rein in my powers. I built a kind of mental shield to keep anybody's shit from getting into my brain or vice versa." He grimaced. "Empathic shit."

Oh, that explained a few things. "That's what I felt when we traveled. You somehow included me in your shields to keep the bad guys from sensing us."

"Yeah."

"Was it safe to take a peek? I mean, what if the psychics these terrorists are using noticed?"

"I doubt it." Sean slid off the bed and unfurled his body to full height. "It was a split second, and just a sliver of a crack in my shields."

Kira shimmied to the bed's edge, her legs dangling. "Do you think that Nathan man is the one helping them? Maybe he caused Edward's heart attack."

"Maybe." Sean rubbed his chin. "But I'm not sure that guy has powers."

"How can you tell?"

"Intuition." Sean shrugged. "Or maybe it's a wild guess. One can feel just like the other. The more important thing we learned is that Tesler was kidnapping people long before he and Jackson Tennant took over ALI. Ferrell said Tesler had been holding Nathan prisoner for at least a decade. Tesler didn't become chief mad scientist at ALI until six years ago."

"Thought Tesler only kidnapped psychics."

"So did I."

Kira gave him an exasperated look. "Doesn't that mean Nathan must have powers?"

"If I know anything about my sweet grandfather," Sean said, his gaze going flinty, "it's that he would do anything to anyone if it helped him achieve his goals. This Nathan guy has a kid. Maybe the kid has powers, and that's why Tesler took Nathan—to torture him into saying where his kid is. Ferrell seems to have picked up Tesler's research where he left off."

Kira shimmied farther forward, about to jump off the bed, but Sean held out his hands to her. When she clasped his hands, he hoisted her to her feet.

"That doesn't make sense," she said. "Ferrell talked about Nathan's son, but she also said Nathan had been a prisoner for more than a decade. Any child Nathan might've had would be a teenager, maybe even an adult, by now. How could Nathan know where his son is today when he's been a prisoner for all these years?"

"Maybe Tesler told him."

"Which makes no sense either. If Tesler knew where the kid is, why keep Nathan alive?"

Sean let out a frustrated sigh. "I don't know. I may be psychic, but I don't read minds. Gramps liked torturing people. Maybe he kept Nathan around for fun, or maybe he thought he could use the guy as leverage to get the kid to do whatever he wanted."

A chill of knowing shivered through Kira. "The way Ferrell and her gang are doing with Caleb. They took him as leverage."

"Exactly like that." Sean clasped his hands at his nape. "It's pretty obvious now we're dealing with the remnants of Tesler's research. We thought Jackson Tennant's death put an end to it, but Tesler survived him. Then we thought Tesler's death put an end to it, but somebody must've had a copy of his research. The sweet and huggable Dr. Ferrell must've gotten her mitts on it, or maybe Tesler shared his data with her. She might've been his protégé."

Too many unknowns. Too many questions they didn't know to ask.

"We know one thing we didn't know before," she said.

"Yeah, my grandfather's research is the monster that won't die, like Dracula in all those movies."

"No." Kira laid her hands on his chest, angling her head back to meet his gaze. "We know where they are."

He crimped his lips. "We know they're in a bunker, that's all."

"And we have their address." She patted his chest, smiling with what felt like a bit of smugness. She'd earned the right to crow a little. "I saw an address on the console over there. I'm sure it's the location of this property. So I memorized it."

Chapter Sixteen

H E COULD'VE KISSED HER. SERIOUSLY, HE COULD'VE DRAGGED HER into his arms and kissed her like she'd offered him the keys to Fort Knox. But he didn't. He could've hauled her down onto the bed and taken her in a frenzy like they were the last two people on the planet. But he didn't. Mostly because he'd lost the ability to move or speak.

Luckily, his voice came back after a few seconds of gaping at her. "You did what?"

"I memorized the address." She tapped her head with one finger.

"You're amazing," he said with an awestruck tone because she'd awed him at every turn. "I didn't even think of that. Didn't see any addresses, anyway."

She glided her hands up to his shoulders. "You were distracted by bad memories. That's why we're good together. I fill in when you're freaked out and vice versa."

Good together. Them. Him and her. Together.

Kira talked like they were a couple, two average people involved in a romance.

That's when it hit him like a bolt of lightning slamming into the top of his head, splitting him in two. He shouldn't be doing this with her—or anyone. He shouldn't have dragged her into his messed-up world. She didn't need him. Her powers were strong enough to get her where she needed to go to save her brother.

"I'm no good for you," he said, taking a step away from her though he wanted to pull her into his arms and never let go. "You've been amazing, and I need your help, but you get nothing from me. I'm so messed up I don't think I can ever get back to normal. Whatever 'normal' means."

"Of course you can." She moved toward him, but he held up a hand in warning. "Sean, stop it. We're in this together."

"You're strong all by yourself. Go save Caleb and that Nathan guy. I'd get in the way."

She shook her head, a small movement that conveyed more emotion than he cared to figure out. "I'm not going without you. Where is this coming from? We just had a big success with our joint excursion. Is this because of what we saw in the bunker? In the isolation room? I get that it brought up bad memories for you, but—"

"You know nothing." He suppressed a flinch at the frozen edge in his voice. "I kidnapped you, have you forgotten?"

"No, I haven't."

He expected to hear anger in her voice, but instead, she sounded…sympathetic.

Dammit, he could've handled anger. But caring was too much. Way too much.

"I am not a good person," he told her. "I kidnapped you. I tied you up. I'm not sure what I would've done to get information out of you. Don't you get it? I'm exactly like my grandfather, stopping at nothing to get what I want. I'm like that Ferrell bitch too. And like Gabriel Amador. That whackjob abducted a teenage girl and did God knows what to her until she caved and used her powers to torment Grace, all so Amador could get what he wanted. That's what I did to you."

Kira watched him, her eyes shimmering with unshed tears, but she made no move toward him. The look on her face, it bit into him like cold metal teeth.

"Don't you get it?" he hissed through clenched teeth, his body quivering from head to toe. "Once, I was Nathan. A prisoner. A test subject. I was tortured until I caved and told Tesler…I don't even know what I might've told him. And something inside me got broken, something that will never heal. I'm so fucked up I kidnapped you and vowed to myself I'd do whatever it took to find out the truth, even if that meant hurting you. I am my grandfather. I am Amador."

She said nothing, her gaze trained on him.

He jabbed a finger toward the motel-room door. "Get out of here. Go rescue your brother. But stay as far away from me as you possibly can. I will bring you down."

Blue eyes glistening, she shook her head.

With his finger still aimed at the door, he glared at her.

She exhaled a deep breath, wiped her eyes with the backs of her hands, and squared her shoulders. "No."

His jaw dropped. His arm fell to his side. "What? Were you not listening?"

"I heard everything you said." She marched up to him, her faced tilted up to his, her expression defiant. "But you are full of crap. I understand you've been through a horrific experience, and I can't imagine what that did to you. But I know you, Sean, and you are not a monster."

"You know me? We met yesterday."

"Doesn't matter. I know what kind of man you are." She captured his face in her soft, warm hands. "You never hurt me. When those zip ties scraped my wrists, you put padding under them. You let me go because you realized you'd made a mistake out of desperation and fear. I could've run, but I didn't. I chose to stay with you."

"Because you thought you needed my help. You don't."

"Yes I do." An intense certainty imbued her voice with a depth of emotion he hadn't heard from her before. She sounded resolute, like he never had been about anything. "Together, we're strong enough to stop these scumbags, and we have less than eighteen hours to do it. Now you want to abandon me? No way. You're sticking around, buster, whether you like it or not."

One corner of his mouth twitched in what felt like a smile trying to take hold but failing miserably. "Whether I like it or not? Are you planning to tie me up?"

Her sexy little mouth formed a sexy little smile. "Only if you want me to."

"Kira..." He tried to back away again, but her hands rooted him in place. "I was never this powerful before, only with you. That means the power boost is coming from you, which means you don't need me. You're as strong as Grace, maybe stronger."

"Baloney. I was never this strong before either." She hopped up onto the tips of her toes to level their gazes, and though he tried to look away, her sapphire eyes captured him. "We are powerful together."

He couldn't tear his focus away from her eyes. They'd begun to glow faintly with a lighter-blue fire, a sign she'd tapped into her powers. Though the scientists at ALI had assumed the paranormal fire in the eyes of psychics occurred only when they traveled, Sean had learned a long time ago that wasn't true. Anytime a psychic tapped into their powers, their eyes would glow, faintly if they used latent power, more strongly if they accessed the crossroads to engage their higher abilities. Kira seemed to open up her powers without thinking about it whenever she experienced strong emotions.

To experience her emotions right now...He battled the impulse to crack open his shields and let a piece of her inside. *Bad idea.* If he tasted her soul, he'd never want to stop.

"Do it," she whispered, "feel what I'm feeling. I want you to. Maybe then you'll understand why I'm not letting you run away."

He hiked up one brow. "If I do that, we'll wind up naked on that bed again."

She looped her arms around his neck, her luscious body plastered to him. "Maybe that's what you need right now. A quickie to temper your high-voltage stress."

"We can't. No time."

"That's why I said a quickie." She unhooked the button of his jeans and dragged the zipper down, then sneaked her hand inside. When he sucked in a choked gasp, she smirked. "This is therapy."

Maybe he should've said no, but his mind blanked the second her warm hand closed over his dick.

And he gave in.

———

KIRA GUIDED THE RENTAL CAR DOWN ROADS LEADING AWAY FROM the city and out into the wilds where fields of cultivated wheat gave way to grassy hills. They'd ditched their phones and bought a new, throwaway smartphone nobody could trace with any luck. Sean had left Amador's credit card at the motel, using what little cash he had to buy the new phone. He'd looked up the bunker's address on the "burner phone," as he'd called it, using an app to find their way.

Her suggestion for stress relief had worked like a charm, and he now smiled and joked with her, even sang along with the radio a few times. She had no illusions that she was so good in bed she'd cured him of his guilt and fear. Sex with him was hot and made more intimate by their psychic connection, but she knew sex with anybody would've relaxed him.

This guy had turned stressed-out into an Olympic sport. And he'd won the gold medal.

When he wasn't stressed, he could be so…nice.

Maybe his rough charm and sense of humor explained why she'd invited him to read her emotions. She couldn't think of a single valid reason for letting him do that because, although he'd refused to do it, she'd wanted him to do it more than she'd ever wanted anything. What would he find out if he took a peek? The possible answers should've frightened her, but she had never feared him or what he could do. Even when he'd held her hostage, she hadn't been afraid of him.

Sean brought out the phone and peered at its screen. "Got a signal. Three bars. That oughta work."

"Work for what?" she asked, easing the car around a curve in the bumpy dirt road.

"I need to call Grace and David."

"Shouldn't you leave them alone? They've been through a lot the past couple days."

"Yeah, but they've got a flash drive that used to belong to Jackson Tennant." Sean curled his hand around the phone, and she could sense a wisp of his anxiety rippling through the air between them. "I need to have Grace do a search for me in those files. To find out if Nathan what's-his-name is in the list of travelers involved in Project Outreach. Grace and David can sense when a person has powers, but I've never been very good at that. I don't think Nathan has powers, but this is the only way I know of to find out for sure if he's a psychic or just a normal guy being used as a pawn to get to his kid."

"What if he's not in the files?"

Sean shrugged. "Then we won't know for sure either way."

"Is it weird that I'm getting used to everything being a mystery?"

"You're a woman of mystery, for sure." He flashed her a mischievous smile. "And I like it."

Why did her tummy flutter whenever he smiled at her? What bothered her most was the pain in her chest she'd started to get when he looked at her that way. "Make your call, Casanova."

Sean dialed up his friends—his family, he'd called them—and played the audio through the car's stereo. When a man answered, he said, "David, I've got you on speaker with me and Kira. We—"

"Grace and Abby are gone," David said.

"What?" Sean bolted upright, his head bumping the car's roof.

Kira glanced at him, her pulse quickening, but he was staring out the windshield at nothing.

"Someone took them," David said, "They shot a cannister through the living-room window and gassed us. Some kind of knockout drug. When I woke up, Edward was here but Grace and Abby were gone."

Sean squeezed words out between his clenched teeth. "How long ago did this happen?"

"An hour. I tried to call you, but there was no answer."

"We switched phones." Sean squinted his entire face, squeezing his eyes shut for a second. "I'm sorry. This is my fault."

"It's their fault," David snarled. "The bastards who made those bombs. They did this, and you have to find them. Find Grace and Abby. Took me a while to charter a jet, but we're about to take off for Great Falls."

"Where the hell's Amador? He's got a jet."

"I don't know where he is. He's not answering his phone either."

Gabriel Amador was missing too? Something was up, for sure, Kira realized. Something bad.

"Can't you travel to Grace?" Sean asked. "Manifest and get her and Abby away from whoever took them."

"I can't." David hesitated. "My powers are gone."

Sean's eyes flared wide.

Kira pulled the car over to the side of the road.

"How is that possible?" Sean asked. "I've only ever seen it with an EM field."

"I would've felt that," David said. "Besides, I would've had to stay within the EM field for that to work. This isn't electromagnetic. I don't know what it is."

"We're going to find Grace and Abby," Sean said. "We're on our way to the bunker where these lunatics are holed up. Kira and I RV'd the place and saw her brother. I'm betting that's where they're taking Grace and Abby too."

Sean rattled off his new phone number and gave David an abridged recap of events today.

"I hate to ask this," Sean said, "but are you where you can plug into the flash drive?"

"Yes, I have it with me and I have a laptop. What do you need?"

"Search for a traveler called Nathan. Don't know his last name."

"Give me a minute."

The sound of fingers tapping keys ensued. After a moment, David said, "I'm not seeing anyone called Nathan." He fell silent for a moment, then said, "If these people have an isolation room…"

"No one's hurting them," Sean said, his dark tone saying more than his words could. "I'll make sure of it."

"I know you will," David said. "I'll call when I get to Great Falls. Be careful, Sean. Both of you be careful."

"We will." Sean disconnected the call. "Get us back on the road."

Kira steered the car back onto the dirt road, glancing at Sean while the vehicle rolled down a straight stretch. He stared out the side window, giving her a great view of the back of his head. The anxiety that had wafted out of him a few minutes ago had become a churning sea of tension between them. It swirled around her, cold and sharp, nicking her psyche. He believed he held everything inside his mental shields, and at first, she hadn't been able to perceive anything from him. She'd assumed it was because she had no empathic abilities. After learning about his shields, she'd assumed she couldn't sense anything from him because she wasn't an empath and he had barriers to protect himself.

Both times they'd made love, she felt him. The real Sean, the one he guarded closely, letting no one touch that part of him. Whether he'd meant to or not, he'd shared himself with her during their intimate encounters.

And now, she realized she could perceive his emotions—despite having no empathic powers before today. Maybe it wasn't empathic sensing. Maybe it was the intensity of their emotional bond carving out a channel between them for their powers to flow down. She had no idea, really, and asking Sean seemed like a bad idea right now. He was stressed again. And who could blame him? The villains had abducted the woman he clearly viewed as a mother figure. They'd taken her daughter too.

Sean faced forward, his expression grim. "We need to stop before we get any closer to the bunker. They might've already seen us coming, but we can't risk getting any closer. We'll RV from here."

"Is it safe to do that? What if they come grab us while we're out of our bodies?"

"Have to hope they don't."

She threw him a sidelong look. "A nice, vague answer. Totally helpful."

"Excuse me for not knowing everything. I doubt they can track us, anyway, with our burner phone."

They lapsed into silence as the car sped down the road. She decided to cut him some slack considering the circumstances. A vague answer would do for now.

"Pull over there," Sean finally said.

He pointed at a two-track road on the right. Weeds poked up between the twin trails etched by car tires.

Kira squinted at the road, slowing down as they approached it. A gate closed off the two-track with a sign on it that read "No Trespassing." She let the car roll to a stop alongside the overgrown road. "This is a driveway, not a road. Somebody might live down there."

"I'll find out." He whipped out his phone again and tapped items on the screen.

"How are you going to find out?" she asked, helpless to keep the skepticism out of her voice.

"RV." He used his thumb and forefinger to zoom in on something on his phone's screen, then tapped once. "I pulled up a satellite image of the property. Not great resolution, but good enough to get me there."

"What if the owner went to the grocery store? You might think the place is unoccupied when—"

He relaxed into his seat, his gaze going distant.

The jerk had gone on an excursion in the middle of their conversation.

Kira huffed, barring her arms over her chest and glaring out the windshield since she couldn't glare at him. Not with any effect, at least. He was out of his body, traveling through the metaphysical plane. She wanted to follow him just so she could punch him for bailing on their conversation and making a decision without asking how she felt about it.

She glanced at his vacant body. No more sex for you, mister, no matter how uptight you get.

In the passenger seat, Sean's body jerked. He gurgled like someone being strangled.

Her heart raced, and adrenaline spiked through her. What if the bad guys used another psychic to get to Sean in the crossroads? Was that even possible? She reached for him, about to shake the heck out of him until he came back to her, but then he went motionless.

She held motionless too, her torso twisted toward him, her hands clamped over the center console. *Please be okay, please.*

His chest heaved with a sudden, deep inhalation. He blinked rapidly, cleared his throat, and sat up straighter. "The place isn't in use. The furniture's covered with sheets and there's no electricity. The windows are covered up with shutters. It's the perfect place to hide while we RV the bunker."

She eyed him up and down, her body still twisted to face him. "Are you okay? Your body seemed to be in distress for a minute there."

"I'm peachy." He gave her a placid smile. "Everything's fine. Chill, Kira."

Chill? Peachy? She'd never heard him talk that way except in sarcasm. Granted, she'd known him for little more than a day, but she felt like she knew him pretty well. For now, she'd have to let it go.

"We have less than fourteen hours," she said, easing the car into the driveway, forced to stop at the closed gate. "What if we can't stop them in time? What if they order us to murder everyone in Great Falls or they'll kill our families?"

"Deal with that if it happens."

"Aren't you worried they'll kill us and get somebody else to do their bidding? And what about Grace and Abby? And David's lack of powers?"

He shrugged one shoulder. "One thing at a time. We can't worry about everything at once or we'll never get anything done."

Suddenly he was pragmatic. *Terrific.*

Kira waved at the gate and the conspicuous padlock holding it shut. "What about that?"

He rolled his eyes at her. "You're telekinetic, baby. Bust that thing open."

Baby. The word tripped her up for a minute while she struggled to decipher the meaning of those two syllables. Was he being sarcastic? Or was he really calling her by a pet name?

She rolled down the window, thrust her arm out, and flicked her fingers toward the padlock. It burst open, flying off its chain to plunk onto the ground.

"Good job," Sean said, hitting her with a sly smile. "Now let's go whup these dirtbags."

His abrupt switch to enthusiastic optimism left her with a gnawing, burning-acid sensation in her stomach.

"Take it easy," he said. "We've got this, baby."

Her tummy fluttered every time he called her "baby." Why did he say it? Didn't matter.

The odds were high they wouldn't survive to see tomorrow.

Chapter Seventeen

THE TIRES CRUNCHED OVER ROCKS IN THE TWO-TRACK DRIVEWAY as the car raced closer and closer to the cabin Sean knew was hidden among the trees. They would find the bunker and stop the bad guys. He knew this too, with a certainty that should've disturbed him, but he didn't care if it was irrational. He recognized the truth. He felt it in his soul.

Kira kept giving him funny looks. She didn't understand his newfound optimism.

He didn't either, but he was going with it. When he'd flown through the crossroads to remote view this property, something had rushed through him. Oh, not just anything, no. Power, warm and viscous and seductive, had flowed through his psyche and tingled down his metaphysical nerves, enlivening him, filling up his psychic energy reserves, depleted by everything he'd done today. The power had beckoned him to linger in the crossroads, to consume more and more and more fuel. Talon-like shards of energy had dug into him, pulling him back while he fought to keep moving, all the while tempted to slide back into the unknown force that craved him as much as he craved it.

Breaking away from it had taken a split second that yawned like an eternity.

In the crossroads, time seemed to have little relevance. It was a metaphysical plane, not the real world.

Twice before, he'd experienced something like that. Talons. Power. A massive source of energy reaching out for him. The first time, he'd almost given in and tapped into it to find Kira's brother—except he'd realized at the last second he might lose himself to that power. It hungered. Grace had warned him, but he'd never really thought he'd be desperate enough to consider ignoring her warnings.

But the second time the power had touched him, seeking him with its greasy talons, he'd assumed it was nothing but another psychic sensing his and Kira's intrusion into the bunker. Now, he had to wonder.

No, he didn't need to wonder about anything. He knew. The ultimate source of psychic power had tried to ensnare him again.

The Golden Power had tasted him, and it hungered for more.

His shields wouldn't keep it out forever. They'd almost crumbled when he traveled moments ago. *Be careful,* David had said. Sean had thought David meant don't get killed. But maybe he'd also meant it as a warning against giving in to the Golden Power. Sean hadn't told David about his previous encounters with it, but his friend knew enough about the Golden Power to worry as much as Grace did.

The driveway opened out into a small clearing with a log cabin situated at its center. Shutters concealed the windows.

"Park behind the house," he said. "Under the trees."

Kira obeyed without even making a snide remark about his bossiness. Unhooking her seatbelt, she asked, "What now?"

"We can either go inside or stay on the porch. Doesn't matter to me where we do this."

"On the porch." She pushed her door open. "Rather not invade someone's home."

Sean grinned. "If the owners show up and get mad, I'll just make them forget they ever saw us."

With one foot out the door, she paused to fix her unblinking gaze on him. "That's not funny. Manipulating people's minds for our convenience? I can't believe you'd even joke about that."

He was kind of surprised too, but he didn't see what was wrong with it. The owners would never know anything had happened.

Kira's mouth fell open. "You still think it's a good idea, don't you?"

Oh shit. He did. The Golden Power had infected him.

She climbed out of the car and slammed the driver's door.

Numbly, Sean clambered out of his side and jogged to catch up to Kira. She was stalking toward the covered porch and stomping up the wooden steps. He sped up and snagged her arm as she turned left to head for a wooden swing suspended from the porch ceiling at the far end.

She aimed her bleak gaze at him.

A shiver sidled up his spine, rousing every fine hair on his body.

"I'm sorry," he said, releasing her arm. "I think, uh, something's happening to me. Something not good."

"Whatever it is, it started when you traveled to check out this place."

"Yeah." He shoved a hand into his hair, dragging it down to his nape. "I think maybe the Golden Power got inside me. A little bit."

"Inside you?" She leaned back a touch like she wanted to back away but wasn't sure he'd let her. "The way you described this Golden Power, it sounds like pure evil. You called it a living, breathing, ravenous energy that nearly destroyed Grace."

"I said it feels like that. It's energy, pure and simple, which means I can control it."

"Do you even realize how crazy you sound?"

"Sure, but—" He cut himself off because he'd been about to defend the Golden Power, to claim it didn't feel that bad inside him and maybe they could use it to their advantage. "Jesus, I'm poisoned with it."

"Shake it off."

"Not sure I can."

"I'm sure." She hesitated, her mouth tight, then marched up to him and slanted her head back to meet his gaze. "You are strong and good. You can shake off this poisonous power. Do it, Sean. Do it quick before the Golden Power gets too deep inside you."

He needed to do it. Wanted to do it. But he could think of only one way to burn out the infection.

Get this crap out of you by any means necessary.

"Dammit," he hissed.

Sean hauled Kira into him and crushed his mouth to hers.

A riot of sensations flooded over him. The warmth of her lips. The softness of her skin. The womanly scent of her that enveloped him. The heat of desire, hers mingling with his. A sweet, gentle feeling of...belonging. The sensation swelled in his chest, a blooming warmth that spread outward into his entire body while the soft yet solid core of it remained rooted in his chest, over his heart.

In his heart.

His pulse sped up at the realization, though he couldn't comprehend what it meant, not consciously. He slipped his tongue inside her mouth, reveling in the taste of her, the slick softness of her tongue as she answered his movements with her own. She opened wider for him, and he took more, took as much as she would give, drowning in the pleasure of their kiss.

The sliver of oily power, shaved off the ultimate source of psychic energy, crumbled away in the presence of her.

Sean broke the kiss, breathing hard, but couldn't make himself let go of her or pull back. Their mouths lingered a hair's breadth apart. She gazed up at him with a dazed expression, her blue irises burning with a preternatural fire and the pupils large and black, a door to the unknown recesses of her soul, a place he'd gladly dive into without reservation.

A lazy smile curved her kiss-swollen lips. "You're looking at me like I'm the answer to your prayers."

You are, he thought but couldn't manage to say. His voice wouldn't co-operate. That he wanted to say those words, that he understood the truth of them deep in his soul, raked a shiver down his spine. Not a chill. Not really hot, either. The shiver embodied something in between, something indescribable.

He brushed his fingertips down her cheek, awed by this incredible woman who, for some reason he couldn't comprehend, wanted him. Trusted him. Saved him.

"It's gone," he finally said, his voice rough. "The sliver of the Golden Power that got wedged inside me. It's gone."

She'd gotten inside him and obliterated that sliver. Had his shields popped a leak? The thought spiked cold through him until he took a sec-ond to inspect his mental vault and realized it was intact. He hadn't slipped up. She had penetrated his shields because he'd let her inside them, ex-panding them to protect her. And because she could get to him when no one else could. His surrogate family, Grace and David, they'd tried to get through to him, but he hadn't listened. Then Kira blasted into his life, and he couldn't ignore her.

More than her powers got to him. She made him feel again, whether he'd wanted to or not.

He hadn't wanted to, but now, he couldn't imagine not feeling this way.

She smiled again, her eyes sparkling. "I'm glad it's gone. You don't need that nasty power to get the job done. We can do it together."

He nodded, because he couldn't figure out how to explain what she'd done to him—or how much he needed it. Needed her.

Kira touched her lips to his, the kiss feather-light and achingly sweet.

"It's time," he said. "Let's take down those bastards."

A FIELD OF INKY DARKNESS SURROUNDED THEM, SPRINKLED WITH white stars, pinpoints that marked someone or someplace within the universe. Kira hung suspended in the crossroads with Sean, unable to see him but sensing him close by along with the strange feeling he was holding her hand. In the real world, they both sat on the porch swing of a stranger's house, eyes closed and hands linked. Here in the metaphysical world, they were joined in a different and far more intimate way.

Their powers had become one.

She sensed it but couldn't explain the feeling. Connection. Belonging. Even those words failed to describe it.

A star pulsed, and they rocketed toward it.

Down the tunnel they sped, bursting out into a dimly lit space.

Their astral bodies had landed inside the bunker in the room where they'd found Caleb last time. Now, the barrel-roofed space stood vacant.

A chill scraped along her nerves. *Something's off,* her intuition warned, but she had no idea what precisely she'd detected. Not a smell, not a sound, not a physical sensation.

"You feel it," Sean said, "don't you?"

She nodded. "Not sure what *it* is, though."

"For me, it's a feeling. Kind of dark and squiggly, cold but spiked with heat."

Yes, that described what she was experiencing rather well. Realization tingled through her. "I know what it is."

He glanced at her, a question in his eyes.

She swallowed against a lump in her throat. "Foreboding."

"Yeah, you're right." He assumed a posture and an expression of acute alertness as if observing and analyzing everything. "I'd say it's more like impending doom."

"That's what happens if we fail. Let's not do that."

He gave a sharp, decisive nod.

Then he took hold of her astral hand—would she ever get used to having no body but seeming to have a body at the same time?—and guided her toward the door to the isolation room. He ducked his head through the door just enough to peek inside.

"Nobody in there," he said.

They checked the file-cabinet area but found nothing there either.

"Must be another door," she said. "One we missed the first time."

Sean led her around the room's periphery, but they discovered no other entrances or exits. When they circled back around to the isolation-room door, Sean glanced at it, glanced away, then focused on it again and swallowed visibly.

He exhaled a long breath through his parted lips. "Guess it's through there, then."

Anxiety rolled off him in psychic waves.

She squeezed his hand. "We could go through one of the walls and see what's on the other side. We don't have bodies after all. Walls don't limit us."

"Might be solid rock on the other side, or solid dirt." He shook his head. "Flailing around blindly isn't the answer. The most expedient method is to follow the doors we can see."

He was right, of course, but she knew he didn't want to go into the isolation room. Her heart hurt for him, for what he'd endured in the past and for what he had to do now. She admired his tenacity in going through with this, despite his fears. He was brave and selfless, not at all the arrogant jerk she'd taken him for when they first met.

In her defense, he had been kidnapping her at the time.

Bygones. She understood him now, understood his motivations and fears.

They marched through the closed door into the isolation room. Lights flashed on the equipment banks. Hard drives whirred. A chilly draft wafted over them from the ventilation system. On the opposite side of the room, a door hung open.

She flashed back to the guards dragging Nathan through that door. That could've been her brother. It still might be.

"Let's go," Sean said, and they hurried through the other door.

It took them into a corridor with cracked and worn linoleum floors, gray walls, and bare white bulbs affixed to the ceiling at regular intervals. The odor of disinfectant permeated the space.

She tried not to think about why they'd needed to disinfect the corridor.

Head turning right and left, Sean screwed up his mouth. "Which way?"

"Take a guess. Let your intuition guide you."

"Maybe we should listen to yours, not mine."

She exhaled a frustrated noise. "Fine. This way."

With her hand around his, she headed left down the corridor. No doors except the one to the isolation room. No signs indicating…anything. Had she really expected a literal sign? Red-painted letters with a big red arrow next to them announcing "bad guys this-a-way"?

Maybe not an actual sign. But a psychic one…

Kira halted.

Sean gave her a confused look.

"Is there a way," she said, "for us to look around and see if anybody's here? And if so, where they are?"

"Grace can do that. I tried, but I couldn't pull it off."

"Let's try now."

"We're not Grace."

Kira growled in frustration this time. "Jeez, you really have an inferiority complex about Grace, don't you? We've got the power of two psychics to work with. If she could do it alone, we can do it together for sure."

One side of his mouth kicked up. "You're a real can-do person, aren't you?"

"Better than being a doomsayer." She raised her eyebrows. "You were all 'la-dee-da, everything's cool' when you had that piece of the Golden Power influencing you. If I'd suggested this then, you would've jumped at the chance. Probably would've fist-pumped and told me 'we are the awesomest and we can do anything,' but now you're back to thinking Grace is the only one who can do anything."

"Awesomest?" He shook his head. "I would never say that. I might say 'we rock.' I wouldn't fist-pump either."

"Not the point." She took his hands and looked straight into his eyes. "Help me create psychic radar."

"If we're looking for people, it'd be more like thermal imaging."

She threw her head back and growled again.

He chuckled softly. "Let's do this."

Their gazes locked, and power sizzled between them. She focused on the task, creating a visual means of detecting human bodies, zeroing her psychic senses in on the idea like a laser sighting in on a target. Sean's eyes glowed bright green, rims of fire around his dark, shrinking pupils. In those ever-narrowing disks of blackness, she spied a reflection of her own eyes blazing blue.

Energy poured into them from the crossroads, not the bad kind, but the good and necessary kind that fueled their powers. They hadn't traveled back to the crossroads, but she felt the latent connection to that place like a power line funneling electricity. This line surged with psychic energy, imbuing them both with what they needed to accomplish this feat.

Find human bodies. Living, human bodies, she amended.

No, she did not want to find the corpses of innocent people these villains had murdered.

Something shifted inside her like a switch flicked to the "on" position. She tore her gaze away from Sean to scan the corridor.

Everything looked different. Walls came through as dark slabs, and though they stayed in focus, with a tiny release of power she could peer through the walls and then zoom back out to see them again. She noted pipes in the walls and shimmering white lines that must've been electric wires as well as the chasms of ventilation shafts.

"Are you seeing this?" she asked in a hushed voice, amazed at what they'd done.

"Yeah," Sean said, his voice equally amazed. "We did it."

Holding his astral hand in hers, she towed him down the corridor.

Wait. They were holding hands? On their previous excursion, they couldn't touch each other. Something had changed between them.

"Sean," she said as they kept moving down the corridor, "how are we touching each other?"

He slowed his pace, his brows knitting together, and glanced at their hands. "Not sure. Our shared power has gotten stronger, I guess."

"But why?"

"Don't know. Don't care right now."

A lot of things had changed since they'd first met. They'd experienced each other's powers, they'd had sex, and they'd bonded on a deeper level because of it and also because of the secrets they revealed to each other.

But Sean was right. They had more important concerns at the moment.

They wandered past yard after yard of walls with nothing behind them. Nothing under the floors, either. Above, she saw ventilation shafts and wiring and pipes. If there was another floor above this one, she couldn't see through to it. Wall, wall, wall after gray wall. She observed nothing else.

Kira turned her gaze to the end of the corridor.

And stopped dead.

"I see it too," Sean said.

Human-shaped blobs—revealed in shades of red, yellow, and blue—moved around somewhere beyond the wall. Pipes and vents and wiring obscured her view, but she recognized those shapes as human. She ran to the wall, running her hands over its surface in search of any indication of a doorway but finding nothing. Another corridor began where the first one ended, shooting off to the right.

"Door must be down there," she said, and without waiting for Sean, she sprinted down the corridor.

Their footfalls slapped on the linoleum floor. She wondered briefly how astral feet clad in nonexistent shoes could make any noise, but she'd realized a while ago trying to make mundane sense of psychic stuff was pointless. She'd give herself a headache but gain no insight.

Another corridor branched off this one, so Kira swerved left down that path.

Sean grabbed her shoulders from behind, forcing her to halt.

"Slow up," he growled in her ear. "You're not paying attention. Look, you can see them right there."

He raised one arm to point to her left a few feet ahead of where they stood.

The hairs on her arms lifted and her skin prickled. Beyond the wall, human-shaped blobs moved, glowing like infrared footage she'd seen in movies. Sean was right. This ability was more like thermal imaging than X-ray. Four blobs held motionless, posted in a semicircle around another person who seemed to be sitting in a chair, though her human-only infrared couldn't show her the furniture. The other three blobs shifted this way and that, bent down, gesticulated. One person threw his or her hands up as if frustrated.

"Ready to go in?" Sean asked.

"Yes."

He took her hand, leading her straight through the wall.

They emerged inside a laboratory. Unlike the isolation room, this room featured no electronic equipment. It held medical paraphernalia, everything from devices to measure vital signs to an open cabinet full of hospital gowns—and of course, tools. Scalpels. Needles. Blood pressure cuffs. A small saw.

Kira's attention stalled on the saw. What were they cutting with that thing?

Sean noticed her staring at the serrated implement and murmured, "Tesler thought he could mine powers from people's brains by cutting them out."

"Cutting out their brains?" Her voice was barely a whisper. She couldn't fathom how anyone could do such a horrific thing.

"Yeah," Sean said. "He wanted to cut out Grace's brain."

Oh God, she prayed Dr. Ferrell hadn't tried that.

Kira tore her attention away from the saw to peruse the rest of the room. Four guards stood sentinel in a semicircle around a chair identical to the one in the isolation room, guarding the man strapped into the chair. Nathan had his eyes closed, his muscles slack as if he slept or had been drugged unconscious. In front of their prisoner, Ferrell and two lackeys loitered, all dressed in lab coats. Ferrell drummed the toe of one sensible shoe on the linoleum floor, arms crossed over her chest and one finger tapping, as she watched her underlings scurrying around to gather tools.

"Hurry up," she hissed. "He wants the contingency in place before the retrieval begins."

Kira wanted to ask Sean what a retrieval was, but she didn't want to miss anything Ferrell said or did. Everything seemed important, even the way she snatched a ballpoint pen from her breast pocket and twirled it between her fingers. Any little thing might provide a vital clue.

Right. Like Kira Magnusson was a crack detective. Sherlock Holmes with boobs.

One of the lackeys, the one she'd called Watkins earlier, cast a wary glance at Nathan. "We've tried this before, but he always resists the process. Can't we do without the contingency?"

"No." Ferrell strode up to the lackey, towering over the short, lanky man. "Watkins, you disappoint me. And our leader will be severely disappointed in your lack of commitment to the cause. Should I call him in here so you can explain why you refuse to activate the contingency?"

Watkins' skin turned a shade paler, and he flapped his head meekly.

"I didn't think so," Ferrell said, and she stalked to the chair. She tilted her head side to side, examining her prisoner with dispassionate interest, the scientist mulling her specimen. After a moment, she sighed and planted one hand atop Nathan's arm. Leaning her weight into his flesh and bone, she raised her other hand and smacked his cheek. She struck him hard enough to redden the skin. "Wake up, Nathan. I know you're only pretending to sleep. Your boy is almost here, and soon he'll be in our custody. How does it feel to know you've lost? After so many years of protecting your son at the expense of your own freedom?"

Nathan's lips warped into a grimace. He opened his eyes, spearing Ferrell with a glare as hot and sharp as a steel spike thrust into a smelting furnace.

"You don't have him yet," Nathan said, his voice calm but laced with something dangerous. "If you did, you wouldn't be making vague threats and talking about your beloved contingency plan."

"He's nearby, darling." She leaned more weight into her hold on his arm, earning a wince from Nathan. "Thanks to David Ransom, we know they're coming here and that they'll find a place not far away to hunker down. They plan to breach this facility. We will be ready for them."

What did Ferrell mean about David? Had they bugged David's phone and overheard him talking to Sean earlier?

Kira had no time to puzzle out the answer because the rest of what the scientist had said penetrated her mind at last. They. Ferrell spoke of more than one person. And she said "they" were hiding close to the bunker intending to breach…Her thoughts trailed off as a cold realization shuddered through her.

Ferrell was talking about her and Sean.

She sensed the truth sinking into Sean's mind too, a detached but no less disturbing shiver of understanding. Nathan's son…

"That's right," Ferrell said like she'd read Kira's mind, though she was speaking to her prisoner. "Nathan Vandenbrook will finally be reunited with his son."

A bolt of shock erupted from Sean to slam into Kira. She gasped, whirling toward him.

His face had gone ashen, and his jaw was slack. Not blinking, he gaped at the man strapped into the chair. His father.

CHAPTER EIGHTEEN

SEAN STOOD PARALYZED, HIS ASTRAL BODY COLD AND STIFF, HIS heart hammering with such force his chest hurt. He couldn't breathe. Couldn't think. This man was his father? No, no, his dad took off for no good reason, abandoning him and his mom without so much as a goodbye. Mom never talked about it, but Sean deduced the truth from the anguish in her eyes whenever he'd asked about his dad. For her to be that broken up about it even years later, the bastard must've done something awful.

Nathan angled his head the slightest bit, and for the first time, Sean got a clear view of the man's eyes. The green irises gleamed in the light of the sterile bulbs suspended from the ceiling.

Green eyes. His mom's had been gray-blue. His grandfather, Tesler, had dark-brown eyes.

No, no, no, no. Sean scuffled backward a couple steps, suddenly breathing hard, almost hyperventilating. This man couldn't be his father. If he was, that meant Tesler had abducted his dad, ripping him away from his family and imprisoning him for seventeen years. Why? Sean swallowed hard, his breaths shortening into staccato gasps. His ears rang. His face tingled with numbness. Why do this to his father? Why?

Kira's hand slipped into his. She threaded their fingers, clasping his hand.

"You'll never get him," Nathan told Ferrell. "Sean is brave and smart. Sophie was a good mother, and even after everything Tesler put him through—" Nathan's voice broke, but he pulled in a breath and fortified his tone. "Even after the torture and the drugs, Sean grew into a strong and good man. He'll fight you, and he'll win."

Strong and good? This man, his supposed father, couldn't know anything about him. Tesler had held Nathan hostage, presumably in a different facility from Sean, for seventeen years. Sean had never seen his father, much less spoken to him. This man wasn't present when sweet Gramps beat and burned and cut Sean, then injected him with enough of JT's poison serum to make him half mad. Somehow, Sean had survived those trials without going totally nuts, but he wasn't normal either.

Not strong. Not good. He'd screwed up too many times to qualify for either adjective.

Kira brushed a lock of hair from his forehead, and he marveled at the fact they could touch in astral form. Why they could this time, he had no clue. This connection with her, it was more than psychic or sexual. He recognized that, but he didn't understand why it should be.

And he didn't deserve her tenderness or the bond they shared.

"The contingency," Ferrell said, leaning in to glower at Nathan from inches away. "You will implement it, or Caleb Magnusson dies."

Nathan gritted his teeth, his lip curling with a hatred Sean understood. He'd hated Tesler that much.

Kira's hand clutched his.

They had to rescue Caleb first before they tried to take down Ferrell and whatever psycho she called her boss.

Ferrell had said "thanks to David Ransom" they'd found where Sean and Kira had hidden. Whether her goons really had found them, he didn't know. David had no knowledge of their hideout, and he wouldn't betray them, anyway. Unless Ferrell threatened to hurt Abby. Or unless they'd tapped David's phone.

Someone had abducted Grace and Abby. It must've been Ferrell and her cohorts.

He and Kira needed to find Grace and her daughter too.

"You know what we want," Ferrell said. "Do it now."

Nathan spat in her face. "Fuck you."

Sean pulled Kira tight against him. "We have to get Caleb now. Then we need to find out where Grace and Abby are."

"But your father—"

"Can obviously handle himself. We'll come back for him."

Sean prayed getting some distance from the man would ease the deep-down itch inside him, the unease that made him so antsy he thought he might pop out of his own skin. But when they materialized in the barrel-ceilinged room, the itch got worse instead of better.

Caleb slouched on the overstuffed couch. He looked so small and helpless perched on the big cushions, knees drawn up, hugging himself while—

Oh jeez. The kid was crying.

With a glance, no words required, he and Kira agreed on a plan. They made themselves visible to her brother.

Caleb's head shot up, his bleary eyes wide. "Kiki?"

Sean couldn't even manage a sarcastic comment about the nickname. Yeah, things had gone beyond bad straight into horrifying.

Leaping off the couch, Caleb ran to Kira and tried to hug her. His arms passed right through her. "Kira?"

"It's me," she said, kneeling before her brother. "I don't have time to explain right now, but it's really me. I need you to trust me and do what I say. Can you do that?"

The boy bit his bottom lip and nodded.

Kira raised a hand as if to touch him, then lowered it. "This is my friend, Sean. He's going to help us get you out of here."

Caleb nodded again, biting his lip harder.

"We have to move," Sean said.

Kira rose. "I know."

"You'll need to do something about that door." He pointed toward the sealed entrance to the isolation room.

She lifted a hand, clamped her fingers tight, and shot them straight.

The door exploded open, thwacking into the wall inside the other room and bouncing back to a halfway-closed position.

Sean moved toward the door. "Follow me. And watch out for bad guys."

With Sean in the lead, they wended their way through the bunker facility single file with Caleb between him and Kira. The kid had serious mettle. Despite being kidnapped and having his life threatened, Caleb marched down the corridors as fast as his legs could go, no longer crying, not even complaining about the breakneck speed of their escape. Nathan had called Sean brave, but that was crap. He'd crumbled under pressure more than once. Tesler had stormed into his life when he was fifteen. Caleb was only eight, but he evinced an inner strength Sean had never achieved.

Though she'd blown open the first door, Kira dialed it back after that, releasing the locks and then engaging them again after Caleb got through the doors. The psychic thermal imaging he and Kira had created let Sean check for enemies before they led Caleb through any doorway or into any new corridor. How much time did they have before Ferrell and her cohorts discovered Caleb was gone? *Not enough.*

A clock ticked in Sean's head, counting down the seconds until all hell broke loose. It was a clock with no hands, no digital readout. He had no clue how long they had.

They reached a door that looked different from the others. It was dark-gray metal with a lever handle and clearly thicker than the other doors they'd breached. Sean thrust his head through the door—and sunlight blinded him. Through the brilliance, he spotted trees.

Sean pulled back into the building. "This is the exit. Take Caleb and find him a spot where he can hide until we come for him."

"What about you?" Kira asked.

"I'll hang back to keep watch and scan for more warm bodies. You go with Caleb."

She watched him for a moment. "Okay. But I'm coming back as soon as he's hunkered down."

"Fine." He'd known it wouldn't be that easy to get rid of her, but he also knew he had to do it. His messed-up life would not hurt anyone else.

Kira unlocked the door and eased it open with her powers, raising her hand palm out to nudge it. She exited first, with Caleb close behind.

The kid paused to look back at Sean, then followed Kira outside.

Once Kira had shut and locked the door, Sean flew back to the room where Ferrell held Nathan. He was slumped in his chair, eyes glassy, mouth open.

The doctor patted Nathan's cheek. "I knew you'd see reason. The serum always makes you more pliable."

Serum. Sean tensed, his nerves bristled by the word. By what it meant. Ferrell must've employed the drug developed by Jackson Tennant, which he'd called a serum. The drug Tesler had given Sean.

Burning agony. His mind on fire. Muscles cramping with convulsive force.

And Ferrell had done that to his father how many times? *Seventeen years.*

"It's time," Ferrell said to Nathan. "Activate the contingency."

A wave of searing energy shot through Sean, shattering his astral body, obliterating his connection to Kira.

He hurtled back into his physical body with the force of a skydiver slamming into the earth because his chute hadn't opened. Bones shattering. Skull fracturing. The agony of a thousand shards of glass gored him from head to toe.

And he screamed.

His entire body throbbed. His vision was blurry and wobbling like his eyes had turned into vibrating jelly. The paralysis lasted a few minutes that seemed like hours, but gradually, he regained movement in his fingers, then his arms, then his legs. His vision settled and swam back into focus.

Gasping for air, he gaped at the wood ceiling above him. The cabin. The porch.

Kira.

He rolled onto his side, realized he was lying on the porch floor, and heaved himself into a sitting position with more effort than it would've taken to lift a one-ton rock. His muscles burned and ached. He blinked rapidly, focusing in on the lump on the wooden swing.

Sean scrambled closer.

Kira lay in a heap on the swing, her feet dangling over the edge, her eyes shut. With shaking fingers, he checked her wrist for a pulse. There it was, strong and steady. He nearly collapsed from relief but forced himself to stay upright. He stroked her cheek, swept hair from her face, and closed his hand around one of hers.

"Don't move!"

Sean swung his head to the right and tightened his grip on Kira's hand.

Men dressed in camouflage outfits and wielding big guns had surrounded the cabin. One of them stood at the bottom of the porch steps, his weapon trained on Sean.

"You can't get away," the man hollered, louder than necessary. "Come quietly, or we will shoot you. Not dead, but it'll hurt like hell. Either way, you're coming with us."

Sean tried to tap into his powers, any of them, but he met a yawning vacancy in his own mind. No remote viewing. No healing, though he desperately tried to use that power on Kira. No empathic sensing either. He had zilch.

The lead commando clomped up the steps. "I'm sure you've realized by now your powers are gone. You can't fight us. If you try, your girl will get hurt—and we'll take you both anyway."

What could he do? He had no weapons, not even a big stick. He was powerless.

Sean got to his feet, hands raised, and spoke the words he'd sworn never to utter. "I surrender."

CHAPTER NINETEEN

THE GROUND TREMBLED BENEATH KIRA, ROUSING HER FROM A DEEP and groggy slumber. A rumbling accompanied the shaking. An earthquake? Did they have those in…Where was she? Montana, that was it. She and Sean had flown to Montana on Gabriel Amador's jet and…What had they done here? Everything was fuzzy.

Kira peeled her lids apart, wincing at the brightness of sunlight in her eyes. Her cheek rested on fabric—denim, she realized. She was lying on her side with her head propped up on…someone's thigh. She blinked repeatedly to clear her vision, and the surroundings came into focus. She was in a vehicle. In front of her, two large seats bracketed a center console, and two large men occupied those seats. They wore all black and stared straight ahead with a purpose and resolve indicative of men following orders.

An arm draped over her with one big hand resting on her elbow.

Warmth sifted through her. Sean's thigh pillowed her head and his hand cupped her elbow. The protectiveness of the posture softened her unease, but only a smidgen, because the memory of what happened flared in her mind. Scorching energy had slammed into her, disintegrating her astral form and plummeting her back into her body at the cabin. The agonizing force of her ejection from the bunker had knocked her unconscious.

She pushed up into a half-sitting position, held up by one straight arm. Sean's hand slid down to her hip, shifted by her movement. His body faced forward, but he'd turned his head toward the window, hiding his expression and eyes from her. Though his hand on her hip seemed relaxed, the rest of his body was strung taut.

"How are you feeling?" he asked without looking at her, his voice flat.

"Okay." She swung her legs off the bench seat, her feet coming to rest on the floor of the bulky SUV. It was black, of course, with a dark-gray interior. "How long was I out?"

"Ten minutes, eighteen seconds."

An awfully specific length of time. He didn't wear a watch.

Kira wriggled to get situated on the seat close to Sean, their thighs touching.

He lifted his arm to accommodate her, then settled it around her shoulders.

She studied his profile, wishing to hell he'd look at her. "How do you know the minutes and seconds?"

Moving only his index finger, he pointed toward the front, into the gap between the passenger seat and the door. Kira leaned over his lap to squint into the space. The black-clad guard seated there had his right elbow braced on the door's armrest with his hand raised, fingers tapping the glass. On his wrist, he wore a big digital watch. The numbers glowed green.

"I can count," Sean whispered, "and that guy's had his hand like that the whole time."

Ah. At least that explained how he knew the specific length of time she'd been out. But she had another question about that.

Leaning back into the seat, into the sanctuary of Sean's arm, she asked, "Why were you keeping track of exactly how long I stayed unconscious?"

At last, he swung his head toward her and speared her with a look of such intense longing it made her throat constrict. "Because I needed to know."

His voice was intense too, rife with things she didn't dare consider right now.

They had bigger problems than whether he…had feelings for her. Or vice versa.

"Are they taking us to the bunker?" she asked.

"I'm guessing yeah." He tugged her closer. "We have no powers."

"What?" *Not possible,* her logical brain insisted. But when she flicked her fingers toward the man in the passenger seat, intending to shove his seat forward, nothing happened. She got a faint zing of psychic energy, but then it fizzled out and flicking her fingers again produced nothing. No zing. No fizzle. Just a yawning emptiness where her powers should've been. "What do we do?"

"Nothing, for the moment. Wait for an opening or something." He pulled her tight against him and dipped his mouth to her ear to murmur, "Caleb?"

"Safe, for now," she said sotto voce, speaking out of the corner of her mouth in case the guards up front could read lips in the rear-view mirror. These days, nothing seemed impossible. "I got him hunkered down before—What the hell happened to us? It was like I got torn out of remote-viewing mode and stuffed back into my body."

"More like a bomb detonating in your psyche, I'd say. That's what I felt, anyway."

Though he sounded calm, she perceived the dark tension in him and didn't like it one bit. His demeanor reminded her of the night they'd met, when he'd been hell-bent on punishing the person who set off the bomb at the cafe. He couldn't bring himself to hurt her, though. She had a sick feeling he might lose those compunctions when confronted with the mastermind of this terror spree.

If he tapped into the Golden Power again...

Dread shuddered through her, cold and viscous.

She rested her head on his shoulder and winced at a soreness on her scalp. "Must've hit my head when I passed out. Got a sore spot."

His arm around her stiffened. "Are you okay? Do you feel any dizziness or pain?"

"No, I'm fine."

Though his arm slackened a bit, he gusted out a sigh. "I can't even heal you."

"I'm fine." She found his other hand, the fingers of which he'd bent into his thigh, and took hold of it. "How could we lose our powers?"

"No frigging idea." He exhaled a slow breath. "Electromagnetic fields tuned to a particular frequency can dampen psychic abilities, but even that can't erase them altogether. David said his powers are gone. These people must've used the same method on us, to cancel out our abilities."

"You think our powers are gone for good?"

"Don't know." He slid his hand up and down her arm, caressing tenderly. "Dr. Ferrell kept talking about a contingency plan. Maybe this is it."

"Knocking out our powers? I guess that would solve the problem of us remote viewing their bunker, but so far, they've wanted us to use our powers to do things for them." She picked up his hand, sandwiching it between both of hers. "Why would they suddenly want us de-powered?"

"No idea."

The vehicle crested a hill, and the driver steered it off the road and onto a two-track. The dirt road sloped downhill, heading into a forested area. Shadows closed in around the SUV, plunging the interior into a false twilight, the sudden gloom making Kira clasp Sean's hand more firmly. Her pulse accelerated more the closer they got to wherever they were being taken. The bunker, she knew that. She'd exited the place and glimpsed its exterior, but having the powers ripped out of her mind had turned her flight with Caleb into a blurry rush. She remembered getting her brother settled into a hiding spot in the woods. Everything else had become hazy.

Concrete steps. Yes, she recalled that. The door had opened into a concrete stairwell that led up to ground level. Trees, she remembered that too. Lots and lots of trees.

The SUV rolled to a stop.

Kira straightened and peered out the windshield, but she couldn't see anything.

Bushes, she abruptly remembered. Right, there had been bushes concealing the stairwell.

Damn, some seriously paranoid weirdos had built this bunker. She couldn't see any hint of it, even when the guards ushered them out of the vehicle. A second SUV had followed them, a fact she hadn't noted until they climbed out of the vehicle that had brought them here. The second one must've trailed close behind, since it arrived at the same time.

Four guards piled out of the second SUV. They joined the first two to shepherd Kira and Sean toward a clump of bushes. Only when they drew up parallel to the steps did she notice the yawning maw of the concrete stairwell. Trees shielded it from overhead viewing.

Seriously paranoid people, for sure.

The two guards from the first SUV tromped down the steps to the door hidden under a concrete overhang, masked by shadows. Keys jangled. A lock chunked.

A door swung inward.

"Bring 'em in," a guard said.

His four buddies nudged Kira and Sean toward the stairwell. They descended into the shadows, through the open doorway into a lighted corridor. This was the way she and Sean had brought Caleb on their flight from the facility. Now, they were being herded into its bowels. Powerless. Captive.

Fear shot through her. When Sean had kidnapped her, she hadn't feared for her safety. With these lunatics, she had no idea what to expect. They tortured people. Orchestrated bombings. Would they kill too? Yes, her intuition warned. Yes, they would.

Kira lost track of how many times they turned into a different corridor. She lost track of everything, her mind reeling from the sequence of events that led her to this moment. How had these maniacs found her to begin with? How had they taken Caleb? She'd gone to pick him up after school only to find him missing, and minutes later, she'd received the first call. *Wait for instructions*, they'd said. *Tell no one or your brother dies.* She'd obeyed, too stunned to think of what to do. Then came the tests, the practicing, and after that...

The cafe. Sean. The movie theater. Sean. Healing David. Flying to Montana. Those brief moments of bliss with Sean, followed by finding his long-lost father and freeing Caleb only to have their powers stripped away.

Why had any of this happened? What did it all mean?

So much didn't make sense. Terrorists claimed responsibility for their attacks. These people hadn't. They'd left the world wondering how and why these tragedies occurred. The first bomb had no trigger, nothing to clue police in to the origins of the device. The second one had a trigger and had detonated without a psychic push. The villains must've guessed she and Sean would try to find the second bomb and dispose of it without causing an explosion. They'd built a failsafe into the device that time, so they could set it off remotely.

And still, they hadn't claimed responsibility.

The guards unlocked a door and ushered Sean and Kira inside a room.

Kira gulped back a gasp. The isolation room.

Sean had gone stony, his body taut and his gaze glued to the chair at the room's center.

Nathan was strapped to the chair with leather restraints and shackles, the double bindings a clear sign these people feared him. Or feared his powers. They must've brought him back to this room so they'd have the added protection of the dual restraints.

But Sean said he couldn't sense any psychic energy in his father. Something else that didn't add up.

Dr. Ferrell stood by the banks of equipment, her hip braced against the wall, arms folded over her chest. She observed the newcomers with detached interest, once again the scientist examining her specimens.

Her assistant hovered nearby, his eyes large, hands clamped over his belly, fingers scratching his skin.

Jeez, how badass was Nathan to inspire this kind of anxiety?

Unless...they feared someone else.

The assistant had his gaze nailed to a single person, the same individual Ferrell's scientific interest had settled on.

Sean.

But he had no powers anymore. *Right now,* he didn't. Maybe they knew he'd regain his abilities soon.

God, she prayed he did. She prayed her powers came back too. Together, they could stop these lunatics.

The door to the barrel-ceilinged room pivoted open, and a figure strode into the isolation room.

Kira froze.

Gabriel Amador smiled. "Welcome to my sanctuary."

SEAN STARED AT AMADOR, HIS BRAIN STRUGGLING TO COMPREHEND what he saw. It couldn't be. As much as Sean disliked Amador, he never would've thought the guy could become the mastermind of a terrorist organization bent on…doing things that made no sense. Yeah, that fact alone should've made him suspicious Amador was involved. The guy had a handful of screws loose inside that skull of his. They must've jangled whenever he shook his head.

No, this was impossible. Amador lacked the coherence to mastermind his own life, much less a bizarre plot of this magnitude.

Then again, Amador had founded and helmed an international venture capital firm. He'd gotten rich that way and kept the company going even after his son and wife died and he'd descended into revenge-driven madness.

Amador had seemed almost happy about David being in a coma—and disappointed when Sean and Kira healed David. Amador had stayed by Grace's side, offering a smarmy kind of comfort. The guy had kindled a torch for her ever since they'd met five years ago, though Grace swore he'd gotten over those feelings. *Yeah, right.* A fruitcake didn't shed its fruit.

He should've seen this coming.

Right, he should've guessed the nutjob who adored Grace would get hold of his long-missing father and orchestrate a nefarious plot to do crazy things that seemed to have no purpose.

Sean's gaze tracked from Amador to Nathan. His father stared up at the ceiling, his breathing heavy, his body limp. What had Amador done to Nathan?

"You are curious," Amador said, one hand in the pocket of his gray slacks. He wore a crisp white dress shirt, long-sleeve, with gold cuff links that glinted in the light of the bare bulbs suspended from the ceiling. "You wonder why I've done all of this."

Sean snorted. "No shit."

"The world needs to understand. I am showing them."

"Understand what? How whacked-out you are?"

Amador's mouth curved in a creepily satisfied smile. "They need to understand psychic faculties exist. Only when they accept the existence of such powers will they comprehend the danger posed by the individuals who possess them."

The guy had to be kidding. Insane-o dude on the loose, remember?

"Let me see if I've got the gist of this," Sean said, trying for the calmest tone he could muster, which wasn't real calm. "You kidnap and torture psychics, then blackmail Kira into setting off bombs as part of a plan to convince the world we're the bad guys? You set off the second bomb, not us. You abducted a little boy, and I'd bet a trillion dollars you took Grace and Abby too. Why would anyone believe a word you say? Nobody's going to accept psychic powers made a bomb go off." Sean shook his head, so baffled he couldn't think of words for a few seconds. "I thought you wanted Grace to, you know, fall for you or something. She's a psychic, bonehead. If you vilify all of us, you vilify her too."

"She will understand," Amador said, "once my plan is fully executed. She will be grateful I saved her from a life of constant fear of discovery and constant anxiety about the Golden Power."

"Jeez, Gabe, that's—" No other word for it, so Sean plowed ahead. "That's crazy, man. Like, one-hundred-percent bonkers, nutcrackers insane."

Amador sighed like a man forced to exercise extreme patience with a slow child. "Sean, you fail to see the wider picture. Sometimes violence is the only action that will gain the world's attention. Only when forced to see the truth will they do so."

"The truth? You're showing the world you're a terrorist." Sean stopped as a realization struck him. "But nobody's taken responsibility for these bombings. Nobody knows how they were done either, which means nobody realizes this has anything to do with psychics. Your plan is toast."

"We begin the final phase shortly." Amador strolled over to Nathan's chair, resting his hand on the back next to the other man's head. "Once that begins, everyone will know the truth. And the final phase begins with you."

Sean jerked his head back. "Me?"

"Actually," Amador said, "this begins with your father and ends with you."

Sean couldn't wrap his mind around anything Amador had said. He shook his head dumbly.

"Your father was the key to entrapping you," Amador said. "Now that we have you, the rest of the plan may be enacted."

Sean glanced at Nathan.

His father raised his head and focused on Sean. "I'm sorry."

For what, Sean wanted to ask. His voice wouldn't cooperate.

Amador patted Nathan's head. "Your father is a null."

Sean felt his forehead wrinkle as his brows cinched together. "A what?"

"He's one of a rare breed known as nulls." Amador circled behind the chair, trailing his fingers along the top of its back. "Other psychics can't detect a null's power, but more importantly, a null has the ability to cancel out the powers of another psychic. This is how we captured you and Kira, and Grace and Abby. Nathan sent out a nullifying pulse aimed specifically at the Ransoms, eliminating Grace and David's powers. Later, he fired off another pulse directed at the two of you."

Amador gestured at Sean and Kira.

Nullifying power? That…wasn't…possible.

Was it?

"You have never heard of this ability," Amador said, "have you? I'm not surprised. It is rare, and few have seen it, much less studied it. Buried deep in Tesler's records, which Grace permitted me to examine over the years, I discovered a one-paragraph statement about nulls. The only scientist to have studied one died in nineteen twenty-three, but he left behind tantalizing clues about these rare and coveted individuals."

Sean could do nothing except shake his head again.

"Tesler never realized your father had this ability," Amador continued. "Dr. Ferrell, though once his protégé, had taken control of an ALI facility here in Montana. She began secret experiments to determine if any of the travelers in her domain might be nulls. Tesler had taken your father to study his known psychic talents, but his powers were too weak to be of much value. This was before Jackson Tennant developed the power-enhancing serum. Since Nathan seemed useless, Tesler sent him to Ferrell. She was to keep him in custody until Tesler could get you transferred to his aegis."

Custody? Aegis? Sean stared at Amador without blinking. "I don't get—I mean, why would Tesler want me? I didn't come into my powers until I was fifteen, long after my mom ran away from her father because he was such a scumbag."

"No, Sean. You evinced paranormal abilities long before then." Amador laid his palm atop Nathan's head. "That is why your mother fled with you and hid from her father. Tesler had witnessed your nascent powers and wanted to study you, but your mother at last realized what 'study' meant to her father. She would not allow him to harm you, so she and Nathan fled with you and tried to hide." Amador smiled wistfully. "But Nathan made the mistake of returning to your former home to retrieve your favorite toy. Tesler's men were lying in wait and captured him."

His father had gotten caught because of him. Sean rocked back on his heels, his mind spinning with colliding thoughts. It was his fault. His fault.

"Unfortunately," Amador said, "your father managed to call your mother just before Tesler's men apprehended him. He'd sensed someone following him and feared for the safety of you and your mother, so he instructed her to run. She did. You were only five at the time. Sophie did an excellent job of hiding you both, that is why Tesler couldn't find you for years."

Sean didn't want to know, but he couldn't stop himself from asking. "How did he find us?"

"Ask your father."

Nathan dropped his chin to his chest, his shoulders caving in.

"What do you want from me?" Sean asked Amador.

The bastard rolled his shoulders back and lifted his chin. "You will become the face of the movement, the one who forces the world to recognize the reality and dangers of psychic phenomena."

"How the hell do I do that?"

"By taking responsibility for the attacks."

Chapter Twenty

THE FACE OF THE MOVEMENT. SEAN STILL COULDN'T MOVE ANY PART of his body except his mouth, which he couldn't seem to shut up. Amador meant Sean would become an avowed terrorist. So far, the bombings hadn't killed anyone, and the second event hadn't resulted in any injuries, but the sinking feeling in the pit of Sean's stomach warned him Amador wasn't done yet. Did this wacko actually believe terrorism would make the world believe in psychic powers?

"Your plan sucks," Sean said. "Even if I do what you want, it won't have the effect you're hoping for. Nobody's going to believe in the paranormal because we claim to have set off a bomb with telekinesis."

"You will demonstrate for them. In the video you will make and we will distribute."

"Sure, because everybody knows videos can't be faked. Totally convincing." No point in arguing, Sean realized. Amador would never give up his crazy plan. So, he asked the question he'd been wondering about since Amador made his grand entrance. "Why did you keep telling me not to investigate? Sounds like you wanted me here to play patsy for you."

"I do, and it was my plan from the start. David's injuries would push you to hunt for the perpetrator, I knew this because you crave vengeance the same as I have."

"But the first bombing could've injured or killed me."

The whackjob shrugged one shoulder. "A risk worth taking. If you had died, I could have easily made Kira the face of the movement."

Blame whatever psychic was handy. *Awesome.*

Sean straightened, determined to appear strong in front of his nemesis—and that's what Amador had become, his enemy. "You said your master plan starts with my dad. Tell me how."

Amador shrugged, his attention wandering along with his gaze.

"Wake up," Sean growled, snapping his fingers to regain the man's attention. "I talked to David a while ago. I know Grace and Abby have been kidnapped." Sean fisted his hands, then forced himself to loosen them. Calmness and strength, that's what he needed to convey. "You took them, admit it."

"Yes, I have them," Amador said, "or I soon will. They should arrive any moment. Four psychics with no powers have less than no chance of besting me. Once you accept you have no other recourse, Sean, you will do as I command."

He could've pointed out no one could have "less than no chance" of anything, but logic no longer held any sway over Amador.

"You seriously think," Sean said, "I'll claim responsibility for the bombings."

Amador wagged one finger like a metronome. "More than that, I'm afraid. You will also take responsibility for the worst act of terrorism in recorded history."

Cold swept through Sean, and a steel ball of dread solidified in his gut. His fingers crooked into his palms, the nails digging into his skin. "What are you talking about?"

He knew it would be bad, whatever Amador had cooked up for his final phase. It would be really bad. Colossal. But he couldn't have imagined how terrible until the man voiced his scheme.

"It's quite simple," Amador said as if discussing a football game. "Malmstrom Air Force Base is not far from here. The base houses intercontinental ballistic missiles with nuclear rockets inside them. You will launch one of these missiles and destroy a significant portion of the eastern seaboard of the United States."

Sean stumbled backward a step, unable to blink or breathe. He shook his head. His brain had gone into its own little nuclear meltdown as he struggled to comprehend Amador's words. ICBM. Rockets. Launch. Destroy.

Amador wanted to nuke the East Coast. To get revenge on psychics, he'd sacrifice millions of innocent people.

His son had been psychic. The single thought broke through the melee in Sean's mind. Why would Amador punish others like his son? *Think, man, get a grip fast. No time for panic.*

Sean glanced at Kira. Wide eyed and pale, she met his gaze head-on, and he knew. They couldn't let this happen. If they had to die in the effort, they must stop Amador from enacting his plan.

Without letting on they were sabotaging him.

Kira nodded as if she'd heard his thoughts or guessed them. Two people shouldn't know each other this well after a couple days, but they did. Circumstance had forced them together, but something else linked them. Something he didn't have time to consider.

To Amador, Sean said, "Your son, Evander, had psychic abilities. How can you hate all of us when your son had the same kind of powers we have?"

"Do not mention my son. Do not speak his name." Amador's face turned crimson, his lips warped and quivering as he snarled his words. "Powers killed my son. If he had been a normal child, Karl Tesler would never have taken him, and he would never have died. My wife and son would still be with me."

"Okay, but—"

"Stop speaking!" Amador roared. "You are the grandson of the man who tortured and murdered my child. Tesler stole my son's life, but he let you live. You do not deserve the life you have been given, do not appreciate it, believe you have suffered more than anyone else. You have no conception of what suffering truly is. Only I know!"

The last three words thundered through the contained space, reverberating off the walls and vibrating in Sean's ears. Amador had gone so far off the deep end he must've sunk straight to the bottom of the ocean. Sean had never claimed he suffered more than anyone else. Maybe he hadn't appreciated what he had as much as he should, but that didn't make him evil. The weirdest part of this whole experience was that it had shown him he deserved the life he had, the loved ones he had, the powers he had. Kira proved all of that to him.

Amador had no clue about anything.

"I will have my vengeance," Amador hissed, raising his fists to shake them in the air. "Innocent blood must be spilled to convince the world of the true danger."

"What exactly do you think will happen if you nuke the East Coast?"

"Everyone will believe. Everyone will see the truth."

"Then what?"

Amador's fury dissolved into a blank expression.

"You don't know," Sean said. "If the final phase of your plan is launching an ICBM, that means you have no clue what to do after that. Nuke the East Coast, blame the psychics, and that's the sum total of your plan."

"I need no further actions after that," Amador said with a confused expression. "I will have made my point."

"Don't you realize the authorities will start an all-out, no-holds-barred hunt for the terrorists who murdered millions of people? They'll come for all of us, you included."

"They will come for you, the one who confesses to these crimes."

"And I'll give you up." Sean scratched his neck, unsure how to proceed when Amador wouldn't admit to the lunacy of his plan. Take another tack, he decided. "I'm not doing jack for you. Cancel your statement to the world because I will not be the face of your crazy movement."

"Will you watch Kira and Nathan suffer and die?"

Of course he wouldn't, but Amador absolutely would hurt them to hammer his point into Sean's brain. The point being "I'm a nutjob bent on destruction." Sean needed a plan of his own, but so far nothing had come to him. Refusing to do Amador's bidding hadn't worked.

Should've gotten a degree in psychology, not math.

"Let me talk to my dad," Sean said. "Alone."

"You may speak to him, but only in my presence."

"Uh-uh. I talk to him alone or you can forget about Malmstrom and the East Coast apocalypse." Not that Sean would ever launch a nuke, no way, but he needed Amador to believe he might do it. He would die before he'd nuke an entire country or even a single acre of land. He had no choice but to reiterate his threat, channeling the anger that had simmered inside him before Kira showed him how to let it go. "Leave me alone with my dad or no dice. You can find somebody else to launch your ICBM, and I'll watch you torture Kira and Nathan. I mean, I don't even know my dad. And Kira, well, I kidnapped her because she blew up my best friend. Do you really think I care what happens to them?"

Amador pursed his lips, his gaze narrowed on Sean. "But you hold her hand."

"To make sure she doesn't run away." Sean hesitated. "It's not like I can use my powers to escape with my daddy. I've got no mojo, thanks to the nullifying trick. I'm as harmless as a kitten, right?"

Even kittens had claws and sharp teeth, though.

Amador huffed. "As you wish. But you will have five minutes, not one second more."

"Fine." Sean waved toward the sweet lady doctor. "And take Ferrell and the goons with you. Kira stays."

Kira looked surprised but stayed silent.

Amador squinted at Sean. "If you don't care for her, why do you wish her to stay?"

"Because I do." Damn, he really sucked at this manipulation crap. Luckily for him, Amador was too screwy to realize it. "Do what I say if you want your doomsday to happen."

Lips squashed into a sharp line, Amador nodded. "You are not to remove Nathan's restraints. We will be watching on the monitors in the control room across the hall."

He gestured for the others to follow him, and they trooped out of the room into the corridor, shutting the door.

Alone with his father, Sean suddenly had no clue what to say. He clomped up to the chair, itching to tear off the restraints, but Amador would be watching. Sean had to leave the restraints in place.

"It's all right," his father said. "I know you can't set me free, not with Amador keeping an eye on you."

"Can you read my mind?"

His father laughed without even a hint of humor. "No, I wouldn't even if I could. But I can't, anyway. You were staring at the restraints, so I assumed you wanted to free me."

Sean glanced at the leather straps and metal shackles again. The heat of anger swelled in his chest, and he couldn't tamp it down. Nullifying his powers seemed to have stripped away his natural ability to repress emotions, and the calm Kira had imbued into him had been tapped out when he had to pretend he'd let Amador butcher her and his dad. He'd relied on his empathic ability to keep his emotions in check. He didn't know how to repress without paranormal assistance.

He'd have to feel it. Push through the anger and pain, and somehow, get through this ordeal.

Dead or alive.

Kira came up beside him and slipped her hand into his. The simple gesture evoked a storm of emotions inside him, things he couldn't sort out even if he had the time. Mostly good things. She'd gotten through his psychic defenses to make him feel again, so of course, she got through his normal defenses too. He couldn't hide from her.

"Mom never talked about you," Sean said to his father. "I thought you walked out on us. When I came into my powers, I figured you must've known I'd be a freak and you left because of me."

Nathan gave him a sad smile. "I never wanted to leave you or your mother. I loved you both. I never stopped loving you."

Sean's throat constricted, but he squeezed the words out. "It was my fault you got caught. You went back for my toy."

"It wasn't your fault. I should've known better than to go back there, but you were so distraught about leaving your favorite bear behind. After taking you away from the only home you'd ever known…" Nathan shut his eyes briefly. "I had to do one small thing to make it better for you. I made a mistake, Sean. You did nothing wrong."

Maybe not back then, but lately…Yeah, he'd messed up enough for one lifetime.

No more.

His father bent toward him as far as possible with the restraints holding him down. His expression and his voice conveyed wrenching emotion. "It's my fault, Sean, not yours. I betrayed you twice. I tried not to, but they have ways of breaking even the strongest person, and I was never the strongest. Not like you and your mother. They broke me, and I told them where to find you."

Tiny arcs of electricity sparked across Sean's skin, the physical manifestation of a shock too deep to repress, even if he'd had the capacity to do that. He knew of one surefire way to break the strongest psychics.

"JT's serum," Sean said. "The one they gave you earlier today. They've given it to you before, haven't they? That's how they broke you."

"Yes. I fought it as hard as I could…"

"Nobody can fight that poison." A memory barreled through his mind, of the searing agony and the mind-melting power of the serum. "I've had it. I know what it's like."

Nathan stared at him, eyes wide. He opened his mouth to speak but seemed incapable of piecing together words, his jaw working.

The horror and concern on his father's face triggered a hard pang in Sean's chest. All his life he'd believed his dad abandoned him and his mom—for no good reason, or else because of Sean's latent powers. He'd finally learned the truth.

Just in time for both of them to die.

Kira squeezed his hand, and he squeezed hers right back.

Then he spoke to his father. "Are my powers gone for good?"

"No, they'll come back."

"How long?"

His dad shrugged, wincing as the restraints bit into his muscles. "It varies. Six hours at most, based on past experience. Could be less, though."

Sean prayed it would be a lot less. They needed their powers back now.

What Nathan had said a moment ago resurfaced in Sean's mind. "You said you told Amador and his buddies where to find me. How did you know?"

A bitter smile tightened Nathan's mouth. "Traveling. I've been keeping an eye on you for as long as I've been a prisoner of Tesler and the ones who came after him. No one noticed. I found ways to disguise my activities by checking on you when they thought I was asleep or during scheduled excursions. My powers aren't particularly strong, but I have limited remote-viewing abilities. It was enough to let me keep tabs on you." He shut his eyes again, swallowed hard, and looked straight at Sean. "When Tesler got his hands on you, I tried to intervene. But I don't have that kind of power. I'm sorry, Sean."

He didn't know what to say to that or how to feel about it. Maybe his dad wasn't the prick he'd thought he was, or maybe this was an act instigated by Ferrell and Amador to trick Sean into doing things he would never do without coercion. They might've decided subtle coercion, of the emotional kind, would work better than blackmail or threats of violence.

With his empathic ability crippled, Sean couldn't get a read on Nathan. He'd have to trust his instincts about the man, but he was too confused to do that. He'd trusted Grace and David as soon as he met them, despite knowing nothing about either of them. His instincts urged him to believe in their good intentions, and he'd been right to take that advice. David had been a prisoner of Tesler and JT when Sean met him, and Grace had been on the run from the same two villains. Neither of them, however, had been a prisoner for seventeen years.

Could someone held for that long stay true to his own nature? Nathan must've been tortured, drugged, and who-knew-what else. What if he'd been worn down? Broken and then reshaped into whatever Tesler and now Ferrell wanted him to become?

What better weapon to use against Sean than his own father?

"You don't know if you should trust me," Nathan said. "I understand. You're smart to doubt me. I doubt myself sometimes, after all these years as a prisoner. But I've always tried to protect you the best I could, though I didn't always succeed."

Sean wanted to believe him so badly.

Despite knowing the answer wouldn't make him feel better, he had to ask. "How bad was it? The things they did to you, I mean. Being a prisoner for so long."

"There were unpleasant times, but I spent most of my days in fairly decent quarters reading or watching TV. I have an old photograph of you, me, and your mom. I'd look at it whenever I needed to remember why I'm fighting them." Nathan sighed, seeming older and more exhausted all of a sudden. "I assumed I'd never get out of here. The torture was occasional, but it's the drugs that bother me the most. I can withstand pain a lot better than chemicals that turn my brain to jelly."

"We'll get you out of here somehow."

Nathan shook his head. "Don't bother about me. Whatever happens, whatever they threaten, you cannot give them what they want."

"I know."

Sean would make sure Amador never got his way, no matter the cost. If Sean had to die to stop the madman, he'd make the sacrifice without hesitation.

Chapter Twenty-One

A LOCK CLUNKED, AND THE DOOR SWUNG OPEN. KIRA BACKED away from Nathan, with Sean following her, as Amador and his co-horts marched into the room. The revelations so far had proved shocking, and she couldn't imagine what Sean must have been feeling right now. His father was alive. Nathan had never willingly abandoned his family. Kira was happy for Sean that he'd learned the truth, but she worried about what might come next. Amador was far from done with them.

She sensed it in a way she couldn't explain. The certainty rang in her soul.

Kira and Sean backed up to within ten feet of the door to the barrel-ceilinged room. Her hand found his, and she clasped it tightly. He returned the gesture, though neither of them looked at the other. Their gazes stayed trained on Amador.

The lunatic aimed a benevolent smile at Sean. "I permitted you to speak with your father. You should now realize the gravity of your situation. If you refuse to obey my commands, your father will suffer. Kira will suffer."

Sean glared at Amador. "They can handle it. I am not launching a nuke for you."

"Perhaps Kira can convince you."

Kira shook her head. "Forget it. I'm not telling Sean to kill millions of people."

"That's unfortunate. I had hoped to avoid this, but you leave me no choice." Amador waved to the guards. "Retrieve the surprise."

Two guards departed, and the door shut behind them with a *chunk*.

"Do you wonder," Amador said, "how we found you, Kira?"

She had wondered about that a lot, but suddenly she was sure she didn't want to know.

He told her anyway. "Your boyfriend wasn't the only witness to your display of psychic power. Onlookers not only watched but also recorded your outburst on their cellular telephones. Two of them posted the videos online."

Kira bit down on her lip but even the slight pain couldn't keep her focused. Videos? Online?

"None of them believed your display had been paranormal in nature," Amador said. "No, they thought it a prank instigated by one of those practical-joke shows on television. But the keywords they used when describing the incident attracted the attention of our search bots. When we viewed the videos, we knew you must have powers. One of the witnesses named you, even tagged you in the social media post. That is how we found you."

Tagged her? Kira didn't remember that, but then, she'd avoided social media after her boyfriend posted a rant about what an evil witch she was. The videos must've been posted after that.

Jesus. Videos. Social media ruined her life, literally.

The door burst open, and the guards ushered two people into the room. The prisoners had black hoods over their heads, but she could tell the couple included a man and a woman.

One guard shut the door while the other nodded to Amador.

He spoke to Kira. "You needed the proper motivation to undertake the tasks ahead of you. I gave you that motivation."

With a jerk of his head, he commanded the guards.

They whipped the hoods off the prisoners' heads.

Kira gasped, stumbling backward.

Her parents blinked rapidly as if clearing their vision in the sudden brightness. When they focused on her at last, they both began to cry. Her mom tried to rush to her, but a guard slung out an arm to bar her way.

"Kira, sweetie," Mom said, "are you okay? Where's Caleb?"

She couldn't speak for a moment, a span of a second or two when time seemed to have stopped. The room swayed around her once. She took a couple slow breaths and marshaled all her self-control to remain calm. "I'm okay. Caleb's okay too."

As far as she knew. She'd left him in the woods, tucked inside a hollow, dead tree trunk that had fallen to the ground. He would stay there because she'd asked him to, and Caleb was a good boy.

The start of tears pricked at the backs of her eyes. She breathed in through her nose, deep and slow, and blew the breath out through her mouth. No time for crying. She needed answers pronto.

"I thought you were in Africa," she said, hoping her voice didn't betray her bitterness. "You said that's where you'd be when you walked away without a second thought. When you abandoned your eight-year-old son."

Her father winced. Her mother looked stricken.

"Please believe us," her father said, "we never wanted this."

Don't hate us, we never wanted this. That's what their note had said.

Gabriel Amador sauntered up beside her parents, a smug smile on his lips. "They tell the truth, Kira. Your parents would never have left of their own volition, despite learning of your telekinetic abilities. I tried to convince them to come with me voluntarily, but they refused to leave their beloved children. They required a greater motivation."

Dread coiled in her chest like a snake about to strike, sinking its cold, razor-sharp teeth into her heart. She resisted the impulse to hug herself because she suspected Amador wanted her unsettled. No way in hell would she give him what he craved.

"I don't understand," she said in the calmest tone she could muster. "What did you do to them?"

"To them? Nothing." Amador cast his gaze on her parents, then focused on her again. "I merely told them if they wanted to prevent their children from enduring painful and extended torture, they must do precisely as I say. They agreed."

You evil, insane son of a bitch. Kira's fists clenched at her sides, and she fought with all her strength to keep from hurling her body at him and clawing his eyes out. She didn't give a damn what he'd suffered, what reasons he had for going nuts and tormenting others. Nothing justified the things he'd done.

"Now you see," Amador said, "what is at stake. I did this for you, Kira. The proper motivation is vital to completing the mission. I know from experience loss and pain are a powerful impetus for taking action most would consider immoral but which is crucial to changing the world, remaking it into a place free of criminals with unspeakable power."

Criminals? She supposed she was one after the things she'd done lately, but only because this man had forced her to do it. Not every psychic was a criminal, though. But why argue with the man? He was beyond reason, beyond logic, entrenched in a crazed fantasy that painted him as a hero. What he believed he was saving, she had no idea.

Amador was obsessed with Grace. Maybe he thought he was saving her. He had claimed she'd be grateful once he'd fully executed his plan.

"I don't get it," Kira said. "You went to all this trouble just to terrify the world into believing psychic phenomena are real. And you think Grace will want you after that? She won't be grateful you ruined her life and the lives of countless other people."

"All will become clear, eventually. I have what I need now—you and Kira and Nathan." Amador rubbed his jaw. "I do have multiple contingencies in case you require further motivation, but I would prefer you cooperate willingly."

Contingencies for what? Nathan had been a contingency, with his nullifying ability. Kira couldn't think about what else Amador might have up his sleeve. Too many other things to worry about, and besides, he might be lying. Crazy people liked to do that.

"You claim you got Sean involved on purpose," she said, "but you couldn't have known he'd go to that cafe."

"Of course I did." Amador clasped his hands behind his back, bouncing on his heels. "I've been watching Sean for some time, waiting for the moment when he would be at his weakest and most desperate. Only then would he insert himself into the plan. By urging him not to become involved, I ensured he would. I believe it's known as reverse psychology."

Sean looked as confused as Kira felt. "How did you know I'd be at the cafe?"

Amador reverted to his most patient tone. "I'd installed listening devices in Grace and David's home as well as in your apartment. The Ransoms and Edward McLean have become lax in their security measures, and they stopped sweeping their home for surveillance devices six months ago. They at last felt safe in their new home, which made this the perfect time to enact my plan. I overheard David speaking to Grace about his planned 'intervention' with you that morning and that the cafe was a fine place to talk."

"But..." Sean shook his head slowly, his brows drawn together. "You wouldn't have had time to plant the bomb and tell Kira to go there."

Amador smiled in that smugly satisfied way again, rocking on his heels. "One of my agents was watching you, and he had the device with him. The moment you and David left to walk to the cafe, a journey that takes ten minutes, my agent drove there to plant the device. At that time of day, the restaurant is busy. No one noticed another man dressed as a waiter. While my agent placed the bomb, another of my people called Kira to give her instructions."

Sean stared into space, his gaze distant. "But she would've had to be close by."

"They'd called me an hour earlier," Kira said, "and told me to wait in an alley. Turned out that was a block from the cafe."

She'd forgotten about that until now, what with her life being threatened every other minute and an apocalypse looming.

"At last, you see," Amador told Sean, "how perfectly I planned all of this."

"Oh yes," Kira said, "you're a bona fide genius. Congratulations on wounding all those innocent bystanders."

Amador's chest puffed up, clear evidence he hadn't grasped the snide tone of her comments. He really believed he'd done a good thing. Saving the world from psychics. Getting his revenge.

"Sean," Amador said, "it's time for you to speak to the world and take responsibility for these incidents. The final phase begins now."

CHAPTER TWENTY-TWO

AKE RESPONSIBILITY FOR TERRORIST ATTACKS THAT WOUNDED IN-
nocent people? Sean gritted his teeth. No way. He would never do that. If
he refused outright, Amador might hurt Caleb or Kira's parents—or Grace
and Abby, maybe even David. What the hell was Sean supposed to do? He
had no powers, no weapons, no way to fight back except with his big, snarky
mouth.

And that didn't seem to be working. Not for him, not for Kira. No
matter what they said, Amador wouldn't budge in his nutso conviction he
was saving the world. The guy had sunk so deep into his delusions he might
never crawl back out.

Much as Sean hated to admit it, he'd thought Amador got better over
the past five years. Sure, for all these years the guy had wandered in and
out of a psychiatric clinic. One particular clinic, actually. The one Amador had bought five years ago to help victims of Tesler's worst tactics, men
who had been turned into mindless automatons, an army of zombie-like
soldiers. Amador had also signed himself in to the same clinic and had
spent a good part of the past five years in treatment there, off and on,
seeming to make progress but apparently backsliding too. Why else would
he have kept returning to the clinic as a patient?

His mind must've been too far gone for treatment to work. He'd endured losing his son to Tesler, a madman who abducted and tortured the
twelve-year-old Evander Amador and finally slit the boy's throat when he
served no useful purpose to Tesler's research. Then, Amador's wife committed suicide, and the man had no one left. No reason to keep going. No
purpose in life except to seek vengeance.

That was how Grace had met Amador. He'd planned to use her as a tool
in his quest for retribution. Sure, in the end Amador had helped Grace,

David, and Sean stop Tesler and his cronies. But he'd started out using Grace. Drugging her. Tormenting a teenage girl to coerce her into using her powers to stalk and terrorize Grace.

Karl Tesler had, ultimately, set in motion the events leading to this moment—to Amador's madness and the debacle it instigated. Sean's grandfather had created this monster.

A thread of knowing, too slender and ethereal to grab on to, flittered in Sean's mind. He must understand this. Right this second. The fates of so many people depended on it.

Sean took slow, deliberate steps toward Amador, halting an arm's length away.

The other man watched him with that bizarre calmness in his demeanor and that creepy little pleased smile on his lips.

Need those powers back. But Sean knew he couldn't count on them anytime soon.

"I want to understand this," Sean said. He fought through the shock and anger, determined to sound reasonable and give Amador no call to lash out. "Tesler—My grandfather was a monster. He did unspeakable things to men, women, and children whose only crime was having abilities most people don't have and can't believe exist. He killed your son. You want someone to pay for that, I get it. Maybe you really want the world to accept psychic phenomena as real because then they'd be accepting your son too, in a way. You want justice for Evander. Mass murder isn't the way to get it."

Amador's body snapped taut and ramrod straight. He narrowed his eyes, his lips tightening into a slash. "I told you never to speak my son's name."

"I'm sorry for what happened to you. Maybe I can't really understand what you went through, but I'm trying to understand you now. What is it you really want? Why was it so important to get me involved in all this? You said you want to punish me because Tesler let me live but he killed your son. I don't think that's the whole reason I'm here, though, is it?"

The question hung in the air like an invisible, fetid fog. Sean had the weird sensation if he took a single breath, if he heard the answer to his question, he'd ingest a toxin nothing could eradicate. The toxic cost of knowing.

Amador didn't move or speak, his features frozen in that expression of barely contained fury.

Silence blanketed them like the invisible fog Sean had imagined. It surrounded them and cloyed to their skin. He felt it on his flesh, chilly and sticky, raising the hairs on his arms.

"You are like me," Amador said coolly, speaking each syllable with the care of a man determined to make his thoughts known without any misunderstanding. "We share more in common than you realize, Sean. Your father was torn from you just as my son was taken from me. Tesler abused your father in much the same way he abused my son. Your mother died, and so did my wife. The difference, however, is that my wife chose to take her life. But they both died as a direct result of Tesler's actions."

"My mom died in a car accident."

The hard line of Amador's mouth softened the tiniest bit, kinking into the barest of smiles. "Yes, she died while in a car, but it was no accident. Your grandfather orchestrated it."

Sean's feet wanted to stumble backward, to carry him away from Amador, but he held his position. No way would he show any more fear or shock to this man. "The cops told me it was an accident. A tire blew out, she lost control, and the car hit a utility pole. She died instantly."

"No," Amador said with a pity-laden shake of his head. "Tesler ordered a traveler, one of his inmates, to destroy the tire in such a way your mother would lose control and strike that pole. He wanted her dead because she knew too much. Your mother had discovered the truth about her father's so-called research project, and she was horrified. She'd threatened to go to the authorities. Since she had evidence to support her claims, in the form of files she'd stolen from Tesler, he had to rid himself of her for good."

Sean stared at Amador. No, even Tesler couldn't have been that vile, having his own daughter murdered.

I did love her once. The thought pierced his brain, a memory of that recurring dream. This time when a fragment of the nightmare came back to him, the words were spoken in Karl Tesler's voice. Grace had believed Tesler cared about Sean in his own twisted way. Had the dream always been about Tesler? Why did he keep dreaming about his grandfather saying he loved "her"?

"We are alike in many ways," Amador said. "You abducted Kira just as I abducted your friend, Cari. What would you have done if I hadn't intervened and forced the two of you to work together?"

Not what Amador had done, Sean wanted to say. It would've been a lie. He couldn't claim he would've stopped short of hurting Kira because he'd been teetering on a desperate edge.

You wouldn't have hurt me, Kira had told him later. She believed it, believed in him.

"And of course," Amador said, still not shutting the hell up, "I betrayed Grace by alerting Tesler to her location. We have that in common as well."

"Who are you claiming I betrayed?" Sean asked.

"Grace."

What the frigging hell? Sean drew his head back. "I never did that."

Amador canted his head, eying Sean with a baffled expression. "You truly don't know, do you? I suppose Grace believed she was protecting you by not revealing your actions. While JT was still alive, Tesler tried to make David reveal the true identity of the traveler known only as Janet Austen. David knew the traveler was Grace and that her parents had secreted her away somewhere before their deaths. David would not be broken, though." Amador waved a finger at Sean. "You, however, required little coercion to comply. You exposed Grace and led Tesler and JT to her."

Now that he wanted to step away from this bastard, Sean's body refused to budge even one millimeter. He couldn't speak or think or look away from Amador. The man was lying. He had to be.

Yeah, someone had betrayed Grace years ago and led the bad guys to her. No one ever figured out who it was, or at least, no one would tell Sean if they did know. He'd sensed, thanks to his empathic ability, Grace and David kept something from him years ago when they told him Tesler was his grandfather. Since he'd had other things to worry about then, like getting a handle on his newly emerged empathic power, he'd decided to forget about it. Couldn't have been important, or else they would've told him what it was.

I did love her once.

The words catapulted him into a memory of the dream. No, not a dream. It had always been a memory of a real event, one too traumatic for his mind to hold on to, so his subconscious had repressed it. The truth emerged in fragments in a dream, pieces he couldn't tape back together.

Until this moment.

The here and now faded away as the past engulfed him.

Sean lies strapped to a chair in an isolation room, tears streaming down his cheeks, blood trickling down his forehead into his eyes. Cuts and burns, raw and blistered, have turned his arms into a red, seeping mess. The pain racks his body, his mind, too intense to let him think, let him understand. How could anyone do this to another human being? Why do they do this to him? He's never hurt anyone, but they demand answers he can't give.

An ALI technician hovers over him, lips pursed, scrutinizing Sean's face.

The door bursts inward, and Karl Tesler storms into the room.

Sean glimpses the scientist through a haze of blood-tinged tears. The two men speak to each other, but he can't focus on their words, can't focus on anything except the searing agony.

Tesler shouts at his underling, and the technician flees the room.

Sean sobs. He hates crying, but he's powerless to stem the tears.

Karl Tesler approaches the chair and leans in, his hand on the chair's arm way too close to Sean's arm. The man's hand floats up as if he might touch Sean's face.

He yanks his hand away, scowling at Sean. "I did love her once. You may not believe it, but I did. So very much. I wish this could be another way..." Tesler steps back, squares his shoulders, and his expression mutates into ice . His voice is equally chilled. "But there is no other way to deal with your kind. I need Janet Austen, and you will give her to me."

Footsteps. The technician returns and hands Tesler a syringe. "The serum, sir."

Tesler snatches the syringe from the technician's grasp and lowers it to Sean's arm. He hesitates, his brows pinched. With an annoyed sigh, he stabs the needle into Sean's arm, depressing the plunger.

Sean flinches at the burst of pain, but tears choke his voice. He can't beg for mercy even if he wanted to. Sean convulses as the serum scorches through his veins. His eyes bulge. He drags in one wheezing breath, his body ablaze with a new, deeper agony. His body slumps in the chair of its own volition.

Tesler bends near Sean's face. "Now, track David Ransom."

"Can't…" Sean's voice is slightly slurred. Why is Tesler asking him to do this? "Not my power."

"I just gave you more power than a weakling like you deserves. Track David Ransom."

Sean moans.

Tesler slaps him across the face.

His entire body jerks.

"Do it," Tesler hisses. "That's an order."

Sean has no choice. The serum warps his mind, his will, until he must do as he's told. He flies through the crossroads faster than ever before, spots a pulsing star, and races to the destination at light speed. He emerges inside a house. David is nearby, he senses it. Compelled by the serum and Tesler's command, Sean tracks David into the bedroom of the house where a woman lies on the bed, asleep.

Grace Powell.

Sean hesitates, afraid David will notice him, but his friend remains focused on Grace. David loves her, Sean knows. Sean loves her too, like a mother or a sister, and remembers all the times she talked with him about his powers and helped him accept what he is. Now, she doesn't remember any of it. David had told him Grace developed amnesia after her parents' deaths.

A thought explodes in his mind. He knows the answer to the question Tesler's lackey asked him earlier, over and over while cutting and burning him. He knows, but he cannot let Tesler know.

The serum melts away his resolve, but he must not tell.

Sean returns to his body, rousing in a groggy haze.

Tesler grips Sean's chin and wrenches his head. "Who is she?"

Sean clamps his teeth shut. He won't tell. He won't.

The serum scorches, weakens, annihilates.

"You. Will. Tell. Me." Tesler smacks him. Sean's head snaps back, and his mouth pops open. "Who is Janet Austen?"

"She... ahhh..." No, no, no, he will not say it.

"Tell me!" Tesler seizes Sean's shoulders and rattles him hard.

Sean's jaw quivers. Tears stream down his cheeks. He fights the serum as hard as he can, but it's not enough. His mind dissolves, his will dissolves, and a sharp sob racks him. "Grace Powell."

A sickening grin splits Tesler's mouth. His eyes sparkle with a dark glee. To his assistant, he says, "Make sure the boy remembers nothing."

The present reeled back into focus around him, and Sean staggered backward a single step. It was true. He betrayed Grace.

But that did not make him like Amador. A few days ago, he might've believed that. Today, he saw everything more clearly.

Amador reached Sean in one large step and grasped his shoulders. "We are the same. This is why I know you will do as I command and tell the world you orchestrated the bombings. You will also issue a warning about a far worse calamity to come. I have written a statement for you to read."

"Why would I do any of that?"

"Because like me you will do anything, no matter how heinous, to save the ones you love." He glanced at Ferrell. "Have they arrived?"

She brought out a phone and tapped its screen several times. "Yes. We've apprehended Grace and Abigail Ransom, and they've arrived at the facility."

Amador grinned. "You see? It all comes together. Soon, the world will see psychics the way I wish them to, and Tesler's true legacy will be exposed. Grace will understand even if you do not."

Grace would understand what?

Sean went stiff and cold inside as a dozen gears, once disassembled and scattered in his brain, clicked into position one by one.

Amador, unhinged as he was, had revealed the clues without meaning to. Little things he'd said shed light on his actions, his plans, his real purpose.

He'd hoped David would die in the first explosion. He'd been annoyed when Sean and Kira healed David. He believed Sean was just like him, driven by rage and a need for revenge too powerful to deny. Amador had dragged Sean into this cockamamie plot on purpose, and Sean saw only one reason for it.

Tesler's true legacy would be exposed, Amador had said.

And finally, Sean realized what this man wanted. He intended to kill David, convince everyone Sean was a madman like his grandfather, and probably kill him too. Like he'd already admitted, he would expose psychics as dangerous enemies. But he didn't want to convince the world. He needed just one person to believe.

Ferrell had said Grace and Abby had arrived at "the facility." She must've meant this underground bunker. Had Grace really lost her powers? Nathan said the nullification was temporary. Could she have regained her powers already? If she had, she would've escaped with Abby. Ferrell might've lied, and they might be safe.

If he had his powers, he'd know for sure.

He supposed this was what they called irony. He'd repressed his powers for so long, prayed they might just go away if he ignored them, and now he needed them desperately.

Sean had to know one last thing before he'd be sure of his realization. So, he looked straight into Amador's eyes and asked, "My father can nullify powers. You think you can use him to permanently strip a psychic's powers, don't you?"

"Yes."

Amador wouldn't strip Sean's or Kira's powers, not yet. He had one target in mind, the one person in the world he coveted enough to go to these outrageously insane lengths.

Grace.

Chapter Twenty-Three

THE FINAL PHASE. KIRA'S BRAIN HAD GOTTEN STUCK ON THAT phrase several minutes ago when Amador stated that "the final phase begins now." Whether he would really stop after nuking the East Coast was another question altogether. Who knew with someone as unbalanced as Gabriel Amador? In the past ten minutes, he'd shocked her and Sean with enough revelations to knock them off kilter for a good while. Exactly what he'd intended to do, of course.

Her gaze traveled to her parents for the umpteenth time. She still couldn't wrap her head around the idea they hadn't willingly abandoned her and Caleb. They'd surrendered to Amador to protect their children. Why had Amador taken them and left Kira to her own devices for sixteen months? The man seemed to have the patience of a snail, inching toward his goal one millimeter at a time, certain he would reach that goal one day, certain vengeance would be his.

Tesler was long gone. Punishing Sean probably seemed like the best alternative, to destroy the only living relative of the man who'd been responsible for his son's death. Amador kept insisting Sean was just like him, but he was dead wrong. When the choice came down to hurting her, he'd pulled back. Despite his desperation, Sean couldn't cross the line Amador had charged past a long time ago.

Did Amador really have Grace and Abby?

Kira glanced at Sean, standing beside her but his gaze distant. He'd gone stoic, and she couldn't blame him for that. Finding out your captor planned to force you to take the blame for terrorist attacks would turn anyone into a stone statue. If he had betrayed Grace like Amador claimed, that would explain the pallor of his face. She couldn't look away from him, wishing with all her mental might that she could sense his emotions and know if he was all right inside that stiff, stone-faced shell. She didn't have empathic powers, but with him she'd been able to detect some of his feelings as if they could share their powers. She needed that connection more than ever.

A tingling swept through her, light and brief but enough to raise the hairs on her arms and her nape.

What the…She just repressed a shiver as the sensation rushed through her again. No, it couldn't be, not yet. Then again, Nathan had said six hours at most and that it varied. She covered her right hand with her left, holding them in front of her casually, and flicked the index finger of her right hand against her thumb.

A spark snapped to life for a split second, then fizzled out.

Eureka. She fought the impulse to jump up and down pumping her fists in the air. Never in her life before today would she have believed she'd celebrate having her powers. She had to lose them to appreciate how much she needed, and yes, wanted them. They were a part of her.

She looked at Sean again. He was a part of her too, the part she'd been missing but never realized it until today.

With a slow breath, in and out, she relaxed into her returning powers.

Her mind touched Sean's. His only reaction was a faint widening of his eyes for half a second, followed by the briefest tightening of his lips. It had seemed like he was trying not to smile.

Maybe he'd figured out their powers were coming back online.

And then it happened. She sensed his emotions, or a taste of them, and her heart swelled with pride and…affection. What did he feel right now? Resolve, steady and sure. Yes, underneath she detected fear, anger, disgust, and a little bit of shame directed at himself. His overriding attitude, though, was an unbreakable resolve to find a way to stop Amador and thwart his plan. When she'd first touched his mind, he'd given off a hint of anxiety. Now, he believed with complete conviction they could succeed.

She clasped his hand, and power sizzled between them.

He locked down his shields, sealing them both off from prying minds.

Amador was in the corner with Ferrell, engaged in a heated discussion.

Nathan, slumped in the chair, suddenly swung his head toward Sean and Kira. His lips curved up for a heartbeat, then he covered his delight with a neutral expression. He knew their powers had returned. And he was glad.

Kira knew how he felt. She wanted to belt out a chorus of "Hallelujah."

Instead, she sank into the connection with Sean, into the power coursing between them through their linked hands. It hummed inside her, tingled through her, stronger than before. She wondered what they could do with this newly potent connection and decided to test it.

By sending a thought to him.

Can you hear me? She imbued the thought with the fervent energy of her hope. *If you can hear me, squeeze my hand.*

Sean gave her hand a light squeeze. His eyes rotated toward her, and at the instant their gazes intersected, she knew he'd heard her. It didn't seem to bother him in the least.

Do they really have Grace and Abby? she asked.

I don't know.

We need to check.

He aimed his gaze forward, so she followed suit, shifting her attention in the general direction of her parents. A phantom fist gripped her chest. She hadn't even been able to hug them.

Sean's hand tightened around hers, a gentle gesture of reassurance.

You check on Grace and Abby, he told her in her mind.

Me? I don't have a connection with them.

Through me, you do. We're connected.

And that didn't bother her at all either. She'd grown fond of this link with him, never having had anything close to it with anyone else. Close to it? No, nothing she'd shared with anyone else came within a million miles of this.

I'll try, she told him.

Eyes open, she soared out of her body and into the crossroads, rocketing through the tunnel in a nanosecond. Suspended in the field of stars, she let go of her thoughts and waited for a sign.

A star pulsed.

She flew toward it, straight through its brilliant light and down another dark tunnel. Her astral self popped out inside the bunker facility, inside a corridor she recognized because she and Sean had brought Caleb this way earlier.

Grace and Abby Ransom were being herded by two armed guards.

The men took them into a room furnished with a metal table and metal folding chairs. One guard waved for them to sit down, and they complied.

Grace looped her arm around Abby's shoulders. She was talking to the guards, but Kira couldn't hear the words. Floating nearer to them, she focused on sharpening her astral hearing.

"—could at least tell me where we are," Grace said. "Who are you working for?"

"You'll find out soon enough." The guard sneered. "You're the next surprise."

The guards exited the room. A lock chunked into position as they shut the door.

"What's going on, Mommy?" Abby asked, her blue eyes shining darker in the fluorescent lighting.

"It's okay," Grace said, kissing the top of her daughter's head. "Daddy will come for us, or Uncle Sean will. Everything will work out."

"When can we go home?"

"Soon, I promise."

A pain thudded in Kira's chest. She'd spoken the same words to Caleb, and she had yet to make good on them. She hadn't lied to her brother, and Grace was not lying to her daughter. Kira would make sure they both kept their promises.

"Why are we here?" Abby asked.

"I don't know, sweetie," Grace said. "I don't know."

Kira let out an explosive growl, the embodiment of her frustration. "You're here because Gabriel Amador is a goddamn liar and a lunatic."

Grace and Abby swiveled their gazes to Kira, their eyes wide.

Looking at her. They were *looking* at her.

Kira opened her mouth but couldn't make words come out.

Grace leaped up. "Kira."

"Amador is a liar," Kira repeated. "He's the mastermind behind this whole insane plot."

Grace's forehead wrinkled as if she could not comprehend Kira's words.

"David never trusted him," Grace said, "and I had my doubts too sometimes. But I never imagined…I mean, this is…"

She shook her head, and her mouth fell open then clapped shut.

"I know," Kira said. "Sean didn't like Amador, but he couldn't believe the man was capable of this either."

"What on earth is happening here?"

Faster than she'd ever spoken in her life, Kira spelled out the details she and Sean had learned from Amador. Well, almost everything. Two things she still couldn't decide whether to reveal.

Grace laid a hand on her forehead. "Oh dear God. Why didn't I see this before?"

"I don't see how you could have. It's total lunacy, and you're a sane person."

"Guess you're right."

"There's one more thing," Kira said. "Sean and I are in this building. And, um, I left something out when I told you about Nathan. He's—" Kira didn't know if she should be the one to tell Grace, but she suddenly realized the woman ought to know so she'd understand the full picture. "Nathan is Sean's father."

Grace stared blankly at Kira. "His father? Sean always said his dad ran out on him and his mom."

"That's what Sean thought. Turns out Nathan's been a captive for seventeen years, first held by Tesler, now by Tesler's protégé and Amador." Kira hesitated again, gnawing the inside of her cheek. This next bit, well, she still had no idea if informing Grace was a good idea. Once again, though, Kira decided the woman needed to know. "Amador told Sean he was the one who betrayed you to Tesler way back when."

"Oh Jesus," Grace said, shutting her eyes briefly. She flattened her lips, then sighed and relaxed as if she'd accepted an uncomfortable truth. "David and I knew. We found out five years ago, but we didn't tell Sean. He was still coming to terms with his empathic ability, and he'd just found out Tesler was his grandfather. Maybe we should've told him the rest, but we figured he'd never find out." Grace laid a palm on her forehead, rubbing the heel in the space between her eyebrows. "We never imagined we'd all get roped into another mess like this."

"Sean doesn't blame you for not telling him," Kira said, moving closer to the table. "He understands, and he forgives you."

And it was the truth. Through her connection to Sean, she perceived his feelings about the matter. He loved Grace and David like family, and he understood why they hadn't told him.

Grace straightened, lifted her chin, and with a steely glint in her eyes said, "We have to get out of here. Can you unlock the door?"

"Your powers haven't come back yet?"

"No. I feel an inkling of them, but not enough to work with."

Grace glanced down and raised her brows.

Kira followed Grace's eye movement down to her own foot. It tapped against the leg of the metal table. It *touched* the table.

"You didn't realize you're manifesting," Grace said. "I'm guessing this is the first time you've done it."

Speechless, Kira nodded. After a few seconds, she managed to say, "Sean told me only you can manifest. Other people need your help to do it."

Grace smiled with the exasperated affection of a mother. "Sean still underestimates himself, doesn't he? But this is all you, Kira, hey?"

"No." Kira gave a single, sharp shake of her head. "This is us. I can do more because Sean and I have a connection, it supercharges our powers."

Grace smiled again with a kind of knowing only someone older than twenty-two could achieve. "Guess there's a new power couple in town."

"Oh, we're not a couple," Kira said, "not officially. We haven't really talked about it. Anyway, I can bust the door open with a telekinetic shot."

Kira held up her hand and flicked her fingers.

The door popped inward with a *thwack*.

A guard jumped and spun around, waving his gun wildly.

With another flick, Kira zapped him with a jolt of electricity that bowled him over and sent him skidding across the floor. He lay dazed for a second before passing out.

"Nice," Grace said. "Wish I could do that."

"Better get moving," Kira said.

Grace and Abby followed her into the corridor. No other guards were in sight, but they needed to know for sure where everyone was.

"I'll scope out the facility," Kira said. "To check for bad guys."

She tried to zip back through the crossroads, to get into that thermal-imaging mode and scan the building for warm bodies, but nothing happened. She gazed down at her manifested body.

"It's anchoring you," Grace said. "Your artificially created body. You have to disperse it."

"Uh...What now?"

"Disperse it," Grace said with a faint laugh. "Let go of it. Your mind is holding on, keeping the molecules glued together. Release the manifestation."

"Sure. Piece of cake."

"You can do it, Kira."

The conviction in Grace's voice was genuine and unwavering. For a virtual stranger to believe in her...Well, Kira couldn't let Grace down.

She shut her eyes and exhaled, releasing her hold on everything with a whoosh of breath. The physical body she'd unwittingly created vanished, replaced by her astral form. Free of the anchor weighing her down, she opened up her senses and switched into thermal-imaging mode. Without any conscious decision to do it, she soared up through the ceiling to peer down on the facility concealed inside the hill. Blips of human shapes appeared in her vision. Most of them loitered in the isolation room, except for Grace and Abby—and several shapes she thought must be more guards. They waited in a space near the isolation room. In separate quarters distant from the isolation room and the guards, two individual blobs lingered.

Prisoners? Lackeys? She had no idea, but they were nowhere near the room in which Grace and Abby waited.

No one lingered in the vicinity of Grace and Abby, save for the unconscious guard.

Kira pulled back into her astral form, still inside the corridor with Grace and her daughter. "I can tell you how to get outside, so you can hide with my brother. I got him out of this place earlier."

"But you and Sean—"

"Please, Grace, we need to know you and the kids are safe. David's on his way, but I don't know when he'll get here. And his powers are gone too."

"They'll come back soon." Grace stood, and Abby got up too, wrapping her little arms around her mother. Placing a hand on Abby's shoulder, Grace said, "We'll find your brother and stay with him."

"His name is Caleb. Tell him Kiki sent you." Kira glanced at the open doorway. "I'll see you as far as the exit."

In silence, they hurried down the corridors to the door that led outside. Kira busted open the door and trailed Grace and Abby up the concrete steps to the outdoors. She watched until the mother and daughter vanished into the gloom of the woods. With her cool new thermal vision, she tracked them until they met up with Caleb.

She and Sean would stop this madness right now and free their loved ones, free the world, from the threat of impending cataclysm.

Unless they died. Of course, considering their powers, they might find a way to contact their friends and family even after death. *Not going to happen.* They would survive—and defeat their enemies.

They had to.

Kira released her astral form and flew back to the isolation room, settling into her real body with a surprisingly soft landing. Her actual eyes were still open, and her hand remained locked around Sean's. He didn't glance at her, though he must've sensed her return.

She beamed a single thought to him. Grace and Abby are fine and hiding with Caleb, which means Amador has two less bits of leverage.

He did dart his gaze to her then for the briefest moment. *Good. Time to stop Mr. Let's Nuke America.*

Kira held back the smile that itched to surface. *Got a plan?*

Yep. His lips ticked up at the corners, an expression so fleeting no one else would've noticed. *Let's kick his ass.*

How? My parents and your dad…

Sean twined their fingers, gripping her hand tight. *We're saving everyone. Right now.*

For a second, she wondered if the Golden Power had sneaked inside him again, fueling him with so much tainted power he believed he could do anything.

As if he'd read her mind, which he absolutely could have done if he'd wanted—hello, psychics here—he tugged her hand enough to draw her an eensy bit closer and whispered into her mind. *This is all me, not the Golden Power. We can do this if you believe it too.*

The truth rushed through her in a dizzying wave. *I believe it. I believe in us.*

Gabriel Amador ended his conversation with Ferrell and strode up to Sean and Kira. "It is time for your statement, Sean. It will be simulcast on television, radio, and the internet. Every signal will be hijacked, thanks to a certain traveler I have in residence here who turned out to be an accomplished hacker whose powers converge with his natural talents. Quite convenient, no?"

"Yeah, you really rock," Sean said. "Forcing more innocent people to do your bidding. How much did you torture this one to get what you wanted?"

A muscle jumped in Amador's jaw. He snagged the wrist of Kira's free arm, the one not currently held fast by Sean's hand around hers.

"Kira stays with me," Amador said.

Sean's eyes narrowed to slits, his nostrils flaring the tiniest bit. "She stays with me or you can forget this whole thing. You can't nuke anybody without our help."

"I have your loved ones. They will suffer if you fail to comply."

"Kira stays with me or this is over, and you can kill us all if you want."

What was he up to? Kira didn't have a chance to ask him telepathically because Amador released her wrist and said, "As you wish."

The man spoke words of acquiescence, but his expression conveyed pure arrogance. He believed he had them right where he wanted.

Amador gestured to the guards, and Kira and Sean were escorted out of the isolation room.

I hope you really have a plan, Kira told Sean through their link as they hurried down the corridor with guards surrounding them and Amador in the lead.

Sean's thought beamed into her, warm and full of assurance. *Today, we save the world.*

They crossed the hall to a room on the other side. The second they walked into the control room, Kira's stomach plunged downward with a sickening rush. A bank of black-and-white video monitors displayed various parts of the bunker facility. Many of the rooms were empty, but four contained human beings locked up in various kinds of cells. In one video feed, Nathan wriggled in his dentist-like chair, seemingly testing his bonds while a pair of guards observed without expression. Another feed showed her parents returning to their room, a slightly nicer version of a prison cell with a bed and bare-bones sofa as well as a Spartan bathroom.

A third feed showed a woman sleeping, or seeming to sleep, on a cot. The fourth monitor displayed images of a small room darkened by a false twilight, thanks to the weak, bare bulb suspended from the ceiling. A young man, maybe the same age as Kira and Sean, paced the width of the square cell, running his hand along the concrete wall.

These prisoners must've been the unknown blobs she'd spotted earlier.

Gabriel Amador pointed to the feed showing the young man. "This is Danny, our resident hacker. He has a talent for breaking into electronic systems, with assistance from his psychic powers."

"Why do you need me," Sean said, "if you've got this guy? He could launch your nuke for you."

"No, he can't." Amador tapped the video monitor. "Danny has never breached a network as highly secured as that of a nuclear facility. He tried once, with a site less secure than Malmstrom, and almost got caught. Without an electronic link to the target, his powers fail. We cannot risk that. You will handle this task for us."

Besides, Amador wanted to punish Sean for the crime of being related to Tesler.

Kira glanced around the room to note its other contents. Besides the monitors, it also housed equipment for recording video—a camera connected to a computer and equipped with a large, fuzzy microphone. A stool chair sat in front of the camera, and a blank wall provided the backdrop for Amador's video.

Sean's video. The loon was about to make Sean take the fall.

Without looking at him, she asked Sean in her mind, *What do we do?*

He clinched her hand tighter. *Zap their equipment.*

She sank her teeth into her bottom lip. Destroying the equipment would tick off Amador, and who knew what he'd do then. *What about your dad and my parents? Grace and the kids? And the other prisoners?*

Leave that to me.

Kira bit her lip harder, so hard pain cut through her flesh.

Trust me, Sean said in her mind.

With a rush of tingling awareness, she realized one vital fact. She did trust him. Completely.

She curled the fingers of her free hand into her palm and pulled in a deep breath. Energy crackled in her palm, silent and invisible yet palpable. With their minds connected and their hands joined, their powers had also become linked like a two-way electrical path coursing energy back and forth in a loop that supercharged their powers. The potency of it grew stronger and stronger, more than ever before. It fed into her enough strength to intensify the telekinetic energy contained in her palm, making it crackle and sizzle on her skin, under her skin, lifting every fine hair on her body.

She flung up her hand, fingers spread, and hurled the energy at the bank of monitors.

CHAPTER TWENTY-FOUR

SEAN CHOKED ON A GASP AS THE ENERGY OF KIRA'S TELEKINETIC blast tugged on his powers and crashed into the wall of monitors. The ball of electrical power erupted into miniature bolts of lightning that lashed out in multiple directions. The energy crackled and snapped, sizzled and hissed, diving deep into the circuits hidden within the electronics. Bolts lanced through the air to fry the video camera and singe the wire leading to the computer. The PC exploded, shards spewing through the room.

His veins burned with a heady rush of adrenaline and psychic power.

Mini bolts of lightning lanced the walls, seeking out electrical lines.

The lights went out.

Seconds. He had seconds to save everyone, or this was all for nothing.

Fueled by the double whammy of his powers and Kira's, Sean blasted through the crossroads, barely noticing the stars that blurred into elongated lines as he shot past them. He emerged in the isolation room, an arm's length from where his father sat in the torture chair. The emergency lighting painted the room in shades of blood red.

"You need to get out of here," Sean said. "We just pissed off a whackjob, and he'll be coming for you to punish me."

Nathan blinked once in slow motion, his lips parted.

"Hurry up," Sean said.

Nathan shook his head as if shedding the lingering memory of a strange dream and wriggled his hands inside the leather restraints. "I'm not going anywhere. Help the others."

No, no, no, he hadn't found his dad only to leave him behind in this hellhole. But he didn't have the kind of power necessary to shatter the restraints.

Or did he?

The energy surging through him carried with it the flavor of Kira's power. Telekinesis.

He threw open the floodgates of his mind, letting her power pour into him. Energy sparked on his skin, tiny explosions of kinetic power.

Nathan stared at him, unblinking. "I had no idea you could do that."

"Yeah, neither did I."

The energy gathered at his fingertips, shimmering and snapping.

Sean thrust out a hand, firing tiny bolts at the chair.

Metal buckles that secured the leather restraints popped open. The shackles burst apart.

"Did I hurt you?" Sean asked, his heartbeats thudding in his chest and in his ears.

"No." His father clambered out of the chair slowly like he couldn't quite believe he was free. Nathan faced his son, his smile evincing shock and pride. "Thank you."

A strange warmth radiated through his chest, but Sean had no time to figure out what it was. "Can you find your own way out? I have to hurry to help the others."

"I'll be fine. You go, save the world."

Sean hesitated for the briefest moment, staring at his father, over-whelmed by the bizarre but comforting warmth in his chest—around his heart.

Then he left.

He didn't need the crossroads this time. Somehow, he just…thought his way to his destination. He wanted to find Kira's parents, and zoom, he was in their room. The red light of the emergency bulbs provided minimal illumination, enough to move around with care. Sean didn't need to move, though. The Magnussons huddled in the corner, eyes darting, arms around each other.

Sean couldn't blame them for being afraid. They'd spent sixteen months in the tender loving care of Gabriel Amador. Who knew what the whackjob had done to them.

With a single thought, Sean made himself visible.

The Magnussons jerked in unison.

"It's okay," Sean said, holding his hands up, palms out. "I'm here to help. I'm Kira's friend, Sean. You saw me in the, uh, other room."

The torture chamber. Sean's stomach roiled at the memory, but he forced himself to stay calm.

Well, as calm as possible under the circumstances.

"Come with me," he said, "and I'll help you get out of this place."

"Where's Kira?" Mr. Magnusson asked.

"She's okay." Sean sensed her like a warm and steady breeze wafting over him, carrying with it the sweet scent of tropical things. He gestured for them to follow him. "Hurry, please."

I need more power.

The thought shivered through him. Kira's thought, not his own. He fired off his response even as he guided her parents into the corridor, flinging the door open with a burst of power borrowed from Kira. *You don't need to ask, just do it. This is our power now.*

A wave of heat rushed through him. It was like a steamy embrace from Kira, and it knocked him off kilter for one second too long. He stumbled, slapped a hand on the corridor wall, and fought for breath as a burst of vertigo whirled in his head. When it ceased, he heard a sound all too familiar to him.

The *ka-chunk* of a round being chambered in a large-caliber weapon.

Mrs. Magnusson shrieked.

Sean shoved away from the wall just as the solitary guard swung his weapon in Sean's direction.

"Don't move," the guy said, his voice slightly shaky. "I've got orders to take you alive, but I can shoot them if that's what it takes."

The guard swerved his weapon—an AK-47, maybe—toward the Magnussons.

Sean didn't want to hurt the guy. The guard's eyes were wide, and his whole body was shaking. He might've been forced to obey Amador, or maybe he'd signed on for the gig but didn't realize how totally nutso crazy his boss was until it was too late.

Either way, Sean preferred not to kill anybody unless he had no choice.

He tapped into Kira's power, and with his arms at his sides, he flicked one finger.

A mini bolt zapped the guard. He crumpled to the floor, his gun clattering on the linoleum.

Sean bent to check the man's neck for a pulse. It surged against his finger. *Thank God.*

He snatched up the gun.

Only then did he realize what he'd done.

A tingle rushed over his skin, awareness of the fact he'd failed to note until this very second. He'd manifested.

Holy smokes. He'd manifested all on his own, thanks to the boost from Kira's power.

Yeah, he felt like jumping up and down, hooting, pumping his fists. No time for celebration, though. He had to get these people out of here.

"Let's go," he told the Magnussons.

Kira's parents followed him without question, though they seemed kind of dazed. While he plotted out the best escape route in his mind, soaring out of his manifested body to view the network of corridors from above, he simultaneously shepherded the Magnussons through the facility. He had no clue how he managed the dual tasks, but he had no time to wonder or to marvel at it.

They rounded a corner.

A ripping noise inside the walls raced up the corridor. In its wake, black lines marked the singed electrical lines and cables buried in the walls. The black lines shot past them, around the corner, trailing the noise Kira's power created as she destroyed every last shred of technology in this place. Electronics not connected to the bunker's systems might've survived Kira's assault, but he doubted that would give the bad guys much to work with.

The emergency power might go soon too. Better hurry it up.

He mentally selected the fastest route out of the facility and urged Kira's parents to move faster.

The other prisoners.

Sean skidded to a stop, frozen by the thought. He'd forgotten about them. How could he forget? *Got to save them.* Adrenaline heightened his senses and coursed through his veins. He lost his grip on the overhead view of the corridors, lost his path to freedom for the Magnussons.

Get a grip, numbskull.

He couldn't do three things at once. Find the right corridors, guide the Magnussons, save the other prisoners. He would fail at all of it if he tried. And what about Kira? Amador might—

Fear zinged through him, cold and sharp and stinging.

Sean spotted a doorway and sprinted toward it, throwing the door open.

A supply closet.

Good enough for the moment.

He waved for Kira's parents to approach. "Hide in this closet. I need to check on Kira, but you should be safe in here."

Like he had even a shred of a clue if they would be. But he had no choice. Returning to Kira meant releasing his manifested body and his hold on this location.

The Magnussons hurried into the closet.

A cold weight settled in Sean's gut as he shut the door—and prayed he was doing the right thing.

He let go of the manifestation and slammed back into his body.

Gabriel Amador cradled his left arm, breathing hard. Sweat sheened his face.

The lunatic reached for Kira.

And got zapped big time by the glittering field of kinetic energy that surrounded her and Sean.

Sean glanced at her, and awe shimmered through his psyche. Her dark hair fluttered around her face in slow motion as if buoyed by static electricity. Her eyes glowed a deep and incandescent blue, like sapphires set ablaze.

The red emergency lights had gone out, but the shimmering white of her telekinetic power lit the room.

Amador stumbled backward, grimacing and bellowing at the burst of energy that had zapped him.

The guards had retreated into the corner furthest from Kira, faces pale, eyes bulging. Now, they bolted from the room.

Amador screamed at them in Spanish, probably a slew of curses. Nasty ones, by the tone of his voice. With his undamaged hand, he dug a phone out of his pocket.

Did you get them all? Kira asked through their telepathic link.

No. My dad's free, and I hid your parents in a closet. But I couldn't get the others. Not enough power.

Her anxiety filtered into him, tensing his muscles. She worried for her parents, he knew.

Amador fumbled with his phone.

What should we do with him? Kira asked.

Knock him out. Give us time to figure out the rest.

She lifted her hand, power sparking between her fingers.

"No!" Amador shouted, his eyes wild. "I have my finger on a button that will release a poisonous gas into this facility and kill everyone. If I cannot have my revenge on the world, I will exact it on you."

The whackjob hovered one finger over the phone's screen.

Kira curled her fingers, about to unleash a bolt.

Amador squashed his finger onto the phone's screen. "You are too late."

Chapter Twenty-Five

T HE ROOM STANK OF SCORCHED WALLS AND FRIED WIRES. KIRA stared unseeing in Amador's direction, her mind spinning with thoughts that crashed into each other, shattering and reforming over and over while she fought to make sense of what was happening. Amador released poison gas. Into the whole facility? Into the cells where he kept his prisoners? Was he even telling the truth?

Her pulse raced faster than a hummingbird's heart. She felt lightheaded, her knees weak. This couldn't be how things ended. *Mom, Dad, please forgive me.*

No, no, no, this was not the end.

She glanced at Sean, but his grim expression matched her emotions. They'd expended a hell of a lot of energy on destroying the facility's electrical system and trying to rescue the prisoners. Even with their combined powers, they lacked the capability to stop the gas.

"In case you are wondering," Amador said, staggering backward to slump against the bank of monitors, "we will survive. The gas affects the guest wing, not the control room."

Guest wing? Seriously? Those people were prisoners.

We need more power.

Kira jumped at the sensation of Sean's words injected into her brain. She'd gotten used to sharing thoughts with him, but her nerves had been scraped raw. Everyone would die unless they did something. What? More power, they needed more power. Fast.

And she knew of just one way to acquire it.

She turned toward Sean, and as if he'd sensed her intention, he turned to face her at the same instant. They clutched each other's hands, forming a complete circle of psychic energy with their joined palms. This time, they spoke aloud.

"No," he said. "It's too dangerous."

"We have no choice. That lunatic—" She jerked her head in Amador's direction. The man had sagged to the floor, his expression dreamily crazed. "He's killing everyone. We have to do this, no matter the cost."

"The power will eat us alive."

She inched closer, her head tilted back to meet his burning green gaze. "You told me it acts like a living, breathing, ravenous thing, but it's not alive. It can't control us unless we let it. So, don't let it. We can fight together, for each other, for what we need to get this done. Trust me, like I trust you."

He stared into her eyes, the intensity of it shivering heat through her body. With a fierce determination she'd never heard from him before, he said, "I trust you."

Amador laughed, the sound almost hysterical. "It's too late for whatever you're planning. Too late, too long, too far."

The sing-song tone of the last bit made Kira cringe inside. The man had lost the last thread tying his sanity together.

Sean pulled her into his arms, hugging her to his firm, warm body. "If we hold on to each other, nothing will tear us apart."

It sounded silly, but she believed him. She wrapped her arms around his torso and nestled her face against his chest.

"Close your eyes," Sean told her. "And follow me."

Kira shut her eyes and held on.

Every other time, they had traveled as separate astral entities linked by their hands. Now, they soared up into the crossroads as one, their minds mingled, their powers merged, and broke out into the field of stars. She'd hardly noticed the tunnel. They hovered amid the blackness, surrounded by glittering points of light. They didn't seek a star, though, or the connection it might offer to a place or a person in the real world. No, they sought a far more elusive quarry.

They acted in unison, throwing out ropes of energy, hunting for their prey, lashing out into the furthest reaches of the crossroads. A barrier reflected their questing ropes back at them, and oily talons clawed at their minds, but they funneled everything they had into the barrier to punch through it. A concussion, like a blast of astral wind, pummeled them. They steeled themselves against it and dived through the gap they'd blasted open straight into the pulsating core of the ultimate power.

Energy. Glistening, golden energy.

It engulfed and infused them, fueled and emboldened them. The power surged into their minds with overwhelming speed and intensity, a tidal wave of the most potent psychic energy in the universe. It was the universe. It was the essence of power.

And it belonged to them.

The Golden Power shot through their astral bodies straight down into their physical bodies. It energized them with the heady ecstasy of an orgasm, but the climax of their union with the Golden Power had no physical effect. They imagined it did because it permeated their beings.

Kira exploded back into her body, ablaze with more power than she'd ever dreamed she could achieve, alive with an energy too potent to deny.

Sean's chest heaved beneath her head. His heart pounded under her ear.

He pushed her away just enough to grasp her shoulders and aim his blazing eyes at her. Shimmering green energy outlined his body, and when she glanced down at herself, she discovered the same green fire glittered around her.

"We did it," he said, breathless.

She nodded, struggling to catch her own breath. "Let's do this."

They shot out of their bodies once again, soaring through the walls of the facility to locate the endangered men and women trapped inside. They found her parents first, still hiding in the supply closet where Sean had left them. He hadn't told Kira where he left them. She just knew. The incredible power coursing through them both joined their minds like never before. She understood what he wanted without asking, knew what he knew without a word spoken—and vice versa.

Her parents startled when she and Sean materialized in front of them.

"Are you okay?" Kira asked.

"We're...fine." Her dad spoke slowly, his astonished gaze aimed at her. Mom looked the same, awestruck but not afraid of her or Sean.

"Hang on," Sean said.

Kira let him take them both out of their manifested bodies—an out-of-body-experience once removed?—to hover above the facility for a bird's-eye view. Instead of looking down on the surroundings, though, they gazed down on the interior of the underground building. The roof vanished, the ceilings of the rooms inside vanished, and they entered a kind of altered reality that revealed things invisible to the naked eye.

Streams of dark-gray smoke unfurled inside one section of the building.

No, not smoke. The tendrils of writhing, expanding grayness represented the invisible poison gas. The stuff emerged inside four rooms, spreading outward into the corridors.

Her parents and Nathan had escaped the gas so far, but inside two of the rooms, human-shaped blobs pounded on the doors of their cells. The rooms had filled with gas.

Are we too late? The thought, though her own, ripped into her soul.

No, dammit.

Had Sean thought that, or had she? The lines between them had begun to blur.

But the power, it infused them.

They raced to one of the rooms.

A tawny-haired woman sagged against the door, too weak to pound on it any longer. She sobbed and wailed, her cries suffused with anger and hopelessness. She wheezed, gagged, her eyes flaring wide.

Sean and Kira dispersed the gas with a burst of power, realigning the molecules until the poison became an inert gas. She had no idea how they'd done it, only that they had. The woman slumped to the floor, her face ashen, gasping for breath. Sean and Kira surrounded her, unseen and without form, ghosts embracing her with their power. White light enveloped the woman, and Kira sensed the damage to her body reversing, repairing, healing.

Before they left the woman, they opened the door for her and Kira whispered into the woman's ear the directions for getting out of the bunker.

They hadn't manifested or made their presences known, but the woman understood their instructions on a subconscious level. She hustled out of the room.

Next, they healed and freed the hacker-slash-psychic.

A quick overhead scan told them every last molecule of the poison had been eradicated, even the reserves Amador hadn't released yet. They also discovered Nathan had broken out of the facility and was ushering the other two prisoners out the door through which Sean and Kira had entered earlier. Amador's guards fled out another exit on the opposite side of the hill that concealed the bunker.

Gabriel Amador still huddled on the floor in the control room.

When they returned to the supply closet, dropping back into their manifested bodies, her parents no longer seemed shell-shocked. Instead, they wore looks of determination colored by exhaustion. She and Sean escorted them out of the building to meet up with Nathan and the others. They had no time for family reunions. Kira told Nathan where she'd left Grace and the kids, and he vowed to find them.

She believed he would do it. Though she'd just met both Sean and his father, she realized they shared the same stalwart conviction to help others and do the right thing. Just like Sean would've given his life to save someone else, Nathan would risk his own safety to find and protect Caleb, Grace, and Abby.

After quick farewells—not goodbye, but "see you soon"—Kira and Sean returned to their real bodies inside the control room. The green energy still glimmered around them like a body-size halo, but she didn't worry about that. She worried about their prisoner.

Gabriel Amador lay sprawled on the floor, his neck bent at a ninety-degree angle thanks to his head being lodged against the bank of monitors while his body lay perpendicular to the wall. Sweat slicked his face and matted his hair. His body trembled. The whites of his wide eyes shone a sickly color in the pale-green glow of the power halo around Sean and Kira.

Their halo provided the sole source of illumination.

Amador laughed weakly. "The world will know my vengeance."

Sean stepped toward the man, eying him with a pinched expression. "It's over, Gabriel. You lost."

"No, no, it's a setback only." Amador tried to push up off the floor but his arms gave out, and he crumpled again. "The ICBM. It will show them. Everyone will see."

With a gusty sigh, Sean knelt beside Amador. "No, they won't. You wanted everyone to know how dangerous psychics are, didn't you? Your son was one of us, so why would—"

"He was not one of you," Amador spat. "Evander had no powers until Tesler abducted him and pumped him full of drugs to induce psychic experiences."

"You told Grace your son had powers, and that's why Tesler took him."

"No, no, no!" Amador flung his body into a slouched sitting position, his arms dangling loose at his sides. "Evander did not travel. Tesler invented the story because he needed an excuse to take my child. He wanted younger subjects to study. I don't care what your grandfather said. Evander never traveled to the facility through remote viewing. He never sensed other psychics and went to them. It did not happen."

Sean threw Kira a confused look. She must've worn the same expression. The man before them, once cocky in his belief he had the upper hand, had dissolved into a lump of craziness.

"During my treatments at the hospital," Amador said, seeming unable to stop talking now that he'd started, "I had visions of the truth. The doctors called them hallucinations, but I knew the universe was gifting me with the truth. I realized Evander did not have powers after all, but that he was chosen for induction because of me. Tesler hoped to ransom him for the money he needed to continue his secret research since JT had never known about what he and Ferrell had planned. He did not even know Tesler and his cohort had abducted your father."

"But, uh," Sean began, rubbing his jaw, "did they ever ask for ransom money? I mean, I thought Evander was experimented on and then killed."

Amador sprang to his feet, roaring so loud it vibrated Kira's eardrums. "They would have ransomed him! I saw the truth!"

Oh jeez. The man had hallucinated the only truth he could accept—that his son had no powers and therefore was not like Sean or Kira or any of the others. Amador needed to believe his son had been taken for ransom, though the facts belied that belief.

Amador burst into sobs, doubling over, clutching his belly.

Sean strode back to Kira. "This guy has lost more than the plot. He's lost the whole frigging book and the library too."

"What do we do with him?"

"Lock him in one of the cells here and come back for him after we get everybody else to safety." Sean clenched his fists. "And we have to find Ferrell."

They half dragged Amador out of the control room, Kira holding one of his arms while Sean held the other. The man leaned on them heavily, his sobs mutating into moans. They dropped him off in one of the cells and locked the door, then headed out the same exit their families and the other prisoners had gone out of earlier.

Four guards awaited them, arrayed in a semicircle around the top of the concrete stairwell. Each man brandished a weapon that looked like an AK-47 but also had a pistol strapped to his hip.

Sean and Kira froze at the base of the steps.

The eyes of every guard went wide at the sight of the green halo around Sean and Kira, but each man held his position. Four guns stayed trained on them.

Well, they must've seen weird things before. They worked in a facility that held psychics.

Let's knock them out, Kira told Sean through their mental link.

He gave a sharp nod.

They stretched out their shared power, lashing it at the guards.

And slammed into a granite-hard barrier. The force of the impact flung their powers back at them and hurled them to the concrete. Stars burst in Kira's vision while pain webbed out through her skull. She winced, gasped, and lay there prone, paralyzed by the shock.

Sean groaned, pushing up onto his elbows, dazed.

Kira heaved her body up into a sitting position. Her head throbbed. She ached all over, but nothing seemed broken and she saw no cuts or abrasions on her or on Sean. What she did detect disturbed her far more than injuries might have.

She sensed a gaping maw of nothingness inside her, devoid of psychic energy.

And her connection to Sean had been severed.

Kira glanced at him, but his gaze had gone bleary and unfocused.

A slender figure pushed between the middle two guards at the top of the stairs.

"EM," Sean muttered. "She used…"

His voice trailed off, and he squeezed his eyes shut like he was struggling to stay awake.

"Yes," Ferrell said, "he understands. I've implemented another of our contingencies, an electromagnetic field tuned to the precise frequency of psychic powers. You have nothing."

Kira scrambled to her knees. "Only as long as you keep that field up. Since I destroyed the electrical systems in your facility, I'm guessing you got your EM field up and running with battery power. It won't last forever."

"Long enough, though."

Ferrell stopped at the edge of the top step. She'd shed her lab coat, but she clasped the handle of a canvas bag with a zipper closure. She waved a hand in the air.

The four guards moved aside. Behind, two more guards kept their weapons aimed at a group of prisoners.

Kira opened her mouth, but the gasp lodged in her throat. She recognized these people.

The guards watched over the two prisoners she and Sean had freed as well as Kira's parents, Sean's father, Caleb, and Grace and Abby Ransom.

"Congratulations," Ferrell said. "You failed."

Chapter Twenty-Six

Y OU DON'T HAVE DAVID," SEAN SAID, BECAUSE IT WAS THE ONLY thing he could think of to say when he at last regained enough physical energy to speak and move. "David's a powerful traveler, and he'll be here any minute to clobber you."

In all the commotion, he'd forgotten about Ferrell. Hadn't looked for her at all. Made sure to keep track of Amador, believing him to be the biggest threat, but overlooked the deceptively pretty mad scientist. The face of an angel, the heart of a demon. That was Dr. Ferrell. Dear old Grandpa would be so proud of his disciple.

Sean had also forgotten about EM fields. *Idiot.* When he'd found out they used Nathan's power to cancel out his and Kira's, he'd stupidly assumed that was Ferrell's only trick. Amador had mentioned "multiple contingencies," but Sean hadn't realized what that meant.

He clambered to his feet and helped Kira up.

Ferrell surveyed her entourage—the guards and the prisoners—with self-satisfaction. "I have your father, and David's wife and child. You'll play your part to protect Nathan and these innocent bystanders. If David Ransom arrives, he'll do as I say too—unless he prefers to watch his family die painful deaths."

"You're as bonkers as Amador."

"Biel is right about you." She took half a step closer, a dark glee shimmering in her eyes. "You betrayed a woman you think of as a surrogate mother, leading her enemies straight to her and causing untold suffering. That makes you as twisted as Biel and as malleable too."

Malleable? Like hell.

She'd called Amador by his nickname, Biel. It had to mean something.

Acid ate away at his gut, giving rise to a gnawing dread, but Sean folded his arms over his chest and kept his chin up. "Don't you want to know where your boyfriend is?"

Ferrell's brows scrunched.

"Gabriel Amador," Sean said. "Your sweet Biel. He's gone way far over the edge, inches away from turning into a drooling idiot. His plans are toast, and so is his brain."

The woman's eyes narrowed, and her upper lip twitched. She shouted for her minions to bring Sean and Kira out of the stairwell, and two guards trotted down the steps to retrieve them. One man snagged Kira's arm and hauled her up the stairs roughly, making her trip twice. Sean clenched his fists, desperate to slug the creep for manhandling a woman. The other guard grabbed Sean's arm and tried to drag him in the same manner but didn't have the strength to do it. He settled for herding Sean up the stairs.

Once they were on the surface, across the little clearing from the other prisoners, Ferrell stalked up to Sean. "Where is Gabriel Amador?"

Sean considered lying, to make her believe he'd killed the guy, but decided that might piss her off to the point of being super dangerous. So, he told the truth. "We locked him up in one of the cells he used to imprison innocent people so the two of you could abuse them at your leisure. Seemed appropriate to confine the nutjob in his own prison."

"Which cell?" Ferrell spoke each syllable with exaggerated lip movements, her teeth clamped together.

"Don't remember."

What are you doing? Kira's question reverberated in his mind, but he didn't dare glance at her. He had a plan. Sort of. Right now, a half-assed scheme was the best option.

Follow my lead, he told her.

He sensed her anxiety, but she kept quiet, sending him a pulse of…He repressed a weird shiver. Kira had given him a taste of something sweet and warm and gentle. Affection? He wasn't sure he could recognize that emotion anymore. Yet his chest ached with a sensation not unlike what Kira had communicated to him without a word or a gesture, simply with her heart.

She was awesome. In her personality and in her powers.

Oh God. Did he—he couldn't—no way.

The realization he couldn't acknowledge, wouldn't acknowledge, got him choked up nonetheless. He gulped against the constriction in his throat, refusing to let Dr. Ferrell see any emotion, any weakness, in him.

Even if it had shown, Ferrell wouldn't have noticed. She was busy railing about her beloved Biel and how brilliant he was. Wow, Sean hadn't realized she actually had feelings for the loony-tunes guy. Maybe he could use that to his advantage.

Then she shattered his misconception.

Ferrell looked Sean straight in the eye and said, "Gabriel Amador is insane. You're correct on that point. If you think to hold him hostage as a means of getting your way, forget it. Kill him if you want."

"Thought the two of you were tight."

"We were lovers, yes, but only as a means to placate him. He is brilliant, but in the way of an idiot savant. Sex makes him easier to handle and more pliable."

Oh man. He got it now. Of course the crazy guy hadn't done all this on his own.

"You let him think he was in charge," Sean said, "but you were running the show. This nutso scheme to expose psychics as a threat to humanity was your idea. You used Amador's vengeance plot because it meshed with what you wanted. Nuking the East Coast must've been his idea, but the rest of it was you, right?"

"Most of it, yes." She stepped back, lifting the black bag. "I've brought some of my best tools. If you don't do as I say, I'll use them on your friends and loved ones."

Sean didn't point out he'd just met his father a few hours ago and hardly knew the man. Besides, Ferrell had Grace and Abby too, and Kira. He couldn't let this woman hurt anybody.

"What is it you want?" he asked.

"Essentially the same thing Biel wanted. You will make a public statement claiming responsibility for the bombings. Your statement, the one I've prepared for you, will make it clear psychics are a threat and are determined to take over the world."

Sean spluttered, trying not to laugh. He didn't feel amused, though. He felt dumbfounded and a little bit sick. Take over the world? Right, because all the psychics of the world had united into an army. Sheesh, would anybody believe that?

"You will, of course, offer proof," Ferrell said. "Gabriel's idea about launching an ICBM may be extreme, but it will get the job done."

Everything inside Sean went cold, doused with an icy bucket of reality. Ferrell was as crazy as Amador.

"Each ICBM," she went on, "carries multiple rockets. You will target various cities around the world and issue this threat in your broadcast. If the world's leaders accede to your demands, you'll disable the rockets."

"And what are my demands?"

"Ten billion dollars."

He spluttered again. Jeez, this woman had nerve. "Why would anyone believe this malarkey?"

"Because you will make them believe. You will kill the Vice President of the United States."

"Wh—How am I supposed to do that?"

Ferrell tapped her long fingernails on the canvas bag. "You and Kira clearly tapped into the Golden Power. Use that to enhance your own abilities and strangle the Vice President. He's currently giving a commencement speech at Vanderbilt University. Thousands will see it happen. Be sure to make it showy, so no one will doubt the attack is paranormal in nature."

Showy. Attack. Kill the VP.

No way in hell.

He needed her to believe he'd do this, though.

"Guess you've got me where you want," he said. "One problem. Your fancy control room is rubble now."

"Oh, you won't need that." She smiled, the expression not in the least friendly or happy. "You are going to commandeer Malmstrom Air Force Base."

Sean opened his mouth but couldn't make any sounds come out. Take over a military base? What, all by himself? "I need help to do that."

"You go alone."

"At least let Kira—"

"No."

"You'll have to take down the EM field."

"Nice try, but no," Ferrell said. "My men will escort you outside the field, but not before I dose you with my favorite serum. It will make you...cooperative."

The serum. Sean tried to swallow, but his mouth and throat had gone dry.

Ferrell gestured to the guard who stood beside Kira. When the man hauled her to the scientist, Ferrell extracted a syringe and a small glass vial from her bag. Setting down the bag, she filled the syringe and tapped out the bubbles, squirting a brief jet of liquid. Satisfied, she told the guard, "Restrain her."

The second the guard reached for Kira's wrists, she kicked out with one foot and landed a solid shot in the guy's groin. The guard doubled over, gasping.

Ferrell shouted, "Bring her to me!"

Just as Kira rammed her elbow backward into the guard behind her, another guard sprinted up alongside her and smacked the butt of his gun into her head. The *crack* of its impact echoed in the clearing.

Kira crumpled to the ground.

"No!" Kira's mother shrieked.

Sean's heart pounded so hard and fast he felt lightheaded. He started to run for Kira, but three more guards joined the one already posted beside him, swarming around him with guns aimed at his chest. He no longer had the capacity to stop them. His link to Kira was gone. The telekinetic power she'd shared with him had snuffed out when the EM field encompassed them.

No, no, no. He ground his teeth until his jaw ached, glancing around in a desperate search for a way out, something he could do, some way to get to Kira and make sure she wasn't…His jaw quivered. She wasn't dead. She couldn't be.

Between the guards' bodies, he spotted Kira's limp form on the ground.

If he ran for her, if he tried to get a weapon away from one of the guards, the others would shoot him. Maybe not dead, since that would blow up Ferrell's plans, but they'd make sure he couldn't fight anymore. A shot to the leg or the shoulder would do the trick.

Ferrell knelt beside Kira, feeling for a pulse in her throat. "She's alive. For now. But she won't be offering any aid to you, Sean." Ferrell jabbed the needle she still held into Kira's neck and depressed the plunger. "The strong sedative I'm giving her will make certain she'll be of no help even if the EM field goes down."

The scientist tossed the empty syringe aside. She brought out a fresh syringe and filled it with liquid from a small vial, then she strolled up to Sean.

"Maybe I'll just kill you right now," Sean snarled, "with my bare hands."

"You won't." Ferrell smiled again in that creepy way. "You don't have the power. Not psychically, not physically. Guns trump muscles, but the serum trumps everything."

Ferrell was right. Even if he could knock out the EM field, he wouldn't have the power. Not without Kira. She'd made him strong in more than his psychic abilities. She'd made him a stronger man, a better man, and he wouldn't let any harm come to her or the other prisoners. What could he do?

The EM field had dampened his powers to the point of being useless. But though the Golden Power had faded, its seductive energy simmered deep inside him. Even the dampening field hadn't eradicated it completely. If he tapped into it again…Without Kira to ground him, could he come back from it this time?

Grace had done it. But she'd also sworn never to use the Golden Power again, and she'd made Sean swear he wouldn't either. Now, he'd used it twice. Grace would rip him a new one for that alone. If he did it again, she'd kill him.

Dammit, he wasn't a kid anymore. He made his own choices. And Grace, as smart and powerful as she was, didn't know everything about the psychic world. The Golden Power hadn't consumed him this time, not with Kira beside him.

She was out cold. He'd have to do it alone. If it destroyed him, well, at least the others would survive and he'd take Ferrell down with him.

"You're right," he told Ferrell. "On my own, I don't have enough power to stop you."

But he could access more power. Though Ferrell had guessed he and Kira used the Golden Power, she clearly thought he couldn't access it inside the EM field. Good. *Powers dampened, not destroyed.*

Ferrell stabbed the needle into his neck, and searing acid scorched through his veins. It annihilated his willpower, his determination, everything that kept him from doing what she wanted. He fought against the serum even as it scoured out his mind and convulsed his muscles, refusing to collapse, refusing to give in.

The scientist got another syringe out of her bag and filled it from a different vial. "This will make Kira's heart stop beating instantly. One wrong move and she dies."

Yeah, the woman also thought only Kira could use telekinesis. *Keep underestimating me, you slimy, arrogant snake.*

Sean cleared his throat. "I need to RV the base to get the lay of the land. I've never seen pictures of Malmstrom, much less been there."

The woman squinted at him, angling her head. "All right. But remember, Kira will die if you pull anything—and should the serum fail for any reason, I can take your father outside of the EM field and have him nullify your powers at any time."

Sean glanced at his father. The second their eyes met, he knew—though he couldn't explain how—his father would never, ever again do that to him. No matter what Ferrell did or said.

Ferrell instructed one of the guards to retrieve Amador, then she told Sean, "No tricks, or Kira dies."

"I know."

The scientist studied Nathan, her gaze glinting with the light of keen understanding.

"Ah," Ferrell said, all but cooing the syllable, "I see I can no longer trust Nathan to do as I say. His fatherly instincts have gone into overdrive, haven't they? Well, I suppose you'll need a greater motivation."

"You've got Kira, and Grace and Abby. I'll do what I said."

If David showed up…Sean cursed himself silently for thinking his friend would arrive and save them all. This time, it was up to Sean.

"Best to be certain," Ferrell said. She rose and snatched the pistol from the holster of the nearest guard. "It's the scientific way."

She leveled the gun at Kira where she lay prone and unconscious on the ground.

A certainty of what was about to go down, almost a premonition, jolted through Sean. "No, you don't have to—"

Ferrell pulled the trigger. The shot detonated in the clearing, deafening and shocking.

Kira twitched. Red liquid oozed down her forehead from the bullet hole at its center.

Sean roared with a fury that scorched out reason, thought, intention—and the serum. It evaporated from his blood on a tide of his own healing power. He didn't give a damn that he'd finally healed himself and done it despite the EM field too. He surged forward determined to rip Ferrell's head from her body with his bare hands.

A guard punched the butt of his AK-47 into Sean's chest.

The impact slammed him to the ground backward. The breath exploded out of his lungs, and he couldn't suck in more air. Blackness dotted his vision. If he didn't regain his breath soon, he'd pass out—and be no good to anyone.

Kira. He could heal her. But when he tried, his mind slammed into a wall.

The fucking EM field. He could heal his own body but not hers? Dammit, he needed more power.

Don't let on the serum isn't working, he reminded himself.

He dragged in a wheezing breath, his lungs burning. And he glared at the bitch smiling down at him.

"Now you're properly motivated," she said. "Complete your task, and I will lower the EM field so you can heal Kira. Assuming you hurry. It's my understanding a healer can use his power only on a body whose soul hasn't departed yet."

Souls? He'd never considered that idea in relation to his power, but he had no time to think about it.

Two guards took up positions on either side of him, their weapons trained on him.

Ferrell wagged her finger. "Tick tock, Sean."

His gaze fell on Kira. The wound. The gunshot. His chest constricted, his heart seemingly squeezed by a phantom pressure. His jaw quivered from more than gritting his teeth. And in that instant, he realized exactly what he had to do.

Sean tried to fly out of his body, but the EM field ensnared him. *Shit.* He had to relax. Sure, with the woman he loved lying dead a few feet away. He loved her? Yeah, holy heaven, he did. The revelation rocked him, but he clung to the emotion, to the power of it, as he sought out the thread of the Golden Power that lingered inside him. He latched onto it. Tugged. Seized it with all his willpower and yanked.

A tiny hole, a pinprick, popped open in the EM field.

Power trickled into him. Not much, but enough.

He soared up into the crossroads and straight into the heart of the universe—straight into the purest, most potent energy that had ever existed.

And he devoured it all.

Chapter Twenty-Seven

THE ENERGY FLOWED INTO HIM, AROUND HIM, IGNITING THE GREEN halo once more. The glow shimmered a millimeter above his skin, its energy tingling over his flesh even as its counterpart inside him crackled and suffused his psychic senses. The power wanted to overwhelm him—that seemed to be its natural tendency, like the way a deluge of rain would coalesce into a flash flood when it gushed down a hillside—but he refused to give the power an unimpeded path to his mind. He threw up dams, redirecting the flow to the place where he needed it to go.

He controlled the Golden Power.

Grace had been right when she said it was energy, nothing more, not a living thing that could seize control. The power could inundate a person's mind unless they seized it. Grace's fears had held her back and allowed the energy to consume her like it had him the first time.

When this was over, he'd show her how to take command of the power.

First, save Kira. Then, kill Ferrell.

Yeah, today he could commit murder no problem.

Sean dived out of the crossroads toward his body but halted above the woods, hovering there as an invisible spirit. He surveyed the landscape and the life-forms below. The bunker appeared as a small hill to the naked eye. He peered through the earth into the interior, searching the corridors for blips that would indicate life. One blip appeared, inside the cell where Sean and Kira had left Amador, while a blip outside the door indicated the guard Ferrell had dispatched to retrieve Amador.

Outside the bunker, he spotted the blips of the guards, the prisoners, and Ferrell crouched beside Kira where she lay prone on the ground.

Dead on the ground.

The weight on his chest grew heavier.

His astral form floated a few feet above the heads of the men and women congregated in the clearing.

Nathan veered his gaze toward his son, and Sean had the weirdest sensation his dad was looking straight at him, seeing him though he had no visible form. For anyone to see a traveler, they needed to share a connection. Sean had met his father earlier today. How could they have a bond? It was crazy.

And yet, his father was watching him. Nathan's lips kinked into a slight smile.

Sean glanced at Kira, but she still lay lifeless on the ground.

Ferrell, kneeling beside Kira, stood and marched up to Sean where he rested on the grass. It was weird to see his own body, his vacant expression. The scientist grabbed his chin and shook it but received no reaction. She pursed her lips, one hand fisted at her side, and slapped him with the other hand. Still no reaction. Sean sensed the slap, not as a physical sensation but as a snap in his psychic tether to his body.

The scientist glared into the vacant eyes of Sean's body. "If you don't come back soon, Kira will stay dead."

He summoned the power, gathering the diverging streams into a river of energy that obeyed his command.

Ferrell crouched beside Kira again.

Sean unleashed the torrent. Psychic energy poured down in a widening deluge no one could see but everyone experienced. The green power, sparkling with golden flecks, rained down on the group below, spreading outward from the center positioned directly over Kira and Ferrell. The scientist jerked, dropping the syringe. Her eyes went wide.

She collapsed, unconscious.

The guards crumpled next.

As the energy rushed outward, Sean redirected it away from the prisoners, like a sluice guiding the flow where he wanted. The power fizzled out at the edge of the woods and at the earth-covered wall of the bunker.

Next, he sought out the device generating the EM field. Though he had no clue where it was or what it was, he located it anyway. With a spurt of power, he disabled the EM field.

Kira is still dead.

The truth gripped him in its frigid claws. He'd done so much from outside his body, but to save Kira, he had to be in his physical form. He couldn't explain how he knew, but he understood what was required. Flesh and blood to restore flesh and blood.

Sean dropped back into his body. The switch from astral vision to the real thing made him dizzy for a second, but as his senses settled down, his gaze found Kira.

Peripherally, he noticed he'd knocked out all the bad guys.

His attention glued to Kira, he scrambled across the ground to her. He raised his shaking hands to her head, bracketing it with his palms over her ears. The green halo around him blanketed her. It crackled on her skin, poured into her through her nostrils, escalated until it enveloped them both in a blinding, sparkling veil of energy.

The power fled his body through his hands, streaming into her, healing the damage. The bullet emerged from the wound little by little as the tissues knit together in its wake. The slug rolled off her forehead and fell to the ground. Cells repaired themselves. Neurons reconnected. Her heart fluttered and thumped once, twice, three times, regaining its natural and strong rhythm. Blood coursed through her veins, enlivening and nourishing her flesh.

As the last iota of power vacated him, she opened her eyes.

"Sean," Kira said, her voice suffused with wonder, "how did you—"

He collapsed to the ground, and everything went black.

———

KIRA SPRANG TO HER KNEES. IN THE BACK OF HER MIND, SHE REALIZED something incredible had just occurred, but she had no chance to appreciate it. Sean lay slumped on the ground, out cold.

What had he done?

She pressed a finger to his wrist, praying for a pulse. Nothing. Struggling not to panic, she jammed her finger into his neck. Nothing. No, goddammit, he would not die in her place. Exchange one life for another? Like hell she'd let him get away with that.

"You're not leaving me," she said, tears pooling in her eyes, blurring her vision. "I won't let you do this, not for me."

She flipped him onto his back and laid her palms on his chest. Energy lingered within him, she sensed it. The energy of the Golden Power. That's what he had done to save her. He'd invited the ultimate power into his mind and body, not caring if it destroyed him.

For her. He'd sacrificed himself for her.

The EM field was gone. She recognized that fact. With every ounce of psychic energy inside her, she reached for the Golden Power within him.

And she tapped into his healing ability.

He wasn't dead, not quite yet. If she hurried…

So hurry, idiot.

Kira channeled his power through her own and back into his body, something she hadn't known she could do. Instinct took over, and she let it guide her powers. Her hands on his chest began to glow faintly green.

Sean moaned. His head lolled.

Relief gushed through her. She caught his face in her hands. "Wake up, you jerk. You don't get to leave me yet. We're stuck together, remember?"

His eyelids opened halfway, and he gave her a dazed smile. "You sure are bossy. I'm trying to die heroically here, and you can't stop telling me what to do."

Tears spilled down her cheeks. "Dying heroically is overrated. The people who love you, we'd rather you stick around."

"We?" He pushed up onto his elbows, his smile turning sexy. "You included yourself there. Guess that means you've got a thing for me."

"Shut up so I can kiss you."

Kira crushed her mouth to his in a quick, fierce kiss.

Nathan rushed up to Sean and Kira, his expression awed and proud at the same time. "You have amazing control, Sean. I thought you weren't very adept with your powers yet, but what do I know? I haven't seen you since you were five." He clapped a hand on Sean's shoulder. "Good work, son."

Sean's chest puffed up a little when his father called him "son." The dad he'd thought abandoned him had praised him for doing a good thing, and Kira understood the pride he must feel at knowing his father loved him after all. Until today he'd cursed his deadbeat dad, and she'd cursed her deadbeat parents. Maybe that's what Ferrell, and Tesler before her, had intended—to make them both weaker and more malleable by taking away their families, convincing them their parents hadn't wanted to be with them. But his father had fought every day for seventeen years, determined never to betray his kid. And her parents had made a desperate choice believing it would spare her and Caleb a horrible fate.

Their parents had done the best they could. She and Sean had done the best they could, and somehow, they'd emerged victorious.

"What should we do with them?" Nathan asked, indicating the guards and Ferrell with a sweep of his arm.

"I've got an idea," Sean said, "but I need Kira's help."

Sean raised a hand to cup her face. His skin was warm. His powers came alive, sizzling between them, awakening her own powers along with a damp ache between her thighs. She wanted him, yes. More than that, she needed him. She needed more than his powers and the ferocious potency of their merged psychic energy. She needed him, the man, the jerk who'd turned out to be a strong and caring person who'd taken her powers into himself despite not knowing her and despite the fact she'd tried to trick him repeatedly so she could escape. He trusted her even after that, and she'd learned she could trust him too. With her life. With her heart.

Crazy as it sounded when they'd known each other such a short time, she recognized the truth. She loved him, and the realization shivered through her, sultry and sweet.

With his palm on her cheek, he said, "We need to finish this. What do you say?"

"I'm with you. Whenever, wherever, whatever."

They both got to their feet. He brushed hair from her face, trailing his fingers down her cheek.

She glanced around, her brows lifting when she saw the unconscious baddies. Her gaze returned to Sean, and she touched his face. "You took out all the bad guys."

"Yeah, but it's not quite over yet. They're out cold, but not dead." He hooked an arm around her waist. "We have one more thing to do. It ought to set things right, but it won't be pretty."

"What are you talking about?"

"Ferrell and Amador were right about one part of their plan. Somebody has to take responsibility for the bombings, to close that case and let the world move on from it." He looked at the limp form of Dr. Ferrell and sighed. "It's the only way to make sure they're locked up for good, someplace they can't escape from."

Kira caught his face in her hands. "You're going to have to explain your plan to me."

"It's simple, really." He pulled in a deep breath. "We're going to manipulate their minds with thought projection. They are going to take responsibility for the attacks."

"First, we'd better lock up these guards."

"I'll do that," Nathan said.

Kira's eyes flew wide when her parents approached and announced, "We'll help Nathan."

Grace walked up then with Abby and Caleb in tow. "I should take the kids someplace less scary."

A horrible thought popped into Kira's mind, and she asked, "Did they see what just went down?"

"No. There were guards in front of us blocking our view."

Kira's shoulders slumped with relief. "Thank goodness for that."

Caleb rushed at her, latching his arms around her waist, forcing Sean to relinquish his hold on her. "Kiki! Kiki! Are you okay? I'm okay. Mom and Dad are here, did you see?"

"Yeah, kiddo, I saw." She tousled his hair. "They have to help me out for a little bit. Go with Grace and Abby, okay? Me and Mom and Dad will come get you soon, I promise."

"Okay," he said with the sort of annoyed tone only a child could make sound endearing.

Caleb ran to their parents and squeezed each of them in turn, his hugs fierce and quick. Their mom lifted him up into her arms for a fuller hug, kissed his cheek, and murmured to him. Dad chucked Caleb's chin and said something Kira couldn't hear. Her brother trotted back to Grace.

"Take them to the cabin," Kira said. "The one where Sean and I hid. It's a few miles away—"

"I can find it," Grace told her. She tapped a finger on her temple. "Psychic, remember? I'll scout the place with RV. We'll take one of the SUVs parked around the other side of the hill."

Everyone must have gotten their powers back. The EM field had been disabled several minutes ago.

Sean slung an arm around her waist again, tugging her close.

Grace went rigid, her gaze sharpening on a sight to the left of the bunker's recessed door.

Kira followed the track of Grace's gaze.

A blond man traipsed out of the woods.

"David!" Grace shouted.

She bolted for her husband, flung her arms around his neck, and lavished him with kisses hot enough to make Kira blush. David Ransom wrapped his arms around his wife.

Abby sprinted to her parents and clamped her little arms around her father's leg.

When his wife surrendered his mouth, David glanced around and said, "Looks like I missed the party."

"It was a dud, anyway," Grace said. "Amador didn't get his nuclear-fallout jamboree."

"Amador?" David said, seeming confused.

Grace patted his cheek. "I'll explain later. Right now, you should help Sean and Kira—and Sean's father."

David's brows shot up. "Father?"

"Explain later, honey. Help now."

Grace waved to Kira's mother. "Mrs. Magnusson, why don't you come with me and the kids? David will help wrangle the baddies. He's really good at that."

"I am?" David said with a faint smirk.

"Oh yes, honey, you are."

Kira's mom gave her a quick hug, then accompanied Grace and the kids to the rented SUV David had driven here. He'd hidden it in the woods a few hundred yards away, but they'd all agreed it was safer for Grace to take the rented car rather than the closer ones owned and operated by villains. Better to exercise excessive caution, he'd said. Everyone had agreed with him.

While the grumble of the vehicle engine faded away, David, Nathan, and Kira's dad gathered up the weapons belonging to the unconscious guards. Kira had asked to have one of the handguns, though she couldn't explain why she'd wanted it. Her intuition niggled at her, but she had no idea what it was trying to tell her. Sean took a pistol as well. Before rousing and corralling the guards, the other men took time to introduce themselves to the two prisoners Kira and Sean had freed.

Kira faced Sean, who had his back to the unconscious Ferrell. "How long will they stay knocked out?"

"Not sure." Sean tucked his gun inside his waistband. "Never knocked anybody out with my powers before."

A sensation shivered through her, cold and sharp like a blanket of needles pricking her skin. She curled her hand around the grip of the gun she'd commandeered, her finger hovering over the trigger.

"What is it?" Sean asked.

"Don't know." Kira stepped sideways. Ferrell still sprawled limp on the ground, eyes closed, but the sensation on her skin grew stronger. "Sean—"

"Ahhh!" a male voice hollered.

Kira whipped her head around to see a guard floundering to his feet, dazed, striking his fists out blindly. David landed a kick to the guard's gut, sending him tumbling to the earth again.

Something rustled behind Sean.

Kira swung her head toward the ground behind Sean.

Dr. Ferrell had clambered to her feet. She staggered forward with a scalpel in her white-knuckle grip. The scientist raised the scalpel, its blade targeted on Sean's neck.

"No!" Kira shouted.

She veered her gun up and pulled the trigger.

The shot boomed in the clearing. The bullet struck Ferrell smack in the chest. She jerked, eyes bulging.

Kira fired again and again.

Ferrell toppled to the ground, a lump of flesh, her eyes wide and vacant. Blood stained her white shirt, spreading outward.

Sometime between Kira shouting and when she'd fired the gun, Sean had whirled around to see what had frightened her. He stared down at the dead scientist without expression.

Kira dropped the gun. It plunked onto the earth. "I had to—She was about to—"

"I know." Sean pulled her into his arms. "You saved my life again. Thank you."

Despite the shock of killing another human being, Kira couldn't muster any regret for what she'd done or pity for the woman whose life she'd taken. Ferrell had shot Kira in the head. The woman deserved what she'd gotten. Besides, the so-called scientist had tortured God-knew-how-many innocent men, women, and probably children too.

The world was a better place without Dr. Ferrell in it.

From across the clearing, David called out, "What happened?"

"Kira saved my ass again," Sean said with a glimmer of humor in his green eyes.

"Oh, is that all?" David said, his voice rife with the same humor. "Not sure his ass is worth the effort, Kira."

"Man, you are not funny," Sean said, "no matter how hard you try. Stick to rounding up the bad guys. Your wife says that's all you're good for."

Kira peeked around Sean's thick bicep. David, Nathan, and her father had found zip ties on some of the guards, and now they used those very restraints to hobble the uniformed men.

"You're my hero," Sean said.

Kira rolled her eyes at him.

"I'm serious." He hooked a finger under her chin, urging her to meet his gaze. "You are an amazing, smart, and feisty woman. You talked back to me when I kidnapped you instead of playing the meek victim, and you believed in me when you really shouldn't have. I gave you no reason to trust me, but you did. You showed me my powers aren't dangerous, that I'm not dangerous unless I want to be. You made me feel human again. You made me feel, period. I owe you everything."

The way he was looking at her, she knew he meant all of it.

Footfalls clapped in the stairwell.

Sean and Kira swung their guns up and aimed them toward the concrete entrance to the bunker.

A solitary guard led a wild-eyed and haggard Gabriel Amador up the steps. When the guard noted his buddies tied up and the weapons Kira and Sean aimed at him, he dropped his gun and raised his hands in surrender.

Gabriel Amador laughed. Not arrogant laughter, either. Panicked, hysterical sounds.

"Okay," Sean said. "Time for Gabe here to confess in front of the world."

Chapter Twenty-Eight

KIRA WATCHED SEAN AND NATHAN SET UP THE VIDEO EQUIPMENT in the clearing. Her telekinetic pulse had wiped out the electrical wiring and computers in the bunker—plus any devices connected to them. They'd found a backup camera and laptop computer in a storage room that hadn't been connected to the system and therefore hadn't been affected.

A few minutes ago, a realization had struck her, and she'd burst out laughing. Everyone had looked at her funny, but Sean had been the one to speak up.

"Why are you laughing?" he'd asked. "Did getting resurrected make you demented?"

"No." She shook her head, still chuckling. "I just realized I haven't even thought about lighting up a cigarette since we left that crappy hotel room in Kansas. I don't want one at all."

"Okay, resurrection didn't make you crazy. It cured you of smoking?"

She'd wandered closer to him to whisper so only he would hear. "Maybe it's you that cured me. I haven't craved a smoke since the first time we kissed."

At that, he'd grinned with supreme self-satisfaction.

Grace had called from the cabin to assure Kira her mom and Caleb were doing fine. According to Grace, Caleb and Abby were building a stick fort on the lawn. Both kids seemed to have shed all the weight of the trauma they'd endured lately. Children were resilient, though Kira hadn't realized how resilient until now. How amazing that under these circumstances a child could still have a good time.

Despite having spent seventeen years believing his father was a deadbeat, after less than a day with his dad Sean already looked at the man with a touch of hero worship in his gaze.

The men had locked the guards in separate cells inside the bunker and moved Dr. Ferrell's body into a storage room located inside the bunker next to the exit. Thanks to Ferrell's little bag of goodies, they'd been able to sedate Amador enough to keep him from trying anything. Not that the man seemed capable of causing trouble. It was a precaution, nothing more. Amador was too far gone to do much more than breathe. Kira and Sean hadn't bothered to secure the man with zip ties.

The two former prisoners had become part of the team. Danny, the hacker-slash-psychic, sat on the ground with the undamaged computer on his lap doing things he'd explained but that Kira did not understand. The woman they'd rescued, Eva, guarded the prisoners. She brandished a large gun and looked like she'd have no qualms about shooting any villains who might appear.

Kira's dad, never the hugging type before, seized her in a bear hug. "I can't believe you're here. This is a miracle, an honest-to-goodness miracle."

Her father had hugged her five times in the past twenty minutes. She didn't mind at all. In fact, she couldn't keep from smiling every time.

"All set," Sean called out to the group. "Danny, are you ready?"

"Good to go," the young man replied. "The funds have been moved, the feed is set up, and the documents are in place."

Sean had insisted they take a good chunk of Amador's fortune and allocate it to a bank account in the Cayman Islands. From there, once the dust settled, they'd distribute the funds to victims of the bombings and to psychics abused by Amador, Ferrell, and Tesler. Grace and David had found a number of those psychics over the past five years, and each deserved compensation. So did the bombing victims. They'd left Amador enough of a bank balance to make it plausible he could've funded a terrorist group.

Danny had also planted documents on Amador's computer system at his home, accessing it remotely from here in the Montana woods. Turned out Danny's powers supercharged his hacking talents just like Amador had claimed, letting him make brand-new files seem like they'd existed for years. The files planted on Amador's computer revealed his insane plot and his motivations, as well as Ferrell's complicity. In crafting the evidence, they had all agreed to omit Tesler's involvement—not to spare the dead man's reputation, but to spare Sean from becoming the grandson of an infamous madman. Sean had balked at the idea at first, though Kira had insisted on it. He'd relented when his father threw his support behind the plan.

He listened to his dad. It was sweet.

Sean hauled Amador to his feet, bracing the man with two strong hands on his slumped shoulders. Then, Sean used his healing power to eradicate the sedative. Amador blinked rapidly, his gaze clearing but his mind remaining addled.

This was the dangerous part. Amador needed to be clear of mind to make the video, which meant Kira and Sean had a brief window in which to manipulate his mind.

She knew Sean hated using thought projection. The idea bothered her too, but Amador had done much worse to so many people. This was justice.

Nathan and Eva stood behind Amador but out of range of the camera, guarding in case any of Amador and Ferrell's lackeys had escaped before they'd rounded up the lot of them.

Side by side in front of Amador, Kira and Sean linked their hands. Power crackled between them, and then they did it.

They reshaped a man's mind.

⸺

"I AND MY GROUP ARE RESPONSIBLE FOR THE BOMBS DETONATED IN THE cafe and the movie theater," Gabriel Amador said without a trace of remorse in his voice or his expression. "Jackson Tennant murdered my son, and the world allowed this to happen. I sought to punish everyone because everyone is guilty. I regret nothing. My path is just, exacting vengeance on a world that permits evil to exist provided the evildoers have money and power. It's not right, and we intend to stop the madness."

Amador paused, but his gaze remained fixed on the camera, unflinching and cold.

"Our next target," Amador said, "will be of global import. We will launch an intercontinental ballistic missile from Malmstrom Air Force Base in Montana. No one can stop us."

The television picture switched to a woman reporter standing outside the gates of Malmstrom.

"Earlier today," the reporter said, "Spanish billionaire Gabriel Amador was apprehended while attempting to break into Missile Command here at Malmstrom Air Force Base. Six coconspirators were also arrested at a defunct bunker in the mountains. They had apparently tried to destroy the bunker to cover their tracks but only managed to fry the electrical system. Amador claims to have psychic powers that allowed him to commit the attacks and that would've let his group launch an ICBM. However, authorities found a large amount of data on Amador's home computer that incriminates him and his coconspirators in a bizarre plot described as 'staggeringly unhinged.' The small terrorist cell helmed by Amador and the late Dr. Helena Ferrell, whom Amador admits to murdering, seems to have consisted of just six other individuals, all of whom are in custody and reportedly will testify against Amador. Evidence from Amador's computer reportedly shows how the cell members detonated the first bomb without using a trigger, but authorities won't share that information at this time."

The video changed to a scene of Amador, handcuffed, being shoved into a police car by men wearing FBI jackets.

The reporter said, "This audacious and ill-conceived terrorist plot has been disrupted with no lives lost. I'm Crystal Jones reporting from Malmstrom Air Force Base near Great Falls, Montana."

EPILOGUE

Three Months Later

SEAN LAY ON AN OVERSIZE BEACH TOWEL SURROUNDED BY GOLDEN sand with golden sunshine warming his skin. Since he wore only swim trunks, the heat of the tropical sun warmed most of his body. The sight beside him heated up the rest of him.

Kira sprawled across the other half of the towel wearing a skimpy bikini. The strings that held it together were tied in little bows. The way she reclined there made her breasts mound up. The bikini bottoms accentuated her hips. The outfit and the pose showed off every one of her lush curves to best effect and made his groin ache. Her dark hair sprayed over the towel and onto the sand while sunglasses concealed her eyes.

Her lips curved into a satisfied smile. "I like the Caribbean."

"Me too." Sean rolled onto his side, braced on one elbow, and his gaze landed on the mouthwatering slopes of her breasts. "I also like that nobody's tried to abduct or murder us for three whole months. How long do you think the peace will last?"

"You worry too much." She splayed a hand over his cheek, her thumb rubbing the corner of his mouth. "I thought you'd learned to kick back and enjoy life."

"I backslide once in a while. Maybe I need a refresher lesson."

"Mm, I like giving you refreshers." She reached up to graze her fingers over his hair. "I like you as a redhead. You're not hiding from the past anymore."

Yeah, he'd made peace with the past, with the fact he couldn't change who his grandfather had been or what the man had done. None of that tainted Sean. Not anymore.

The sound of splashing drew their attention to the water. Caleb giggled as he jumped around in the knee-high waves. His parents had dropped to their knees to let their son splash them relentlessly. The three of them grinned and laughed, and Mr. Magnusson lifted Caleb above his head. The family had been reunited for three months, and though recovering from what had happened took time, they'd reforged their family bond quickly.

Sean glanced over his shoulder at his family. His dad lounged in a beach chaise alongside Edward, who sat in a matching chair. Grace and David relaxed on a beach towel while Abby played in the sand. David sat up to help her make a little tower for her sandcastle. Grace observed with a smile lighting up her face.

Everyone was happy these days. Their group vacation to Aruba had begun a week ago, and they had another week before they went home. Then, they'd continue their mission to find and help psychics who were abused by Jackson Tennant, Tesler, Ferrell, and Amador. Considering JT and his lackeys had created two dozen facilities around the world, this mission could take the rest of their lives.

Saving people was never a waste of time.

As for Gabriel Amador, he'd spend the rest of his life in a high-security mental institution. Nobody could save that man.

They'd each taken a bit of Amador's money. When Sean had asked if stealing from a crazy guy was immoral, David had told him, "It's not stealing. It's compensation for what he took from us. You and I were locked up and tortured in the Mojave Desert facility."

"But JT locked us up," Sean had pointed out, "and then Tesler after that."

"We can't get to JT's money. Amador abused a lot of people, including you and Grace. He used the same tactics as JT and Tesler. It's not wrong to make him pay for our pain and suffering."

Sean decided he could live with that. Besides, the bulk of what they'd taken from Amador had gone to the bombing victims and psychics abused by JT, Tesler, and Amador. Sean and his extended family took just enough to make life a little easier.

"Hey," Kira said, tickling his chin. "What are you thinking about?"

With a long, satisfied sigh, he told her, "How lucky we are."

"Yes, we are that." She sat up and stretched. "Ready for that refresher?"

"Absolutely." Sean jumped up, then bent to grab her around the waist and lift her up too. She squeaked when he set her feet down in the sun-baked sand. He kept his arm around her, and that lithe body pinned to his, when he twisted sideways to wave at his father. When his dad noticed, Sean shouted, "We're going for a walk."

Nathan Vandenbrook flashed a knowing grin. "Have fun."

Sean led Kira down a well-maintained path for a ways until he saw the smaller trail he'd scouted earlier. "Scouting" meant he'd RV'd the trail to find the perfect spot. They emerged from the trees into a clearing around a small waterfall. The pool at the base of the falls shimmered a crystalline blue.

"This is beautiful," Kira said, smiling broadly as she surveyed the surroundings.

He pulled her tight against him and kissed her, exploring her mouth with his lips and his tongue, diving deep to savor the taste of her and the way she responded with silken strokes of her own tongue. "The scenery's not as beautiful as you. Nothing could be."

"I love it when you shower me with compliments."

"Plan on showering you with something else right now." He stripped off his swim trunks, then fingered the bow of one bikini string. "Sorry, but nudity is required for this event."

A flush tinted her cheeks, though not from embarrassment. Her nipples pearled, jutting against the flimsy fabric of her bikini top, and her breaths shortened.

He untied the strings of her bikini one by one. The top fell off first, fluttering to the ground, followed swiftly by the bottoms.

"What now?" she asked, touching her fingertips to his chest.

"You'll see."

He swept her up in his arms, strode to the pool, and tossed her into the middle of it.

Kira shrieked as she plunked into the water with a big splash.

Sean leaped in after her, water shooting up around him. He caught her around the waist. "Time for grown-up water games."

He slid a hand between their bodies, gliding it down her belly and between her thighs. When he slipped his fingers between her folds, she gasped. When he began stroking her flesh, her eyes drifted half shut and her mouth fell open on a long, low moan. He caressed her until she was writhing against him, held in place by his arm, her moans becoming louder and hungrier. The second her body tensed, he devoured her mouth, swallowing her cries as she climaxed.

She sagged against him, her head on his shoulder.

"I have to ask you a question," he murmured into her ear.

"Huh?" She sounded dazed, which he took as a compliment.

Sean rubbed her back in slow circles and nuzzled her wet hair. "I said I need to ask you a question."

With an irritated little noise, she lifted her head to gaze at him. "Can it wait? We haven't gotten to the best part yet."

He nipped her chin. "We'll get there, trust me."

She crossed her arms, resting them on his collarbone. Her nose bumped his. "Okay, ask your question."

"Um…" Suddenly, he couldn't make the words come out. He brushed the backs of his fingers over her cheek, mesmerized by her jewel-bright eyes. "I love you, Kira. Will you marry me?"

The wattage of her smile could've powered the lights for an entire city. "Yes."

He grinned. "Thank you."

She laughed. "You don't have to thank me for saying yes to your proposal."

"But I'm grateful." He placed a light kiss on her lips. "The ring is in our room at the hotel. I was going to hold off asking until later, but I couldn't wait a second longer."

She wriggled her hips. "Show me how grateful you are."

He took hold of her hips, and she wound her legs around him. The water lapped around them as he plunged inside her with one smooth thrust. Tiny waves splashed against their bodies while he took her slowly, sweetly, relishing every sensation. He fit inside her like she'd been made for him, and he knew they'd been made for each other. Psychic energy sizzled inside them and on their skin. He glided in and out, in and out, her soft wetness welcoming him, his hard-on throbbing with a mounting need to spill himself inside her. She clung to him, panting into his ear, her fingers clawing at his scalp. He thrust harder, faster, lost in the rapture of taking the woman he loved.

Her sheath tightened around him, and her body went rigid.

The moment her climax hit, he surrendered to the sensations, his release pulsating out of him and into her, melding their bodies even as the glittering, tingling energy of their powers merged. He let out a hoarse cry.

She kissed his neck and his cheek, her lips feathery on his skin. "I love you, Sean. Can't wait to marry you."

"Neither can I. We should do the deed before you start classes again." He combed his fingers through her drenched hair while her drenched sex stayed snug around him. "I'm proud of you for going back to college."

"It's not an amazing feat. I filled out some paperwork, that's all."

"After what you've been through, it takes guts to get your life back in order."

"You're the brave one." She ran a finger over his lips. "You went through way worse things than I did. I'm in awe of your strength and determination."

Right then and there, he knew he would love this woman forever.

He squeezed her ass with both hands. "Whatever happened to that refresher course in relaxation?"

She pushed away from him, swimming backward while crooking a finger at him. "Follow me."

He would follow her anywhere, even into the heart of the universe.

And for them, that wasn't a metaphor.

to subscribe to her newsletter

for updates on forthcoming books
&
to receive exclusive content!

ANNA DURAND IS A BESTSELLING, MULTI-AWARD-WINNING AUTHOR OF contemporary and paranormal romance. Her books have earned best-seller status on every major retailer and wonderful reviews from readers around the world. But that's the boring spiel. Here are some really cool things you want to know about Anna!

Born on Lackland Air Force Base in Texas, Anna grew up moving here, there, and everywhere thanks to her dad's job as an instructor pilot. She's lived in Texas (twice), Mississippi, California (twice), Michigan (twice), and Alaska—and now Ohio.

As for her writing, Anna has always made up stories in her head, but she didn't write them down until her teen years. Those first awful books went into the trash can a few years later, though she learned a lot from those stories. Eventually, she would pen her first romance novel, the paranormal romance *Willpower*, and she's never looked back since.

Want even more details about Anna? Sign up for her newsletter to get exclusive content and updates on forthcoming books.

VISIT ANNADURAND.COM TO SIGN UP.